PENGUIN TWENTIETH-CENTURY CLASSICS

SELECTED STORIES

William Sydney Porter (1862–1910) published all of his work—a novel and some 300 short stories—under the pseudonym O. Henry. His talent for vivid caricature, local tone, narrative agility, and compassion tempered by irony made him a vastly popular writer in the last decade of his life. He was born in Greensboro, North Carolina, to ordinary middle-class parents and worked in an uncle's drugstore as a youth, becoming a certified pharmacist. Like many Southerners after the Civil War, he sought his fortune in the West, holding various jobs (newspaper work, clerking in a land office, a teller at an Austin bank). Charged with embezzlement in 1894, he fled to Honduras, returning in 1897 to be with his ill and dying wife. His conviction was caused more by his eluding trial than by the conflicting evidence of theft. In the Ohio State Penitentiary (1898–1901), he began to write the stories that made him famous. He moved to New York, remarried, and kept his identity a secret from all but a few friends. He is buried in Asheville, North Carolina. He is universally honored for his mastery of the short story and for his humane spirit.

Guy Davenport, a critic and writer of fiction, is best known for two books of essays, *The Geography of the Imagination* and *Every Force Evolves a Form*. He has published seven collections of short stories and numerous translations of early Greek poets and playwrights. Now retired, he was a professor of English at the University of Kentucky from 1964 to 1990. He is also a painter and illustrator.

PENGUIN TWENTIETH-CENTURY CLASSICS

SELECTED STORIES

[illegible] Sydney Porter (1862–1910) published [illegible] novel and [illegible] short stories [illegible] pseudonym [illegible] [illegible] [illegible] [illegible] [illegible] [illegible] [illegible] [illegible] Honduras [illegible] Ohio State Penitentiary [illegible] [illegible] stories [illegible] New York [illegible] [illegible] short story and [illegible]

[illegible] and [illegible] The [illegible] short stories [illegible] [illegible] [illegible] professor of English at the University [illegible] from 1904 to 1909 [illegible]

O. HENRY

Selected Stories

Edited and with an Introduction by

GUY DAVENPORT

PENGUIN BOOKS

PENGUIN BOOKS
Published by the Penguin Group
Penguin Books USA Inc., 375 Hudson Street,
New York, New York 10014, U.S.A.
Penguin Books Ltd, 27 Wrights Lane, London W8 5TZ, England
Penguin Books Australia Ltd, Ringwood, Victoria, Australia
Penguin Books Canada Ltd, 10 Alcorn Avenue,
Toronto, Ontario, Canada M4V 3B2
Penguin Books (N.Z.) Ltd, 182–190 Wairau Road,
Auckland 10, New Zealand

Penguin Books Ltd, Registered Offices:
Harmondsworth, Middlesex, England

This collection edited and introduced by
Guy Davenport first published in Penguin Books 1993

7 9 10 8

LIBRARY OF CONGRESS CATALOGING IN PUBLICATION DATA

Henry, O., 1862–1910
[Selections. 1993]
Selected stories/ O. Henry; edited and with an introduction by Guy Davenport.
p. cm.
ISBN 0 14 01.8688 3
I. Davenport, Guy. II. Title.
PS2649.P5A6 1993 92-39604
813'.52—dc20

Printed in the United States of America
Set in Bembo
Designed by Cheryl L. Cipriani

CONTENTS

FROM *Heart of the West* (1907)

FROM *The Voice of the City* (1908)

FROM *The Gentle Grafter* (1908)

FROM *Roads of Destiny* (1909)

FROM *Options* (1909)

FROM *Sctrictly Business* (1910)

INTRODUCTION

It was only toward the end of the first decade of this century that the shy and amiable North Carolinian who had published some three hundred stories under the pen name O. Henry consented to be photographed. He had, as we know, his reasons: he also refused to be interviewed. One of his editors at Doubleday, Page, and Co., Harry Steger, persuaded him to be photographed by William M. van der Weyde, whose portraits of O. Henry are some of the finest of any American writer. Steger remembered in later years that it took two hours to cajole O. Henry into getting dressed and walking two blocks, from the Hotel Caledonia to van der Weyde's studio.

The unique interview, by George MacAdam, was also at the insistence of his publishers. But here O. Henry was in his element and had only to become one of his own characters (the master confidence man Jeff Peters) to bluff his way through it. He made himself a Texas newspaper man—true enough—to account for his familiarity with the West. Of his job as a teller in an Austin bank, he said nothing.

"Then a friend of mine who had a little money (wonderful thing, that—isn't it?—a friend with a little money) suggested that I join him in a trip to Central America, whither he was going with the intention of entering the fruit business."

We can hear that *whither.* If you're speaking fiction, you might as well make it literary. William Sidney Porter was in Honduras because he had been charged with embezzlement in Austin and had jumped bail (married man that he was, with a daughter) and sailed to Central America from New Orleans. He could not have been in New Orleans for more than a few days, yet the stories he set there have the color and tone of a native's familiarity.

"The banana plantation faded into nothing; I drifted back to Texas." There had never been a banana plantation, and O. Henry returned to Texas, after two years in Trujillo, because he learned that his wife was very ill. She died on July 25, 1897, and O. Henry was tried in February of the next year—on the same day that Émile Zola stood before judges in a Parisian court (he jumped bail too and sat out his troubles in London) for accusing the army and government of falsely condemning Captain Dreyfus in that notorious *affaire*. O. Henry and Dreyfus were probably equally innocent. One of the charges against O. Henry was for a day when he wasn't in Austin, and the others may have been due to inept bookkeeping. There has always been a rumor that O. Henry was shielding someone else, and he wrote many stories about embezzlement, false charges, and one friend's taking the rap for another.

"I went to New Orleans and took up literary work in earnest." He went to the Ohio State Penitentiary on April 25, 1898, to serve a five-year sentence. He was released, after time off for good behavior and exemplary deportment as a pharmacist in the infirmary, on July 24, 1901.

In prison he changed his middle name from Sidney to Sydney (a city that began as Botany Bay). Throughout his work we can find concealed references to his felony. The pseudonym that he began to write under in prison is constructed from the *oh* of *Ohio* and the *en* and *ry* in *penitentiary* (he gives the code for this in the story "The Man Higher Up," in which a con man named Alfred E. Ricks is caught but returns to the game as A. L. Fredericks).

In an age of triple names, when even P. G. Wodehouse had to be Pelham Grenville Wodehouse, the name O. Henry sounded puckishly plain and humble. It was an Odyssean *Nobody*. To every query about it, O. Henry gave a different answer: "*O.* is the easiest letter to write." Sometimes he said the *O.* was for *Olivier,* "the French for Oliver, you know."

From prison O. Henry made a stop in Pittsburgh and almost immediately moved to New York, where his stories were beginning to be talked about and were in demand. For the next ten years, until his death (under the pseudonym Will S. Parker) in 1910, he kept magazines and newspapers supplied with short stories in a style unmistakably his own, a handful of which have always been staple selections in anthologies. He was one of the most popular of American writers. The year of his death saw two collections, *Strictly Business* and *Whirligigs*. *Sixes and Sevens* came out in 1911, and stories were still being collected into books as late as 1917 (*Waifs and Strays*). The biography of his childhood playmate C. Alphonso Smith was published in 1916, disclosing the truth of O. Henry's life and making him not so much a character in one of his own stories as one from Conrad. To those friends who knew his past, O. Henry always compared himself to Lord Jim.

His first book, the novel *Cabbages and Kings,* is strangely like *Nostromo*: both are intricately plotted novels about the misappropriation of large sums of money in a Latin American republic.

The year of O. Henry's (as well as Tolstoy's and Mark Twain's) death, 1910, was also the year when, after a vigorous adolescence, Modernism came to full maturity. Neither America nor Europe was as aware of this transatlantic renaissance as history would have us believe. Modernism was a secret enterprise. If O. Henry was unaware of Stieglitz's 291 Gallery, so was Ezra Pound.

O. Henry wrote with the frontier at his back. For him modernity was being able to buy a New York suit (only three years out of date) in Houston or to hear John Philip Sousa on a phonograph in Honduras. His modern architecture was not Wright's Robie house (1909) but the Flat Iron Building. He mentions Alberto Santos-Dumont twice, but not the Wright brothers. Yet for all his being, like Kipling, an avuncular presence in a new age of revolutionary nieces and nephews, he seemed to Europeans to be a radically new kind of American writer.

Cesare Pavese considered him an innovator and energizer of narrative English: "He ended sentences the way no one had ever before ended them, except Rabelais." Pavese credited him with opening a vein of new ore: *del bizzarro e del cosmopolitico,* the finding of a strange beauty in the mundane business of a city. To the Russians of the Konstruktivist movement, he was a writer whose constant wit, terseness, and irony was—like ragtime, the automobile, and pragmatism—the essence of American vitality. Boris Ejxenbaum distinguished between the sentimental, sweet stories and those of harsh frontier and city life, which he preferred, and praised them for their vigorous comic spirit and sardonic detachment. The analogy to ragtime is not far-fetched. If Washington Irving, whom O. Henry admired and thought of as an ancestor in the matter of writing about New Yorkers, wrote for the harpsichord, and Poe for the cello, then O. Henry was the Scott Joplin of prose stylists.

With two exceptions, O. Henry's stories display a remarkable family resemblance. These two, "Roads of Destiny" and "The Enchanted Kiss," are instructive in that they show how wayward O. Henry might have been far more often, and how wise he was in keeping to what he could do best. "Roads of Destiny" is set in France (the only time he tried *that*), in a romanticized past (or *that*), and is—not to put too fine a point on it—a plagiarism of Robert Louis Stevenson's "The Sire de Malétroit's Door." But it is a generous plagiarism, as O. Henry triples Stevenson's plot. It is a skillful story. When Stevenson's ground for O. Henry's variations was first published, its title was "The Sire de Malétroit's Mousetrap"—and O. Henry in a notable letter about a novel he never wrote, as well as in several stories, refers to the human condition as "a mousetrap." And the collection of Stevenson's in which it appeared in 1882 is *New Arabian Night's Entertainment*. Eventually O. Henry would evolve the metaphor of the writer as a Haroun al-Raschid moving in disguise among his subjects.

The other exception to "the O. Henry story" is a flirtation with Poe, the supernatural, and drugs. That he did not repudiate these cuckoos in the nest is evidence that he was ambitious to abandon his typical kind of story. The last, unfinished, story was, consciously or unconsciously, an echo of Ambrose Bierce's "The Incident at Owl Creek" and thus an analogue of Borges's "The Secret Miracle": in all three stories a man at the moment of death experiences a dilation of time in which he lives for a considerable while.

When O. Henry said that life is a mousetrap, he was thinking of the traps of habit and convention. He wrote several stories in which a person resolves to break free from his dull round, yet returns to it at the first opportunity. William James, a devoted reader of O. Henry, may have been influenced by him in his chapter on habit in *The Principles of Psychology*.

A more apt image than the mousetrap would be a maze or labyrinth, for O. Henry built some of his best stories ("The Higher Abdication" and "The Church with the Overshot Wheel" for example) around the possibility of finding a lost past in a maze. Luck and coincidence are very real, and credulity is taxed far more by reality than by fiction. Fiction, however, has to explain itself. The famous "O. Henry ending" is always plausible and logical. O. Henry's characters are never pawns of fate; they carry their destiny within themselves. Some—the tricksters—are aware of this and become masters in the art of making things happen. Others—the innocent and helpless—are usually lucky or wander around unharmed in the magic of their own unawareness of evil. Kidnappers are defeated by the innocence of the kidnapped ("Hostages to Momus" and "The Ransom of Red Chief"); the biter is bit. The more elaborate the plot to deceive, the more hilarious the failure.

It is not, however, the plot that the reader who has come to like O. Henry reads him for; it is the charm of his comic eye, the accuracy of his ear, and, in this day and age, the rude honesty of his moral sense. Bret Harte's "The Postmistress of Laurel Run" might well be by O. Henry. The style and plot are similar, but no one would mistake it for an O. Henry story: it is not in his idiom. It lacks the epigrams O. Henry (like Mark Twain) tucked into the narrative. Consider:

> Thrice in a lifetime may woman walk upon clouds—once when she trippeth to the altar, once when she first enters Bohemian halls [to dine with artists in Greenwich Village], the last when she marches back across her first garden with the dead hen of her neighbor in her hand.
>
> As for children, no one understands them except old maids, hunchbacks, and shepherd dogs.
>
> We may achieve climate, but weather is thrust upon us.
>
> The full moon is a witch.
>
> All of life, as we know it, moves in little, unavailing circles.
>
> Man is too thoroughly an egoist not to be also an egotist.
>
> All cities say the same thing. When they get through saying it there is an echo from Philadelphia.
>
> When a poor man finds a long-hidden silver dollar that has slipped through a rip in his vest-lining, he sounds the pleasure of life with a deeper plummet than any millionaire can hope to cast.
>
> But in time truth and science and nature will adapt themselves to art.
>
> When we begin to move in straight lines and turn sharp corners our natures begin to change. The consequence is that Nature, being more adaptive than Art, tries to conform to its sterner regulations. The result is often a rather curious product—for instance: A prize chrysanthemum, wood alcohol whiskey, a Republican Missouri, cauliflower *au gratin,* and a New Yorker.

One of the few authors O. Henry mentions in his own voice is Montaigne. He also admired Lamb and Hazlitt, and the one successful writer among his characters is an essayist. When academia began to dismiss O. Henry as a scribbler of light fiction for the semiliterate, they complained that he wrote in slang and hinted that he was vulgar. He was indeed a master of many vernaculars—of the cattle ranch, of Southerners black and white, of the Bowery—and his own prose sometimes ran to epidemics of puns (usually good, like "a peroxide Juno," which I would have to explain to my students, unless they had just read a translation of Homer with "ox-eyed Juno" in it) and to outrageous periphrasis. But look at a scene that's happening in O. Henry's own territory, written in the Naturalist manner:

> A very little boy stood upon a heap of gravel for the honor of Rum Alley. He was throwing stones at howling urchins from Devil's Row who were circling madly about the heap and pelting at him.
>
> His infantile countenance was livid with fury. His small body was writhing in the delivery of great, crimson oaths.
>
> "Run, Jimmie, run! Dey'll get yehs," screamed a retreating Rum Alley child.
>
> "Naw," responded Jimmie with a valiant roar, "dese micks can't make me run."
>
> Howls of renewed wrath went up from Devil's Row throats. Tattered gamins on the right made a furious assault on the gravel heap.

That's the opening paragraphs of Stephen Crane's *Maggie: A Girl of the Streets* (1893).

O. Henry would have found a way around *circling madly, infantile countenance, livid with fury, crimson oaths,* and *tattered gamins*. And there are more dime-novel formulae than Crane would have liked to see pointed out. Crane's style would evolve into the tense, imagistic prose of *The Red Badge* and "The Open Boat." The modernity of *Maggie* is in its beginning, with a scene of brisk action, as if it were a moving picture.

When the cinema began in the hands of Lumière, Edison, and Méliès, it had to return to the most archaic moment of theatre: the mime. O. Henry begins and ends his novel *Cabbages and Kings* with silent images. The first shows us the plot of the novel by carefully misleading us as to what's actually going on; the second is offered as "a vitagraphoscope," the kind of short film one saw at Coney Island by leaning into a viewer while turning a crank. The classical mime appeared in Greece simultaneously with New Comedy. Old Comedy, which may have developed from the raucous and gloriously obscene satyr play, was harshly satiric and *ad hominem*: Aristophanes's "The Clouds" is about Socrates and his philosophy, caricatured in broadest humor and reduced to the ridiculous.

In New Comedy the characters are all types (the Old Grouch, the Stupid Servant, the Young Lovers, the Athenian Cook, the Miser). The Greek word "character" means trademark—a potter's mark on the underside of a vase—and was used by Aristotle's student Theophrastos in his study of psychological types. The fun of types is that they are predictable, trapped, with mechanistic responses. This brilliant invention of the fifth century B.C. proved to be the most durable of the arts. It must have existed in culture as the folk art of the joke before Menander shaped it for the stage. Its twin, but lesser, art, the mime (acted at dinner parties and in city squares by a single actor taking all the parts) was a short skit. The actor had to establish in a matter of seconds that he was a rube from the sticks, or a near idiotic schoolteacher, or a portly matron trying on all the shoes at the cobbler's. In our time, the mime became the silent film (Laurel and Hardy, Buster Keaton, Chaplin), while New Comedy flourished both on the stage and in the short story. Miserable as our century is, we can still boast that for seventy years of it we had P. G. Wodehouse, the Menander *de nos jours,* and for ten years O. Henry. There have been many others, of course, but none—with the possible exception of the exotic and manic S. J. Perelman and the gentle, whimsical Thurber—whose whole art was cast in the masterfully styled puppetry of New Comedy.

Yevgeny Zamyatin saw O. Henry's stories as the art of brevity and speed proper to America. Like the country most take place in, they are democratic, optimistic, proletarian. O. Henry's stories were published in newspapers and magazines; they could be read on the subway, in restaurants, in any odd fifteen minutes.

To comedy alone is character in its original sense meaningful and necessary. Achilles is not a type, nor Hector; the weather of their minds, while rich in heroic sunlight and sweet with affections and loyalties, is unpredictable and infinitely variable. New Comedy was born as a psychological theory about minds of limited means: the young in love for the first time, people trapped by ideas and passions, or in human bondage to prejudices and greed. O. Henry is fascinated by programmed minds. In "The Duplicity of Hargraves" the stock character is a proud, boastful old Alabama gentleman living in Washington and in reduced means with his daughter. Hargraves, a young actor, duplicates him in a play about just such a character. The old gentleman sees the play and is outraged. So far we have a story that, in other prose and with different slants of light, Henry James might have written, or Chekhov. O. Henry, however, has only laid his ground. The old Alabaman is distracted from his outrage by the wholly unexpected arrival of a faithful black retainer, a child when last seen. He has become a successful farmer in "Newbraska," where he is a citizen of some prominence, and is in Washington for a Baptist convention. He has come to repay money the family gave him after the war, to start a new life in the West. The old gentleman, in tears, accepts the money; more important, his antique values, which Hargraves's play had ridiculed, are restored by the freed slave's loyalty and respect. But this black prodigy of Roman virtue is also the actor Hargraves, as only we and the daughter know. O. Henry has shown how versatility, a liberty of spirit, can dance any dance it wants to around rigidity: this mobility is the very essence of comedy.

Hence the very many stories O. Henry wrote about confidence men, together with the high comedy of confidence men gulling, and being gulled by, other confidence men. A variant of this theme is that of humble people assuming, for an evening, the status of the rich (itself a variant of the Haroun al-Raschid theme of the rich and powerful disguised as nobodies). These stories are the richer for our knowing that O. Henry himself was a man in disguise—in more ways, I suspect, than the biographers have appreciated. He kept his past to himself, even his image. He refused to play the one role in which he was famous, that of writer. In his one interview he said that he thought little of his stories, even when they had the dignity of the collected volumes. One wonders how honest he was with himself when he said that he wanted to be a serious writer, to abandon the elaborate jokes that an enormous public admired as lively and wise short stories.

The novel he planned, and never wrote, was to be about a perfectly ordinary man "caught in his mousetrap." He wanted to be as minutely realistic as a writer can be. Flaubert had the same ambition, "to write a book in which nothing happens."

Joyce fulfilled both projects in *Ulysses.* O. Henry's ideal novel remains among possibilities. Publishers call such books ghosts—projected works that never got written. (Milton's was a "Macbeth" with which he got no further than the title.) In a sense, all of O. Henry's stories add up to the unwritten novel. They cover American life at the turn of the century from the West to New York, the South and Central America—Teddy Roosevelt's geography, if you will; the Mississippi belonged to Mark Twain. In a perfect world with perfect books, we might have O. Henry's western tales illustrated by Frederic Remington and the New York tales by John Sloan and George Bellows.

Is it humility or satire that has O. Henry mention a bargain lot in a junkshop that's "Henry James's works, six talking-machine records, one pair of tennis shoes, two bottles of horse radish, and a rubber plant," all for $1.89? We can imagine William James's chuckle. We know that O. Henry bridled at being compared to Maupassant ("smutty"), but we have no information as to how he thought of himself among writers. His New York is contiguous with that of Edith Wharton, who entered doors closed to William Sydney Porter. The truth is, literary history has forgotten O. Henry's world. There is a story, "The Snow Man," that O. Henry had one Harris Merton Lyon finish for him. Lyon is Theodore Dreiser's "De Maupassant, Junior" in *Twelve Men,* a bohemian failure "who sometimes wrote like O. Henry." Of the New York literary people with whom he worked—Robert H. Davis, Richard Duffy, William Johnston, Gilman Hall—only the name of Witter Bynner has not drowned in the ocean of time. It was Bynner who, fresh out of Harvard, showed O. Henry how various stories could be fitted together to make the novel *Cabbages and Kings.*

O. Henry's literary companions were ones he never met: Robert Louis Stevenson, Kipling, Mark Twain, and the unknown writer of *The Thousand Nights and One Night.* The wonder is that their influence was so invisibly absorbed. From all of them (along with Omar Khayyam) he took the understanding that a story is a calculation of fate, independent of a philosophy or religion, and that the art of tale-telling is a high skill deriving from observation, experience, and insight into human character. He did not challenge any of the writers he admired on their own ground (except for the one Stevensonian *hommage*). Nor did he ever write an autobiographical line. All of his work is a miracle of imaginative projection.

He probably never saw the many boardinghouse rooms of the working girls that he described so convincingly. He never met a South American dictator, a New York millionaire, or a Mexican bandit. He knew one confidence man (the original of Jeff Peters). His being a registered pharmacist turns up regularly when he shows off his expertise in *materia medica* and prescriptions.

His prose style is by now historical and can be compared in energy to that of Thom Nashe or Thomas Urquhart, as you will, or to other literary vernaculars, whether Artemus Ward or Damon Runyon. It is a narrative (and expository) style of wonderful flexibility, as useful for pathos as for satire. What's most admirable in it is its constant attention to telling specifics: the comfort of a cool iron bedstead against which to press tired feet, the furniture on a summer resort in the Blue Ridge mountains, the art of cooking for cowboys on a roundup. Real history, a wise historian has said, is in novels. The age encapsulated by O. Henry is an American cultural myth. There is no erasure of history in believing in his fresh-faced freckled girls or his frank, good-natured young men (Hemingway continued them, having deleted their sense of humor) or cowpunchers as tough as whang leather and gentle as a baby. Nature allows everything. That there is one prostitute in all of O. Henry, no clergy, and no odors can be explained by the genteel tradition that policed the arts not so much as a puritan interdiction (though there was that, too) as a code of well-bred manners, of which writing was considered to be an arbiter.

O. Henry's myth addressed itself to good nature, honesty, fair play, compassion, love, and friendship. His culture demanded these of him; he was heartily willing to comply. But one has not read far into him before one realizes that he is mischievously subversive, that he admires rascals and bare-faced liars and those who have opted out of the rat race. It is the trickster who survives in a world that is legally dishonest (governments, banks, lawyers). Virtue is *virtú*: outmaneuver or be stepped on.

Twice in O. Henry artists destroy very lucrative work with which they are dissatisfied, and the hack writer is treated as a villain. Sharpshooters, safe crackers, successful revolutionaries, titled lords who can cook good grub for cowboys—skill is success in O. Henry. If he had a philosophy, it was that to be good you have to be good at something. And for something. He himself was very good at writing stories.

SUGGESTIONS FOR FURTHER READING

Books by O. Henry

Cabbages and Kings	(1904)
The Four Million	(1906)
The Trimmed Lamp	(1907)
The Voice of the City	(1908)
The Gentle Grafter	(1908)
Roads of Destiny	(1909)
Options	(1909)
Strictly Business	(1910)
Whirligigs	(1910)
Let Me Feel Your Pulse	(1910)
Sixes and Sevens	(1911)
Rolling Stones	(1912)
Waifs and Strays	(1917)

Books and Articles about O. Henry

Clarkson, Paul S., "A Decomposition of *Cabbages and Kings*," *American Literature* VII (1935), pp. 195–202.

Davis, Robert H., and Arthur B. Maurice, *The Caliph of Bagdad, Being Arabian Nights Flashes of the Life, Letters, and Work of O. Henry* (New York: D. Appleton, 1931).

Ejxenbaum, Boris M., "O. Henry and the Theory of the Short

Story," *Readings in Russian Poetics: Formalist and Structuralist Views,* edited by Ladislav Matejka and Krystyna Pomorska (Cambridge: MIT Press, 1971).

Jennings, Al, *Through the Shadows with O. Henry* (New York: The H. K. Fly Company, 1921).

Long, Eugene Hudson, *O. Henry: The Man and His Work* (New York: Russell and Russell, 1949).

O'Connor, Richard, *O. Henry: The Legendary Life of William S. Porter* (New York: Doubleday, 1970).

Smith, C. Alphonso, *O. Henry Biography* (New York: Doubleday, Page, 1916).

Zamyatin, Yevgeny, "O. Henry," *A Soviet Heretic,* edited and translated by Mirra Ginsburg (Chicago: University of Chicago Press, 1970).

Selected Stories

The Coming-Out of Maggie

Every Saturday night the Clover Leaf Social Club gave a hop in the hall of the Give and Take Athletic Association on the East Side. In order to attend one of these dances you must be a member of the Give and Take—or, if you belong to the division that starts off with the right foot in waltzing, you must work in Rhinegold's paper-box factory. Still, any Clover Leaf was privileged to escort or be escorted by an outsider to a single dance. But mostly each Give and Take brought the paper-box girl that he affected; and few strangers could boast of having shaken a foot at the regular hops.

Maggie Toole, on account of her dull eyes, broad mouth and left-handed style of footwork in the two-step, went to the dances with Anna McCarty and her "fellow." Anna and Maggie worked side by side in the factory, and were the greatest chums ever. So Anna always made Jimmy Burns take her by Maggie's house every Saturday night so that her friend could go to the dance with them.

The Give and Take Athletic Association lived up to its name. The hall of the association in Orchard Street was fitted out with muscle-making inventions. With the fibres thus builded up the members were wont to engage the police and rival social athletic organizations in joyous combat. Between these more serious occupations the Saturday night hops with the paper-box factory girls came as a refining influence and as an efficient screen. For sometimes the tip went 'round, and if you were among the elect that tiptoed up the dark back stairway you might see as neat and satisfying a little welter-weight affair to a finish as ever happened inside the ropes.

On Saturdays Rhinegold's paper-box factory closed at 3 P.M. On one such afternon Anna and Maggie walked homeward together. At Maggie's door Anna said, as usual: "Be ready at seven sharp, Mag, and Jimmy and me'll come by for you."

But what was this? Instead of the customary humble and grateful thanks from the non-escorted one there was to be perceived a high poised head, a prideful dimpling at the corners of a broad mouth, and almost a sparkle in a dull brown eye.

"Thanks, Anna," said Maggie; "but you and Jimmy needn't bother to-night. I've a gentleman friend that's coming round to escort me to the hop."

The comely Anna pounced upon her friend, shook her, chided and beseeched her. Maggie Toole catch a fellow! Plain, dear, loyal, unattractive Maggie, so sweet as a chum, so unsought for a two-step or a moonlit bench in the little park. How was it? When did it happen? Who was it?

"You'll see to-night," said Maggie, flushed with the wine of the first grapes she had gathered in Cupid's vineyard. "He's swell all right. He's two inches taller than Jimmy, and an up-to-date dresser. I'll introduce him, Anna, just as soon as we get to the hall."

Anna and Jimmy were among the first Clover Leafs to arrive that evening. Anna's eyes were brightly fixed upon the door of the hall to catch the first glimpse of her friend's "catch."

At 8:30 Miss Toole swept into the hall with her escort. Quickly her triumphant eye discovered her chum under the wing of her faithful Jimmy.

"Oh, gee!" cried Anna, "Mag ain't made a hit—oh, no! Swell fellow? well, I guess! Style? Look at 'um."

"Go as far as you like," said Jimmy, with sandpaper in his voice. "Cop him out if you want him. These new guys always win out with the push. Don't mind me. He don't squeeze all the lines, I guess. Huh!"

"Shut up, Jimmy. You know what I mean. I'm glad for Mag. First fellow she ever had. Oh, here they come."

Across the floor Maggie sailed like a coquettish yacht convoyed by a stately cruiser. And truly, her companion justified the encomiums of the faithful chum. He stood two inches taller than the average Give and Take athlete; his dark hair curled; his eyes and his teeth flashed whenever he bestowed his frequent smiles. The young men of the Clover Leaf Club pinned not their faith to the graces of person as much as they did to its prowess, its achievements in hand-to-hand conflicts, and its preservation from the legal duress that constantly menaced it. The member of the association who would bind a paper-box maiden to his conquering chariot scorned to employ Beau Brummell airs. They were not considered honorable methods of warfare. The swelling biceps, the coat straining at its buttons over the chest, the air of conscious conviction of the supereminence of the male in the cosmogony of creation, even a calm display of bow legs as subduing and enchanting agents in the gentle tourneys of Cupid—these were the approved arms and ammunition of the Clover Leaf gallants. They viewed, then, the genuflexions and alluring poses of this visitor with their chins at a new angle.

"A friend of mine, Mr. Terry O'Sullivan," was Maggie's formula of introduction. She led him around the room, presenting him to each new-arriving Clover Leaf. Almost was she pretty now, with the unique luminosity in her eyes that comes to a girl with her first suitor and a kitten with its first mouse.

"Maggie Toole's got a fellow at last," was the word that went round among the paper-box girls. "Pipe Mag's floor-walker"—thus the Give and Takes expressed their indifferent contempt.

Usually at the weekly hops Maggie kept a spot on the wall warm with her back. She felt and showed so much gratitude whenever a self-sacrificing partner invited her to dance that his pleasure was cheapened and diminished. She had even grown used to noticing Anna joggle the reluctant Jimmy with her elbow as a signal for him to invite her chum to walk over his feet through a two-step.

But to-night the pumpkin had turned to a coach and six. Terry O'Sullivan was a victorious Prince Charming, and Maggie Toole winged her first butterfly flight. And though our tropes of fairyland be mixed with those of entomology they shall not spill one drop of ambrosia from the rose-crowned melody of Maggie's one perfect night.

The girls besieged her for introduction to her "fellow." The Clover Leaf young men, after two years of blindness, suddenly perceived charms in Miss Toole. They flexed their compelling muscles before her and bespoke her for the dance.

Thus she scored; but to Terry O'Sullivan the honors of the evening fell thick and fast. He shook his curls; he smiled and went easily through the seven motions for acquiring grace in your own room before an open window ten minutes each day. He danced like a faun; he introduced manner and style and atmosphere; his words came trippingly upon his tongue, and—he waltzed twice in succession with the paper-box girl that Dempsey Donovan brought.

Dempsey was the leader of the association. He wore a dress suit, and could chin the bar twice with one hand. He was one of "Big Mike" O'Sullivan's lieutenants, and was never troubled by trouble. No cop dared to arrest him. Whenever he broke a pushcart man's head or shot a member of the Heinrick B. Sweeney Outing and Literary Association in the kneecap, an officer would drop around and say:

"The Cap'n'd like to see ye a few minutes round to the office whin ye have time, Dempsey, me boy."

But there would be sundry gentlemen there with large gold fob chains and black cigars; and somebody would tell a funny story, and then Dempsey would go back and work half an hour with the six-pound dumbbells. So, doing a tight-rope act on a wire stretched across Niagara was a safe terpsichorean performance compared with waltzing twice with Dempsey Donovan's paper-box girl. At 10 o'clock the jolly round face of "Big Mike" O'Sullivan shone at the door for five minutes upon the scene. He always looked in for five minutes, smiled at the girls and handed out real perfectos to the delighted boys.

Dempsey Donovan was at his elbow instantly, talking rapidly. "Big Mike" looked carefully at the dancers, smiled, shook his head and departed.

The music stopped. The dancers scattered to the chairs along the walls. Terry O'Sullivan, with his entrancing bow, relinquished a pretty girl in blue to her partner and started back to find Maggie. Dempsey intercepted him in the middle of the floor.

Some fine instinct that Rome must have bequeathed to us caused nearly every one to turn and look at them—there was a subtle feeling that two gladiators had met in the arena. Two or three Give and Takes with tight coat sleeves drew nearer.

"One moment, Mr. O'Sullivan," said Dempsey. "I hope you're enjoying yourself. Where did you say you lived?"

The two gladiators were well matched. Dempsey had, perhaps, ten pounds of weight to give away. The O'Sullivan had breadth and quickness. Dempsey had a glacial eye, a dominating slit of mouth, an indestructible jaw, a complexion like a belle's and the coolness of a champion. The visitor showed more fire in his contempt and less control over his conspicuous sneer. They were enemies by the law written when the rocks were molten. They were each too splendid, too mighty, too incomparable to divide pre-eminence. One only must survive.

"I live on Grand," said O'Sullivan, insolently; "and no trouble to find me at home. Where do you live?"

Dempsey ignored the question.

"You say your name's O'Sullivan," he went on. "Well, 'Big Mike' says he never saw you before."

"Lots of things he never saw," said the favorite of the hop.

"As a rule," went on Dempsey, huskily sweet, "O'Sullivans in this district know one another. You escorted one of our lady members here, and we want a chance to make good. If you've got a family tree let's see a few historical O'Sullivan buds come out on it. Or do you want us to dig it out of you by the roots?"

"Suppose you mind your own business," suggested O'Sullivan, blandly.

Dempsey's eye brightened. He held up an inspired forefinger as though a brilliant idea had struck him.

"I've got it now," he said, cordially. "It was just a little mistake. You ain't no O'Sullivan. You are a ring-tailed monkey. Excuse us for not recognizing you at first."

O'Sullivan's eye flashed. He made a quick movement, but Andy Geoghan was ready and caught his arm.

Dempsey nodded at Andy and William McMahan, the secretary of the club, and walked rapidly toward a door at the rear of the hall. Two other members of the Give and Take Association swiftly joined the little group. Terry O'Sullivan was now in the hands of the Board of Rules and Social Referees. They spoke to him briefly and softly, and conducted him out through the same door at the rear.

This movement on the part of the Clover Leaf members requires a word of elucidation. Back of the association hall was a small room rented by the club. In this room personal difficulties that arose on the ballroom floor were settled, man to man, with the weapons of nature, under the supervision of the Board. No lady could say that she had witnessed a fight at a Clover Leaf hop in several years. Its gentlemen members guaranteed that.

So easily and smoothly had Dempsey and the Board done their preliminary work that many in the hall had not noticed the checking of the fascinating O'Sullivan's social triumph. Among these was Maggie. She looked about for her escort.

"Smoke up!" said Rose Cassidy. "Wasn't you on? Demps Donovan picked a scrap with your Lizzie-boy, and they've waltzed out to the slaughter room with him. How's my hair look done up this way, Mag?"

Maggie laid a hand on the bosom of her cheese-cloth waist.

"Gone to fight with Dempsey!" she said, breathlessly. "They've got to be stopped. Dempsey Donovan can't fight him. Why, he'll—he'll kill him!"

"Ah, what do you care?" said Rosa. "Don't some of 'em fight every hop?"

But Maggie was off, darting her zig-zag way through the maze of dancers. She burst through the rear door into the dark hall and then threw her solid shoulder against the door of the room of single combat. It gave way, and in the instant that she entered her eye caught the scene—the Board standing about with open watches; Dempsey Donovan in his shirt sleeves dancing light-footed, with the wary grace of the modern pugilist, within easy reach of his adversary; Terry O'Sullivan standing with arms folded and a murderous look in his dark eyes. And without slacking the speed of her entrance she leaped forward with a scream—leaped in time to catch and hang upon the arm of O'Sullivan that was suddenly uplifted, and to whisk from it the long, bright stiletto that he had drawn from his bosom.

The knife fell and rang upon the floor. Cold steel drawn in the rooms of the Give and Take Association! Such a thing had never happened before. Every one stood motionless for a minute. Andy Geoghan kicked the stiletto with the toe of his shoe curiously, like an antiquarian who has come upon some ancient weapon unknown to his learning.

And then O'Sullivan hissed something unintelligible between his teeth. Dempsey and the Board exchanged looks. And then Dempsey looked at O'Sullivan without anger, as one looks at a stray dog, and nodded his head in the direction of the door. "The back stairs, Giuseppi," he said, briefly. "Somebody'll pitch your hat down after you."

Maggie walked up to Dempsey Donovan. There was a brilliant spot of red in her cheeks, down which slow tears were running. But she looked him bravely in the eye.

"I knew it, Dempsey," she said, as her eyes grew dull even in their tears. "I knew he was a Guinea. His name's Tony Spinelli. I hurried in when they told me you and him was scrappin'. Them Guineas always carries knives. But you don't understand, Dempsey. I never had a fellow in my life. I got tired of comin' with Anna and Jimmy every night, so I fixed it with him to call himself O'Sullivan, and brought him along. I knew there'd be nothin' doin' for him if he came as a Dago. I guess I'll resign from the club now."

Dempsey turned to Andy Geoghan.

"Chuck that cheese slicer out of the window," he said, "and tell 'em inside that Mr. O'Sullivan has had a telephone message to go down to Tammany Hall."

And then he turned back to Maggie.

"Say, Mag," he said, "I'll see you home. And how about next Saturday night? Will you come to the hop with me if I call around for you?"

It was remarkable how quickly Maggie's eyes could change from dull to a shining brown.

"With you, Dempsey?" she stammered. "Say—will a duck swim?"

A Service of Love

When one loves one's Art no service seems too hard.

That is our premise. This story shall draw a conclusion from it, and show at the same time that the premise is incorrect. That will be a new thing in logic, and a feat in story-telling somewhat older than the great wall of China.

Joe Larrabee came out of the post-oak flats of the Middle West pulsing with a genius for pictorial art. At six he drew a picture of the town pump with a prominent citizen passing it hastily. This effort was framed and hung in the drug-store window by the side of the ear of corn with an uneven number of rows. At twenty he left for New York with a flowing necktie and a capital tied up somewhat closer.

Delia Caruthers did things in six octaves so promisingly in a pine-tree village in the South that her relatives chipped in enough in her chip hat for her to go "North" and "finish." They could not see her f——, but that is our story.

Joe and Delia met in an atelier where a number of art and music students had gathered to discuss chiaroscuro, Wagner, music, Rembrandt's works, pictures, Waldteufel, wall paper, Chopin and Oolong.

Joe and Delia became enamored one of the other, or each of the other, as you please, and in a short time were married—for (see above), when one loves one's Art no service seems too hard.

Mr. and Mrs. Larrabee began housekeeping in a flat. It was a lonesome flat—something like the A sharp way down at the left-hand end of the keyboard. And they were happy; for they had their Art, and they had each other. And my advice to the rich young man would be—sell all thou hast, and give it to the poor—janitor for the privilege of living in a flat with your Art and your Delia.

Flat-dwellers shall indorse my dictum that theirs is the only true happiness. If a home is happy it cannot fit too close—let the dresser collapse and become a billiard table; let the mantel turn to a rowing machine, the escritoire to a spare bedchamber, the washstand to an upright piano; let the four walls come together, if they will, so you and your Delia are between. But if home be the other kind, let it be wide and long—enter you at the Golden Gate, hang your hat on Hatteras, your cape on Cape Horn and go out by the Labrador.

Joe was painting in the class of the great Magister—you know his fame. His fees are high; his lessons are light—his high-lights have brought him renown. Delia was studying under Rosenstock—you know his repute as a disturber of the piano keys.

They were mighty happy as long as their money lasted. So is every—but I will not be cynical. Their aims were very clear and defined. Joe was to become capable very soon of turning out pictures that old gentlemen with thin side-whiskers and thick pocketbooks would sandbag one another in his studio for the privilege of buying. Delia was to become familiar and then contemptuous with Music, so that when she saw the orchestra seats and boxes unsold she could have sore throat and lobster in a private dining-room and refuse to go on the stage.

But the best, in my opinion, was the home life in the little flat—the ardent, voluble chats after the day's study; the cozy dinners and fresh, light breakfasts; the interchange of ambitions—ambitions interwoven each with the other's or else inconsiderable—the mutual help and inspiration; and—overlook my artlessness—stuffed olives and cheese sandwiches at 11 P.M.

But after a while Art flagged. It sometimes does, even if some switchman doesn't flag it. Everything going out and nothing coming in, as the vulgarians say. Money was lacking to pay Mr. Magister and Herr Rosenstock their prices. When one loves one's Art no service seems too hard. So, Delia said she must give music lessons to keep the chafing dish bubbling.

For two or three days she went out canvassing for pupils. One evening she came home elated.

"Joe, dear," she said, gleefully, "I've a pupil. And, oh, the loveliest people. General—General A. B. Pinkney's daughter—on Seventy-first Street. Such a splendid house, Joe—you ought to see the front door! Byzantine I think you would call it. And inside! Oh, Joe, I never saw any thing like it before.

"My pupil is his daughter Clementina. I dearly love her already. She's a delicate thing—dresses always in white; and the sweetest, simplest manners! Only eighteen years old. I'm to give three lessons a week; and, just think, Joel, $5 a lesson. I don't mind it a bit; for when I get two or three more pupils I can resume my lessons with Herr Rosenstock. Now, smooth out that wrinkle between your brows, dear, and let's have a nice supper."

"That's all right for you, Dele," said Joe, attacking a can of peas with a carving knife and a hatchet, "but how about me? Do you think I'm going to let you hustle for wages while I philander in the regions of high art? Not by the bones of Benvenuto Cellini! I guess I can sell papers or lay cobblestones, and bring in a dollar or two."

Delia came and hung about his neck.

"Joe, dear, you are silly. You must keep on at your studies. It is not as if I had quit my music and gone to work at something else. While I teach I learn. I am always with my music. And we can live as happily as millionaires on $15 a week. You mustn't think of leaving Mr. Magister."

"All right," said Joe, reaching for the blue scalloped vegetable dish. "But I hate for you to be giving lessons. It isn't Art. But you're a trump and a dear to do it."

"When one loves one's Art no service seems too hard," said Delia.

"Magister praised the sky in that sketch I made in the park," said Joe. "And Tinkle gave me permission to hang two of them in his window. I may sell one if the right kind of a moneyed idiot sees them."

"I'm sure you will," said Delia, sweetly. "And now let's be thankful for Gen. Pinkney and this veal roast."

During all of the next week the Larrabees had an early breakfast. Joe was enthusiastic about some morning-effect sketches he was doing in Central Park, and Delia packed him off breakfasted, coddled, praised and kissed at 7 o'clock. Art is an engaging mistress. It was most times 7 o'clock when he returned in the evening.

At the end of the week Delia, sweetly proud but languid, triumphantly tossed three five-dollar bills on the 8 × 10 (inches) centre table of the 8 × 10 (feet) flat parlor.

"Sometimes," she said, a little wearily, "Clementina tries me. I'm afraid she doesn't practice enough, and I have to tell her the same things so often. And then she always dresses entirely in white, and that does get monotonous. But Gen. Pinkney is the dearest old man! I wish you could know him, Joe. He comes in sometimes when I am with Clementina at the piano—he is a widower, you know—and stands there pulling his white goatee. 'And how are the semiquavers and the demisemiquavers progressing?' he always asks.

"I wish you could see the wainscoting in that drawing room, Joe! And those Astrakhan rug portières. And Clementina has such a funny little cough. I hope she is stronger than she looks. Oh, I really am getting attached to her, she is so gentle and high bred. Gen. Pinkney's brother was once Minister to Bolivia."

And then Joe, with the air of Monte Cristo, drew forth a ten, a five, a two and a one—all legal tender notes—and laid them beside Delia's earnings.

"Sold that watercolor of the obelisk to a man from Peoria," he announced, overwhelmingly.

"Don't joke with me," said Delia—"not from Peoria!"

"All the way. I wish you could see him, Dele. Fat man with a woolen muffler and a quill toothpick. He saw the sketch in Tinkle's window and thought it was a windmill at first. He was game, though, and bought it anyhow. He ordered another—an oil sketch of the Lackawanna freight depot—to take back with him. Music lessons! Oh, I guess Art is still in it."

"I'm so glad you've kept on," said Delia, heartily. "You're bound to win, dear. Thirty-three dollars! We never had so much to spend before. We'll have oysters to-night."

"And filet mignon with champignons," said Joe. "Where is the olive fork?"

On the next Saturday evening Joe reached home first. He spread his $18 on the parlor table and washed what seemed to be a great deal of dark paint from his hands.

Half an hour later Delia arrived, her right hand tied up in a shapeless bundle of wraps and bandages.

"How is this?" asked Joe after the usual greetings. Delia laughed, but not very joyously.

"Clementina," she explained, "insisted upon a Welsh rabbit after her lesson. She is such a queer girl. Welsh rabbits at 5 in the afternoon. The General was there. You should have seen him run for the chafing dish, Joe, just as if there wasn't a servant in the house. I know Clementina isn't in good health; she is so nervous. In serving the rabbit she spilled a great lot of it, boiling hot, over my hand and wrist. It hurt awfully, Joe. And the dear girl was so sorry! But Gen. Pinkney!—

Joe, that old man nearly went distracted. He rushed downstairs and sent somebody—they said the furnace man or somebody in the basement—out to a drug store for some oil and things to bind it up with. It doesn't hurt so much now."

"What's this?" asked Joe, taking the hand tenderly and pulling at some white strands beneath the bandages.

"It's something soft," said Delia, "that had oil on it. Oh, Joe, did you sell another sketch?" She had seen the money on the table.

"Did I?" said Joe; "just ask the man from Peoria. He got his depot to-day, and he isn't sure but he thinks he wants another parkscape and a view on the Hudson. What time this afternoon did you burn your hand, Dele?"

"Five o'clock, I think," said Dele, plaintively. "The iron—I mean the rabbit came off the fire about that time. You ought to have seen Gen. Pinkney, Joe, when—"

"Sit down here a moment, Dele," said Joe. He drew her to the couch, sat beside her and put his arm across her shoulders.

"What have you been doing for the last two weeks, Dele?" he asked.

She braved it for a moment or two with an eye full of love and stubbornness, and murmured a phrase or two vaguely of Gen. Pinkney; but at length down went her head and out came the truth and tears.

"I couldn't get any pupils," she confessed. "And I couldn't bear to have you give up your lessons; and I got a place ironing shirts in that big Twenty-fourth Street laundry. And I think I did very well to make up both General Pinkney and Clementina, don't you, Joe? And when a girl in the laundry set down a hot iron on my hand this afternoon I was all the way home making up that story about the Welsh rabbit. You're not angry, are you, Joe? And if I hadn't got the work you mightn't have sold your sketches to that man from Peoria."

"He wasn't from Peoria," said Joe, slowly.

"Well, it doesn't matter where he was from. How clever you are, Joe—and—kiss me, Joe—and what made you ever suspect that I wasn't giving music lessons to Clementina?"

"I didn't," said Joe, "until to-night. And I wouldn't have then, only I sent up this cotton waste and oil from the engine-room this afternoon for a girl upstairs who had her hand burned with a smoothing-iron. I've been firing the engine in that laundry for the last two weeks."

"And then you didn't——"

"My purchaser from Peoria," said Joe, "and Gen. Pinkney are both creations of the same art—but you wouldn't call it either painting or music."

And then they both laughed, and Joe began:

"When one loves one's Art no service seems——"

But Delia stopped him with her hand on his lips. "No," she said—"just 'When one loves.' "

Between Rounds

The May moon shone bright upon the private boarding-house of Mrs. Murphy. By reference to the almanac a large amount of territory will be discovered upon which its rays also fell. Spring was in its heyday, with hay fever soon to follow. The parks were green with new leaves and buyers for the Western and Southern trade. Flowers and summer-resort agents were blowing; the air and answers to Lawson were growing milder; hand-organs, fountains and pinochle were playing everywhere.

The windows of Mrs. Murphy's boarding-house were open. A group of boarders were seated on the high stoop upon round, flat mats like German pancakes.

In one of the second-floor front windows Mrs. McCaskey awaited her husband. Supper was cooling on the table. Its heat went into Mrs. McCaskey.

At nine McCaskey came. He carried his coat on his arm and his pipe in his teeth; and he apologized for disturbing the boarders on the steps as he selected spots of stone between them on which to set his size 9, width Ds.

As he opened the door of his room he received a surprise. Instead of the usual stove-lid or potato-masher for him to dodge, came only words.

Mr. McCaskey reckoned that the benign May moon had softened the breast of his spouse.

"I heard ye," same the oral substitutes for kitchenware. "Ye can apollygize to riff-raff of the streets for settin' yer unhandy feet on the tails of their frocks, but ye'd walk on the neck of yer wife the length of a clothesline without so much as a 'Kiss me fut,' and I'm sure it's that long from rubberin' out the windy for ye and the victuals cold such as there's money to buy after drinkin' up yer wages at Gallegher's every Saturday evenin', and the gas man here twice to-day for his."

"Woman," said Mr. McCaskey, dashing his coat and hat upon a chair, "the noise of ye is an insult to me appetite. When ye run down politeness ye take the mortar from between the bricks of the foundations of society. 'Tis no more than exercisin' the acrimony of a gentleman when we ask the dissent of ladies blockin' the way for steppin' between them. Will ye bring the pig's face of ye out of the windy and see to the food?"

Mrs. McCaskey arose heavily and went to the stove. There was something in her manner that warned Mr. McCaskey. When the corners of her mouth went down suddenly like a barometer it usually foretold a fall of crockery and tinware.

"Pig's face, is it?" said Mrs. McCaskey, and hurled a stewpan full of bacon and turnips at her lord.

Mr. McCaskey was no novice at repartee. He knew what should follow the entrée. On the table was a roast sirloin of pork, garnished with shamrocks. He retorted with this, and drew the appropriate return of a bread pudding in an earthen dish. A hunk of Swiss cheese accurately thrown by her husband struck Mrs. McCaskey below one eye. When she replied with a well-aimed coffee-pot full of a hot, black, semi-fragrant liquid the battle, according to courses, should have ended.

But Mr. McCaskey was no 50-cent *table d'hôter.* Let cheap Bohemians consider coffee the end, if they would. Let them make that *faux pas.* He was foxier still. Finger-bowls were not beyond the compass of his experience. They were not to be had in the Pension Murphy; but their equivalent was at hand. Triumphantly he sent the granite-ware wash-basin at the head of his matrimonial adversary. Mrs. McCaskey dodged in time. She reached for a flatiron, with which, as a sort of cordial, she hoped to bring the gastronomical duel to a close. But a loud, wailing scream downstairs caused both her and Mr. McCaskey to pause in a sort of involuntary armistice.

On the sidewalk at the corner of the house Policeman Cleary was standing with one ear upturned, listening to the crash of household utensils.

" 'Tis Jawn McCaskey and his missis at it again," meditated the policeman. "I wonder shall I go up and stop the row. I will not. Married folks they are: and few pleasures they have. 'Twill not last long. Sure, they'll have to borrow more dishes to keep it up with."

And just then came the loud scream below stairs, betokening fear or dire extremity. " 'Tis probably the cat," said Policeman Cleary, and walked hastily in the other direction.

The boarders on the steps were fluttered. Mr. Toomey, an insurance solicitor by birth and an investigator by profession, went inside to analyze the scream. He returned with the news that Mrs. Murphy's little boy, Mike, was lost. Following the messenger, out bounced Mrs. Murphy—two hundred pounds in tears and hysterics, clutching the air and howling to the sky for the loss of thirty pounds of freckles and mischief. Bathos, truly; but Mr. Toomey sat down at the side of Miss Purdy, millinery, and their hands came together in sympathy. The two old maids, Misses Walsh, who complained every day about the noise in the halls, inquired immediately if anybody had looked behind the clock.

Major Griggs, who sat by his fat wife on the top step, arose and buttoned his coat. "The little one lost?" he exclaimed. "I will scour the city." His wife never allowed him out after dark. But now she said: "Go, Ludovic!" in a baritone voice. "Whoever can look upon that mother's grief without springing to her relief has a heart of stone." "Give me some thirty or—sixty cents, my love," said the Major. "Lost children sometimes stray far. I may need car-fares."

Old man Denny, hall room, fourth floor back, who sat on the lowest step, trying to read a paper by the street lamp, turned over a page to follow up the article about the carpenter's strike. Mrs. Murphy shrieked to the moon: "Oh, ar-r-Mike, f'r Gawd's sake, where is me little bit av a boy?"

"When'd ye see him last?" asked old man Denny, with one eye on the report of the Building Trades League.

"Oh," wailed Mrs. Murphy, " 'twas yisterday, or maybe four hours ago! I dunno. But it's lost he is, me little boy Mike. He was playin' on the sidewalk only this mornin'—or was it Wednesday? I'm that busy with work, 'tis hard to keep up with dates. But I've looked the house over from top to cellar, and it's gone he is. Oh, for the love av Hiven——"

Silent, grim, colossal, the big city has ever stood against its revilers. They call it hard as iron; they say that no pulse of pity beats in its bosom; they compare its streets with lonely forests and deserts of lava. But beneath the hard crust of the lobster is found a delectable and luscious food. Perhaps a different simile would have been wiser. Still, nobody should take offence. We would call no one a lobster without good and sufficient claws.

No calamity so touches the common heart of humanity as does the straying of a little child. Their feet are so uncertain and feeble; the ways are so steep and strange.

Major Griggs hurried down to the corner, and up the avenue into Billy's place. "Gimme a rye-high," he said to the servitor. "Haven't seen a bow-legged, dirty-faced little devil of a six-year-old lost kid around here anywhere, have you?"

Mr. Toomey retained Miss Purdy's hand on the steps. "Think of that dear dear little babe," said Miss Purdy, "lost from his mother's side—perhaps already fallen beneath the iron hoofs of galloping steeds—oh, isn't it dreadful?"

"Ain't that right?" agreed Mr. Toomey, squeezing her hand. "Say I start out and help look for um!"

"Perhaps," said Miss Purdy, "you should. But, oh, Mr. Toomey, you are so dashing—so reckless—suppose in your enthusiasm some accident should befall you, then what——"

Old man Denny read on about the arbitration agreement, with one finger on the lines.

In the second floor front Mr. and Mrs. McCaskey came to the window to recover their second wind. Mr. McCaskey was scooping turnips out of his vest with a crooked forefinger, and his lady was wiping an eye that the salt of the roast pork had not benefited. They heard the outcry below, and thrust their heads out of the window.

" 'Tis little Mike is lost," said Mrs. McCaskey, in a hushed voice, "the beautiful, little, trouble-making angel of a gossoon!"

"The bit of a boy mislaid?" said Mr. McCaskey, leaning out of the window. "Why, now, that's bad enough, entirely. The childer, they be different. If 'twas a woman I'd be willin', for they leave peace behind 'em when they go."

Disregarding the thrust, Mrs. McCaskey caught her husband's arm.

"Jawn," she said, sentimentally, "Missis Murphy's little bye is lost. 'Tis a great city for losing little boys. Six years old he was. Jawn, 'tis the same age our little bye would have been if we had had one six years ago."

"We never did," said Mr. McCaskey, lingering with the fact.

"But if we had, Jawn, think what sorrow would be in our hearts this night, with our little Phelan run away and stolen in the city nowheres at all."

"Ye talk foolishness," said Mr. McCaskey. " 'Tis Pat he would be named, after me old father in Cantrim."

"Ye lie!" said Mrs. McCaskey, without anger. "Me brother was worth tin dozen bog-trotting McCaskeys. After him would the bye be named." She leaned over the window-sill and looked down at the hurrying and bustle below.

"Jawn," said Mrs. McCaskey, softly, "I'm sorry I was hasty wid ye."

" 'Twas hasty puddin', as ye say," said her husband, "and hurry-up turnips and get-a-move-on-ye coffee. "Twas what ye would call a quick lunch, all right, and tell no lie."

Mrs. McCaskey slipped her arm inside her husband's and took his rough hand in hers.

"Listen at the cryin' of poor Mrs. Murphy," she said. " 'Tis an awful thing for a bit of a bye to be lost in this great big city. If 'twas our little Phelan, Jawn, I'd be breakin' me heart."

Awkwardly Mr. McCaskey withdrew his hand. But he laid it around the nearing shoulder of his wife.

" 'Tis foolishness, of course," said he, roughly, "but I'd be cut up some meself if our little—Pat was kidnapped or anything. But there never was any children for us. Sometimes I've been ugly and hard with ye, Judy. Forget it."

They leaned together, and looked down at the heart-drama being acted below.

Long they sat thus. People surged along the sidewalk, crowding, questioning, filling the air with rumors, and inconsequent surmises. Mrs. Murphy plowed back and forth in their midst, like a soft mountain down which plunged an audible cataract of tears. Couriers came and went.

Loud voices and a renewed uproar were raised in front of the boarding-house.

"What's up now, Judy?" asked Mr. McCaskey.

" 'Tis Missis Murphy's voice," said Mrs. McCaskey, harking. "She says she's after finding little Mike asleep behind the roll of linoleum under the bed in her room."

Mr. McCaskey laughed loudly.

"That's yer Phelan," he shouted, sardonically. "Divil a bit would a Pat have done that trick. If the bye we never had is strayed and stole, by the powers, call him Phelan, and see him hide out under the bed like a mangy pup."

Mrs. McCaskey arose heavily, and went toward the dish closet, with the corners of her mouth drawn down.

Policeman Cleary came back around the corner as the crowd dispersed. Surprised, he upturned an ear toward the McCaskey apartment, where the crash of irons and chinaware and the ring of hurled kitchen utensils seemed as loud as before. Policeman Cleary took out his timepiece.

"By the deported snakes!" he exclaimed. "Jawn McCaskey and his lady have been fightin' for an hour and a quarter by the watch. The missis could give him forty pounds weight. Strength to his arm."

Policeman Cleary strolled back around the corner.

Old man Denny folded his paper and hurried up the steps just as Mrs. Murphy was about to lock the door for the night.

An Unfinished Story

We no longer groan and heap ashes upon our heads when the flames of Tophet are mentioned. For, even the preachers have begun to tell us that God is radium, or ether or some scientific compound, and that the worst we wicked ones may expect is a chemical reaction. This is a pleasing hypothesis; but there lingers yet some of the old, goodly terror of orthodoxy.

There are but two subjects upon which one may discourse with a free imagination, and without the possibility of being controverted. You may talk of your dreams; and you may tell what you heard a parrot say. Both Morpheus and the bird are incompetent witnesses; and your listener dare not attack your recital. The baseless fabric of a vision, then, shall furnish my theme—chosen with apologies and regrets instead of the more limited field of pretty Polly's small talk.

I had a dream that was so far removed from the higher criticism that it had to do with the ancient, respectable, and lamented bar-of-judgment theory.

Gabriel had played his trump; and those of us who could not follow suit were arraigned for examination. I noticed at one side a gathering of professional bondsmen in solemn black and collars that buttoned behind; but it seemed there was some trouble about their real estate titles; and they did not appear to be getting any of us out.

A fly cop—an angel policeman—flew over to me and took me by the left wing. Near at hand was a group of very prosperous-looking spirits arraigned for judgment.

"Do you belong with that bunch?" the policeman asked.

"Who are they?" was my answer.

"Why," said he, "they are——"

But this irrelevant stuff is taking up space that the story should occupy.

Dulcie worked in a department store. She sold Hamburg edging, or stuffed peppers, or automobiles, or other little trinkets such as they keep in department stores. Of what she earned, Dulcie received six dollars per week. The remainder was credited to her and debited to somebody else's account in the ledger kept by G—— Oh, primal energy, you say, Reverend Doctor—— Well, then, in the Ledger of Primal Energy.

During her first year in the store, Dulcie was paid five dollars per week. It would be instructive to know how she lived on that amount. Don't care? Very well; probably you are interested in larger amounts. Six dollars is a larger amount. I will tell you how she lived on six dollars per week.

One afternoon at six, when Dulcie was sticking her hat pin within an eighth of an inch of her *medulla oblongata,* she said to her chum, Sadie—the girl that waits on you with her left side:

"Say, Sade, I made a date for dinner this evening with Piggy."

"You never did!" exclaimed Sadie, admiringly. "Well, ain't you the lucky one? Piggy's an awful swell; and he always takes a girl to swell places. He took Blanche up to the Hoffman House one evening, where they have swell music, and you see a lot of swells. You'll have a swell time, Dulce."

Dulcie hurried homeward. Her eyes were shining, and her cheeks showed the delicate pink of life's—real life's—approaching dawn. It was Friday; and she had fifty cents left of her week's wages.

The streets were filled with the rush-hour floods of people. The electric lights of Broadway were glowing—calling moths from miles, from leagues, from hundreds of leagues out of darkness around to come in and attend the singeing school. Men in accurate clothes, with faces like those carved on cherry stones by the old salts in sailors' homes, turned and stared at Dulcie as she sped, unheeding, past them. Manhattan, the night-blooming cereus, was beginning to unfold its dead-white, heavy-odored petals.

Dulcie stopped in a store where goods were cheap and bought an imitation lace collar with her fifty cents. That money was to have been spent otherwise—fifteen cents for supper, ten cents for breakfast, ten cents for lunch. Another dime was to be added to her small store of savings; and five cents was to be squandered for licorice drops—the kind that made your cheek look like the toothache, and last as long. The licorice was an extravagance—almost a carouse—but what is life without pleasures?

Dulcie lived in a furnished room. There is this difference between a furnished room and a boarding-house. In a furnished room, other people do not know it when you go hungry.

Dulcie went up to her room—the third-floor-back in a West Side brownstone-front. She lit the gas. Scientists tell us that the diamond is the hardest substance known. Their mistake. Landladies know of a compound beside which the diamond is as putty. They pack it in the tips of gas-burners; and one may stand on a chair and dig at it in vain until one's fingers are pink and bruised. A hairpin will not remove it; therefore let us call it immovable.

So Dulcie lit the gas. In its one-fourth-candle-power glow we will observe the room.

Couch-bed, dresser, table, washstand, chair—of this much the landlady was guilty. The rest was Dulcie's. On the dresser were her treasures—a gilt china vase presented to her by Sadie, a calendar issued by a pickle works, a book on the divination of dreams, some rice powder in a glass dish, and a cluster of artificial cherries tied with a pink ribbon.

Against the wrinkly mirror stood pictures of General Kitchener, William Muldoon, the Duchess of Marlborough, and Benvenuto Cellini. Against one wall was a plaster of Paris plaque of an O'Callahan in a Roman helmet. Near it was a violent oleograph of a lemon-colored child assaulting an inflammatory butterfly. This was Dulcie's final judgment in art; but it had never been upset. Her rest had never been disturbed by whispers of stolen copes; no critic had elevated his eyebrows at her infantile entomologist.

Piggy was to call for her at seven. While she swiftly makes ready, let us discreetly face the other way and gossip.

For the room, Dulcie paid two dollars per week. On week-days her breakfast cost ten cents; she made coffee and cooked an egg over the gaslight while she was dressing. On Sunday mornings she feasted royally on veal chops and pineapple fritters at "Billy's" restaurant, at a cost of twenty-five cents—and tipped the waitress ten cents. New York presents so many temptations for one to run into extravagance. She had her lunches in the department-store restaurant at a cost of sixty cents for the week; dinners were $1.05. The evening papers—show me a New Yorker going without his daily paper!—came to six cents; and two Sunday papers—one for the personal column and the other to read—were ten cents. The total amounts to $4.76. Now, one has to buy clothes, and——

I give it up. I hear of wonderful bargains in fabrics, and of miracles performed with needle and thread; but I am in doubt. I hold my pen poised in vain when I would add to Dulcie's life some of those joys that belong to woman by virtue of all the unwritten, sacred, natural, inactive ordinances of the equity of heaven. Twice she had been to Coney Island and had ridden the hobby-horses. 'Tis a weary thing to count your pleasures by summers instead of by hours.

Piggy needs but a word. When the girls named him, an undeserving stigma was cast upon the noble family of swine. The words-of-three-letters lesson in the old blue spelling book begins with Piggy's biography. He was fat; he had the soul of a rat, the habits of a bat, and the magnanimity of a cat. . . . He wore expensive clothes; and was a connoisseur in starvation. He could look at a shop-girl and tell you to an hour how long it had been since she had eaten anything more nourishing than marshmallows and tea. He hung about the shopping districts, and prowled around in department stores with his invitations to dinner. Men who escort dogs upon the streets at the end of a string look down upon him. He is a type; I can dwell upon him no longer; my pen is not the kind intended for him; I am no carpenter.

At ten minutes to seven Dulcie was ready. She looked at herself in the wrinkly mirror. The reflection was satisfactory. The dark blue dress, fitting without a wrinkle, the hat with its jaunty black feather, the but-slightly-soiled gloves—all representing self-denial, even of food itself—were vastly becoming.

Dulcie forgot everything else for a moment except that she was beautiful, and that life was about to lift a corner of its mysterious veil for her to observe its wonders. No gentleman had ever asked her out before. Now she was going for a brief moment into the glitter and exalted show.

The girls said that Piggy was a "spender." There would be a grand dinner, and music, and splendidly dressed ladies to look at and things to eat that strangely twisted the girls' laws when they tried to tell about them. No doubt she would be asked out again.

There was a blue pongee suit in a window that she knew—by saving twenty cents a week instead of ten in—let's see—— Oh, it would run into years! But there was a second-hand store in Seventh Avenue where——

Somebody knocked at the door. Dulcie opened it. The landlady stood there with a spurious smile, sniffing for cooking by stolen gas.

"A gentleman's downstairs to see you," she said. "Name is Mr. Wiggins."

By such epithet was Piggy known to unfortunate ones who had to take him seriously.

Dulcie turned to the dresser to get her handkerchief; and then she stopped still, and bit her underlip hard. While looking in her mirror she had seen fairyland and herself, a princess, just awakening from a long slumber. She had forgotten one that was watching her with sad, beautiful, stern eyes—the only one there was to approve or condemn what she did. Straight and slender and tall, with a look of sorrowful reproach on his handsome, melancholy face, General Kitchener fixed his wonderful eyes on her out of his gilt photograph frame on the dresser.

Dulcie turned like an automatic doll to the landlady.

"Tell him I can't go," she said, dully. "Tell him I'm sick, or something. Tell him I'm not going out."

After the door was closed and locked, Dulcie fell upon her bed, crushing her black tip, and cried for ten minutes. General Kitchener was her only friend. He was Dulcie's ideal of a gallant knight. He looked as if he might have a secret sorrow, and his wonderful moustache was a dream, and she was a little afraid of that stern yet tender look in his eyes. She used to have little fancies that he would call at the house sometime, and ask for her, with his sword clanking against his high boots. Once, when a boy was rattling a piece of chain against a lamp post she had opened the window and looked out. But there was no use. She knew that General Kitchener was away over in Japan, leading his army against the savage Turks; and he would never step out of his gilt frame for her. Yet one look from him had vanquished Piggy that night. Yes, for that night.

When her cry was over Dulcie got up and took off her best dress, and put on her old blue kimono. She wanted no dinner. She sang two verses of "Sammy." Then she became intensely interested in a little red speck on the side of her nose. And after that was attended to, she drew up a chair to the rickety table, and told her fortune with an old deck of cards.

"The horrid, impudent thing!" she said aloud. "And I never gave him a word or a look to make him think it!"

At nine o'clock Dulcie took a tin box of crackers and a little pot of raspberry jam out of her trunk and had a feast. She offered General Kitchener some jam on a cracker; but he only looked at her as the sphinx would have looked at a butterfly—if there are butterflies in the desert.

"Don't eat if you don't want to," said Dulcie. "And don't put on so many airs and scold so with your eyes. I wonder if you'd be so superior and snippy if you had to live on six dollars a week."

It was not a good sign for Dulcie to be rude to General Kitchener. And then she turned Benvenuto Cellini face downward with a severe gesture. But that was not inexcusable; for she had always thought he was Henry VIII, and she did not approve of him.

At half-past nine Dulcie took a last look at the pictures on the dresser, turned out the light and skipped into bed. It's an awful thing to go to bed with a good-night look at General Kitchener, William Muldoon, the Duchess of Marlborough, and Benvenuto Cellini.

This story doesn't really get anywhere at all. The rest of it comes later—sometime when Piggy asks Dulcie again to dine with him, and she is feeling lonelier than usual, and General Kitchener happens to be looking the other way; and then——

As I said before, I dreamed that I was standing near a crowd of prosperous-looking angels, and a policeman took me by the wing and asked if I belonged with them.

"Who are they?" I asked.

"Why," said he, "they are the men who hired working-girls, and paid 'em five or six dollars a week to live on. Are you one of the bunch?"

"Not on your immortality," said I. "I'm only a fellow that set fire to an orphan asylum, and murdered a blind man for his pennies."

After Twenty Years

The policeman on the beat moved up the avenue impressively. The impressiveness was habitual and not for show, for spectators were few. The time was barely 10 o'clock at night, but chilly gusts of wind with a taste of rain in them had well nigh depeopled the streets.

Trying doors as he went, twirling his club with many intricate and artful movements, turning now and then to cast his watchful eye adown the pacific thoroughfare, the officer, with his stalwart form and slight swagger, made a fine picture of a guardian of the peace.

The vicinity was one that kept early hours. Now and then you might see the lights of a cigar store or of an all-night lunch counter; but the majority of the doors belonged to business places that had long since been closed.

When about midway of a certain block the policeman walked up to him the man spoke up quickly.

"It's all right, officer," he said, reassuringly. "I'm just waiting for a friend. It's an appointment made twenty years ago. Sounds a little funny to you, doesn't it? Well, I'll explain if you'd like to make certain it's all straight. About that long ago there used to be a restaurant where this store stands—'Big Joe' Brady's restaurant."

"Until five years ago," said the policeman. "It was torn down then."

The man in the doorway struck a match and lit his cigar. The light showed a pale, square-jawed face with keen eyes, and a little white scar near his right eyebrow. His scarfpin was a large diamond, oddly set.

"Twenty years ago to-night," said the man, "I dined here at 'Big Joe' Brady's with Jimmy Wells, my best chum, and the finest chap in the world. He and I were raised here in New York, just like two brothers, together. I was eighteen and Jimmy was twenty. The next morning I was to start for the West to make my fortune. You couldn't have dragged Jimmy out of New York; he thought it was the only place on earth. Well, we agreed that night that we would meet here again exactly twenty years from that date and time, no matter what our conditions might be or from what distance we might have to come. We figured that in twenty years each of us ought to have our destiny worked out and our fortunes made, whatever they were going to be."

"It sounds pretty interesting," said the policeman. "Rather a long time between meets, though, it seems to me. Haven't you heard from your friend since you left?"

"Well, yes, for a time we corresponded," said the other. "But after a year or two we lost track of each other. You see, the West is a pretty big proposition, and I kept hustling around over it pretty lively. But I know Jimmy will meet me here if he's alive, for he always was the truest, stanchest old chap in the world. He'll never forget. I came a thousand miles to stand in this door to-night, and it's worth it if my old partner turns up."

The waiting man pulled out a handsome watch, the lids of it set with small diamonds.

"Three minutes to ten," he announced. "It was exactly ten o'clock when we parted here at the restaurant door."

"Did pretty well out West, didn't you?" asked the policeman.

"You bet! I hope Jimmy has done half as well. He was a kind of plodder, though, good fellow as he was. I've had to compete with some of the sharpest wits going to get my pile. A man gets in a groove in New York. It takes the West to put a razor-edge on him."

The policeman twirled his club and took a step or two.

"I'll be on my way. Hope your friend comes around all right. Going to call time on him sharp?"

"I should say not!" said the other. "I'll give him half an hour at least. If Jimmy is alive on earth he'll be here by that time. So long, officer."

"Good-night, sir," said the policeman, passing on along his beat, trying doors as he went.

There was now a fine, cold drizzle falling, and the wind had risen from its uncertain puffs into a steady blow. The few foot passengers astir in that quarter hurried dismally and silently along with coat collars turned high and pocketed hands. And in the door of the hardware store the man who had come a thousand miles to fill an appointment, uncertain almost to absurdity, with the friend of his youth, smoked his cigar and waited.

About twenty minutes he waited, and then a tall man in a long overcoat, with collar turned up to his ears, hurried across from the opposite side of the street. He went directly to the waiting man.

"Is that you, Bob?" he asked, doubtfully.

"Is that you, Jimmy Wells?" cried the man in the door.

"Bless my heart!" exclaimed the new arrival, grasping both the other's hands with his own. "It's Bob, sure as fate. I was certain I'd find you here if you were still in existence. Well, well, well!—twenty years is a long time. The old restaurant's gone, Bob; I wish it had lasted, so we could have had another dinner there. How has the West treated you, old man?"

"Bully; it has given me everything I asked it for. You've changed lots, Jimmy. I never thought you were so tall by two or three inches."

"Oh, I grew a bit after I was twenty."

"Doing well in New York, Jimmy?"

"Moderately. I have a position in one of the city departments. Come on, Bob; we'll go around to a place I know of, and have a good long talk about old times."

The two men started up the street, arm in arm. The man from the

West, his egotism enlarged by success, was beginning to outline the history of his career. The other, submerged in his overcoat, listened with interest.

At the corner stood a drug store, brilliant with electric lights. When they came into this glare each of them turned simultaneously to gaze upon the other's face.

The man from the West stopped suddenly and released his arm.

"You're not Jimmy Wells," he snapped. "Twenty years is a long time, but not long enough to change a man's nose from a Roman to a pug."

"It sometimes changes a good man into a bad one," said the tall man. "You've been under arrest for ten minutes, 'Silky' Bob. Chicago thinks you may have dropped over our way and wires us she wants to have a chat with you. Going quietly, are you? That's sensible. Now, before we go to the station here's a note I was asked to hand to you. You may read it here at the window. It's from Patrolman Wells."

The man from the West unfolded the little piece of paper handed him. His hand was steady when he began to read, but it trembled a little by the time he had finished. The note was rather short.

> Bob: I was at the appointed place on time. When you struck the match to light your cigar I saw it was the face of the man wanted in Chicago. Somehow I couldn't do it myself, so I went around and got a plain clothes man to do the job.
>
> Jimmy

By Courier

It was neither the season nor the hour when the Park had frequenters; and it is likely that the young lady, who was seated on one of the benches at the side of the walk, had merely obeyed a sudden impulse to sit for a while and enjoy a foretaste of coming Spring.

She rested there, pensive and still. A certain melancholy that touched her countenance must have been of recent birth, for it had not yet altered the fine and youthful contours of her cheek, nor subdued the arch though resolute curve of her lips.

A tall young man came striding through the park along the path near which she sat. Behind him tagged a boy carrying a suit-case. At sight of the young lady, the man's face changed to red and back to pale again. He watched her countenance as he drew nearer, with hope and anxiety mingled on his own. He passed within a few yards of her, but he saw no evidence that she was aware of his presence or existence.

Some fifty yards further on he suddenly stopped and sat on a bench at one side. The boy dropped the suit-case and stared at him with wondering, shrewd eyes. The young man took out his handkerchief and wiped his brow. It was a good handkerchief, a good brow, and the young man was good to look at. He said to the boy:

"I want you to take a message to that young lady on that bench. Tell her I am on my way to the station, to leave for San Francisco, where I shall join that Alaska moose-hunting expedition. Tell her that, since she has commanded me neither to speak nor to write to her, I take this means of making one last appeal to her sense of justice, for the sake of what has been. Tell her that to condemn and discard one who has not deserved such treatment, without giving him her reasons or a chance to explain is contrary to her nature as I believe it to be. Tell her that I have thus, to a certain degree, disobeyed her injunctions, in the hope that she may yet be inclined to see justice done. Go, and tell her that."

The young man dropped a half-dollar into the boy's hand. The boy looked at him for a moment with bright, canny eyes out of a dirty, intelligent face and then set off at a run. He approached the lady on the bench a little doubtfully, but unembarrassed. He touched the brim of an old plaid bicycle cap perched on the back of his head. The lady looked at him coolly, without prejudice or favor.

"Lady," he said, "dat gent on de oder bench sent yer a song and dance by me. If yer don't know de guy, and he's tryin' to do de Johnny act, say de word, and I'll call a cop in t'ree minutes. If yer does know him, and he's on de square, w'y I'll spiel yer de bunch of hot air he sent yer."

The young lady betrayed a faint interest.

"A song and dance!" she said, in a deliberate, sweet voice that semed to clothe her words in a diaphanous garment of impalpable irony. "A new idea—in the troubadour line, I suppose. I—used to know the gentleman who sent you so I think it will hardly be necessary to call the police. You may execute your song and dance, but do not sing too loudly. It is a little early yet for open-air vaudeville, and we might attract attention."

"Awe," said the boy, with a shrug down the length of him, "yer know what I mean, lady. 'Tain't a turn, it's wind. He told me to tell yer he's got his collars and cuffs in dat grip for a scoot clean out to 'Frisco. Den he's goin' to shoot snow-birds in de Klondike. He says yer told him not to send 'round no more pink notes nor come hangin' over de garden gate, and he takes dis means of puttin' yer wise. He says yer refereed him out like a has-been, and never give him no chance to kick at de decision. He says yer swiped him, and never said why."

The slightly awakened interest in the young lady's eyes did not abate. Perhaps it was caused by either the originality or the audacity of the snow-bird hunter, in thus circumventing her express commands against the ordinary modes of communication. She fixed her eye on a statue standing disconsolate in the dishevelled park, and spoke into the transmitter:

"Tell the gentleman that I need not repeat to him a description of my ideals. He knows what they have been and what they still are. So far as they touch on this case, absolute loyalty and truth are the ones paramount. Tell him that I have studied my own heart as well as one can, and I know its weakness as well as I do its needs. That is why I decline to hear his pleas, whatever they may be. I did not condemn him through hearsay or doubtful evidence, and that is why I made no charge. But, since he persists in hearing what he already well knows, you may convey the matter.

"Tell him that I entered the conservatory that evening from the rear, to cut a rose for my mother. Tell him I saw him and Miss Ashburton beneath the pink oleander. The tableau was pretty, but the pose and juxtaposition were too eloquent and evident to require explanation. I left the conservatory, and, at the same time, the rose and my ideal. You may carry that song and dance to your impressario."

"I'm shy on one word, lady. Jux—jux—put me wise on that, will yer?"

"Juxtaposition—or you may call it propinquity—or, if you like, being rather too near for one maintaining the position of an ideal."

The gravel spun from beneath the boy's feet. He stood by the other bench. The man's eyes interrogated him, hungrily. The boy's were shining with the impersonal zeal of the translator.

"De lady says dat she's on to de fact dat gals is dead easy when a feller come spielin' ghost stories and tryin' to make up, and dat's why she won't listen to no soft-soap. She says she caught yer dead to rights, huggin' a bunch o' calico in de hot-house. She side-stepped in to pull some posies and yer was squeezin' der oder gal to beat de band. She says it looked cute, all right all right, but it made her sick. She says yer better git busy, and make a sneak for de train."

The young man gave a low whistle and his eyes flashed with a sudden thought. His hand flew to the inside pocket of his coat, and drew out a handful of letters. Selecting one, he handed it to the boy, following it with a silver dollar from his vest-pocket.

"Give that letter to the lady," he said, "and ask her to read it. Tell her that it should explain the situation. Tell her that, if she had mingled a little trust with her conception of the ideal, much heartache might have been avoided. Tell her that loyalty she prizes so much has never wavered. Tell her I am waiting for an answer."

The messenger stood before the lady.

"De gent says he's had de ski-bunk put on him widout no cause. He says he's no bum guy; and, lady, yer read dat letter, and I'll bet yer he's a white sport, all right."

The young lady unfolded the letter, somewhat doubtfully, and read it.

> Dear Dr. Arnold: I want to thank you for your most kind and opportune aid to my daughter last Friday evening, when she was overcome by an attack of her old heart-trouble in the conservatory at Mrs. Waldron's reception. Had you not been near to catch her as she fell and to render proper attention, we might have lost her. I would be glad if you would call and undertake the treatment of her case.
>
> Gratefully yours,
> Robert Ashburton

The young lady refolded the letter, and handed it to the boy.

"De gent wants an answer," said the messenger. "What's de word?"

The lady's eyes suddenly flashed on him, bright, smiling and wet.

"Tell that guy on the other bench," she said, with a happy, tremulous laugh, "that his girl wants him."

The Pendulum

"Eighty-first Street—let 'em out, please," yelled the shepherd in blue.

A flock of citizen sheep scrambled out and another flock scrambled aboard. Ding-ding! The cattle cars of the Manhattan Elevated rattled away, and John Perkins drifted down the stairway of the station with the released flock.

John walked slowly toward his flat. Slowly, because in the lexicon of his daily life there was no such word as "perhaps." There are no surprises awaiting a man who has been married two years and lives in a flat. As he walked John Perkins prophesied to himself with gloomy and downtrodden cynicism the foregone conclusions of the monotonous day.

Katy would meet him at the door with a kiss flavored with cold cream and butter-scotch. He would remove his coat, sit upon a macadamized lounge and read, in the evening paper, of Russians and Japs slaughtered by the deadly linotype. For dinner there would be pot roast, a salad flavored with a dressing warranted not to crack or injure the leather, stewed rhubarb and the bottle of strawberry marmalade blushing at the certificate of chemical purity on its label. After dinner Katy would show him the new patch in her crazy quilt that the iceman had cut for her off the end of his four-in-hand. At half-past seven they would spread newspapers over the furniture to catch the pieces of plastering that fell when the fat man in the flat overhead began to take his physical culture exercises. Exactly at eight Hickey & Mooney, of the vaudeville team (unbooked) in the flat across the hall, would yield to the gentle influence of delirium tremens and begin to overturn chairs under the delusion that Hammerstein was pursuing them with a five-hundred-dollar-a-week contract. Then the gent at the window across the air-shaft would get out his flute; the nightly gas leak would steal forth to frolic in the highways; the dumbwaiter would slip off its trolley; the janitor would drive Mrs. Zanowitski's five children once more across the Yalu; the lady with the champagne shoes and the Skye terrier would trip downstairs and paste her Thursday name over her bell and letter-box—and the evening routine of the Frogmore flats would be under way.

John Perkins knew these things would happen. And he knew that at a quarter past eight he would summon his nerve and reach for his hat, and that his wife would deliver this speech in a querulous tone:

"Now, where are you going, I'd like to know, John Perkins?"

"Thought I'd drop up to McCloskey's," he would answer, "and play a game or two of pool with the fellows."

Of late such had been John Perkins's habit. At ten or eleven he would return. Sometimes Katy would be asleep; sometimes, waiting up, ready to melt in the crucible of her ire a little more gold plating from the wrought steel chains of matrimony. For these things Cupid will have to answer when he stands at the bar of justice with his victims from the Frogmore flats.

To-night John Perkins encountered a tremendous upheaval of the commonplace when he reached his door. No Katy was there with her affectionate, confectionate kiss. The three rooms seemed in portentous disorder. All about lay her things in confusion. Shoes in the middle of the floor, curling tongs, hair bows, kimonos, powder box, jumbled together on dresser and chairs—this was not Katy's way. With a sinking heart John saw the comb with a curling cloud of her brown hair among its teeth. Some unusual hurry and perturbation must have possessed her, for she always carefully placed these combings in the little blue vase on the mantel to be some day formed into the coveted feminine "rat."

Hanging conspicuously to the gas jet by a string was a folded paper. John seized it. It was a note from his wife running thus:

Dear John:

I just had a telegram saying mother is very sick. I am going to take the 4:30 train. Brother Sam is going to meet me at the depot there. There is cold mutton in the icebox. I hope it isn't her quinzy again. Pay the milkman 50 cents. She had it bad last spring. Don't forget to write to the company about the gas meter, and your good socks are in the top drawer. I will write to-morrow.

Hastily,

Katy

Never during their two years of matrimony had he and Katy been separated for a night. John read the note over and over in a dumbfounded way. Here was a break in a routine that had never varied, and it left him dazed.

There on the back of a chair hung, pathetically empty and formless, the red wrapper with black dots that she always wore while getting the meals. Her week-day clothes had been tossed here and there in her haste. A little paper bag of her favorite butter-scotch lay with its string yet unwound. A daily paper sprawled on the floor, gaping rectangularly where a railroad time-table had been clipped from it. Everything in the room spoke of a loss, of an essence gone, of its soul and life departed. John Perkins stood among the dead remains with a queer feeling of desolation in his heart.

He began to set the rooms tidy as well as he could. When he touched her clothes a thrill of something like terror went through him. He had never thought what existence would be without Katy. She had become so thoroughly annealed into his life that she was like the air he breathed—necessary but scarcely noticed. Now, without warning, she was gone, vanished, as completely absent as if she had never existed. Of course it would be only for a few days, or at most a week or two, but it seemed to him as if the very hand of death had pointed a finger at his secure and uneventful home.

John dragged the cold mutton from the ice-box, made coffee, and sat down to a lonely meal face to face with the strawberry marmalade's shameless certificate of purity. Bright among withdrawn blessings now appeared to him the ghosts of pot roasts and the salad with tan polish dressing. His home was dismantled. A quinzied mother-in-law had knocked his lares and penates sky-high. After his solitary meal John sat at a front window.

He did not care to smoke. Outside the city roared to him to come join in its dance of folly and pleasure. The night was his. He might go forth unquestioned and thrum the strings of jollity as free as any gay bachelor there. He might carouse and wander and have his fling until dawn if he liked; and there would be no wrathful Katy waiting for him, bearing the chalice that held the dregs of his joy. He might play pool at McCloskey's with his roistering friends until Aurora dimmed the electric bulbs if he chose. The hymeneal strings that had curbed him always when the Frogmore flats had palled upon him were loosened. Katy was gone.

John Perkins was not accustomed to analyzing his emotions. But as he sat in his Katy-bereft 10 × 12 parlor he hit unerringly upon the keynote of his discomfort. He knew now that Katy was necessary to his happiness. His feeling for her, lulled into unconsciousness by the dull round of domesticity, had been sharply stirred by the loss of her presence. Has it not been dinned into us by proverb and sermon and fable that we never prize the music till the sweet-voiced bird has flown—or in other no less florid and true utterances?

"I'm a double-dyed dub," mused John Perkins, "the way I've been treating Katy. Off every night playing pool and bumming with the boys instead of staying home with her. The poor girl here all alone with nothing to amuse her, and me acting that way! John Perkins, you're the worst kind of a shine. I'm going to make it up for the little girl. I'll take her out and let her see some amusement. And I'll cut out the McCloskey gang right from this minute."

Yes, there was the city roaring outside for John Perkins to come dance in the train of Momus. And at McCloskey's the boys were knocking the balls idly into the pockets against the hour for the nightly game. But no primrose way nor clicking cue could woo the remorseful soul of Perkins the bereft. The thing that was his, lightly held and half scorned, had been taken away from him, and he wanted it. Backward to a certain man named Adam, whom the cherubim bounced from the orchard, could Perkins, the remorseful, trace his descent.

Near the right hand of John Perkins stood a chair. On the back of it stood Katy's blue shirtwaist. It still retained something of her contour. Midway of the sleeves were fine, individual wrinkles made by the movements of her arms in working for his comfort and pleasure. A delicate but impelling odor of bluebells came from it. John took it and looked long and soberly at the unresponsive grenadine. Katy had never been unresponsive. Tears:—yes, tears—came into John Perkins's eyes. When she came back things would be different. He would make up for all his neglect. What was life without her?

The door opened. Katy walked in carrying a little hand satchel. John stared at her stupidly.

"My! I'm glad to get back," said Katy. "Ma wasn't sick to amount to anything. Sam was at the depot, and said she just had a little spell, and got all right soon after they telegraphed. So I took the next train back. I'm just dying for a cup of coffee."

Nobody heard the click and rattle of the cogwheels as the third-floor-front of the Frogmore flats buzzed its machinery back into the Order of Things. A band slipped, a spring was touched, the gear was adjusted and the wheels revolve in their old orbit.

John Perkins looked at the clock. It was 8.15. He reached for his hat and walked to the door.

"Now, where are you going, I'd like to know, John Perkins?" asked Katy, in a querulous tone.

"Thought I'd drop up to McCloskey's," said John, "and play a game or two of pool with the fellows."

The Buyer from Cactus City

It is well that hay fever and colds do not obtain in the healthful vicinity of Cactus City, Texas, for the dry goods emporium of Navarro & Platt, situated there, is not to be sneezed at.

Twenty thousand people in Cactus City scatter their silver coin with liberal hands for the things that their hearts desire. The bulk of this semi-precious metal goes to Navarro & Platt. Their huge brick building covers enough ground to graze a dozen head of sheep. You can buy of them a rattlesnake-skin necktie, an automobile, or an eighty-five dollar, latest style, lady's tan coat in twenty different shades. Navarro & Platt first introduced pennies west of the Colorado River. They had been ranchmen with business heads, who saw that the world did not necessarily have to cease its revolutions after free grass went out.

Every Spring, Navarro, senior partner, fifty-five, half-Spanish, cosmopolitan, able, polished, had "gone on" to New York to buy goods. This year he shied at taking up the long trail. He was undoubtedly growing older; and he looked at his watch several times a day before the hour came for his siesta.

"John," he said, to his junior partner, "you shall go on this year to buy the goods."

Platt looked tired.

"I'm told," said he, "that New York is a plumb dead town; but I'll go. I can take a whirl in San Antone for a few days on my way and have some fun."

Two weeks later a man in a Texas full dress suit—black frock coat, broad-brimmed soft white hat, and lay-down collar 3-4 inch high, with black, wrought-iron necktie—entered the wholesale cloak and suit establishment of Zizzbaum & Son, on lower Broadway.

Old Zizzbaum had the eye of an osprey, the memory of an elephant, and a mind that unfolded from him in three movements like the puzzle of the carpenter's rule. He rolled to the front like a brunette polar bear, and shook Platt's hand.

"And how is the good Mr. Navarro in Texas?" he said. "The trip was too long for him this year, so? We welcome Mr. Platt instead."

"A bull's eye," said Platt, "and I'd give forty acres of unirrigated Pecos County land to know how you did it."

"I knew," grinned Zizzbaum, "just as I know that the rainfall in

El Paso for the year was 28.5 inches, or an increase of 15 inches, and that therefore Navarro & Platt will buy a $15,000 stock of suits this spring instead of $10,000, as in a dry year. But that will be to-morrow. There is first a cigar in my private office that will remove from your mouth the taste of the ones you smuggled across the Rio Grande and like—because they are smuggled."

It was late in the afternoon and business for the day had ended. Zizzbaum left Platt with a half-smoked cigar, and came out of the private office to Son, who was arranging his diamond scarfpin before a mirror, ready to leave.

"Abey," he said, "you will have to take Mr. Platt around to-night and show him things. They are customers for ten years. Mr. Navarro and I we played chess every moment of spare time when he came. That is good, but Mr. Platt is a young man and this is his first visit to New York. He should amuse easily."

"All right," said Abey, screwing the guard tightly on his pin. "I'll take him on. After he's seen the Flatiron and the head waiter at the Hotel Astor and heard the phonograph play 'Under the Old Apple Tree' it'll be half-past ten, and Mr. Texas will be ready to roll up in his blanket. I've got a supper engagement at 11:30, but he'll be all to the Mrs. Winslow before then."

The next morning at 10 Platt walked into the store ready to do business. He had a bunch of hyacinths pinned on his lapel. Zizzbaum himself waited on him. Navarro & Platt were good customers, and never failed to take their discount for cash.

"And what did you think of our little town?" asked Zizzbaum, with the fatuous smile of the Manhattanite.

"I shouldn't care to live in it," said the Texan. "Your son and I knocked around quite a little last night. You've got good water, but Cactus City is better lit up."

"We've got a few lights on Broadway, don't you think, Mr. Platt?"

"And a good many shadows," said Platt. "I think I like your horses best. I haven't seen a crowbait since I've been in town."

Zizzbaum led him upstairs to show the samples of suits.

"Ask Miss Asher to come," he said to a clerk.

Miss Asher came, and Platt, of Navarro & Platt, felt for the first time the wonderful bright light of romance and glory descend upon him. He stood still as a granite cliff above the cañon of the Colorado, with his wide-open eyes fixed upon her. She noticed his look and flushed a little, which was contrary to her custom.

Miss Asher was the crack model of Zizzbaum & Son. She was of the blond type known as "medium," and her measurements even went the required 38-25-42 standard a little better. She had been at Zizzbaum's two years, and knew her business. Her eye was bright, but cool; and had she chosen to match her gaze against the optic of the famed basilisk, that fabulous monster's gaze would have wavered and softened first. Incidentally, she knew buyers.

"Now, Mr. Platt," said Zizzbaum, "I want you to see these princess gowns in the light shades. They will be the thing in your climate. This first, if you please, Miss Asher."

Swiftly in and out of the dressing-room the prize model flew, each time wearing a new costume and looking more stunning with every change. She posed with absolute self-possession before the stricken buyer, who stood, tongue-tied and motionless, while Zizzbaum orated oilily of the styles. On the model's face was her faint, impersonal professional smile that seemed to cover something like weariness or contempt.

When the display was over Platt seemed to hesitate. Zizzbaum was a little anxious, thinking that his customer might be inclined to try elsewhere. But Platt was only looking over in his mind the best building sites in Cactus City, trying to select one on which to build a house for his wife-to-be—who was just then in the dressing-room taking off an evening gown of lavender and tulle.

"Take your time, Mr. Platt," said Zizzbaum. "Think it over to-night. You won't find anybody else meet our prices on goods like these. I'm afraid you're having a dull time in New York, Mr. Platt. A young man like you—of course, you miss the society of the ladies. Wouldn't you like a nice young lady to take out to dinner this evening? Miss Asher, now, is a very nice young lady; she will make it agreeable for you."

"Why, she doesn't know me," said Platt, wonderingly. "She doesn't know anything about me. Would she go? I'm not acquainted with her."

"Would she go?" repeated Zizzbaum, with uplifted eyebrows. "Sure, she would go. I will introduce you. Sure, she would go."

He called Miss Asher loudly.

She came, calm and slightly contemptuous, in her white shirt waist and plain black skirt.

"Mr. Platt would like the pleasure of your company to dinner this evening," said Zizzbaum, walking away.

"Sure," said Miss Asher, looking at the ceiling. "I'd be much pleased. Nine-eleven West Twentieth Street. What time?"

"Say seven o'clock."

"All right, but please don't come ahead of time. I room with a school teacher, and she doesn't allow any gentleman to call in the room. There isn't any parlor, so you'll have to wait in the hall. I'll be ready."

At half-past seven Platt and Miss Asher sat at a table in a Broadway restaurant. She was dressed in a plain, filmy black. Platt didn't know that it was all a part of her day's work.

With the unobtrusive aid of a good waiter he managed to order a respectable dinner, minus the usual Broadway preliminaries.

Miss Asher flashed upon him a dazzling smile.

"Mayn't I have something to drink?" she asked.

"Why, certainly," said Platt. "Anything you want."

"A dry Martini," she said to the waiter.

When it was brought and set before her Platt reached over and took it away.

"What is this?" he asked.

"A cocktail, of course."

"I thought it was some kind of tea you ordered. This is liquor. You can't drink this. What is your first name?"

"To my intimate friends," said Miss Asher, freezingly, "it is 'Helen.' "

"Listen, Helen," said Platt, leaning over the table. "For many years every time the spring flowers blossomed out on the prairies I got to thinking of somebody that I'd never seen or heard of. I knew it was you the minute I saw you yesterday. I'm going back home to-morrow, and you're going with me. I know it, for I saw it in your eyes when you first looked at me. You needn't kick, for you've got to fall into line. Here's a little trick I picked out for you on my way over."

He flicked a two-carat diamond solitaire ring across the table. Miss Asher flipped it back to him with her fork.

"Don't get fresh," she said, severely.

"I'm worth a hundred thousand dollars," said Platt. "I'll build you the finest house in west Texas."

"You can't buy me, Mr. Buyer," said Miss Asher, "if you had a hundred million. I didn't think I'd have to call you down. You didn't look like the others to me at first, but I see you're all alike."

"All who?" asked Platt.

"All you buyers. You think because we girls have to go out to dinner with you or lose our jobs that you're privileged to say what you please. Well, forget it. I thought you were different from the others, but I see I was mistaken."

Platt struck his fingers on the table with a gesture of sudden, illuminating satisfaction.

"I've got it!" he exclaimed, almost hilariously—"the Nicholson place, over on the north side. There's a big grove of live oaks and a natural lake. The old house can be pulled down and the new one set further back."

"Put out your pipe," said Miss Asher. "I'm sorry to wake you up, but you fellows might as well get wise, once for all, to where you stand. I'm supposed to go to dinner with you and help jolly you along so you'll trade with old Zizzy, but don't expect to find me in any of the suits you buy."

"Do you mean to tell me," said Platt, "that you go out this way with customers, and they all—they all ask you like I have?"

"They all make plays," said Miss Asher. "But I must say that you've got 'em beat in one respect. They generally talk diamonds, while you've actually dug one up."

"How long have you been working, Helen?"

"Got my name pat, haven't you? I've been supporting myself for eight years. I was a cash girl and a wrapper and then a shop girl until I was grown, and then I got to be a suit model. Mr. Texas Man, don't you think a little wine would make this dinner a little less dry?"

"You're not going to drink wine any more, dear. It's awful to think how——I'll come to the store to-morrow and get you. I want you to pick out an automobile before we leave. That's all we need to buy here."

"Oh, cut that out. If you knew how sick I am of hearing such talk."

After the dinner they walked down Broadway and came upon Diana's little wooded park. The trees caught Platt's eye at once, and he must turn along under the winding walk beneath them. The lights shone upon two bright tears in the model's eyes.

"I don't like that," said Platt. "What's the matter?"

"Don't you mind," said Miss Asher. "Well, it's because—well, I didn't think you were that kind when I first saw you. But you are all alike. And now will you take me home, or will I have to call a cop?"

Platt took her to the door of her boarding-house. They stood for a minute in the vestibule. She looked at him with such scorn in her eyes that even his heart of oak began to waver. His arm was halfway around her waist, when she struck him a stinging blow on the face with her open hand.

As he stepped back a ring fell from somewhere and bounded on the tiled floor. Platt groped for it and found it.

"Now, take your useless diamond and go, Mr. Buyer," she said.

"This was the other one—the wedding ring," said the Texan, holding the smooth gold band on the palm of his hand.

Miss Asher's eyes blazed upon him in the half darkness.

"Was that what you mean?—did you——"

Somebody opened the door from inside the house.

"Good-night," said Platt. "I'll see you at the store to-morrow."

Miss Asher ran up to her room and shook the school teacher until she sat up in bed ready to scream "Fire!"

"Where is it?" she cried.

"That's what I want to know," said the model. "You've studied geography, Emma, and you ought to know. Where is a town called Cac—Cac—Carac—Caracas City, I think they called it?"

"How dare you wake me up for that?" said the school teacher. "Caracas is in Venezuela, of course."

"What's it like?"

"Why, it's principally earthquakes and Negroes and monkeys and malarial fever and volcanoes."

"I don't care," said Miss Asher, blithely; "I'm going there tomorrow."

Brickdust Row

Blinker was displeased. A man of less culture and poise and wealth would have sworn. But Blinker always remembered that he was a gentleman—a thing that no gentleman should do. So he merely looked bored and sardonic while he rode in a hansom to the centre of disturbance, which was the Broadway office of Lawyer Oldport, who was agent for the Blinker estate.

"I don't see," said Blinker, "why I should be always signing confounded papers. I am packed, and was to have left for the North Woods this morning. Now I must wait until to-morrow morning. I hate night trains. My best razors are, of course, at the bottom of some unidentifiable trunk. It is a plot to drive me to bay rum and a monologuing, thumb-handed barber. Give me a pen that doesn't scratch. I hate pens that scratch."

"Sit down," said double-chinned, gray Lawyer Oldport. "The worst has not been told you. Oh, the hardships of the rich! The papers are not yet ready to sign. They will be laid before you to-morrow at eleven. You will miss another day. Twice shall the barber tweak the helpless nose of a Blinker. Be thankful that your sorrows do not embrace a haircut."

"If," said Blinker, rising, "the act did not involve more signing of papers I would take my business out of your hands at once. Give me a cigar, please."

"If," said Lawyer Oldport, "I had cared to see an old friend's son gulped down at one mouthful by sharks I would have ordered you to take it away long ago. Now, let's quit fooling, Alexander. Besides the grinding task of signing your name some thirty times to-morrow, I must impose upon you the consideration of a matter of business—of business, and I may say humanity or right. I spoke to you about this five years ago, but you would not listen—you were in a hurry for a coaching trip, I think. The subject has come up again. The property——"

"Oh, property!" interrupted Blinker. "Dear Mr. Oldport, I think you mentioned to-morrow. Let's have it all at one dose to-morrow—signatures and property and snappy rubber bands and that smelly sealing-wax and all. Have luncheon with me? Well, I'll try to remember to drop in at eleven to-morrow. Morning."

The Blinker wealth was in lands, tenements, and hereditaments, as the legal phrase goes. Lawyer Oldport had once taken Alexander in his little pulmonary gasoline runabout to see the many buildings and rows of buildings that he owned in the city. For Alexander was sole heir. They had amused Blinker very much. The houses looked so incapable of producing the big sums of money that Lawyer Oldport kept piling up in banks for him to spend.

In the evening Blinker went to one of his clubs, intending to dine. Nobody was there except some old fogies playing whist who spoke to him with grave politeness and glared at him with savage contempt. Everybody was out of town. But here he was kept in like a schoolboy to write his name over and over on pieces of paper. His wounds were deep.

Blinker turned his back on the fogies, and said to the club steward who had come forward with some nonsense about cold fresh salmon roe:

"Symons, I'm going to Coney Island." He said it as one might say: "All's off, I'm going to jump into the river."

The joke please Symons. He laughed within a sixteenth of a note of the audibility permitted by the laws governing employees.

"Certainly, sir," he tittered. "Of course, sir, I think I can see you at Coney, Mr. Blinker."

Blinker got a paper and looked up the movements of Sunday steamboats. Then he found a cab at the first corner and drove to a North River pier. He stood in line, as democratic as you or I, and bought a ticket, and was trampled upon and shoved forward until, at last, he found himself on the upper deck of the boat staring brazenly at a girl who sat alone upon a camp stool. But Blinker did not intend to be brazen; the girl was so wonderfully good looking that he forgot for one minute that he was the prince incog, and behaved just as he did in society.

She was looking at him, too, and not severely. A puff of wind threatened Blinker's straw hat. He caught it warily and settled it again. The movement gave the effect of a bow. The girl nodded and smiled, and in another instant he was seated at her side. She was dressed all in white, she was paler than Blinker imagined milkmaids and girls of humble stations to be, but she was as tidy as a cherry blossom, and her steady, supremely frank gray eyes looked out from the intrepid depths of an unshadowed and untroubled soul.

"How dare you raise your hat to me?" she asked, with a smile-redeemed severity.

"I didn't," Blinker said, but he quickly covered the mistake by extending it to "I didn't know how to keep from it after I saw you."

"I do not allow gentlemen to sit by me to whom I have not been introduced," she said with a sudden haughtiness that deceived him. He rose reluctantly, but her clear, teasing laugh brought him down to his chair again.

"I guess you weren't going far," she declared, with beauty's magnificent self-confidence.

"Are you going to Coney Island?" asked Blinker.

"Me?" She turned upon him wide-open eyes full of bantering surprise. "Why, what a question! Can't you see that I'm riding a bicycle in the park?" Her drollery took the form of impertinence.

"And I'm laying bricks on a tall factory chimney," said Blinker.

"Mayn't we see Coney together? I'm all alone and I've never been there before."

"It depends," said the girl "on how nicely you behave. I'll consider your application until we get there."

Blinker took pains to provide against the rejection of his application. He strove to please. To adopt the metaphor of his nonsensical phrase, he laid brick upon brick on the tall chimney of his devoirs until, at length, the structure was stable and complete. The manners of the best society come around finally to simplicity; and as the girl's way was that naturally, they were on a mutual plane of communication from the beginning.

He learned that she was twenty, and her name was Florence; that she trimmed hats in a millinery shop; that she lived in a furnished room with her best chum Ella, who was cashier in a shoe store; and that a glass of milk from the bottle on the window-sill and an egg that boils itself while you twist up your hair makes a breakfast good enough for any one. Florence laughed when she heard "Blinker."

"Well," she said. "It certainly shows that you have imagination. It gives the 'Smiths' a chance for a little rest, anyhow."

They landed at Coney, and were dashed on the crest of a great human wave of mad pleasure-seekers into the walks and avenues of Fairyland gone into vaudeville.

With a curious eye, a critical mind, and a fairly withheld judgment Blinker considered the temples, pagodas and kiosks of popularized delights. Hoi polloi trampled, hustled, and crowded him. Basket parties bumped him; sticky children tumbled, howling, under his feet, candying his clothes. Insolent youths strolling among the booths with hard-won canes under one arm and easily won girls on the other, blew defiant smoke from cheap cigars into his face. The publicity gentlemen with megaphones, each before his own stupendous attraction, roared like Niagara in his ears. Music of all kinds that could be tortured from brass, reed, hide, or string, fought in the air to gain space for its vibrations against its competitors. But what held Blinker in awful fascination was the mob, the multitude, the proletariat shrieking, struggling, hurrying, panting, hurling itself in incontinent frenzy, with unabashed abandon, into the ridiculous sham palaces of trumpery and tinsel pleasures. The vulgarity of it, its brutal overriding of all the tenets of repression and taste that were held by his caste, repelled him strongly.

In the midst of his disgust he turned and looked down at Florence by his side. She was ready with her quick smile and upturned, happy eyes, as bright and clear as the water in trout pools. The eyes were saying that they had the right to be shining and happy, for was their owner not with her (for the present) Man, her gentleman Friend and holder of the keys to the enchanted city of fun.

Blinker did not read her look accurately, but by some miracle he suddenly saw Coney aright.

He no longer saw a mass of vulgarians seeking gross joys. He now looked clearly upon a hundred thousand true idealists. Their offenses were wiped out. Conterfeit and false though the garish joys of these spangled temples were, he perceived that deep under the gilt surface they offered saving and apposite balm and satisfaction to the restless human heart. Here, at least, was the husk of Romance, the empty but shining casque of Chivalry, the breath-catching though safe-guarded dip and flight of Adventure, the magic carpet that transports you to the realms of fairyland, though its journey be through but a few poor yards of space. He no longer saw a rabble, but his brothers seeking the ideal. There was no magic of poesy here or of art; but the glamour of their imagination turned yellow calico into cloth of gold and the megaphone into the silver trumpets of joy's heralds.

Almost humbled, Blinker rolled up the shirt sleeves of his mind and joined the idealists.

"You are the lady doctor," he said to Florence. "How shall we go about doing this jolly conglomeration of fairy tales, incorporated?"

"We will begin there," said the Princess, pointing to a fun pagoda on the edge of the sea, "and we will take them all in, one by one."

They caught the eight o'clock returning boat and sat, filled with pleasant fatigue, against the rail in the bow, listening to the Italians' fiddle and harp. Blinker had thrown off all care. The North Woods seemed to him an uninhabitable wilderness. What a fuss he had made over signing his name—pooh! he could sign it a hundred times. And her name was as pretty as she was—"Florence," he said it to himself a great many times.

As the boat was nearing its pier in the North River a two-funnelled, drab, foreign-looking sea-going steamer was dropping down toward the bay. The boat turned its nose in towards its slip. The steamer veered as if to seek mid-stream, and then yawed, seemed to increase its speed and struck the Coney boat on the side near the stern, cutting into it with a terrifying shock and crash.

While the six hundred passengers on the boat were mostly tumbling about the decks in a shrieking panic the captain was shouting at the steamer that it should not back off and leave the rent exposed for the water to enter. But the steamer tore its way out like a savage sawfish and cleaved its heartless way, full speed ahead.

The boat began to sink at its stern, but moved slowly toward the slip. The passengers were a frantic mob, unpleasant to behold.

Blinker held Florence tightly until the boat had righted itself. She made no sound or sign of fear. He stood on a camp stool, ripped off the slats above his head and pulled down a number of the life preservers. He began to buckle one around Florence. The rotten canvas split and the fraudulent granulated cork came pouring out in a stream. Florence caught a handful of it and laughed gleefully.

"It looks like breakfast food," she said. "Take it off. They're no good."

She unbuckled it and threw it on the deck. She made Blinker sit down and sat by his side and put her hand in his. "What'll you bet we don't reach the pier all right?" she said, and began to hum a song.

And now the captain moved among the passengers and compelled order. The boat would undoubtedly make her slip, he said, and ordered the women and children to the bow, where they would land first. The boat, very low in the water at the stern, tried gallantly to make his promise good.

"Florence," said Blinker, as she held him close by an arm and hand, "I love you."

"That's what they all say," she replied, lightly.

"I am not one of 'they all,' " he persisted. "I never knew any one I could love before. I could pass my life with you and be happy every day. I am rich. I can make things all right for you."

"That's what they all say," said the girl again, weaving the words into her little, reckless song.

"Don't say that again," said Blinker in a tone that made her look at him in frank surprise.

"Why shouldn't I say it?" she asked, calmly. "They all do."

"Who are 'they'?" he asked, jealous for the first time in his existence.

"Why, the fellows I know."

"Do you know so many?"

"Oh, well, I'm not a wall flower," she answered with modest complacency.

"Where do you see these—these men? At your home?"

"Of course not. I meet them just as I did you. Sometimes on the boat, sometimes in the park, sometimes on the street. I'm a pretty good judge of a man. I can tell in a minute if a fellow is one who is likely to get fresh."

"What do you mean by 'fresh'?"

"Who try to kiss you—me, I mean."

"Do any of them try that?" asked Blinker, clenching his teeth.

"Sure. All men do. You know that."

"Do you allow them?"

"Some. Not many. They won't take you out anywhere unless you do."

She turned her head and looked searchingly at Blinker. Her eyes were as innocent as a child's. There was a puzzled look in them, as though she did not understand him.

"What's wrong about my meeting fellows?" she asked, wonderingly.

"Everything," he answered, almost savagely. "Why don't you entertain your company in the house where you live? Is it necessary to pick up Tom, Dick, and Harry on the street?"

She kept her absolutely ingenuous eyes upon his.

"If you could see the place where I live you wouldn't ask that. I live in Brickdust Row. They call it that because there's red dust from the bricks crumbling over everything. I've lived there for more than four years. There's no place to receive company. You can't have anybody come to your room. What else is there to do? A girl has got to meet the men, hasn't she?"

"Yes," he said hoarsely. "A girl has got to meet a—has got to meet the men."

"The first time one spoke to me on the street," she continued, "I ran home and cried all night. But you get used to it. I meet a good many nice fellows at church. I go on rainy days and stand in the vestibule until one comes up with an umbrella. I wish there was a parlor, so I could ask you to call, Mr. Blinker—are you really sure it isn't 'Smith,' now?"

The boat landed safely. Blinker had a confused impression of walking with the girl through quiet crosstown streets until she stopped at a corner and held out her hand.

"I live just one more block over," she said. "Thank you for a very pleasant afternoon."

Blinker muttered something and plunged northward till he found a cab. A big, gray church loomed slowly at his right. Blinker shook his fist at it through the window.

"I gave you a thousand dollars last week," he cried under his breath, "and she meets them in your very doors. There is something wrong; there is something wrong."

At eleven the next day Blinker signed his name thirty times with a new pen provided by Lawyer Oldport.

"Now let me get to the woods," he said, surlily.

"You are not looking well," said Lawyer Oldport. "The trip will do you good. But listen, if you will, to that little matter of business of which I spoke to you yesterday, and also five years ago. There are some buildings, fifteen in number, of which there are new five-year leases to be signed. Your father contemplated a change in the lease provisions, but never made it. He intended that the parlors of these houses should not be sublet, but that the tenants should be allowed to use them for reception rooms. These houses are in the shopping districts, and are mainly tenanted by young working girls. As it is they are forced to seek companionship outside. This row of red brick——"

Blinker interrupted him with a loud, discordant laugh.

"Brickdust Row for an even hundred," he cried. "And I own it. Have I guessed right?"

"The tenants have some such name for it," said Lawyer Oldport.

Blinker arose and jammed his hat down to his eyes.

"Do what you please with it," he said, harshly. "Remodel it, burn it, raze it to the ground. But, man, it's too late, I tell you. It's too late. It's too late. It's too late."

The Foreign Policy of Company 99

John Byrnes, hose-cart driver of Engine Company No. 99, was afflicted with what his comrades called Japanitis.

Byrnes had a war map spread permanently upon a table in the second story of the engine-house, and he could explain to you at any hour of the day or night the exact positions, conditions and intentions of both the Russian and Japanese armies. He had little clusters of pins stuck in the map which represented the opposing forces, and these he moved about from day to day in conformity with the war news in the daily papers.

Wherever the Japs won a victory John Byrnes would shift his pins, and then he would execute a war dance of delight, and the other firemen would hear him yell: "Go it, you blamed little, sawed-off, huckleberry-eyed, monkey-faced hot tamales! Eat 'em up, you little sleight-o'-hand, bow-legged bull terriers—give 'em another of them Yalu looloos, and you'll eat rice in St. Petersburg. Talk about your Russians—say, wouldn't they give you painsky when it comes to a scrapovitch?"

Not even on the fair island of Nippon was there a more enthusiastic champion of the Mikado's men. Supporters of the Russian cause did well to keep clear of Engine House No. 99.

Sometimes all thoughts of the Japs left John Byrnes's head. That was when the alarm of fire had sounded and he was strapped in his driver's seat on the swaying cart, guiding Erebus and Joe, the finest team in the whole department—according to the crew of 99.

Of all the codes adopted by man for regulating his actions toward his fellow-mortals, the greatest are these—the code of King Arthur's Knights of the Round Table, the Constitution of the United States and the unwritten rules of the New York Fire Department. The Round Table methods are no longer practicable since the invention of street cars and breach-of-promise suits, and our Constitution is being found more and more unconstitutional every day, so the code of our firemen must be considered in the lead, with the Golden Rule and Jeffries's new punch trying for place and show.

The Constitution says that one man is as good as another; but the Fire Department says he is better. This is a too generous theory, but the law will not allow itself to be construed otherwise. All of which comes perilously near to being a paradox, and commends itself to the attention of the S.P.C.A.

One of the transatlantic liners dumped out at Ellis Island a lump of protozoa which was expected to evolve into an American citizen. A steward kicked him down the gangway, a doctor pounced upon his eyes like a raven, seeking for trachoma or ophthalmia; he was hustled ashore and ejected into the city in the name of Liberty—perhaps, theoretically, thus inoculating against kingocracy with a drop of its own virus. This hypodermic injection of Europeanism wandered happily into the veins of the city with the broad grin of a pleased child. It was not burdened with baggage, cares or ambitions. Its body was lithely built and clothed in a sort of foreign fustian; its face was brightly vacant, with a small, flat nose, and was mostly covered by a thick, ragged, curling beard like the coat of a spaniel.

In the pocket of the imported Thing were a few coins—denarii—scudi—kopecks—pfennings—pilasters—whatever the financial nomenclature of his unknown country may have been.

Prattling to himself, always broadly grinning, pleased by the roar and movement of the barbarous city into which the steamship cut-rates had shunted him, the alien strayed away from the sea, which he hated, as far as the district covered by Engine Company No. 99. Light as a cork, he was kept bobbing along by the human tide, the crudest atom in all the silt of the stream that emptied into the reservoir of Liberty.

While crossing Third Avenue he slowed his steps, enchanted by the thunder of the elevated trains above him and the soothing crash of the wheels on the cobbles. And then there was a new, delightful chord in the uproar—the musical clanging of a gong and a great shining juggernaut belching fire and smoke, that people were hurrying to see.

This beautiful thing, entrancing to the eye, dashed past, and the protoplasmic immigrant stepped into the wake of it with his broad, enraptured, uncomprehending grin. And so stepping, stepped into the path of No. 99's flying hose-cart, with John Byrnes gripping, with arms of steel, the reins over the plunging backs of Erebus and Joe.

The unwritten constitutional code of the fireman has no exceptions or amendments. It is a simple thing—as simple as the rule of three. There was the needless unit in the right of way; there was the hose-cart, and the iron pillar of the elevated railroad.

John Byrnes swung all his weight and muscle on the left rein. The team and cart swerved that way and crashed like a torpedo into the pillar. The men on the cart went flying like skittles. The driver's strap burst, the pillar rang with a shock, and John Byrnes fell on the car track with a broken shoulder twenty feet away, while Erebus—beautiful, raven-black, best-loved Erebus—lay whickering in the harness with a broken leg.

In consideration for the feelings of Engine Company No. 99 the details will be lightly touched. The company does not like to be reminded of that day. There was a great crowd, and hurry calls were sent in; and while the ambulance gong was clearing the way the men of No. 99 heard the crack of the S.P.C.A. agent's pistol, and turned their heads away, not daring to look toward Erebus again.

When the firemen got back to the engine-house they found that one of them was dragging by the collar the cause of their desolation and grief. They set it in the middle of the floor and gathered grimly about it. Through its whiskers the calamitous object chattered effervescently and waved its hands.

"Sounds like a seidlitz powder," said Mike Dowling, disgustedly, "and it makes me sicker than one. Call that a man!—that hoss was worth a steamer full of such two-legged animals. It's a immigrant—that's what it is."

"Look at the doctor's chalk mark on its coat," said Reilly, the desk man. "It's just landed. It must be a kind of a Dago or a Hun or one of them Finns, I guess. That's the kind of truck that Europe unloads onto us."

"Think of a thing like that getting in the way and laying John up in hospital and spoiling the best fire team in the city," groaned another fireman. "It ought to be taken down to the dock and drowned."

"Somebody go around and get Sloviski," suggested the engine driver, "and let's see what nation is responsible for this conglomeration of hair and head noises."

Sloviski kept a delicatessen store around the corner on Third Avenue, and was reputed to be a linguist.

One of the men fetched him—a fat, cringing man, with a discursive eye and the odors of many kinds of meats upon him.

"Take a whirl at this importation with your jaw-breakers, Sloviski," requested Mike Dowling. "We can't quite figure out whether he's from the Hackensack bottoms or Hongkong-on-the-Ganges."

Sloviski addressed the stranger in several dialects, that ranged in rhythm and cadence from the sounds produced by a tonsillitis gargle to the opening of a can of tomatoes with a pair of scissors. The immigrant replied in accents resembling the uncorking of a bottle of ginger ale.

"I have you his name," reported Sloviski. "You shall not pronounce it. Writing of it in paper is better." They gave him paper, and he wrote, "Demetre Svangvsk."

"Looks like short hand," said the desk man.

"He speaks some language," continued the interpreter, wiping his forehead, "of Austria and mixed with a little Turkish. And, den, he have some Magyar words and a Polish or two, and many like the Roumanian, but not without talk of one tribe in Bessarabia. I do not quite understand."

"Would you call him a Dago or a Polocker, or what?" asked Mike, frowning at the polyglot description.

"He is a"—answered Sloviski—"he is a—I dink he come from—

I dink he is a fool," he concluded, impatient at his linguistic failure, "and if you pleases I will go back at mine delicatessen."

"Whatever he is, he's a bird," said Mike Dowling; "and you want to watch him fly."

Taking by the wing the alien fowl that had fluttered into the nest of Liberty, Mike led him to the door of the engine-house and bestowed upon him a kick hearty enough to convey the entire animus of Company 99. Demetre Svangvsk hustled away down the sidewalk, turning once to show his ineradicable grin to the aggrieved firemen.

In three weeks John Byrnes was back at his post from the hospital. With great gusto he proceeded to bring his war map up to date. "My money on the Japs every time," he declared. "Why, look at them Russians—they're nothing but wolves. Wipe 'em out, I say—and the little old jiu-jitsu gang are just the cherry blossoms to do the trick, and don't you forget it!"

The second day after Byrnes's reappearance came Demetre Svangvsk, the unidentified, to the engine-house, with a broader grin than ever. He managed to convey the idea that he wished to congratulate the hose-cart driver on his recovery and to apologize for having caused the accident. This he accomplished by so many extravagant gestures and explosive noises that the company was diverted for half an hour. Then they kicked him out again, and on the next day he came back grinning. How or where he lived no one knew. And then John Byrnes's nine-year-old son, Chris, who brought him convalescent delicacies from home to eat, took a fancy to Svangvsk, and they allowed him to loaf about the door of the engine-house occasionally.

One afternoon the big drab automobile of the Deputy Fire Commissioner buzzed up to the door of No. 99 and the Deputy stepped inside for an informal inspection. The men kicked Svangvsk out a little harder than usual and proudly escorted the Deputy around 99, in which everything shone like my lady's mirror.

The Deputy respected the sorrow of the company concerning the loss of Erebus, and he had come to promise it another mate for Joe that would do him credit. So they let Joe out of his stall and showed the Deputy how deserving he was of the finest mate that could be in horsedom.

While they were circling around Joe confabbing, Chris climbed into the Deputy's auto and threw the power full on. The men heard a monster puffing and a shriek from the lad, and sprang out too late. The big auto shot away, luckily taking a straight course down the street. The boy knew nothing of its machinery; he sat clutching the cushions and howling. With the power on nothing could have stopped the auto except a brick house, and there was nothing for Chris to gain by such a stoppage.

Demetre Svangvsk was just coming in again with a grin for another kick when Chris played his merry little prank. While the others sprang for the door Demetre sprang for Joe. He glided upon the horse's bare back like a snake and shouted something at him like the crack of a dozen whips. One of the firemen afterward swore that Joe answered him back in the same language. Ten seconds after the auto started the big horse was eating up the asphalt behind it like a strip of macaroni.

Some people two blocks and a half away saw the rescue. They said that the auto was nothing but a drab noise with a black speck in the middle of it for Chris, when a big bay horse with a lizard lying on its back cantered up alongside of it, and the lizard reached over and picked the black speck out of the noise.

Only fifteen minutes after Svangvsk's last kicking at the hands—or rather the feet—of Engine Company No. 99 he rode Joe back through the door with the boy safe, but acutely conscious of the licking he was going to receive.

Svangvsk slipped to the floor, leaned his head against Joe's and made a noise like a clucking hen. Joe nodded and whistled loudly through his nostrils, putting to shame the knowledge of Sloviski, of the delicatessen.

John Byrnes walked up to Svangvsk, who grinned, expecting to be kicked. Byrnes gripped the outlander so strongly by the hand that Demetre grinned anyhow, conceiving it to be a new form of punishment.

"The heathen rides like a Cossack," remarked a fireman who had seen a Wild West show—"they're the greatest riders in the world."

The word seemed to electrify Svangvsk. He grinned wider than ever.

"Yas—yas—me Cossack," he spluttered, striking his chest.

"Cossack!" repeated John Byrnes, thoughtfully, "ain't that a kind of a Russian?"

"They're one of the Russian tribes, sure," said the desk man, who read books between fire alarms.

Just then Alderman Foley, who was on his way home and did not know of the runaway, stopped at the door of the engine-house and called to Byrnes.

"Hello there, Jimmy, me boy—how's the war coming along? Japs still got the bear on the trot, have they?"

"Oh, I don't know," said John Byrnes, argumentatively, "them Japs haven't got any walkover. You wait till Kuropatkin gets a good whack at 'em and they won't be knee-high to a puddle-dusksky."

The Count and the Wedding Guest

One evening when Andy Donovan went to dinner at his Second Avenue boarding-house, Mrs. Scott introduced him to a new boarder, a young lady, Miss Conway. Miss Conway was small and unobtrusive. She wore a plain, snuffy-brown dress, and bestowed her interest, which seemed languid, upon her plate. She lifted her diffident eyelids and shot one perspicuous, judicial glance at Mr. Donovan, politely murmured his name, and returned to her mutton. Mr. Donovan bowed with the grace and beaming smile that were rapidly winning for him social, business and political advancement, and erased the snuffy-brown one from the tablets of his consideration.

Two weeks later Andy was sitting on the front steps enjoying his cigar. There was a soft rustle behind and above him and Andy turned his head—and had his head turned.

Just coming out of the door was Miss Conway. She wore a night-black dress of *crêpe de—crêpe de*—oh, this thin black goods. Her hat was black, and from it drooped and fluttered an ebony veil, filmy as a spider's web. She stood on the top step and drew on black silk gloves. Not a speck of white or a spot of color about her dress anywhere. Her rich golden hair was drawn, with scarcely a ripple, into a shining, smooth knot low on her neck. Her face was plain rather than pretty, but it was now illuminated and made almost beautiful by her large gray eyes that gazed above the houses across the street into the sky with an expression of the most appealing sadness and melancholy.

Gather the idea, girls—all black, you know, with the preference for *crêpe de*—oh, *crêpe de Chine*—that's it. All black, and that sad, faraway look, and the hair shining under the black veil (you have to be a blonde, of course), and try to look as if, although your young life had been blighted just as it was about to give a hop-skip-and-a-jump over the threshold of life, a walk in the park might do you good, and be sure to happen out the door at the right moment, and—oh, it'll fetch 'em every time. But it's fierce, now, how cynical I am, ain't it?—to talk about mourning costumes this way.

Mr. Donovan suddenly reinscribed Miss Conway upon the tablets of his consideration. He threw away the remaining inch and a quarter of his cigar, that would have been good for eight minutes yet, and quickly shifted his center of gravity to his low-cut patent leathers.

"It's a fine, clear evening, Miss Conway," he said; and if the Weather Bureau could have heard the confident emphasis of his tones it would have hoisted the square white signal, and nailed it to the mast.

"To them that has the heart to enjoy it, it is, Mr. Donovan," said Miss Conway, with a sigh.

Mr. Donovan, in his heart, cursed fair weather. Heartless weather! It should hail and blow and snow to be consonant with the mood of Miss Conway.

"I hope none of your relatives—I hope you haven't sustained a loss?" ventured Mr. Donovan.

"Death has claimed," said Miss Conway, hesitating—"not a relative, but one who—but I will not intrude my grief upon you, Mr. Donovan."

"Intrude?" protested Mr. Donovan. "Why, say, Miss Conway, I'd be delighted, that is, I'd be sorry—I mean I'm sure nobody could sympathize with you truer than I would."

Miss Conway smiled a little smile. And oh, it was sadder than her expression in repose.

" 'Laugh, and the world laughs with you; weep, and they give you the laugh,' " she quoted. "I have learned that, Mr. Donovan. I have no friends or acquaintances in this city. But you have been kind to me. I appreciate it highly."

He had passed her the pepper twice at the table.

"It's tough to be alone in New York—that's a cinch," said Mr. Donovan. "But, say—whenever this little old town does loosen up and get friendly it goes the limit. Say you took a little stroll in the park, Miss Conway—don't you think it might chase away some of your mullygrubs? And if you'd allow me—"

"Thanks, Mr. Donovan. I'd be pleased to accept of your escort if you think the company of one whose heart is filled with gloom could be anyways agreeable to you."

Through the open gates of the iron-railed, old, downtown park, where the elect once took the air, they strolled, and found a quiet bench.

There is this difference between the grief of youth and that of old age; youth's burden is lightened by as much of it as another shares; old age may give and give, but the sorrow remains the same.

"He was my fiancé," confided Miss Conway, at the end of an hour. "We were going to be married next spring. I don't want you to think that I am stringing you, Mr. Donovan, but he was a real Count. He had an estate and a castle in Italy. Count Fernando Mazzini was his name. I never saw the beat of him for elegance. Papa objected, of course, and once we eloped, but Papa overtook us, and took us back. I thought sure Papa and Fernando would fight a duel. Papa has a livery business—in P'kipsee, you know.

"Finally, Papa came 'round, all right, and said we might be married next spring. Fernando showed him proofs of his title and wealth, and then went over to Italy to get the castle fixed up for us. Papa's very proud and, when Fernando wanted to give me several thousand dollars for my trousseau he called him down something awful. He wouldn't even let me take a ring or any presents from him. And when Fernando sailed I came to the city and got a position as cashier in a candy store.

"Three days ago I got a letter from Italy, forwarded from P'kipsee, saying that Fernando had been killed in a gondola accident.

"That is why I am in mourning. My heart, Mr. Donovan, will remain forever in his grave. I guess I am poor company, Mr. Donovan, but I cannot take any interest in no one. I should not care to keep you from gaiety and your friends who can smile and entertain you. Perhaps you would prefer to walk back to the house?"

Now, girls, if you want to observe a young man hustle out after a pick and shovel, just tell him that your heart is in some other fellow's grave. Young men are grave-robbers by nature. Ask any widow. Something must be done to restore that missing organ to weeping angels in *crêpe de Chine*. Dead men certainly get the worst of it from all sides.

"I'm awful sorry," said Mr. Donovan, gently. "No, we won't walk back to the house just yet. And don't say you haven't no friends in this city, Miss Conway. I'm awful sorry, and I want you to believe I'm your friend, and that I'm awful sorry."

"I've got his picture here in my locket," said Miss Conway, after wiping her eyes with her handkerchief. "I never showed it to anybody; but I will to you, Mr. Donovan, because I believe you to be a true friend."

Mr. Donovan gazed long and with much interest at the photograph in the locket that Miss Conway opened for him. The face of Count Mazzini was one to command interest. It was a smooth, intelligent, bright, almost a handsome face—the face of a strong, cheerful man who might well be a leader among his fellows.

"I have a larger one, framed, in my room," said Miss Conway. "When we return I will show you that. They are all I have to remind me of Fernando. But he ever will be present in my heart, that's a sure thing."

A subtle task confronted Mr. Donovan—that of supplanting the unfortunate Count in the heart of Miss Conway. This his admiration for her determined him to do. But the magnitude of the undertaking did not seem to weigh upon his spirits. The sympathetic but cheerful friend was the rôle he essayed; and he played it so successfully that the next half-hour found them conversing pensively across two plates of ice-cream, though yet there was no diminution of the sadness in Miss Conway's large gray eyes.

Before they parted in the hall that evening she ran upstairs and brought down the framed photograph wrapped lovingly in a white silk scarf. Mr. Donovan surveyed it with inscrutable eyes.

"He gave me this the night he left for Italy," said Miss Conway. "I had the one for the locket made from this."

"A fine-looking man," said Mr. Donovan, heartily. "How would it suit you, Miss Conway, to give me the pleasure of your company to Coney next Sunday afternoon?"

A month later they announced their engagement to Mrs. Scott and the other boarders. Miss Conway continued to wear black.

A week after the announcement the two sat on the same bench in the downtown park, while the fluttering leaves of the trees made a dim kinetoscopic picture of them in the moonlight. But Donovan had worn a look of abstracted gloom all day. He was so silent to-night that love's lips could not keep back any longer the question that love's heart propounded.

"What's the matter, Andy, you are so solemn and grouchy to-night?"

"Nothing, Maggie."

"I know better. Can't I tell? You never acted this way before. What is it?"

"It's nothing much, Maggie."

"Yes it is; and I want to know. I'll bet it's some other girl you are thinking about. All right. Why don't you go get her if you want her? Take your arm away, if you please."

"I'll tell you then," said Andy, wisely, "but I guess you won't understand it exactly. You've heard of Mike Sullivan, haven't you? 'Big Mike' Sullivan, everybody calls him."

"No, I haven't," said Maggie. "And I don't want to, if he makes you act like this. Who is he?"

"He's the biggest man in New York," said Andy, almost reverently. "He can about do anything he wants to with Tammany or any other old thing in the political line. He's a mile high and as broad as East River. You say anything against Big Mike, and you'll have a million men on your collarbone in about two seconds. Why, he made a visit over to the old country awhile back, and the kings took to their holes like rabbits.

"Well, Big Mike's a friend of mine. I ain't more than deuce-high in the district as far as influence goes, but Mike's as good a friend to a little man, or a poor man as he is to a big one. I met him to-day on the Bowery, and what do you think he does? Comes up and shakes hands. 'Andy,' says he, 'I've been keeping cases on you. You've been putting in some good licks over on your side of the street, and I'm proud of you. What'll you take to drink?' He takes a cigar and I take a highball. I told him I was going to get married in two weeks. 'Andy,' says he, 'send me an invitation, so I'll keep in mind of it, and I'll come to the wedding.' That's what Big Mike says to me; and he always does what he says.

"You don't understand it, Maggie, but I'd have one of my hands cut off to have Big Mike Sullivan at our wedding. It would be the proudest day of my life. When he goes to a man's wedding, there's a guy being married that's made for life. Now, that's why I'm maybe looking sore to-night."

"Why don't you invite him, then, if he's so much to the mustard?" said Maggie, lightly.

"There's a reason why I can't," said Andy, sadly. "There's a reason why he mustn't be there. Don't ask me what it is, for I can't tell you."

"Oh, I don't care," said Maggie. "It's something about politics, of course. But it's no reason why you can't smile at me."

"Maggie," said Andy, presently, "do you think as much of me as you did of your—as you did of the Count Mazzini?"

He waited a long time, but Maggie did not reply. And then, suddenly she leaned against his shoulder and began to cry—to cry and shake with sobs, holding his arm tightly, and wetting the *crêpe de Chine* with tears.

"There, there, there!" soothed Andy, putting aside his own trouble. "And what is it, now?"

"Andy," sobbed Maggie, "I've lied to you, and you'll never marry me, or love me any more. But I feel that I've got to tell. Andy, there never was so much as the little finger of a count. I never had a beau in my life. But all the other girls had; and they talked about 'em; and that seemed to make the fellows like 'em more. And, Andy, I look swell in black—you know I do. So I went out to a photograph store and bought that picture, and had a little one made for my locket, and made up all that story about the Count and about his being killed, so I could wear black. And nobody can love a liar, and you'll shake me, Andy, and I'll die for shame. Oh, there never was anybody I liked but you—and that's all."

But instead of being pushed away, she found Andy's arm folding her closer. She looked up and saw his face cleared and smiling.

"Could you—could you forgive me, Andy?"

"Sure," said Andy. "It's all right about that. Back to the cemetery for the Count. You've straightened everything out, Maggie. I was in hopes you would before the wedding-day. Bully girl!"

"Andy," said Maggie, with a somewhat shy smile, after she had been thoroughly assured of forgiveness, "did you believe all that story about the Count?"

"Well, not to any large extent," said Andy, reaching for his cigar case; "because it's Big Mike Sullivan's picture you've got in that locket of yours."

The Country of Elusion

The cunning writer will choose an indefinable subject; for he can then set down his theory of what it is; and next, at length, his conception of what it is not—and lo! his paper is covered. Therefore let us follow the prolix and unmapable trail into the mooted country, Bohemia.

Grainger, sub-editor of *Doc's Magazine,* closed his roll-top desk, put on his hat, walked into the hall, punched the "down" button, and waited for the elevator.

Grainger's day had been trying. The chief had tried to ruin the magazine a dozen times by going against Grainger's ideas for running it. A lady whose grandfather had fought with McClellan had brought a portfolio of poems in person.

Grainger was curator of the Lion's House of the magazine. That day he had "lunched" an Arctic explorer, a short-story writer, and the famous conductor of a slaughter-house exposé. Consequently his mind was in a whirl of icebergs, Maupassant, and trichinosis.

But there was a surcease and a recourse; there was Bohemia. He would seek distraction there; and, let's see—he would call by for Mary Adrian.

Half an hour later he threaded his way like a Brazilian orchid-hunter through the palm forest in the tiled entrance hall of the "Idealia" apartment-house. One day the christeners of apartment-houses and the cognominators of sleeping-cars will meet, and there will be some jealous and sanguinary knifing.

The clerk breathed Grainger's name so languidly into the house telephone that it seemed it must surely drop, from sheer inertia, down to the janitor's regions. But, at length, it soared dilatorily up to Miss Adrian's ear. Certainly, Mr. Grainger was to come up immediately.

A colored maid with an Eliza-crossing-the-ice expression opened the door of the apartment for him. Grainger walked sideways down the narrow hall. A bunch of burnt-umber hair and a sea-green eye appeared in the crack of a door. A long, white, undraped arm came out, barring the way.

"So glad you came, Ricky, instead of any of the others," said the eye. "Light a cigarette and give it to me. Going to take me to dinner? Fine. Go into the front room till I finish dressing. But don't sit in your usual chair. There's pie in it—meringue. Kappelman threw it at Reeves last evening while he was reciting. Sophy has just come to straighten up. Is it lit? Thanks. There's Scotch on the mantel—oh, no, it isn't—that's chartreuse. Ask Sophy to find you some. I won't be long."

Grainger escaped the meringue. As he waited his spirits sank still lower. The atmosphere of the room was as vapid as a zephyr wandering over a Vesuvian lava-bed. Relics of some feast lay about the room, scattered in places where even a prowling cat would have been surprised to find them. A straggling cluster of deep red roses in a marmalade jar bowed their heads over tobacco ashes and unwashed goblets. A chafing dish stood on the piano; a leaf of sheet music supported a stack of sandwiches in a chair.

Mary came in, dressed and radiant. Her gown was of that thin, black fabric whose name through the change of a single vowel seems to summon visions ranging between the extremes of man's experiences. Spelled with an *"ê"* it belongs to Gallic witchery and diaphanous dreams: with an *"a"* it drapes lamentation amd woe.

That evening they went to the Café André. And, as people would confide to you in a whisper that André's was the only truly Bohemian restaurant in town, it may be well to follow them.

André began his professional career as a waiter in a Bowery ten-cent eating-house. Had you seen him there you would have called him tough—to yourself. Not aloud, for he would have "soaked" you as quickly as he would have soaked his thumb in your coffee. He saved money and started a basement *table d'hôte* in Eighth (or Ninth) Street. One afternoon André drank too much absinthe. He announced to his startled family that he was the Grand Lama of Thibet, therefore requiring an empty audience hall in which to be worshiped. He moved all the tables and chairs from the restaurant into the back yard, wrapped a red tablecloth around himself, and sat on a step-ladder for a throne. When the diners began to arrive, Madame, in a flurry of despair, laid cloths and ushered them, trembling, outside. Between the tables clothes-lines were stretched, bearing the family wash. A party of Bohemia hunters greeted the artistic innovation with shrieks and acclamations of delight. That week's washing was not taken in for two years. When André came to his senses he had the menu printed on stiffly starched cuffs, and served the ices in little wooden tubs. Next he took down his sign and darkened the front of the house. When you went there to dine you fumbled for an electric button and pressed it. A lookout slid open a panel in the door, looked at you suspiciously, and asked if you were acquainted with Senator Herodotus Q. McMilligan, of the Chickasaw Nation. If you were you were admitted and allowed to dine. If you were not, you were admitted and allowed to dine. There you have one of the abiding principles of Bohemia. When André had accumulated $20,000 he moved uptown, near Broadway, in the fierce light that beats upon the thrown-down. There we find him and leave him, with customers in pearls and automobile veils, striving to catch his excellently graduated nod of recognition.

There is a large round table in the northeast corner of André's at which six can sit. To this table Grainger and Mary Adrian made their way. Kappelman and Reeves were already there. And Miss Tooker, who designed the May cover for the *Ladies' Notathome Magazine*. And Mrs. Pothunter, who never drank anything but black-and-white highballs, being in mourning for her husband, who—oh, I've forgotten what he did—died, like as not.

Spaghetti-weary reader, wouldst take one penny-in-the-slot peep into the fair land of Bohemia? Then look; and when you think you have seen it you have not. And it is neither thimbleriggery nor astigmatism.

The walls of the Café André were covered with original sketches by the artists who furnished much of the color and sound of the place. Fair woman furnished the theme for the bulk of the drawings. When you say "sirens and siphons" you come near to estimating the alliterative atmosphere of André's.

First, I want you to meet my friend, Miss Adrian. Miss Tooker and Mrs. Pothunter you already know. While she tucks in the fingers of her elbow gloves you shall have her daguerreotype. So faint and uncertain shall the portrait be:

Age, somewhere between twenty-seven and high-neck evening dresses. Camaraderie in large bunches—whatever the fearful word may mean. Habitat—anywhere from Seattle to Tierra del Fuego. Temperament uncharted—she let Reeves squeeze her hand after he recited one of his poems; but she counted the change after sending him out with a dollar to buy some pickled pigs' feet. Deportment 75 out of a possible 100. Morals 100.

Mary was one of the princesses of Bohemia. In the first place, it was a royal and a daring thing to have been named Mary. There are twenty Fifines and Héloïses to one Mary in the Country of Elusion.

Now her gloves are tucked in. Miss Tooker has assumed a June poster pose; Mrs. Pothunter has bitten her lips to make the red show; Reeves has several times felt his coat to make sure that his latest poem is in the pocket. (It had been neatly typewritten; but he had copied it on the back of letters with a pencil.) Kappelman is underhandedly watching the clock. It is ten minutes to nine. When the hour comes it is to remind him of a story. Synopsis: A French girl says to her suitor: "Did you ask my father for my hand at nine o'clock this morning, as you said you would?" "I did not," he replies. "At nine o'clock I was fighting a duel with swords in the Bois de Boulogne." "Coward!" she hisses.

The dinner was ordered. You know how long the Bohemian feast of reason keeps up with the courses. Humor with the oysters; wit with the soup; repartee with the entrée; brag with the roast; knocks for Whistler and Kipling with the salad; songs with the coffee, the slapsticks with the cordials.

Between Miss Adrian's eyebrows was the pucker that shows the intense strain it requires to be at ease in Bohemia. Pat must come each sally, *mot,* and epigram. Every second of deliberation upon a reply costs you a bay leaf. Fine as a hair, a line began to curve from her nostrils to her mouth. To hold her own not a chance must be missed. A sentence addressed to her must be as a piccolo, each word of it a stop, which she must be prepared to seize upon and play. And she must always be quicker than a Micmac Indian to paddle the light canoe of conversation away from the rocks in the rapids that flow from the Pierian spring. For, plodding reader, the handwriting on the wall in the banquet hall of Bohemia is *"laisser faire."* The gray ghost that sometimes peeps through the rings of smoke is that of slain old King Convention. Freedom is the tyrant that holds them in slavery.

As the dinner waned, hands reached for the pepper cruet rather than for the shaker of Attic salt. Miss Tooker, with an elbow to business, leaned across the table toward Grainger, upsetting her glass of wine.

"Now, while you are fed and in good humor," she said, "I want to make a suggestion to you about a new cover."

"A good idea," said Grainger, mopping the tablecloth with his napkin. "I'll speak to the waiter about it."

Kappelman, the painter, was the cut-up. As a piece of delicate Athenian wit he got up from his chair and waltzed down the room with a waiter. The dependent, no doubt an honest, pachydermatous, worthy, tax-paying art-despising biped, released himself from the unequal encounter, carried his professional smile back to the dumb-waiter and dropped it down the shaft to eternal oblivion. Reeves began to make Keats turn in his grave. Mrs. Pothunter told the story of the men who met the widow on the train. Miss Adrian hummed what is still called a *chanson* in the cafés of Bridgeport. Grainger edited each individual effort with his assistant editor's smile, which meant: "Great! but you'll have to send them in through the regular channels. If I were the chief now—but you know how it is."

And soon the head waiter bowed before them, desolated to relate that the closing hour had already become chronologically historical; so out all trooped into the starry midnight, filling the street with gay laughter, to be barked at by hopeful cabmen and enviously eyed by the dull inhabitants of an uninspired world.

Grainger left Mary at the elevator in the trackless palm forest of the Idealia. After he had gone she came down again carrying a small handbag, 'phoned for a cab, drove to the Grand Central Station, boarded a 12.55 commuter's train, rode four hours with her burnt-umber head bobbing against the red-plush back of the seat, and landed during a fresh, stinging, glorious sunrise at a deserted station, the size of a peach crate, called Crocusville.

She walked a mile and clicked the latch of a gate. A bare, brown cottage stood twenty yards back; an old man with a pearl-white, Calvinistic face and clothes dyed blacker than a raven in a coal-mine was washing his hands in a tin basin on the front porch.

"How are you, Father?" said Mary timidly.

"I am as well as Providence permits, Mary Ann. You will find your mother in the kitchen."

In the kitchen a cryptic, gray woman kissed her glacially on the forehead, and pointed out the potatoes which were not yet peeled for breakfast. Mary sat in a wooden chair and decorticated spuds, with a thrill in her heart.

For breakfast there were grace, cold bread, potatoes, bacon, and tea.

"You are pursuing the same avocation in the city concerning which you have advised us from time to time by letter, I trust," said her father.

"Yes," said Mary. "I am still reviewing books for the same publication."

After breakfast she helped wash the dishes, and then all three sat in straight-back chairs in the barefloored parlor.

"It is my custom," said the old man, "on the Sabbath day to read aloud from the great work entitled the 'Apology for Authorized and Set Forms of Liturgy,' by the ecclesiastical philosopher and revered theologian Jeremy Taylor."

"I know it," said Mary blissfully, folding her hands.

For two hours the numbers of the great Jeremy rolled forth like the notes of an oratorio played on the violoncello. Mary sat gloating in the new sensation of racking physical discomfort that the wooden chair brought her. Perhaps there is no happiness in life so perfect as the martyr's. Jeremy's minor chords soothed her like the music of tom-tom. "Why, oh why," she said to herself, "does some one not write words to it?"

At eleven they went to church in Crocusville. The back of the pine bench on which she sat had a penitential forward tilt that would have brought St. Simeon down, in jealousy, from his pillar. The preacher singled her out, and thundered upon her vicarious head the damnation of the world. At each side of her an adamant parent held her rigidly to the bar of judgment. An ant crawled upon her neck, but she dared not move. She lowered her eyes before the congregation—a hundred-eyed Cerberus that watched the gates through which her sins were fast thrusting her. Her soul was filled with a delirious, almost a fanatic joy. For she was out of the clutch of the tyrant, Freedom. Dogma and creed pinioned her with beneficent cruelty, as steel braces bind the feet of a crippled child. She was hedged, adjured, shackled, shored up, strait-jacketed, silenced, ordered. When they came out the minister stopped to greet them. Mary could only hang her head and answer "Yes, sir," and "No, sir," to his questions. When she saw that the other women carried their hymn-books at their waists with their left hands, she blushed and moved hers there, too, from her right.

She took the three-o'clock train back to the city. At nine she sat at the round table for dinner in the Café André. Nearly the same crowd was there.

"Where have you been to-day?" asked Mrs. Pothunter. "I 'phoned to you at twelve."

"I have been away in Bohemia," answered Mary, with a mystic smile.

There! Mary has given it away. She has spoiled my climax. For I was to have told you that Bohemia is nothing more than the little country in which you do not live. If you try to obtain citizenship in it, at once the court and retinue pack the royal archives and treasure and move away beyond the hills. It is a hillside that you turn your head to peer at from the windows of the Through Express.

At exactly half-past eleven Kappelman, deceived by a new softness and slowness of *riposte* and parry in Mary Adrian, tried to kiss her. Instantly she slapped his face with such strength and cold fury that he shrank down, sobered, with the flaming red print of a hand across his leering features. And all sounds ceased, as when the shadows of great wings come upon a flock of chattering sparrows. One had broken the paramount law of sham-Bohemia—the law of *"Laisser faire."* The shock came not from the blow delivered, but from the blow received. With the effect of a schoolmaster entering the play-room of his pupils was that blow administered. Women pulled down their sleeves and laid prim hands against their ruffled side locks. Men looked at their watches. There was nothing of the effect of a brawl about it; it was purely the still panic produced by the sound of the ax of the fly cop, Conscience, hammering at the gambling-house doors of the Heart.

With their punctilious putting on of cloaks, with their exaggerated pretense of not having seen or heard, with their stammering exchange of unaccustomed formalities, with their false show of a light-hearted exit I must take leave of my Bohemian party. Mary has robbed me of my climax; and she may go.

But I am not defeated. Somewhere there exists a great vault miles broad and miles long—more capacious than the champagne caves of France. In that vault are stored the anti-climaxes that should have been tagged to all the stories that have been told in the world. I shall cheat that vault of one deposit.

Minnie Brown, with her aunt, came from Crocusville down to the city to see the sights. And because she had escorted me to fishless trout streams and exhibited to me open-plumbed waterfalls and broken my camera while I Julyed in her village, I must escort her to the hives containing the synthetic clover honey of town.

Especially did the custom-made Bohemia charm her. The spaghetti wound its tendrils about her heart; the free red wine drowned her belief in the existence of commercialism in the world; she was dazed and enchanted by the rugose wit that can be churned out of California claret.

But one evening I got her away from the smell of halibut and linoleum long enough to read to her the manuscript of this story, which then ended before her entrance into it. I read it to her because I knew that all the printing-presses in the world were running to try to please her and some others. And I asked her about it. "I didn't quite catch the trains," said she. "How long was Mary in Crocusville?"

"Ten hours and five minutes," I replied.

"Well, then the story may do," said Minnie. "But if she had stayed there a week Kappelman would have got his kiss."

The Ransom of Mack

Me and old Mack Lonsbury, we got out of that Little Hide-and-Seek gold mine affair with about $40,000 apiece. I say "old" Mack; but he wasn't old. Forty-one, I should say; but he always seemed old.

"Andy," he says to me, "I'm tired of hustling. You and me have been working hard together for three years. Say we knock off for a while, and spend some of this idle money we've coaxed our way."

"The proposition hits me just right," says I. "Let's be nabobs a while and see how it feels. What'll we do—take in the Niagara Falls, or buck at faro?"

"For a good many years," says Mack, "I've thought that if I ever had extravagant money I'd rent a two-room cabin somewhere, hire a Chinaman to cook, and sit in my stocking feet and read Buckle's History of Civilization."

"That sounds self-indulgent and gratifying without vulgar ostentation," says I; "and I don't see how money could be better invested. Give me a cuckoo clock and a Sep Winner's Self-Instructor for the Banjo, and I'll join you."

A week afterward me and Mack hits this small town of Piña, about thirty miles out from Denver, and finds an elegant two-room house that just suits us. We deposited half-a-peck of money in the Piña bank and shook hands with every one of the 340 citizens in the town. We brought along the Chinaman and the cuckoo clock and Buckle and the Instructor with us from Denver; and they made the cabin seem like home at once.

Never believe it when they tell you riches don't bring happiness. If you could have seen old Mack sitting in his rocking-chair with his blue-yarn sock feet up in the window and absorbing in that Buckle stuff through his specs you'd have seen a picture of content that would have made Rockefeller jealous. And I was learning to pick out "Old Zip Coon" on the banjo, and the cuckoo was on time with his remarks, and Ah Sing was messing up the atmosphere with the handsomest smell of ham and eggs that ever laid the honeysuckle in the shade. When it got too dark to make out Buckle's nonsense and the notes in the Instructor, me and Mack would light our pipes and talk about science and pearl diving and sciatica and Eygpt and spelling and fish and trade-winds and leather and gratitude and eagles, and a lot of subjects that we'd never had time to explain our sentiments about before.

One evening Mack spoke up and asked me if I was much apprised in the habits and policies of women folks.

"Why, yes," says I, in a tone of voice; "I know 'em from Alfred to Omaha. The feminine nature and similitude," says I, "is as plain to my sight as the Rocky Mountains is to a blue-eyed burro. I'm onto all their little sidesteps and punctual discrepancies."

"I tell you, Andy," says Mack, with a kind of sigh. "I never had the least amount of intersection with their predispositions. Maybe I might have had a proneness in respect to their vicinity, but I never took the time. I made my own living since I was fourteen; and I never seemed to get my ratiocinations equipped with the sentiments usually depicted toward the sect. I sometimes wish I had," says old Mack.

"They're an adverse study," says I, "and adapted to points of view. Although they vary in rationale, I have found 'em quite often obviously differing from each other in divergences of contrast."

"It seems to me," goes on Mack, "that a man had better take 'em in and secure his inspirations of the sect when he's young and so preordained. I let my chance go by; and I guess I'm too old now to go hopping into the curriculum."

"Oh, I don't know," I tells him. "Maybe you better credit yourself with a barrel of money and a lot of emancipation from a quantity of uncontent. Still, I don't regret my knowledge of 'em," I says. "It takes a man who understands the symptoms and by-plays of women-folks to take care of himself in this world."

We stayed on in Piña because we liked the place. Some folks might enjoy their money with noise and rapture and locomotion; but me and Mack we had had plenty of turmoils and hotel towels. The people were friendly; Ah Sing got the swing of the grub we liked; Mack and Buckle were as thick as two body-snatchers, and I was hitting out a cordial resemblance to "Buffalo Gals, Can't You Come Out To-night," on the banjo.

One day I got a telegram from Speight, the man that was working a mine I had an interest in out in New Mexico. I had to go out there; and I was gone two months. I was anxious to get back to Piña and enjoy life once more.

When I struck the cabin I nearly fainted. Mack was standing in the door; and if angels ever wept, I saw no reason why they should be smiling then.

That man was a spectacle. Yes; he was worse; he was a spyglass; he was the great telescope in the Lick Observatory. He had on a coat and shiny shoes and a white vest and a high silk hat; and a geranium as big as an order of spinach was spiked onto his front. And he was smirking and warping his face like an infernal storekeeper or a kid with colic.

"Hello, Andy," says Mack, out of his face. "Glad to see you back. Things have happened since you went away."

"I know it," says I, "and a sacrilegious sight it is. God never made you that way, Mack Lonsbury. Why do you scarify His works with this presumptious kind of ribaldry?"

"Why, Andy," said he, "they've elected me justice of the peace since you left."

I looked at Mack close. He was restless and inspired. A justice of the peace ought to be disconsolate and assuaged.

Just then a young woman passed on the sidewalk; and I saw Mack kind of half snicker and blush, and then he raised up his hat and smiled and bowed, and she smiled and bowed, and went on by.

"No hope for you," says I, "if you've got the Mary-Jane infirmity at your age. I thought it wasn't going to take on you. And patent leather shoes! All this in two little short months!"

"I'm going to marry the young lady who just passed to-night," says Mack, in a kind of a flutter.

"I forgot something at the post-office," says I, and walked away quick.

I overtook that young woman a hundred yards away. I raised my hat and told her my name. She was about nineteen; and young for her age. She blushed, and then looked at me cool, like I was the snow scene from the "Two Orphans."

"I understand you are to be married to-night," I said.

"Correct," says she. "You got any any objections?"

"Listen, sissy," I begins.

"My name is Miss Rebosa Reed," says she in a pained way.

"I know it," says I. "Now, Rebosa, I'm old enough to have owed money to your father. And that old, specious, dresssed-up, garbled, seasick ptomaine prancing around avidiously like an irremediable turkey gobbler with patent leather shoes on is my best friend. Why did you go and get him invested in this marriage business?"

"Why, he was the only chance there was," answered Miss Rebosa.

"Nay," says I, giving a sickening look of admiration at her complexion and style of features; "with your beauty you might pick any kind of a man. Listen, Rebosa. Old Mack ain't the man you want. He was twenty-two when you were *née* Reed, as the papers say. This bursting into bloom won't last with him. He's all ventilated with oldness and rectitude and decay. Old Mack's down with a case of Indian summer. He overlooked his bet when he was young; and now he's suing Nature for the interest on the promissory note he took from Cupid instead of the cash. Rebosa, are you bent on having this marriage occur?"

"Why, sure I am," says she, oscillating the pansies on her hat, "and so is somebody else, I reckon."

"What times is it to take place?" I asks.

"At six o'clock," says she.

I made up my mind right away what to do. I'd save old Mack if I could. To have a good, seasoned, ineligible man like that turn chicken for a girl that hadn't quit eating slate pencils and buttoning in the back was more than I could look on with easiness.

"Rebosa," says I, earnest, drawing upon my display of knowledge concerning the feminine intuitions of reason—"ain't there a young man in Piña—a nice young man that you think a heap of?"

"Yep," says Rebosa, nodding her pansies—"Sure there is! What do you think! Gracious!"

"Does he like you?" I asks. "How does he stand in the matter?"

"Crazy," says Rebosa. "Ma has to wet down the front steps to keep him from sitting there all the time. But I guess that'll be all over after tonight," she winds up with a sigh.

"Rebosa," says I, "you don't really expeience any of this adoration called love for old Mack, do you?"

"Lord! no," says the girl, shaking her head. "I think he's as dry as a lava bed. The idea!"

"Who is this young man that you like, Rebosa?" I inquires.

"It's Eddie Bayles," says she. "He clerks in Crosby's grocery. But he don't make but thirty-five a month. Ella Noakes was wild about him once."

"Ol Mack tells me," I says, "that he's going to marry you at six o'clock this evening."

"That's the time," says she. "It's to be at our house."

"Rebosa," says I, "listen to me. If Eddie Bayles had a thousand dollars cash—a thousand dollars, mind you, would buy him a store of his own—if you and Eddie had that much to excuse matrimony on, would you consent to marry him this evening at five o'clock?"

The girl looks at me a minute; and I can see these inaudible cogitations going on inside of her, as women will.

"A thousand dollars?" says she. "Of course I would."

"Come on," says I. "We'll go and see Eddie."

We went up to Crosby's store and called Eddie outside. He looked to be estimable and freckled; and he had chills and fever when I made my proposition.

"At five o'clock?" says he, "for a thousand dollars? Please don't wake me up! Well, you *are* the rich uncle retired from the spice business in India. I'll buy out old Crosby and run the store myself."

We went inside and got old man Crosby apart and explained it. I wrote my check for a thousand dollars and handed it to him. If Eddie and Rebosa married each other at five he was to turn the money over to them.

And then I gave 'em my blessing, and went to wander in the wildwood for a season. I sat on a log and made cogitations on life and old age and the zodiac and the ways of women and all the disorder that goes with a lifetime. I passed myself congratulations that I had probably saved my old friend Mack from his attack of Indian summer. I knew when he got well of it and shed his infatuation and his patent leather shoes, he would feel grateful. "To keep old Mack disinvolved," thinks I, "from relapses like this, is worth more than a thousand dollars." And most of all I was glad that I'd made a study of women, and wasn't to be deceived any by their means of conceit and evolution.

It must have been half-past five when I got back home. I stepped in; and there sat old Mack on the back of his neck in his old clothes with his blue socks on the window and the History of Civilization propped up on his knees.

"This don't look like getting ready for a wedding at six," I says, to seem innocent.

"Oh," says Mack, reaching for his tobacco, "that was postponed back to five o'clock. They sent me a note saying the hour had been changed. It's all over now. What made you stay away so long, Andy?"

"You heard about the wedding?" I asks.

"I operated it," says he. "I told you I was justice of the peace. The preacher is off East to visit his folks, and I'm the only one in town that can perform the dispensations of marriage. I promised Eddie and Rebosa a month ago I'm marry 'em. He's a busy lad; and he'll have a grocery of his own some day."

"He will," says I.

"There was lots of women at the wedding," says Mack, smoking up. "But I didn't seem to get any ideas from 'em. I wish I was informed in the structure of their attainments like you said you was."

"That was two months ago," says I, reaching up for the banjo.

The Higher Abdication

Curly the tramp sidled toward the free-lunch counters. He caught a fleeting glance from the bartender's eye, and stood still, trying to look like a business man who had just dined at the Menger and was waiting for a friend who had promised to pick him up in his motor car. Curly's histrionic powers were equal to the impersonation; but his make-up was wanting.

The bartender rounded the bar in a casual way, looking up at the ceiling as though he was pondering some intricate problem of kalsomining, and then fell upon Curly so suddenly that the roadster had no excuses ready. Irresistibly, but so composedly that it seemed almost absentmindedness on his part, the dispenser of drinks pushed Curly to the swinging doors and kicked him out, with a nonchalance that almost amounted to sadness. That was the way of the Southwest.

Curly arose from the gutter leisurely. He felt no anger or resentment toward his ejector. Fifteen years of tramphood spent out of the twenty-two years of his life had hardened the fibres of his spirit. The slings and arrows of outrageous fortune fell blunted from the buckler of his armored pride. With especial resignation did he suffer contumely and injury at the hands of bartenders. Naturally, they were his enemies; and unnaturally, they were often his friends.He had to take his chances with them. But he had not yet learned to estimate these cool, languid, southwestern knights of the bung-starter, who had the manners of an Earl of Pawtucket, and who, when they disapproved of your presence, moved you with the silence and despatch of a chess automaton advancing a pawn.

Curly stood a few moments in the narrow, mesquite-paved street. San Antonio puzzled and disturbed him. Three days he had been a non-paying guest of the town, having dropped off there from a box car of an I. & G.N. freight, because Greaser Johnny had told him in Des Moines that the Alamo City was manna fallen, gathered, cooked, and served free with cream and sugar. Curly had found the tip partly a good one. There was hospitality in plenty of a careless, liberal, irregular sort. But the town itself was a weight upon his spirits after his experience with the rushing, business-like, systematized cities of the North and East. Here he was often flung a dollar, but too frequently a good-natured kick would follow it. Once a band of hilarious cowboys had roped him on Military Plaza and dragged him across the black soil until no respectable rag-bag would have stood sponsor for his clothes. The winding, doubling streets, leading nowhere, bewildered him. And then there was a little river, crooked as a pot-hook that crawled through the middle of the town, crossed by a hundred little bridges so nearly alike that they got on Curly's nerves. And the last bartender wore a number nine shoe.

The saloon stood on a corner. The hour was eight o'clock. Home-farers and outgoers jostled Curly on the narrow stone sidewalk. Between the buildings to his left he looked down a cleft that proclaimed itself another thoroughfare. The alley was dark except for one patch of light. Where there was a light there were sure to be human beings. Where there were human beings after nightfall in San Antonio there might be food, and there was sure to be drink. So Curly headed for the light.

The illumination came from Schwegel's Café. On the sidewalk in front of it Curly picked up an old envelope. It might have contained a check for a million. It was empty; but the wanderer read the address, "Mr. Otto Schwegel," and the name of the town and State. The postmark was Detroit.

Curly entered the saloon. And now in the light it could be perceived that he bore the stamp of many years of vagabondage. He had none of the tidiness of the calculating and shrewd professional tramp. His wardrobe represented the cast-off specimens of half a dozen fashions and eras. Two factories had combined their efforts in providing shoes for his feet. As you gazed at him there passed through your mind vague impressions of mummies, wax figures, Russian exiles, and men lost on desert islands. His face was covered almost to his eyes with a curly brown beard that he kept trimmed short with a pocket-knife, and that had furnished him with his *nom de route*. Light-blue eyes, full of sullenness, fear, cunning, impudence, and fawning, witnessed the stress that had been laid upon his soul.

The saloon was small, and in its atmosphere the odor of meat and drink struggled for the ascendency. The pig and the cabbage wrestled with hydrogen and oxygen. Behind the bar Schwegel labored with an assistant whose epidermal pores showed no signs of being obstructed. Hot wiernerwurst and sauerkraut were being served to purchasers of beer. Curly shuffled to the end of the bar, coughed hollowly, and told Schwegel that he was a Detroit cabinet-maker out of a job.

It followed as the night the day that he got his schooner and lunch.

"Was you acquainted maybe mit Heinrich Strauss in Detroit?" asked Schwegel.

"Did I know Heinrich Strauss?" repeated Curly, affectionately. "Why, say, 'Bo, I wish I had a dollar for every game of pinochle me and Heine has played on Sunday afternoons."

More beer and a second plate of steaming food was set before the diplomat. And then Curly, knowing to a fluid-drachm how far a "con" game would go, shuffled out into the unpromising street.

And now he began to perceive the inconveniences of this stony Southern town. There was none of the outdoor gaiety and brilliancy and music that provided distraction even to the poorest in the cities of the North. Here, even so early, the gloomy, rock-walled houses were closed and barred against the murky dampness of the night. The streets were mere fissures through which flowed gray wreaths of river mist. As he walked he heard laughter and the chink of coin and chips behind darkened windows, and music coming from every chink of wood and stone. But the diversions were selfish; the day of popular pastimes had not yet come to San Antonio.

But at length Curly, as he strayed, turned the sharp angle of another lost street and came upon a rollicking band of stockmen from the outlying ranches celebrating in the open in front of an ancient wooden hotel. One great roisterer from the sheep country who had just instigated a movement toward the bar, swept Curly in like a stray goat with the rest of his flock. The princes of kine and wool hailed him as a new zoölogical discovery, and uproariously strove to preserve him in the diluted alcohol of their compliments and regards.

An hour afterward Curly staggered from the hotel barroom, dismissed by his fickle friends, whose interest in him had subsided as quickly as it had risen. Full—stoked with alcoholic fuel and cargoed with food, the only question remaining to disturb him was that of shelter and bed.

A drizzling, cold Texas rain had begun to fall—an endless, lazy, unintermittent downfall that lowered the spirits of men and raised a reluctant steam from the warm stones of the streets and houses. Thus comes the "norther" dousing gentle spring and amiable autumn with the chilling salutes and adieux of coming and departing winter.

Curly followed his nose down the first tortuous street into which his irresponsible feet conducted him. At the lower end of it, on the bank of the serpentine stream, he perceived an open gate in a cemented rock wall. Inside he saw camp fires and a row of low wooden sheds built against three sides of the enclosing wall. He entered the enclosure. Under the sheds many horses were champing at their oats and corn. Many wagons and buckboards stood about with their teams' harness thrown carelessely upon the shafts and doubletrees. Curly recognized the place as a wagon yard, such as is provided by merchants for their out-of-town friends and customers. No one was in sight. No doubt the drivers of those wagons were scattered about the town "seeing the elephant and hearing the owl." In their haste to become patrons of the town's dispensaries of mirth and good cheer the last ones to depart must have left the great wooden gate swinging open.

Curly had satisfied the hunger of an anaconda and the thirst of a camel, so he was neither in the mood nor the condition of an explorer. He zigzagged his way to the first wagon that his eyesight distinguished in the semi-darkness under the shed. It was a two-horse wagon with a top of white canvas. The wagon was half filled with loose piles of wool sacks, two or three great bundles of gray blankets, and a number of bales, bundles, and boxes. A reasoning eye would have estimated the load at once as ranch supplies, bound on the morrow for some outlying hacienda. But to the drowsy intelligence of Curly they represented only warmth and softness and protection against the cold humidity of the night. After several unlucky efforts, at last he conquered gravity so far as to climb over a wheel and pitch forward upon the best and warmest bed he had fallen upon in many a day. Then he became instinctively a burrowing animal, and dug his way like a prairie-dog down among the sacks and blankets, hiding himself from the cold air as snug and safe as a bear in his den. For three nights sleep had visited Curly only in broken and shivering doses. So now, when Morpheus condescended to pay him a call, Curly got such a strangle hold on the mythological old gentleman that it was a wonder that any one else in the whole world got a wink of sleep that night.

Six cow-punchers of the Cibolo Ranch were waiting around the door of the ranch store. Their ponies cropped grass near by, tied in the Texas fashion—which is not tied at all. Their bridle reins had been dropped to the earth, which is a more effectual way of securing them (such is the power of habit and imagination) than you could devise out of a half-inch rope and a live-oak tree.

These guardians of the cow lounged about, each with a brown cigarette paper in his hand, and gently but unceasingly cursed Sam Revell, the storekeeper. Sam stood in the door, snapping the red elastic bands on his pink madras shirtsleeves and looking down affectionately at the only pair of tan shoes within a forty-mile radius. His offence had been serious, and he was divided between humble apology and admiration for the beauty of his raiment. He had allowed the ranch stock of "smoking" to become exhausted.

"I thought sure there was another case of it under the counter, boys," he explained. "But it happened to be catterdges."

"You've sure got a case of happendicitis," said Poky Rodgers, fence rider of the Largo Verde *potrero*. "Somebody ought to happen to give you a knock on the head with the butt end of a quirt. I've rode in nine miles for some tobacco; and it don't appear natural and seemly that you ought to be allowed to live."

"The boys was smokin' cut plug and dried mesquite leaves mixed when I left," sighed Mustang Taylor, horse wrangler of the Three Elm camp. "They'll be lookin' for me back by nine. They'll be settin' up, with their papers ready to roll a whiff of the real thing before bedtime. And I've got to tell 'em that this pink-eyed, sheep-headed, sulphur-footed, shirt-waisted son of a calico broncho, Sam Revell, hasn't got no tobacco on hand."

Gregorio Falcon, Mexican vaquero and best thrower of the rope on the Cibolo, pushed his heavy, silver-embroidered straw sombrero back upon his thicket of jet-black curls and scraped the bottoms of his pockets for a few crumbs of the precious weed.

"Ah, Don Samuel," he said, reproachfully, but with his touch of Castilian manners, "escuse me. Dthey say dthe jackrabbeet and dthe sheep have the most leetle *sesos*—haw you call dthem—brain-es? Ah, don't believe dthat, Don Samuel—escuse me. Ah dthink people w'at don't keep esmokin' tobacco, dthey—bot you weel escuse me, Don Samuel."

"Now, what's the use of chewin' the rag, boys," said the untroubled Sam, stooping over to rub the toes of his shoes with a red-and-yellow handkerchief. "Ranse took the order for some more smokin' to San Antone with him Tuesday. Pancho rode Ranse's hoss back yesterday; and Ranse is goin' to drive the wagon back himself. There wa'n't much of a load—just some woolsacks and blankets and nails and canned peaches an a few things we was out of. I look for Ranse to roll in to-day sure. He's a early starter and a hell-to-split driver, and he ought to be here not far from sundown."

"What plugs is he drivin'?" asked Mustang Taylor, with a smack of hope in his tones.

"The buckboard grays," said Sam.

"I'll wait a spell, then," said the wrangler. "Them plugs eat up a trail like a road-runner swallowin' a whip snake. And you may bust me open a can of green-gage plums, Sam, while I'm waitin' for somethin' better."

"Open me some yellow clings," ordered Poky Rodgers. "I'll wait, too."

The tobaccoless punchers arranged themselves comfortably on the steps of the store. Inside Sam chopped open with a hatchet the tops of the cans of fruit.

The store, a big, white wooden building like a barn, stood fifty yards from the ranch-house. Beyond it were the horse corrals; and still farther the wool sheds and the brush-topped shearing pens—for the Rancho Cibolo raised both cattle and sheep. Behind the store, at a little distance, were the grass-thatched *jacals* of the Mexicans who bestowed their allegiance upon the Cibolo.

The ranch-house was composed of four large rooms, with plastered adobe walls, and a two-room wooden ell. A twenty-feet-wide "gallery" circumvented the structure. It was set in a grove of immense live-oaks and water-elms near a lake—a long, not very wide, and tremendously deep lake in which, at nightfall, great gars leaped to the surface and plunged with the noise of hippopotamuses frolicking at their bath. From the trees hung garlands and massive pendants of the melancholy gray moss of the South. Indeed, the Cibolo ranch-house seemed more of the South than of the West. It looked as if old "Kiowa" Truesdell might have brought it with him from the lowlands of Mississippi when he came to Texas with his rifle in the hollow of his arm in '55.

But, though he did not bring the family mansion, Truesdell did bring something in the way of a family inheritance that was more lasting than brick or stone. He brought one end of the Truesdell-Curtis family feud. And when a Curtis bought the Rancho de los Olmos, sixteen miles from the Cibolo, there were lively times on the pear flats and in the chaparral thickets of the Southwest. In those days Truesdell cleaned the brush of many a wolf and tiger cat and Mexican lion; and one or two Curtises fell heirs to notches on his rifle stock. Also he buried a brother with a Curtis bullet in him on the bank of the lake at Cibolo. And then the Kiowa Indians made their last raid upon the ranches between the Frio and the Rio Grande, and Truesdell at the head of his rangers rid the earth of them to the last brave, earning his sobriquet. Then came prosperity in the form of waxing herds and broadening lands. And then old age and bitterness, when he sat, with his great mane of hair as white as the Spanish-dagger blossoms and his fierce, pale-blue eyes, on the shaded gallery at Cibolo, growling like the pumas that he had slain. He snapped his fingers at old age; the bitter taste of life did not come from that. The cup that stuck at his lips was that his only son Ransom wanted to marry a Curtis, the last youthful survivor of the other end of the feud.

For a while the only sounds to be heard at the store were the rattling of the tin spoons and the gurgling intake of the juicy fruits by the cowpunchers, the stamping of the grazing ponies, and the singing of a doleful song by Sam as he contentedly brushed his stiff auburn hair for the twentieth time that day before a crinkly mirror.

From the door of the store could be seen the irregular, sloping stretch of prairie to the south, with its reaches of light-green, billowing mesquite flats in the lower places, and its rises crowned with nearly black masses of short chaparral. Through the mesquite flat wound the ranch road that, five miles away, flowed into the old government trail to San Antonio. The sun was so low that the gentlest elevation cast its gray shadow miles into the green-gold of sunshine.

That evening ears were quicker than eyes.

The Mexican held up a tawny finger to still the scraping of tin against tin.

"One waggeen," said he, "cross the Arroyo Hodo. Ah hear dthe wheel. Verree rockee place, dthe Hondo."

"You've got good ears, Gregorio," said Mustang Taylor. "I never heard nothin' but the song-bird in the bush and the zephyr skally-hootin' across the peaceful dell."

In ten minutes Taylor remarked: "I see the dust of a wagon risin' right above the fur end of the flat."

"You have verree good eyes, señor," said Gregorio smiling.

Two miles away they saw a faint cloud dimming the green ripples of the mesquites. In twenty minutes they heard the clatter of horses' hoofs: in five minutes more the gray plugs dashed out of the thicket, whickering for oats and drawing the light wagon behind them like a toy.

From the *jacals* came a cry of: *"El Amo! El Amo!"* Four Mexican youths raced to unharness the grays. The cow-punchers gave a yell of greeting and delight.

Ranse Truesdell, driving, threw the reins to the ground and laughed.

"It's under the wagon sheet, boys," he said. "I know what you're waiting for. If Sam lets it run out again we'll use them yellow shoes of his for a target. There's two cases. Pull 'em out and light up. I know you'll want a smoke."

After striking dry country Ranse had removed the wagon sheet from the bows and thrown it over the goods in the wagon. Six pairs of hasty hands draged it off and grabbled beneath the sacks and blankets for the cases of tobacco.

Long Collins, tobacco messenger from the San Gabriel outfit, who rode with the longest stirrups west of the Mississippi, delved with an arm like the tongue of a wagon. He caught something harder than a blanket and pulled out a fearful thing—a shapeless, muddy bunch of leather tied together with wire and twine. From its ragged end, like the head and claws of a disturbed turtle, protruded human toes.

"Who-ee!" yelled Long Collins. "Ranse, are you a-packin' around of corpuses? Here's a—howlin' grasshoppers!"

Up from his long slumber popped Curly, like some vile worm from its burrow. He clawed his way out and sat blinking like a disreputable, drunken owl. His face was as bluish red and puffed and seamed and crosslined as the cheapest round steak of the butcher. His eyes were swollen slits; his nose a pickled beet; his hair would have made the wildest thatch of a Jack-in-the-box look like the satin poll of a Cléo de Mérode. The rest of him was scarecrow done to the life.

Ranse jumped down from his seat and looked at his strange cargo with wide-open eyes.

"Here, you maverick, what are you doing in my wagon? How did you get in there?"

The punchers gathered around in delight. For the time they had forgotten tobacco.

Curly looked around him slowly in every direction. He snarled like a Scotch terrier through his ragged beard.

"Where is this," he rasped through his parched throat. "It's a damn farm in an old field. What'd you bring me here for—say? Did I say I wanted to come here? What are you Reubs rubberin' at—hey? G'wan or I'll punch some of your faces."

"Drag him out, Collins," said Ranse.

Curly took a slide and felt the ground rise up and collide with his shoulder blades. He got up and sat on the steps of the store shivering from outraged nerves, hugging his knees and sneering. Taylor lifted out a case of tobacco and wrenched off its top. Six cigarettes began to glow, bringing peace and forgiveness to Sam.

"How'd you come in my wagon?" repeated Ranse, this time in a voice that drew a reply.

Curly recognized the tone. He had heard it used by freight brakemen and large persons in blue carrying clubs.

"Me?" he growled. "Oh, was you talkin' to me? Why, I was on my way to the Menger, but my valet had forgot to pack my pajamas. So I crawled into that wagon in the wagon-yard—see? I never told you to bring me out to this bloomin' farm—see?"

"What is it, Mustang?" asked Poky Rodgers, almost forgetting to smoke in his ecstasy. "What do it live on?"

"It's a galliwampus, Poky," said Mustang. "It's the thing that hollers 'williwallo' up in ellum trees in the low grounds of nights. I don't know if it bites."

"No, it ain't, Mustang," volunteered Long Collins. "Them galliwampuses has fins on their backs, and eighteen toes. This here is a hicklesnifter. It lives under the ground and eats cherries. Don't stand so close to it. It wipes out villages with one stroke of its prehensile tail."

Sam, the cosmopolite, who called bartenders in San Antone by their first name, stood in the door. He was a better zoölogist.

"Well, ain't that a Willie for your whiskers?" he commented. "Where'd you dig up the hobo, Ranse? Goin' to make an auditorium for inbreviates out of the ranch?"

"Say," said Curly, from whose panoplied breast all shafts of wit fell blunted. "Any of you kiddin' guys got a drink on you? Have your fun. Say, I've been hittin' the stuff till I don't know straight up."

He turned to Ranse. "Say, you shanghaied me on your d—d old prairie schooner—did I tell you to drive me to a farm? I want a drink. I'm goin' all to little pieces. What's doin'?"

Ranse saw that the tramp's nerves were racking him. He despatched one of the Mexican boys to the ranch-house for a glass of whisky. Curly gulped it down; and into his eyes came a brief, grateful glow—as human as the expression in the eye of a faithful setter dog.

"Thanky, boss," he said, quietly.

"You're thirty miles from a railroad, and forty miles from a saloon," said Ranse.

Curly fell back weakly against the steps.

"Since you are here," continued the ranchman, "come along with me. We can't turn you out on the prairie. A rabbit might tear you to pieces."

He conducted Curly to a large shed where the ranch vehicles were kept. There he spread out a canvas cot and brought blankets.

"I don't suppose you can sleep," said Ranse, "since you've been pounding your ear for twenty-four hours. But you can camp here till morning. I'll have Pedro fetch you up some grub."

"Sleep!" said Curly. "I can sleep a week. Say, sport, have you got a coffin nail on you?"

Fifty miles had Ransom Truesdell driven that day. And yet this is what he did.

Old "Kiowa" Truesdell sat in his great wicker chair reading by the light of an immense oil lamp. Ranse laid a bundle of newspapers fresh from town at his elbow.

"Back, Ranse?" said the old man, looking up.

"Son," old "Kiowa" continued, "I've been thinking all day about a certain matter that we have talked about. I want you to tell me again. I've lived for you. I've fought wolves and Indians and worse white men to protect you. You never had any mother that you can remember. I've taught you to shoot straight, ride hard, and live clean. Later on I've worked to pile up dollars that'll be yours. You'll be a rich man, Ranse, when my chunk goes out. I've made you. I've licked you into shape like a leopard cat licks its cubs. You don't belong to yourself—you've got to be a Truesdell first. Now, is there to be any more nonsense about this Curtis girl?"

"I'll tell you once more," said Ranse, slowly. "As I am a Truesdell and as you are my father, I'll never marry a Curtis."

"Good boy," said old "Kiowa." "You'd better go get some supper."

Ranse went to the kitchen at the rear of the house. Pedro, the Mexican cook, sprang up to bring the food he was keeping warm in the stove.

"Just a cup of coffee, Pedro," he said, and drank it standing. And then:

"There's a tramp on a cot in the wagon-shed. Take him something to eat. Better make it enough for two."

Ranse walked out toward the *jacals.* A boy came running.

"Manuel, can you catch Vaminos, in the little pasture, for me?"

"Why not, señor? I saw him near the *puerta* but two hours past. He bears a drag-rope."

"Get him and saddle him as quick as you can."

"Prontito, señor."

Soon mounted, on Vaminos, Ranse leaned in the saddle, pressed with his knees, and galloped eastward past the store, where sat Sam trying his guitar in the moonlight.

Vaminos shall have a word—Vaminos the good dun horse. The Mexicans, who have a hundred names for the colors of a horse, called him *gruyo.* He was a mouse-colored, slate-colored, flea-bitten roan-dun, if you can conceive it. Down his back from his mane to his tail went a line of black. He would live forever; and surveyors have not laid off as many miles in the world as he could travel in a day.

Eight miles east of the Cibolo ranch-house Ranse loosened the pressure of his knees, and Vaminos stopped under a big ratama tree. The yellow ratama blossoms showered fragrance that would have undone the roses of France. The moon made the earth a great concave bowl with a crystal sky for a lid. In a glade five jack-rabbits leaped and played together like kittens. Eight miles farther east shone a faint star that appeared to have dropped below the horizon. Night riders, who often steered their course by it, knew it to be the light in the Rancho de los Olmos.

In ten minutes Yenna Curtis galloped to the tree on her sorrel pony Dancer. The two leaned and clasped hands heartily.

"I ought to have ridden nearer your home," said Ranse. "But you never will let me."

Yenna laughed. And in the soft light you could see her strong white teeth and fearless eyes. No sentimentality there, in spite of the moonlight, the odor of the ratamas, and the admirable figure of Ranse Truesdell, the lover. But she was there, eight miles from her home, to meet him.

"How often have I told you, Ranse," she said, "that I am your half-way girl? Always half-way."

"Well?" said Ranse, with a question in his tones.

"I did," said Yenna, with almost a sigh. "I told him after dinner when I thought he would be in a good humor. Did you ever wake up a lion, Ranse, with the mistaken idea that he would be a kitten? He almost tore the ranch to pieces. It's all up. I love my daddy, Ranse, and I'm afraid—I'm afraid of him, too. He ordered me to promise that I'd never marry a Truesdell. I promised. That's all. What luck did you have?"

"The same," said Ranse, slowly. "I promised him that his son would never marry a Curtis. Somehow I couldn't go against him. He's mighty old. I'm sorry, Yenna."

The girl leaned in her saddle and laid one hand on Ranse's, on the horn of his saddle.

"I never thought I'd like you better for giving me up," she said ardently, "but I do. I must ride back now, Ranse. I slipped out of the house and saddled Dancer myself. Good-night, neighbor."

"Good-night," said Ranse. "Ride carefully over them badger holes."

They wheeled and rode away in opposite directions. Yenna turned in her saddle and called clearly:

"Don't forget I'm your half-way girl, Ranse."

"Damn all family feuds and inherited scraps," muttered Ranse vindictively to the breeze as he rode back to the Cibolo.

Ranse turned his horse into the small pasture and went to his own room. He opened the lowest drawer of an old bureau to get out the packet of letters that Yenna had written him one summer when she had gone to Mississippi for a visit. The drawer stuck, and he yanked at it savagely—as a man will. It came out of the bureau, and bruised both his shins—as a drawer will. An old, folded yellow letter without an envelope fell from somewhere—probably from where it had lodged in one of the upper drawers. Ranse took it to the lamp and read it curiously.

Then he took his hat and walked to one of the Mexican *jacals*.

"Tía Juana," he said, "I would like to talk with you awhile."

An old, old Mexican woman, white-haired and wonderfully wrinkled, rose from a stool.

"Sit down," said Ranse, removing his hat and taking the one chair in the *jacal*. "Who am I, Tía Juana?" he asked, speaking Spanish.

"Don Ransom, our good friend and employer. Why do you ask?" answered the old woman wonderingly.

"Tía Juana, who am I?" he repeated, with his stern eyes looking into hers.

A frightened look came in the old woman's face. She fumbled with her black shawl.

"Who am I, Tía Juana?" said Ranse once more.

"Thirty-two years I have lived on the Rancho Cibolo," said Tía Juana. "I thought to be buried under the coma mott beyond the garden before these things should be known. Close the door, Don Ransom, and I will speak. I see in your face that you know."

An hour Ranse spent behind Tía Juana's closed door. As he was on his way back to the house Curly called to him from the wagon-shed.

The tramp sat on his cot, swinging his feet and smoking.

"Say, sport," he grumbled. "This is no way to treat a man after kidnappin' him. I went up to the store and borrowed a razor from that fresh guy and had a shave. But that ain't all a man needs. Say—can't you loosen up for about three fingers more of that booze? I never asked you to bring me to your d—d farm."

"Stand up out here in the light," said Ranse, looking at him closely.

Curly got up sullenly and took a step or two.

His face, now shaven smooth, seemed transformed. His hair had been combed, and it fell back from the right side of his forehead with a peculiar wave. The moonlight charitably softened the ravages of drink; and his aquiline, well-shaped nose and small, square-cleft chin almost gave distinction to his looks.

Ranse sat on the foot of the cot and looked at him curiously.

"Where did you come from . . . have you got any home or folks anywhere?"

"Me? Why, I'm a dook," said Curly. "I'm Sir Reginald—oh, cheese it. No; I don't know anything about my ancestors. I've been a tramp ever since I can remember. Say, old pal, are you going to set 'em up again tonight or not?"

"You answer my questions and maybe I will. How did you come to be a tramp?"

"Me," answered Curly. "Why, I adopted that profession when I was an infant. Case of had to. First thing I can remember, I belonged to a big, lazy hobo called Beefsteak Charley. He sent me around to houses to beg. I wasn't hardly big enough to reach the latch of a gate."

"Did he ever tell you how he got you?" asked Ranse.

"Once when he was sober he said he bought me for an old six-shooter and six bits from a band of drunken Mexican sheep-shearers. But what's the diff? That's all I know."

"All right," said Ranse. "I reckon you're a maverick for certain.

I'm going to put the Rancho Cibolo brand on you. I'll start you to work in one of the camps to-morrow."

"Work!" sniffed Curly, disdainfully. "What do you take me for? Do you think I'd chase cows, and hop-skip-and-jump around after crazy sheep like that pink-and-yellow guy at the store says these Reubs do? Forget it."

"Oh, you'll like it when you get used to it," said Ranse. "Yes. I'll send you up one more drink by Pedro. I think you'll make a first-class cow-puncher before I get through with you."

"Me?" said Curly. "I pity the cows you set me to chaperon. They can go chase themselves. Don't forget my nightcap, please, boss."

Ranse paid a visit to the store before going to the house. Sam Revell was taking off his tan shoes regretfully and preparing for bed.

"Any of the boys from the San Gabriel camp riding in early in the morning?" asked Ranse.

"Long Collins," said Sam, briefly. "For the mail."

"Tell him," said Ranse, "to take that tramp out to camp with him and keep him till I get there."

Curly was sitting on his blankets in the San Gabriel camp cursing talentedly when Ranse Truesdell rode up and dismounted on the next afternoon. The cow-punchers were ignoring the stray. He was grimy with dust and black dirt. His clothes were making their last stand in favor of the conventions.

Ranse went up to Buck Rabb, the camp boss, and spoke briefly.

"He's a plum buzzard," said Buck. "He won't work, and he's the low-downest passel of inhumanity I ever see. I didn't know what you wanted done with him, Ranse, so I just let him set. That seems to suit him. He's been condemned to death by the boys a dozen times, but I told 'em maybe you was savin' him for torture."

Ranse took off his coat.

"I've got a hard job before me, Buck, I reckon, but it has to be done. I've got to make a man out of that thing. That's what I've come to camp for."

He went up to Curly.

"Brother," he said, "don't you think if you had a bath it would allow you to take a seat in the company of your fellow-man with less injustice to the atmosphere?"

"Run away, farmer," said Curly, sardonically. "Willie will send for nursey when he feels like having his tub."

The *charco,* or water hole, was twelve yards away. Ranse took one of Curly's ankles and dragged him like a sack of potatoes to the brink.

Then with the strength and sleight of a hammer-thrower he hurled the offending member of society far into the lake.

Curly crawled out and up the bank spluttering like a porpoise.

Ranse met him with a piece of soap and a coarse towel in his hands.

"Go to the other end of the lake and use this," he said. "Buck will give you some dry clothes at the wagon."

The tramp obeyed without protest. By the time supper was ready he had returned to camp. He was hardly to be recognized in his new blue shirt and brown duck clothes. Ranse observed him out of the corner of his eye.

"Lordy, I hope he ain't a coward," he was saying to himself. "I hope he won't turn out to be a coward."

His doubts were soon allayed. Curly walked straight to where he stood. His light-blue eyes were blazing.

"Now I'm clean," he said, meaningly, "maybe you'll talk to me. Think you've got a picnic here, do you? You clodhoppers think you can run over a man because you know he can't get away. All right. Now, what do you think of that?"

Curly planted a stinging slap against Ranse's left cheek. The print of his hand stood out a dull red against the tan.

Ranse smiled happily.

The cow-punchers talk to this day of the battle that followed.

Somewhere in his restless tour of the cities Curly had acquired the art of self-defence. The ranchman was equipped only with the splendid strength and equilibrium of perfect health and the endurance conferred by decent living. The two attributes nearly matched. There were no formal rounds. At last the fibre of the clean liver prevailed. The last time Curly went down from one of the ranchman's awkward but powerful blows he remained on the grass, but looking up with an unquenched eye.

Ranse went to the water barrel and washed the red from a cut on his chin in the stream from the faucet.

On his face was a grin of satisfaction.

Much benefit might accrue to educators and moralists if they could know the details of the curriculum of reclamation through which Ranse put his waif during the month that he spent in the San Gabriel camp. The ranchman had no fine theories to work out—perhaps his whole stock of pedagogy embraced only a knowledge of horse-breaking and a belief in heredity.

The cow-punchers saw that their boss was trying to make a man out of the strange animal that he had sent among them; and they tacitly organized themselves into a faculty of assistants. But their system was their own.

Curly's first lesson stuck. He became on friendly and then on intimate terms with soap and water. And the thing that pleased Ranse most was that his "subject" held his ground at each successive higher step. But the steps were sometimes far apart.

Once he got at the quart bottle of whisky kept sacredly in the grub tent for rattlesnake bites, and spent sixteen hours on the grass, magnificently drunk. But when he staggered to his feet his first move was to find his soap and towel and start for the *charco*. And once, when a treat came from the ranch in the form of a basket of fresh tomatoes and young onions, Curly devoured the entire consignment before the punchers reached the camp at supper time.

And then the punchers punished him in their own way. For three days they did not speak to him, except to reply to his own questions or remarks. And they spoke with absolute and unfailing politeness. They played tricks on one another; they pounded one another hurtfully and affectionately; they heaped upon one another's heads friendly curses and obloquy; but they were polite to Curly. He saw it, and it stung him as much as Ranse hoped it would.

Then came a night that brought a cold, wet norther. Wilson, the youngest of the outfit, had lain in camp two days, ill with a fever. When Joe got up at daylight to begin breakfast he found Curly sitting asleep against a wheel of the grub wagon with only a saddle blanket around him, while Curly's blankets were stretched over Wilson to protect him from the rain and wind.

Three nights after that Curly rolled himself in his blanket and went to sleep. Then the other punchers rose up softly and began to make preparations. Ranse saw Long Collins tie a rope to the horn of a saddle. Others were getting out their six-shooters.

"Boys," said Ranse, "I'm much obliged. I was hoping you would. But I didn't like to ask."

Half a dozen six-shooters began to pop—awful yells rent the air—Long Collins galloped wildly across Curly's bed, dragging the saddle after him. That was merely their way of gently awaking their victim. Then they hazed him for an hour, carefully and ridiculously, after the code of cow camps. Whenever he uttered protest they held him stretched over a roll of blankets and thrashed him woefully with a pair of leather leggins.

And all this meant that Curly had won his spurs, that he was receiving the punchers' accolade. Nevermore would they be polite to him. But he would be their "pardner" and stirrup-brother, foot to foot.

When the fooling was ended all hands made a raid on Joe's big coffeepot by the fire for a Java nightcap. Ranse watched the new knight carefully to see if he understood and was worthy. Curly limped with his cup of coffee to a log and sat upon it. Long Collins followed and sat by his side. Buck Rabb went and sat at the other. Curly—grinned.

And then Ranse furnished Curly with mounts and saddle and equipment, and turned him over to Buck Rabb, instructing him to finish the job.

Three weeks later Ranse rode from the ranch into Rabb's camp, which was then in Snake Valley. The boys were saddling for the day's ride. He sought out Long Collins among them.

"How about that bronco?" he asked.

Long Collins grinned.

"Reach out your hand, Ranse Truesdell," he said, "and you'll touch him. And you can shake his'n, too, if you like, for he's plumb white and there's none better in no camp."

Ranse looked again at the clear-faced, bronzed, smiling cow-puncher who stood at Collins's side. Could that be Curly? He held out his hand, and Curly grasped it with the muscles of a bronco-buster.

"I want you at the ranch," said Ranse.

"All right, sport," said Curly, heartily. "But I want to come back again. Say, pal, this is a dandy farm. And I don't want any better fun than hustlin' cows with this bunch of guys. They're all to the merry merry."

At the Cibolo ranch-house they dismounted. Ranse bade Curly wait at the door of the living room. He walked inside. Old "Kiowa" Truesdell was reading at a table.

"Good-morning, Mr. Truesdell," said Ranse.

The old man turned his white head quickly.

"How is this?" he began. "Why do you call me 'Mr.—'?"

When he looked at Ranse's face he stopped, and the hand that held his newspaper shook slightly.

"Boy," he said slowly, "how did you find it out?"

"It's all right," said Ranse, with a smile. "I made Tía Juana tell me. It was kind of by accident, but it's all right."

"You've been like a son to me," said old "Kiowa," trembling.

"Tía Juana told me all about it," said Ranse. "She told me how you adopted me when I was knee-high to a puddle duck out of a wagon train of prospectors that was bound West. And she told me how the kid—your own kid, you know—got lost or was run away with. And she said it was the same day that the sheep-shearers got on a bender and left the ranch."

"Our boy strayed from the house when he was two years old," said the old man. "And then along came these emigrant wagons with a youngster they didn't want; and we took you. I never intended you to know, Ranse. We never heard of our boy again."

"He's right outside, unless I'm mightly mistaken," said Ranse, opening the door and beckoning.

Curly walked in.

No one could have doubted. The old man and the young had the same sweep of hair, the same nose, chin, line of face, and prominent light-blue eyes.

Old "Kiowa" rose eagerly.

Curly looked about the room curiously. A puzzled expression came over his face. He pointed to the wall opposite.

"Where's the tick-tock?" he asked, absentmindedly.

"The clock," cried old "Kiowa" loudly. "The eight-day clock used to stand there. Why———"

He turned to Ranse, but Ranse was not there.

Already a hundred yards away, Vaminos, the good flea-bitten dun, was bearing him eastward like a racer through dust and chaparral towards the Rancho de los Olmos.

A Call Loan

In those days the cattlemen were the anointed. They were the grandees of the grass, kings of the kine, lords of the lea, barons of beef and bone. They might have ridden in gold chariots had their tastes so inclined. The cattleman was caught in a stampede of dollars. It seemed to him that he had more money than was decent. But when he had bought a watch with precious stones set in the case so large that they hurt his ribs, and a California saddle with silver nails and Angora skin *suaderos,* and ordered everybody up to the bar for whisky—what else was there for him to spend money for?

Not so circumscribed in expedient for the reduction of surplus wealth were those lairds of the lariat who had womenfolk to their name. In the breast of the rib-sprung sex the genius of purse lightening may slumber through years of inopportunity, but never, my brothers, does it become extinct.

So, out of the chaparral came Long Bill Longley from the Bar Circle Branch on the Frio—a wife-driven man—to taste the urban joys of success. Something like half a million dollars he had, with an income steadily increasing.

Long Bill was a graduate of the camp and trail. Luck and thrift, a cool head, and a telescopic eye for mavericks had raised him from cowboy to be a cowman. Then came the boom in cattle, and Fortune, stepping gingerly among the cactus thorns, came and emptied her cornucopia at the doorstep of the ranch.

In the little frontier city of Chaparosa, Longley built a costly residence. Here he became a captive, bound to the chariot of social existence. He was doomed to become a leading citizen. He struggled for a time like a mustang in his first corral, and then he hung up his quirt and spurs. Time hung heavily on his hands. He organized the First National Bank of Chaparosa, and was elected its president.

One day a dyspeptic man, wearing double-magnifying glasses, inserted an official-looking card between the bars of the cashier's window of the First National Bank. Five minutes later the bank force was dancing at the beck and call of a national bank examiner.

This examiner, Mr. J. Edgar Todd, proved to be a thorough one.

At the end of it all the examiner put on his hat, and called the president, Mr. William R. Longley, into the private office.

"Well, how do you find things?" asked Longley, in his slow, deep tones. "Any brands in the round-up you didn't like the looks of?"

"The bank checks up all right, Mr. Longley," said Todd; "and I find your loans in very good shape—with one exception. You are carrying one very bad bit of paper—one that is so bad that I have been thinking that you surely do not realize the serious position it places you in. I refer to a call loan of $10,000 made to Thomas Merwin. Not only is the amount in excess of the maximum sum the bank can loan any individual legally, but it is absolutely without endorsement or security. Thus you have doubly violated the national banking laws, and have laid yourself open to criminal prosecution by the Government. A report of the matter to the Comptroller of the Currency—which I am bound to make—would, I am sure, result in the matter being turned over to the Department of Justice for action. You see what a serious thing it is."

Bill Longley was leaning his lengthy, slowly moving frame back in his swivel chair. His hands were clasped behind his head, and he turned a little to look the examiner in the face. The examiner was surprised to see a smile creep about the rugged mouth of the banker, and a kindly twinkle in his light-blue eyes. If he saw the seriousness of the affair, it did not show in his countenance.

"Of course, you don't know Tom Merwin," said Longley, almost genially. "Yes, I know about that loan. It hasn't any security except Tom Merwin's word. Somehow, I've always found that when a man's word is good, it's the best security there is. Oh, yes, I know the Government doesn't think so. I guess I'll see Tom about that note."

Mr. Todd's dyspepsia seemed to grow suddenly worse. He looked at the chaparral banker through his double-magnifying glasses in amazement.

"You see," said Longley, easily explaining the thing away, "Tom heard of 2,000 head of two-year-olds down near Rocky Ford on the Rio Grande that could be had for $8 a head. I reckon 'twas one of old Laendro Garcia's outfits that he had smuggled over, and he wanted to make a quick turn on 'em. Those cattle are worth $15 on the hoof in Kansas City. Tom knew it and I knew it. He had $6,000, and I let him have the $10,000 to make the deal with. His brother Ed took 'em on to market three weeks ago. He ought to be back 'most any day now with the money. When he comes Tom'll pay that note."

The bank examiner was shocked. It was, perhaps, his duty to step out to the telegraph office and wire the situation to the Comptroller. But he did not. He talked pointedly and effectively to Longley for three minutes. He succeeded in making the banker understand that he stood upon the border of a catastrophe. And then he offered a tiny loophole of escape.

"I am going to Hilldale's to-night," he told Longley, "to examine a bank there. I will pass through Chaparosa on my way back. At twelve tomorrow I shall call at this bank. If this loan has been cleared out of the way by that time it will not be mentioned in my report. If not—I will have to do my duty."

With that the examiner bowed and departed.

The President of the First National lounged in his chair half an hour longer, and then he lit a mild cigar, and went over to Tom Merwin's house. Merwin, a ranchman in brown duck, with a contemplative eye, sat with his feet upon a table, plaiting a rawhide quirt.

"Tom," said Longley, leaning against the table, "you heard anything from Ed yet?"

"Not yet," said Merwin, continuing his plaiting. "I guess Ed'll be along back now in a few days."

"There was a bank examiner," said Longley, "nosing around our place to-day, and he bucked a sight about the note of yours. You know I know it's all right, but the thing *is* against the banking laws. I was pretty sure you'd have paid it off before the bank was examined again, but the son-of-a-gun slipped in on us, Tom. Now, I'm short of cash myself just now, or I'd let you have the money to take it up with. I've got till twelve o'clock to-morrow, and then I've got to show the cash in place of that note or———"

"Or what, Bill?" asked Merwin, as Longley hesitated.

"Well, I suppose it means be jumped on with both of Uncle Sam's feet."

"I'll try to raise the money for you on time," said Merwin, interested in his plaiting.

"All right, Tom," concluded Longley, as he turned toward the door; "I knew you would if you could."

Merwin threw down his whip and went to the only other bank in town, a private one, run by Cooper & Craig.

"Cooper," he said, to the partner by that name, "I've got to have $10,000 to-day or to-morrow. I've got a house and lot here that's worth about $6,000 and that's all the actual collateral. But I've got a cattle deal on that's sure to bring me in more than that much profit within a few days."

Cooper began to cough.

"Now, for God's sake don't say no," said Merwin. "I owe that much money on a call loan. It's been called, and the man that called it is a man I've laid on the same blanket with in cow-camps and ranger-camps for ten years. He can call anything I've got. He can call the blood out of my veins and it'll come. He's got to have the money. He's in a devil of a———Well, he needs the money, and I've got to get it for him. You know my word's good, Cooper."

"No doubt of it," assented Cooper, urbanely, "but I've a partner, you know. I'm not free in making loans. And even if you had the best security in your hands, Merwin, we couldn't accommodate you in less than a week. We're just making a shipment of $15,000 to Myer Brothers in Rockdell, to buy cotton with. It goes down on the narrow gauge to-night. That leaves our cash quite short at present. Sorry we can't arrange it for you."

Merwin went back to his little bar office and plaited at his quirt again. About four o'clock in the afternoon he went to the First National and leaned over the railing of Longley's desk.

"I'll try to get that money for you to-night—I mean to-morrow, Bill."

"All right, Tom," said Longley, quietly.

At nine o'clock that night Tom Merwin stepped cautiously out of the small frame house in which he lived. It was near the edge of the little town, and few citizens were in the neighborhood at that hour. Merwin wore two six-shooters in a belt and a slouch hat. He moved swiftly down a lonely street, and then followed the sandy road that ran parallel to the narrow-gauge track until he reached the water-tank, two miles below the town. There Tom Merwin stopped, tied a black silk handkerchief about the lower part of his face, and pulled his hat down low.

In ten minutes the night train for Rockdell pulled up at the tank, having come from Chaparosa.

With a gun in each hand Merwin raised himself from behind a clump of chaparral and started for the engine. But before he had taken three steps, two long, strong arms clasped him from behind, and he was lifted from his feet and thrown, face downward, upon the grass. There was a heavy knee pressing against his back, and an iron hand grasping each of his wrists. He was held thus, like a child, until the engine had taken water, and until the train had moved, with accelerating speed, out of sight. Then he was released, and rose to his feet to face Bill Longley.

"The case never needed to be fixed up this way, Tom," said Longley. "I saw Cooper this evening, and he told me what you and him talked about. Then I went down to your house to-night and saw you come out with your guns on, and I followed you. Let's go back, Tom."

They walked away together, side by side.

" 'Twas the only chance I saw," said Merwin, presently. "You called your loan, and I tried to answer you. Now, what'll you do, Bill, if they sock it to you?"

"What would you have done if they'd socked it to you?" was the answer Longley made.

"I never thought I'd lay in a bush to stick up a train," remarked Merwin; "but a call loan's different. A call's a call with me. We've got twelve hours yet, Bill, before this spy jumps onto you. We've got to raise them spondulicks somehow. Maybe we can—Great Sam Houston! do you hear that?"

Merwin broke into a run, and Longley kept with him, hearing only a rather pleasing whistle somewhere in the night rendering the lugubrious air of "The Cowboy's Lament."

"It's the only tune he knows," shouted Merwin, as he ran. "I'll bet———"

They were at the door of Merwin's house. He kicked it open and fell over an old valise lying in the middle of the floor. A sunburned, firm-jawed youth, stained by travel, lay upon the bed puffing at a brown cigarette.

"What's the word, Ed?" gasped Merwin.

"So, so," drawled that capable youngster. "Just got in on the 9:30. Sold the bunch for fifteen, straight. Now, buddy, you want to quit kickin' a valise around that's got $29,000 in greenbacks in its in'ards."

The Princess and the Puma

There had to be a king and queen, of course. The king was a terrible old man who wore six-shooters and spurs, and shouted in such a tremendous voice that the rattlers on the prairie would run into their holes under the prickly pear. Before there was a royal family they called the man "Whispering Ben." When he came to own 50,000 acres of land and more cattle than he could count, they called him O'Donnell "the Cattle King."

The queen had been a Mexican girl from Laredo. She made a good, mild, Coloradoclaro wife, and even succeeded in teaching Ben to modify his voice sufficiently while in the house to keep the dishes from being broken. When Ben got to be king she would sit on the gallery of Espinosa Ranch and weave rush mats. When wealth became so irresistible and oppressive that upholstered chairs and a centre table were brought down from San Antone in the wagons, she bowed her smooth, dark head, and shared the fate of the Danaë.

To avoid *lèse-majesté* you have been presented first to the king and queen. They do not enter the story, which might be called "The

Chronicle of the Princess, the Happy Thought, and Lion that Bungled his Job."

Josefa O'Donnell was the surviving daughter, the princess. From her mother she inherited warmth of nature and a dusky, semi-tropic beauty. From Ben O'Donnell the royal she acquired a store in intrepidity, common sense, and the faculty of ruling. The combination was worth going miles to see. Josefa while riding her pony at a gallop could put five out of six bullets through a tomato-can swinging at the end of a string. She could play for hours with a white kitten she owned, dressing it in all manner of absurd clothes. Scorning a pencil, she could tell you out of her head what 1545 two-year-olds would bring on the hoof, at $8.50 per head. Roughly speaking, the Espinosa Ranch is forty miles long and thirty broad—but mostly leased land. Josefa, on her pony, had prospected over every mile of it. Every cow-puncher on the range knew her by sight and was a loyal vassal. Ripley Givens, foreman of one of the Espinosa outfits, saw her one day, and made up his mind to form a royal matrimonial alliance. Presumptuous? No. In those days in the Neuces country a man was a man. And, after all, the title of cattle king does not presuppose blood royal. Often it only signifies that its owner wears the crown in token of his magnificent qualities in the art of cattle stealing.

One day Ripley Givens rode over to the Double Elm Ranch to inquire about a bunch of strayed yearlings. He was late in setting out on his return trip, and it was sundown when he struck the White Horse Crossing of the Nueces. From there to his own camp it was sixteen miles. To the Espinosa ranch-house it was twelve. Givens was tired. He decided to pass the night at the Crossing.

There was a fine water hole in the river-bed. The banks were thickly covered with great trees, undergrown with brush. Back from the water hole fifty yards was a stretch of curly mesquite grass—supper for his horse and bed for himself. Givens staked his horse, and spread out his saddle blankets to dry. He sat down with his back against a tree and rolled a cigarette. From somewhere in the dense timber along the river came a sudden, rageful, shivering wail. The pony danced at the end of his rope and blew a whistling snort of comprehending fear. Givens puffed at his cigarette, but he reached leisurely for his pistol-belt, which lay on the grass, and twirled the cylinder of his weapon tentatively. A great gar plunged with a loud splash into the water hole. A little brown rabbit skipped around a bunch of catclaw and sat twitching his whiskers and looking humorously at Givens. The pony went on eating grass.

It is well to be reasonably watchful when a Mexican lion sings soprano along the arroyos at sundown. The burden of his song may be that young calves and fat lambs are scarce, and that he has a carnivorous desire for your acquaintance.

In the grass lay an empty fruit can, cast there by some former sojourner. Givens caught sight of it with a grunt of satisfaction. In his coat pocket tied behind his saddle was a handful or two of ground coffee. Black coffee and cigarettes! What ranchero could desire more?

In two minutes he had a little fire going clearly. He started, with his can, for the water hole. When within fifteen yards of its edge he saw, between the bushes, a side-saddled pony with down-dropped reins cropping grass a little distance to his left. Just rising from her hands and knees on the brink of the water hole was Josefa O'Donnell. She had been drinking water, and she brushed the sand from the palms of her hands. Ten yards away, to her right, half concealed by a clump of sacuista, Givens saw the crouching form of the Mexican lion. His amber eyelids glared hungrily; six feet from them was the tip of the tail stretched straight, like a pointer's. His hind-quarters rocked with the motion of the cat tribe preliminary to leaping.

Givens did what he could. His six-shooter was thirty-five yards away lying on the grass. He gave a loud yell, and dashed between the lion and the princess.

The "rucus," as Givens called it afterward, was brief and somewhat confused. When he arrived on the line of attack he saw a dim streak in the air, and heard a couple of faint cracks. Then a hundred pounds of Mexican lion plumped down upon his head and flattened him, with a heavy jar, to the ground. He remembered calling out: "Let up, now—no fair gouging!" and then he crawled from under the lion like a worm, with his mouth full of grass and dirt, and a big lump on the back of his head where it had struck the root of a water-elm. The lion lay motionless. Givens, feeling aggrieved, and suspicious of fouls, shook his fist at the lion, and shouted: "I'll rastle you again for twenty———" and then he got back to himself.

Josefa was standing in her tracks, quietly reloading her silver-mounted .38. It had not been a difficult shot. The lion's head made an easier mark than a tomato-can swinging at the end of a string. There was a provoking, teasing, maddening smile upon her mouth and in her dark eyes. The would-be-rescuing knight felt the fire of his fiasco burn down to his soul. Here had been his chance, the chance that he had dreamed of; and Momus, and not Cupid, had presided over it. The satyrs in the wood were, no doubt, holding their sides in hilarious, silent laughter. There had been something like vaudeville—say Signor Givens and his funny knockabout act with the stuffed lion.

"Is that you, Mr. Givens?" said Josefa, in her deliberate, saccharine contralto. "You nearly spoiled my shot when you yelled. Did you hurt your head when you fell?"

"Oh, no," said Givens, quietly; "that didn't hurt." He stooped ignominiously and dragged his best Stetson hat from under the beast. It was crushed and wrinkled to a fine comedy effect. Then he knelt down and softly stroked the fierce, open-jawed head of the dead lion.

"Poor old Bill!" he exclaimed, mournfully.

"What's that?"asked Josefa, sharply.

"Of course you didn't know, Miss Josefa," said Givens, with an air of one allowing magnanimity to triumph over grief. "Nobody can blame you. I tried to save him, but I couldn't let you know in time."

"Save who?"

"Why, Bill. I've been looking for him all day. You see, he's been our camp pet for two years. Poor old fellow, he wouldn't have hurt a cottontail rabbit. It'll break the boys all up when they hear about it. But you couldn't tell of course, that Bill was just trying to play with you."

Josefa's black eyes burned steadily upon him. Ripley Givens met the test successfully. He stood rumpling the yellow-brown curls on his head pensively. In his eyes was regret, not unmingled with a gentle reproach. His smooth features were set to a pattern of indisputable sorrow. Josefa wavered.

"What was your pet doing here?" she asked, making a last stand. "There's no camp near the White Horse Crossing."

"The old rascal ran away from camp yesterday," answered Givens, readily. "It's a wonder the coyotes didn't scare him to death. You see, Jim Webster, our horse wrangler, brought a little terrier pup into camp last week. The pup made life miserable for Bill—he used to chase him around and chew his hind legs for hours at a time. Every night when bedtime came Bill would sneak under one of the boys' blankets and sleep to keep the pup from finding him. I reckon he must have been worried pretty desperate or he wouldn't have run away. He was always afraid to get out of sight of camp."

Josefa looked at the body of the fierce animal. Givens gently patted one of the formidable paws that could have killed a yearling calf with one blow. Slowly a red flush widened upon the dark olive face of the girl. Was it the signal of shame of the true sportsman who has brought down ignoble quarry? Her eyes grew softer, and the lowered lids drove away all their bright mockery.

"I'm very sorry," she said, humbly; "but he looked so big, and jumped so high that———"

"Poor old Bill was hungry," interrupted Givens, in quick defence of the deceased. "We always made him jump for his supper in camp. He would lie down and roll over for a piece of meat. When he saw you he thought he was going to get something to eat from you."

Suddenly Josefa's eyes opened wide.

"I might have shot you!" she exclaimed. "You ran right in between. You risked your life to save your pet! That was fine, Mr. Givens. I like a man who is kind to animals."

Yes; there was even admiration in her gaze now. After all, there was a hero rising out of the ruins of the anti-climax. The look on Givens's face would have secured him a high position in the S.P.C.A.

"I always loved 'em," said he; "horses, dogs, Mexican lions, cows, alligators———"

"I hate alligators," instantly demurred Josefa; "crawly, muddy things!"

"Did I say alligators?" said Givens. "I meant antelopes, of course."

Josefa's conscience drove her to make further amends. She held out her hand penitently. There was a bright, unshed drop in each of her eyes.

"Please forgive me, Mr. Givens, won't you? I'm only a girl, you know, and I was frightened at first. I'm very, very sorry I shot Bill. You don't know how ashamed I feel. I wouldn't have done it for anything."

Givens took the proffered hand. He held it for a time while he allowed the generosity of his nature to overcome his grief at the loss of Bill. At last it was clear that he had forgiven her.

"Please don't speak of it any more, Miss Josefa. 'Twas enough to frighten any young lady the way Bill looked. I'll explain it all right to the boys."

"Are you really sure you don't hate me?" Josefa came closer to him impulsively. Her eyes were sweet—oh, sweet and pleading with gracious penitence. "I would hate any one who would kill my kitten. And how daring and kind of you to risk being shot when you tried to save him! How very few men would have done that!" Victory wrested from defeat! Vaudeville turned into drama! Bravo, Ripley Givens!

It was now twilight. Of course Miss Josefa could not be allowed to ride on to the ranch-house alone. Givens resaddled his pony in spite of that animal's reproachful glances, and rode with her. Side by side they galloped across the smooth grass, the princess and the man who was kind to animals. The prairie odors of fruitful earth and delicate bloom were thick and sweet around them. Coyotes yelping over there on the hill! No fear. And yet———

Josefa rode closer. A little hand seemed to grope. Givens found it with his own. The ponies kept an even gait. The hands lingered together, and the owner of one explained.

"I never was frightened before, but just think! How terrible it would be to meet a really wild lion! Poor Bill! I'm so glad you came with me!"

O'Donnell was sitting on the ranch gallery.

"Hello, Rip!" he shouted—"that you?"

"He rode in with me," said Josefa. "I lost my way and was late."

"Much obliged," called the cattle king. "Stop over, Rip, and ride to camp in the morning."

But Givens would not. He would push on to camp. There was a bunch of steers to start off on the trail at daybreak. He said good-night, and trotted away.

An hour later, when the lights were out, Josefa, in her night-robe, came to her door and called to the king in his own room across the brick-paved hallway:

"Say, Pop, you know that old Mexican lion they call the 'Gotch-eared Devil'—the one that killed Gonzales, Mr. Martin's sheep herder, and about fifty calves on the Salada range? Well, I settled his hash this afternoon over at the White Horse Crossing. Put two balls in his head with my .38 while he was on the jump. I knew him by the slice gone from his left ear that old Gonzales cut off with his machete. You couldn't have made a better shot yourself, Daddy."

"Bully for you!" thundered Whispering Ben from the darkness of the royal chamber.

The Indian Summer of Dry Valley Johnson

Dry Valley Johnson shook the bottle. You have to shake the bottle before using; for sulphur will not dissolve. Then Dry Valley saturated a small sponge with the liquid and rubbed it carefully into the roots of his hair. Besides sulphur there was sugar of lead in it and tincture of nux vomica and bay rum. Dry Valley found the recipe in a Sunday newspaper. You must next be told why a strong man came to fall a victim to a Beauty Hint.

Dry Valley had been a sheepman. His real name was Hector, but he had been rechristened after his range to distinguish him from "Elm Creek" Johnson, who ran sheep further down the Frio.

Many years of living face to face with sheep on their own terms wearied Dry Valley Johnson. So, he sold his ranch for eighteen thousand dollars and moved to Santa Rosa to live a life of gentlemanly ease. Being a silent and melancholy person of thirty-five—or perhaps thirty-eight—he soon became that cursed and earthcumbering thing—an elderlyish bachelor with a hobby. Some one gave him his first strawberry to eat, and he was done for.

Dry Valley bought a four-room cottage in the village, and a library on strawberry culture. Behind the cottage was a garden of which he made a strawberry patch. In his old gray woolen shirt, his brown duck trousers and high-heeled boots he sprawled all day on a canvas cot under a live-oak tree at his back door studying the history of the seductive scarlet berry.

The school teacher, Miss De Witt, spoke of him as "a fine, presentable man, for all his middle age." But the focus of Dry Valley's eyes embraced no women. They were merely beings who flew skirts as a signal for him to lift awkwardly his heavy, round-crowned, broad-brimmed felt Stetson whenever he met them, and then hurry past to get back to his beloved berries.

And all this recitative by the chorus is only to bring us to the point where you may be told why Dry Valley shook up the insoluble sulphur in the bottle. So long-drawn and inconsequential a thing is history—the anamorphous shadow of a milestone reaching down the road between us and the setting sun.

When his strawberries were beginning to ripen Dry Valley bought the heaviest buggy whip in the Santa Rosa store. He sat for many hours under the live-oak tree plaiting and weaving in an extension to its lash. When it was done he could snip a leaf from a bush twenty feet away with the cracker. For the bright, predatory eyes of Santa Rosa youth were watching the ripening berries, and Dry Valley was arming himself against their expected raids. No greater care had he taken of his tender lambs during his ranching days than he did of his cherished fruit, warding it from the hungry wolves that whistled and howled and shot their marbles and peered through the fence that surrounded his property.

In the house next to Dry Valley's lived a widow with a pack of children that gave the husbandman frequent anxious misgivings. In the woman there was a strain of the Spanish. She had wedded one of the name of O'Brien. Dry Valley was a connoisseur in cross strains; and he foresaw trouble in the offspring of this union.

Between the two homesteads ran a crazy picket fence overgrown with morning glory and wild gourd vines. Often he could see little heads with mops of black hair and flashing dark eyes dodging in and out between the pickets, keeping tabs on the reddening berries.

Late one afternoon Dry Valley went to the post office. When he came back, like Mother Hubbard he found the deuce to pay. The descendants of Iberian bandits and Hibernian cattle raiders had swooped down upon his strawberry patch. To the outraged vision of Dry Valley there seemed to be a sheep corral full of them; perhaps they numbered five or six. Between the rows of green plants they were stooped, hopping about like toads, gobbling silently and voraciously his finest fruit.

Dry Valley slipped into the house, got his whip, and charged the marauders. The lash curled about the legs of the nearest—a greedy ten-year-old—before they knew they were discovered. His screech gave warning; and the flock scampered for the fence like a drove of *javelis* flushed in the chaparral. Dry Valley's whip drew a toll of two more elfin shrieks before they dived through the vine-clad fence and disappeared.

Dry Valley, less fleet, followed them nearly to the pickets. Checking his useless pursuit, he rounded a bush, dropped his whip and stood, voiceless, motionless, the capacity of his powers consumed by the act of breathing and preserving the perpendicular.

Behind the bush stood Panchita O'Brien, scorning to fly. She was nineteen, the oldest of the raiders. Her night-black hair was gathered back in a wild mass and tied with a scarlet ribbon. She stood, with reluctant feet, yet nearer the brook than to the river; for childhood had environed and detained her.

She looked at Dry Valley Johnson for a moment with magnificent insolence, and before his eyes slowly crunched a luscious berry between her white teeth. Then she turned and walked slowly to the fence with a swaying, conscious motion, such as a duchess might make use of in leading a promenade. There she turned again and grilled Dry Valley Johnson once more in the dark flame of her audacious eyes, laughed a trifle school-girlishly, and twisted herself with pantherish quickness between the pickets to the O'Brien side of the wild gourd vine.

Dry Valley picked up his whip and went into the house. He stumbled as he went up the two wooden steps. The old Mexican woman who cooked his meals and swept his house called him to supper as he went through the rooms. Dry Valley went on, stumbled down the front steps, out the gate and down the road into a mesquite thicket at the edge of town. He sat down in the grass and laboriously plucked the spines from a prickly pear, one by one. This was his attitude of thought, acquired in the days when his problems were only those of wind and wool and water.

A thing had happened to the man—a thing that, if you are eligible, you must pray may pass you by. He had become enveloped in the Indian Summer of the Soul.

Dry Valley had had no youth. Even his childhood had been one of dignity and seriousness. At six he had viewed the frivolous gambols of the lambs on his father's ranch with disapproval. His life as a young man had been wasted. The divine fires and impulses, the glorious exaltations and despairs, the glow and enchantment of youth had passed above his head. Never a thrill of Romeo had he known; he was but a melancholy Jaques of the forest with a rudder philosophy lacking the bitter-sweet flavor of experience that tempered the veteran years of the rugged ranger of Arden. And now in his sere and yellow leaf one scornful look from the eyes of Panchita O'Brien had flooded the autumnal landscape with a tardy and delusive summer heat.

But a sheepman is a hardy animal. Dry Valley Johnson had weathered too many northers to turn his back on a late summer, spiritual or real. Old? He would show them.

By the next mail went an order to San Antonio for an outfit of the latest clothes, colors and styles and prices no object. The next day went the recipe for the hair restorer clipped from a newspaper;

for Dry Valley's sunburned auburn hair was beginning to turn silvery above his ears.

Dry Valley kept indoors closely for a week except for frequent sallies after youthful strawberry snatchers. Then, a few days later, he suddenly emerged brilliantly radiant in the hectic glow of his belated midsummer madness.

A jay-bird-blue tennis suit covered him outwardly, almost as far as his wrists and ankles. His shirt was ox-blood; his collar winged and tall; his necktie a floating oriflamme; his shoes a venomous bright tan, pointed and shaped on penitential lasts. A little flat straw hat with a striped band desecrated his weather-beaten head. Lemon-colored kid gloves protected his tough hands from the benignant May sunshine. This sad and optic-smiting creature teetered out of its den, smiling foolishly and smoothing its gloves for men and angels to see. To such a pass had Dry Valley Johnson been brought by Cupid, who always shoots game that is out of season with an arrow from the iver of Momus. Reconstructing mythology, he had risen, a prismatic macaw, from the ashes of the gray-brown phoenix that had folded its tired wings to roost under the tree of Santa Rosa.

Dry Valley paused in the street to allow Santa Rosans within sight of him to be stunned; and then deliberately and slowly, as his shoes required, entered Mrs. O'Brien's gate.

Not until the eleven months' drought did Santa Rosa cease talking about Dry Valley Johnson's courtship of Panchita O'Brien. It was an unclassifiable procedure; something like a combination of cake-walking, deaf-and-dumb oratory, postage stamp flirtation, and parlor charades. It lasted two weeks and then came to a sudden end.

Of course Mrs. O'Brien favored the match as soon as Dry Valley's intentions were disclosed. Being the mother of a woman child, and therefore a charter member of the Ancient Order of the Rat-trap, she joyfully decked out Panchita for the sacrifice. The girl was temporarily dazzled by having her dresses lengthened and her hair piled up on her head, and came near forgetting that she was only a slice of cheese. It was nice, too, to have as good a match as Mr. Johnson paying you attentions and to see the other girls fluttering the curtains at their windows to see you go by with him.

Dry Valley bought a buggy with yellow wheels and a fine trotter in San Antonio. Every day he drove out with Panchita. He was never seen to speak to her when they were walking or driving. The consciousness of his clothes kept his mind busy; the knowledge that he could say nothing of interest kept him dumb; the feeling that Panchita was there kept him happy.

He took her to parties and dances, and to church. He tried—oh, no man ever tried so hard, to be young as Dry Valley did. He could not dance; but he invented a smile which he wore on these joyous occasions, a smile that, in him, was as great a concesson to mirth and gaiety as turning hand-springs would be in another. He began to seek the company of the young men in the town—even of the boys. They accepted him as a decided damper, for his attempts at sportiveness were so forced that they might as well have essayed their games in a cathedral. Neither he nor any other could estimate what progress he had made with Panchita.

The end came suddenly in one day, as often disappears the false afterglow before a November sky and wind.

Dry Valley was to call for the girl one afternoon at six for a walk. An afternoon walk in Santa Rosa was a feature of social life that called for the pink of one's wardrobe. So Dry Valley began gorgeously to array himself; and so early that he finished early, and went over to the O'Brien cottage. As he neared the porch on the crooked walk from the gate he heard sounds of revelry within. He stopped and looked through the honeysuckle vines in the open door.

Panchita was amusing her younger brothers and sisters. She wore a man's clothes—no doubt those of the late Mr. O'Brien. On her head was the smallest bother's straw hat decorated with an ink-striped paper band. On her hands were flapping yellow cloth gloves, roughly cut out and sewn for the masquerade. The same material covered her shoes, giving them the semblance of tan leather. High collar and flowing necktie were not omitted.

Panchita was an actress. Dry Valley saw his affectedly youthful gait, his limp where the right shoe hurt him, his forced smile, his awkward simulation of a gallant air, all reproduced with startling fidelity. For the first time a mirror had been held up to him. The corroboration of one of the youngsters calling, "Mamma, come and see Pancha do like Mr. Johnson," was not needed.

As softly as the caricatured tans would permit, Dry Valley tiptoed back to the gate and home again.

Twenty minutes after the time appointed for the walk Panchita tripped demurely out her gate in a thin, trim white lawn and sailor hat. She strolled up the sidewalk and slowed her steps at Dry Valley's gate, her manner expressing wonder at his unusual delinquency.

Then out of his door and down the walk strode—not the polychromatic victim of a lost summer time, but the sheepman, rehabilitated. He wore his old gray woolen shirt, open at the throat, his brown duck trousers stuffed into his run-over boots, and his white felt sombrero on the back of his head. Twenty years or fifty he might look; Dry Valley cared not. His light blue eyes met Panchita's dark ones with a cold flash in them. He came as far as the gate. He pointed with his long arm to her house.

"Go home," said Dry Valley. "Go home to your mother. I wonder lightnin' don't strike a fool like me. Go home and play in the sand. What business have you got cavortin' around with grown men? I reckon I was locoed to be makin' a he poll-parrot out of myself for a kid like you. Go home and don't let me see you no more. Why I done it, will somebody tell me? Go home, and let me try and forget it."

Panchita obeyed and walked slowly toward her home, saying nothing. For some distance she kept her head turned and her large eyes fixed intrepidly upon Dry Valley's. At her gate she stood for a moment looking back at him, then ran suddenly and swiftly into the house.

Old Antonia was building a fire in the kitchen stove. Dry Valley stopped at the door and laughed harshly.

"I'm a pretty looking old rhinoceros to be gettin' stuck on a kid ain't I, 'Tonia?" said he.

"Not verree good thing," agreed Antonia, sagely, "for too much old man to likee *muchacha*."

"You bet it ain't," said Dry Valley, grimly. "It's dum foolishness; and, besides, it hurts."

He brought at one armful the regalia of his aberration—the blue tennis suit, shoes, hat, gloves, and all, and threw them in a pile at Antonia's feet.

"Give them to your old man," said he, "to hunt antelope in."

Just as the first star presided palely over the twilight Dry Valley got his biggest strawberry book and sat on the back steps to catch the last of the reading light. He thought he saw the figure of someone in his strawberry patch. He laid aside the book, got his whip, and hurried forth to see.

It was Panchita. She had slipped through the picket fence and was halfway across the patch. She stopped when she saw him and looked at him without wavering.

A sudden rage—a humiliating flush of unreasoning wrath—came

over Dry Valley. For this child he had made himself a motley to the view. He had tried to bribe Time to turn backward for himself; he had been made a fool of. At last he had seen his folly. There was a gulf between him and youth over which he could not build a bridge even with yellow gloves to protect his hands. And the sight of his torment coming to pester him with her elfin pranks—coming to plunder his strawberry vines like a mischievous school-boy—roused all his anger.

"I told you to keep away from here," said Dry Valley. "Go back to your home."

Panchita moved slowly toward him.

Dry Valley cracked his whip.

"Go back home," said Dry Valley, savagely, "and play theatricals some more. You'd make a fine man. You've made a fine one of me."

She came a step nearer, silent, and with that strange, defiant, steady shine in her eye that had always puzzled him. Now it stirred his wrath.

His whiplash whistled through the air. He saw a red streak suddenly come out through her white dress above her knee where it had struck.

Without flinching and with the same unchanging dark glow in her eyes, Panchita came steadily toward him through the strawberry vines. Dry Valley's trembling hand released his whip handle. When within a yard of him Panchita stretched out her arms.

"God kid!" stammered Dry Valley, "do you mean———?"

But the seasons are versatile; and it may have been Springtime after all, instead of Indian Summer, that struck Dry Valley Johnson.

The Reformation of Calliope

Calliope Catesby was in his humors again. Ennui was upon him. This goodly promontory, the earth—particularly that portion of it known as Quicksand—was to him no more than a pestilent congregation of vapors. Overtaken by the megrims, the philosopher may seek relief in soliloquy; my lady find solace in tears; the flaccid Easterner scold at the millinery bills of his women folk. Such recourse was insufficient to the denizens of Quicksand. Calliope, especially, was wont to express his ennui according to his lights.

Over night Calliope had hung out signals of approaching low spirits. He had kicked his own dog on the porch of the Occidental Hotel, and refused to apologize. He had become capricious and fault-finding in conversation. While strolling about he reached often for twigs of mesquite and chewed the leaves fiercely. That was always an ominous act. Another symptom alarming to those who were familiar with the different stages of his doldrums was his increasing politeness and a tendency to use formal phrases. A husky softness succeeded the usual penetrating drawl in his tones. A dangerous courtesy marked his manners. Later, his smile became crooked, the left side of his mouth slanting upward, and Quicksand got ready to stand from under.

At this stage Calliope generally began to drink. Finally, about midnight, he was seen going homeward, saluting those whom he met with exaggerated but inoffensive courtesy. Not yet was Calliope's melancholy at the danger point. He would seat himself at the window of the room he occupied over Silvester's tonsorial parlors and there chant lugubrious and tuneless ballads until morning, accompanying the noises by appropriate maltreatment of a jingling guitar. More magnanimous than Nero, he would thus give musical warning of the forthcoming municipal upheaval that Quicksand was scheduled to endure.

A quiet, amiable man was Calliope Catesby at other times—quiet to indolence, and amiable to worthlessness. At best he was a loafer and a nuisance; at worst he was the Terror of Quicksand. His ostensible occupation was something subordinate in the real estate line; he drove the beguiled Easterner in buckboards out to look over lots and ranch property. Originally he came from one of the Gulf States, his lank six feet, slurring rhythm of speech, and sectional idioms giving evidence of his birthplace.

And yet, after taking on Western adjustments, this languid pine-box whittler, cracker barrel hugger, shady corner lounger of the cotton fields and sumac hills of the South became famed as a bad man among men who had made a life-long study of the art of truculence.

At nine the next morning Calliope was fit. Inspired by his own barbarous melodies and the contents of his jug, he was ready primed to gather fresh laurels from the diffident brow of Quicksand. Encircled and criss-crossed with cartridge belts, abundantly garnished with revolvers, and copiously drunk, he poured forth into Quicksand's main street. Too chivalrous to surprise and capture a town by silent sortie, he paused at the nearest corner and emitted his slogan—that fearful, brassy yell, so reminiscent of the steam piano, that had gained for him the classic appellation that had superseded his own baptismal name. Following close upon his vociferation came three shots from his forty-five by way of limbering up the guns and testing his aim. A yellow dog, the personal property of Colonel Swazey, the proprietor of the Occidental, fell feet upward in the dust with one farewell yelp. A Mexican who was crossing the street from the Blue Front grocery, carrying in his hand a bottle of kerosene, was stimulated to a sudden and admirable burst of speed, still grasping the neck of the shattered bottle. The new gilt weathercock on Judge Riley's lemon and ultra-marine two-story residence shivered, flapped, and hung by a splinter, the sport of the wanton breezes.

The artillery was in trim. Calliope's hand was steady. The high, calm ecstasy of habitual battle was upon him, though slightly embittered by the sadness of Alexander in that his conquests were limited to the small world of Quicksand.

Down the street went Calliope, shooting right and left. Glass fell like hail; dogs vamosed; chickens flew, squawking; feminine voices shrieked concernedly to youngsters at large. The din was perforated at intervals by the *staccato* of the Terror's guns, and was drowned periodically by the brazen screech that Quicksand knew so well. The occasion of Calliope's low spirits were legal holidays in Quicksand. All along the main street in advance of his coming clerks were putting up shutters and closing doors Business would languish for a space. The right of way was Calliope's, and as he advanced, observing the dearth of opposition and the few opportunities for distraction, his ennui perceptibly increased.

But some four squares farther down lively preparations were being made to minister to Mr. Catesby's love for interchange of compliments and repartee. On the previous night numerous messengers had hastened to advise Buck Patterson, the city marshal, of Calliope's impending eruption. The patience of that official, often strained in extending leniency toward the disturber's misdeeds, had been overtaxed. In Quicksand some indulgence was accorded the natural ebullition of human nature. Providing that the lives of the more useful citizens were not recklessly squandered, or too much property needlessly laid waste, the community sentiment was against a too strict enforcement of the law. But Calliope had raised the limit. His outbursts had been too frequent and too violent to come within the classification of a normal and sanitary relaxation of spirit.

Buck Patterson had been expecting and awaiting in his little ten-by-twelve frame office that preliminary yell announcing that Calliope was feeling blue. When the signal came the City Marshal rose to his feet and buckled on his guns. Two deputy sheriffs and three citizens who had proven the edible qualities of fire also stood up, ready to bandy with Calliope's leaden jocularities.

"Gather that fellow in," said Buck Patterson, setting forth the lines of the campaign. "Don't have no talk, but shoot as soon as you can get a show. Keep behind cover and bring him down. He's a no good 'un. It's up to Calliope to turn up his toes this time, I reckon. Go to him all spraddled out, boys. And don't git too reckless, for what Calliope shoots at he hits."

Buck Patterson, tall, muscular, and solemn-faced, with his bright "City Marshal" badge shining on the breast of his blue flannel shirt, gave his posse directions for the onslaught upon Calliope. The plan was to accomplish the downfall of the Quicksand Terror without loss to the attaching party, if possible.

The splenetic Calliope, unconscious of retributive plots, was steaming down the channel, cannonading on either side, when he suddenly became aware of breakers ahead. The City Marshal and one of the deputies rose up behind some dry-goods boxes half a square to the front and opened fire. At the same time the rest of the posse, divided, shelled him from two side streets up which they were cautiously manœuvring from a well-executed detour.

The first volley broke the lock of one of Calliope's guns, cut a neat underbit in his right ear, and exploded a cartridge in his crossbelt, scorching his ribs as it burst. Feeling braced up by this unexpected tonic to his spiritual depression, Calliope executed a fortissimo note from his upper registers, and returned the fire like an echo. The upholders of the law dodged at his flash, but a trifle too late to save one of the deputies a bullet just above the elbow, and the marshal a bleeding cheek from a splinter that a ball tore from a box he had ducked behind.

And now Calliope met the enemy's tactics in kind. Choosing with a rapid eye the street from which the weakest and least accurate fire had come, he invaded it at double-quick, abandoning the unprotected middle of the street. With rare cunning the opposing force in that direction—one of the deputies and two of the valorous volunteers—waited, concealed by beer barrels, until Calliope had passed their retreat, and then peppered him from the rear. In another moment they were reinforced by the marshal and his other men, and then

Calliope felt that in order to successfully prolong the delights of the controversy he must find some means of reducing the great odds against him. His eye fell upon a structure that seemed to hold out this promise, providing he could reach it.

Not far away was the little railroad station, its building a strong box house, ten by twenty feet, resting upon a platform four feet above ground. Windows were in each of its walls. Something like a fort it might become to a man thus sorely pressed by superior numbers.

Calliope made a bold and rapid spurt for it, the marshal's crowd "smoking" him as he ran. He reached the haven in safety, the station agent leaving the building by a window, like a flying squirrel, as the garrison entered the door.

Patterson and his supporters halted under protection of a pile of lumber and held consultations. In the station was an unterrified desperado who was an excellent shot and carried an abundance of ammunition. For thirty yards on each side of the besieged was a stretch of bare, open ground. It was a sure thing that the man who attempted to enter that unprotected area would be stopped by one of Calliope's bullets.

The City Marshal was resolved. He had decided that Calliope Catesby should no more wake the echoes of Quicksand with his strident whoop. He had so announced. Officially and personally he felt imperatively bound to put the soft pedal on that instrument of discord. It played bad tunes.

Standing near was a hand truck used in the manipulation of small freight. It stood by a shed full of sacked wool, a consignment from one of the sheep ranches. On this truck the marshal and his men piled three heavy sacks of wool. Stooping low, Buck Patterson started for Calliope's fort, slowly pushing this loaded truck before him for protection. The posse, scattering broadly, stood ready to nip the besieged in case he should show himself in an effort to repel the juggernaut of justice that was creeping upon him. Only once did Calliope make demonstration. He fired from a window and some tufts of wool spurted from the marshal's trustworthy bulwark. The return shots from the posse pattered against the window frame of the fort. No loss resulted on either side.

The marshal was too deeply engrossed in steering his protected battleship to be aware of the approach of the morning train until he was within a few feet of the platform. The train was coming up on the other side of it. It stopped only one minute at Quicksand. What an opportunity it would offer to Calliope! He had only to step out the other door, mount the train, and away.

Abandoning his breastworks, Buck, with his gun ready, dashed up the steps and into the room, driving open the closed door with one heave of his weighty shoulder. The members of the posse heard one shot fired inside, and then there was silence.

At length the wounded man opened his eyes. After a blank space he again could see and hear and feel and think. Turning his eyes about, he found himself lying on a wooden bench. A tall man with a perplexed countenance, wearing a big badge with "City Marshal" engraved upon it, stood over him. A little old woman in black, with a wrinkled face and sparkling black eyes was holding a wet handkerchief against one of his temples. He was trying to get these facts fixed in his mind and connected with past events, when the old woman began to talk.

"There now, great, big, strong man! That bullet never tetched ye! Jest skeeted along the side of your head and sort of paralyzed ye for a spell. I've heerd of sech things afor! con-cussion is what they names it. Abel Wadkins used to kill squirrels that way—barkin' em, Abe called it. You jest been barked, sir, and you'll be all right in a little bit. Feel lots better already, don't ye! You just lay still a while longer and let me bathe your head. You don't know me, I reckon, and 'tain't surprisin' that you shouldn't. I come in on that train from Alabama to see my son. Big son, ain't he? Lands! you wouldn't hardly think he'd ever been a baby, would ye? This is my son, sir."

Half turning, the old woman looked up at the standing man, her worn face lighting with a proud and wonderful smile. She reached out one veined and calloused hand and took one of her son's. Then smiling cheerily down at the prostrate man, she continued to dip the handkerchief in the waiting-room tin washbasin and gently apply it to his temple. She had the benevolent garrulity of old age.

"I ain't seen my son before," she continued, "in eight years. One of my nephews, Elkanah Price, he's a conductor on one of them railroads, and he got me a pass to come out here. I can stay a whole week on it, and then it'll take me back again. Jest think, now, that little boy of mine has got to be a officer—a city marshal of a whole town! That's something like a constable, ain't it? I never knowed he was a officer; he didn't say nothin' about it in his letters. I reckon he thought his old mother'd be skeered about the danger he was in. But, laws! I never was much of a hand to git skeered. 'Tain't no use. I heard them guns a-shootin' while I was gittin' off them cars, and I see smoke a-comin' out of the depot, but I jest walked right along. Then I see son's face lookin' out through the window. I knowed him at oncet. He met me at the door, and squeezed me 'most to death. And there you was, sir, a-lyin' there jest like you was dead, and I 'lowed we'd see what might be done to help sot you up."

"I think I'll sit up now," said the concussion patient. "I'm feeling pretty fair by this time."

He sat, somewhat weakly yet, leaning against the wall. He was a rugged man, big-boned and straight. His eyes, steady and keen, seemed to linger upon the face of the man standing so still above him. His look wandered often from the face he studied to the marshal's badge upon the other's breast.

"Yes, yes, you'll be all right," said the old woman, patting his arm, "if you don't get to cuttin' up agin, and havin' folks shootin' at you. Son told me about you, sir, while you was layin' senseless on the floor. Don't you take it as meddlesome fer an old woman with a son as big as you to talk about it. And you mustn't hold no grudge ag'in my son for havin' to shoot at ye. A officer has got to take up for the law—it's his duty—and them that acts bad and lives wrong has to suffer. Don't blame my son any, sir—'tain't his fault. He's always been a good boy—good when he was growin' up, and kind and 'bedient and well-behaved. Won't you let me advise you, sir, not to do so no more? Be a good man, and leave liquor alone and live peaceably and godly. Keep away from bad company and work honest and sleep sweet."

The black-mittened hand of the old pleader gently touched the breast of the man she addressed. Very earnest and candid her old, worn face looked. In her rusty black dress and antique bonnet she sat, near the close of a long life, and epitomized the experience of the world. Still the man to whom she spoke gazed above her head, contemplating the silent son of the old mother.

"What does the marshal say?" he asked. "Does he believe the advice is good? Suppose the marshal speaks up and says if the talk's all right?"

The tall man moved uneasily. He fingered the badge on his breast for a moment, and then he put an arm around the old woman and drew her close to him. She smiled the unchanging mother smile of three-score years, and patted his big brown hand with her crooked, mittened fingers while her son spake.

"I say this," he said, looking squarely into the eyes of the other man, "that if I was in your place I'd follow it. If I was a drunken, desp'rate character, without shame or hope, I'd follow it. If I was in your place and you was in mine I'd say: 'Marshal, I'm willin' to swear if you'll give me the chance I'll quit the racket. I'll drop the tanglefoot and the gun play, and won't play hoss no more. I'll be a good citizen and go to work and quit my foolishness. So help me God!' That's what I'd say to you if you was marshal and I was in your place."

"Hear my son talkin'," said the old woman, softly. "Hear him, sir. You promise to be good and he won't do you no harm. Forty-one year ago his heart first beat ag'in mine, and it's beat true ever since."

The other man rose to his feet, trying his limbs and stretching his muscles.

"Then," said he, "if you was in my place and said that, and I was marshal, I'd say: 'Go free, and do your best to keep your promise.' "

"Lawsy!" exclaimed the old woman, in a sudden flutter, "ef I didn't clear forget that trunk of mine! I see a man settin' it on the platform jest as I seen son's face in the window, and it went plum out of my head. There's eight jars of home-made quince jam in that trunk that I made myself. I wouldn't have nothin' happen to them jars for a red apple."

Away to the door she trotted, spry and anxious, and then Calliope Catesby spoke out to Buck Patterson:

"I just couldn't help it, Buck. I seen her through the window a-comin' in. She had never heard a word 'bout my tough ways. I didn't have the nerve to let her know I was a worthless cuss bein' hunted down by the community. There you was lyin' where my shot laid you, like you was dead. The idea struck me sudden, and I just took your badge off and fastened it onto myself, and I fastened my reputation onto you. I told her I was the marshal and you was a holy terror. You can take your badge back now, Buck."

With shaking fingers Calliope began to unfasten the disc of metal from his shirt.

"Easy there!" said Buck Patterson. "You keep that badge right where it is, Calliope Catesby. Don't you dare to take it off till the day your mother leaves this town. You'll be city marshal of Quicksand as long as she's here to know it. After I stir around town a bit and put 'em on I'll guarantee that nobody won't give the thing away to her. And say, you leather-headed, rip-roarin', low-down son of a locoed cyclone, you follow that advice she gave me! I'm goin' to take some of it myself, too."

"Buck," said Calliope, feelingly, "ef I don't I hope I may———"

"Shut up," said Buck. "She's a-comin' back."

The Complete Life of John Hopkins

There is a saying that no man has tasted the full flavor of life until he has known poverty, love, and war. The justness of this reflection commends it to the lover of condensed philosophy. The three conditions embrace about all there is in life worth knowing. A surface thinker might deem that wealth should be added to the list. Not so. When a poor man finds a long-hidden quarter-dollar that has slipped through a rip into his vest lining, he sounds the pleasure of life with a deeper plummet than any millionaire can hope to cast.

It seems that the wise executive power that rules life has thought best to drill man in these three conditions; and none may escape all three. In rural places the terms do not mean so much. Poverty is less pinching; love is temperate; war shrinks to contests about boundary lines and the neighbors' hens. It is in the cities that our epigram gains in truth and vigor; and it has remained for one John Hopkins to crowd the experience into a rather small space of time.

The Hopkins flat was like a thousand others. There was a rubber plant in one window; a flea-bitten terrier sat in the other, wondering when he was to have his day.

John Hopkins was like a thousand others. He worked at $20 per week in a nine-story, red-brick building at either Insurance, Buckle's Hoisting Engines, Chiropody, Loans, Pulleys, Boas Renovated, Waltz Guaranteed in Five Lessons, or Artificial Limbs. It is not for us to wring Mr. Hopkins's avocation from these outward signs that be.

Mrs. Hopkins was like a thousand others. The auriferous tooth, the sedentary disposition, the Sunday afternoon wanderlust, the draught upon the delicatessen store for home-made comforts, the furor for department store marked-down sales, the feeling of superiority to the lady in the third-floor front who wore genuine ostrich tips and had two names over her bell, the mucilaginous hours during which she remained glued to the window sill, the vigilant avoidance of the instalment man, the tireless patronage of the acoustics of the dumb-waiter shaft—all the attributes of the Gotham flat-dweller were hers.

One moment yet of sententiousness and the story moves.

In the Big City large and sudden things happen. You round a corner and thrust the rib of your umbrella into the eye of your old friend from Kootenai Falls. You stroll out to pluck a Sweet William in the park—and lo! bandits attack you—you are ambulanced to the hospital—you marry your nurse; are divorced—get squeezed while short on U.P.S. and D.O.W.N.S.—stand in the bread line—marry an heiress, take out your laundry and pay your club dues—seemingly all in the wink of an eye. You travel the streets, and a finger beckons to you, a handkerchief is dropped for you, a brick is dropped upon you, the elevator cable or your bank breaks, a table d'hôte or your wife disagrees with you, and Fate tosses you about like cork crumbs in wine opened by an un-feed waiter. The City is a sprightly youngster, and you are red paint upon its toy, and you get licked off.

John Hopkins sat, after a compressed dinner, in his glove-fitting straight-front flat. He sat upon a hornblende couch and gazed, with satiated eyes, at Art Brought Home to the People in the shape of "The Storm" tacked against the wall. Mrs. Hopkins discoursed droningly of the dinner smells from the flat across the hall. The flea-bitten terrier gave Hopkins a look of disgust and showed a man-hating tooth.

Here was neither poverty, love, nor war; but upon such barren stems may be grafted those essentials of a complete life.

John Hopkins sought to inject a few raisins of conversation into the tasteless dough of existence. "Putting a new elevator in at the office," he said, discarding the nominative noun, "and the boss has turned out his whiskers."

"You don't mean it!" commented Mrs. Hopkins.

"Mr. Whipples," continued John, "wore his new spring suit down today. I liked it fine. It's a gray with———" He stopped, suddenly stricken by a need that made itself known to him. "I believe I'll walk down to the corner and get a five-cent cigar," he concluded.

John Hopkins took his hat and picked his way down the musty halls and stairs of the flat-house.

The evening air was mild, and the streets shrill with the careless cries of children playing games controlled by mysterious rhythms and phrases. Their elders held the doorways and steps with leisurely pipe and gossip. Paradoxically, the fire-escapes supported lovers in couples who made no attempt to fly the mounting conflagration they were there to fan.

The corner cigar store aimed at by John Hopkins was kept by a man named Freshmayer, who looked upon the earth as a sterile promontory.

Hopkins, unknown in the store, entered and called genially for his "bunch of spinach, carfare grade." This imputation deepened the pessimism of Freshmayer; but he set out a brand that came perilously near to filling the order. Hopkins bit off the roots of his purchase, and lighted up at the swinging gas jet. Feeling in his pockets to make payment, he found not a penny there.

"Say, my friend," he explained, frankly, "I've come out without any change. Hand you that nickel first time I pass."

Joy surged in Freshmayer's heart. Here was corroboration of his belief that the world was rotten and man a peripatetic evil. Without a word he rounded the end of his counter and made earnest onslaught upon his customer. Hopkins was no man to serve as a punching-bag for a pessimistic tobacconist. He quickly bestowed upon Freshmayer a colorado-maduro eye in return for the ardent kick that he received from the dealer in goods for cash only.

The impetus of the enemy's attack forced the Hopkins line back to the sidewalk. There the conflict raged; the pacific wooden Indian, with his carven smile, was overturned, and those of the street who delighted in carnage pressed round to view the zealous joust.

But then came the inevitable cop and imminent inconvenience for both the attacker and attacked. John Hopkins was a peaceful citizen, who worked at rebuses of nights in a flat, but he was not without the fundamental spirit of resistance that comes with the battle-rage. He knocked the policeman into a grocer's sidewalk display of goods and gave Freshmayer a punch that caused him temporarily to regret that he had not made it a rule to extend a five-cent line of credit to certain customers. Then Hopkins took spiritedly to his heels down the sidewalk, closely followed by the cigar-dealer and the policeman, whose uniform testified to the reason in the grocer's sign that read: "Eggs cheaper than anywhere else in the city."

As Hopkins ran he became aware of a big, low, red, racing automobile that kept abreast of him in the street. This auto steered in to the side of the sidewalk, and the man guiding it motioned to Hopkins to jump into it. He did so without slackening his speed, and fell into the turkey-red upholstered seat beside the chauffeur. The big machine, with a diminuendo cough, flew away like an albatross down the avenue into which the street emptied.

The driver of the auto sped his machine without a word. He was masked beyond guess in the goggles and diabolic garb of the chauffeur.

"Much obliged, old man," called Hopkins, gratefully. "I guess you've got sporting blood in you, all right, and don't admire the sight of two men trying to soak one. Little more and I'd have been pinched."

The chauffeur made no sign that he had heard. Hopkins shrugged a shoulder and chewed at his cigar, to which his teeth had clung grimly throughout the mêlée.

Ten minutes and the auto turned into the open carriage entrance of a noble mansion of brown stone, and stood still. The chauffeur leaped out, and said:

"Come quick. The lady, she will explain. It is the great honor you will have, monsieur. Ah, that milady could call upon Armand to do this thing! But, no, I am only one chauffeur."

With vehement gestures the chauffeur conducted Hopkins into the house. He was ushered into a small but luxurious reception chamber. A lady, young, and possessing the beauty of visions, rose from a chair. In her eyes smouldered a becoming anger. Her high-arched, thread-like brows were ruffled into a delicious frown.

"Milady," said the chauffeur, bowing low, "I have the honor to relate to you that I went to the house of Monsieur Long and found him to be not at home. As I came back I see this gentleman in combat against—how you say—greatest odds. He is fighting with five—ten—thirty men—genadarmes, *aussi.* Yes, milady, he what you call 'swat' one—three—eight policemans. If the Monsieur Long is out I say to myself this gentleman he will serve milady so well, and I bring him here."

"Very well, Armand," said the lady, "you may go." She turned to Hopkins.

"I sent my chauffeur," she said, "to bring my cousin, Walter Long. There is a man in this house who has treated me with insult and abuse. I have complained to my aunt, and she laughs at me. Armand says you are brave. In these prosaic days men who are both brave and chivalrous are few. May I count upon your assistance?"

John Hopkins thrust the remains of his cigar into his coat pocket. He looked upon this winning creature and felt his first thrill of romance. It was a knightly love, and contained no disloyalty to the flat with the flea-bitten terrier and the lady of his choice. He had married her after a picnic of the Lucy Label Stickers' Union, Lodge No. 2, on a dare and a bet of new hats and chowder all around with his friend, Billy McManus. This angel who was begging him to come to her rescue was something too heavenly for chowder, and as for hats—golden, jewelled crowns for her!

"Say," said John Hopkins, "just show me the guy that you've got the grouch at. I've neglected my talents as a scrapper heretofore, but this is my busy night."

"He is in there," said the lady, pointing to a closed door. "Come. Are you sure that you do not falter or fear?"

"Me?" said John Hopkins. "Just give me one of those roses in the bunch you are wearing, will you?"

The lady gave him a red, red rose. John Hopkins kissed it, stuffed it into his vest pocket, opened the door and walked into the room. It was a handsome library, softly but brightly lighted. A young man was there, reading.

"Books on etiquette is what you want to study," said John Hopkins, abruptly. "Get up here, and I'll give you some lessons. Be rude to a lady, will you?"

The young man looked mildly surprised. Then he arose languidly, dextrously caught the arms of John Hopkins and conducted him irresistibly to the front door of the house.

"Beware, Ralph Branscombe," cried the lady, who had followed, "what you do to the gallant man who has tried to protect me."

The young man shoved John Hopkins gently out the door and then closed it.

"Bess," he said calmly, "I wish you would quit reading historical novels. How in the world did that fellow get in here?"

"Armand brought him," said the young lady. "I think you are awfully mean not to let me have that St. Bernard. I sent Armand for Walter. I was so angry with you."

"Be sensible, Bess," said the young man, taking her arm. "That dog isn't safe. He has bitten two or three people around the kennels. Come now, let's go tell auntie we are in good humor again."

Arm in arm, they moved away.

John Hopkins walked to his flat. The janitor's five-year-old daughter was playing on the steps. Hopkins gave her a nice, red rose and walked upstairs.

Mrs. Hopkins was philandering with curl-papers.

"Get your cigar?" she asked, disinterestedly.

"Sure," said Hopkins, "and I knocked around a while outside. It's a nice night."

He sat upon the hornblende sofa, took out the stump of his cigar, lighted it, and gazed at the graceful figures in "The Storm" on the opposite wall.

"I was telling you," said he, "about Mr. Whipple's suit. It's a gray, with an invisible check, and it looks fine."

Dougherty's Eye-Opener

Big Jim Dougherty was a sport. He belonged to that race of men. In Manhattan it is a distinct race. They are the Caribs of the North—strong, artful, self-sufficient, clannish, honorable within the laws of their race, holding in lenient contempt neighboring tribes who bow to the measure of Society's tape-line. I refer, of course, to the titled nobility of sportdom. There is a class which bears as a qualifying adjective the substantive belonging to a wind instrument made of a cheap and base metal. But the tin mines of Cornwall never produced the material for manufacturing descriptive nomenclature for "Big Jim" Dougherty.

The habitat of the sport is the lobby or the outside corner of certain hotels and combination restaurants and cafés. They are mostly men of different sizes, running from small to large; but they are unanimous in the possession of a recently shaven, blue-black cheek and chin and dark overcoats (in season) with black velvet collars.

Of the domestic life of the sport little is known. It has been said that Cupid and Hymen sometimes take a hand in the game and copper the queen of hearts to lose. Daring theorists have averred—not content with simply saying—that a sport often contracts a spouse, and even incurs descendants. Sometimes he sits in the game of politics; and then at chowder picnics there is a revelation of a Mrs. Sport and little Sports in glazed hats with tin pails.

But mostly the sport is Oriental. He believes his women-folk should not be too patent. Somewhere behind grilles or flower-ornamented fire escapes they await him. There, no doubt, they tread on rugs from Teheran and are diverted by the bulbul and play upon the dulcimer and feed upon sweetmeats. But away from his home the sport is an integer. He does not, as men of other races in Manhattan do, become the convoy in his unoccupied hours of fluttering laces and high heels that tick off delectably the happy seconds of the evening parade. He herds with his own race at corners, and delivers a commentary in his Carib lingo upon the passing show.

"Big Jim" Dougherty had a wife, but he did not wear a button portrait of her upon his lapel. He had a home in one of those brownstone, iron-railed streets on the west side that look like a recently excavated bowling alley of Pompeii.

To this home of his Mr. Dougherty repaired each night when the hour was so late as to promise no further diversion in the arch domains of sport. By that time the occupant of the monogamistic harem would be in dreamland, the bulbul silenced and the hour propitious for slumber.

"Big Jim" always arose at twelve, meridian, for breakfast, and soon afterward he would return to the rendezvous of his "crowd."

He was always vaguely conscious that there was a Mrs. Dougherty. He would have received without denial the charge that the quiet, neat, comfortable little woman across the table at home was his wife. In fact, he remembered pretty well that they had been married for nearly four years. She would often tell him about the cute tricks of Spot, the canary, and the light-haired lady that lived in the window of the flat across the street.

"Big Jim" Dougherty even listened to this conversation of hers sometimes. He knew that she would have a nice dinner ready for him every evening at seven when he came for it. She sometimes went to matinées, and she had a talking machine with six dozen records. Once when her Uncle Amos blew in on a wind from up-state she went with him to the Eden Musée. Surely these things were diversions enough for any woman.

One afternoon Mr. Dougherty finished his breakfast, put on his hat and got away fairly for the door. When his hand was on the knob he heard his wife's voice.

"Jim" she said, firmly, "I wish you would take me out to dinner this evening. It has been three years since you have been outside the door with me."

"Big Jim" was astounded. She had never asked anything like this before. It had the flavor of a totally new proposition. But he was a game sport.

"All right," he said. "You be ready when I come at seven. None of this 'wait two minutes till I primp an hour or two' kind of business, now, Dele."

"I'll be ready," said his wife, calmly.

At seven she descended the stone steps in the Pompeian bowling alley at the side of "Big Jim" Dougherty. She wore a dinner gown made of a stuff that the spiders must have woven, and of a color that a twilight sky must have contributed. A light coat with many admirably unnecessary capes and adorably inutile ribbons floated downward from her shoulders. Fine feathers do make fine birds; and the only reproach in the saying is for the man who refuses to give up his earnings for the ostrich-tip industry.

"Big Jim" Dougherty was troubled. There was a being at his side whom he did not know. He thought of the sober-hued plumage that this bird of paradise was accustomed to wear in her cage, and this winged revelation puzzled him. In some way she reminded him of the Delia Cullen that he had married four years before. Shyly and rather awkwardly he stalked at her right hand.

"After dinner I'll take you back home, Dele," said Mr. Dougherty, "and then I'll drop back up to Seltzer's with the boys. You can have swell chuck to-night if you want it. I made a winning on Anaconda yesterday so you can go as far as you like."

Mr. Dougherty had intended to make the outing with his unwonted wife an inconspicuous one. Uxoriousness was a weakness that the precepts of the Caribs did not countenance. If any of his friends of the track, the billiard cloth or the square circle had wives they had never complained of the fact in public. There were a number of table d'hôte places on the cross streets near the broad and shining way; and to one of these he had proposed to escort her, so that the bushel might not be removed from the light of his domesticity.

But while on the way Mr. Dougherty altered those intentions. He had been casting stealthy glances at his attractive companion and he was seized with the conviction that she was no selling plater. He resolved to parade with his wife past Seltzer's café, where at this time a number of his tribe would be gathered to view the daily evening processions. Yes; and he would take her to dine at Hoogley's, the swellest slow-lunch warehouse on the line, he said to himself.

The congregation of smooth-faced tribal gentlemen were on watch at Seltzer's. As Mr. Dougherty and his reorganized Delia passed they stared, momentarily petrified, and then removed their hats—a performance as unusual to them as was the astonishing innovation presented to their gaze by "Big Jim." On the latter gentleman's impassive face there appeared a slight flicker of triumph—a faint flicker, no more to be observed than the expression called there by the draft of little casino to a four-card spade flush.

Hoogley's was animated. Electric lights shone—as, indeed, they were expected to do. And the napery, the glassware, and the flowers also meritoriously performed the spectacular duties required of them. The guests were numerous, well-dressed, and gay.

A waiter—not necessarily obsequious—conducted "Big Jim" Dougherty and his wife to a table.

"Play that menu straight across for what you like, Dele," said "Big Jim." "It's you for a trough of the gilded oats to-night. It strikes me that maybe we've been sticking too fast to home fodder."

"Big Jim's" wife gave her order. He looked at her with respect. She had mentioned truffles; and he had not known that she knew what truffles were. From the wine list she designated an appropriate and desirable brand. He looked at her with some admiration.

She was beaming with the innocent excitement that woman derives from the exercise of her gregariousness. She was talking to him about a hundred things with animation and delight. And as the meal progressed her cheeks, colorless from a life indoors, took on a delicate flush. "Big Jim" looked around the room and saw that none of the women there had her charm. And then he thought of the three years she had suffered immurement, uncomplaining, and a flush of shame warmed him, for he carried fair play as an item in his creed.

But when the Honorable Patrick Corrigan, leader in Dougherty's district and a friend of his, saw them and came over to the table, matters got to the three-quarter stretch. The Honorable Patrick was a gallant man, both in deeds and words. As for the Blarney stone, his previous actions toward it must have been pronounced. Heavy damages for breach of promise could surely have been obtained had the Blarney stone seen fit to sue the Honorable Patrick.

"Jimmy, old man!" he called; he clapped Dougherty on the back; he shone like a midday sun upon Delia.

"Honorable Mr. Corrigan . . . Mrs. Dougherty," said "Big Jim."

The Honorable Patrick became a fountain of entertainment and admiration. The waiter had to fetch a third chair for him; he made another at the table, and the wineglasses were refilled.

"You selfish old rascal!" he exclaimed, shaking an arch finger at "Big Jim," "to have kept Mrs. Dougherty a secret from us."

And then "Big Jim" Dougherty, who was no talker, sat dumb, and saw the wife who had dined every evening for three years at home, blossom like a fairy flower. Quick, witty, charming, full of light and ready talk, she received the experienced attack of the Honorable Patrick on the field of repartee and surprised, vanquished, delighted him. She unfolded her long-closed petals and around her the room became a garden. They tried to include "Big Jim" in the conversation, but he was without a vocabulary.

And then a stray bunch of politicians and good fellows who lived for sport came into the room. They saw "Big Jim" and the leader, and over they came and were made acquainted with Mrs. Dougherty. And in a few minutes she was holding a salon. Half a dozen men surrounded her, courtiers all, and six found her capable of charming. "Big Jim" sat, grim, and kept saying to himself: "Three years, three years!"

The dinner came to an end. The Honorable Patrick reached for Mrs. Dougherty's cloak; but that was a matter of action instead of words, and Dougherty's big hand got it first by two seconds.

While the farewells were being said at the door the Honorable Patrick smote Dougherty mightily between the shoulders.

"Jimmy, me boy," he declared, in a giant whisper, "the madam is a jewel of the first water. Ye're a lucky dog."

"Big Jim" walked homeward with his wife. She seemed quite as pleased with the lights and show windows in the streets as with the admiration of the men in Hoogley's. As they passed Seltzer's they heard the sound of many voices in the café. The boys would be starting the drinks around now and discussing past performances.

At the door of their home Delia paused. The pleasure of the outing radiated softly from her countenance. She could not hope for Jim of evenings, but the glory of this one would lighten her lonely hours for a long time.

"Thank you for taking me out, Jim," she said, gratefully. "You'll be going back to Seltzer's now, of course."

"To——with Seltzer's," said "Big Jim," emphatically. "And d——Pat Corrigan! Does he think I haven't got any eyes?"

And the door closed behind both of them.

While the Auto Waits

Promptly at the beginning of twilight, came again to that quiet corner of that quiet, small park the girl in gray. She sat upon a bench and read a book, for there was yet to come a half hour in which print could be accomplished.

To repeat: Her dress was gray, and plain enough to mask its impeccancy of style and fit. A large-meshed veil imprisoned her turban hat and a face that shone through it with a calm and unconscious beauty. She had come there at the same hour on the day previous, and on the day before that; and there was one who knew it.

The young man who knew it hovered near, relying upon burnt sacrifices to the great joss, Luck. His piety was rewarded, for, in turning a page, her book slipped from her fingers and bounded from the bench a full yard away.

The young man pounced upon it with instant avidity, returning it to its owner with that air that seems to flourish in parks and public places—a compound of gallantry and hope, tempered with respect for the policeman on the beat. In a pleasant voice, he risked an inconsequent remark upon the weather—that introductory topic responsible for so much of the world's unhappiness—and stood poised for a moment, awaiting his fate.

The girl looked him over leisurely; at his ordinary, neat dress and his features distinguished by nothing particular in the way of expression.

"You may sit down, if you like," she said, in a full, deliberate contralto. "Really, I would like to have you do so. The light is too bad for reading. I would prefer to talk."

The vassal of Luck slid upon the seat by her side with complaisance.

"Do you know," he said, speaking the formula with which park chairmen open their meetings, "that you are quite the stunningest girl I have seen in a long time? I had my eye on you yesterday. Didn't know somebody was bowled over by those pretty lamps of yours, did you, honeysuckle?"

"Whoever you are," said the girl, in icy tones, "you must remember that I am a lady. I will excuse the remark you have just made because the mistake was, doubtless, not an unnatural one—in your circle. I asked you to sit down; if the invitation must constitute me your honeysuckle, consider it withdrawn."

"I earnestly beg your pardon," pleaded the young man. His expression of satisfaction had changed to one of penitence and humility. "It was my fault, you know—I mean, there are girls in parks, you know—that is, of course, you don't know, but———"

"Abandon the subject, if you please. Of course I know. Now, tell me about these people passing and crowding, each way, along these paths. Where are they going? Why do they hurry so? Are they happy?"

The young man had promptly abandoned his air of coquetry. His cue was now for a waiting part; he could not guess the rôle he would be expected to play.

"It *is* interesting to watch them," he replied, postulating her mood. "It is the wonderful drama of life. Some are going to supper and some to—er—other places. One wonders what their histories are."

"I do not," said the girl; "I am not so inquisitive. I come here to sit because here, only, can I be near the great, common, throbbing heart of humanity. My part in life is cast where its beats are never felt. Can you surmise why I spoke to you, Mr.———?"

"Parkenstacker," supplied the young man. Then he looked eager and hopeful.

"No," said the girl, holding up a slender finger, and smiling slightly. "You would recognize it immediately. It is impossible to keep one's name out of print. Or even one's portrait. This veil and this hat of my maid furnish me with an *incog*. You should have seen the chauffeur stare at it when he thought I did not see. Candidly, there are five or six names that belong in the holy of holies, and mine, by the accident of birth, is one of them. I spoke to you, Mr. Stackenpot———"

"Parkenstacker," corrected the young man, modestly.

"—Mr. Parkenstacker, because I wanted to talk, for once, with a natural man—one unspoiled by the despicable gloss of wealth and supposed social superiority. Oh! you do not know how weary I am of it—money, money, money! And of the men who surround me, dancing like little marionettes all cut by the same pattern. I am sick of pleasure, of jewels, of travel, of society, of luxuries of all kinds."

"I always had an idea," ventured the young man, hesitatingly, "that money must be a pretty good thing."

"A competence is to be desired. But when you have so many millions that———!" She concluded the sentence with a gesture of despair. "It is the monotony of it," she continued, "that palls. Drives, dinners, theatres, balls, suppers, with the gilding of superfluous wealth over it all. Sometimes the very tinkle of the ice in my champagne glass nearly drives me mad."

Mr. Parkenstacker looked ingenuously interested.

"I have always liked," he said, "to read and hear about the ways of wealthy and fashionable folks. I suppose I am a bit of a snob. But I like to have my information accurate. Now, I had formed the opinion that champagne is cooled in the bottle and not by placing ice in the glass."

The girl gave a musical laugh of genuine amusement.

"You should know," she explained, in an indulgent tone, "that we of the non-useful class depend for our amusement upon departure from precedent. Just now it is a fad to put ice in champagne. The idea was originated by a visiting Prince of Tartary while dining at the Waldorf. It will soon give some other whim. Just as at a dinner party this week on Madison Avenue a green kid glove was laid by the plate of each guest to be put on and used while eating olives."

"I see," admitted the young man, humbly. "These special diversions of the inner circle do not become familiar to the common public."

"Sometimes," continued the girl, acknowledging his confession of error by a slight bow, "I have thought that if I ever should love a man it would be one of lowly station. One who is a worker and not a drone. But, doubtless, the claims of caste and wealth will prove stronger than my inclination. Just now I am besieged by two. One is a Grand Duke of a German principality. I think he has, or has had, a wife, somewhere, driven mad by his intemperance and cruelty. The other is an English Marquis, so cold and mercenary that I even prefer the diabolism of the Duke. What is it that impels me to tell you these things, Mr. Packenstacker?"

"Parkenstacker," breathed the young man. "Indeed, you cannot know how much I appreciate your confidences."

The girl contemplated him with a calm, impersonal regard that befitted the difference in their stations.

"What is your line of business, Mr. Parkenstacker?" she asked.

"A very humble one. But I hope to rise in the world. Were you really in earnest when you said that you could love a man of lowly position?"

"Indeed I was. But I said 'might.' There is the Grand Duke and the Marquis, you know. Yes; no calling could be too humble were the man what I would wish him to be."

"I work," declared Mr. Parkenstacker, "in a restaurant."

The girl shrank slightly.

"Not as a waiter?" she said, a little imploringly. "Labor is noble, but—personal attendance, you know—valets and———"

"I am not a waiter. I am cashier in"—on the street they faced that bounded the opposite side of the park was the brilliant electric sign "RESTAURANT"—"I am cashier in that restaurant you see there."

The girl consulted a tiny watch set in a bracelet of rich design upon her left wrist, and rose, hurriedly. She thrust her book into a glittering reticule suspended from her waist, for which, however, the book was too large.

"Why are you not at work?" she asked.

"I am on the night turn," said the young man; "it is yet an hour before my period begins. May I not hope to see you again?"

"I do not know. Perhaps—but the whim may not seize me again. I must go quickly now. There is a dinner, and a box at the play—and, oh! the same old round. Perhaps you noticed an automobile at the upper corner of the park as you came. One with a white body."

"And red running gear?" asked the young man, knitting his brows reflectively.

"Yes. I always come in that. Pierre waits for me there. He supposes me to be shopping in the department store across the square. Conceive of the bondage of the life wherein we must deceive even our chauffeurs. Goodnight."

"But it is dark now," said Mr. Parkenstacker, "and the park is full of rude men. May I not walk———?"

"If you have the slightest regard for my wishes," said the girl, firmly, "you will remain at this bench for ten minutes after I have left. I do not mean to accuse you, but you are probably aware that autos generally bear the monogram of their owner. Again, goodnight."

Swift and stately she moved away through the dusk. The young man watched her graceful form as she reached the pavement at the park's edge, and turned up along it toward the corner where stood the automobile. Then he treacherously and unhesitatingly began to dodge and skim among the park trees and shrubbery in a course parallel to her route, keeping her well in sight.

When she reached the corner she turned her head to glance at the motor car, and then passed it, continuing on across the street. Sheltered behind a convenient standing cab, the young man followed her movements closely with his eyes. Passing down the sidewalk of the street opposite the park, she entered the restaurant with the blazing sign. The place was one of those frankly glaring establishments, all white paint and glass, where one may dine cheaply and conspicuously. The girl penetrated the restaurant to some retreat at its rear, whence she quickly emerged without her hat and veil.

The cashier's desk was well to the front. A red-haired girl on the stool climbed down, glancing pointedly at the clock as she did so. The girl in gray mounted in her place.

The young man thrust his hands into his pockets and walked slowly back along the sidewalk. At the corner his foot struck a small, paper-covered volume lying there, sending it sliding to the edge of the turf. By its picturesque cover he recognized it as the book the girl had been reading. He picked it up carelessly, and saw that its title was "New Arabian Nights," the author being of the name of Stevenson. He dropped it again upon the grass, and lounged, irresolute, for a minute. Then he stepped into the automobile, reclined upon the cushions, and said two words to the chauffeur:

"Club, Henri."

The Defeat of the City

Robert Walmsley's descent upon the city resulted in a Kilkenny struggle. He came out of the fight victor by a fortune and a reputation. On the other hand, he was swallowed up by the city. The city gave him what he demanded and then branded him with its brand. It remodelled, cut, trimmed, and stamped him to the pattern it approves. It opened its social gates to him and shut him in on a close-cropped, formal lawn with the select herd of ruminants. In dress, habits, manners, provincialism, routine, and narrowness he acquired that charming insolence, that irritating completeness, that sophisticated crassness, that over-balanced poise that makes the Manhattan gentleman so delightfully small in his greatness.

One of the up-state rural counties pointed with pride to the successful young metropolitan lawyer as a product of its soil. Six years earlier this county had removed the wheat straw from between its huckleberry-stained teeth and emitted a derisive and bucolic laugh as old man Walmsley's freckle-faced "Bob" abandoned the certain three-per-diem meals of the one-horse farm for the discontinuous quick lunch counters of the three-ringed metropolis. At the end of the six years no murder trial, coaching party, automobile accident or cotillion was complete in which the name of Robert Walmsley did not figure. Tailors waylaid him in the street to get a new wrinkle from the cut of his unwrinkled trousers. Hyphenated fellows in the clubs and members of the oldest subpœnaed families were glad to clap him on the back and allow him three letters of his name.

But the Matterhorn of Robert Walmsley's success was not scaled until he married Alicia Van Der Pool. I cite the Matterhorn, for just so high and cool and white and inaccessible was this daughter of the old burghers. The social Alps that ranged about her—over whose bleak passes a thousand climbers struggled—reached only to her knees. She towered in her own atmosphere, serene, chaste, prideful, wading in no fountains, dining no monkeys, breeding no dogs for bench shows. She was a Van Der Pool. Fountains were made to play for her; monkeys were made for other people's ancestors; dogs, she understood, were created to be companions of blind persons and objectionable characters who smoked pipes.

This was the Matterhorn that Robert Walmsley accomplished. If he found, with the good poet with the game foot and artificially curled hair, that he who ascends to mountain tops will find the loftiest peaks most wrapped in clouds and snow, he concealed his chillblains beneath a brave and smiling exterior. He was a lucky man and knew it, even though he were imitating the Spartan boy with an ice-cream freezer beneath his doublet frappéeing the region of his heart.

After a brief wedding tour abroad, the couple returned to create a decided ripple in the calm cistern (so placid and cool and sunless it is) of the best society. They entertained at their red brick mausoleum of ancient greatness in an old square that is a cemetery of crumbled glory. And Robert Walmsley was proud of his wife; although while one of his hands shook his guests' the other held tightly to his alpenstock and thermometer.

One day Alicia found a letter written to Robert by his mother. It was a unerudite letter, full of crops and motherly love and farm notes. It chronicled the health of the pig and the recent red calf, and asked concerning Robert's in return. It was a letter direct from the soil, straight from home, full of biographies of bees, tales of turnips, pæans of new-laid eggs, neglected parents and the slump in dried apples.

"Why have I not been shown your mother's letters?" asked Alicia.

There was always something in her voice that made you think of lorgnettes, of accounts at Tiffany's, of sledges smoothly gliding on the trail from Dawson to Forty Mile, of the tinkling of pendent prisms on your grandmothers' chandeliers, of snow lying on a convent roof; of a police sergeant refusing bail. "Your mother," continued Alicia, "invites us to make a visit to the farm. I have never seen a farm. We will go there for a week or two, Robert."

"We will," said Robert, with the grand air of an associate Supreme Justice concurring in an opinion. "I did not lay the invitation before you because I thought you would not care to go. I am much pleased at your decision."

"I will write to her myself," answered Alicia, with a faint foreshadowing of enthusiasm. "Félice shall pack my trunks at once. Seven, I think, will be enough. I do not suppose that your mother entertains a great deal. Does she give many house parties?"

Robert arose, and as attorney for rural places filed a demurrer against six of the seven trunks. He endeavored to define, picture, elucidate, set forth and describe a farm. His own words sounded strange in his ears. He had not realized how thoroughly urbsidized he had become.

A week passed and found them landed at the little country station five hours out from the city. A grinning, stentorian, sarcastic youth driving a mule to a spring wagon hailed Robert savagely.

"Hallo, Mr. Walmsley. Found your way back at last, have you? Sorry I couldn't bring in the automobile for you, but dad's bull-tonguing the ten-acre clover patch with it to-day. Guess you'll excuse my not wearing a dress suit over to meet you—it ain't six o'clock yet, you know."

"I'm glad to see you, Tom," said Robert, grasping his brother's hand. "Yes, I've found my way at last. You've a right to say 'at last.' It's been over two years since the last time. But it will be oftener after this, my boy."

Alicia, cool in the summer heat as an Arctic wraith, white as a Norse snow maiden in her flimsy muslin and fluttering lace parasol, came round the corner of the station; and Tom was stripped of his assurance. He became chiefly eyesight clothed in blue jeans, and on the homeward drive to the mule alone did he confide in language the inwardness of his thoughts.

They drove homeward. The low sun dropped a spendthrift flood of gold upon the fortunate fields of wheat. The cities were far away.

The road lay curling around wood and dale and hill like a ribbon lost from the robe of careless summer. The wind followed like a whinnying colt in the track of Phœbus's steeds.

By and by the farmhouse peeped gray out of its faithful grove; they saw the long lane with its convoy of walnut trees running from the road to the house; they smelled the wild rose and the breath of cool, damp willows in the creek's bed. And then in unison all the voices of the soil began a chant addressed to the soul of Robert Walmsley. Out of the tilted aisles of the dim wood they came hollowly; they chirped and buzzed from the parched grass; they trilled from the ripples of the creek ford; they floated up in clear Pan's pipe notes from the dimming meadows; the whippoorwills joined in as they pursued midges in the upper air; slow-going cow-bells struck out a homely accompaniment—and this was what each one said: "You've found your way back at last, have you?"

The old voices of the soil spoke of him. Leaf and bud and blossom conversed with him in the old vocabulary of his careless youth—the inanimate things, the familiar stones and rails, the gates and furrows and roofs and turns of road had an eloquence, too, and a power in the transformation. The country had smiled and he had felt the breath of it, and his heart was drawn as if in a moment back to his old love. The city was far away.

This rural atavism, then, seized Robert Walmsley and possessed him. A queer thing he noticed in connection with it was that Alicia, sitting at his side, suddenly seemed to him a stranger. She did not belong to this recurrent phase. Never before had she seemed so remote, so colorless and high—so intangible and unreal. And yet he had never admired her more than when she sat there by him in the rickety spring wagon, chiming no more with his mood and with her environment than the Matterhorn chimes with a peasant's cabbage garden.

That night when the greetings and the supper were over, the entire family, including Buff, the yellow dog, bestrewed itself upon the front porch. Alicia, not haughty but silent, sat in the shadow dressed in an exquisite pale-gray tea gown. Robert's mother discoursed to her happily concerning marmalade and lumbago. Tom sat on the top step; Sisters Millie and Pam on the lowest step to catch the lightning bugs. Mother had the willow rocker. Father sat in the big armchair with one of its arms gone. Buff sprawled in the middle of the porch in everybody's way. The twilight pixies and pucks stole forth unseen and plunged other poignant shafts of memory into the heart of Robert. A rural madness entered his soul. The city was far away.

Father sat without his pipe, writhing in his heavy boots, a sacrifice to rigid courtesy. Robert shouted: "No, you don't!" He fetched the pipe and lit it; he seized the old gentleman's boots and tore them off. The last one slipped suddenly, and Mr. Robert Walmsley, of Washington Square, tumbled off the porch backward with Buff on top of him, howling fearfully. Tom laughed sarcastically.

Robert tore off his coat and vest and hurled them into a lilac bush.

"Come out here, you landlubber," he cried to Tom, "and I'll put grass seed on your back. I think you called me a 'dude' a while ago. Come along and cut your capers."

Tom understood the invitation and accepted it with delight. Three times they wrestled on the grass, "side holds," even as the giants of the mat. And twice was Tom forced to bite grass at the hands of the distinguished lawyer. Dishevelled, panting, each still boasting of his own prowess, they stumbled back to the porch. Millie cast a pert reflection upon the qualities of a city brother. In an instant Robert had secured a horrid katydid in his fingers and bore down upon her. Screaming wildly, she fled up the lane pursued by the avenging glass of form. A quarter of a mile and they returned, she full of apology to the victorious "dude." The rustic mania possessed him unabatedly.

"I can do up a cowpenful of you slow hayseeds," he proclaimed, vaingloriously. "Bring on your bulldogs, your hired men, and your logrollers."

He turned handsprings on the grass that prodded Tom to envious sarcasm. And then, with a whoop, he clattered to the rear and brought back Uncle Ike, a battered colored retainer of the family, with his banjo, and strewed sand on the porch and danced "Chicken in the Bread Tray" and did buck-and-wing wonders for half an hour longer. Incredibly wild and boisterous things he did. He sang, he told stories that set all but one shrieking, he played the yokel, the humorous clodhopper; he was mad, mad with the revival of the old life in his blood.

He became so extravagant that once his mother sought gently to reprove him. Then Alicia moved as though she were about to speak, but she did not. Through it all she sat immovable, a slim, white spirit in the dusk that no man might question or read.

By and by she asked permission to ascend to her room, saying that she was tired. On her way she passed Robert. He was standing in the door, the figure of vulgar comedy, with ruffled hair, reddened face and unpardonable confusion of attire—no trace there of the immaculate Robert Walmsley, the courted clubman and ornament of select circles. He was doing a conjuring trick with some household utensils, and the family, now won over to him without exception, was beholding him with worshipful admiration.

As Alicia passed in Robert started suddenly. He had forgotten for the moment that she was present. Without a glance at him she went on upstairs.

After that the fun grew quiet. An hour passed in talk, and then Robert went up himself.

She was standing by the window when he entered their room. She was still clothed as when they were on the porch. Outside and crowding against the window was a giant apple tree, full blossomed.

Robert sighed and went near the window. He was ready to meet his fate. A confessed vulgarian, he foresaw the verdict of justice in the shape of that still, whiteclad form. He knew the rigid lines that a Van Der Pool would draw. He was a peasant gambling indecorously in the valley, and the pure, cold, white, unthawed summit of the Matterhorn could not but frown on him. He had been unmasked by his own actions. All the polish, the poise, the form that the city had given him had fallen from him like an ill-fitting mantle at the first breath of a country breeze. Dully he awaited the approaching condemnation.

"Robert," said the calm, cool voice of his judge, "I thought I married a gentleman."

Yes, it was coming. And yet, in the face of it, Robert Walmsley was eagerly regarding a certain branch of the apple tree upon which he used to climb out of that very window. He believed he could do it now. He wondered how many blossoms there were on the tree—ten millions? But here was someone speaking again:

"I thought I married a gentleman," the voice went on, "but———"

Why had she come and was standing so close by his side?

"But I find that I have married"—was this Alicia talking?—"something better—a man—Bob, dear, kiss me, won't you?"

The city was far away.

The Plutonian Fire

There are a few editor men with whom I am privileged to come in contact. It has not been long since it was their habit to come in contact with me. There is a difference.

They tell me that with a large number of the manuscripts that are submitted to them come advices (in the way of a boost) from the author asseverating that the incidents in the story are true. The destination of such contributions depends wholly upon the question of the inclosure of stamps. Some are returned, the rest are thrown on the floor in a corner on top of a pair of gum shoes, an overturned statuette of the Winged Victory, and a pile of old magazines containing a picture of the editor in the act of reading the latest copy of *Le Petit Journal,* right side up—you can tell by the illustrations. It is only a legend that there are waste baskets in editors' offices.

Thus the truth is held in disrepute. But in time truth and science and nature will adapt themselves to art. Things will happen logically, and the villain be discomfited instead of being elected to the board of directors. But in the meantime fiction must not only be divorced from fact, but must pay alimony and be awarded custody of the press dispatches.

This preamble is to warn you off the grade crossing of a true story. Being that, it shall be told simply, with conjuctions substituted for adjectives wherever possible, and whatever evidences of style may appear in it shall be due to the linotype man. It is a story of the literary life in a great city, and it should be of interest to every author within a 20-mile radius of Gosport, Ind., whose desk holds a MS. story beginning thus: "While the cheers following his nomination were still ringing through the old court-house, Harwood broke away from the congratulating handclasps of his henchmen and hurried to Judge Creswell's house to find Ida."

Pettit came up out of Alabama to write fiction. The Southern papers had printed eight of his stories under an editorial caption identifying the author as the son of "the gallant Major Pettingill Pettit, our former County Attorney and hero of the battle of Lookout Mountain."

Pettit was a rugged fellow, with a kind of shame-faced culture, and my good friend. His father kept a general store in a little town called Hosea. Pettit had been raised in the pine-woods and broom-sedge fields adjacent thereto. He had in his gripsack two manuscript novels of the adventures in Picardy of one Gaston Laboulaye, Vicomte de

Montrepos, in the year 1329. That's nothing. We all do that. And some day when we make a hit with the little sketch about a newsy and his lame dog, the editor prints the other one for us—or "on us," as the saying is—and then—and then we have to get a big valise and peddle those patent air-draft gas burners. At $1.25 everybody should have 'em.

I took Pettit to the red-brick house which was to appear in an article entitled "Literary Landmarks of Old New York," some day when we got through with it. He engaged a room there, drawing on the general store for his expenses. I showed New York to him, and he did not mention how much narrower Broadway is than Lee Avenue in Hosea. This seemed a good sign, so I put the final test.

"Suppose you try your hand at a descriptive article," I suggested, "giving your impressions of New York as seen from the Brooklyn Bridge. The fresh point of view, the———"

"Don't be a fool," said Pettit. "Let's go have some beer. On the whole, I rather like the city."

We discovered and enjoyed the only true Bohemia. Every day and night we repaired to one of those palaces of marble and glass and tilework, where goes on a tremendous and sound epic of life. Valhalla itself could not be more glorious and sonorous. The classic marble on which we ate, the great, light-flooded, vitreous front, adorned with snow-white scrolls; the grand Wagnerian din of clanking cups and bowls, the flashing staccato of brandishing cutlery, the piercing recitative of the white-aproned grub-maidens at the morgue-like banquet tables; the recurrent leit-motif of the cash-register—it was a gigantic, triumphant wedding of art and sound, a deafening, soul-uplifting pageant of heroic and emblematic life. And the beans were only ten cents. We wondered why our fellow-artists care to dine at sad little tables in their so-called Bohemian restaurants; and we shuddered lest they should seek out our resorts and make them conspicuous with their presence.

Pettit wrote many stories, which the editors returned to him. He wrote love stories, a thing I have always kept free from, holding the belief that the well-known and popular sentiment is not properly a matter for publication, but something to be privately handled by the alienists and florists. But the editors had told him that they wanted love stories, because they said the women read them.

Now, the editors are wrong about that, of course. Women do not read the love stories in the magazines. They read the poker-game stories and the recipes for cucumber lotion. The love stories are read by fat cigar drummers and little ten-year-old girls. I am not criticizing the judgment of editors. They are mostly very fine men, but a man can be but one man, with individual opinions and tastes. I knew two associate editors of a magazine who were wonderfully alike in almost everything. And yet one of them was very fond of Flaubert, while the other preferred gin.

Pettit brought me his returned manuscripts, and we looked them over together to find out why they were not accepted. They seemed to me pretty fair stories, written in a good style, and ended, as they should, at the bottom of the last page.

They were well constructed and the events were marshalled in orderly and logical sequence. But I thought I detected a lack of living substance—it was much as if I gazed at a symmetrical array of presentable clamshells from which the succulent and vital inhabitants had been removed. I intimated that the author might do well to get better acquainted with his theme.

"You sold a story last week," said Pettit, "about a gun fight in an Arizona mining town in which the hero drew his Colt's .45 and shot seven bandits as fast as they came in the door. Now, if a six-shooter could———"

"Oh, well," said I, "that's different. Arizona is a long way from New York. I could have a man stabbed with a lariat or chased by a pair of chaparreras if I wanted to, and it wouldn't be noticed until the usual error-sharp from around McAdams Junction isolates the erratum and writes in to the papers about it. But you are up against another proposition. This thing they call love is as common around New York as it is in Sheboygan during the young onion season. It may be mixed here with a little commercialism—they read Byron, but they look up Bradstreet's, too, while they're among the Bs, and Brigham also if they have time—but it's pretty much the same old internal disturbance everywhere. You can fool an editor with a fake picture of a cowboy mounting a pony with his left hand on the saddle horn, but you can't put him up a tree with a love story. So, you've got to fall in love and then write the real thing."

Pettit did. I never knew whether he was taking my advice or whether he fell an accidental victim.

There was a girl he had met at one of these studio contrivances—a glorious, impudent, lucid, open-minded girl with hair the color of Culmbacher, and a good-natured way of despising you. She was a New York girl.

Well (as the narrative style permits us to say infrequently), Pettit went to pieces. All those pains, those lover's doubts, those heart-burnings and tremors of which he had written so unconvincingly were his. Talk about Shylock's pound of flesh! Twenty-five pounds Cupid got from Pettit. Which is the usurer?

One night Pettit came to my room exalted. Pale and haggard but exalted. She had given him a jonquil.

"Old Hoss," said he, with a new smile flickering around his mouth, "I believe I could write that story to-night—the one, you know, that is to win out. I can feel it. I don't know whether it will come out or not, but I can feel it."

I pushed him out of my door. "Go to your room and write it," I ordered. "Else I can see your finish. I told you this must come first. Write it to-night and put it under my door when it is done. Put it under my door to-night when it is finished—don't keep it until tomorrow."

I was reading my bully old pal Montaigne at two o'clock when I heard the sheets rustle under my door. I gathered them up and read the story.

The hissing of geese, the languishing cooing of doves, the braying of donkeys, the chatter of irresponsible sparrows—these were in my mind's ear as I read. "Suffering Sappho!" I exclaimed to myself. "Is this the divine fire that is supposed to ignite genius and make it practical and wage-earning?"

The story was sentimental drivel, full of whimpering soft-heartedness and gushing egoism. All the art that Pettit had acquired was gone. A perusal of its buttery phrases would have made a cynic of a sighing chamber-maid.

In the morning Pettit came to my room. I read him his doom mercilessly. He laughed idiotically.

"All right, Old Hoss," he said, cheerily, "make cigar-lighters of it. What's the difference? I'm going to take her to lunch at Claremont today."

There was about a month of it. And then Pettit came to me bearing an invisible mitten, with the fortitude of a dish-rag. He talked of the grave and South America and prussic acid; and I lost an afternoon getting him straight. I took him out and saw that large and curative doses of whiskey were administered to him. I warned you this was a true story—'ware your white ribbons if you follow this tale. For two weeks I fed him whiskey and Omar, and read to him regularly every evening the column in the evening paper that reveals the secrets of female beauty. I recommend the treatment.

After Pettit was cured he wrote more stories. He recovered his old-time facility and did work just short of good enough. Then the curtain rose on the third act.

A little, dark-eyed, silent girl from New Hampshire, who was studying applied design, fell deeply in love with him. She was the intense sort, but externally *glacée,* such as New England sometimes fools us with. Pettit liked her mildly, and took her about a good deal. She worshipped him, and now and then bored him.

There came a climax when she tried to jump out of a window, and he had to save her by some perfunctory, unmeant wooing. Even I was shaken by the depths of the absorbing affection she showed. Home, friends, traditions, creeds went up like thistle-down in the scale against her love. It was really discomposing.

One night again Pettit sauntered in, yawning. As he had told me before, he said he felt that he could do a great story, and as before I hunted him to his room and saw him open his inkstand. At one o'clock the sheets of paper slid under my door.

I read that story, and I jumped up, late as it was, with a whoop of joy. Old Pettit had done it. Just as though it lay there, red and bleeding, a woman's heart was written into the lines. You couldn't see the joining, but art, exquisite art, and pulsing nature had been combined into a love story that took you by the throat like the quinsy. I broke into Pettit's room and beat him on the back and called him names—names high up in the galaxy of the immortals that we admired. And Pettit yawned and begged to be allowed to sleep.

On the morrow, I dragged him to an editor. The great man read, and rising, gave Pettit his hand. That was a decoration, a wreath of bay, and a guarantee of rent.

And then old Pettit smiled slowly. I call him Gentleman Pettit now to myself. It's a miserable name to give a man, but it sounds better than it looks in print.

"I see," said old Pettit, as he took up his story and began tearing it into small strips. "I see the game now. You can't write with ink, and you can't write with your own heart's blood, but you can write with the heart's blood of someone else. You have to be a cad before you can be an artist. Well, I am for old Alabama and the Major's store. Have you got a light, Old Hoss?"

I went with Pettit to the depot and died hard.

"Shakespeare's sonnets?" I blurted, making a last stand. "How about him?"

"A cad," said Pettit. "They give it to you, and you sell it—love, you know. I'd rather sell ploughs for father."

"But," I protested, "you are reversing the decision of the world's greatest———"

"Good-bye, Old Hoss," said Pettit.

"Critics," I continued. "But—say if the Major can use a fairly good salesman and book-keeper down there in the store, let me know, will you?"

Squaring the Circle

At the hazard of wearying youth this tale of vehement emotions must be prefaced by a discourse on geometry.

Nature moves in circles; Art in straight lines. The natural is rounded; the artificial is made up of angles. A man lost in the snow wanders, in spite of himself, in perfect circles; the city man's feet, denaturalized by rectangular streets and floors, carry him ever away from himself.

The round eyes of childhood typify innocence; the narrow line of the flirt's optic proves the invasion of art. The horizontal mouth is the mark of determined cunning; who has not read Nature's most spontaneous lyric in lips rounded for the candid kiss?

Beauty is Nature in perfection; circularity is its chief attribute. Behold the full moon, the enchanting gold ball, the domes of splendid temples, the huckleberry pie, the wedding ring, the circus ring, the ring for the waiter, and the "round" of drinks.

On the other hand, straight lines show that Nature has been deflected. Imagine Venus's girdle transformed into a "straight front!"

When we began to move in straight lines and turn sharp corners our natures begin to change. The consequence is that Nature, being more adaptive than Art, tries to conform to its sterner regulations. The result is often a rather curious product—for instance: A prize chrysanthemum, wood alcohol whiskey, a Republican Missouri, cauliflower *au gratin,* and a New Yorker.

Nature is lost quickest in a big city. The cause is geometrical, not moral. The straight lines of its streets and architecture, the rectangularity of its laws and social customs, the undeviating pavements, the hard, severe, depressing, uncompromising rules of all its ways—even of its recreation and sports—coldly exhibit a sneering defiance of the curved line of Nature.

Wherefore, it may be said that the big city has demonstrated the problem of squaring the circle. And it may be added that this mathematical introduction precedes an account of the fate of a Kentucky feud that was imported to the city that has a habit of making its importations conform to its angles.

The feud began in the Cumberland Mountains between the Folwell and the Harkness families. The first victim of the homespun vendetta was a 'possum dog belonging to Bill Harkness. the Harkness family evened up this dire loss by laying out the chief of the Folwell clan. The Folwells were prompt at repartee. They oiled up their squirrel rifles and made it feasible for Bill Harkness to follow his dog to a land where the 'possums come down when treed without the stroke of an ax.

The feud flourished for forty years. Harknesses were shot at the plough, through their lamp-lit cabin windows, coming from camp-meetings, asleep, in duello, sober and otherwise, singly and in family groups, prepared and unprepared. Folwells had the branches of their family tree lopped off in similar ways, as the traditions of their country prescribed and authorized.

By and by the pruning left but a single member of each family. And then Cal Harkness, probably reasoning that further pursuance of the controversy would give a too decided personal flavor to the feud, suddenly disappeared from the relieved Cumberlands, baulking the avenging hand of Sam, the ultimate opposing Folwell.

A year afterward Sam Folwell learned that his hereditary, unsuppressed enemy was living in New York City. Sam turned over the big iron washpot in the yard, scraped off some of the soot, which he mixed with lard and shined his boots with the compound. He put on his store clothes of butternut dyed black, a white shirt and collar, and packed a carpet-sack with Spartan *lingerie*. He took his squirrel rifle from its hooks, but put it back again with a sigh. However ethical and plausible the habit might be in the Cumberlands, perhaps New York would not swallow his pose of hunting squirrels among the skyscrapers along Broadway. An ancient but reliable Colt's revolver that he resurrected from a bureau drawer seemed to proclaim itself the pink of weapons for metropolitan adventure and vengeance. This and a hunting-knife in a leather sheath, Sam packed in the carpet-sack. As he started, muleback, for the lowland railroad station the last Folwell turned in his saddle and looked grimly at the little cluster of white-pine slabs in the clump of cedars that marked the Folwell burying-ground.

Sam Folwell arrived in New York in the night. Still moving and living in the free circles of nature, he did not perceive the formidable, pitiless, restless, fierce angles of the great city waiting in the dark to close about the rotundity of his heart and brain and mould him to the form of its millions of reshaped victims. A cabby picked him out of the whirl, as Sam himself had often picked a nut from a bed of wind-tossed autumn leaves, and whisked him away to a hotel commensurate to his boots and carpet-sack.

On the next morning the last of the Folwells made his sortie into the city that sheltered the last Harkness. The Colt was thrust beneath his coat and secured by a narrow leather belt; the hunting-knife hung between his shoulder-blades, with the haft an inch below his coat collar. He knew this much—that Cal Harkness drove an express wagon somewhere in that town, and that he, Sam Folwell, had come to kill him. And as he stepped upon the sidewalk the red came into his eye and the feud-hate into his heart.

The clamor of the central avenues drew him thitherward. He had half expected to see Cal coming down the street in his shirt-sleeves with a jug and a whip in his hand, just as he would have seen him in Frankfort or Laurel City. But an hour went by and Cal did not appear. Perhaps he was waiting in ambush, to shoot him from a door or a window. Sam kept a sharp eye on doors and windows for a while.

About noon the city tired of playing with its mouse and suddenly squeezed him with its straight lines.

Sam Folwell stood where two great, rectangular arteries of the city cross. He looked four ways, and saw the world hurled from its orbit and reduced by spirit level and tape to an edged and cornered plane. All life moved on tracks, in grooves, according to system, within boundaries, by rote. The root of life was the cube root; the measure of existence was square measure. People streamed by in straight rows; the horrible din and crash stupefied him.

Sam leaned against the sharp corner of a stone building. Those faces passed him by thousands, and not one of them were turned toward him. A sudden foolish fear that he had died and was a spirit, and that they could not see him, seized him. And then the city smote him with loneliness.

A fat man dropped out of the stream and stood a few feet distant, waiting for his car. Sam crept to his side and shouted above the tumult into his ear:

"The Rankinses' hogs weighed more'n ourn a whole passel, but the mast in thar neighborhood was a fine chance better than what it was down———"

The fat man moved away unostentatiously, and bought roasted chestnuts to cover his alarm.

Sam felt the need of a drop of mountain dew. Across the street men passed in and out through swinging doors. Brief glimpses could be had of a glistening bar and its bedeckings. The feudist crossed and essayed to enter. Again had Art eliminated the familiar circle. Sam's hand found no door-knob—it slid, in vain, over a rectangular brass plate and polished oak with nothing even so large as a pin's head upon which his fingers might close.

Abashed, reddened, heartbroken, he walked away from the bootless door and sat upon a step. A locust club tickled him in the ribs.

"Take a walk for yourself," said the policeman. "You've been loafing around here long enough."

At the next corner a shrill whistle sounded in Sam's ear. He wheeled around and saw a black-browed villain scowling at him over peanuts heaped on a steaming machine. He started across the street. An immense engine, running without mules, with the voice of a bull and the smell of a smoky lamp, whizzed past, grazing his knee. A cab-driver bumped him with a hub and explained to him that kind words were invented to be used on other occasions. A motorman clanged his bell wildly and, for once in his life, corroborated a cab-driver. A large lady in a changeable silk waist dug an elbow into his back, and a newsy pensively pelted him with banana rinds, murmuring, "I hates to do it—but if anybody seen me let it pass!"

Cal Harkness, his day's work over and his express wagon stabled, turned the sharp edge of the building that, by the cheek of architects, is modelled upon a safety razor. Out of the mass of hurrying people his eye picked up, three yards away, the surviving bloody and implacable foe of his kith and kin.

He stopped short and wavered for a moment, being unarmed and sharply surprised. But the keen mountaineer's eye of Sam Folwell had picked him out.

There was a sudden spring, a ripple in the steam of passers-by and the sound of Sam's voice crying:

"Howdy, Cal! I'm durned glad to see ye."

And in the angles of Broadway, Fifth Avenue, and Twenty-third Street the Cumberland feudists shook hands.

The Fool-Killer

Down South whenever any one perpetrates some particularly monumental piece of foolishness everybody says: "Send for Jesse Holmes."

Jesse Holmes is the Fool-Killer. Of course he is a myth, like Santa Claus and Jack Frost and General Prosperity and all those concrete conceptions that are supposed to represent an idea that Nature had failed to embody. The wisest of the Southrons cannot tell you whence comes the Fool-Killer's name; but few and happy are the households from the Roanoke to the Rio Grande in which the name Jesse Holmes has not been pronounced or invoked. Always with a smile, and often with a tear, is he summoned to his official duty. A busy man is Jesse Holmes.

I remember the clear picture of him that hung on the walls of my fancy during my barefoot days when I was dodging his oft-threatened devoirs. To me he was a terrible old man, in gray clothes, with a long, ragged, gray beard, and reddish, fierce eyes. I looked to see him come stumping up the road in a cloud of dust, with a white oak staff in his hand and his shoes tied with leather thongs. I may yet——

But this is a story, not a sequel.

I have taken notice with regret that few stories worth reading have been written that did not contain drink of some sort. Down go the fluids, from Arizona Dick's three fingers of red pizen to the inefficacious Oolong that nerves Lionel Monstresser to repartee in the "Dotty Dialogues." So, in such good company I may introduce an absinthe drip—one absinthe drip, dripped through a silver dripper, orderly, opalescent, cool, green-eyed—deceptive.

Kerner was a fool. Besides that, he was an artist and my good friend. Now, if there is one thing on earth utterly despicable to another, it is an artist in the eyes of an author whose story he has illustrated. Just try it once. Write a story about a mining camp in Idaho. Sell it. Spend the money, and then, six months later, borrow a quarter (or a dime), and buy the magazine containing it. You find a full-page wash drawing of your hero, Black Bill, the cowboy. Somewhere in your story you employed the word "horse." Aha! the artist has grasped the idea. Black Bill has on the regulation trousers of the M. F. H. of the Westchester County Hunt. He carries a parlor rifle, and wears a monocle. In the distance is a section of Forty-second

Street during a search for a lost gas-pipe, and the Taj Mahal, the famous mausoleum in India.

Enough! I hated Kerner, and one day I met him and we became friends. He was young and gloriously melancholy because his spirits were so high and life had so much in store for him. Yes, he was almost riotously sad. That was his youth. When a man begins to be hilarious in a sorrowful way you can bet a million that he is dyeing his hair. Kerner's hair was plentiful and carefully matted as an artist's thatch should be. He was a cigaretteur, and he audited his dinners with red wine. But, most of all, he was a fool. And, wisely, I envied him, and listened patiently while he knocked Velasquez and Tintoretto. Once he told me that he liked a story of mine that he had come across in an anthology. He described it to me, and I was sorry that Mr. Fitz James O'Brien was dead and could not learn of the eulogy of his work. But mostly Kerner made few breaks and was a consistent fool.

I'd better explain what I mean by that. There was a girl. Now, a girl, as far as I am concerned, is a thing that belongs in a seminary or an album; but I conceded the existence of the animal in order to retain Kerner's friendship. He showed me her picture in a locket—she was a blonde or a brunette—I have forgotten which. She worked in a factory for eight dollars a week. Lest factories quote this wage by way of vindication, I will add that the girl had worked for five years to reach that supreme elevation of remuneration, beginning at $1.50 per week.

Kerner's father was worth a couple of millions. He was willing to stand for art, but he drew the line at the factory girl. So Kerner disinherited his father and walked out to a cheap studio and lived on sausages for breakfast and on Farroni for dinner. Farroni had the artistic soul and a line of credit for painters and poets, nicely adjusted. Sometimes Kerner sold a picture and bought some new tapestry, a ring and a dozen silk cravats, and paid Farroni two dollars on account.

One evening Kerner had me to dinner with himself and the factory girl. They were to be married as soon as Kerner could slosh paint profitably. As for the ex-father's two millions—pouf!

She was a wonder. Small and halfway pretty, and as much at her ease in that cheap café as though she were only in the Palmer House, Chicago, with a souvenir spoon already safely hidden in her shirt waist. She was natural. Two things I noticed about her especially. Her belt buckle was exactly in the middle of her back, and she didn't tell us that a large man with a ruby stick-pin had followed her up all the way from Fourteenth Street. Was Kerner such a fool? I wondered. And then I thought of the quantity of striped cuffs and blue glass beads that $2,000,000 can buy for the heathen, and I said to myself that he was. And then Elise—certainly that was her name—told us, merrily, that the brown spot on her waist was caused by her landlady knocking at the door while she (the girl—confound the English language) was heating an iron over the gas jet, and she hid the iron under the bedclothes until the coast was clear, and there was a piece of chewing gum stuck to it when she began to iron the waist and—well, I wondered how in the world the chewing gum came to be there—don't they ever stop chewing it?

A while after that—don't be impatient, the absinthe drip is coming now—Kerner and I were dining at Farroni's. A mandolin and a guitar were being attacked; the room was full of smoke in nice, long crinkly layers just like the artists draw the steam from a plum pudding on Christmas posters and a lady in a blue silk and gasolined gauntlets was beginning to hum an air from the Catskills.

"Kerner," said I, "you are a fool."

"Of course," said Kerner, "I wouldn't let her go on working. Not my wife. What's the use to wait? She's willing. I sold that water color of the Palisades yesterday. We could cook on a two-burner gas stove. You know the ragouts I can throw together. Yes, I think we will marry next week."

"Kerner," said I, "you are a fool."

"Have an absinthe drip?" said Kerner, grandly. "To-night you are a guest of Art in paying quantities. I think we will get a flat with a bath."

"I never tried one—I mean an absinthe drip," said I.

The waiter brought it and poured the water slowly over the ice in the dipper.

"It looks exactly like the Mississippi River water in the big bend below Natchez," said I, fascinated, gazing at the be-muddled drip.

"There are such flats for eight dollars a week," said Kerner.

"You are a fool," said I, and began to sip the filtration. "What you need," I continued, "is the official attention of one Jesse Holmes."

Kerner, not being a Southerner, did not comprehend, so he sat, sentimental, figuring on his flat in his sordid, artistic way, while I gazed into the green eyes of the sophisticated Spirit of Wormwood.

Presently I noticed casually that a procession of bacchantes limned on the wall immediately below the ceiling had begun to move, traversing the room from right to left in a gay and spectacular pilgrimage.

I did not confide my discovery to Kerner. The artistic temperament is too high-strung to view deviations from the natural laws of the art of kalsomining. I sipped my absinthe drip and sawed wormwood.

One absinthe drip is not much—but I said again to Kerner, kindly: "You are a fool." And then, in the vernacular: "Jesse Holmes for yours."

And then I looked around and saw the Fool-Killer, as he had always appeared to my imagination, sitting at a nearby table, and regarding us with his reddish, fatal, relentless eyes. He was Jesse Holmes from top to toe; he had the long, gray, ragged beard, the gray clothes of ancient cut, the executioner's look, and the dusty shoes of one who had been called from afar. His eyes were turned fixedly upon Kerner. I shuddered to think that I had invoked him from his assiduous southern duties. I thought of flying, and then I kept my seat, reflecting that many men had escaped his ministrations when it seemed that nothing short of an appointment as Ambassador to Spain could save them from him. I had called my brother Kerner a fool and was in danger of hell fire. That was nothing; but I would try to save him from Jesse Holmes.

The Fool-Killer got up from his table and came over to ours. He rested his hands upon it, and turned his burning, vindictive eyes upon Kerner, ignoring me.

"You are a hopeless fool," he said to the artist. "Haven't you had enough of starvation yet? I offer you one more opportunity. Give up this girl and come back to your home. Refuse, and you must take the consequences."

The Fool-Killer's threatening face was within a foot of his victim's; but to my horror, Kerner made not the slightest sign of being aware of his presence.

"We will be married next week," he muttered absent-mindedly. "With my studio furniture and some second-hand stuff we can make out."

"You have decided your own fate," said the Fool-Killer, in a low but terrible voice. "You may consider yourself as one dead. You have had your last chance."

"In the moonlight," went on Kerner, softly, "we will sit under the skylight with our guitar and sing away the false delights of pride and money."

"On your own head be it," hissed the Fool-Killer, and my scalp prickled when I perceived that neither Kerner's eyes nor his ears took the slightest cognizance of Jesse Holmes. And then I knew that for some reason the veil had been lifted for me alone, and that I had been elected to save my friend from destruction at the Fool-Killer's hand. Something of the fear and wonder of it must have showed itself in my face.

"Excuse me," said Kerner, with his wan, amiable smile; "was I talking to myself? I think it is getting to be a habit with me."

The Fool-Killer turned and walked out of Farroni's.

"Wait here for me," said I, rising; "I must speak to that man. Had you no answer for him? Because you are a fool must you die like a mouse under his foot? Could you not utter one squeak in your own defence?"

"You are drunk," said Kerner, heartlessly. "No one addressed me."

"The destroyer of your mind," said I, "stood above you just now and marked you for his victim. You are not blind or deaf."

"I recognize no such person," said Kerner. "I have seen no one but you at this table. Sit down. Hereafter you shall have no more absinthe drips."

"Wait here," said I, furious; "if you don't care for your own life, I will save it for you."

I hurried out and overtook the man in gray halfway down the block. He looked as I had seen him in my fancy a thousand times—truculent, gray and awful. He walked with the white oak staff, and but for the street-sprinkler the dust would have been flying under his tread.

I caught him by the sleeve and steered him to a dark angle of a building. I knew he was a myth, and I did not want a cop to see me conversing with vacancy, for I might land in Bellevue minus my silver matchbox and diamond ring.

"Jesse Holmes," said I, facing him with apparent bravery, "I know you. I have heard of you all my life. I know now what a scourge you have been to your country. Instead of killing fools you have been murdering the youth and genius that are necessary to make a people live and grow great. You are a fool yourself, Holmes; you began killing off the brightest and best of your countrymen three generations ago, when the old and obsolete standards of society and honor and orthodoxy were narrow and bigoted. You proved that when you put your murderous mark upon my friend Kerner—the wisest chap I ever knew in my life."

The Fool-Killer looked at me grimly and closely.

"You're a queer jag," said he curiously. "Oh, yes; I see who you are now. You were sitting with him at the table. Well, if I'm not mistaken, I heard you call him a fool, too."

"I did," said I. "I delight in doing so. It is from envy. By all the standards that you know he is the most egregious and grandiloquent and gorgeous fool in all the world. That's why you want to kill him."

"Would you mind telling me who or what you think I am?" asked the old man.

I laughed boisterously and then stopped suddenly, for I remembered that it would not do to be seen so hilarious in the company of nothing but a brick wall.

"You are Jesse Holmes, the Fool-Killer," I said, solemnly, "and you are going to kill my friend Kerner. I don't know who rang you up, but if you do kill him I'll see that you get pinched for it. That is," I added, despairingly, "if I can get a cop to see you. They have a poor eye for mortals, and I think it would take the whole force to round up a myth murderer."

"Well," said the Fool-Killer, briskly, "I must be going. You had better go home and sleep it off. Good-night."

At this I was moved at a sudden fear for Kerner to a softer and more pleading mood. I leaned agianst the gray man's sleeve and besought him:

"Good Mr. Fool-Killer, please don't kill little Kerner. Why can't you go back South and kill Congressmen and clay-eaters and let us alone? Why don't you go up on Fifth Avenue and kill millionaires that keep their money locked up and won't let young fools marry because one of 'em lives on the wrong street? Come and have a drink, Jesse. Will you never get on to your job?"

"Do you know this girl that your friend has made himself a fool about?" asked the Fool-Killer.

"I have the honor," said I, "and that's why I called Kerner a fool. He is a fool because he has waited so long before marrying her. He is a fool because he has been waiting in the hopes of getting the consent of some absurd two-million-dollar-fool parent or something of the sort."

"Maybe," said the Fool-Killer—"maybe I—I might have looked at it differently. Would you mind going back to the restaurant and bringing your friend Kerner here?"

"Oh, what's the use, Jesse," I yawned. "He can't see you. He didn't know you were talking to him at the table. You are a fictitious character, you know."

"Maybe he can this time. Will you go fetch him?"

"All right," said I, "but I've a suspicion that you're not strictly sober, Jesse. You seem to be wavering and losing your outlines. Don't vanish before I get back."

I went back to Kerner and said:

"There's a man with an invisible homicidal mania waiting to see you outside. I believe he wants to murder you. Come along. You won't see him, so there's nothing to be frightened about."

Kerner looked anxious.

"Why," said he, "I had no idea one absinthe would do that. You'd better stick to Wurzburger. I'll walk home with you."

I led him to Jesse Holmes's.

"Rudolph," said the Fool-Killer, "I'll give in. Bring her up to the house. Give me your hand, boy."

"Good for you, dad," said Kerner, shaking hands with the old man. "You'll never regret it after you know her."

"So, you did see him when he was talking to you at the table?" I asked Kerner.

"We hadn't spoken to each other in a year," said Kerner. "It's all right now."

I walked away.

"Where are you going?" called Kerner.

"I am going to look for Jesse Holmes," I answered, with dignity and reserve.

Transients in Arcadia

There is a hotel on Broadway that has escaped discovery by the summer-resort promoters. It is deep and wide and cool. Its rooms are finished in dark oak of a low temperature. Home-made breezes and deep-green shrubbery give it the delights without the inconveniences of the Adirondacks. One can mount its broad staircases or glide dreamily upward in its aërial elevators, attended by guides in brass buttons, with a serene joy that Alpine climbers have never attained. There is a chef in its kitchen who will prepare for you brook trout better than the White Mountains ever served, sea food that would turn Old Point Comfort—"by Gad, sah!"—green with envy, and Maine venison that would melt the official heart of the game warden.

A few have found out this oasis in the July desert of Manhattan. During that month you will see the hotel's reduced array of guests scattered luxuriously about in the cool twilight of its lofty dining-room, gazing at one another across the snowy waste of unoccupied tables, silently congratulatory.

Superfluous, watchful, pneumatically moving waiters hover near, supplying every want before it is expressed. The temperature is perpetual April. The ceiling is painted in water colors to counterfeit a summer sky across which delicate clouds drift and do not vanish as those of nature do to our regret.

The pleasing, distant roar of Broadway is transformed in the imagination of the happy guests to the noise of a waterfall filling the woods with its restful sound. At every strange footstep the guests turn an anxious ear, fearful lest their retreat be discovered and invaded by the restless pleasure-seekers who are forever hounding Nature to her deepest lairs.

Thus in the depopulated caravansary the little band of connoisseurs jealously hide themselves during the heated season, enjoying to the uttermost delights of mountain and seashore that art and skill have gathered and served to them.

In this July came to the hotel one whose card that she sent to the clerk for her name to be registered read "Mme. Héloise D'Arcy Beaumont."

Madame Beaumont was a guest such as the Hotel Lotus loved. She possessed the fine air of the élite, tempered and sweetened by a cordial graciousness that made the hotel employées her slaves. Bell-boys fought for the honor of answering her ring; the clerks, but for the question of ownership, would have deeded to her the hotel and its contents; the other guests regarded her as the final touch of feminine exclusiveness and beauty that rendered the entourage perfect.

This super-excellent guest rarely left the hotel. Her habits were consonant with the customs of the discriminating patrons of the Hotel Lotus. To enjoy that delectable hostelry one must forego the city as though it were leagues away. By night a brief excursion to the nearby roofs is in order; but during the torrid day one remains in the umbrageous fastnesses of the Lotus as a trout hangs poised in the pellucid sanctuaries of his favorite pool.

Though alone in the Hotel Lotus, Madame Beaumont preserved the state of a queen whose loneliness was of position only. She breakfasted at ten, a cool, sweet, leisurely, delicate being who glowed softly in the dimness like a jasmine flower in the dusk.

But at dinner was Madame's glory at its height. She wore a gown as beautiful and immaterial as the mist from an unseen cataract in a mountain gorge. The nomenclature of this gown is beyond the guess of the scribe. Always pale-red roses reposed against its lace-garnished front. It was a gown that the head-waiter viewed with respect and met at the door. You thought of Paris when you saw it, and maybe of mysterious countesses, and certainly of Versailles and rapiers and Mrs. Fiske and rouge-et-noir. There was an untraceable rumor in the Hotel Lotus that Madame was a cosmopolite, and that she was pulling with her slender white hands certain strings between the nations in the favor of Russia. Being a citizeness of the world's smoothest roads it was small wonder that she was quick to recognize in the refined purlieus of the Hotel Lotus the most desirable spot in America for a restful sojourn during the heat of midsummer.

On the third day of Madame Beaumont's residence in the hotel a young man entered and registered himself as a guest. His clothing—to speak of his points in approved order—was quietly in the mode; his features good and regular; his expression that of a poised and sophisticated man of the world. He informed the clerk that he would remain three or four days, inquired concerning the sailing of European steamships, and sank into the blissful inanition of the nonpareil hotel with the contented air of a traveller in his favorite inn.

The young man—not to question the veracity of the register—was Harold Farrington. He drifted into the exclusive and calm current of life in the Lotus so tactfully and silently that not a ripple alarmed his fellow-seekers after rest. He ate in the Lotus and of its patronym, and was lulled into blissful peace with the other fortunate mariners. In one day he acquired his table and his waiter and the fear lest the panting chasers after repose that kept Broadway warm should pounce upon and destroy this contiguous but covert haven.

After dinner on the next day after the arrival of Harold Farrington Madame Beaumont dropped her handkerchief in passing out. Mr. Farrington recovered and returned it without the effusiveness of a seeker after acquaintance.

Perhaps there was a mystic freemasonry between the discriminating guests of the Lotus. Perhaps they were drawn one to another by the fact of their common good fortune in discovering the acme of summer resorts in a Broadway hotel. Words delicate in courtesy and tentative in departure from formality passed between the two. And, as if in the expedient atmosphere of a real summer resort, an acquaintance grew, flowered and fructified on the spot as does the mystic plant of the conjuror. For a few moments they stood on a balcony upon which the corridor ended, and tossed the feathery ball of conversation.

"One tires of the old resorts," said Madame Beaumont, with a faint but sweet smile. "What is the use to fly to the mountains or the seashore to escape noise and dust when the very people that make both follow us there?"

"Even on the ocean," remarked Farrington sadly, "the Philistines be upon you. The most exclusive steamers are getting to be scarcely more than ferry boats. Heaven help us when the summer resorter discovers that the Lotus is further away from Broadway than Thousand Islands or Mackinac."

"I hope our secret will be safe for a week, anyhow," said Madame, with a sigh and a smile. "I do not know where I would go if they should descend upon the dear Lotus. I know of but one place so delightful in summer, and that is the castle of Count Polinski, in the Ural Mountains."

"I hear that Baden-Baden and Cannes are almost deserted this season," said Farrington. "Year by year the old resorts fall in disrepute. Perhaps many others, like ourselves, are seeking out the quiet nooks that are overlooked by the majority."

"I promise myself three days more of this delicious rest," said Madame Beaumont. "On Monday the *Cedric* sails."

Harold Farrington's eyes proclaimed his regret. "I too must leave on Monday," he said, "but I do not go abroad."

Madame Beaumont shrugged one round shoulder in a foreign gesture.

"One cannot hide here forever, charming though it may be. The château has been in preparation for me longer than a month. Those house parties that one must give—what a nuisance! But I shall never forget my week in the Hotel Lotus."

"Nor shall I," said Farrington in a low voice, "and I shall never *forgive* the *Cedric*."

On Sunday evening, three days afterward, the two sat at a little table on the same balcony. A discreet waiter brought ices and small glasses of claret cup.

Madame Beaumont wore the same beautiful evening gown that she had worn each day at dinner. She seemed thoughtful. Near her hand on the table lay a small chatelaine purse. After she had eaten her ice she opened the purse and took out a one-dollar bill.

"Mr. Farrington," she said, with the smile that had won the Hotel Lotus, "I want to tell you something. I'm going to leave before breakfast in the morning, because I've got to go back to my work. I'm behind the hosiery counter at Casey's Mammoth Store, and my vacation's up at eight o'clock tomorrow. That paper dollar is the last cent I'll see till I draw my eight dollars salary next Saturday night. You're a real gentleman, and you've been good to me, and I wanted to tell you before I went.

"I've been saving up out of my wages for a year just for this vacation. I wanted to spend one week like a lady if I never do another one. I wanted to get up when I please instead of having to crawl out at seven every morning; and I wanted to live on the best and be waited on and ring bells for things just like rich folks do. Now I've done it, and I've had the happiest time I ever expect to have in my life. I'm going back to my work and my little hall bedroom satisfied for another year. I wanted to tell you about it, Mr. Farrington, because I—I thought you kind of liked me, and I—I liked you. But, oh, I couldn't help deceiving you up till now, for it was all just like a fairy tale to me. So I talked about Europe and the things I've read about in other countries, and made you think I was a great lady.

"This dress I've got on—it's the only one I have that's fit to wear—I bought from O'Dowd & Levinsky on the instalment plan.

"Seventy-five dollars is the price, and it was made to measure. I paid $10 down, and they're to collect $1 a week till it's paid for. That'll be about all I have to say, Mr. Farrington, except that my name is Mamie Siviter instead of Madame Beaumont, and I thank you for your attentions. This dollar will pay the instalment due on the dress to-morrow. I guess I'll go up to my room now."

Harold Farrington listened to the recital of the Lotus's loveliest guest with an impassive countenance. When she had concluded he drew a small book like a checkbook from his coat pocket. He wrote upon a blank form in this with a stub of pencil, tore out the leaf, tossed it over to his companion and took up the paper dollar.

"I've got to go to work, too, in the morning," he said, "and I might as well begin now. There's a receipt for the dollar instalment. I've been a collector for O'Dowd & Levinsky for three years. Funny, ain't it, that you and me both had the same idea about spending our vacation? I've always wanted to put up at a swell hotel, and I saved up out of my twenty per, and did it. Say, Mame, how about a trip to Coney Saturday night on the boat—what?"

The face of the pseudo Madame Héloise D'Arcy Beaumont beamed.

"Oh, you bet I'll go, Mr. Farrington. The store closes at twelve on Saturdays. I guess Coney'll be all right even if we did spend a week with the swells."

Below the balcony the sweltering city growled and buzzed in the July night. Inside the Hotel Lotus the tempered, cool shadows reigned, and the solicitous waiter single-footed near the low windows, ready at a nod to serve Madame and her escort.

At the door of the elevator Farrington took his leave, and Madame Beaumont made her last ascent. But before they reached the noiseless cage he said: "Just forget that 'Harold Farrington,' will you?—McManus is the name—James McManus. Some call me Jimmy."

"Good-night, Jimmy," said Madame.

Extradited from Bohemia

From near the village of Harmony, at the foot of the Green Mountains, came Miss Medora Martin to New York with her color-box and easel.

Miss Medora resembled the rose which the autumnal frosts had spared the longest of all her sister blossoms. In Harmony, when she started alone to the wicked city to study art, they said she was a mad, reckless, headstrong girl. In New York, when she first took her seat at a West Side boarding-house table, the boarders asked: "Who is the nice-looking old maid?"

Medora took heart, a cheap hall bedroom, and two art lessons a week from Professor Angelini, a retired barber who had studied his profession in a Harlem dancing academy. There was no one to set her right, for here in the big city they do it unto all of us. How many of us are badly shaved daily and taught the two-step imperfectly by ex-pupils of Bastien Le Page and Gérôme? The most pathetic sight in New York—except the manners of the rush-hour crowds—is the dreary march of the hopeless army of Mediocrity. Here Art is no benignant goddess, but a Circe who turns her wooers into mewing Toms and Tabbies who linger about the doorsteps of her abode, unmindful of the flying brickbats and boot-jacks of the critics. Some of us creep back to our native villages to the skim-milk of "I told you so"; but most of us prefer to remain in the cold courtyard of our mistress's temple, snatching the scraps that fall from her divine table d'hôte. But some of us grow weary at last of the fruitless service. And then there are two fates open to us. We can get a job driving a grocer's wagon, or we can get swallowed up in the Vortex of Bohemia. The latter sounds good; but the former really pans out better. For, when the grocer pays us off we can rent a dress suit and—the capitalized system of humor describes it best—Get Bohemia On the Run.

Miss Medora chose the Vortex and thereby furnishes us with our little story.

Professor Angelini praised her sketches excessively. Once, when she had made a neat study of a horse-chestnut tree in the park, he declared she would become a second Rosa Bonheur. Again—a great artist has his moods—he would say cruel and cutting things. For example, Medora had spent an afternoon patiently sketching the statue and the architecture at Columbus Circle. Tossing it aside with a sneer, the professor informed her that Giotto had once drawn a perfect circle with one sweep of his hand.

One day it rained, the weekly remittance from Harmony was overdue, Medora had a headache, the professor had tried to borrow two dollars from her, her art dealer had sent back all her water-colors unsold and—Mr. Binkley asked her out to dinner.

Mr. Binkley was the gay boy of the boarding-house. He was forty-nine, and owned a fish-stall in a downtown market. But after six o'clock he wore an evening suit and whooped things up connected with the beaux arts. The young men said he was an "Indian." He was supposed to be an accomplished habitué of the inner circles of Bohemia. It was no secret that he had once loaned $10 to a young man who had had a drawing printed in *Puck*. Often has one thus obtained his entrée into the charmed circle, while the other obtained both his entrée and roast.

The other boarders enviously regarded Medora as she left at Mr. Binkley's side at nine o'clock. She was as sweet as a cluster of dried autumn grasses in her pale blue—oh—er—that very thin stuff—in her pale blue Comstockized silk waist and box-pleated voile skirt, in her soft pink glow on her thin cheeks and the tiniest bit of rouge powder on her face, with her handkerchief and room key in her brown walrus, pebble-grain hand-bag.

And Mr. Binkley looked imposing and dashing with his red face and gray mustache, and his tight dress coat, that made the back of his neck roll up just like a successful novelist's.

They drove in a cab to the Café Terence, just off the most glittering part of Broadway, which, as everyone knows, is one of the most popular and widely patronized, jealously exclusive Bohemian resorts in the city.

Down between the rows of little tables tripped Medora, of the Green Mountains, after her escort. Thrice in a lifetime may woman walk upon clouds—once when she trippeth to the altar, once when she first enters Bohemian halls, the last when she marches back across her first garden with the dead hen of her neighbor in her hand.

There was a table set, with three or four about it. A waiter buzzed around it like a bee, and silver and glass shone upon it. And, preliminary to the meal, as the prehistoric granite strata heralded the protozoa, the bread of Gaul, compounded after the formula of the recipe for the eternal hills, was there set forth to the hand and tooth of a long-suffering city, while the gods lay beside their nectar and home-made biscuits and smiled, and the dentists leaped for joy in their gold-leafy dens.

The eye of Binkley fixed a young man at his table with the Bohemian gleam, which is a compound of the look of the Basilisk, the shine of a bubble of Würzburger, the inspiration of genius and the pleading of a panhandler.

The young man sprang to his feet. "Hello, Bink, old boy!" he shouted. "Don't tell me you were going to pass our table. Join us—unless you've another crowd on hand."

"Don't mind, old chap," said Binkley, of the fish-stall. "You know how I like to butt up against the fine arts. Mr. Vandyke—Mr. Madder—er—Miss Martin, one of the elect also in art—er———"

The introduction went around. There were also Miss Elise and Miss Toinette. Perhaps they were models, for they chattered of the St. Regis decorations and Henry James—and they did it not badly.

Medora sat in transport. Music—wild, intoxicating music made by troubadours direct from a rear basement room in Elysium—set her thoughts to dancing. Here was a world never before penetrated by her warmest imagination or any of the lines controlled by Harriman. With the Green Mountains' external calm upon her she sat, her soul flaming in her with the fire of Andalusia. The tables were filled with Bohemia. The room was full of the fragrance of flowers—

both mille and cauli. Questions and corks popped; laughter and silver rang; champagne flashed in the pail, wit flashed in the pan.

Vandyke ruffled his long, black locks, disarranged his careless tie and leaned over to Madder.

"Say, Maddy," he whispered, feelingly, "sometimes I'm tempted to pay this Philistine his ten dollars and get rid of him."

Madder ruffled his long, sandy locks and disarranged his careless tie.

"Don't think of it, Vandy," he replied. "We are short, and Art is long."

Medora ate strange viands and drank elderberry wine that they poured in her glass. It was just the color of that in the Vermont home. The waiter poured something in another glass that seemed to be boiling, but when she tasted it it was not hot. She had never felt so lighthearted before. She thought lovingly of Green Mountain farm and its fauna. She leaned, smiling, to Miss Elise.

"If I were at home," she said, beamingly, "I could show you the cutest little calf!"

"Nothing for you in the White Lane," said Miss Elise. "Why don't you pad?"

The orchestra played a wailing waltz that Medora had learned from the hand-organs. She followed the air with nodding head in a sweet soprano hum. Madder looked across the table at her, and wondered in what strange waters Binkley had caught her in this seine. She smiled at him, and they raised glasses and drank of the wine that boiled when it was cold.

Binkley had abandoned art and was prating of the unusual spring catch of shad. Miss Elise arranged the palette-and-maul-stick tie pin of Mr. Vandyke. A Philistine at some distant table was maundering volubly either about Jerome or Gérôme. A famous actress was discoursing excitably about monogrammed hosiery. A hose clerk from a department store was loudly proclaiming his opinions of the drama. A writer was abusing Dickens. A magazine editor and a photographer were drinking a dry brand at a reserved table. A 36-25-42 young lady was saying to an eminent sculptor: "Fudge for your Prax Italys! Bring one of your Venus Anno Dominus down to Cohen's and see how quickly she'd be turned down for a cloak model. Back to the quarries with your Greeks and Dagos!"

Thus went Bohemia.

At eleven Mr. Binkley took Medora to the boarding-house and left her, with a society bow, at the foot of the hall stairs. She went up to her room and lit the gas.

And then, as suddenly as the dreadful genie arose in vapor from the copper vase of the fisherman, arose in that room the formidable shape of the New England Conscience. The terrible thing that Medora had done was revealed to her in its full enormity. She had sat in the presence of the ungodly and looked upon the wine both when it was red and effervescent.

At midnight she wrote this letter:

Mr. Beriah Hoskins, Harmony, Vermont

Dear Sir: Henceforth, consider me as dead to you forever. I have loved you too well to blight your career by bringing into it my guilty and sin-stained life. I have succumbed to the insidious wiles of this wicked world and have been drawn into the vortex of Bohemia. There is scarcely any depth of glittering iniquity that I have not sounded. It is hopeless to combat my decision. There is no rising from the depths to which I have sunk. Endeavor to forget me. I am lost forever in the fair but brutal maze of awful Bohemia. Farewell.

Once your Medora

On the next day Medora formed her resolutions. Beelzebub, flung from heaven, was no more cast down. Between her and the apple blossoms of Harmony there was a fixed gulf. Flaming cherubim warded her from the gates of her lost paradise. In one evening, by the aid of Binkley and Mumm, Bohemia had gathered her into its awful midst.

There remained to her but one thing—a life of brilliant but irremediable error. Vermont was a shrine that she never would dare to approach again. But she would not sink—there were great and compelling ones in history upon whom she would model her meteoric career—Camille, Lola Montez, Royal Mary, Zaza—such a name as one of these would that of Medora Martin be to future generations.

For two days Medora kept to her room. On the third she opened a magazine at the portrait of the King of Belgium, and laughed sardonically. If that far-famed breaker of women's hearts should cross her path, he would have to bow before her cold and imperious beauty. She would not spare the old or the young. All America—all Europe should do homage to her sinister but compelling charm.

As yet she could not bear to think of the life she had once desired—a peaceful one in the shadow of the Green Mountains with Beriah at her side, and orders for expensive oil paintings coming in by each mail from New York. Her one fatal misstep had shattered that dream.

On the fourth day Medora powdered her face and rouged her lips. Once she had seen Carter in "Zaza." She stood before the mirror in a reckless attitude and cried: *"Zut! zut!"* She rhymed it with "nut," but with the lawless word Harmony seemed to pass away forever. The Vortex had her. She belonged to Bohemia for evermore. And never would Beriah———

The door opened and Beriah walked in.

" 'Dory," said he, "what's all that chalk and pink stuff on your face, honey?"

Medora extended an arm.

"Too late," she said solemnly. "The die is cast. I belong to another world. Curse me if you will—it is your right. Go, and leave me in the path I have chosen. Bid them all at home never to mention my name again. And sometimes, Beriah, pray for me when I am revelling in the gaudy, but hollow, pleasures of Bohemia."

"Get a towel, 'Dory," said Beriah, "and wipe that paint off your face. I came as soon as I got your letter. Them pictures of yours ain't amounting to anything. I've got tickets for both of us back on the evening train. Hurry and get your things in your trunk."

"Fate was too strong for me, Beriah. Go while I am strong to bear it."

"How do you fold this easel, 'Dory?—now begin to pack, so we have time to eat before train time. The maples is all out in full-grown leaves, 'Dory—you just ought to see 'em!"

"Not this early, Beriah?"

"You ought to see 'em, 'Dory; they're like an ocean of green in the morning sunlight!"

"Oh, Beriah!"

On the train she said to him suddenly:

"I wonder why you came when you got my letter."

"Oh, shucks!" said Beriah. "Did you think you could fool me? How could you be run away to that Bohemia country like you said when your letter was postmarked New York as plain as day?"

From Each According to His Ability

Vuyning left his club, cursing it softly, without any particular anger. From ten in the morning until eleven it had bored him immeasurably. Kirk with his fish story, Brooks with his Porto Rico cigars, old Morrison with his anecdote about the widow, Hepburn with his invariable luck at billiards—all these afflictions had been repeated without change of bill or scenery. Besides these morning evils Miss Allison had refused him again on the night before. But that was a chronic trouble. Five times she had laughed at his offer to make her Mrs. Vuyning. He intended to ask her again the next Wednesday evening.

Vuyning walked along Forty-fourth Street to Broadway, and then drifted down the great sluice that washes out the dust of the gold-mines of Gotham. He wore a morning suit of light gray, low, dull kid shoes, a plain, finely woven straw hat, and his visible linen was the most delicate possible shade of heliotrope. His necktie was the blue-gray of a November sky, and its knot was plainly the outcome of a lordly carelessness combined with an accurate conception of the most recent dictum of fashion.

Now, to write of a man's haberdashery is a worse thing than to write a historical novel "around" Paul Jones, or to pen a testimonial to a hay-fever cure.

Therefore, let it be known that the description of Vuyning's apparel is germane to the movements of the story, and not to make room for the new fall stock of goods.

Even Broadway that morning was a discord in Vuyning's ears; and in his eyes it paralleled for a few dreamy, dreary minutes a certain howling, scorching, seething, malodorous slice of street that he remembered in Morocco. He saw the struggling mass of dogs, beggars, fakirs, slavedrivers and veiled women in carts without horses, the sun blazing brightly among the bazaars, the piles of rubbish from ruined temples in the street—and then a lady passing jabbed the ferrule of a parasol in his side and brought him back to Broadway.

Five minutes of his stroll brought him to a certain corner, where a number of silent, pale-faced men are accustomed to stand, immovably, for hours, busy with the file blades of their penknives, with their hat brims on a level with their eyelids. Wall Street speculators, driving home in their carriages, love to point out these men to their visiting friends and tell them of this rather famous lounging-place of the "crooks." On Wall Street the speculators never use the file blades of their knives.

Vuyning was delighted when one of this company stepped forth and addressed him as he was passing. He was hungry for something out of the ordinary, and to be accosted by this smooth-faced, keen-eyed, low-voiced, athletic member of the under world, with his grim yet pleasant smile, had all the taste of an adventure to the convention-weary Vuyning.

"Excuse me, friend," said he. "Could I have a few minutes' talk with you—on the level?"

"Certainly," said Vuyning, with a smile. "But, suppose we step aside to a quieter place. There is a divan—a café over here that will do. Schrumm will give us a private corner."

Schrumm established them under a growing palm, with two seidls between them. Vuyning made a pleasant reference to meteorological conditions, thus forming a hinge upon which might be swung the door leading from the thought repository of the other.

"In the first place," said his companion, with the air of one who presents his credentials, "I want you to understand that I am a crook. Out West I am known as Rowdy the Dude. Pickpocket, supper man, second-story man, yeggman, boxman, all-round burglar, card-sharp and slickest con man west of the Twenty-third Street ferry landing—that's my history. That's to show I'm on the square—with you. My name's Emerson."

"Confound old Kirk with his fish stories," said Vuyning to himself, with silent glee as he went through his pockets for a card. "It's pronounced 'Vining,' " he said, as he tossed it over to the other. "And I'll be as frank with you. I'm just a kind of a loafer, I guess, living on my daddy's money. At the club they call me 'Left-at-the-Post.' I never did a day's work in my life; and I haven't the heart to run over a chicken when I'm motoring. It's a pretty shabby record, altogether."

"There's one thing you can do," said Emerson, admiringly; "you can carry duds. I've watched you several times pass on Broadway. You look the best-dressed man I've seen. And I'll bet you a gold mine I've got $50 worth more gent's furnishings on my frame than you have. That's what I wanted to see you about. I can't do the trick. Take a look at me. What's wrong?"

"Stand up," said Vuyning.

Emerson arose, and slowly revolved.

"You've been 'outfitted,' " declared the clubman. "Some Broadway window-dresser has misused you. That's an expensive suit, though, Emerson."

"A hundred dollars," said Emerson.

"Twenty too much," said Vuyning. "Six months old in cut, one inch too long, and half an inch too much lapel. Your hat is plainly dated one year ago, although there's only a sixteenth of an inch lacking in the brim to tell the story. That English poke in your collar is too short by the distance between Troy and London. A plain gold link cuff-button would take all the shine out of those pearl ones with diamond settings. Those tan shoes would be exactly the articles to work into the heart of a Brooklyn school-ma'am on a two weeks' visit to Lake Ronkonkoma. I think I caught a glimpse of a blue silk sock embroidered with russet lilies of the valley when you—improperly—drew up your trousers as you sat down. There are always plain ones to be had in stores. Have I hurt your feelings, Emerson?"

"Double the ante!" cried the criticized one, greedily. "Give me more of it. There's a way to tote the haberdashery, and I want to get wise to it. Say, you're the right kind of swell. Anything else to the queer about me?"

"Your tie," said Vuyning, "is tied with absolute precision and correctness."

"Thanks," gratefully—"I spent over half an hour at it before I—"

"Thereby," interrupted Vuyning, "completing your resemblance to a dummy in a Broadway store window."

"Yours truly," said Emerson, sitting down again. "It's bully of you to put me wise. I knew there was something wrong, but I couldn't just put my finger on it. I guess it comes by nature to know how to wear clothes."

"Oh, I suppose," said Vuyning, with a laugh, "that my ancestors picked up the knack while they were peddling clothes from house to house a couple of hundred years ago. I'm told they did that."

"And mine," said Emerson, cheerfully, "were making their visits at night, I guess, and didn't have a chance to catch on to the correct styles."

"I tell you what," said Vuyning, whose ennui had taken wings, "I'll take you to my tailor. He'll eliminate the mark of the beast from your exterior. That is, if you care to go on further in the way of expense."

"Play 'em to the ceiling," said Emerson, with a boyish smile of joy. "I've got a roll as big around as a barrel of black-eyed peas and as loose as the wrapper of a two-for-fiver. I don't mind telling you that I was not touring among the Antipodes when the burglar-proof safe of the Farmers' National Bank of Butterville, Ia., flew open some moonless nights ago to the tune of $16,000."

"Aren't you afraid," asked Vuyning, "that I'll call a cop and hand you over?"

"You tell me," said Emerson, coolly, "why I didn't keep them."

He laid Vuyning's pocketbook and watch—the Vuyning 100-year-old family watch—on the table.

"Man," said Vuyning, revelling, "did you ever hear the tale Kirk tells about the six-pound trout and the old fisherman?"

"Seems not," said Emerson, politely, "I'd like to."

"But you won't," said Vuyning. "I've heard it scores of times. That's why I won't tell you. I was just thinking how much better this is than a club. Now, shall we go to my tailor?"

"Boys, and elderly gents," said Vuyning, five days later at his club, standing up against the window where his coterie was gathered, and keeping out the breeze, "a friend of mine from the West will dine at our table this evening."

"Will he ask if we have heard the latest from Denver?" said a member, squirming in his chair.

"Will he mention the new twenty-three-story Masonic Temple, in Quincy, Ill.?" inquired another, dropping his nose-glasses.

"Will he spring one of those Western Mississippi River catfish stories, in which they use yearling calves for bait?" demanded Kirk fiercely.

"Be comforted," said Vuyning. "He has none of the little vices. He is a burglar and safe-blower, and a pal of mine."

"Oh, Mary Ann!" said they. "Must you always adorn every statement with your alleged humor?"

It came to pass that at eight in the evening a calm, smooth, brilliant, affable man sat at Vuyning's right hand during dinner. And when the ones who pass their lives in city streets spoke of skyscrapers or of the little Czar on his far, frozen throne, or of insignificant fish from inconsequential streams, this big, deep-chested man, faultlessly clothed, and eyed like an Emperor, disposed of their Lilliputian chatter with a wink of his eyelash.

And then he painted for them with hard, broad strokes a marvellous lingual panorama of the West. He stacked snow-topped mountains on the table, freezing the hot dishes of the waiting diners. With a wave of his hand he swept the clubhouse into a pine-crowned gorge, turning the waiters into a grim posse, and each listener into a blood-stained fugitive, climbing with torn fingers upon the ensanguined rocks. He touched the table and spoke, and the five panted as they gazed on barren lava beds, and each man took his tongue between his teeth and felt his mouth bake at the tale of a land empty of water and food. As simply as Homer sang, while he dug a tine of his fork leisurely into the tablecloth, he opened a new world to their view, as does one who tells a child of the Looking-Glass Country.

As one of his listeners might have spoken of tea too strong at a Madison Square "afternoon" so he depicted the ravages of "redeye" in a border town when the caballeros of the lariat and "forty-five" reduced ennui to a minimum.

And then, with a sweep of his white, unringed hands, he dismissed Melpomene, and forthwith Diana and Amaryllis footed it before the mind's eye of the clubmen.

The savannas of the continent spread before them. The wind, humming through a hundred leagues of sage brush and mesquite, closed their ears to a city's staccato noises. He told them of camps, of ranches marooned in a sea of fragrant prairie blossoms, of gallops in the stilly night that Apollo would have forsaken his daytime steeds to enjoy; he read them the great, rough epic of the cattle and the hills that had not been spoiled by the hand of man, the mason. His words were a telescope to the city men, whose eyes had looked upon Youngstown, O., and whose tongues had called it "West."

In fact, Emerson had them "going."

The next morning at ten he met Vuyning, by appointment, at a Forty-second Street café.

Emerson was to leave for the West that day. He wore a suit of dark cheviot that looked to have been draped upon him by an ancient Grecian tailor who was a few thousand years ahead of the styles.

"Mr. Vuyning," said he, with the clear, ingenuous smile of the successful "crook," "it's up to me to go the limit for you any time I can do so. You're the real thing; and if I can ever return the favor, you bet your life I'll do it."

"What was the cow-puncher's name?" asked Vuyning, "who used to catch a mustang by the nose and mane, and throw him till he put the bridle on?"

"Bates," said Emerson.

"Thanks," said Vuyning. "I thought it was Yates. Oh, about that toggery business—I'd forgotten that."

"I've been looking for some guy to put me on the right track for years," said Emerson. "You're the goods, duty free, and halfway to the warehouse in a red wagon."

"Bacon, toasted on a green willow switch over red coals, ought to put broiled lobsters out of business," said Vuyning. "And you say a horse at the end of a thirty-foot rope can't pull a ten-inch stake out of wet prairie? Well, good-bye, old man, if you must be off."

At one o'clock Vuyning had luncheon with Miss Allison by previous arrangement.

For thirty minutes he babbled to her, unaccountably, of ranches, horses, cañons, cyclones, round-ups, Rocky Mountains, and beans and bacon. She looked at him with wondering and half-terrified eyes.

"I was going to propose again to-day," said Vuyning, cheerily, "but I won't. I've worried you often enough. You know dad has a ranch in Colorado. What's the good of staying here? Jumping jonquils! but it's great out there. I'm going to start next Tuesday."

"No, you won't," said Miss Allison.

"What?" said Vuyning.

"Not alone," said Miss Allison, dropping a tear upon her salad. "What do you think?"

"Betty!" exclaimed Vuyning, "what do you mean?"

"I'll go too," said Miss Allison, forcibly.

Vuyning filled her glass with Apollinaris.

"Here's to Rowdy the Dude!" he gave—a toast mysterious.

"Don't know him," said Miss Allison; "but if he's your friend, Jimmy—here goes!"

The Memento

Miss Lynnette D'Armande turned her back on Broadway. This was but tit for tat, because Broadway had often done the same thing to Miss D'Armande. Still, the "tats" seemed to have it, for the ex-leading lady of the "Reaping the Whirlwind" company had everything to ask of Broadway, while there was no vice-versa.

So Miss Lynnette D'Armade turned the back of her chair to her window that overlooked Broadway, and sat down to stitch in time the lisle-thread heel of a black silk stocking. The tumult and glitter of the roaring Broadway beneath her window had no charm for her; what she greatly desired was the stifling air of a dressing-room on that fairyland street and the roar of an audience gathered in that capricious quarter. In the meantime, those stockings must not be neglected. Silk does wear out so, but—after all, isn't it just the only goods there is?

The Hotal Thalia looks on Broadway as Marathon looks on the sea. It stands like a gloomy cliff above the whirlpool where the tides of two great thoroughfares clash. Here the player-bands gather at the end of their wanderings to loosen the buskin and dust the sock. Thick in the streets around it are booking-offices, theatres, agents, schools, and the lobster-palaces to which those thorny paths lead.

Wandering through the eccentric halls of the dim and fusty Thalia, you seem to have found yourself in some great ark or caravan about to sail, or fly, or roll away on wheels. About the house lingers a sense of unrest, of expectation, of transientness, even of anxiety and apprehension. The halls are a labyrinth. Without a guide, you wander like a lost soul in a Sam Lloyd puzzle.

Turning any corner, a dressing-sack or a *cul-de-sac* may bring you up short. You meet alarming tragedians talking in bath-robes in search of rumored bathrooms. From hundreds of rooms come the buzz of talk, scraps of new and old songs, and the ready laughter of the convened players.

Summer has come; their companies have disbanded, and they take their rest in their favorite caravansary, while they besiege the managers for engagements for the coming season.

At this hour of the afternoon the day's work of tramping the rounds of the agents' offices is over. Past you, as you ramble distractedly through the mossy halls, flit audible visions of houris, with veiled, starry eyes, flying tag-ends of things and a swish of silk, bequeathing to the dull hallways an odor of gaiety and a memory of *frangipanni*. Serious young comedians, with versatile Adam's apples, gather in doorways and talk of Booth. Far-reaching from somewhere comes the smell of ham and red cabbage, and the crash of dishes on the American plan.

The indeterminate hum of life in the Thalia is enlivened by the discreet popping—at reasonable and salubrious intervals—of beer-bottle corks. Thus punctuated, life in the genial hostel scans easily—the comma being the favorite mark, semicolons frowned upon, and periods barred.

Miss D'Armande's room was a small one. There was room for her rocker between the dresser and the wash-stand if it were placed longitudinally. On the dresser were its usual accoutrements, plus the ex-leading lady's collected souvenirs of road engagements and photographs of her dearest and best professional friends.

At one of these photographs she looked twice or thrice as she darned, and smiled friendily.

"I'd like to know where Lee is just this minute," she said, half-aloud.

If you had been privileged to view the photograph thus flattered, you would have thought at the first glance that you saw the picture of a many-petalled white flower, blown through the air by a storm. But the floral kingdom was not responsible for that swirl of petalous whiteness.

You saw the filmy, brief skirt of Miss Rosalie Ray as she made a complete heels-over-head turn in his wisteria-entwined swing, far out from the stage, high above the heads of the audience. You saw the camera's inadequate representation of the graceful, strong kick, with which she, at this exciting moment, sent flying, high and far, the yellow silk garter that each evening spun from her agile limb and descended upon the delighted audience below.

You saw, too, amid the black-clothed, mainly masculine patrons of select vaudeville a hundred hands raised with the hope of staying the flight of the brilliant aërial token.

Forty weeks of the best circuits this act had brought Miss Rosalie Ray, for each of two years. She did other things during her twelve minutes—a song and dance, imitations of two or three actors who are but imitations of themselves, and a balancing feat with a step-ladder and feather-duster; but when the blossom-decked swing was let down from the flies, and Miss Rosalie sprang smiling into the seat, with the golden circlet conspicuous in the place whence it was soon to slide and become a soaring and coveted guerdon—then it was that the audience rose in its seat as a single man—or presumably so—and indorsed the specialty that made Miss Ray's name a favorite in the booking-offices.

At the end of two years Miss Ray suddenly announced to her dear friend, Miss D'Armande, that she was going to spend the summer at an antediluvian village on the north shore of Long Island, and that the stage would see her no more.

Seventeen minutes after Miss Lynnette D'Armande had expressed her wish to know the whereabouts of her old chum, there were sharp raps at her door.

Doubt not that it was Rosalie Ray. At the shrill command to enter she did so, with something of a tired flutter, and dropped a heavy hand-bag on the floor. Upon my word, it was Rosalie, in a loose, travel-stained automobileless coat, closely tied brown veil with yard-long flying ends, gray walking suit, and tan oxfords with lavender over-gaiters.

When she threw off her veil and hat, you saw a pretty enough face, now flushed and disturbed by some unusual emotion, and restless, large eyes with discontent marring their brightness. A heavy pile of dull auburn hair, hastily put up, was escaping in crinkly, waving strands and curling, small locks from the confining combs and pins.

The meeting of the two was not marked by the effusion vocal, gymnatical, osculatory, and catechetical that distinguishes the greetings of their unprofessional sisters in society. There was a brief clinch, two simultaneous labial dabs, and they stood on the same footing of the old days. Very much like the short salutations of soldiers or of travellers in foreign wilds are the welcomes between the strollers at the corners of their criss-cross roads.

"I've got the hall-room two flights up above yours," said Rosalie, "but I came straight to see you before going up. I didn't know you were here till they told me."

"I've been in since the last of April," said Lynnette. "And I'm going on the road with a 'Fatal Inheritance' Company. We open next week in Elizabeth. I thought you'd quit the stage, Lee. Tell me about yourself."

Rosalie settled herself with a skilful wriggle on the top of Miss D'Armande's wardrobe trunk, and leaned her head against the papered wall. From long habit, thus can peripatetic leading ladies and their sisters make themselves as comfortable as though the deepest armchairs embraced them.

"I'm going to tell you, Lynn," she said, with a strangely sardonic and yet carelessly resigned look on her youthful face. "And then to-morrow I'll strike the old Broadway trail again, and wear some more paint off the chairs in the agents' offices. If anybody had told me any time in the last three months up to four o'clock this afternoon that

I'd ever listen to that 'Leave-your-name-and-address' rot of the booking bunch again, I'd have given 'em the real Mrs. Fiske laugh. Loan me a handkerchief, Lynn. Gee! but those Long Island trains are fierce. I've got enough soft-coal cinders on my face to go on and play *Topsy* without using the cork. And, speaking of corks—got anything to drink, Lynn?"

Miss D'Armande opened a door of the washstand and took out a bottle.

"There's nearly a pint of Manhattan. There's a cluster of carnations in the drinking glass, but———"

"Oh, pass the bottle. Save the glass for company. Thanks! That hits the spot. The same to you. My first drink in three months!

"Yes, Lynn, I quit the stage at the end of last season. I quit it because I was sick of the life. And especially because my heart and soul were sick of men—of the kind of men we stage people have to be up against. You know what the game is to us—it's a fight against 'em all the way down the line from the manager who wants us to try his new motor-car to the bill-posters who want to call us by our front names.

"And the men we have to meet after the show are the worst of all. The stage-door kind, and the manager's friends who take us to supper and show their diamonds and talk about seeing 'Dan' and 'Dave' and 'Charlie' for us. They're beasts, and I hate 'em.

"I tell you, Lynn, it's the girls like us on the stage that ought to be pitied. It's girls from good homes that are honestly ambitious and work hard to rise in the profession, but never do get there. You hear a lot of sympathy sloshed around on chorus girls and their fifteen dollars a week. Piffle! There ain't a sorrow in the chorus that a lobster cannot heal.

"If there's any tears to shed, let 'em fall for the actress that gets a salary of from thirty to forty-five dollars a week for taking a leading part in a bum show. She knows she'll never do any better but she hangs on for years, hoping for the 'chance' that never comes.

"And the fool plays we have to work in! Having another girl roll you around the stage by the hind legs in a 'Wheelbarrow Chorus' in a musical comedy is dignified drama compared with the idiotic things I've had to do in the thirty-centers.

"But what I hated most was the men—the men leering and blathering at you across tables, trying to buy you with Würzburger or Extra Dry, according to their estimate of your price. And the men in the audiences, clapping, yelling, snarling, crowding, writhing, gloating—like a lot of wild beasts, with their eyes fixed on you, ready to eat you up if you come in reach of their claws. Oh how I hate 'em!

"Well, I'm not telling you much about myself, am I, Lynn?

"I had two hundred dollars saved up, and I cut the stage the first of the summer. I went over on Long Island and found the sweetest little village that ever was, called Soundport, right on the water. I was going to spend the summer there, and study up on elocution, and try to get a class in the fall. There was an old widow lady with a cottage near the beach who sometimes rented a room or two just for company, and she took me in. She had another boarder, too—the Reverend Arthur Lyle.

"Yes, he was the head-liner. You're on, Lynn. I'll tell you all of it in a minute. It's only a one-act play.

"The first time he walked on, Lynn, I felt myself going; the first lines he spoke, he had me. He was different from the men in audiences. He was tall and slim, and you never heard him come in the room, but you *felt* him. He had a face like a picture of a knight—like one of that Round Table bunch—and a voice like a 'cello solo. And his manners!

"Lynn, if you'd take John Drew in his best drawing-room scene and compare the two, you'd have John arrested for disturbing the peace.

"I'll spare you the particulars; but in less than a month Arthur and I were engaged. He preached at a little one-night stand of a Methodist church. There was to be a parsonage the size of a lunch-wagon, and hens and honeysuckles when we were married. Arthur used to preach to me a good deal about Heaven, but he never could get my mind quite off those honeysuckles and hens.

"No; I didn't tell him I'd been on the stage. I hated the business and all that went with it; I'd cut it out forever, and I didn't see any use of stirring things up. I was a good girl, and I didn't have anything to confess, except being an elocutionist, and that was about all the strain my conscience would stand.

"Oh, I tell you, Lynn, I was happy. I sang in the choir and attended the sewing society, and recited that 'Annie Laurie' thing with the whistling stunt in it, 'in a manner bordering upon the professional,' as the weekly village paper reported it. And Arthur and I went rowing, and walking in the woods and clamming, and that poky little village seemed to me the best place in the world. I'd have been happy to live there always, too, if———

"But one morning old Mrs. Gurley, the widow lady, got gossipy while I was helping her string beans on the back porch, and began to gush information, as folks who rent out their rooms usually do. Mr. Lyle was her idea of a saint on her earth—as he was mine, too. She went over all his virtues and graces, and wound up by telling me that Arthur had had an extremely romantic love-affair, not long before, that had ended unhappily. She didn't seem to be on to the details, but she knew that he had been hit pretty hard. He was paler and thinner, she said, and he had some kind of a remembrance or keepsake of the lady in a little rosewood box that he kept locked in his desk drawer in his study.

" 'Several times,' says she, 'I've seen him gloomerin' over that box of evenings, and he always locks it up right away if anybody comes into the room.'

"Well, you can imagine how long it was before I got Arthur by the wrist and led him down stage and hissed in his ear.

"That same afternoon we were lazying around in a boat among the waterlilies at the edge of the bay.

" 'Arthur,' says I, 'you never told me you'd had another love-affair. But Mrs. Gurley did,' I went on, to let him know I knew. I hate to hear a man lie.

" 'Before you came,' says he, looking me frankly in the eye, 'there was a previous affection—a strong one. Since you know of it, I will be perfectly candid with you.'

" 'I am waiting,' says I.

" 'My dear Ida,' says Arthur—of course I went by my real name, while I was in Soundport—'this former affection was a spiritual one, in fact. Although the lady aroused my deepest sentiments, and was, as I thought, my ideal woman, I never met her, and never spoke to her. It was an ideal love. My love for you, while no less ideal, is different. You wouldn't let that come between us.'

" 'Was she pretty?' I asked.

" 'She was very beautiful,' said Arthur.

" 'Did you see her often?' I asked.

" 'Something like a dozen times,' says he.

" 'Always from a distance?' says I.

" 'Always from quite a distance,' says he.

" 'And you loved her?' I asked.

" 'She seemed my ideal of beauty and grace—and soul,' says Arthur.

" 'And this keepsake that you keep under lock and key, and moon over at times, is that a remembrance from her?'

" 'A memento,' says Arthur, 'that I have treasured.'

" 'Did she send it to you?'

" 'It came from her,' says he.

" 'In a roundabout way?' I asked.

" 'Somewhat roundabout,' says he, 'and yet rather direct.'

" 'Why didn't you ever meet her?' I asked. 'Were your positions in life so different?'

" 'She was far above me,' says Arthur. 'Now, Ida,' he goes on, 'this is all of the past. You're not going to be jealous, are you?'

" 'Jealous!' says I. 'Why, man, what are you talking about? It makes me think ten times as much of you as I did before I knew about it.'

"And it did, Lynn—if you can understand it. That ideal love was a new one on me, but it struck me as being the most beautiful and glorious thing I'd ever heard of. Think of a man loving a woman he'd never even spoken to, and being faithful just to what his mind and heart pictured her! Oh, it sounded great to me. The men I'd always known come at you with either diamonds, knock-out drops, or a raise of salary—and their ideals—well, we'll say no more.

"Yes, it made me think more of Arthur than I did before. I couldn't be jealous of that far-away divinity that he used to worship, for I was going to have him myself. And I began to look upon him as a saint on earth, just as old lady Gurley did.

"About four o'clock this afternoon a man came to the house for Arthur to go and see somebody that was sick among his church bunch. Old lady Gurley was taking her afternoon snore on the couch, so that left me pretty much alone.

"In passing by Arthur's study I looked in, and saw his bunch of keys hanging in the drawer of his desk, where he'd forgotten 'em. Well, I guess we're all to the Mrs. Bluebeard now and then, ain't we, Lynn? I made up my mind I'd have a look at that memento he kept so secret. Not that I cared what it was—it was just curiosity.

"While I was opening the drawer I imagined one or two things it might be. I thought it might be a dried rosebud she'd dropped down to him from a balcony, or maybe a picture of her he'd cut out of a magazine, she being so high up in the world.

"I opened the drawer, and there was the rosewood casket about the size of a gent's collar box. I found the little key in the bunch that fitted it, and raised the lid.

"I took one look at that memento, and then I went to my room and packed my trunk. I threw a few things into my grip, gave my hair a flirt or two with a side-comb, put on my hat, and went in and gave the old lady's foot a kick. I'd tried awfully hard to use proper and correct language while I was there for Arthur's sake, and I had the habit down pat, but it left me then.

" 'Stop sawing gourds,' says I, 'and sit up and take notice. The ghost's about to walk. I'm going away from here, and I owe you eight dollars. The expressman will call for my trunk.'

"I handed her the money.

" 'Dear me, Miss Crosby!' said she. 'Is anything wrong? I thought you were pleased here. Dear me, young women are so hard to understand, and so different from what you expect 'em to be.'

" 'You're damn right,' says I. 'Some of 'em are. But you can't say that about men. *When you know one man you know 'em all!* That settles the human race question.'

"And then I caught the four-thirty-eight, soft-coal unlimited; and here I am."

"You didn't tell me what was in that box, Lee," said Miss D'Armande, anxiously.

"One of those yellow silk garters that I used to kick off my leg into the audience during that old vaudeville swing act of mine. Is there any of the cocktail left, Lynn?"

Jeff Peters as a Personal Magnet

Jeff Peters has been engaged in as many schemes for making money as there are recipes for cooking rice in Charleston, S. C.

Best of all I like to hear him tell of his earlier days when he sold liniments and cough cures on street corners, living hand to mouth, heart to heart with the people, throwing heads or tails with fortune for his last coin.

"I struck Fisher Hill, Arkansaw," said he, "in buckskin suit, moccasins, long hair and a thirty-carat diamond ring that I got from an actor in Texarkana. I don't know what he ever did with the pocket knife I swapped him for it.

"I was Dr. Waugh-hoo, the celebrated Indian medicine man. I carried only one best bet just then, and that was Resurrection Bitters. It was made of life-giving plants and herbs accidentally discovered by Ta-qua-la, the beautiful wife of the chief of the Choctaw Nation, while gathering truck to garnish a platter of boiled dog for the annual corn dance.

"Business hadn't been good at the last town, so I only had five dollars. I went to the Fisher Hill druggist and he credited me for a half gross of eight ounce bottles and corks. I had the labels and ingredients in my valise, left over from the last town. Life began to look rosy again after I got in my hotel room with the water running from the tap, and the Resurrection Bitters lining up on the table by the dozen.

"Fake? No, sir. There was two dollars' worth of fluid extract of cinchona and a dime's worth of aniline in that half-gross of bitters. I've gone through towns years afterwards and had folks ask for 'em again.

"I hired a wagon that night and commenced selling the bitters on Main Street. Fisher Hill was a low, malarial town; and a compound hypothetical pneumo-cardiac anti-scorbutic tonic was just what I diagnosed the crowd as needing. The bitters started off like sweetbreads-on-toast at a vegetarian dinner. I had sold two dozen at fifty cents apiece when I felt somebody pull my coat tail. I knew what that meant; so I climbed down and sneaked a five-dollar bill into the hand of a man with a German silver star on his lapel.

" 'Constable,' says I, 'it's a fine night.'

" 'Have you got a city license,' he asked, 'to sell this illegitimate essence of spooju that you flatter by the name of medicine?'

" 'I have not,' says I. 'I didn't know you had a city. If I can find it tomorrow I'll take one out if it's necessary.'

" 'I'll have to close you up till you do,' says the constable.

"I quit selling and went back to the hotel. I was talking to the landlord about it.

" 'Oh, you won't stand no show in Fisher Hill,' says he. 'Dr. Hoskins, the only doctor here, is a brother-in-law of the Mayor, and they won't allow no fake doctors to practice in town.'

" 'I don't practice medicine,' says I, 'I've got a State peddler's license, and I take out a city one wherever they demand it.'

"I went to the Mayor's office the next morning and they told me he hadn't showed up yet. They didn't know when he'd be down. So Doc Waugh-hoo hunches down again in a hotel chair and lights a jimpson-weed regalia, and waits.

"By and by a young man in a blue necktie slips into the chair next to me and asks the time.

" 'Half-past ten' says I, 'and you are Andy Tucker. I've seen you work. Wasn't it you that put up the Great Cupid Combination package on the Southern States? Let's see, it was a Chilian diamond engagement ring, a wedding ring, a potato masher, a bottle of soothing syrup and Dorothy Vernon—all for fifty cents.'

"Andy was pleased to hear that I remembered him. He was a good street man; and he was more than that—he respected his profession, and he was satisfied with 300 per cent profit. He had plenty of offers to go into the illegitimate drug and garden seed business; but he was never to be tempted off of the straight path.

"I wanted a partner, so Andy and me agreed to go out together. I told him about the situation on Fisher Hill and how finances was low on account of the local mixture of politics and jalap. Andy had just got in on the train that morning. He was pretty low himself, and was going to canvass the town for a few dollars to build a new battleship by popular subscription at Eureka Springs. So we went out and sat on the porch and talked it over.

"The next morning at eleven o'clock when I was sitting there alone, an Uncle Tom shuffles into the hotel and asked for the doctor to come and see Judge Banks, who, it seems, was the mayor and a mighty sick man.

" 'I'm no doctor,' says I. 'Why don't you go and get the doctor?'

" 'Boss,' says he. 'Doc Hoskin am done gone twenty miles in the country to see some sick persons. He's de only doctor in de town, and Massa Banks am powerful bad off. He sent me to ax you to please, suh, come.'

" 'As man to man,' says I, 'I'll go and look him over.' So I put a bottle of Resurrection Bitters in my pocket and goes up on the hill to the mayor's mansion, the finest house in town, with a mansard roof and two cast-iron dogs on the lawn.

"This Mayor Banks was in bed all but his whiskers and feet. He was making internal noises that would have had everybody in San Francisco hiking for the parks. A young man was standing by the bed holding a cup of water.

" 'Doc,' says the Mayor. 'I'm awful sick. I'm about to die. Can't you do nothing for me?'

" 'Mr. Mayor,' says I, 'I'm not a regular preordained disciple of S. Q. Lapius, I never took a course in a medical college,' says I. 'I've just come as a fellow man to see if I could be of any assistance.'

" 'I'm deeply obliged,' says he. 'Doc Waugh-hoo, this is my nephew, Mr. Biddle. He has tried to alleviate my distress, but without success. Oh, Lordy! Ow-ow-ow!!' he sings out.

"I nods at Mr. Biddle and sets down by the bed and feels the mayor's pulse. 'Let me see your liver—your tongue, I mean,' says I. Then I turns up the lids of his eyes and looks close at the pupils of 'em.

" 'How long have you been sick?' I asked.

" 'I was taken down—ow-ouch—last night,' says the Mayor. 'Gimme something for it, Doc, won't you?'

" 'Mr. Fiddle,' says I, 'raise the window shade a bit, will you?'

" 'Biddle,' says the young man. 'Do you feel like you could eat some ham and eggs, Uncle James?'

" 'Mr. Mayor,' says I, after laying my ear to his right shoulder blade and listening, 'you've got a bad attack of super-inflammation of the right clavicle of the harpsichord!'

" 'Good Lord!' says he, with a groan. 'Can't you rub something on it, or set it or anything?'

"I picks up my hat and starts for the door.

" 'You ain't going, Doc?' says the Mayor with a howl. 'You ain't going away and leave me to die with this—superfluity of the clapboards, are you?'

" 'Common humanity, Dr. Whoa-ha,' says Mr. Biddle, 'ought to prevent your deserting a fellow-human in distress.'

" 'Dr. Waugh-hoo, when you get through plowing,' says I. And then I walks back to the bed and throws back my long hair.

" 'Mr. Mayor,' says I, 'there is only one hope for you. Drugs will do you no good. But there is another power higher yet, although drugs are high enough,' says I.

" 'And what is that?' says he.

" 'Scientific demonstrations,' says I. 'The triumph of mind over sarsaparilla. The belief that there is no pain and sickness except what is produced when we ain't feeling well. Declare yourself in arrears. Demonstrate.'

" 'What is this paraphernalia you speak of, Doc?' says the Mayor. 'You ain't a Socialist, are you?'

" 'I am speaking,' says I, 'of the great doctrine of psychic financiering—of the enlightened school of long-distance, subconscientious treatment of fallacies and meningitis—of that wonderful in-door sport known as personal magnetism.'

" 'Can you work it, Doc?' asks the Mayor.

" 'I'm one of the Sole Sanhedrims and Ostensible Hooplas of the Inner Pulpit,' says I. 'The lame talk and the blind rubber whenever I make a pass at 'em. I am a medium, a coloratura hypnotist and a spirituous control. It was only through me at the recent seances at Ann Arbor that the last president of the Vinegar Bitters Company could revisit the earth to communicate with his sister Jane. You see me peddling medicine on the streets,' says I, 'to the poor. I don't practice personal magnetism on them. I do not drag it in the dust,' says I, 'because they haven't got the dust.'

" 'Will you treat my case?' asks the Mayor.

" 'Listen,' says I. 'I've had a good deal of trouble with medical societies everywhere I've been. I don't practice medicine. But, to save your life, I'll give you the psychic treatment if you'll agree as mayor not to push the license question.'

" 'Of course I will,' says he. 'And now get to work, Doc, for them pains are coming on again.'

" 'My fee will be $250.00, cure guaranteed in two treatments,' says I.

" 'All right,' says the Mayor. 'I'll pay it. I guess my life's worth that much.'

"I sat down by the bed and looked him straight in the eye.

" 'Now,' says I, 'get your mind off the disease. You ain't sick. You haven't got a heart or a clavicle or a funny bone or brains or anything. You haven't got any pain. Declare error. Now you feel the pain that you didn't have leaving, don't you?'

" 'I do feel some little better, Doc,' says the Mayor, 'darned if I don't. Now state a few lines about my not having this swelling in my left side, and I think I could be propped up and have some sausage and buckwheat cakes.'

"I made a few passes with my hands.

" 'Now,' says I, 'the inflammation's gone. The right lobe of the perihelion has subsided. You're getting sleepy. You can't hold your eyes open any longer. For the present the disease is checked. Now, you are asleep.'

"The Mayor shut his eyes slowly and began to snore.

" 'You observe, Mr. Tiddle,' says I, 'the wonder of modern science.'

" 'Biddle,' says he. 'When will you give uncle the rest of the treatment, Dr. Pooh-pooh?'

" 'Waugh-hoo,' says I. 'I'll come back at eleven to-morrow. When he wakes up give him eight drops of turpentine and three pounds of steak. Good morning.'

"The next morning I went back on time. 'Well, Mr. Riddle,' says I, when he opened the bedroom door, 'and how is uncle this morning?'

" 'He seems much better,' says the young man.

"The Mayor's color and pulse was fine. I gave him another treatment, and he said the last of the pain left him.

" 'Now,' says I, 'you'd better stay in bed for a day or two, and you'll be all right. It's a good thing I happened to be in Fisher Hill, Mr. Mayor,' says I, 'for all the remedies in the cornucopia that the regular schools of medicine use couldn't have saved you. And now that error has flew and pain proved a perjurer, let's allude to a cheerfuller subject—say the fee of $250. No checks, please, I hate to write my name on the back of a check almost as bad as I do on the front.'

" 'I've got the cash here,' says the Mayor, pulling a pocket book from under his pillow.

"He counts out five fifty-dollar notes and holds 'em in his hand.

" 'Bring the receipt,' he says to Biddle.

"I signed the receipt and the Mayor handed me the money. I put it in my inside pocket careful.

" 'Now do your duty, officer,' says the Mayor, grinning much unlike a sick man.

"Mr. Biddle lays his hand on my arm.

" 'You're under arrest, Dr. Waugh-hoo, alias Peters,' says he, 'for practising medicine without authority under the State law.'

" 'Who are you?' I asks.

" 'I'll tell you who he is,' says the Mayor, sitting up in bed. 'He's a detective employed by the State Medical Society. He's been following you over five counties. He came to me yesterday and we fixed up this scheme to catch you. I guess you won't do any more doctoring around these parts, Mr. Fakir. What was it you said I had, Doc?' the Mayor laughs, 'compound—well it wasn't softening of the brain, I guess, anyway.'

" 'A detective,' says I.

" 'Correct,' says Biddle. 'I'll have to turn you over to the sheriff.'

" 'Let's see you do it,' says I, and I grabs Biddle by the throat and half throws him out the window, but he pulls a gun and sticks it under my chin, and I stand still. Then he puts handcuffs on me, and takes the money out of my pocket.

" 'I witness,'' says he, 'that they're the same bills that you and I marked, Judge Banks. I'll turn them over to the sheriff when we get to his office, and he'll send you a receipt. They'll have to be used as evidence in the case.'

" 'All right, Mr. Biddle,' says the Mayor. 'And now, Doc Waughhoo,' he goes on, 'why don't you demonstrate? Can't you pull the cork out of your magnetism with your teeth and hocus-pocus them handcuffs off?'

" 'Come on, officer,' says I, dignified. 'I may as well make the best of it.' And then I turns to old Banks and rattles my chains.

" 'Mr. Mayor,' says I, 'the time will come soon when you'll believe that personal magnetism is a success. And you'll be sure that it succeeded in this case, too.'

"And I guess it did.

"When we got nearly to the gate, I says: 'We might meet somebody now, Andy. I reckon you better take 'em off, and———' Hey? Why, of course it was Andy Tucker. That was his scheme; and that's how we got the capital to go into business together."

Modern Rural Sports

Jeff Peters must be reminded. Whenever he is called upon, pointedly, for a story, he will maintain that his life has been as devoid of incident as the longest of Trollope's novels. But lured, he will divulge. Therefore I cast many and divers flies upon the current of his thoughts before I feel a nibble.

"I notice," says I, "that the Western farmers, in spite of their prosperity, are running after their old populistic idols again."

"It's the running season," said Jeff, "for farmers, shad, maple trees and the Connemaugh River. I know something about farmers. I thought I struck one once that had got out of the rut; but Andy Tucker proved to me I was mistaken. 'Once a farmer, always a sucker,' said Andy. 'He's the man that's shoved into the front row among bullets, ballots and the ballet. He's the funny-bone and gristle of the country,' said Andy, 'and I don't know who we would do without him.'

"One morning me and Andy wakes up with sixty-eight cents between us in a yellow pine hotel on the edge of the predigested hoecake belt of southern Indiana. How we got off the train there the night before I can't tell you; for she went through the village so fast that what looked like a saloon to us through the car window turned out to be a composite view of a drug store and a water tank two blocks apart. Why we got off at the first station we could, belongs to a little oroide gold watch and Alaska diamond deal we failed to pull off the day before, over the Kentucky line.

"When I woke up I heard roosters crowing, and smelt something like the fumes of nitro-muriatic acid and heard something heavy fall on the floor below us, and a man swearing.

" 'Cheer up, Andy,' says I. 'We're in a rural community. Somebody has just tested a gold brick downstairs. We'll go out and get what's coming to us from a farmer; and then yoicks! and away.'

"Farmers was always a kind of reserve fund to me. Whenever I was in hard luck I'd go to the crossroads, hook a finger in a farmer's suspender, recite the prospectus of my swindle in a mechanical kind of way, look over what he had, give him back his keys, whetstone, and papers that was of no value except to owner, and stroll away without asking any questions. Farmers are not fair game to me as high up in our business as me and Andy was; but there was times when we found 'em useful just as Wall Street does the Secretary of the Treasury now and then.

"When we went downstairs we saw we was in the midst of the finest farming section we ever see. About two miles away on a hill was a big white house in a grove surrounded by a widespread agricultural agglomeration of fields and barns and pastures and outhouses.

" 'Whose house is that?' we asked the landlord.

" 'That,' says he, 'is the domicile and the arboreal, terrestrial and horticultural accessories of Farmer Ezra Plunkett, one of our county's most progressive citizens.'

"After breakfast me and Andy, with eight cents capital left, casts the horoscope of the rural potentate.

" 'Let me go alone,' says I. 'Two of us against one farmer would look as onesided as Roosevelt using both hands to kill a grizzly.'

" 'All right,' says Andy. 'I like to be a true sport even when I'm only collecting redates from the rutabag raisers. What bait are you going to use for this Ezra thing?' Andy asks me.

" 'Oh,' says I, 'the first thing that come to hand in the suit case. I reckon I'll take along some of the new income tax receipts; and the recipe for making clover honey out of clabber and apple peelings; and the order blanks for the McGuffey's readers, which afterwards turn out to be McCormick reapers; and the pearl necklace found on the train; and a pocket-size goldbrick; and a———"

" 'That'll be enough,' says Andy. 'Any one of the lot ought to land on Ezra. And, say, Jeff, make that succotash fancier give you nice, clean new bills. It's a disgrace to our Department of Agriculture, Civil Service and Pure Food Law the kind of stuff some of these farmers hand out to us. I've had to take rolls from 'em that looked like bundles of microbe cultures captured out of a Red Cross ambulance.'

"So, I goes to a livery stable and hires a buggy on my looks. I drove out to the Plunkett farm and hitched. There was a man sitting on the front steps of the house. He had on a white flannel suit, a diamond ring, golf cap and a pink ascot tie. 'Summer boarder,' says I to myself.

" 'I'd like to see Farmer Ezra Plunkett,' says I to him.

" 'You see him,' says he. 'What seems to be on your mind?'

"I never answered a word. I stood still, repeating to myself the rollicking lines of that merry jingle, 'The Man with the Hoe.' When I looked at this farmer, the little devices I had in my pocket for buncoing the pushed-back brows seemed as hopeless as trying to shake down the Beef Trust with a mittimus and a parlor rifle.

" 'Well,' says he, looking at me close, 'speak up. I see the left pocket of your coat sags a good deal. Out with the goldbrick first. I'm rather more interested in the bricks than I am in the trick sixty-day notes and the lost silver mine story.'

"I had a kind of cerebral sensation of foolishness in my ideas of ratiocination; but I pulled out the little brick and unwrapped my handkerchief off it.

" 'One dollar and eighty cents,' says the farmer, hefting it in his hand. 'Is it a trade?'

" 'The lead in it is worth more than that,' says I, dignified. I put it back in my pocket.

" 'All right,' says he. 'But I sort of wanted it for the collection I'm starting. I got a $5000 one last week for $2.10.'

"Just then a telephone bell rings in the house.

" 'Come in, Bunk,' says the farmer, 'and look at my place. It's kind of lonesome here sometimes. I think that's New York calling.'

"We went inside. The room looked like a Broadway stockbroker's—light-oak desks, two 'phones, Spanish leather upholstered chairs and couches, oil paintings in gilt frames a foot deep and a ticker hitting off the news in one corner.

" 'Hello, hello!' says the funny farmer. 'Is that the Regent Theatre? Yes; this is Plunkett, of Woodbine Centre. Reserve four orchestra seats for Friday evening—my usual ones. Yes; Friday—good-bye.'

" 'I run over to New York every two weeks to see a show,' says the farmer, hanging up the receiver. 'I catch the eighteen-hour flyer at Indianapolis, spend ten hours in the heyday of night on the Yappian Way, and get home in time to see the chickens go to roost forty-eight hours later. Oh, the pristine Hubbard squasherino of the cave-dwelling period is getting geared up some for the annual meeting of the Don't-Blow-Out-the-Gas Association, don't you think, Mr. Bunk?'

" 'I seem to perceive,' says I, 'a kind of hiatus in the agrarian traditions in which, heretofore, I have reposed confidence.'

" 'Sure, Bunk' says he. 'The yellow primrose on the river's brim is getting to look to us Reubs like a holiday edition de luxe of the Language of Flowers with deckle edges and frontispiece.'

"Just then the telephone calls him again.

" 'Hello, hello!' says he. 'Oh, that's Perkins, at Milldale. I told you $800 was too much for that horse. Have you got him there? Good. Let me see him. Get away from the transmitter. Now make him trot in a circle. Faster. Yes, I can hear him. Keep on—faster yet. . . . That'll do. Now lead him up to the phone. Closer. Get his nose nearer. There. Now wait. No; I don't want that horse. What? No; not at any price. He interferes; and he's windbroken. Good-bye.'

" 'Now, Bunk,' says the farmer, 'do you begin to realize that agriculture has had a hair cut? You belong in a bygone era. Why, Tom Lawson himself knows better than to try to catch an up-to-date agriculturist napping. It's Saturday, the Fourteenth, on the farm, you bet. Now, look here, and see how we keep up with the day's doings.'

"He shows me a machine on a table with two things for your ears like the penny-in-the-slot affairs. I puts it on and listens. A female voice starts up reading headlines of murders, accidents, and other political casualties.

" 'What you hear,' says the farmer, 'is a synopsis of to-day's news in the New York, Chicago, St. Louis and San Francisco papers. It is wired in to our rural News Bureau and served hot to subscribers. On this table you see the principal dailies and weeklies of the country. Also a special service of advance sheets of the monthly magazines.'

"I picks up one sheet and sees that it's headed: 'Special Advance Proofs. In July, 1909, the *Century* will say'—and so forth.

"The farmer rings up somebody—his manager, I reckon—and tells him to let the herd of 15 Jerseys go at $600 a head; and to sow the 900-acre field in wheat: and to have 200 extra cans ready at the station for the milk trolley car. Then he passes the Henry Clays and sets out a bottle of green chartreuse, and goes over and looks at the ticker tape.

" 'Consolidated Gas up two points,' says he. 'Oh, very well.'

" 'Ever monkey with copper?' I asks.

" 'Stand back!' says he, raising his hand, 'or I'll call the dog. I told you not to waste your time.'

"After a while he says: 'Bunk, if you don't mind my telling you, your company begins to cloy slightly. I've got to write an article on the Chimera of Communism for a magazine, and attend a meeting of the Race Track Association this afternoon. Of course you understand by now that you can't get my proxy for your Remedy, whatever it may be.'

"Well, sir, all I could think of to do was to go out and get in the buggy. The horse turned round and took me back to the hotel. I hitched him and went in to see Andy. In his room I told him about this farmer, word for word; and I sat picking at the table cover like one bereft of sagaciousness.'

" 'I don't understand it,' say I, humming a sad and foolish little song to cover my humiliation.

"Andy walks up and down the room for a long time, biting the left end of his mustache as he does when in the act of thinking.

" 'Jeff,' says he, finally, 'I believe your story of this expurgated rustic; but I am not convinced. It looks incredulous to me that he could not have inoculated himself against all the preordained systems of bucolic bunco. Now, you never regarded me as a man of special religious proclivities, did you, Jeff?' says Andy.

" 'Well,' says I, 'No. But,' says I, not to wound his feelings, 'I have also observed many church members whose said proclivities were not so outwardly developed that they would show on a white handkerchief if you rubbed 'em with it.'

" 'I have always been a deep student of nature from creation down,' says Andy, 'and I believe in an ultimatum design of Providence.

Farmers was made for a purpose; and that was to furnish a livelihood to men like me and you. Else why was we given brains? It is my belief that the manna that the Israelites lived on for forty years in the wilderness was only a figurative word for farmers; and they kept up the practice to this day. And now,' says Andy, 'I am going to test my theory "Once a farmer, always a come-on," in spite of the veneering and the orifices that a spurious civilization has brought to him.'

" 'You'll fail, same as I did,' says I. 'This one's shook off the shackles of the sheep-fold. He's entrenched behind the advantages of electricity, education, literature and intelligence.'

" 'I'll try,' said Andy. 'There are certain Laws of Nature that Free Rural Delivery can't overcome.'

"Andy fumbles around awhile in the closet and comes out dressed in a suit with brown and yellow checks as big as your hand. His vest is red with blue dots, and he wears a high silk hat. I noticed he'd soaked his sandy mustache in a kind of blue ink.

" 'Great Barnums?' says I. 'You're a ringer for a circus thimblerig man.'

" 'Right,' says Andy. 'Is the buggy outside? Wait here till I come back. I won't be long.'

"Two hours afterwards Andy steps in the room and lays a wad of money on the table.

" 'Eight hundred and sixty dollars,' says he. 'Let me tell you. He was in. He looked me over and began to guy me. I didn't say a word, but got out the walnut shells and began to roll the little ball on the table. I whistled a tune or two, and then I started up the old formula.

" 'Step up lively, gentleman,' says I, 'and watch the little ball. It costs you nothing to look. There you see it, and there you don't. Guess where the little joker is. The quickness of the hand deceives the eye.'

" 'I steals a look at the farmer man. I see the sweat coming out on his forehead. He goes over and closes the front door and watches me some more. Directly he says: "I'll bet you twenty I can pick the shell the ball's under now."

" 'After that,' goes on Andy, 'there is nothing new to relate. He only had $860 in cash in the house. When I left he followed me to the gate. There was tears in his eyes when he shook hands.

" ' "Bunk," ' says he, ' "thank you for the only real pleasure I've had in years. It brings up happy old days when I was only a farmer and not an agriculturist. God bless you." ' "

Here Jeff Peters ceased, and I inferred that his story was done.

"Then you think———" I began.

"Yes," said Jeff. "Something like that. You let the farmers go ahead and amuse themselves with politics. Farming's a lonesome life; and they've been against the shell game before."

The Man Higher Up

Across our two dishes of spaghetti, in a corner of Provenzano's restaurant, Jeff Peters was explaining to me the three kinds of graft.

Every winter Jeff comes to New York to eat spaghetti, to watch the shipping in East River from the depths of his chinchilla overcoat, and to lay in a supply of Chicago-made clothing at one of the Fulton Street stores. During the other three seasons he may be found further west—his range is from Spokane to Tampa. In his profession he takes a pride which he supports and defends with a serious and unique philosophy of ethics. His profession is no new one. He is an incorporated, uncapitalized, unlimited asylum for the reception of the restless and unwise dollars of his fellow men.

In the wilderness of stone in which Jeff seeks his annual lonely holiday he is glad to palaver of his many adventures, as a boy will whistle after sundown in a wood. Wherefore, I mark on my calendar the time of his coming, and open a question of privilege at Provenzano's concerning the little wine-stained table in the corner between the rakish rubber plant and the framed palazzio della something on the wall.

"There are two kinds of grafts," said Jeff, "that ought to be wiped out by law. I mean Wall Street speculation, and burglary."

"Nearly everybody will agree with you as to one of them," said I, with a laugh.

"Well, burglary ought to be wiped out, too," said Jeff; and I wondered whether the laugh had been redundant.

"About three months ago," said Jeff, "it was my privilege to become familiar with a sample of each of the aforesaid branches of illegitimate art. I was *sine qua grata* with a member of the housebreakers' union and one of the John D. Napoleons of finance at the same time."

"Interesting combination," said I, with a yawn. "Did I tell you I bagged a duck and a ground squirrel at one shot last week over in the Ramapos?" I knew well how to draw Jeff's stories.

"Let me tell you first about these barnacles that clog the wheels of society by poisoning the springs of rectitude with their upas-like eye," said Jeff, with the pure gleam of the muck-raker in his own.

"As I said, three months ago I got into bad company. There are two times in a man's life when he does this—when he's dead broke, and when he's rich.

"Now and then the most legitimate business runs out of luck. It was out in Arkansas I made the wrong turn at a cross-road, and drives into this town of Peavine by mistake. It seems I had already assaulted and disfigured Peavine the spring of the year before. I had sold $600 worth of young fruit trees there—plums, cherries, peaches and pears. The Peaviners were keeping an eye on the country road and hoping I might pass that way again. I drove down Main Street as far as the Crystal Palace drug-store before I realized I had committed ambush upon myself and my white horse Bill.

"The Peaviners took me by surprise and Bill by the bridle and began a conversation that wasn't entirely disassociated with the subject of fruit trees. A committee of 'em ran some trace-chains through the armholes of my vest and escorted me through their gardens and orchards.

"Their fruit trees hadn't lived up to their labels. Most of 'em had turned out to be persimmons and dogwoods, with a grove or two of blackjacks and poplars. The only one that showed any signs of bearing anything was a fine young cottonwood that had put forth a hornet's nest and half of an old corset-cover.

"The Peaviners protracted our fruitless stroll to the edge of town. They took my watch and money on account; and they kept Bill and the wagon as hostages. They said the first time one of them dogwood trees put forth an Amsden's June peach I might come back and get my things. Then they took off the trace-chains and jerked their thumbs in the direction of the Rocky Mountains; and I struck a Lewis and Clark lope for the swollen rivers and impenetrable forests.

"When I regained intellectualness I found myself walking into an unidentified town on the A., T. & S. F. railroad. The Peaviners hadn't left anything in my pockets except a plug of chewing—they wasn't after my life—and that saved it. I bit off a chunk and sits down on a pile of ties by the track to recogitate my sensations of thought and perspicacity.

"And then along comes a fast freight which slows up a little at the town; and off it drops a black bundle that rolls for twenty yards in a cloud of dust and then gets up and begins to spit soft coal and interjections. I see it is a young man broad across the face, dressed more for Pullmans than freights, and with a cheerful kind of smile in spite of it all that made Phoebe Snow's job look like a chimney-sweep's.

" 'Fall off?' says I.

" 'Nunk,' says he. 'Got off. Arrived at my destination. What town is this?'

" 'Haven't looked it up on the map yet,' says I. 'I got in about five minutes before you did. How does it strike you?'

" 'Hard,' says he, twisting one of his arms around. 'I believe that shoulder—no, it's all right.'

"He stoops over to brush the dust off his clothes, when out of his pocket drops a fine, nine-inch burglar's steel jimmy. He picks it up and looks at me sharp, and then grins and holds out his hand.

" 'Brother,' says he, 'greetings. Didn't I see you in Southern Missouri last summer selling colored sand at half-a-dollar a teaspoonful to put into lamps to keep the oil from exploding?'

" 'Oil,' says I, 'never explodes. It's the gas that forms that explodes.' But I shakes hands with him, anyway.

" 'My name's Bill Bassett,' says he to me, 'and if you'll call it professional pride instead of conceit, I'll inform you that you have the pleasure of meeting the best burglar that ever set a gum-shoe on ground drained by the Mississippi River.'

"Well, me and this Bill Bassett sits on the ties and exchanges brags as artists in kindred lines will do. It seems he didn't have a cent, either, and we went into close caucus. He explained why an able burglar sometimes had to travel on freights by telling me that a servant girl had played him false in Little Rock, and he was making a quick get-away.

" 'It's part of my business,' says Bill Bassett, 'to play up to the ruffles when I want to make a riffle as Raffles. 'Tis loves that makes the bit go 'round. Show me a house with a swag in it and a pretty parlor-maid, and you might as well call the silver melted down and sold, and me spilling truffles and that Château stuff on the napkin under my chin, while the police are calling it an inside job just because the old lady's nephew teaches a Bible class. I first make an impression on the girl,' says Bill, 'and when she lets me inside I make an impression on the locks. But this one in Little Rock done me,' says he. 'She saw me taking a trolley ride with another girl, and when I came 'round on the night she was to leave the door open for me it was fast. And I had keys made for the doors upstairs. But, no sir. She had sure cut off my locks. She was a Delilah,' says Bill Bassett.

"It seems that Bill tried to break in anyhow with his jimmy, but the girl emitted a succession of bravura noises like the top-riders of a tally-ho, and Bill had to take all the hurdles between there and the depot. As he had no baggage they tried hard to check his departure, but he made a train that was just pulling out.

" 'Well,' says Bill Bassett, when we had exchanged memoirs of our dead lives, 'I could eat. This town don't look like it was kept under a Yale lock. Suppose we commit some mild atrocity that will bring in temporary expense money. I don't suppose you've brought along any hair tonic or rolled gold watch-chains, or similar law-defying swindles that you could sell on the plaza to the pikers of the paretic populace, have you?'

" 'No,' says I, 'I left an elegant line of Patagonian diamond earrings and rainy-day sunbursts in my valise at Peavine. But they're to stay there till some of them black-gum trees begin to glut the market with yellow clings and Japanese plums. I reckon we can't count on them unless we take Luther Burbank in for a partner.'

" 'Very well,' says Bassett, 'we'll do the best we can. Maybe after dark I'll borrow a hairpin from some lady, and open the Farmers and Drovers Marine Bank with it.'

"While we were talking, up pulls a passenger train to the depot near by. A person in a high hat gets off on the wrong side of the train and comes tripping down the track towards us. He was a little, fat man with a big nose and rat's eyes, but dressed expensive, and carrying a hand-satchel careful, as if it had eggs or railroad bonds in it. He passes by us and keeps on down the track, not appearing to notice the town.

" 'Come on,' says Bill Bassett to me, starting after him.

" 'Where?' I asks.

" 'Lordy!' says Bill, 'had you forgot you was in the desert? Didn't you see Colonel Manna drop down right before your eyes? Don't you hear the rustling of General Raven's wings? I'm surprised at you, Elijah.'

"We overtook the stranger in the edge of some woods, and as it was after sun-down and in a quiet place, nobody saw us stop him. Bill takes the silk hat off the man's head and brushes it with his sleeve and puts it back.

" 'What does this mean, sir?' says the man.

" 'When I wore one of these,' says Bill, 'and felt embarrassed, I always done that. Not having one now I had to use yours. I hardly know how to begin, sir, in explaining our business with you, but I guess we'll try your pockets first.'

"Bill Bassett felt in all of them, and looked disgusted.

" 'Not even a watch,' he says. 'Ain't you ashamed of yourself, you whited sculpture? Going about dressed like a head-waiter, and financed like a Count. You haven't even got carfare. What did you do with your transfer?'

"The man speaks up and says he has no assets or valuables of any sort. But Bassett takes his hand-satchel and opens it. Out comes some collars and socks and a half page of a newspaper clipped out. Bill reads the clipping careful, and holds out his hand to the held-up party.

" 'Brother,' says he, 'greetings! Accept the apologies of friends. I am Bill Bassett, the burglar. Mr. Peters, you must make the acquaintance of Mr. Alfred E. Ricks. Shake hands. Mr. Peters,' says Bill, 'stands about halfway between me and you, Mr. Ricks, in the line of havoc and corruption. He always gives something for the money he gets. I'm glad to meet you, Mr. Ricks—you and Mr. Peters. This is the first time I ever attended a full gathering of the National Synod of Sharks—housebreaking, swindling, and financiering all represented. Please examine Mr. Ricks' credentials, Mr. Peters.'

"The piece of newspaper that Bill Bassett handed me had a good picture of this Ricks on it. It was a Chicago paper, and it had obloquies of Ricks in every paragraph. By reading it over I harvested the intelligence that said alleged Ricks had laid off all that portion of the State of Florida that lies under water into town lots and sold 'em to alleged innocent investors from his magnificently furnished offices in Chicago. After he had taken in a hundred thousand or so dollars one of these fussy purchasers that are always making trouble (I've had 'em actually try gold watches I've sold 'em with acid) took a cheap excursion down to the land where it is always just before supper to look at his lot and see if it didn't need a new paling or two on the fence, and market a few lemons in time for the Christmas present trade. He hires a surveyor to find his lot for him. They run the line out and find the flourishing town of Paradise Hollow, so advertised, to be about 40 rods and 16 poles S., 27° E. of the middle of Lake Okeechobee. This man's lot was under thirty-six feet of water, and, besides, had been preëmpted so long by the alligators and gars that his title looked fishy.

"Naturally, the man goes back to Chicago and makes it as hot for Alfred E. Ricks as the morning after a prediction of snow by the weather bureau. Ricks denied the allegation, but he couldn't deny the alligators. One morning the papers came out with a column about it, and Ricks came out by the fire-escape. It seems the alleged authorities had beat him to the safe-deposit box where he kept his winnings, and Ricks has to westward ho! with only feetwear and a dozen 15½ English pokes in his shopping bag. He happened to have some mileage left in his book, and that took him as far as the town in the wilderness where he was spilled out on me and Bill Bassett as Elijah III with not a raven in sight for any of us.

"Then this Alfred E. Ricks lets out a squeak that he is hungry, too, and denies the hypothesis that he is good for the value, let alone the price, of a meal. And so, there was the three of us, representing, if we had a mind to draw syllogisms and parabolas, labor and trade and capital. Now, when trade has no capital there isn't a dicker to be made. And when capital has no money there's a stagnation in steak and onions. That put it up to the man with the jimmy.

" 'Brother bushrangers,' says Bill Bassett, 'never yet, in trouble, did I desert a pal. Hard by, in yon wood, I seem to see unfurnished lodgings. Let us go there and wait till dark.'

"There was an old, deserted cabin in the grove, and we three took possession of it. After dark Bill Bassett tells us to wait, and goes out for half an hour. He comes back with an armful of bread and spare ribs and pies.

" 'Panhandled 'em at a farmhouse on Washita Avenue,' says he. 'Eat, drink, and be leary.'

"The full moon was coming up bright, so we sat on the floor of the cabin and ate in the light of it. And this Bill Bassett begins to brag.

" 'Sometimes,' says he, with his mouth full of country produce, 'I lose all patience with you people that think you are higher up in the profession than I am. Now, what could either of you have done in the present emergency to set us on our feet again? Could you do it, Ricksy?'

" 'I must confess, Mr. Bassett,' says Ricks, speaking nearly inaudible out of a slice of pie, 'that at this immediate juncture I could not, perhaps, promote an enterprise to relieve the situation. Large operations, such as I direct, naturally require careful preparation in advance. I———'

" 'I know, Ricksy,' breaks in Bill Bassett. 'You needn't finish. You need $500 to make the first payment on a blond typewriter, and four roomsful of quartered oak furniture. And you need $500 more for advertising contracts. And you need two weeks' time for the fish to begin to bite. Your line of relief would be about as useful in an emergency as advocating municipal ownership to cure a man suffocated by eighty-cent gas. And your graft ain't much swifter, Brother Peters,' he winds up.

" 'Oh,' says I, 'I haven't seen you turn anything into gold with your wand yet, Mr. Good Fairy. 'Most anybody could rub the magic ring for a little leftover victuals.'

" 'That was only getting the pumpkin ready,' says Bassett, braggy and cheerful. 'The coach and six'll drive up to the door before you know it, Miss Cinderella. Maybe you've got some scheme under your sleeve-holders that will give us a start.'

" 'Son,' says I, 'I'm fifteen years older than you are, and young enough yet to take out an endowment policy. I've been broke before. We can see the lights of that town not half a mile away. I learned under Montague Silver, the greatest street man that ever spoke from a wagon. There are hundreds of men walking those streets this moment with grease spots on their clothes. Give me a gasoline lamp, a dry-goods box, and a two-dollar bar of white castile soap, cut into little———'

" 'Where's your two dollars?' snickered Bill Bassett into my discourse. There was no use arguing with that burglar.

" 'No,' he goes on; 'you're both babes-in-the-wood. Finance has closed the mahogany desk, and trade has put the shutters up. Both of you look to labor to start the wheels going. All right. You admit it. To-night I'll show you what Bill Bassett can do.'

"Bassett tells me and Ricks not to leave the cabin till he comes back, even if it's daylight, and then he starts off toward town, whistling gay.

"This Alfred E. Ricks pulls off his shoes and his coat, lays a silk handkerchief over his hat, and lays down on the floor.

" 'I think I will endeavor to secure a little slumber,' he squeaks. 'The day has been fatiguing. Good-night, my dear Mr. Peters.'

" 'My regards to Morpheus,' says I. 'I think I'll sit up a while.'

"About two o'clock, as near as I could guess by my watch in Peavine, home comes our laboring man and kicks up Ricks, and calls us to the streak of bright moonlight shining in the cabin door. Then he spreads out five packages of one thousand dollars each on the floor, and begins to cackle over the nest-egg like a hen.

" 'I'll tell you a few things about that town,' says he. 'It's named Rocky Springs, and they're building a Masonic temple, and it looks like the Democratic candidate for mayor is going to get soaked by a Pop, and Judge Tucker's wife, who has been down with pleurisy, is some better. I had a talk on these lilliputian thesises before I could get a siphon in the fountain of knowledge that I was after. And there's a bank there called the Lumberman's Fidelity and Plowman's Savings Institution. It closed for business yesterday with $23,000 cash on hand. It will open this morning with $18,000—all silver—that's the reason I didn't bring more. There you are, trade and capital. Now, will you be bad?'

" 'My young friend,' says Alfred E. Ricks, holding up his hands, 'have you robbed this bank? Dear me, dear me!'

" 'You couldn't call it that,' says Bassett. ' "Robbing" sounds harsh. All I had to do was to find out what street it was on. That town is so quiet that I could stand on the corner and hear the tumblers clicking in that safe lock—"right to 45, left twice to 80; right once to 60; left to 15"—as plain as the Yale captain giving orders in the football dialect. Now, boys,' says Bassett, 'this is an early rising town. They tell me the citizens are all up and stirring before daylight. I asked what for, and they said because breakfast was ready at that time. And what of merry Robin Hood? It must be Yoicks! and away with the tinkers' chorus. I'll stake you. How much do you want? Speak up. Capital.'

" 'My dear young friend,' says this ground squirrel of a Ricks, standing on his hind legs and juggling nuts in his paws, 'I have friends in Denver who would assist me. If I had a hundred dollars I———'

"Bassett unpins a package of the currency and throws five twenties to Ricks.

" 'Trade, how much?' he says to me.

" 'Put your money up, Labor,' says I. 'I never yet drew upon honest toil for its hard-earned pittance. The dollars I get are surplus ones that are burning the pockets of damfools and greenhorns. When I stand on a street corner and sell a solid gold diamond ring to a yap for $3.00, I make just $2.60. And I know he's going to give it to a girl in return for all the benefits accruing from a $125.00 ring. His profits are $122.00. Which of us is the biggest fakir?'

" 'And when you sell a poor woman a pinch of sand for fifty cents to keep her lamp from exploding,' says Bassett, 'what do you figure her gross earnings to be, with sand at forty cents a ton?'

" 'Listen,' says I. 'I instruct her to keep her lamp clean and well filled. If she does that it can't burst. And with the sand in it she knows it can't and she don't worry. It's kind of Industrial Christian Science. She pays fifty cents, and gets both Rockefeller and Mrs. Eddy on the job. It ain't everybody that can let the gold-dust twins do their work.'

"Alfred E. Ricks all but licks the dust off of Bill Bassett's shoes.

" 'My dear young friend,' says he, 'I will never forget your generosity. Heaven will reward you. But let me implore you to turn from your ways of violence and crime.'

" 'Mousie,' says Bill, 'the hole in the wainscoting for yours. Your dogmas and inculcations sound to me like the last words of a bicycle pump. What has your high moral, elevator-service system of pillage brought you to? Penuriousness and want. Even Brother Peters, who insists upon contaminating the art of robbery with theories of commerce and trade, admitted he was on the lift. Both of you live by the gilded rule. Brother Peters,' says Bill, 'you'd better choose a slice of this embalmed currency. You're welcome.'

"I told Bill Bassett once more to put this money in his pocket. I never had the respect for burglary that some people have. I always gave something for the money I took, even if it was only some little trifle of a souvenir to remind 'em not to get caught again.

"And then Alfred E. Ricks grovels at Bill's feet again, and bids us adieu. He says he will have a team at a farmhouse, and drive to the station below, and take the train for Denver. It salubrified the atmosphere when that lamentable boll-worm took his departure. He was a disgrace to every non-industrial profession in the country. With all his big schemes and fine offices he had wound up unable even to get an honest meal except by the kindness of a strange and maybe unscrupulous burglar. I was glad to see him go, though I felt a little sorry for him, now that he was ruined forever. What could such a man do without a big capital to work with? Why, Alfred E. Ricks, as we left him, was as helpless as a turtle on its back. He couldn't have worked a scheme to beat a little girl out of a penny slate-pencil.

"When me and Bill Bassett was left alone I did a little sleight-of-mind turn in my head with a trade secret at the end of it. Thinks I, I'll show this Mr. Burglar Man the difference between business and labor. He had hurt some of my professional self-adulation by casting his Persians upon commerce and trade.

" 'I won't take any of your money as a gift, Mr. Bassett,' says I to him, 'but if you'll pay my expenses as a travelling companion until we get out of the danger zone of the immoral deficit you have caused in this town's finances to-night I'll be obliged.'

"Bill Bassett agreed to that, and we hiked westward as soon as we could catch a safe train.

"When we got to a town in Arizona called Los Perros I suggested that we once more try our luck on terra-cotta. That was the home of Montague Silver, my old instructor, now retired from business. I knew Monty would stake me to web money if I could show him a fly buzzing 'round in the locality. Bill Bassett said all towns looked alike to him as he worked mainly in the dark. So we got off the train in Los Perros, a fine little town in the silver region.

"I had an elegant little sure thing in the way of a commercial sling shot that I intended to hit Bassett behind the ear with. I wasn't going to take his money while he was asleep, but I was going to leave him with a lottery ticket that would represent in experience to him $4,755—I think that was the amount he had when we got off the train. But the first time I hinted to him about an investment, he turns on me and disencumbers himself of the following terms and expressions.

" 'Brother Peters,' says he, 'it ain't a bad idea to go into an enterprise of some kind, as you suggest. I think I will. But if I do it will be such a cold proposition that nobody but Robert E. Peary and Charlie Fairbanks will be able to sit on the board of directors.'

" 'I thought you might want to turn your money over,' says I.

" 'I do,' says he, 'frequently. I can't sleep on one side all night. I'll tell you, Brother Peters,' says he, 'I'm going to start a poker room. I don't seem to care for the humdrum in swindling, such as peddling egg-beaters and working off breakfast food on Barnum and Bailey for sawdust to strew in their circus rings. But the gambling business,' says he, 'from the profitable side of the table is a good compromise between swiping silver spoons and selling penwipers at a Waldorf-Astoria charity bazaar.'

" 'Then,' says I, 'Mr. Bassett, you don't care to talk over my little business proposition?"

" 'Why,' says he, 'do you know, you can't get a Pasteur institute to start up within fifty miles of where I live. I bite so seldom.'

"So, Bassett rents a room over a saloon and looks around for some furniture and chromos. The same night I went to Monty Silver's house, and he let me have $200 on my prospects. Then I went to the only store in Los Perros that sold playing cards and bought every deck in the house. The next morning when the store opened I was there bringing all the cards back with me. I said that my partner that was going to back me in the game had changed his mind; and I wanted to sell the cards back again. The storekeeper took 'em at half price.

"Yes, I was seventy-five dollars loser up to that time. But while I had the cards that night I marked every one in every deck. That was labor. And then trade and commerce had their innings, and the bread I had cast upon the waters began to come back in the form of cottage pudding with wine sauce.

"Of course I was among the first to buy chips at Bill Bassett's game. He had bought the only cards there was to be had in town; and I knew the back of every one of them better than I know the back of my head when the barber shows me my haircut in the two mirrors.

"When the game closed I had the five thousand and a few odd dollars, and all Bill Bassett had was the wanderlust and a black cat he had bought for a mascot. Bill shook hands with me when I left.

" 'Brother Peters,' says he, 'I have no business being in business. I was preordained to labor. When a No. 1 burglar tries to make a James out of his jimmy he perpetrates an improfundity. You have a well-oiled and efficacious system of luck at cards,' says he. 'Peace go with you.' And I never afterward sees Bill Bassett again."

"Well, Jeff," said I, when the Autolycan adventurer seemed to have divulged the gist of his tale, "I hope you took care of the money. That would be a respecta—that is a considerable working capital if you should choose some day to settle down to some sort of regular business."

"Me?" said Jeff, virtuously. "You can bet I've taken care of that five thousand."

He tapped his coat over the region of his chest exultantly.

"Gold mining stock," he explained, "every cent of it. Shares par value one dollar. Bound to go up 500 per cent within a year. Non-assessable. The Blue Gopher Mine. Just discovered a month ago. Better get in yourself if you've any spare dollars on hand."

"Sometimes," said I, "these mines are not———"

"Oh, this one's solid as an old goose," said Jeff. "Fifty thousand dollars' worth of ore in sight, and 10 per cent monthly earnings guaranteed."

He drew a long envelope from his pocket and cast it on the table.

"Always carry it with me," said he. "So the burglar can't corrupt or the capitalist break in and water it."

I looked at the beautifully engraved certificate of stock.

"In Colorado, I see," said I. "And, by the way, Jeff, what was the name of the little man who went to Denver—the one you and Bill met at the station?"

"Alfred E. Ricks," said Jeff, "was the toad's designation."

"I see," said I, "the president of this mining company signs himself A. L. Fredericks. I was wondering———"

"Let me see that stock," said Jeff quickly, almost snatching it from me.

To mitigate, even though slightly, the embarrassment I summoned the waiter and ordered another bottle of the Barbera. I thought it was the least I could do.

Hostages to Momus

I

I never got inside of the legitimate line of graft but once. But, one time, as I say, I reversed the decision of the revised statutes and undertook a thing that I'd have to apologize for even under the New Jersey trust laws.

Me and Caligula Polk of Muskogee in the Creek Nation, was down in the Mexican State of Tamaulipas running a peripatetic lottery and monte game. Now, selling lottery tickets is a government graft in Mexico, just like selling forty-eight cents' worth of postage-stamps for forty-nine cents is over here. So Uncle Porfirio he instructs the *rurales* to attend our case.

Rurales? They're a sort of country police; but don't draw any mental crayon portraits of the worthy constable with a tin star and a gray goatee. The *rurales*—well, if we'd mount our Supreme Court on broncos, arm 'em with Winchesters, and start 'em out after John Doe *et al.* we'd have about the same thing.

When the *rurales* started for us we started for the States. They chased us as far as Matamoras. We hid in a brickyard; and that night we swum the Rio Grande, Caligula with a brick in each hand, absent-minded, which he drops upon the soil of Texas, forgetting he had 'em.

From there we migrated to San Antone, and then over to New Orleans where we took a rest. And in that town of cotton bales and other adjuncts to female beauty we made the acquaintance of drinks invented by the Creoles during the period of Louey Cans, in which they are still served at the side doors. The most I can remember of this town is that me and Caligula and a Frenchman name McCarty—wait a minute; Adolph McCarty—was trying to make the French Quarter pay up the back trading-stamps due on the Louisiana Purchase, when somebody hollers that the johndarms are coming. I have an insufficient recollection of buying two yellow tickets through a window; and I seemed to see a man swing a lantern and say "All aboard!" I remembered no more, except that the train butcher was covering me and Caligula up with Augusta J. Evans's works and figs.

When we become revised, we find that we have collided up against the State of Georgia at a spot hitherto unaccounted for in time tables except by an asterisk, which means that trains stop every other Thursday on signal by tearing up a rail. We was waked up in a yellow pine hotel by the noise of flowers and the smell of birds. Yes, sir, for the wind was banging sunflowers as big as buggy wheels against the weatherboarding and the chicken coop was right under the window. Me and Caligula dressed and went downstairs. The landlord was shelling peas on the front porch. He was six feet of chills and fever, and Hongkong in complexion though in other respects he seemed amenable in the exercise of his sentiments and features.

Caligula, who is a spokesman by birth, and a small man, though red-haired and impatient of painfulness of any kind, speaks up.

"Pardner," says he, "good-morning, and be darned to you. Would you mind telling us why we are at? We know the reason we are where, but can't exactly figure out on account of at what place."

"Well, gentlemen," says the landlord, "I reckoned you-all would be inquiring this morning. You all dropped off of the nine-thirty train here last night; and you was right tight. Yes, you was right smart in liquor. I can inform you that you are now in the town of Mountain Valley, in the State of Georgia."

"On top of that," says Caligula, "don't say that we can't have anything to eat."

"Sit down, gentlemen," says the lord, "and in twenty minutes I'll call you to the best breakfast you can get anywhere in town."

That breakfast turned out to be composed of fried bacon and a yellowish edifice that proved up something between pound cake and flexible sandstone. The landlord calls it corn pone; and then he sets out a dish of the exaggerated breakfast food known as hominy; and so me and Caligula makes the acquintance of the celebrated food that enabled every Johnny Reb to lick one and two-thirds Yankees for nearly four years at a stretch.

"The wonder to me is," says Caligula, "that Uncle Robert Lee's boys didn't chase the Grant and Sherman outfit clear up into Hudson's Bay. It would have made me that mad to eat this truck they call mahogany!"

"Hog and hominy," I explains, "is the staple food of this section."

"Then," says Caligula, "they ought to keep it where it belongs. I thought this was a hotel and not a stable. Now, if we was in Muskogee at the St. Lucifer House, I'd show you some breakfast grub. Antelope steaks and fried liver to begin on, and venison cutlets with *chili con carne* and pineapple fritters, and then some sardines and mixed pickles; and top it off with a can of yellow clings and a bottle of beer. You won't find a layout like that on the bill of affairs of any of your Eastern restauraws."

"Too lavish," says I. "I've travelled, and I'm unprejudiced. There'll never be a perfect breakfast eaten until some man grows arms long enough to stretch down to New Orleans for his coffee and over to Norfolk for his rolls, and reaches up to Vermont and digs a slice of butter out of a spring-house, and then turns over a beehive close to a white clover patch out in Indiana for the rest. Then he'd come pretty close to making a meal on the amber that the gods eat on Mount Olympia."

"Too ephemeral," says Caligula. "I'd want ham and eggs, or rabbit stew, anyhow, for a chaser. What do you consider the most edifying and casual in the way of a dinner?"

"I've been infatuated from time to time," I answers, "with fancy ramifications of grub such as terrapins, lobsters, reed birds, jambolaya, and canvas-covered ducks; but after all there's nothing less displeasing to me than a beefsteak smothered in mushrooms on a balcony in sound of the Broadway street cars, with a hand-organ playing down below, and the boys hollering extras about the latest suicide. For the wine, give me a reasonable Pony Cany. And that's all, except a *demi-tasse*."

"Well," says Caligula, "I reckon in New York you get to be a conniseer; and when you go around with a *demi-tasse* you are naturally bound to buy 'em stylish grub."

"It's a great town for epicures," says I. "You'd soon fall into their ways if you was there."

"I've heard it was," says Caligula. "But I reckon I wouldn't. I can polish my fingernails all they need myself."

II

After breakfast we went out on the front porch, lighted up two of the landlord's *flor de upas* perfectos, and took a look at Georgia.

The installment of scenery visible to the eye looked mighty poor. As far as we could see with red hills all washed down with gullies and scattered over with patches of piny woods. Blackberry bushes was all that kept the rail fences from falling down. About fifteen miles over to the north was a little range of well-timbered mountains.

That town of Mountain Valley wasn't going. About a dozen people permeated along the sidewalks; but what you saw mostly was rain-barrels and roosters, and boys poking around with sticks in piles of ashes made by burning the scenery of Uncle Tom shows.

And just then there passes down on the other side of the street a high man in a long black coat and a beaver hat. All the people in sight bowed, and some crossed the street to shake hands with him; folks came out of stores and houses to holler at him; women leaned out of windows and smiled; and all the kids stopped playing to look at him. Our landlord stepped out on the porch and bent himself double like a carpenter's rule, and sung out, "Good-morning, Colonel," when he was a dozen yards gone by.

"And is that Alexander, pa?" says Caligula to the landlord; "and why is he called great?"

"That, gentlemen," says the landlord, "is no less than Colonel Jackson T. Rockingham, the president of the Sunrise & Edenville Tap Railroad, mayor of Mountain Valley, and chairman of the Perry County board of immigration and public improvements."

"Been away a good many years, hasn't he?" I asked.

"No, sir; Colonel Rockingham is going down to the post-office for his mail. His fellow-citizens take pleasure in greeting him thus every morning. The colonel is our most prominent citizen. Besides the height of the stock of the Sunrise & Edenville Tap Railroad, he owns a thousand acres of that land across the creek. Mountain Valley delights, sir, to honor a citizen of such wealth and public spirit."

For an hour that afternoon Caligula sat on the back of his neck on the porch and studied a newspaper, which was unusual in a man who despised print. When he was through he took me to the end of the porch among the sunlight and drying dishtowels. I knew that Caligula had invented a new graft. For he chewed the ends of his mustache and ran the left catch of his suspenders up and down, which was his way.

"What is it now?" I asks. "Just so it ain't floating mining stocks or raising Pennsylvania pinks, we'll talk it over."

"Pennsylvania pinks? Oh, that refers to a coin-raising scheme of the Keystoners. They burn the soles of old women's feet to make them tell where their money's hid."

Caligula's words in business was always few and bitter.

"You see them mountains," said he, pointing. "And you see that colonel man that owns railroads and cuts more ice when he goes to the post-office than Roosevelt does when he cleans 'em out. What we're going to do is to kidnap the latter into the former, and inflict a ransom of ten thousand dollars."

"Illegality," says I, shaking my head.

"I knew you'd say that," says Caligula. "At first sight it does seem to jar peace and dignity. But it don't. I got the idea out of that newspaper. Would you commit aspersions on a equitable graft that the United States itself has condoned and indorsed and ratified?"

"Kidnapping," says I, "is an immoral function in the derogatory list of the statutes. If the United States upholds it, it must be a recent enactment of ethics, along with race suicide and rural delivery."

"Listen," says Caligula, "and I'll explain the case set down in the papers. Here was a Greek citizen named Burdick Harris," says he, "captured for a graft by Africans; and the United States sends two gunboats to the State of Tangiers and makes the King of Morocco give up seventy thousand dollars to Raisuli."

"Go slow," says I. "That sounds too international to take in all at once. It's like 'thimble, thimble, who's got the naturalization papers?' "

" 'Twas press despatches from Constantinople," says Caligula. "You'll see, six months from now. They'll be confirmed by the monthly magazines; and then it won't be long till you'll notice 'em alongside of photos of the Mount Pelee eruption photos in the while-you-get-your-hair-cut weeklies. It's all right, Pick. This African man Raisuli hides Burdick Harris up in the mountains, and advertises his price to the governments of different nations. Now you wouldn't think for a minute," goes on Caligula, "that John Hay would have chipped in and helped his graft along if it wasn't a square game, would you?"

"Why, no," says I. "I've always stood right in with Bryan's policies, and I couldn't consciously say a word against the Republican administration just now. But if Harris was a Greek, on what system of international protocols did Hay interfere?"

"It ain't exactly set forth in the papers," says Caligula. "I suppose it's a matter of sentiment. You know he wrote this poem, 'Little Breeches'; and them Greeks wear little or none. But anyhow, John Hay sends the *Brooklyn* and the *Olympia* over, and they cover Africa with thirty-inch guns. And then Hay cables after the health of the *persona grata*. 'And how are they this morning?' he wires. 'Is Burdick Harris alive yet, or Mr. Raisuli dead?' And the King of Morocco sends up the seventy thousand dollars, and they turn Burdick Harris loose. And there's not half the hard feelings among the nations about this little kidnapping matter as there was about the peace congress. And Burdick Harris says to the reporters, in the Greek language, that he's often heard about the United States, and he admires Roosevelt next to Raisuli, who is one of the whitest and most gentlemanly kidnappers that he ever worked alongside of. So you see, Pick," winds up Caligula, "we've got the law of nations on our side. We'll cut this colonel man out of the herd, and corral him in them little mountains, and stick up heirs and assigns for ten thousand dollars."

"Well, you seldom little red-headed territorial terror," I answers, "you can't bluff your uncle Tecumseh Pickens! I'll be your company in this graft. But I misdoubt if you've absorbed the inwardness of this Burdick Harris case, Calig; and if on any morning we get a telegram from the Secretary of State asking about the health of the scheme, I propose to acquire the most propinquitous and celeritous mule in this section and gallop diplomatically over into the neighboring and peaceful nation of Alabama."

III

Me and Caligula spent the next three days investigating the bunch of mountains into which we proposed to kidnap Colonel Jackson T. Rockingham. We finally selected an upright slice of topography covered with bushes and trees that you could only reach by a secret path that we cut up the side of it. And the only way to reach the mountain was to follow up the bend of a branch that wound among the elevations.

Then I took in hand an important subdivision of the proceedings. I went up to Atlanta on the train and laid in a two-hundred-and-fifty-dollar supply of the most gratifying and efficient lines of grub that money could buy. I always was an admirer of viands in their more palliative and revised stages. Hog and hominy are not only inartistic to my stomach, but they give indigestion to my moral sentiments. And I thought of Colonel Jackson T. Rockingham, president of the Sunrise & Edenville Tap Railroad, and how he would miss the luxury of his home fare as is so famous among wealthy Southerners. So I sunk half of mine and Caligula's capital in as elegant a layout of fresh and canned provisions as Burdick Harris or any other professional kidnappee ever saw in a camp.

I put another hundred in a couple of cases of Bordeaux, two quarts of cognac, two hundred Havana regalias with gold bands, and a camp stove and stools and folding cots. I wanted Colonel Rockingham to be comfortable; and I hoped after he gave up the ten thousand dollars he would give me and Caligula as good a name for gentlemen and entertainers as the Greek man did the friend of his that made the United States his bill collector against Africa. When the goods came down from Atlanta, we hired a wagon, moved them up on the little mountain, and established camp. And then we laid for the colonel.

We caught him one morning about two miles out from Mountain Valley, on his way to look after some of his burnt umber farm land. He was an elegant old gentleman, as thin and tall as a trout rod, with frazzled shirt-cuffs and specs on a black string. We explained to him, brief and easy, what we wanted; and Caligula showed him, careless, the handle of his forty-five under his coat.

"What?" says Colonel Rockingham. "Bandits in Perry County, Georgia! I shall see that the board of immigration and public improvements hears of this!"

"Be so unfoolhardy as to climb into that buggy," says Caligula, "by order of the board of perforation and public depravity. This is a business meeting, and we're anxious to adjourn *sine qua non*."

We drove Colonel Rockingham over the mountain and up the side of it as far as the buggy could go. Then we tied the horse, and took our prisoner on foot up to the camp.

"Now, colonel," I says to him, "we're after the ransom, me and my partner; and no harm will come to you if the King of Mor—if your friends send up the dust. In the meantime, we are gentlemen the same as you. And if you give us your word not to try to escape, the freedom of the camp is yours."

"I give you my word," says the colonel.

"All right," says I; "and now it's eleven o'clock and me and Mr. Polk will proceed to inoculate the occasion with a few well-timed trivialities in the line of grub."

"Thank you," says the colonel; "I believe I could relish a slice of bacon and a plate of hominy."

"But you won't," says I, emphatic. "Not in this camp. We soar in higher regions than them occupied by your celebrated but repulsive dish."

While the colonel read his paper, me and Caligula took off our coats and went in for a little luncheon *de luxe* just to show him. Caligula was a fine cook of the Western brand. He could toast a buffalo or fricassee a couple of steers as easy as a woman could make a cup of tea. He was gifted in the way of knocking together edibles when haste and muscle and quantity was to be considered. He held the record west of the Arkansas River for frying pancakes with his left hand, broiling venison cutlets with his right and skinning a rabbit with his teeth at the same time. But I could do things *en casserole* and *à la creole,* and handle the oil and tabasco as gently and nicely as a French *chef.*

So at twelve o'clock we had a hot lunch ready that looked like a banquet on a Mississippi River steamboat. We spread it on the tops of two or three big boxes, opened two quarts of the red wine, set the olives and a canned oyster cocktail and a ready-made Martini by the colonel's plate, and called him to grub.

Colonel Rockingham drew up his campstool, wiped off his specs, and looked at the things on the table. Then I thought he was swearing; and I felt mean because I hadn't taken more pains with the victuals. But he wasn't; he was asking a blessing; and me and Caligula hung our heads and I saw a tear drop from the colonel's eye into his cocktail.

I never saw a man eat with so much earnestness and application—not hastily like a grammarian or one of the canal, but slow and appreciative, like a anaconda, or a real *vive bonjour.*

In an hour and a half the colonel leaned back. I brought him a pony of brandy and his black coffee, and set the box of Havana regalias on the table.

"Gentlemen," says he, blowing out the smoke and trying to breathe it back again, "when we view the eternal hills and the smiling and beneficent landscape, and reflect upon the goodness of the Creator who———"

"Excuse me, colonel," says I, "but there's some business to attention to now"; and I brought out paper and pen and ink and laid 'em before him. "Who do you want to send to for the money?" I asks.

"I reckon," says he, after thinking a bit, "to the vice-president of our railroad, at the general offices of the Company in Edenville."

"How far is it to Edenville from here?" I asked.

"About ten miles," says he.

Then I dictated these lines, and Colonel Rockingham wrote them out:

> I am kidnapped and held a prisoner by two desperate outlaws in a place which is useless to attempt to find. They demand ten thousand dollars at once for my release. The amount must be raised immediately, and these directions followed. Come alone with the money to Stony Creek, which runs out of Blacktop Mountains. Follow the bed of the creek till you come to a big flat rock on the left bank, on which is marked a cross in red chalk. Stand on the rock and wave a white flag. A guide will come to you and conduct you to where I am held. Lose no time.

After the colonel had finished this, he asked permission to tack on a postscript about how white he was being treated, so the railroad wouldn't feel uneasy in its bosom about him. We agreed to that. He wrote down that he had just had lunch with the two desperate ruffians; and then he set down the whole bill of fare, from cocktails to coffee. He wound up with the remark that dinner would be ready about six, and would probably be a more licentious and intemperate affair than lunch.

Me and Caligula read it, and decided to let it go; for we, being cooks, were amenable to praise, though it sounded out of place on a sight draft for ten thousand dollars.

I took the letter over to Mountain Valley road and watched for a messenger. By and by a colored equestrian came along on horseback, riding toward Edenville. I gave him a dollar to take the letter to the railroad offices; and then I went back to camp.

IV

About four o'clock in the afternoon, Caligula, who was acting as lookout, calls to me:

"I have to report a white shirt signaling on the starboard bow, sir."

I went down the mountain and brought back a fat, red man in an alpaca coat and no collar.

"Gentlemen," says Colonel Rockingham, "allow me to introduce my brother, Captain Duval C. Rockingham, vice-president of the Sunrise & Edenville Tap Railroad."

"Otherwise the King of Morocco," says I. "I reckon you don't mind my counting the ransom, just as a business formality."

"Well, no, not exactly," says the fat man, "not when it comes. I turned that matter over to our second vice-president. I was anxious after Brother Jackson's safetiness. I reckon he'll be along right soon. What does that lobster salad you mentioned taste like, Brother Jackson?"

"Mr. Vice-President," says I, "you'll oblige us by remaining here till the second V. P. arrives. This is a private rehearsal, and we don't want any roadside speculators selling tickets."

In half an hour Caligula sings out again:

"Sail ho! Looks like an apron on a broomstick."

I perambulated down the cliff again, and escorted up a man six foot three, with a sandy beard and no other dimensions that you could notice. Thinks I to myself, if he's got ten thousand dollars on his person it's in one bill and folded lengthwise.

"Mr. Patterson G. Coble, our second vice-president," announces the colonel.

"Glad to know you, gentlemen," says this Coble. "I came up to disseminate the tidings that Major Tallahassee Tucker, our general passenger agent, is now negotiating a peach-crate full of our railroad bonds with the Perry County Bank for a loan. My dear Colonel Rockingham, was that chicken gumbo or cracked goobers on the bill of fare in your note? Me and the conductor of fifty-six was having a dispute about it."

"Another white wings on the rocks!" hollers Caligula. "If I see any more I'll fire on 'em and swear they was torpedo-boats!"

The guide goes down again, and convoys into the lair a person in blue overalls carrying an amount of inebriety and a lantern. I am so sure that this is Major Tucker that I don't even ask him until we are up above; and then I discover that it is Uncle Timothy, the yard switchman at Edenville, who is sent ahead to flag our understandings with the gossip that Judge Prendergast, the railroad's attorney, is in the process of mortgaging Colonel Rockingham's farming lands to make up the ransom.

While he is talking, two men crawl from under the bushes into camp, and Caligula, with no white flag to disinter him from his plain duty, draws his gun. But again, Colonel Rockingham intervenes and introduces Mr. Jones and Mr. Batts, engineer and fireman of train number forty-two.

"Excuse us," says Batts, "but me and Jim have hunted squirrels all over this mounting, and we don't need no white flag. Was that straight, colonel, about the plum pudding and pineapples and real store cigars?"

"Towel on a fishing-pole in the offing!" howls Caligula. "Suppose it's the firing line of the freight conductors and brakeman."

"My last trip down," says I, wiping off my face. "If the S. & E. T. wants to run an excursion up here just because we kidnapped their president, let 'em. We'll put out our sign. 'The Kidnapper's Cafe and Trainsmen's Home.' "

This time I caught Major Tallahassee Tucker by his own confession, and I felt easier. I asked him into the creek, so I could drown him if he happened to be a track-walker or caboose porter. All the way up the mountain he driveled to me about asparagus on toast, a thing that his intelligence in life had skipped.

Up above I got his mind segregated from food and asked if he had raised the ransom.

"My dear sir," says he, "I succeeded in negotiating a loan on thirty thousand dollars' worth of the bonds of our railroad, and———"

"Never mind just now, major," says I. "It's all right, then. Wait till after dinner, and we'll settle the business. All of you gentlemen," I continues to the crowd "are invited to stay to dinner. We have mutually trusted one another, and the white flag is supposed to wave over the proceedings."

"The correct idea," says Caligula, who was standing by me. "Two baggage-masters and a ticket agent dropped out of a tree while you was below the last time. Did the major man bring the money?"

"He says," I answered, "that he succeeded in negotiating the loan."

If any cooks ever earned ten thousand dollars in twelve hours me and Caligula did that day. At six o'clock we spread the top of the mountain with as fine a dinner as the personnel of any railroad ever engulfed. We opened all the wine, and we concocted entrées and *pièces de resistance,* and stirred up little savory *chef de cuisines* and organized a mass of grub such as has seldom instigated out of canned and bottled goods. The railroad gathered around it, and the wassail and diversions was intense.

After the feast me and Caligula, in the line of business, takes Major Tucker to one side and talks ransom. The major pulls out an agglomeration of currency about the size of the price of a town lot in the suburbs of Rabbitville, Arizona, and makes this outcry.

"Gentlemen," says he, "the stock of the Sunrise & Edenville railroad has depreciated some. The best I could do with thirty thousand dollars' worth of bonds was to secure a loan of eighty-seven dollars and fifty cents. On the farming lands of Colonel Rockingham, Judge Prendergast was able to obtain, on a ninth mortgage, the sum of fifty dollars. You will find the amount, one hundred and thirty-seven fifty, correct."

"A railroad president," said I, looking this Tucker in the eye, "and the owner of a thousand acres of land; and yet———"

"Gentlemen," says Tucker, "the railroad is ten miles long. There don't any train run on it except when the crew goes out in the pines and gathers enough lightwood knots to get up steam. A long time ago, when times was good, the net earnings used to run as high as eighteen dollars a week. Colonel Rockingham's land has been sold for taxes thirteen times. There hasn't been a peach crop in this part of Georgia for two years. The wet spring killed the watermelons. Nobody around here has money enough to buy fertilizer; and the land is so poor the corn crop failed, and there wasn't enough grass to support the rabbits. All the people have had to eat in this section for over a year is hog and hominy, and———"

"Pick," interrupts Caligula, mussing up his red hair, "what are you going to do with that chicken-feed?"

I hands the money back to Major Tucker; and then I goes over to Colonel Rockingham and slaps him on the back.

"Colonel," says I, "I hope you've enjoyed our little joke. We don't want to carry it too far. Kidnappers! Well, wouldn't it tickle your uncle? My name's Rhinegelder, and I'm a nephew of Chauncey Depew. My friend's a second cousin of the editor of *Puck*. So you can see. We are down South enjoying ourselves in our humorous way. Now, there's two quarts of cognac to open yet, and then the joke's over."

What's the use to go into details? One or two will be enough. I remember Major Tallahassee Tucker playing on a jew's-harp, and

Caligula waltzing with his head on the watch pocket of a tall baggage-master. I hesitate to refer to the cake-walk done by me and Mr. Patterson G. Coble with Colonel Jackson T. Rockingham between us.

And even on the next morning, when you wouldn't think it possible, there was a consolation for me and Caligula. We knew that Raisuli himself never made half the hit with Burdick Harris that we did with the Sunrise & Edenville Tap Railroad.

The Guardian of the Accolade

Not the least important of the force of the Weymouth Bank was Uncle Bushrod. Sixty years had Uncle Bushrod given of faithful service to the house of Weymouth as chattel, servitor, and friend. Of the color of the mahogany bank furniture was Uncle Bushrod—thus dark was he externally; white as the uninked pages of the bank ledgers was his soul. Eminently pleasing to Uncle Bushrod would the comparison have been; for to him the only institution in existence worth considering was the Weymouth Bank, of which he was something between porter and generalissimo-in-charge.

Weymouth lay, dreamy and unbrageous, among the low foothills along the brow of a Southern valley. Three banks there were in Weymouthville. Two were hopeless, misguided enterprises, lacking the presence and prestige of a Weymouth to give them glory. The third was The Bank, managed by the Weymouths—and Uncle Bushrod. In the old Weymouth homestead—the red brick, white-porticoed mansion, the first to your right as you crossed Elder Creek, coming into town—lived Mr. Robert Weymouth (the president of the bank), his widowed daughter, Mrs. Vesey—called "Miss Letty" by every one—and her two children, Nan and Guy. There, also in a cottage on the grounds, resided Uncle Bushrod and Aunt Malindy, his wife. Mr. William Weymouth (the cashier of the bank) lived in a modern, fine house on the principal avenue.

Mr. Robert was a large, stout man, sixty-two years of age, with a smooth, plump face, long iron-gray hair and fiery blue eyes. He was high-tempered, kind, and generous, with a youthful smile and a formidable, stern voice that did not always mean what it sounded like. Mr. William was a milder man, correct in deportment and absorbed in business. The Weymouths formed The Family of Weymouthville, and were looked up to, as was their right of heritage.

Uncle Bushrod was the bank's trusted porter, messenger, vassal, and guardian. He carried a key to the vault, just as Mr. Robert and Mr. William did. Sometimes there was ten, fifteen, or twenty thousand dollars in sacked silver stacked on the vault floor. It was safe with Uncle Bushrod. He was a Weymouth in heart, honesty, and pride.

Of late Uncle Bushrod had not been without worry. It was on account of Marse Robert. For nearly a year Mr. Robert had been known to indulge in too much drink. Not enough, understand, to become tipsy, but the habit was getting a hold upon him, and every one was beginning to notice it. Half a dozen times a day he would leave the bank and step around to the Merchants' and Planters' Hotel to take a drink. Mr. Robert's usual keen judgment and business capacity became a little impaired. Mr. William, a Weymouth, but not so rich in experience, tried to dam the inevitable backflow of the tide, but with incomplete success. The deposits in the Weymouth Bank dropped from six figures to five. Past-due paper began to accumulate, owing to injudicious loans. No one cared to address Mr. Robert on the subject of temperance. Many of his friends said that the cause of it had been the death of his wife some two years before. Others hesitated on account of Mr. Robert's quick temper, which was extremely apt to resent personal interference of such a nature. Miss Letty and the children noticed the change and grieved about it. Uncle Bushrod also worried, but he was one of those who would not have dared to remonstrate, although he and Marse Robert had been raised almost as companions. But there was a heavier shock coming to Uncle Bushrod than that caused by the bank president's toddies and juleps.

Mr. Robert had a passion for fishing, which he usually indulged whenever the season and business permitted. One day, when reports had been coming in relating to the bass and perch, he announced his intention of making a two- or three-days' visit to the lakes. He was going down, he said, to Reedy Lake with Judge Archinard, an old friend.

Now, Uncle Bushrod was treasurer of the Sons and Daughters of the Burning Bush. Every association he belonged to made him treasurer without hesitation. He stood AA1 in colored circles. He was understood among them to be Mr. Bushrod Weymouth, of the Weymouth Bank.

The night following the day on which Mr. Robert mentioned his intended fishing-trip the old man woke up and rose from his bed at twelve o'clock, declaring he must go down to the bank and fetch the pass-book of the Sons and Daughters, which he had forgotten to bring home. The bookkeeper had balanced it for him that day, put the cancelled checks in it, and snapped two elastic bands around it. He put but one band around other passbooks.

Aunt Malindy objected to the mission at so late an hour, denouncing it as foolish and unnecessary, but Uncle Bushrod was not to be deflected from duty.

"I done told Sister Adaline Hoskins," he said, "to come by here for dat book to-morrow mawnin' at sebin o'clock, for to kar' it to de meetin' of de bo'd of 'rangements, and dat book gwine to be here when she come."

So, Uncle Bushrod put on his old brown suit, got his thick hickory stick, and meandered through the almost deserted streets of Weymouthville. He entered the bank, unlocking the side door, and found the passbook where he had left it in the little back room used for private consultations, where he always hung his coat. Looking about casually, he saw that everything was as he had left it, and was about to start for home when he was brought to a standstill by the sudden rattle of a key in the front door. Some one came quickly in, closed the door softly, and entered the counting-room through the door in the iron railing.

That division of the bank's space was connected with the back room by a narrow passage-way, now in deep darkness.

Uncle Bushrod, firmly gripping his hickory stick, tiptoed gently up this passage until he could see the midnight intruder into the sacred precincts of the Weymouth Bank. One dim gas-jet burned there, but even in its nebulous light he perceived at once that the prowler was the bank's president.

Wondering, fearful, undecided what to do, the old colored man stood motionless in the gloomy strip of hallway, and waited developments.

The vault, with its big iron door, was opposite him. Inside that was the safe, holding the papers of value, the gold and currency of the bank. On the floor of the vault was, perhaps, eighteen thousand dollars in silver.

The president took his key from his pocket, opened the vault and went inside, nearly closing the door behind him. Uncle Bushrod saw, through the narrow aperture, the flicker of a candle. In a minute or two—it seemed an hour to the watcher—Mr. Robert came out, bringing with him a large hand-satchel, handling it in a careful but hurried manner, as if fearful that he might be observed. With one hand he closed and locked the vault door.

With a reluctant theory forming itself beneath his wool, Uncle Bushrod waited and watched, shaking in his concealing shadow.

Mr. Robert set the satchel softly upon a desk, and turned his coat collar up about his neck and ears. He was dressed in a rough suit of gray, as if for travelling. He glanced with frowning intentness at the big office clock above the burning gas-jet, and then looked lingeringly about the bank—lingeringly and fondly, Uncle Bushrod thought, as one who bids farewell to dear and familiar scenes.

Now he caught up his burden again and moved promptly and softly out of the bank by the way he had come locking the front door behind him.

For a minute or longer Uncle Bushrod was as stone in his tracks. Had that midnight rifler of safes and vaults been any other on earth than the man he was, the old retainer would have rushed upon him and struck to save the Weymouth property. But now the watcher's soul was tortured by the poignant dread of something worse than mere robbery. He was seized by an accusing terror that said the Weymouth name and the Weymouth honor was about to be lost. Marse Robert robbing the bank! What else could it mean? The hour of the night, the stealthy visit to the vault, the satchel brought forth full and with expedition and silence, the prowler's rough dress, his solicitous reading of the clock, and noiseless departure—what else could it mean?

And then to the turmoil of Uncle Bushrod's thoughts came the corroborating recollection of preceding events—Mr. Robert's increasing intemperance and consequent many moods of royal high spirits and stern tempers; the casual talk he had heard in the bank of the decrease in business and difficulty in collecting loans. What else could it all mean but that Mr. Robert Weymouth was an absconder—was about to fly with the bank's remaining funds, leaving Mr. William, Miss Letty, little Nan, Guy, and Uncle Bushrod to bear the disgrace?

During one minute Uncle Bushrod considered these things, and then he awoke to sudden determination and action.

"Lawd! Lawd!" he moaned aloud, as he hobbled hastily toward the side door. "Sech a come-off after all dese here years of big doin's and fine doin's. Scan'lous sights upon de yearth when de Weymouth fambly done turn out robbers and 'bezzlers! Time for Uncle Bushrod to clean out somebody's chicken-coop and eben matters up. Oh, Lawd! Marse Robert, you ain't gwine do dat. 'N Miss Letty an' dem chillum so proud and talking' 'Weymouth, Weymouth,' all de time! I'm gwine to stop you ef I can. 'Spec yo shoot Mr. Nigger's head off ef he fool wid you, but I'm gwine stop you ef I can."

Uncle Bushrod, aided by his hickory stick, impeded by his rheumatism, hurried down the street toward the railroad station, where the two lines touching Weymouthville met. As he had expected and feared, he saw there Mr. Robert, standing in the shadow of the building, waiting for the train. He held the satchel in his hand.

When Uncle Bushrod came within twenty yards of the bank president, standing like a huge, gray ghost by the station wall, sudden perturbation seized him. The rashness and audacity of the thing he had come to do struck him fully. He would have been happy could he have turned and fled from the possibilities of the famous Weymouth wrath. But again he saw, in his fancy, the white reproachful face of Miss Letty, and the distressed looks of Nan and Guy, should he fail in his duty and they questioned him as to his stewardship.

Braced by the thought, he approached in a straight line, clearing his throat and pounding his stick so that he might be early recognized. Thus he might avoid the likely danger of too suddenly surprising the sometimes hasty Robert.

"Is that you, Bushrod?" called the clamant, clear voice of the gray ghost.

"Yes, suh, Marse Robert."

"What the devil are you doing out at this time of night?"

For the first time in his life, Uncle Bushrod told Marse Robert a falsehood. He could not repress it. He would have to circumlocute a little. His nerve was not equal to a direct attack.

"I done been down, suh, to see ol' Aunt M'ria Patterson. She taken sick in de night, and I kyar'ed her a bottle of M'lindy's medercine. Yes, suh."

"Humph!" said Robert. "You better get home out of the night air. It's damp. You'll hardly be worth killing to-morrow on account of your rheumatism. Think it'll be a clear day, Bushrod?"

"I 'low it will, suh. De sun sot red las' night."

Mr. Robert lit a cigar in the shadow, and the smoke looked like his gray ghost expanding and escaping into the night air. Somehow, Uncle Bushrod could barely force his reluctant tongue to the dreadful subject. He stood, awkward, shambling, with his feet upon the gravel and fumbling with his stick. But then, afar off—three miles away, at the Jimtown switch—he heard the faint whistle of the coming train, the one that was to transport the Weymouth name into the regions of dishonor and shame. All fear left him. He took off his hat and faced the chief of the clan he served, the great, royal, kind, lofty, terrible Weymouth,—he bearded him there at the brink of the awful thing that was about to happen.

"Marse Robert," he began, his voice quavering a little with the stress of his feelings, "you 'member de day dey-all rode de tunnament at Oak Lawn? De day, suh, dat you win in de ridin', and you crown Miss Lucy de queen?"

"Tournament?" said Mr. Robert, taking his cigar from his mouth. "Yes, I remember very well the—but what the deuce are you talking about tournaments here at midnight for? Go 'long home, Bushrod. I believe you're sleepwalking."

"Miss Lucy tetch you on de shoulder," continued the old man, never heeding, "wid a s'ord, and say: 'I mek you a knight, Suh Robert—rise up, pure and fearless and widout reproach.' Dat what Miss Lucy say. Dat's been a long time ago, but me nor you ain't forgot it. And den dar's another time we ain't forgot—de time when Miss Lucy lay on her las' bed. She sent for Uncle Bushrod, and she say: 'Uncle Bushrod, when I die, I want you to take good care of Mr. Robert. Seem like'—so Miss Lucy say—'he listen to you mo' dan to anybody else. He apt to be mighty fractious sometimes, and maybe he cuss you when you try to 'suade him but he need somebody what understand him to be 'round wid him. He am like a little child sometimes'—so Miss Lucy say, wid her eyes shinin' in her po', thin face—'but he always been'—dem was her words—'my knight, pure and fearless and widout reproach.' "

Mr. Robert began to mask, as was his habit, a tendency to soft-heartedness with a spurious anger.

"You—you old windbag!" he growled through a cloud of swirling cigar smoke. "I believe you are crazy. I told you to go home, Bushrod. Miss Lucy said that, did she? Well, we haven't kept the scutcheon very clear. Two years ago last week, wasn't it, Bushrod, when she died? Confound it! Are you going to stand there all night gabbing like a coffee-colored gander?"

The train whistled again. Now it was at the water tank, a mile away.

"Marse Robert," said Uncle Bushrod, laying his hand on the satchel that the banker held. "For Gawd's sake, don't take dis wid you. I knows what's in it. I knows where you got it in de bank. Don' kyar it wid you. Dey's big trouble in dat valise for Miss Lucy and Miss Lucy's child's chillun. Hit's bound to destroy de name of Weymouth and bow dem dat own it wid shame and triberlation. Marse Robert, you can kill dis ole nigger ef you will, but don't take away dis 'er' valise. If I ever crosses over de Jordan, what I gwine to say to Miss Lucy when she ax me: 'Uncle Bushrod, wharfo' didn' you take good care of Mr. Robert?' "

Mr. Robert Weymouth threw away his cigar and shook free one arm with that peculiar gesture that always preceded his outbursts of irascibility. Uncle Bushrod bowed his head to the expected storm, but he did not flinch. If the house of Weymouth was to fall, he would fall with it. The banker spoke, and Uncle Bushrod blinked with surprise. The storm was there, but it was suppressed to the quietness of a summer breeze.

"Bushrod," said Mr. Robert, in a lower voice than he usually employed, "you have overstepped all bounds. You have presumed upon the leniency with which you have been treated to meddle unpardonably. So you know what is in this satchel! Your long and faithful service is some excuse, but—go home, Bushrod—not another word!"

But Bushrod grasped the satchel with a firmer hand. The headlight of the train was lightening the shadows about the station. The roar was increasing, and folks were stirring about at the track side.

"Marse Robert, gimme dis 'er' valise. I got a right, suh, to talk to you dis 'er' way. I slaved for you and 'tended to you from a child up. I went th'ough de war as yo' body-servant tell we whipped de Yankees and sent 'em back to de No'th. I was at yo' weddin', and I was n' fur away when yo' Miss Letty was bawn. And Miss Letty's chillun, dey watches to-day for Uncle Bushrod when he comes home ever' evenin'. I been a' Weymouth, all 'cept in color and entitlements. Both of us is old, Marse Robert. Tain't goin' to be long tell we gwine to see Miss Lucy and has to give an account of our doin's. De old nigger man won't be 'spected to say much mo' dan he done all he could by de fambly dat owned him. But de Weymouths, dey must say dey been livin' pure and fearless and widout reproach. Gimme dis valise, Marse Robert—I'm gwine to hab it. I'm gwine to take it back to the bank and lock it up in de vault. I'm gwine to do Miss Lucy's biddin'. Turn 'er loose, Marse Robert."

The train was standing at the station. Some men were pushing trucks along the side. Two or three sleepy passengers got off and wandered away into the night. The conductor stepped to the gravel, swung his lantern and called: "Hello, Frank!" at some one invisible. The bell clanged, the brakes hissed, the conductor drawled: "All aboard!"

Mr. Robert released his hold on the satchel. Uncle Bushrod hugged it to his breast with both arms, as a lover clasps his first beloved.

"Take it back with you, Bushrod," said Mr. Robert, thrusting his hands into his pockets. "And let the subject drop—now mind! You've said quite enough. I'm going to take this train. Tell Mr. William I will be back on Saturday. Good-night."

The banker climbed the steps of the moving train and disappeared in a coach. Uncle Bushrod stood motionless, still embracing the precious satchel. His eyes were closed and his lips were moving in thanks to the Master above for the salvation of the Weymouth honor. He knew Mr. Robert would return when he said he would. The Weymouths never lied. Nor now, thank the Lord! could it be said that they embezzled the money in banks.

Then awake to the necessity for further guardianship of Weymouth trust funds, the old man started for the bank with the redeemed satchel.

Three hours from Weymouthville, in the gray dawn, Mr. Robert alighted from the train at a lonely flag-station. Dimly he could see the figure of a man waiting on the platform and the shape of a spring-wagon, team and driver. Half a dozen lengthy bamboo fishing-poles projected from the wagon's rear.

"You're here, Bob," said Judge Archinard, Mr. Robert's old friend and schoolmate. "It's going to be a royal day for fishing. I thought you said—why, didn't you bring along the stuff?"

The president of the Weymouth Bank took off his hat and rumpled his gray locks.

"Well, Ben, to tell the truth, there's an infernally presumptuous old nigger belonging in my family that broke up the arrangement. He came down to the depot and vetoed the whole proceeding. He means all right, and—well, I reckon he is right. Somehow, he had found out what I had along—though I hid it in the bank vault and sneaked it out at midnight. I reckon he has noticed that I've been indulging a little more than a gentleman should, and he laid for me with some reaching arguments.

"I'm going to quit drinking," Mr. Robert concluded. "I've come to the conclusion that a man can't keep it up and be quite what he'd like to be—'pure and fearless and without reproach'—that's the way old Bushrod quoted it."

"Well, I'll have to admit," said the judge, thoughtfully, as they climbed into the wagon, "that the old darkey's argument can't conscientiously be overruled."

"Still," said Mr. Robert, with a ghost of a sigh, "there was two quarts of the finest old silk-velvet Bourbon in that satchel you ever wet your lips with."

Phœbe

"You are a man of many novel adventures and varied enterprises," I said to Captain Patricio Maloné. "Do you believe that the possible element of good luck or bad luck—if there is such a thing as luck—has influenced your career or persisted for or against you to such an extent that you were forced to attribute results to the operation of the aforesaid good luck or bad luck?"

This question (of almost the dull insolence of legal phraseology) was put while we sat in Rousselin's little red-tiled café near Congo Square in New Orelans.

Brown-faced, white-hatted, finger-ringed captains of adventure came often to Rousselin's for the cognac. They came from sea and land, and were chary of relating the things they had seen—not because they were more wonderful than the fantasies of the Ananiases of print, but because they were so different. And I was a perpetual wedding-guest, always striving to cast my buttonhole over the finger of one of these mariners of fortune. This Captain Maloné was a Hiberno-Iberian creole who had gone to and fro in the earth and walked up and down in it. He looked like any other well-dressed man of thirty-five whom you might meet, except that he was hopelessly weather-tanned, and wore on his chain an ancient ivory-and-gold Peruvian charm against evil, which has nothing at all to do with his story.

"My answer to your question," said the captain, smiling, "will be to tell you the story of Bad-Luck Kearny. That is, if you don't mind hearing it."

My reply was to pound on the table for Rousselin.

"Strolling along Tchoupitoulas Street one night," began Captain Maloné, "I noticed, without especially taxing my interest, a small man walking rapidly toward me. He stepped upon a wooden cellar door, crashed through it, and disappeared. I rescued him from a heap of soft coal below. He dusted himself briskly, swearing fluently in a mechanical tone, as an underpaid actor recites the gipsy's curse. Gratitude and the dust in his throat seemed to call for fluids to clear them away. His desire for liquidation was expressed so heartily that I went with him to a café down the street where we had some vile vermouth and bitters.

"Looking across that little table I had my first clear sight of Francis Kearny. He was about five feet seven, but as tough as a cypress knee. His hair was darkest red, his mouth such a mere slit that you wondered how the flood of his words came rushing from it. His eyes were the brightest and lightest blue and the hopefullest that I ever saw. He gave the double impression that he was at bay and that you had better not crowd him further.

" 'Just in from a gold-hunting expedition on the coast of Costa Rica,' he explained. 'Second mate of a banana steamer told me the natives were panning out enough from the beach sands to buy all the rum, red calico, and parlor melodeons in the world. The day I got there a syndicate named Incorporated Jones gets a government concession to all minerals from a given point. For the next choice I take coast fever and count green and blue lizards for six weeks in a grass hut. I had to be notified when I was well, for the reptiles were actually there. Then I shipped back as third cook on a Norwegian tramp that blew up her boiler two miles below Quarantine. I was due to bust through that cellar door here to-night, so I hurried the rest of the way up the river, roustabouting on a lower coast packet that made a landing for every fisherman that wanted a plug of tobacco. And now I'm here for what comes next. And it'll be along, it'll be along,' said this queer Mr. Kearny; 'it'll be along on the beams of my bright but not very particular star.'

"From the first the personality of Kearny charmed me. I saw in him the bold heart, the restless nature, and the valiant front against the buffets of fate that make his countrymen such valuable comrades in risk and adventure. And just then I was wanting such men. Moored at a fruit company's pier I had a 500-ton steamer ready to sail the next day with a cargo of sugar, lumber, and corrugated iron for a port in—well, let us call the country Esperando—it has not been long ago, and the name of Patricio Maloné is still spoken there when its unsettled politics are discussed. Beneath the sugar and iron were packed a thousand Winchester rifles. In Aguas Frias, the capital, Don Rafael Valdevia, Minister of War, Esperando's greatest-hearted and most able patriot, awaited my coming. No doubt you have heard, with a smile, of the insignificant wars and uprisings in those little tropic republics. They make but a faint clamor against the din of great nations' battles; but down there, under all the ridiculous uniforms and petty diplomacy and senseless countermarching and intrigue, are to be found statesmen and patriots. Don Rafael Valdevia was one. His great ambition was to raise Esperando into peace and honest prosperity and the respect of the serious nations. So he waited for my rifles in Aguas Frias. But one would think I am trying to win a recruit in you! No; it was Francis Kearny I wanted. And so I told him, speaking long over our execrable vermouth, breathing the stifling odor from garlic and tarpaulins, which, as you know, is the distinctive flavor of cafés in the lower slant of our city. I spoke of the tyrant President Cruz and the burdens that his greed and insolent cruelty laid upon the people. And at that Kearny's tears flowed. And then I dried them with a picture of the fat rewards that would be ours when the oppressor should be overthrown and the wise and generous Valdevia in his seat. Then Kearny leaped to his feet and wrung my hand with the strength of a roustabout. He was mine, he said, till the last minion of the hated despot was hurled from the highest peaks of the Cordilleras into the sea.

"I paid the score and we went out. Near the door Kearny's elbow overturned an upright glass showcase, smashing it into little bits. I paid the storekeeper the price he asked.

" 'Come to my hotel for the night,' I said to Kearny. 'We sail tomorrow at noon.'

"He agreed; but on the sidewalk he fell to cursing again in the dull, monotonous, glib way that he had done when I pulled him out of the coal cellar.

" 'Captain,' said he, 'before we go any further, it's no more than fair to tell you that I'm known from Baffin's Bay to Tierra del Fuego as "Bad-Luck" Kearny. And I'm It. Everything I get into goes up in the air except a balloon. Every bet I ever made I lost except when I coppered it. Every boat I ever sailed on sank except the submarines. Everything I was ever interested in went to pieces except a patent bombshell that I invented. Everything I ever took hold of and tried to run I ran into the ground except when I tried to plough. And that's why they call me Bad-Luck Kearny. I thought I'd tell you.'

" 'Bad-luck,' said I, 'or what goes by the name, may now and then tangle the affairs of any man. But if it persists beyond the estimate of what we may call the "averages" there must be a cause for it.'

" 'There is,' said Kearny, emphatically, 'and when we walk another square I will show it to you.'

"Surprised, I kept by his side until we came to Canal Street and out into the middle of its great width.

"Kearny seized me by an arm and pointed a tragic fore-finger at a rather brilliant star that shone steadily about thirty degrees above the horizon.

" 'That's Saturn,' said he, 'the star that presides over bad luck and evil and disappointment and nothing doing and trouble. I was born under that star. Every move I make, up bobs Saturn and blocks it. He's the hoodoo planet of the heavens. They say he's 73,000 miles in diameter and no solider body than split-pea soup, and he's got as many disreputable and malignant rings as Chicago. Now, what kind of a star is that to be born under?'

"I asked Kearny where he had obtained all this astonishing knowledge.

" 'From Azrath, the great astrologer of Cleveland, Ohio,' said he. 'That man looked at a glass ball and told me my name before I'd taken a chair. He prophesied the date of my birth and death before I'd said a word. And then he cast my horoscope, and the sidereal system socked me in the solar plexus. It was bad luck for Francis Kearny from A to Izard and for his friends that were implicated with him. For that I gave up ten dollars. This Azrath was sorry, but he respected his profession too much to read the heavens wrong for any man. It was night time, and he showed me which Saturn was, and how to find it in different balconies and longitudes.

" 'But Saturn wasn't all. He was only the man higher up. He furnishes so much bad luck that they allow him a gang of deputy sparklers to help hand it out. They're circulating and revolving and hanging around the main supply all the time, each one throwing the hoodoo on his own particular district.

" 'You see that ugly little red star about eight inches above and to the right of Saturn?' Kearny asked me. 'Well, that's her. That's Phœbe. She's got me in charge. "By the day of your birth," says Azrath to me, "your life is subjected to the influence of Saturn. By the hour and minute of it you must dwell under the sway and direct authority of Phœbe, the ninth satellite." So said this Azrath.' Kearny shook his fist viciously skyward. 'Curse her, she's done her work well,' said he. 'Ever since I was astrologized, bad luck has followed me like my shadow, as I told you. And for many years before. Now, Captain, I've told you my handicap as a man should. If you're afraid this evil star of mine might cripple your scheme, leave me out of it.'

"I reassured Kearny as well as I could. I told him that for the time we would banish both astrology and astronomy from our heads. The manifest valor and enthusiasm of the man drew me. 'Let us see what a little courage and diligence will do against bad luck,' I said. 'We will sail to-morrow for Esperando.'

"Fifty miles down the Mississippi our steamer broke her rudder. We sent for a tug to tow us back and lost three days. When we struck the blue waters of the Gulf, all the storm clouds of the Atlantic seemed to have concentrated above us. We thought surely to sweeten those leaping waves with our sugar, and to stack our arms and lumber on the floor of the Mexican Gulf.

"Kearny did not seek to cast off one iota of the burden of our danger from the shoulders of his fatal horoscope. He weathered every storm on deck, smoking a black pipe, to keep which alight rain and sea-water seemed but as oil. And he shook his fist at the black clouds behind which his baleful star winked its unseen eye. When the skies cleared one evening, he reviled his malignant guardian with grim humor.

" 'On watch, aren't you, you red-headed vixen? Out making it hot for little Francis Kearny and his friends, according to Hoyle. Twinkle, twinkle, little devil! You're a lady, aren't you?—dogging a man with bad luck just because he happened to be born while your boss was floorwalker. Get busy and sink the ship, you one-eyed banshee. Phœbe! H'm! Sounds as mild as a milkmaid. You can't judge a woman by her name. Why couldn't I have had a man star? I can't make the remarks to Phœbe that I could to a man. Oh, Phœbe, you be—blasted!'

"For eight days gales and squalls and water-spouts beat us from our course. Five days only should have landed us in Esperando. Our Jonah swallowed the bad credit of it with appealing frankness; but that scarcely lessened the hardships our cause was made to suffer.

"At last one afternoon we steamed into the calm estuary of the little Rio Escondido. Three miles up this we crept, feeling for the shallow channel between the low banks that were crowded to the edge with gigantic trees and riotous vegetation. Then our whistle gave a little toot, and in five minutes we heard a shout and Carlos—my brave Carlos Quintana—crashed through the tangled vines waving his cap madly for joy.

"A hundred yards away was his camp, where three hundred chosen patriots of Esperando were awaiting our coming. For a month Carlos had been drilling them there in the tactics of war, and filling them with the spirit of revolution and liberty.

" 'My Captain—*compadre mío!*' shouted Carlos, while yet my boat was being lowered. 'You should see them in the drill by *companies*—in the column wheel—in the march by fours—they are superb! Also in the manual of arms—but, alas! performed only with sticks of bamboo. The guns, *captain*—say that you have brought the guns!'

" 'A thousand Winchesters, Carlos,' I called to him. 'And two Gatlings.'

" *'Válgame Dios!'* he cried, throwing his cap in the air. 'We shall sweep the world!'

"At that moment Kearny tumbled from the steamer's side into the river. He could not swim, so the crew threw him a rope and drew him back aboard. I caught his eye and his look of pathetic but still bright and undaunted consciousness of his guilty luck. I told myself that although he might be a man to shun, he was also one to be admired.

"I gave orders to the sailing-master that the arms, ammunition, and provisions were to be landed at once. That was easy in the steamer's boats, except for the two Gatling guns. For their transportation ashore we carried a stout flatboat, brought for the purpose in the steamer's hold.

"In the meantime I walked with Carlos to the camp and made the soldiers a little speech in Spanish, which they received with enthusiasm; and then I had some wine and a cigarette in Carlos's tent. Later we walked back to the river to see how the unloading was being conducted.

"The small arms and provisions were already ashore, and the petty officers had squads of men conveying them to camp. One Gatling had been safely landed; the other was just being hoisted over the side of the vessel as we arrived. I noticed Kearny darting about on board, seeming to have the ambition of ten men, and to be doing the work of five. I think his zeal bubbled over when he saw Carlos and me. A rope's end was swinging loose from some part of the tackle. Kearny leaped impetuously and caught it. There was a crackle and a hiss and a smoke of scorching hemp, and the Gatling dropped straight as a plummet through the bottom of the flatboat and buried itself in twenty feet of water and five feet of river mud.

"I turned my back on the scene. I heard Carlos's loud cries as if from some extreme grief too poignant for words. I heard the complaining murmur of the crew and the maledictions of Torres, the sailing-master—I could not bear to look.

"By night some degree of order had been restored in camp. Military rules were not drawn strictly, and the men were grouped about the fires of their several messes, playing games of chance, singing their native songs, or discussing with voluble animation the contingencies of our march upon the capital.

"To my tent, which had been pitched for me close to that of my chief lieutenant, came Kearny, indomitable, smiling, bright-eyed, bearing no traces of the buffets of his evil star. Rather was his aspect that of a heroic martyr whose tribulations were so high-sourced and glorious that he even took a splendor and a prestige from them.

" 'Well, Captain,' said he, 'I guess you realize that Bad-Luck Kearny is still on deck. It was a shame, now, about that gun. She only needed to be slewed two inches to clear the rail; and that's why I grabbed that rope's end. Who'd have thought that a sailor—even a Sicilian lubber on a banana coaster—would have fastened a line in a bow-knot? Don't think I'm trying to dodge the responsibility, Captain. It's my luck.'

" 'There are men, Kearny,' said I, gravely, 'who pass through life blaming upon luck and chance the mistakes that result from their own faults and incompetency. I do not say that you are such a man. But if all your mishaps are traceable to that tiny star, the sooner we endow our colleges with chairs of moral astronomy, the better.'

" 'It isn't the size of the star that counts,' said Kearny; 'it's the quality. Just the way it is with women. That's why they gave the biggest planets masculine names, and the little stars feminine ones—to even things up when it comes to getting their work in. Suppose they had called my star Agamemnon or Bill McCarty or something like that instead of Phœbe. Every time one of those old boys touched their calamity button and sent me down one of their wireless pieces of bad luck, I could talk back and tell 'em what I thought of 'em in suitable terms. But you can't address such remarks to a Phœbe.'

" 'It pleases you to make a joke of it, Kearny,' said I, without smiling. 'But it is no joke to me to think of my Gatling mired in the river ooze.'

" 'As to that,' said Kearny, abandoning his light mood at once, 'I have already done what I could. I have had some experience in hoisting stone in quarries. Torres and I have already spliced three hawsers and stretched them from the steamer's stern to a tree on shore. We will rig a tackle and have the gun on terra firma before noon to-morrow.'

"One could not remain long at outs with Bad-Luck Kearny.

" 'Once more,' said I to him, 'we will waive this question of luck. Have you ever had experience in drilling raw troops?'

" 'I was first sergeant and drill-master,' said Kearny, 'in the Chilean army for one year. And Captain of artillery for another.'

" 'What became of your command?' I asked.

" 'Shot down to a man,' said Kearny, 'during the revolutions against Balmaceda.'

"Somehow the misfortunes of the evil-starred one seemed to turn to me their comedy side. I lay back upon my goat's-hide cot and laughed until the woods echoed. Kearny grinned. 'I told you how it was,' he said.

" 'To-morrow,' I said, 'I shall detail one hundred men under your command for manual-of-arms drill and company evolutions. You will rank as lieutenant. Now, for God's sake, Kearny,' I urged him, 'try to combat this superstition if it is one. Bad luck may be like any other visitor—preferring to stop where it is expected. Get your mind off stars. Look upon Esperando as your planet of good fortune.'

" 'I thank you, Captain,' said Kearny quietly. 'I will try to make it the best handicap I ever ran.'

"By noon the next day the submerged Gatling was rescued, as Kearny had promised. Then Carlos and Manuel Ortiz and Kearny (my lieutenants) distributed Winchesters among the troops and put them through an incessant rifle drill. We fired no shots, blank or solid, for of all coasts Esperando is the stillest; and we had no desire to sound any warnings in the ear of that corrupt government until they should carry with them the message of Liberty and the downfall of Oppression.

"In the afternoon came a mule-rider bearing a written message to me from Don Rafael Valdevia in the capital, Aguas Frias.

"Whenever that man's name comes to my lips, words of tribute to his greatness, his noble simplicity, and his conspicuous genius follow irrepressibly. He was a traveller, a student of peoples and governments, a master of sciences, a poet, an orator, a leader, a soldier, a critic of the world's campaigns and the idol of the people of Esperando. I had been honored by his friendship for years. It was I who first turned his mind to the thought that he should leave for his monument a new Esperando—a country freed from the rule of unscrupulous tyrants, and a people made happy and prosperous by wise and impartial legislation. When he had consented he threw himself into the cause with the undivided zeal with which he endowed all of his acts. The coffers of his fortune were opened to those of us to whom were entrusted the secret moves of the game. His popularity was already so great that he had practically forced President Cruz to offer him the portfolio of Minister of War.

"The time, Don Rafael said in his letter, was ripe. Success, he prophesied, was certain. The people were beginning to clamor publicly against Cruz's misrule. Bands of citizens in the capital were even going about of nights hurling stones at public buildings and expressing their dissatisfaction. A bronze statue of President Cruz in the Botanical Gardens had been lassoed about the neck and overthrown. It only remained for me to arrive with my force and my thousand rifles, and for himself to come forward and proclaim himself the people's savior, to overthrow Cruz in a single day. There would be but a half-hearted resistance from the six hundred government troops stationed in the capital. The country was ours. He presumed that by this time my steamer had arrived at Quintana's camp. He proposed the eighteenth of July for the attack. That would give us six days in which to strike camp and march to Aguas Frias. In the meantime Don Rafael remained my good friend and *compadre en la causa de la libertad*.

"On the morning of the 14th we began our march toward the sea-following range of mountains, over the sixty-mile trail to the capital. Our small arms and provisions were laden on pack mules. Twenty men harnessed to each Gatling gun rolled them smoothly along the flat, alluvial lowlands. Our troops, well shod and well fed, moved with alacrity and heartiness. I and my three lieutenants were mounted on the tough mountain ponies of the country.

"A mile out of camp one of the pack mules, becoming stubborn, broke away from the train and plunged from the path into the thicket. The alert Kearny spurred quickly after it and intercepted its flight.

Rising in his stirrups, he released one foot and bestowed upon the mutinous animal a hearty kick. The mule tottered and fell with a crash broadside upon the ground. As we gathered around it, it walled its great eyes almost humanly toward Kearny and expired. That was bad; but worse, to our minds, was the concomitant disaster. Part of the mule's burden had been one hundred pounds of the finest coffee to be had in the tropics. The bag burst and spilled the priceless brown mass of the ground berries among the dense vines and weeds of the swampy land. *Mala suerte!* When you take away from an Esperandan his coffee, you abstract his patriotism and 50 per cent of his value as a soldier. The men began to rake up the precious stuff; but I beckoned Kearny back along the trail where they would not hear. The limit had been reached.

"I took from my pocket a wallet of money and drew out some bills.

" 'Mr. Kearny,' said I, 'here are some funds belonging to Don Rafael Valdevia, which I am expending in his cause. I know of no better service it can buy for him than this. Here is one hundred dollars. Luck or no luck, we part company here. Star or no star, calamity seems to travel by your side. You will return to the steamer. She touches at Amotapa to discharge her lumber and iron, and then puts back to New Orleans. Hand this note to the sailing-master, who will give you passage.' I wrote on a leaf torn from my book, and placed it and the money in Kearny's hand.

" 'Good-bye,' I said, extending my own. 'It is not that I am displeased with you; but there is no place in this expedition for—let us say, the Señorita Phœbe.' I said this with a smile, trying to smooth the thing for him. 'May you have better luck, *compañero*.'

"Kearny took the money and the paper.

" 'It was just a little touch,' said he, 'just a little lift with the toe of my boot—but what's the odds?—that blamed mule would have died if I had only dusted his ribs with a powder puff. It was my luck. Well, Captain, I would have liked to be in that little fight with you over in Aguas Frias. Success to the cause. *Adiós!*'

"He turned around and set off down the trail without looking back. The unfortunate mule's pack-saddle was transferred to Kearny's pony, and we again took up the march.

"Four days we journeyed over the foot-hills and mountains, fording icy torrents, winding around the crumbling brows of ragged peaks, creeping along the rocky flanges that overlooked awful precipices, crawling breathlessly over tottering bridges that crossed bottomless chasms.

"On the evening of the seventeenth we camped by a little stream on the bare hills five miles from Aguas Frias. At daybreak we were to take up the march again.

"At midnight I was standing outside my tent inhaling the fresh cold air. The stars were shining bright in the cloudless sky, giving the heavens their proper aspect of illimitable depth in distance when viewed from the vague darkness of the blotted earth. Almost at its zenith was the planet Saturn; and with a half-smile I observed the sinister red sparkle of his malignant attendant—the demon star of Kearny's ill luck. And then my thoughts strayed across the hills to the scene of our coming triumph where the heroic and noble Don Rafael awaited our coming to set a new and shining star in the firmament of nations.

"I heard a slight rustling in the deep grass to my right. I turned and saw Kearny coming toward me. He was ragged and dew-drenched and limping. His hat and one boot were gone. About one foot he had tied some makeshift of cloth and grass. But his manner as he approached was that of a man who knows his own virtues well enough to be superior to rebuffs.

" 'Well, sir,' I said, staring at him coldly, 'if there is anything in persistence, I see no reason why you should not succeed in wrecking and ruining us yet.'

" 'I kept half a day's journey behind,' said Kearny, fishing out a stone from the covering of his lame foot, 'so the bad luck wouldn't touch you. I couldn't help it, Captain; I wanted to be in on this game. It was a pretty tough trip, especially in the department of the commissary. In the low grounds there were always bananas and oranges. Higher up it was worse; but your men left a good deal of goat meat hanging on the bushes in the camps. Here's your hundred dollars. You're nearly there now, Captain. Let me in on the scrapping to-morrow.'

" 'Not for a hundred times a hundred would I have the tiniest thing go wrong with my plans now,' I said, 'whether caused by evil planets or the blunders of mere man. But yonder is Aguas Frias, five miles away, and a clear road. I am of the mind to defy Saturn and all his satellites to spoil our success now. At any rate, I will not turn away to-night as weary a traveller and as good a soldier as you are, Lieutenant Kearny. Manuel Ortiz's tent is there by the brightest fire. Rout him out and tell him to supply you with food and blankets and clothes. We march again at daybreak.'

"Kearny thanked me briefly but with feeling and moved away.

"He had gone scarcely a dozen steps when a sudden flash of bright light illumined the surrounding hills; a sinister, growing, hissing sound like escaping steam filled my ears. Then followed a roar as of distant thunder, which grew louder every instant. This terrifying noise culminated in a tremendous explosion, which seemed to rock the hills as an earthquake would; the illumination waxed to a glare so fierce that I clapped my hands to my eyes to save them. I thought the end of the world had come. I could think of no natural phenomenon that would explain it. My wits were staggering. The deafening explosion trailed off into the rumbling roar that had preceded it; and through this I heard the frightened shouts of my troops as they stumbled from their resting places and rushed wildly about. Also I heard the harsh tones of Kearny's voice crying: 'They'll blame it on me, of course, and what the devil it is, it's not Francis Kearny that can give you an answer.'

"I opened my eyes. The hills were still there, dark and solid. It had not been, then, a volcano or an earthquake. I looked up at the sky and saw a comet-like trail crossing the zenith and extending westward—a fiery trail waning fainter and narrower each moment.

" 'A meteor!' I called aloud. 'A meteor has fallen. There is no danger.'

"And then all other sounds were drowned by a great shout from Kearny's throat. He had raised both hands above his head and was standing tiptoe.

" 'PHŒBE'S GONE!' he cried, with all his lungs. 'She's busted and gone to hell. Look, Captain, the little red-headed hoodoo has blown herself to smithereens. She found Kearny too tough to handle, and she puffed up with spite and meanness till her boiler blew up. It'll be Bad-Luck Kearny no more. Oh, let us be joyful!

"Humpty Dumpty sat on a wall;
Humpty busted, and that'll be all!

"I looked up, wondering, and picked out Saturn in his place. But the small red twinkling luminary in his vicinity, which Kearny had pointed out to me as his evil star, had vanished. I had seen it there but half an hour before; there was no doubt that one of those awful and mysterious spasms of nature had hurled it from the heavens.

"I clapped Kearny on the shoulder.

" 'Little man,' said I, 'let this clear the way for you. It appears that astrology has failed to subdue you. Your horoscope must be cast anew with pluck and loyalty for controlling stars. I play you to win. Now, get to your tent, and sleep. Daybreak is the word.'

"At nine o'clock on the morning of the eighteenth of July I rode into Aguas Frias with Kearny at my side. In his clean linen suit and with his military poise and keen eye he was a model of a fighting adventurer. I had visions of him riding as commander of President Valdevia's bodyguard when the plums of the new republic should begin to fall.

"Carlos followed with the troops and supplies. He was to halt in a wood outside the town and remain concealed there until he received the word to advance.

"Kearny and I rode down the Calle Ancha toward the *residencia* of Don Rafael at the other side of the town. As we passed the superb white buildings of the University of Esperando, I saw at an open window the gleaming spectacles and bald head of Herr Bergowitz, professor of the natural sciences and friend of Don Rafael and of me and of the cause. He waved his hand to me, with his broad, bland smile.

"There was no excitement apparent in Aguas Frias. The people went about leisurely as at all times; the market was thronged with bareheaded women buying fruit and *carne;* we heard the twang and tinkle of string bands in the patios of the *cantinas*. We could see that it was a waiting game that Don Rafael was playing.

"His *residencia* was a large but low building around a great courtyard in grounds crowded with ornamental trees and tropic shrubs. At his door an old woman who came informed us that Don Rafael had not yet risen.

" 'Tell him,' said I, 'that Captain Maloné and a friend wish to see him at once. Perhaps he has overslept.'

"She came back looking frightened.

" 'I have called,' she said, 'and rung his bell many times, but he does not answer.'

"I knew where his sleeping-room was. Kearny and I pushed by her and went to it. I put my shoulder against the thin door and forced it open.

"In an armchair by a great table covered with maps and books sat Don Rafael with his eyes closed. I touched his hand. He had been dead many hours. On his head above one ear was a wound caused by a heavy blow. It had ceased to bleed long before.

"I made the old woman call a *mozo,* and dispatched him in haste to fetch Herr Bergowitz.

"He came, and we stood about as if we were half stunned by the awful shock. Thus can the letting of a few drops of blood from one man's veins drain the life of a nation.

"Presently Herr Bergowitz stooped and picked up a darkish stone the size of an orange which he saw under the table. He examined it closely through his great glasses with the eye of science.

" 'A fragment,' said he, 'of detonating meteor. The most remarkable one in twenty years exploded above this city a little after midnight this morning.'

"The professor looked quickly up at the ceiling. We saw the blue sky through a hole the size of an orange nearly above Don Rafael's chair.

"I heard a familiar sound, and turned. Kearny had thrown himself on the floor and was babbling his compendium of bitter, blood-freezing curses against the star of his evil luck.

"Undoubtedly Phœbe had been feminine. Even when hurtling on her way to fiery dissolution and everlasting doom, the last word had been hers."

Captain Maloné was not unskilled in narrative. He knew the point where a story should end. I sat reveling in his effective conclusion when he aroused me by continuing:

"Of course," said he, "our schemes were at an end. There was no one to take Don Rafael's place. Our little army melted away like dew before the sun.

"One day after I had returned to New Orleans I related this story to a friend who holds a professorship in Tulane University.

"When I had finished he laughed and asked whether I had any knowledge of Kearny's luck afterward. I told him no, that I had seen him no more; but that when he left me, he had expressed confidence that his future would be successful now that his unlucky star had been overthrown.

" 'No doubt,' said the professor, 'he is happier not to know one fact. If he derives his bad luck from Phœbe, the ninth satellite of Saturn, that malicious lady is still engaged in overlooking his career. The star close to Saturn that he imagined to be her was near that planet simply by the chance of its orbit—probably at different times he has regarded many other stars that happened to be in Saturn's neighborhood as his evil one. The real Phœbe is visible only through a very good telescope.'

"About a year afterward," continued Captain Maloné, "I was walking down a street that crossed the Poydras Market. An immensely stout, pink-faced lady in black satin crowded me from the narrow sidewalk with a frown. Behind her trailed a little man laden to the gunwhales with bundles and bags of goods and vegetables.

"It was Kearny—but changed. I stopped and shook one of his hands, which still clung to a bag of garlic and red peppers.

" 'How is the luck old *compañero?*' I asked him. I had not the heart to tell him the truth about his star.

" 'Well,' he said, 'I am married, as you may guess.'

" 'Francis!' called the big lady, in deep tones, 'are you going to stop in the street talking all day?'

" 'I am coming, Phœbe dear,' said Kearny hastening after her."

Captain Maloné ceased again.

"After all, do you believe in luck?" I asked.

"Do you?" answered the captain, with his ambiguous smile shaded by the brim of his soft straw hat.

A Double-Dyed Deceiver

The trouble began in Laredo. It was the Llano Kid's fault, for he should have confined his habit of manslaughter to Mexicans. But the Kid was past twenty; and to have only Mexicans to one's credit at twenty is to blush unseen on the Rio Grande border.

It happened in old Justo Valdos's gambling house. There was a poker game at which sat players who were not all friends, as happens often where men ride in from afar to shoot Folly as she gallops. There was a row over so small a matter as a pair of queens; and when the smoke had cleared away it was found that the Kid had committed an indiscretion, and his adversary had been guilty of a blunder. For, the unfortunate combatant, instead of being a Greaser, was a high-blooded youth from the cow ranches, of about the Kid's own age and possessed of friends and champions. His blunder in missing the

Kid's right ear only a sixteenth of an inch when he pulled his gun did not lessen the indiscretion of the better marksman.

The Kid, not being equipped with a retinue, nor bountifully supplied with personal admirers and supporters—on account of a rather umbrageous reputation, even for the border—considered it not incompatible with his indisputable gameness to perform that judicious traditional act known as "pulling his freight."

Quickly the avengers gathered and sought him. Three of them overtook him within a rod of the station. The Kid turned and showed his teeth in that brilliant but mirthless smile that usually preceded his deeds of insolence and violence, and his pursuers fell back without making it necessary for him even to reach for his weapon.

But in this affair the Kid had not felt the grim thirst for encounter that usually urged him on to battle. It had been a purely chance row, born of the cards and certain epithets impossible for a gentleman to brook that had passed between the two. The Kid had rather liked the slim, haughty, brown-faced young chap whom his bullet had cut off in the first pride of manhood. And now he wanted no more blood. He wanted to get away and have a good long sleep somewhere in the sun on the mesquite grass with his handkerchief over his face. Even a Mexican might have crossed his path in safety while he was in this mood.

The Kid openly boarded the north-bound passenger train that departed five minutes later. But at Webb, a few miles out, where it was flagged to take on a traveller, he abandoned that manner of escape. There were telegraph stations ahead; and the Kid looked askance at electricity and steam. Saddle and spur were his rocks of safety.

The man whom he had shot was a stranger to him. But the Kid knew that he was of the Coralitos outfit from Hidalgo; and that the punchers from that ranch were more relentless and vengeful than Kentucky feudists when wrong or harm was done to one of them. So, with the wisdom that has characterized many great fighters, the Kid decided to pile up as many leagues as possible of chaparral and pear between himself and the retaliation of the Coralitos bunch.

Near the station was a store; and near the store, scattered among the mesquite and elms, stood the saddled horses of the customers. Most of them waited, half asleep, with sagging limbs and drooping heads. But one, a long-legged roan with a curved neck, snorted and pawed the turf. Him the Kid mounted, gripped with his knees, and slapped gently with the owner's own quirt.

If the slaying of the temerarious card-player had cast a cloud over the Kid's standing as a good and true citizen, this last act of his veiled his figure in the darkest shadows of disrepute. On the Rio Grande border if you take a man's life you sometimes take trash; but if you take his horse, you take a thing the loss of which renders him poor, indeed, and which enriches you not—if you are caught. For the Kid there was no turning back now.

With the springing roan under him he felt little care or uneasiness. After a five-mile gallop he drew into the plainsman's jogging trot, and rode north-eastward toward the Nueces River bottoms. He knew the country well—its most tortuous and obscure trails through the great wilderness of brush and pear, and its camps and lonesome ranches where one might find safe entertainment. Always he bore to the east; for the Kid had never seen the ocean, and he had a fancy to lay his hand upon the mane of the great Gulf, the gamesome colt of the greater waters.

So after three days he stood on the shore at Corpus Christi, and looked out across the gentle ripples of a quiet sea.

Captain Boone, of the schooner *Flyaway,* stood near his skiff, which one of his crew was guarding in the surf. When ready to sail he had discovered that one of the necessaries of life, in the parallelogrammatic shape of plug tobacco, had been forgotten. A sailor had been dispatched for the missing cargo. Meanwhile the captain paced the sands, chewing profanely at his pocket store.

A slim, wiry youth in high-heeled boots came down to the water's edge. His face was boyish, but with a premature severity that hinted at a man's experience. His complexion was naturally dark; and the sun and wind of an outdoor life had burned it to a coffee-brown. His hair was as black and straight as an Indian's; his face had not yet been upturned to the humiliation of a razor; his eyes were a cold and steady blue. He carried his left arm somewhat away from his body, for pearl handled .45s are frowned upon by town marshals, and are a little bulky when packed in the left armhole of one's vest. He looked beyond Captain Boone at the gulf with the impersonal and expressionless dignity of a Chinese emperor.

"Thinkin' of buyin' that 'ar gulf, buddy?" asked the captain, made sarcastic by his narrow escape from the tobaccoless voyage.

"Why, no," said the Kid gently, "I reckon not. I never saw it before. I was just looking at it. Not thinking of selling it, are you?"

"Not this trip," said the captain. "I'll send it to you C.O.D. when I get back to Buenas Tierras. Here comes that capstan-footed lubber with the chewin'. I ought to've weighed anchor an hour ago."

"Is that your ship out there?" asked the Kid.

"Why, yes," answered the captain, "if you want to call a schooner a ship, and I don't mind lyin'. But you better say Miller and Gonzales, owners, and ordinary plain, Billy-be-damned old Samuel K. Boone, skipper."

"Where are you going to?" asked the refugee.

"Buenas Tierras, coast of South America—I forget what they called the country the last time I was there. Cargo—lumber, corrugated iron, and machetes."

"What kind of a country is it?" asked the Kid—"hot or cold?"

"Warmish, buddy," said the captain. "But a regular Paradise Lost for elegance of scenery and be-yooty of geography. Ye're wakened every morning by the sweet singin' of red birds with seven purple tails, and the sighin' of breezes in the posies and roses. And the inhabitants never work, for they can reach out and pick steamer baskets of the choicest hothouse fruit without gettin' out of bed. And there's no Sunday and no ice and no rent and no troubles and no use and no nothin'. It's a great country for a man to go to sleep with, and wait for somethin' to turn up. The bananys and oranges and hurricanes and pineapples that ye eat comes from there."

"That sounds to me!" said the Kid, at last betraying interest. "What'll the expressage be to take me out there with you?"

"Twenty-four dollars," said Captain Boone; "grub and transportation. Second cabin. I haven't got a first cabin."

"You've got my company," said the Kid, pulling out a buckskin bag.

With three hundred dollars he had gone to Laredo for his regular "blowout." The duel in Valdos's had cut short his season of hilarity, but it had left him with nearly $200 for aid in the flight that it had made necessary.

"All right, buddy," said the captain. "I hope your ma won't blame me for this little childish escapade of yours." He beckoned to one of the boat's crew. "Let Sanchez lift you out to the skiff so you won't get your feet wet."

Thacker, the United States consul at Buenas Tierras, was not yet drunk. It was only eleven o'clock; and he never arrived at his desired state of beatitude—a state where he sang ancient maudlin vaudeville songs and pelted his screaming parrot with banana peels—until the middle of the afternoon. So, when he looked up from his hammock at the sound of a slight cough, and saw the Kid standing in the door of the consulate, he was still in a condition to extend the hospitality and courtesy due from the representative of a great nation. "Don't disturb yourself," said the Kid easily. "I just dropped in. They told me it was customary to light at your camp before starting in to round up the town. I just came in on a ship from Texas."

"Glad to see you, Mr.———," said the consul.

The Kid laughed.

"Sprague Dalton," he said. "It sounds funny to me to hear it. I'm called the Llano Kid in the Rio Grande country."

"I'm Thacker," said the consul. "Take that cane-bottom chair. Now if you've come to invest, you want somebody to advise you. These dingies will cheat you out of the gold in your teeth if you don't understand their ways. Try a cigar?"

"Much obliged," said the Kid, "but if it wasn't for my corn shucks and the little bag in my back pocket I couldn't live a minute." He took out his "makings," and rolled a cigarette.

"They speak Spanish here," said the consul. "You'll need an interpreter. If there's anything I can do, why, I'd be delighted. If you're buying fruit lands or looking for a concession of any sort, you'll want somebody who knows the ropes to look out for you."

"I speak Spanish," said the Kid, "about nine times better than I do English. Everybody speaks it on the range where I come from. And I'm not in the market for anything."

"You speak Spanish?" said Thacker, thoughtfully. He regarded the Kid absorbedly.

"You look like a Spaniard, too," he continued. "And you're from Texas. And you can't be more than twenty or twenty-one. I wonder if you've got any nerve."

"You got a deal of some kind to put through?" asked the Texan, with unexpected shrewdness.

"Are you open to a proposition?" said Thacker.

"What's the use to deny it?" said the Kid. "I got into a little gun frolic down in Laredo, and plugged a white man. There wasn't any Mexican handy. And I come down to your parrot-and-monkey range just for to smell the morning-glories and marigolds. Now, do you *sabe?*"

Thacker got up and closed the door.

"Let me see your hand," he said.

He took the Kid's left hand, and examined the back of it closely.

"I can do it," he said, excitedly. "Your flesh is as hard as wood and as healthy as a baby's. It will heal in a week."

"If it's a fist fight you want to back me for," said the Kid, "don't put your money up yet. Make it gun work, and I'll keep you company. But no bare-handed scrapping, like ladies at a tea-party, for me."

"It's easier than that," said Thacker. "Just step here, will you?"

Through the window he pointed to a two-story white-stuccoed house with wide galleries rising amid the deep-green tropical foliage on a wooded hill that sloped gently from the sea.

"In that house," said Thacker, "a fine old Castilian gentleman and his wife are yearning to gather you into their arms and fill your pockets with money. Old Santos Urique lives there. He owns half the gold-mines in the country."

"You haven't been eating loco weed, have you?" asked the Kid.

"Sit down again," said Thacker, "and I'll tell you. Twelve years ago they lost a kid. No, he didn't die—although most of 'em here do from drinking the surface water. He was a wild little devil, even if he wasn't but eight years old. Everybody knows about it. Some Americans who were through here prospecting for gold had letters to Señor Urique, and the boy who was a favorite with them. They filled his head with big stories about the States; and about a month after they left, the kid disappeared, too. He was supposed to have stowed himself away among the banana bunches on a fruit steamer, and gone to New Orleans. He was seen once afterward in Texas, it was thought, but they never heard anything more of him. Old Urique has spent thousands of dollars having him looked for. The madam was broken up worst of all. The kid was her life. She wears mourning yet. But they say she believes he'll come back to her some day, and never gives up hope. On the back of the boy's left hand was tattooed a flying eagle carrying a spear in his claws. That's old Urique's coat of arms or something that he inherited in Spain."

The Kid raised his left hand slowly and gazed at it curiously.

"That's it," said Thacker, reaching behind the official desk for his bottle of smuggled brandy. "You're not so slow. I can do it. What was I consul at Sandakan for? I never knew till now. In a week I'll have the eagle bird with the frog-sticker blended in so you'd think you were born with it. I brought a set of the needles and ink just because I was sure you'd drop in some day, Mr. Dalton."

"Oh, hell," said the Kid. "I thought I told you my name!"

"All right, 'Kid,' then. I won't be that long. How does 'Señorito Urique' sound, for a change?"

"I never played son any that I remember of," said the Kid. "If I had any parents to mention they went over the divide about the time I gave my first bleat. What is the plan of your round-up?"

Thacker leaned back against the wall and held his glass up to the light.

"We've come now," said he, "to the question of how far you're willing to go in a little matter of the sort."

"I told you why I came down here," said the Kid simply.

"A good answer," said the consul. "But you won't have to go that far. Here's the scheme. After I get the trade-mark tattooed on your hand I'll notify old Urique. In the meantime I'll furnish you with all of your family history I can find out, so you can be studying up points to talk about. You've got the looks, you speak the Spanish, you know the facts, you can tell about Texas, you've got the tattoo mark. When I notify them that the rightful heir has returned and is waiting to know whether he will be received and pardoned what will happen? They'll simply rush down here and fall on your neck, and the curtain goes down for refreshments and a stroll in the lobby."

"I'm waiting," said the Kid. "I haven't had my saddle off in your camp long, pardner, and I never met you before; but if you intend to let it go at a parental blessing, why, I'm mistaken in my man, that's all."

"Thanks," said the consul. "I haven't met anybody in a long time that keeps up with an argument as well as you do. The rest of it is simple. If they take you in only for a while it's long enough. Don't give 'em time to hunt up the strawberry mark on your left shoulder. Old Urique keeps anywhere from $50,000 to $100,000 in his house all the time in a little safe that you could open with a shoe buttoner. Get it. My skill as a tattooer is worth half the boodle. We go halves and catch a tramp steamer for Rio Janeiro. Let the United States go to pieces if it can't get along without my services. *Qué dice, señor?*"

"It sounds to me!" said the Kid, nodding his head. "I'm out for the dust."

"All right, then," said Thacker. "You'll have to keep close until we get the bird on you. You can live in the back room here. I do my own cooking, and I'll make you as comfortable as a parsimonious government will allow me."

Thacker had set the time at a week, but it was two weeks before the design that he patiently tattooed upon the Kid's hand was to his notion. And then Thacker called a *muchacho,* and dispatched this note to the intended victim:

El Señor Don Santos Urique,
Las Casa Blanca,
My Dear Sir:

I beg permission to inform you that there is in my house as a temporary guest a young man who arrived in Buenas Tierras from the United States some days ago. Without wishing to excite any hopes that may not be realized, I think there is a possibility of his being your long-absent son. It might be well for you to call and see him. If he is, it is my opinion that his intention was to return to his home, but upon arriving here, his courage failed him from doubts as to how he would be received. Your true servant,

Thompson Thacker

Half an hour afterward—quick time for Buenas Tierras—Señor Urique's ancient landau drove to the consul's door, with the barefooted coachman beating and shouting at the team of fat, awkward horses.

A tall man with a white moustache alighted, and assisted to the ground a lady who was dressed and veiled in unrelieved black.

The two hastened inside, and were met by Thacker with his best diplomatic bow. By his desk stood a slender young man with clear-cut, sunbrowned features and smoothly brushed black hair.

Señora Urique threw back her heavy veil with a quick gesture. She was past middle age, and her hair was beginning to silver, but her full, proud figure and clear olive skin retained traces of the beauty peculiar to the Basque province. But, once you had seen her eyes, and comprehended the great sadness that was revealed in their deep shadows and hopeless expression, you saw that the woman lived only in some memory.

She bent upon the young man a long look of the most agonized questioning. Then her great black eyes turned, and her gaze rested upon his left hand. And then with a sob, not loud, but seeming to shake the room, she cried *"Hijo mío!"* and caught the Llano Kid to her heart.

A month afterward the Kid came to the consulate in response to a message sent by Thacker.

He looked the young Spanish caballero. His clothes were imported, and the wiles of the jewellers had not been spent upon him in vain.

A more than respectable diamond shone on his finger as he rolled a shuck cigarette.

"What's doing?" asked Thacker.

"Nothing much," said the Kid calmly. "I eat my first iguana steak to-day. They're them big lizards, you *sabe?* I reckon, though, that frijoles and side bacon would do me about as well. Do you care for iguanas, Thacker?"

"No, nor for some other kinds of reptiles," said Thacker.

It was three in the afternoon, and in another hour he would be in his state of beatitude.

"It's time you were making good, sonny," he went on, with an ugly look on his reddened face. "You're not playing up to me square. You've been the prodigal son for four weeks now, and you could have had veal for every meal on a gold dish if you'd wanted it. Now, Mr. Kid, do you think it's right to leave me out so long on a husk diet? What's the trouble? Don't you get your filial eyes on anything that looks like cash in the Casa Blanca? Don't tell me you don't. Everybody knows where old Urique keeps his stuff. It's U. S. currency, too; he don't accept anything else. What's doing? Don't say 'nothing' this time."

"Why, sure," said the Kid, admiring his diamond, "there's plenty of money up there. I'm no judge of collateral in bunches, but I will undertake for to say that I've seen the rise of $50,000 at a time in that tin grub box that my adopted father calls his safe. And he lets me carry the key sometimes just to show me that he knows I'm the real little Francisco that strayed from the herd a long time ago."

"Well, what are you waiting for?" asked Thacker angrily. "Don't you forget that I can upset your apple-cart any day I want to. If old Urique knew you were an impostor, what sort of things would happen to you? Oh, you don't know this country, Mr. Texas Kid. The laws here have got mustard spread between 'em. These people here'd stretch you out like a frog that had been stepped on, and give you about fifty sticks at every corner of the plaza. And they'd wear every stick out, too. What was left of you they'd feed to alligators."

"I might as well tell you now, pardner," said the Kid, sliding down low on his steamer chair, "that things are going to stay just as they are. They're about right now."

"What do you mean?" asked Thacker, rattling the bottom of his glass on his desk.

"The scheme's off," said the Kid. "And whenever you have the pleasure of speaking to me address me as Don Francisco Urique. I'll guarantee I'll answer to it. We'll let Colonel Urique keep his money. His little tin safe is as good as the time-locker in the First National Bank of Laredo as far as you and me are concerned."

"You're going to throw me down, then, are you?" said the consul.

"Sure," said the Kid, cheerfully. "Throw you down. That's it. And now I'll tell you why. The first night I was up at the colonel's house they introduced me to a bedroom. No blankets on the floor—a real room, with a bed and things in it. And before I was asleep, in comes this artificial mother of mine and tucks in the covers. 'Panchito,' she says, 'my little lost one, God has brought you back to me. I bless His name forever.' It was that, or some truck like that, she said. And down comes a drop or two of rain and hits me on the nose. And all that stuck by me, Mr. Thacker. And it's been that way ever since. And it's got to stay that way. Don't you think that it's for what's in it for me, either, that I say so. If you have any such ideas keep 'em to yourself. I haven't had much truck with women in my life, and no mothers to speak of, but here's a lady that we've got to keep fooled. Once she stood it; twice she won't. I'm a low-down wolf, and the devil may have sent me on this trail instead of God, but I'll travel it to the end. And now, don't forget that I'm Don Francisco Urique whenever you happen to mention my name."

"I'll expose you to-day, you—you double-dyed traitor," stammered Thacker.

The Kid arose and, without violence, took Thacker by the throat with a hand of steel, and shoved him slowly into a corner. Then he drew from under his left arm his pearl-handled .45 and poked the cold muzzle of it against the consul's mouth.

"I told you why I come here," he said, with his old freezing smile. "If I leave here, you'll be the reason. Never forget it, pardner. Now, what is my name?"

"Er—Don Francisco Urique," gasped Thacker.

From outside came a sound of wheels, and the shouting of someone, and the sharper thwacks of a wooden whipstock upon the backs of fat horses.

The Kid put up his gun, and walked toward the door. But he turned again and came back to the trembling Thacker, and held up his left hand with its back toward the consul.

"There's one more reason," he said, slowly, "why things have got to stand as they are. The fellow I killed in Laredo had one of them same pictures on his left hand."

Outside, the ancient landau of Don Santos Urique rattled to the door. The coachman ceased his bellowing. Señora Urique, in a voluminous gay gown of white lace and flying ribbons, leaned forward with a happy look in her great soft eyes.

"Are you within, dear son?" she called, in the rippling Castilian.

"*Madre mía, yo vengo* [mother, I come]," answered the young Don Francisco Urique.

A Retrieved Reformation

A guard came to the prison shoe-shop, where Jimmy Valentine was assiduously stitching uppers, and escorted him to the front office. There the warden handed Jimmy his pardon, which had been signed that morning by the governor. Jimmy took it in a tired kind of way. He had served nearly ten months of a four-year sentence. He had expected to stay only about three months, at the longest. When a man with as many friends on the outside as Jimmy Valentine had is received in the "stir" it is hardly worth while to cut his hair.

"Now, Valentine," said the warden, "you'll go out in the morning. Brace up, and make a man of yourself. You're not a bad fellow at heart. Stop cracking safes, and live straight."

"Me?" said Jimmy, in surprise. "Why, I never cracked a safe in my life."

"Oh, no," laughed the warden. "Of course not. Let's see, now. How was it you happened to get sent up on that Springfield job? Was it because you wouldn't prove an alibi for fear of compromising somebody in extremely high-toned society? Or was it simply a case of a mean old jury that had it in for you? It's always one or the other with you innocent victims."

"Me?" said Jimmy, still blankly virtuous. "Why, warden, I never was in Springfield in my life!"

"Take him back, Cronin," smiled the warden, "and fix him up with outgoing clothes. Unlock him at seven in the morning, and let him come to the bull-pen. Better think over my advice, Valentine."

At a quarter past seven on the next morning Jimmy stood in the warden's outer office. He had on a suit of the villainously fitting, ready-made clothes and a pair of the stiff, squeaky shoes that the state furnishes to its discharged compulsory guests.

The clerk handed him a railroad ticket and the five-dollar bill with which the law expected him to rehabilitate himself into good citizenship and prosperity. The warden gave him a cigar, and shook hands. Valentine, 9762, was chronicled on the books "Pardoned by Governor," and Mr. James Valentine walked out into the sunshine.

Disregarding the song of the birds, the waving green trees, and the smell of the flowers, Jimmy headed straight for a restaurant. There he tasted the first sweet joys of liberty in the shape of a broiled chicken and a bottle of white wine—followed by a cigar a grade better than the one the warden had given him. From there he proceeded leisurely to the depot. He tossed a quarter into the hat of a blind man sitting by the door, and boarded his train. Three hours set him down in a little town near the state line. He went to the café of one Mike Dolan and shook hands with Mike, who was alone behind the bar.

"Sorry we couldn't make it sooner, Jimmy, me boy," said Mike. "But we had that protest from Springfield to buck against, and the governor nearly balked. Feeling all right?"

"Fine," said Jimmy. "Got my key?"

He got his key and went upstairs, unlocking the door of a room at the rear. Everything was just as he had left it. There on the floor was still Ben Price's collar-button that had been torn from that eminent detective's shirt-band when they had overpowered Jimmy to arrest him.

Pulling out from the wall a folding-bed, Jimmy slid back a panel in the wall and dragged out a dust-covered suitcase. He opened this and gazed fondly at the finest set of burglar's tools in the East. It was a complete set, made of specially tempered steel, the latest designs in drills, punches, braces and bits, jimmies, clamps, and augers, with two or three novelties invented by Jimmy himself, in which he took pride. Over nine hundred dollars they had cost him to have made at———, a place where they make such things for the profession.

In half an hour Jimmy went downstairs and through the café. He was now dressed in tasteful and well-fitting clothes, and carried his dusted and cleaned suitcase in his hand.

"Got anything on?" asked Mike Dolan, genially.

"Me?" said Jimmy, in a puzzled tone. "I don't understand. I'm representing the New York Amalgamated Short Snap Biscuit Cracker and Frazzled Wheat Company."

This statement delighted Mike to such an extent that Jimmy had to take a seltzer-and-milk on the spot. He never touched "hard" drinks.

A week after the release of Valentine, 9762, there was a neat job of safe-burglary done in Richmond, Indiana, with no clue to the author. A scant eight hundred dollars was all that was secured. Two weeks after that a patented, improved, burglar-proof safe in Logansport was opened like a cheese to the tune of fifteen hundred dollars, currency; securities and silver untouched. That began to interest the rogue-catchers. Then an old-fashioned bank-safe in Jefferson City became active and threw out of its crater an eruption of bank-notes amounting to five thousand dollars. The loses were now high enough to bring the matter up into Ben Price's class of work. By comparing notes, a remarkable similarity in the methods of the burglaries was noticed. Ben Price investigated the scenes of the robberies, and was heard to remark:

"That's Dandy Jim Valentine's autograph. He's resumed business. Look at that combination knob—jerked out as easy as pulling up a radish in wet weather. He's got the only clamps that can do it. And look how clean those tumblers were punched out! Jimmy never has to drill but one hole. Yes, I guess I want Mr. Valentine. He'll do his bit next time without any short-time or clemency foolishness."

Ben Price knew Jimmy's habits. He had learned them while working up the Springfield case. Long jumps, quick get-aways, no confederates, and a taste for good society—these ways had helped Mr. Valentine to become noted as a successful dodger of retribution. It was given out that Ben Price had taken up the trail of the elusive cracksman, and other people with burglar-proof safes felt more at ease.

One afternoon Jimmy Valentine and his suitcase climbed out of the mail-hack in Elmore, a little town five miles off the railroad down in the black-jack country of Arkansas. Jimmy, looking like an athletic young senior just home from college, went down the board sidewalk toward the hotel.

A young lady crossed the street, passed him at the corner and entered a door over which was the sign "The Elmore Bank." Jimmy Valentine looked into her eyes, forgot what he was, and became another man. She lowered her eyes and colored slightly. Young men of Jimmy's style and looks were scarce in Elmore.

Jimmy collared a boy that was loafing on the steps of the bank as if he were one of the stock-holders, and began to ask him questions about the town, feeding him dimes at intervals. By and by the young lady came out, looking royally unconscious of the young man with the suitcase, and went her way.

"Isn't that young lady Miss Polly Simpson?" asked Jimmy, with specious guile.

"Naw," said the boy. "She's Annabel Adams. Her pa owns this bank. What'd you come to Elmore for? Is that a good watch-chain? I'm going to get a bulldog. Got any more dimes?"

Jimmy went to the Palmer Hotel, registered as Ralph D. Spencer, and engaged a room. He leaned on the desk and declared his platform to the clerk. He said he had come to Elmore to look for a location to go into business. How was the shoe business, now, in the town? He had thought of the shoe business. Was there an opening?

The clerk was impressed by the clothes and manner of Jimmy. He, himself, was something of a pattern of fashion to the thinly gilded youth of Elmore, but he now perceived his shortcomings. While trying to figure out Jimmy's manner of tying his four-in-hand he cordially gave information.

Yes, there ought to be a good opening in the shoe line. There wasn't an exclusive shoe-store in the place. The dry-goods and general stores handled them. Business in all lines was fairly good. Hoped Mr. Spencer would decide to locate in Elmore. He would find it a pleasant town to live in, and the people very sociable.

Mr. Spencer thought he would stop over in the town a few days and look over the situation. No, the clerk needn't call the boy. He would carry up his suitcase, himself; it was rather heavy.

Mr. Ralph Spencer, the phœnix that arose from Jimmy Valentine's ashes—ashes left by the flame of a sudden and alternative attack of love—remained in Elmore, and prospered. He opened a shoe-store and secured a good run of trade.

Socially he was also a success, and made many friends. And he accomplished the wish of his heart. He met Miss Annabel Adams, and became more and more captivated by her charms.

At the end of a year the situation of Mr. Ralph Spencer was this: he had won the respect of the community, his shoe-store was flourishing, and he and Annabel were engaged to be married in two weeks. Mr. Adams, the typical, plodding, country banker, approved of Spencer. Annabel's pride in him almost equalled her affection. He was as much at home in the family of Mr. Adams and that of Annabel's married sister as if he were already a member.

One day Jimmy sat down in his room and wrote this letter, which he mailed to the safe address of one of his old friends in St. Louis:

Dear Old Pal:

I want you to be at Sullivan's place, in Little Rock, next Wednesday night at nine o'clock. I want you to wind up some little matters for me. And, also, I want to make you a present of my kit of tools. I know you'll be glad to get them—you couldn't duplicate the lot for a thousand dollars. Say, Billy, I've quit the old business—a year ago. I've got a nice store. I'm making an honest living, and I'm going to marry the finest girl on earth two weeks from now. It's the only life, Billy—the straight one. I wouldn't touch a dollar of another man's money now for a million. After I get married I'm going to sell out and go West, where there won't be so much danger of having old scores brought up against me. I tell you, Billy, she's an angel. She believes in me; and I wouldn't do another crooked thing for the whole world. Be sure to be at Sully's, for I must see you. I'll bring along the tools with me.

Your old friend,

Jimmy

On the Monday night after Jimmy wrote this letter, Ben Price jogged unobtrusively into Elmore in a livery buggy. He lounged about town in his quiet way until he found out what he wanted to know. From the drug-store across the street from Spencer's shoe-store he got a good look at Ralph D. Spencer.

"Going to marry the banker's daughter are you, Jimmy?" said Ben to himself, softly. "Well, I don't know!"

The next morning Jimmy took breakfast at the Adamses. He was going to Little Rock that day to order his wedding-suit and buy something nice for Annabel. That would be the first time he had left town since he came to Elmore. It had been more than a year now since those last professional "jobs," and he thought he could safely venture out.

After breakfast quite a family party went down town together—Mr. Adams, Annabel, Jimmy, and Annabel's married sister with her two little girls, aged five and nine. They came by the hotel where Jimmy still boarded, and he ran up to his room and brought along his suitcase. Then they went on to the bank. There stood Jimmy's horse and buggy and Dolph Gibson, who was going to drive him over to the railroad station.

All went inside the high, carved oak railings into the banking-room—Jimmy included, for Mr. Adams's future son-in-law was welcome anywhere. The clerks were pleased to be greeted by the good-looking, agreeable young man who was going to marry Miss Annabel. Jimmy set his suitcase down. Annabel, whose heart was bubbling with happiness and lively youth, put on Jimmy's hat and picked up the suitcase. "Wouldn't I make a nice drummer?" said Annabel. "My! Ralph, how heavy it is. Feels like it was full of gold bricks."

"Lot of nickel-plated shoe-horns in there," said Jimmy, cooly, "that I'm going to return. Thought I'd save express charges by taking them up. I'm getting awfully economical."

The Elmore Bank had just put in a new safe and vault. Mr. Adams was very proud of it, and insisted on an inspection by every one. The vault was a small one, but it had a new patented door. It fastened with three solid steel bolts thrown simultaneously with a single handle, and had a time-lock. Mr. Adams beamingly explained its workings to Mr. Spencer, who showed a courteous but not too intelligent interest. The two children, May and Agatha, were delighted by the shining metal and funny clock and knobs.

While they were thus engaged Ben Price sauntered in and leaned on his elbow, looking casually inside between the railings. He told the teller that he didn't want anything; he was just waiting for a man he knew.

Suddenly there was a scream or two from the women, and a commotion. Unperceived by the elders, May, the nine-year-old girl, in a spirit of play, had shut Agatha in the vault. She had then shot the bolts and turned the knob of the combination as she had seen Mr. Adams do.

The old banker sprang to the handle and tugged at it for a moment. "The door can't be opened," he groaned. "The clock hasn't been wound nor the combination set."

Agatha's mother screamed again, hysterically.

"Hush!" said Mr. Adams, raising his trembing hand. "All be quiet for a moment, Agatha!" he called as loudly as he could: "Listen to me." During the following silence they could just hear the faint sound of the child wildly shrieking in the dark vault in a panic of terror.

"My precious darling!" wailed the mother. "She will die of fright! Open the door! Oh, break it open! Can't you men do something?"

"There isn't a man nearer than Little Rock who can open that door," said Mr. Adams, in a shaky voice. "My God! Spencer, what shall we do? That child—she can't stand it long in there. There isn't enough air, and, besides, she'll go into convulsions from fright."

Agatha's mother, frantic now, beat the door of the vault with her hands. Somebody wildly suggested dynamite. Annabel turned to Jimmy, her large eyes full of anguish, but not yet despairing. To a woman nothing seems quite impossible to the powers of the man she worships.

"Can't you do something, Ralph—*try*, won't you?"

He looked at her with a queer, soft smile on his lips and in his keen eyes.

"Annabel," he said, "give me that rose you are wearing, will you?"

Hardly believing that she heard him aright, she unpinned the bud from the bosom of her dress, and placed it in his hand. Jimmy stuffed it into his vest-pocket, threw off his coat and pulled up his shirt-sleeves. With that act Ralph D. Spencer passed away and Jimmy Valentine took his place.

"Get away from the door, all of you," he commanded, shortly.

He set his suitcase on the table, and opened it out flat. From that time on he seemed to be unconscious of the presence of any one else. He laid out the shining, queer implements swiftly and orderly, whistling softly to himself as he always did when at work. In a deep silence and immovable, the others watched him as if under a spell.

In a minute Jimmy's pet drill was biting smoothly into the steel door. In ten minutes—breaking his own burglarious record—he threw back the bolts and opened the door.

Agatha, almost collapsed, but safe, was gathered into her mother's arms.

Jimmy Valentine put on his coat, and walked outside the railings toward the front door. As he went he thought he heard a far-away voice that he once knew call "Ralph!" But he never hesitated.

At the door a big man stood somewhat in his way.

"Hello, Ben!" said Jimmy, still with his strange smile. "Got around at last, have you? Well, let's go. I don't know that it makes much difference, now."

And then Ben Price acted rather strangely.

"Guess you're mistaken, Mr. Spencer," he said. "Don't believe I recognize you. Your buggy's waiting for you, ain't it?"

And Ben Price turned and strolled down the street.

Friends in San Rosario

The west-bound stopped at San Rosario on time at 8:20 A.M. A man with a thick black-leather wallet under his arm left the train and walked rapidly up the main street of the town. There were other passengers who also got off at San Rosario, but they either slouched limberly over to the railroad eating-house or the Silver Dollar saloon, or joined the groups of idlers about the station.

Indecision had no part in the movements of the man with the wallet. He was short in stature, but strongly built, with very light, closely trimmed hair, smooth, determined face, and aggressive, gold-rimmed nose glasses. He was well dressed in the prevailing Eastern style. His air denoted a quiet but conscious reserve force, if not actual authority.

After walking a distance of three squares he came to the center of the town's business area. Here another street of importance crossed the main one, forming the hub of San Rosario's life and commerce. Upon one corner stood the postoffice. Upon another Rubensky's Clothing Emporium. The other two diagonally opposing corners were occupied by the town's two banks, the First National and the Stockmen's National. Into the First National Bank of San Rosario the newcomer walked, never slowing his brisk step until he stood at the cashier's window. The bank opened for business at nine, and the working force was already assembled, each member preparing his department for the day's business. The cashier was examining the mail when he noticed the stranger standing at his window.

"Bank doesn't open 'til nine," he remarked, curtly, but without feeling. He had had to make that statement so often to early birds since San Rosario adopted city banking hours.

"I am well aware of that," said the other man, in cool, brittle tones. "Will you kindly receive my card?"

The cashier drew the small spotless parallelogram inside the bars of his wicket, and read:

J.F.C. NETTLEWICK
NATIONAL BANK EXAMINER

"Oh—er—will you walk around inside, Mr.—er—Nettlewick. Your first visit—didn't know your business, of course. Walk right around, please."

The examiner was quickly inside the sacred precincts of the bank, where he was ponderously introduced to each employee in turn by Mr. Edlinger, the cashier—a middle-aged gentleman of deliberation, discretion, and method.

"I was kind of expecting Sam Turner round again, pretty soon," said Mr. Edlinger. "Sam's been examining us now for about four years. I guess you'll find us all right, though considering the tightness in business. Not overly much money on hand, but able to stand the storms, sir, stand the storms."

"Mr. Turner and I have been ordered by the Comptroller to exchange districts," said the examiner, in his decisive, formal tones. "He is covering my old territory in southern Illinois and Indiana. I will take the cash first, please."

Perry Dorsey, the teller, was already arranging his cash on the counter for the examiner's inspection. He knew it was right to a cent, and he had nothing to fear, but he was nervous and flustered. So was every man in the bank. There was something so icy and swift, so impersonal and uncompromising about this man that his very presence seemed an accusation. He looked to be a man who would never make nor overlook an error.

Mr. Nettlewick first seized the currency, and with a rapid, almost juggling motion, counted it by packages. Then he spun the sponge cup toward him and verified the count by bills. His thin, white fingers flew like some expert musician's upon the keys of a piano. He dumped the gold upon the counter with a crash, and the coins whined and sang as they skimmed across the marble slab from the tips of his nimble digits. The air was full of fractional currency when he came to the halves and quarters. He counted the last nickel and dime. He had the scales brought, and he weighed every sack of silver in the vault. He questioned Dorsey concerning each of the cash memoranda—certain checks, charge slips, etc., carried over from the previous day's work—with unimpeachable courtesy, yet with something so mysteriously momentous in his frigid manner, that the teller was reduced to pink cheeks and a stammering tongue.

This newly imported examiner was so different from Sam Turner. It had been Sam's way to enter the bank with a shout, pass the cigars, and tell the latest stories he had picked up on his rounds. His customary greeting to Dorsey had been, "Hello, Perry! Haven't skipped out with the boodle yet, I see." Turner's way of counting the cash had been different too. He would finger the packages of bills in a tired kind of way, and then go into the vault and kick over a few sacks of silver, and the thing was done. Halves and quarters and dimes? Not for Sam Turner. "No chicken feed for me," he would say when they were set before him. "I'm not in the agricultural department." But, then, Turner was a Texan, an old friend of the bank's president, and had known Dorsey since he was a baby.

While the examiner was counting the cash, Major Thomas B. Kingman—known to every one as "Major Tom"—the president of the First National, drove up to the side door with his old dun horse and buggy, and came inside. He saw the examiner busy with the money, and, going into the little "pony corral," as he called it, in which his desk was railed off, he began to look over his letters.

Earlier, a little incident had occurred that even the sharp eyes of the examiner had failed to notice. When he had begun his work at the cash counter, Mr. Edlinger had winked signficantly at Roy Wilson, the youthful bank messenger, and nodded his head slightly toward the front door. Roy understood, got his hat and walked leisurely out, with his collector's book under his arm. Once outside, he made a beeline for the Stockmen's National. That bank was also getting ready to open. No customers had, as yet, presented themselves.

"Say, you people!" cried Roy, with the familiarity of youth and long acquaintance, "you want to get a move on you. There's a new bank examiner over at the First, and he's a stem-winder. He's counting nickels on Perry, and he's got the whole outfit bluffed. Mr. Edlinger gave me the tip to let you know."

Mr. Buckley, president of the Stockmen's National—a stout, elderly man, looking like a farmer dressed for Sunday—heard Roy from his private office at the rear and called him.

"Has Major Kingman come down to the bank yet?" he asked of the boy.

"Yes, sir, he was just driving up as I left," said Roy.

"I want you to take him a note. Put it into his own hands as soon as you get back."

Mr. Buckley sat down and began to write.

Roy returned and handed to Major Kingman the envelope containing the note. The major read it, folded it, and slipped it into his vest pocket. He leaned back in his chair for a few moments as if he were meditating deeply, and then rose and went into the vault. He came out with the bulky, old-fashioned leather note case stamped on the back in gilt letters, "Bills Discounted." In this were the notes due the bank with their attached securities, and the major, in his rough way, dumped the lot upon his desk and began to sort them over.

By this time Nettlewick had finished his count of the cash. His pencil fluttered like a swallow over the sheet of paper on which he had set his figures. He opened his black wallet, which seemed to be also a kind of secret memorandum book, made a few rapid figures in it, wheeled and transfixed Dorsey with the glare of his spectacles. That look seemed to say: "You're safe this time, but . . . "

"Cash all correct," snapped the examiner. He made a dash for the individual bookkeeper, and, for a few minutes there was a fluttering of ledger leaves and a sailing of balance sheets through the air.

"How often do you balance your pass-books?" he demanded, suddenly.

"Er—once a month," faltered the individual bookkeeper, wondering how many years they would give him.

"All right," said the examiner, turning and charging upon the general bookkeeper, who had the statements of his foreign banks and their reconcilement memoranda ready. Everything there was found to be all right. Then the stub book of the certificates of deposit. Flutter—flutter—zip—zip—check! All right, list of over-drafts, please. Thanks. H'm-m. Unsigned bills of the bank next. All right.

Then came the cashier's turn, and easy-going Mr. Edlinger rubbed his nose and polished his glasses nervously under the quick fire of questions concerning the circulation, undivided profits, bank real estate, and stock ownership.

Presently Nettlewick was aware of a big man towering above him at his elbow—a man sixty years of age, rugged and hale, with a rough, grizzled beard, a mass of gray hair, and a pair of penetrating blue eyes that confronted the formidable glasses of the examiner without a flicker.

"Er—Major Kingman, our president—er—Mr. Nettlewick," said the cashier.

Two men of very different types shook hands. One was a finished product of the world of straights lines, conventional methods, and formal affairs. The other was something freer, wider, and nearer to nature. Tom Kingman had not been cut to any pattern. He had been mule-driver, cowboy, ranger, soldier, sheriff, prospector and cattleman. Now, when he was bank president, his old comrades from the prairies, of the saddle, tent, and trail, found no change in him. He had made his fortune when Texas cattle were at the high tide of value, and had organized the First National Bank of San Rosario. In spite of his largeness of heart and sometimes unwise generosity toward his old friends, the bank had prospered, for Major Tom Kingman knew men as well as he knew cattle. Of late years the cattle business had known a depression, and the major's bank was one of the few whose losses had not been great.

"And now," said the examiner, briskly, pulling out his watch, "the last thing is the loans. We will take them up now, if you please."

He had gone through the First National at almost record-breaking speed—but thoroughly, as he did everything. The running order of the bank was smooth and clean, and that had facilitated his work. There was but one other bank in the town. He received from the Government a fee of twenty-five dollars for each bank that he examined. He should be able to go over those loans and discounts in half an hour. If so, he could examine the other bank immediately afterward, and catch the 11:45, the only other train that day in the direction he was working. Otherwise, he would have to spend the night and Sunday in this uninteresting Western town. That was why Mr. Nettlewick was rushing matters.

"Come with me, sir," said Major Kingman, in his deep voice, that united the Southern drawl with the rhythmic twang of the West. "We will go over them together. Nobody in the bank knows those notes as I do. Some of 'em are a little wobbly on their legs, and some are mavericks without extra many brands on their backs, but they'll 'most all pay out at the round-up."

The two sat down at the president's desk. First, the examiner went through the notes at lightning speed, and added up their total, finding it to agree with the amount of loans carried on the book of daily balances. Next, he took up the larger loans, inquiring scrupulously into the condition of their endorsers or securities. The new examiner's mind seemed to course and turn and make unexpected dashes hither and thither like a bloodhound seeking a trail. Finally he pushed aside all the notes except a few, which he arranged in a neat pile before him, and began a dry, formal little speech.

"I find, sir, the condition of your bank to be very good, considering the poor crops and the depresion in the cattle interests of your state. The clerical work seems to be done accurately and punctually. Your past-due paper is moderate in amount, and promises only a small loss. I would recommend the calling in of your large loans, and the making of only sixty and ninety day or call loans until general business revives. And now, there is one thing more, and I will have finished with the bank. Here are six notes aggregating something like $40,000. They are secured, according to their faces, by various stocks, bonds, shares, etc., to the value of $70,000. Those securities are missing from the notes to which they should be attached. I suppose you have them in the safe or vault. You will permit me to examine them."

Major Tom's light-blue eyes turned unflinchingly toward the examiner.

"No, sir," he said, in a low but steady tone; "those securities are neither in the safe nor the vault. I have taken them. You may hold me personally responsible for their absence."

Nettlewick felt a slight thrill. He had not expected this. He had struck a momentous trail when the hunt was drawing to a close.

"Ah!" said the examiner. He waited a moment, and then continued: "May I ask you to explain more definitely?"

"The securities were taken by me," repreated the major. "It was not for my own use, but to save an old friend in trouble. Come in here, sir, and we'll talk it over."

He led the examiner into the bank's private office at the rear, and closed the door. There was a desk, and a table, and half-a-dozen leather-covered chairs. On the wall was the mounted head of a Texas steer with horns five feet from tip to tip. Opposite hung the major's old cavalry saber that he had carried at Shiloh and Fort Pillow.

Placing a chair for Nettlewick, the major seated himself by the window, from which he could see the post-office and the carved limestone front of the Stockman's National. He did not speak at once, and Nettlewick felt, perhaps, that the ice should be broken by something so near its own temperature as the voice of official warning.

"Your statement," he began, "since you have failed to modify it, amounts, as you must know, to a very serious thing. You are aware, also, of what my duty must compel me to do. I shall have to go before the United States Commissioner and make . . ."

"I know, I know," said Major Tom, with a wave of his hand. "You don't suppose I'd run a bank without being posted on national banking laws and the revised statutes! Do your duty. I'm not asking any favors. But I spoke of my friend. I did want you to hear me tell about Bob."

Nettlewick settled himself in his chair. There would be no leaving San Rosario for him that day. He would have to telegraph to the Comptroller of the Currency; he would have to swear out a warrant before the United States Commissioner for the arrest of Major Kingman; perhaps he would be ordered to close the bank on account of the loss of the securities. It was not the first crime the examiner had unearthed. Once or twice the terrible upheaval of human emotions that his investigations had loosed had almost caused a ripple in his official calm. He had seen bank men kneel and plead and cry like women for a chance—an hour's time—the overlooking of a single error. One cashier had shot himself at his desk before him. None of them had taken it with the dignity and coolness of this stern old Westerner. Nettlewick felt that he owed it to him at least to listen if he wished to talk. With his elbow on the arm of his chair, and his square chin resting upon the fingers of his right hand, the bank examiner waited to hear the confession of the president of the First National Bank of San Rosario.

"When a man's your friend," began Major Tom, somewhat didactically, "for forty years, and tried by water, fire, earth, and cyclones, when you can do him a little favor you feel like doing it."

("Embezzle for him $70,000 worth of securities," thought the examiner.)

"We were cowboys together, Bob and I," continued the major, speaking slowly, and deliberately, and musingly, as if his thoughts were rather with the past than the criticial present, "and we prospected together for gold and silver over Arizona, New Mexico, and a good part of California. We were both in the war of sixty-one, but in different commands. We've fought Indians and horse thieves side by side; we've starved for weeks in a cabin in the Arizona mountains, buried twenty feet deep in snow; we've ridden herd together when the wind blew so hard the lightning couldn't strike—well, Bob and I have been through some rough spells since the first time we met in the branding camp of the old Anchor-Bar ranch. And during that time we've found it necessary more than once to help each other out of tight places. In those days it was expected of a man to stick to his friend, and he didn't ask any credit for it. Probably next day you'd need him to get at your back and help stand off a band of Apaches, or put a tourniquet on your leg above a rattlesnake bite and ride for whisky. So, after all, it was give and take, and if you didn't stand square with your pardner, why, you might be shy one when you needed him. But Bob was a man who was willing to go further than that. He never played a limit.

"Twenty years ago I was sheriff of this county and I made Bob my chief deputy. That was before the boom in cattle when we both made our stake. I was sheriff and collector, and it was a big thing for me then. I was married, and we had a boy and a girl—a four and a six year old. There was a comfortable house next to the courthouse, furnished by the county, rent free, and I was saving some money. Bob did most of the office work. Both of us had seen rough times and plenty of rustling and danger, and I tell you it was great to hear the rain and the sleet dashing against the windows of nights, and be warm and safe and comfortable, and know you could get up in the morning and be shaved and have folks call you 'mister.' And then, I had the finest wife and kids that ever struck the range, and my old friend with me enjoying the first fruits of prosperity and white shirts, and I guess I was happy. Yes, I was happy about that time."

The major sighed and glanced casually out of the window. The bank examiner changed his position, and leaned his chin upon his other hand.

"One winter," continued the major, "the money for the county taxes came pouring in so fast that I didn't have time to take the stuff to the bank for a week. I just shoved the checks into a cigar box and the money into a sack, and locked them in the big safe that belonged in the sheriff's office.

"I had been overworked that week, and was about sick, anyway. My nerves were out of order, and my sleep at night didn't seem to rest me. The doctor had some scientific name for it, and I was taking medicine. And so, added to the rest, I went to bed at night with that money on my mind. Not that there was much need of being worried, for the safe was a good one, and nobody but Bob and I knew the combination. On Friday night there was about $6,500 in cash in the bag. On Saturday morning I went to the office as usual. The safe was locked, and Bob was writing at his desk. I opened the safe, and the money was gone. I called Bob, and roused everybody in the courthouse to announce the robbery. It struck me that Bob took it pretty quiet, considering how much it reflected upon both him and me.

"Two days went by and we never got a clew. It couldn't have been burglars, for the safe had been opened by the combination in the proper way. People must have begun to talk, for one aftrnoon in comes Alice—that's my wife—and the boy and girl, and Alice stamps her foot, and her eyes flash, and she cries out, 'The lying wretches—Tom, Tom!' and I catch her in a faint, and bring her 'round little by little, and she lays her head down and cries and cries for the first time since she took Tom Kingman's name and fortunes. And Jack and Zilla—the youngsters—they were always wild as tiger's cubs to rush at Bob and climb all over him whenever they were allowed to come to the courthouse—they stood and kicked their little shoes, and herded together like scared partridges. They were having their first trip down into the shadows of life. Bob was working at his desk, and he got up and went out without a word. The grand jury was in session then, and the next morning Bob went before them and confessed that he stole the money. He said he lost it in a poker game. In fifteen minutes they had found a true bill and sent me the warrant to arrest the man with whom I'd been closer than a thousand brothers for many a year.

"I did it, and then I said to Bob, pointing: 'There's my house, and here's my office, and up there's Maine, and out that way is California, and over there is Florida—and that's your range 'til court meets. You're in my charge, and I take the responsibility. You be here when you're wanted.'

" 'Thanks, Tom,' he said, kind of carelessly; 'I was sort of hoping you wouldn't lock me up. Court meets next Monday, so, if you don't object, I'll just loaf around the office until then. I've got one favor to ask, if it isn't too much. If you'd let the kids come out in the yard once in a while and have a romp I'd like it.'

" 'Why not?' I answered him. 'They're welcome, and so are you. And come to my house the same as ever.' You see, Mr. Nettlewick, you can't make a friend of a thief, but neither can you make a thief of a friend, all at once."

The examiner made no answer. At that moment was heard the shrill whistle of a locomotive pulling into the depot. That was the train on the little, narrow-gauge road that struck into San Rosario from the south. The major cocked his ear and listened for a moment, and looked at his watch. The narrow-gauge was in on time—10:35. The major continued.

"So Bob hung around the office, reading the papers and smoking. I put another deputy to work in his place, and, after a while, the first excitement of the case wore off.

"One day when we were alone in the office Bob came over to where I was sitting. He was looking sort of grim and blue—the same look he used to get when he'd been up watching for Indians all night or herd-riding.

" 'Tom,' says he, 'it's harder than standing off redskins; it's harder than lying in the lava desert forty miles from water; but I'm going to stick it out to the end. You know that's been my style. But if you'd tip me the smallest kind of a sign—if you'd just say, "Bob I understand," why, it would make it lots easier.'

"I was surprised. 'I don't know what you mean, Bob,' I said. 'Of course, you know that I'd do anything under the sun to help you that I could. But you've got me guessing.'

" 'All right, Tom,' was all he said, and he went back to his newspaper and lit another cigar.

"It was the night before the court met when I found out what he meant. I went to bed that night with the same old, light-headed, nervous feeling come back upon me. I dropped off to sleep about midnight. When I woke I was standing half dressed in one of the courthouse corridors. Bob was holding one of my arms, our family doctor the other and Alice was shaking me and half crying. She had sent for the doctor without my knowing it, and when he came they had found me out of bed and missing, and had begun a search.

" 'Sleep-walking,' said the doctor.

"All of us went back to the house, and the doctor told us some remarkable stories about the strange things people had done while in that condition. I was feeling rather chilly after my trip out, and, as my wife was out of the room at the time, I pulled open the door of an old wardrobe that stood in the room and dragged out a big quilt I had seen in there. With it tumbled out the bag of money for stealing which Bob was to be tried—and convicted—in the morning.

" 'How the jumping rattlesnakes did that get there?' I yelled, and all hands must have seen how surprised I was. Bob knew in a flash.

" 'You darned old snoozer,' he said, with the old-time look on his face, 'I saw you put it there. I watched you open the safe and take it out, and I followed you. I looked through the window and saw you hide it in that wardrobe.'

" 'Then, you blankety-blank, flop-eared, sheep-headed coyote, what did you say you took it for?'

" 'Because,' said Bob, simply, 'I didn't know you were asleep.'

"I saw him glance toward the door of the room where Jack and Zilla were, and I knew then what it meant to be a man's friend from Bob's point of view."

Major Tom paused, and again directed his glance out of the window. He saw someone in the Stockmen's National Bank reach and draw a yellow shade down the whole length of its plate-glass, big front window, although the position of the sun did not seem to warrant such a defensive movement against its rays.

Nettlewick sat up straight in his chair. He had listened patiently, but without consuming interest, to the major's story. It had impressed him as irrelevant to the situation, and it could certainly have no effect upon the consequences. Those Western people, he thought, had an exaggerated sentimentality. They were not business-like. They needed to be protected from their friends. Evidently the major had concluded. And what he had said amounted to nothing.

"May I ask," said the examiner, "if you have anything further to say that bears directly upon the question of those abstracted securities?"

"Abstracted securities, sir!" Major Tom turned suddenly in his chair, his blue eyes flashing upon the examiner. "What do you mean, sir?"

He drew from his coat pocket a batch of folded papers held together by a rubber band, tossed them into Nettlewick's hands, and rose to his feet.

"You'll find those securities there, sir, every stock, bond, and share of 'em. I took them from the notes while you were counting the cash. Examine and compare them for yourself."

The major led the way back into the banking room. The examiner, astounded, perplexed, nettled, at sea, followed. He felt that he had been made the victim of something that was not exactly a hoax, but that left him in the shoes of one who had been played upon, used, and then discarded, without even an inkling of the game. Perhaps, also, his official position had been irreverently juggled with. But there was nothing he could take hold of. An official report of the matter would be an absurdity. And, somehow, he felt that he would never know anything more about the matter than he did then.

Frigidly, mechanically, Nettlewick examined the securities, found them to tally with the notes, gathered his black wallet, and rose to depart.

"I will say," he protested, turning the indignant glare of his glasses upon Major Kingman, "that your statements—your misleading statements, which you have not condescended to explain—do not appear to be quite the thing, regarded either as business or humor. I do not understand such motives or actions."

Major Tom looked down at him serenely and not unkindly.

"Son," he said, "there are plenty of things in the chaparral, and on the prairies, and up on the cañons that you don't understand. But I want to thank you for listening to a garrulous old man's prosy story. We old Texans love to talk about our adventures and our old comrades, and the home folks have long ago learned to run when we begin with 'Once upon a time,' so we have to spin our yarns to the stranger within our gates."

The major smiled, but the examiner only bowed coldly, and abruptly quitted the bank. They saw him travel diagonally across the street in a straight line and enter the Stockmen's National Bank.

Major Tom sat down at his desk and drew from his vest pocket the note Roy had given him. He had read it once, but hurriedly, and now, with something like a twinkle in his eyes, he read it again. These were the words he read:

> Dear Tom: I hear there's one of Uncle Sam's greyhounds going through you, and that means that we'll catch him inside of a couple of hours, maybe. Now, I want you to do something for me. We've got just $2,200 in the bank, and the law requires that we have $20,000. I let Ross and Fisher have $18,000 late yesterday afternoon to buy up that Gibson bunch of cattle. They'll realize $40,000 in less than thirty days on the transaction, but that won't make my cash on hand look any prettier to that bank examiner. Now, I can't show him those notes, for they're just plain notes of hand without any security in sight, but you know very well that Pink Ross and Jim Fisher are two of the finest white men God ever made, and they'll do the square thing. You remember Jim Fisher—he was the one who shot that faro dealer in El Paso. I wired Sam Bradshaw's bank to send me $20,000, and it will get in on the narrow-gauge at 10:35. You can't let a bank examiner in to count $2,200 and close your doors. Tom, you hold that examiner. Hold him. Hold him if you have to rope him and sit on his head. Watch our front window after the narrow-gauge gets in, and when we've got the cash inside we'll pull down the shade for a signal. Don't turn him loose till then. I'm counting on you, Tom.
>
> Your Old Pard
> Bob Buckley,
> Prest. Stockmen's National

The major began to tear the note into small pieces and throw them into his waste basket. He gave a satisfied little chuckle as he did so.

"Confounded old reckless cowpuncher!" he growled, contentedly, "that pays him some on account for what he tried to do for me in the sheriff's office twenty years ago."

The Emancipation of Billy

In the old, old, square-porticoed mansion, with the wry window-shutters and the paint peeling off in discolored flakes lived one of the last of the war governors.

The South has forgotten the enmity of the great conflict, but it refuses to abandon its old traditions and idols. In "Governor" Pemberton, as he was still fondly called, the inhabitants of Elmville saw the relic of their state's ancient greatness and glory. In his day he had been a man large in the eye of his country. His state had pressed upon him every honor within its gift. And now when he was old, and enjoying a richly merited repose outside the swift current of public affairs, his townsmen loved to do him reverence for the sake of the past.

The Governor's decaying "mansion" stood upon the main street of Elmville within a few feet of its rickety paling-fence. Every morning the Governor would descend the steps with extreme care and deliberation—on account of his rheumatism—and then the click of his gold-headed cane would be heard as he slowly proceeded up the rugged brick sidewalk. He was now nearly seventy-eight, but he had grown old gracefully and beautifully. His rather long, smooth hair and flowing, parted whiskers were snow-white. His full-skirted frock-coat was always buttoned snugly about his tall, spare figure. He wore a high, well-kept silk hat—known as a "plug" in Elmville—and nearly always gloves. His manners were punctilious, and somewhat overcharged with courtesy.

The Governor's walks up Lee Avenue, the principal street, developed in their course into a sort of memorial, triumphant procession. Everyone he met saluted him with a profound respect. Many would remove their hats. Those who were honored with his personal friendship would pause to shake hands, and then you would see exemplified the genuine *beau idéal* Southern courtesy.

Upon reaching the corner of the second square from the mansion, the Governor would pause. Another street crossed the avenue there, and traffic, to the extent of several farmers' wagons and a peddler's cart or two, would rage about the junction. Then the falcon eye of General Deffenbaugh would perceive the situation, and the General would hasten, with ponderous solicitude, from his office in the First National Bank building to the assistance of his old friend.

When the two exchanged greetings the decay of modern manners would become accusingly apparent. The General's bulky and commanding figure would bend lissomely at a point where you would have regarded its ability to do so with incredulity. The Governor's cherished rheumatism would be compelled, for the moment, to give way before a genuflexion brought down from the days of the cavaliers. The Governor would take the General's arm and be piloted safely between the haywagons and the sprinkling-cart to the other side of the street. Proceeding to the post-office in the care of his friend, the esteemed statesman would there hold an informal levée among the citizens who were come for their morning mail. Here, gathering two or three prominent in law, politics, or family, the pageant would make a stately progress along the Avenue, stopping at the Palace Hotel where, perhaps, would be found upon the register the name of some guest deemed worthy of an introduction to the state's venerable and illustrious son. If any such were found, an hour or two would be spent in recalling the faded glories of the Governor's long-vanished administration.

On the return march the General would invariably suggest that, His Excellency being no doubt fatigued, it would be wise to recuperate for a few minutes at the Drug Emporium of Mr. Appleby R. Fentress (an elegant gentleman, sir—one of the Catham County Fentresses—so many of our best-blooded families have had to go into trade, sir, since the war).

Mr. Appleby R. Fentress was a connoisseur in fatigue. Indeed, if he had not been, his memory alone should have enabled him to prescribe, for the majestic invasion of his pharmacy was a casual happening that had surprised him almost daily for years. Mr. Fentress knew the formula of, and possessed the skill to compound, a certain potion antagonistic to fatigue, the salient ingredient of which he described (no doubt in pharmaceutical terms) as "genuine old hand-made Clover Leaf '59, Private Stock."

Nor did the ceremony of administering the potion ever vary. Mr. Fentress would first compound two of the celebrated mixtures—one for the Governor, and the other for the General to "sample." Then the Governor would make this little speech in his high, piping, quavering voice:

"No, sir—not one drop until you have prepared one for yourself and joined us, Mr. Fentress. Your father, sir, was one of my most valued supporters and friends during My Administration, and any mark of esteem I can confer upon his son is not only a pleasure but a duty, sir."

Blushing with delight at the royal condescension, the druggist would obey, and all would drink to the General's toast: "The prosperity of our grand old state, gentlemen—the memory of her glorious past—the health of her Favorite Son."

Some one of the Old Guard was always at hand to escort the Governor home. Sometimes the General's business duties denied him the privilege, and then Judge Broomfield or Colonel Titus, or one of the Ashford County Slaughters would be on hand to perform the rite.

Such were the observances attendant upon the Governor's morning stroll to the post-office. How much more magnificent, impressive, and spectacular, then, was the scene at public functions when the General would lead forth the silver-haired relic of former greatness, like some rare and fragile waxwork figure, and trumpet his pristine eminence to his fellow citizens!

General Deffenbaugh was the Voice of Elmville. Some said he was Elmville. At any rate, he had no competitor as the Mouthpiece. He owned enough stock in the *Daily Banner* to dictate its utterance, enough shares in the First National Bank to be the referee of its loans, and a war record that left him without a rival for first place at barbecues, school commencements, and Decoration Days. Besides these acquirements he was possessed with endowments. His personality was inspiring and triumphant. Undisputed sway had molded him to the likeness of a fatted Roman emperor. The tones of his voice were not otherwise than clarion. To say that the General was public-spirited would fall short of doing him justice. He had spirit enough for a dozen publics. And as a sure foundation for it all, he had a heart that was big and stanch. Yes; General Deffenbaugh was Elmville.

One little incident that usually occurred during the Governor's morning walk has had its chronicling delayed by more important matters. The procession was accustomed to halt before a small brick office on the Avenue, fronted by a short flight of steep wooden steps. A modest tin sign over the door bore the words: "Wm. B. Pemberton: Attorney-at-Law."

Looking inside, the General would roar: "Hello, Billy, my boy." The less-distinguished members of the escort would call: "Morning, Billy." The Governor would pipe: "Good-morning, William."

Then a patient-looking little man with hair turning gray along the temples would come down the steps and shake hands with each one of the party. All Elmville shook hands when it met.

The formalities concluded, the little man would go back to his table, heaped with law books and papers, while the procession would proceed.

Billy Pemberton was, as his sign declared, a lawyer, by profession. By occupation and common consent he was the Son of his Father. This was the shadow in which Billy lived, the pit out of which he had unsuccessfully striven for years to climb and, he had come to believe, the grave in which his ambitions were destined to be buried. Filial respect and duty he paid beyond the habit of most sons, but he aspired to be known and appraised by his own deeds and worth.

After many years of tireless labor he had become known in certain quarters far from Elmville as a master of the principles of the law. Twice he had gone to Washington and argued cases before the highest tribunal with such acute logic and learning that the silken gowns on the bench had rustled from the force of it. His income from his practice had grown until he was able to support his father, in the old family mansion (which neither of them would have thought of abandoning, rickety as it was) in the comfort and almost the luxury of the old extravagant days. Yet, he remained to Elmville as only "Billy" Pemberton, the son of our distinguished and honored fellow-townsman, "ex-Governor Pemberton." Thus was he introduced at public gatherings where he sometimes spoke, haltingly and prosily, for his talents were too serious and deep for extempore brilliancy; thus was he presented to strangers and to the lawyers who made the circuit of the courts; and so the *Daily Banner* referred to him in print. To be "the son of" was his doom. Whatever he should accomplish would have to be sacrificed upon the altar of this magnificent but fatal parental precedence.

The peculiarity and the saddest thing about Billy's ambition was that the only world he thirsted to conquer was Elmville. His nature was diffident and unassuming. National or State honors might have oppressed him. But, above all things, he hungered for the appreciation of the friends among whom he had been born and raised. He would not have plucked one leaf from the garlands that were so lavishly bestowed upon his father, he merely rebelled against having his own wreaths woven from those dried and self-same branchs. But Elmville "Billied" and "sonned" him to his concealed but lasting chagrin, until at length he grew more reserved and formal and studious than ever.

There came a morning when Billy found among his mail a letter from a very high source, tendering him the appointment to an important judicial position in the new island possessions of our country. The honor was a distinguished one, for the entire nation had discussed the probable recipients of these positions, and had agreed that the situation demanded only men of the highest character, ripe learning, and evenly balanced mind.

Billy could not subdue a certain exultation at this token of the success of his long and arduous labors, but, at the same time, a whimsical smile lingered around his mouth, for he foresaw in which Elmville would place the credit. "We congratulate Governor Pemberton upon the mark of appreciation conferred upon his son"—"Elmville rejoices with our honored citizen, Governor Pemberton, at his son's success"—"Put her there Billy!"—"Judge Billy Pemberton, sir; son of our State's war hero and the people's pride!"—these were the phrases, printed and oral, conjured up by Billy's prophetic fancy. Grandson of his State, and stepchild of Elmville—thus had fate fixed his kinship to the body politic.

Billy lived with his father in the old mansion. The two and an elderly lady—a distant relative—comprised the family. Perhaps, though, old Jeff, the Governor's ancient colored body-servant, should be included. Without doubt, he would have claimed the honor. There were other servants, but Thomas Jefferson Pemberton, sah, was a member of "de fambly."

Jeff was the one Elmvillian who gave to Billy the gold of approval unmixed with the alloy of paternalism. To him "Mars William" was the greatest man in Talbot County. Beaten upon though he was by the shining light that emanates from an ex-war governor, and loyal as he remained to the old *régime*, his faith and admiration were Billy's. As valet to a hero, and a member of the family, he may have had superior opportunities for judging.

Jeff was the first one to whom Billy revealed the news. When he reached home for supper Jeff took his "plug" hat and smoothed it before hanging it upon the hall-rack.

"Dar now!" said the old man: "I knowed it was er comin', I knowed it was gwine ter happen. Er judge, you says, Mars William? Dem Yankees done made you er judge? It's high time, sah, dey was doin' somep'n to make up for dey rescality endurin' de war. I boun' dey holds a confab and says: 'Le's make Mars William Pemberton er judge, and dat'll settle it.' Does you have to go away down to dem Fillypines, Mars William, or kin you judge 'em from here?"

"I'd have to live there most of the time of course," said Billy.

"I wonder what de Gubnor gwine say 'bout dat," speculated Jeff.

Billy wondered too.

After supper, when the two sat in the library, according to their habit, the Governor smoking his clay pipe and Billy his cigar, the son dutifully confessed to having been tendered the appointment.

For a long time the Governor sat, smoking, without making any comment. Billy reclined in his favorite rocker, waiting, perhaps still flushed with satisfaction over the tender that had come to him, unsolicited, in his dingy little office, above the heads of the intriguing, time-serving, clamorous multitude.

At last the Governor spoke; and, though his words were seemingly irrelevant, they were to the point. His voice had a note of martyrdom running through its senile quaver.

"My rheumatism has been growing steadily worse these past months, William."

"I am sorry, Father," said Billy, gently.

"And I am nearly seventy-eight. I am getting to be an old man. I can recall the names of but two or three who were in public life during My Administration. What did you say is the nature of this position that is offered you, William?"

"A Federal judgeship, Father. I believe it is considered to be a somewhat flattering tender. It is outside of politics and wire-pulling, you know."

"No doubt, no doubt. Few of the Pembertons have engaged in professional life for nearly a century. None of them have ever held Federal positions They have been landowners, slave-owners, and planters on a large scale. One or two of the Derwents—your mother's family—were in the law. Have you decided to accept this appointment, William?"

"I am thinking it over," said Billy, slowly, regarding the ash of his cigar.

"You have been a good son to me," continued the Governor, stirring his pipe with the handle of a penholder.

"I've been your son all my life," said Billy, darkly.

"I am often gratified," piped the Governor, betraying a touch of complacency, "by being congratulated upon having a son with such sound and sterling qualities. Especially in this, our native town, is your name linked with mine in the talk of our citizens."

"I never knew anyone to forget the vinculum," murmured Billy, unintelligibly.

"Whatever prestige," pursued the parent, "I may be possessed of, by virtue of my name and services to the state, has been yours to draw upon freely. I have not hesitated to exert it in your behalf whenever opportunity offered. And you have deserved it, William.

You've been the best of sons. And now this appointment comes to take you away from me. I have but a few years left to live. I am almost dependent upon others now, even in walking and dressing. What would I do without you, my son?"

The Governor's pipe dropped to the floor. A tear trickled from his eye. His voice had risen, and crumbled to a weakling falsetto, and ceased. He was an old, old man about to be bereft of the son that cherished him.

Billy rose, and laid his hand upon the Governor's shoulder.

"Don't worry, father," he said, cheerfully. "I'm not going to accept. Elmville is good enough for me. I'll write to-night and decline it."

At the next interchange of devoirs between the Governor and General Deffenbaugh on Lee Avenue, His Excellency, with a comfortable air of self-satisfaction, spoke of the appointment that had been tendered to Billy.

The General whistled.

"That's a plum for Billy," he shouted. "Who'd have thought that Billy—but, confound it, it's been in him all the time. It's a boost for Elmville. It'll send real estate up. It's an honor to our state. It's a compliment to the South. We've all been blind about Billy. When does he leave? We must have a reception. Great Gatlings! that job's eight thousand a year! There's been a car-load of lead-pencils worn to stubs figuring on those appointments. Think of it! Our little wood-sawing, mealy-mouthed Billy! Angel unawares doesn't begin to express it. Elmville is disgraced forever unless she lines up in a hurry for ratification and apology."

The venerable Moloch smiled fatuously. He carried the fire with which to consume all these tributes to Billy, the smoke of which would ascend as an incense to himself.

"Wiliam," said the Governor, with modest pride, "has declined the appointment. He refuses to leave me in my old age. He is a good son."

The General swung around and laid a large forefinger upon the bosom of his friend. Much of the General's success had been due to his dexterity in establishing swift lines of communication between cause and effect.

"Governor," he said, with a keen look in his big, ox-like eyes, "you've been complaining to Billy about your rheumatism."

"My dear General," replied the Governor, stiffly, "my son is forty-two. He is quite capable of deciding such questions for himself. And

I, as his parent, feel it my duty to state that your remark about—er—rheumatism is a mighty poor shot from a very small bore, sir, aimed at a purely personal and private affliction."

"If you will allow me," retorted the General, "you've afflicted the public with it for some time; and 'twas no small bore, at that."

This first tiff between the two old comrades might have grown into something more serious but for the fortunate interruption caused by the ostentatious approach of Colonel Titus and another one of the court retinue from the right county, to whom the General confided the coddled statesman and went his way.

After Billy had so effectually entombed his ambitions, and taken the veil, so to speak, in a sonnery, he was surprised to discover how much lighter of heart and happier he felt. He realized what a long, restless struggle he had maintained, and how much he had lost by failing to cull the simple but wholesome pleasure by the way. His heart warmed now to Elmville and the friends who had refused to set him upon a pedestal. It was better, he began to think, to be "Billy" and his father's son, and to be hailed familiarly by cheery neighbors and grown-up playmates, than to be "Your Honor," and sit among strangers, hearing, maybe, through the arguments of learned counsel, that old man's feeble voice crying: "What would I do without you, my son?"

Billy began to surprise his acquaintances by whistling as he walked up the street; others he astounded by slapping them disrespectfully upon their backs and raking up old anecdotes he had not had the time to recollect for years. Though he hammered away at his law cases as thoroughly as ever, he found more time for relaxation and the company of his friends. Some of the younger set were actually after him to join the golf club. A striking proof of his abandonment to obscurity was his adoption of a most undignified, rakish little soft hat, reserving the "plug" for Sundays and state occasions. Billy was beginning to enjoy Elmville, though that irreverent burgh had neglected to crown him with bay and myrtle.

All the while uneventful peace pervaded Elmville. The Governor continued to make his triumphal parades to the post-office with the General as chief marshal, for the slight squall that had rippled their friendship had, to all indications, been forgotten by both.

But one day Elmville woke to sudden excitement. The news had come that a touring presidential party would honor Elmville by a twenty-minute stop. The Executive had promised a five-minute address from the balcony of the Palace Hotel.

Elmville arose as one man—that man being, of course, General Deffenbaugh—to receive becomingly the chieftain of all the clans. The train with the tiny Stars and Stripes fluttering from the engine pilot arrived. Elmville had done her best. There were bands, flowers, carriages, uniforms, banners, and committees without end. High-school girls in white frocks impeded the steps of the party with roses strewn nervously in bunches. The chieftain had seen it all before—scores of times. He could have pictured it exactly in advance, from the Blue-and-Gray speech down to the smallest rosebud. Yet his kindly smile of interest greeted Elmville's display as if it had been the only and original.

In the upper rotunda of the Palace Hotel the town's most illustrious were assembled for the honor of being presented to the distinguished guests previous to the expected address. Outside, Elmville's inglorious but patriotic masses filled the streets.

Here, in the hotel General Deffenbaugh was holding in reserve Elmville's trump card. Elmville knew; for the trump was a fixed one, and its lead consecrated by archaic custom.

At the proper moment Governor Pemberton, beautifully venerable, magnificently antique, tall, paramount, stepped forward upon the arm of the General.

Elmville watched and harked with bated breath. Never until now—when a Northern President of the United States should clasp hands with ex-war-Governnor Pemberton—would the breach be entirely closed—would the country be made one and indivisible—no North, not much South, very little East, and no West to speak of. So Elmville excitedly scraped kalsomine from the walls of the Palace Hotel with its Sunday best, and waited for the Voice to speak.

And Billy! We had nearly forgotten Billy. He was cast for Son, and he waited patiently for his cue. He carried his "plug" in his hand, and felt serene. He admired his father's striking air and pose. After all, it was a great deal to be son of a man who could so gallantly hold the position of a cynosure for three generations.

General Deffenbaugh cleared his throat. Elmville opened its mouth, and squirmed. The chieftain with the kindly, fateful face was holding out his hand, smiling. Ex-war-Governor Pemberton extended his own across the chasm. But what was this the General was saying?

"Mr. President, allow me to present to you one who has the honor to be the father of our foremost distinguished citizen, learned and honored jurist, beloved townsman, and model Southern gentleman—the Honorable William B. Pemberton."

A Departmental Case

In Texas you may travel a thousand miles in a straight line. If your course is a crooked one, it is likely that both the distance and your rate of speed may be vastly increased. Clouds there sail serenely against the wind. The whippoorwill delivers its disconsolate cry with the notes exactly reversed from those of the Northern brother. Given a drought and a subsequently lively rain, and lo! from a glazed and stony soil will spring in a single night blossomed lilies, miraculously fair. Tom Green County was once the standard of measurement. I have forgotten how many New Jerseys and Rhode Islands it was that could have been stowed away and lost in its chaparral. But the legislative axe has slashed Tom Green into a handful of counties hardly larger than European kingdoms. The legislature convenes at Austin, near the center of the state; and, while the representative from Rio Grande country is gathering his palm leaf fan and his linen duster to set out for the capital, the Pan-handle solon winds his muffler above his well-buttoned overcoat and kicks the snow from his well-greased boots ready for the same journey. All this merely to hint that the big ex-republic of the Southwest forms a sizable star on the flag, and to prepare for the corollary that things sometimes happen there uncut to pattern and unfettered by metes and bounds.

The Commissioner of Insurance, Statistics, and History of the State of Texas was an official of no very great or very small importance. The past tense is used, for now he is Commissioner of Insurance alone. Statistics and history are no longer proper nouns in the government records.

In the year 188–, the governor appointed Luke Coonrod Standifer to be the head of this department. Standifer was then fifty-five years of age, and a Texan to the core. His father had been one of the state's earliest settlers and pioneers. Standifer himself had served the commonwealth as Indian fighter, soldier, ranger, and legislator. Much learning he did not claim, but he had drunk pretty deep of the spring of experience.

If other grounds were less abundant, Texas should be well up in the lists of glory as the grateful republic. For both as republic and state, it has busily heaped honors and solid rewards upon its sons who rescued it from the wilderness.

Wherefore and therefore, Luke Coonrod Standifer, son of Ezra Standifer, ex-Terry ranger, simon-pure democrat, and lucky dweller in an unrepresented portion of the politico-geographical map, was appointed Commissioner of Insurance, Statistics, and History.

Standifer accepted the honor with some doubt as to the nature of the office he was to fill and his capacity for filling it—but he accepted, and by wire. He immedidately set out from the little country town where he maintained (and was scarcely maintained by) a somnolent and unfruitful office of surveying and map-drawing. Before departing, he had looked under the I's, S's, and H's in the "Encyclopaedia Britannica" what information and preparation toward his official duties that those weighty volumes afforded.

A few weeks of incumbency diminished the new commissioner's awe of the great and important office he had been called upon to conduct. An increasing familiarity with its workings soon restored him to his accustomed placid course of life. In his office was an old spectacled clerk—a consecrated, informed, able machine, who held his desk regardless of changes of administrative heads. Old Kauffman instructed his new chief gradually in the knowledge of the department without seeming to do so, and kept the wheels revolving without the slip of a cog.

Indeed, the Department of Insurance, Statistics, and History carried no great heft of the burden of state. Its main work was the regulating of the business done in the state by foreign insurance companies, and the letter of the law was its guide. As for statistics—well, you wrote letters to county officers, and scissored other people's reports, and each year you got out a report of your own about the corn crop and the cotton crop and pecans and pigs and black and white population, and a great many columns of figures headed "bushels" and "acres" and "square miles," etc.—and there you were. History? The branch was purely a receptive one. Old ladies interested in the science bothered you some with long reports of proceedings of their historical societies. Some twenty or thirty people would write you each year that they had secured Sam Houston's pocket-knife or Santa Ana's whisky-flask or Davy Crockett's rifle—all absolutely authenticated—and demanded legislative appropriation to purchase. Most of the work in the history branch went into pigeonholes.

One sizzling August afternoon the commissioner reclined in his office chair, with his feet upon the long, official table covered with green billiard cloth. The commissioner was smoking a cigar, and dreamily regarding the quivering landscape framed by the window that looked upon the treeless capitol grounds. Perhaps he was thinking of the rough and ready life he had led, of the old days of breathless adventure and movement, of the comrades who now trod other paths or had ceased to tread any, of the changes civilization and peace had brought, and, maybe, complacently, of the snug and comfortable camp pitched for him under the dome of the capitol of the state that had not forgotten his services.

The business of the department was lax. Insurance was easy. Statistics were not in demand. History was dead. Old Kauffman, the efficient and perpetual clerk, had requested an infrequent half-holiday, incited to the unusual dissipation by the joy of having successfully twisted the tail of a Connecticut insurance company that was trying to do business contrary to the edicts of the great Lone Star State.

The office was very still. A few subdued noises trickled in through the open door from the other departments—a dull tinkling crash from the treasurer's office adjoining, as a clerk tossed a bag of silver to the floor of the vault—the vague intermittent clatter of a dilatory typewriter—a dull tapping from the state geologist's quarters as if some woodpecker had flown in to bore for his prey in the cool of the massive building—and then a faint rustle, and the light shuffling of the well-worn shoes along the hall, the sounds ceasing at the door toward which the commissioner's lethargic back was presented. Following this, the sound of a gentle voice speaking words unintelligible to the commissioner's somewhat dormant comprehension, but giving evidence of bewilderment and hesitation.

The voice was feminine; the commissioner was of the race of cavaliers who make salaam before the trail of a skirt without considering the quality of its cloth.

There stood in the door a faded woman, one of the numerous sisterhood of the unhappy. She was dressed all in black—poverty's perpetual mourning for lost joys. Her face had the contours of twenty and the lines of forty. She may have lived that intervening score of years in a twelve-month. There was about her yet an aurum of indignant, unappeased, protesting youth that shone faintly through the premature veil of unearned decline.

"I beg your pardon, ma'am," said the commissioner, gaining his feet to the accompaniment of a great creaking and sliding of his chair.

"Are you the governor, sir?" asked the vision of melancholy.

The commissioner hesitated at the end of his best bow, with his hand in the bosom of his double-breasted "frock." Truth at last conquered.

"Well, no, ma'am. I am not the governor. I have the honor to be Commissioner of Insurance, Statistics, and History. Is there anything, ma'am, I can do for you? Won't you have a chair, ma'am?"

The lady subsided into the chair handed her, probably from purely physical reasons. She wielded a cheap fan—last token of gentility to be abandoned. Her clothing seemed to indicate a reduction almost to extreme poverty. She looked at the man who was not the governor, and saw kindliness and simplicity and a rugged, unadorned courtliness emanating from a countenance tanned, and toughened by forty years of outdoor life. Also, she saw that his eyes were clear and strong and blue. Just as they had been when he used them to skim the horizon for raiding Kiowas and Sioux. His moth was as set and firm as it had been on that day when he bearded the old Lion Sam Houston himself, and defied him during that season when secession was the theme. Now, in bearing and dress, Luke Coonrod Standifer endeavored to do credit to the important arts and sciences of Insurance, Statistics, and History. He had abandoned the careless dress of his country home. Now, his broad-brimmed black slouch hat, and his long-tailed "frock" made him not the least imposing of the official family, even if his office was reckoned to stand at the tail of the list.

"You wanted to see the governor, ma'am?" asked the commissioner, with a deferential manner he always used toward the fair sex.

"I hardly know," said the lady, hesitatingly. "I suppose so." And then, suddenly drawn by the sympathetic look of the other, she poured forth the story of her need.

It was a story so common that the public has come to look at its monotony instead of its pity. The old tale of an unhappy married life—made so by a brutal, conscienceless husband, a robber, a spendthrift, a moral coward, and a bully, who failed to provide even the means of the barest existence. Yes, he had come down in the scale so low as to strike her. It happened only the day before—there was the bruise on one temple—she had offended his highness by asking for a little money to live on. And yet she must needs, womanlike, append a plea for her tyrant—he was drinking; he had rarely abused her thus when sober.

"I thought," mourned this pale sister of sorrow, "that maybe the state might be willing to give me some relief. I've heard of such things being done for the families of old settlers. I've heard tell that the state used to give land to the men who fought for it against Mexico, and settled up the country, and helped drive out the Indians. My father did all of that, and he never received anything. He never would take it. I thought the governor would be the one to see, and that's why I came. If Father was entitled to anything, they might let it come to me."

"It's possible, ma'am," said Standifer, "that such might be the case. But 'most all the veterans and settlers got their land certificates issued and located long ago. Stil, we can look that up in the land office and be sure. Your father's name, now, was . . ."

"Amos Colvin, sir."

"Good Lord!" exclaimed Standifer, rising and unbuttoning his tight coat, excitedly. "Are you Amos Colvin's daughter? Why, ma'am, Amos Colvin and me were thicker than two hoss thieves for more than ten years! We fought Kiowas, drove cattle, and rangered side by side nearly all over Texas. I remember seeing you once before now. You were a kid, about seven, a-riding a little yellow pony up and down. Amos and me stopped at your home for a little grub when we were trailing that band of Mexican cattle thieves down through Karnes and Bee. Great tarantulas! and you're Amos Colvin's little girl! Did you ever hear your father mention Luke Standifer—just kind of casually—as if he'd met me once or twice?"

A little pale smile flitted across the lady's white face.

"It seems to me," she said, "that I don't remember hearing him talk about much else. Every day there was some story he had to tell about what he and you had done. Mighty near the last thing I heard him tell was about the time when the Indians wounded him, and you crawled out to him through the grass, with a canteen of water while they———"

"Yes, yes—well—oh, that wasn't anything," said Standifer, "hemming" loudly and buttoning his coat again briskly. "And now, ma'am, who was the infernal skunk—I beg your pardon, ma'am—who was the gentleman you married?"

"Benton Sharp."

The commissioner plumped down again into his chair with a groan. This gentle, sad little woman in the rusty black gown the daughter of his oldest friend, the wife of Benton Sharp! Benton Sharp, one of the most noted "bad" men in that part of the state—a man who had been a cattle thief, an outlaw, a desperado, and was now a gambler, a swaggering bully, who plied his trade in the larger frontier towns, relying upon his record and the quickness of his gun play to maintain his supremacy. Seldom did anyone take the risk of going "up against" Benton Sharp. Even the law officers were content to let him make his own terms of peace. Sharp was a ready and an accurate shot, and as lucky as a brand-new penny at coming clear of scrapes. Standifer wondered how this pillaging eagle ever came to be mated with Amos Colvin's little dove and expressed his wonder.

Mrs. Sharp sighed.

"You see, Mr. Standifer, we didn't know anything about him, and he can be very pleasant and kind when he wants to. We lived down in the little town of Goliad. Benton came riding down that way and stopped there a while. I reckon I was some better looking then than I am now. He was good to me for a whole year after we were married. He insured his life for me for five thousand dollars. But for the last six months he has done everything but kill me. I often wish he had done that, too. He got out of money for a while, and abused me shamefully for not having anything he could spend. Then Father died and left me the little home in Goliad. My husband made me sell that and turned me out into the world. I've barely been able to live, for I'm not strong enough to work. Lately, I heard he was making money in San Antonio, so I went there, and found him, and asked for a little help. This," touching the livid bruise on her temple, "is what he gave me. So I came on to Austin to see the governor. I once heard Father say that there was some land or a pension coming to him from the state that he never would ask for."

Luke Standifer rose to his feet, and pushed his chair back. He looked rather perplexedly around the big office with its handsome furniture.

"It's a long trail to follow," he said, slowly, "trying to get back dues from the government. There's red tape and lawyers and rulings and evidences and courts to keep you waiting. I'm not certain," continued the commissioner, with a profoundly meditative frown, "whether this department that I'm the boss of has any jurisdiction or not. It's only Insurance, Statistics, and History, ma'am, and it don't sound as if it would cover the case. But sometimes a saddle blanket can be made to stretch. You keep your seat, just for a few minutes, ma'am, till I step into the next room and see about it."

The state treasurer was seated within his massive, complicated railings, reading a newspaper. Business for the day was about over. The clerks lolled at their desks, awaiting the closing hour. The Commissioner of Insurance, Statistics, and History entered, and leaned in at the window.

The treasurer, a little, brisk old man, with snow-white moustache and beard, jumped up youthfully and came forward to greet Standifer. They were friends of old.

"Uncle Frank," said the commissioner, using the familiar name by which the historic treasurer was addressed by every Texan, "how much money have you got on hand?"

The treasurer named the sum of the last balance down to the odd cents—something more than a million dollars.

The commissioner whistled lowly, and his eyes grew hopefully bright.

"You know, or else you've heard of, Amos Colvin, Uncle Frank?"

"Knew him well," siad the treasurer, promptly. "A good man. A valuable citizen. One of the settlers in the Southwest."

"His daughter," said Standifer, "is sitting in my office. She's penniless. She's married to Benton Sharp, a coyote and a murderer. He's reduced her to want and broken her heart. Her father helped build up this state, and it's the state's turn to help his child. A couple of thousand dollars will buy back her home and let her live in peace. The State of Texas can't afford to refuse it. Give me the money, Uncle Frank, and I'll give it to her right away. We'll fix up the red-tape business afterward."

The treasurer looked a little bewildered.

"Why, Standifer," he said, "you know I can't pay a cent out of the treasury without a warrant from the comptroller. I can't disburse a dollar without a voucher to show for it."

The commissioner betrayed a slight impatience.

"I'll give you a voucher," he declared. "What's this job they've given me for? Am I just a knot on a mesquite stump? Can't my office stand for it? Charge it up to Insurance and the other two sideshows. Don't Statistics show that Amos Colvin came to this state when it was in the hands of Greasers and rattlesnakes and Comanches, and fought day and night to make a white man's country of it? Don't they show that Amos Colvin's daughter is brought to ruin by a villain who's trying to pull down what you and I and old Texans shed our blood to build up? Don't History show that the Lone Star State never yet failed to grant relief to the suffering and oppressed children of the men who made her the grandest commonwealth in the Union? If Statistics and History don't bear out the claim of Amos Colvin's child I'll ask the next legislature to abolish my office. Come, now, Uncle Frank, let her have the money. I'll sign the papers officially, if you say so; and then if the governor or the comptroller or the janitor or anybody else makes a kick, by the Lord I'll refer the matter to the people and see if they won't indorse the act."

The treasurer looked sympathetic but shocked. The commissioner's voice had grown louder as he rounded off the sentences that, however praiseworthy they might be in sentiment, reflected somewhat upon the capacity of the head of a more or less important department of state. The clerks were beginning to listen.

"Now, Standifer," said the treasurer, soothingly, "you know I'd like to help in this matter, but stop and think a moment, please. Every cent in the treasury is expended only by appropriation made by the legislature, and drawn out by checks issued by the comptroller. I can't control the use of a cent of it. Neither can you. Your department isn't disbursive—it isn't even administrative—it's purely clerical. The only way for the lady to obtain relief is to petition the legislature, and———"

"To the devil with the legislature," said Standifer, turning away.

The treasurer called him back.

"I'd be glad, Standifer, to contribute a hundred dollars personally toward the immediate expenses of Colvin's daughter." He reached for his pocketbook.

"Never mind, Uncle Frank," said the commissioner, in a softer tone. "There's no need of that. She hasn't asked for anything of that sort yet. Besides, her case is in my hands. I see now what a little rag-tag, bob-tail, gotch-eared department I've been put in charge of. It seems to be about as important as an almanac or a hotel register. But while I'm running it, it won't turn away any daughters of Amos Colvin without stretching its jurisdiction to cover, if possible. You want to keep your eye on the Department of Insurance, Statistics, and History."

The commissioner returned to his office, looking thoughtful. He opened and closed an inkstand on his desk many times with extreme and undue attention before he spoke. "Why don't you get a divorce?" he asked, suddenly.

"I haven't the money to pay for it," answered the lady.

"Just at present," announced the commissioner, in a formal tone, "the powers of my department appear to be considerably stringhalted. Statistics seem to be overdrawn at the bank, and History isn't good for a square meal. But you've come to the right place, ma'am. The department will see you through. Where did you say your husband is, ma'am?"

"He was in San Antonio yesterday. He is living there now."

Suddenly the commissioner abandoned his official air. He took the faded little woman's hands in his, and spoke in the old voice he used on the trail and around campfires.

"Your name's Amanda, isn't it?"

"Yes, sir."

"I thought so. I've heard your dad say it often enough. Well, Amanda, here's your father's best friend, the head of a big office in the state government, that's going to help you out of your troubles. And here's the old bush-whacker and cowpuncher that your father has helped out of scrapes time and time again wants to ask you a question. Amanda, have you got enough money to run you for the next two or three days?"

Mrs. Sharp's white face flushed the least bit.

"Plenty, sir—for a few days."

"All right, then, ma'am. Now you go back where you are stopping here, and you come to the office again the day after to-morrow at four o'clock in the afternoon. Very likely by that time there will be something definite to report to you." The commissioner hesitated, and looked a trifle embarrassed. "You said your husband had insured his life for $5,000. Do you know whether the premiums have been kept paid upon it or not?"

"He paid for a whole year in advance about five months ago," said Mrs. Sharp. "I have the policy and receipts in my trunk."

"Oh, that's all right, then," said Standifer. "It's best to look after things of that sort. Some day they may come in handy."

Mrs. Sharp departed, and soon afterward Luke Standifer went down to the little hotel where he boarded and looked up the railroad time-table in the daily paper. Half an hour later he removed his coat and vest, and strapped a peculiarly constructed pistol holster across his shoulder, leaving the receptacle close under his left armpit. Into the holster he shoved a short-barreled .44-calibre revolver. Putting on his clothes again, he strolled down to the station and caught the five-twenty afternoon train for San Antonio.

The San Antonio *Express* of the following morning contained this sensational piece of news:

BENTON SHARP MEETS HIS MATCH

THE MOST NOTED DESPERADO IN SOUTHWEST TEXAS SHOT TO DEATH IN THE GOLD FRONT RESTAURANT—PROMINENT STATE OFFICIAL SUCCESSFULLY DEFENDS HIMSELF AGAINST THE NOTED BULLY—MAGNIFICENT EXHIBITION OF QUICK GUN PLAY.

Last night about eleven o'clock Benton Sharp, with two other men, entered the Gold Front Restaurant and seated themselves at a table. Sharp had been drinking, and was loud and boisterous, as he always was when under the influence of liquor. Five minutes after the party was seated a tall, well-dressed, elderly gentleman entered the restaurant. Few present recognized the Honorable Luke Standifer, the recently appointed Commissioner of Insurance, Statistics, and History.

Going over to the same side where Sharp was, Mr. Standifer prepared to take a seat at the next table. In hanging his hat upon one of the hooks along the wall he let it fall upon Sharp's head. Sharp turned, being in an especially ugly humor, and cursed the other roundly. Mr. Standifer apologized calmly for the accident, but Sharp continued his vituperations. Mr. Standifer was observed to draw near and speak a few sentences to the desperado in so low a tone that no one else caught the words. Sharp sprang up, wild with rage. In the meantime, Mr. Standifer had stepped some yards away, and was standing quietly with his arms folded across the breast of his loosely hanging coat.

With that impetuous and deadly rapidity that made Sharp so dreaded, he reached for the gun he always carried in his hip pocket—a movement that has preceded the death of at least a dozen men at his hands. Quick as the motion was, the bystanders assert that it was met by the most beautiful exhibition of lightning gun-pulling ever witnessed in the Southwest. As Sharp's pistol was being raised—and the act was really quicker than the eye could follow—a glittering .44 appeared as if by some conjuring trick in the right hand of Mr. Standifer, who, without a perceptible movement of his arm, shot Benton Sharp through the heart. It seems that the new Commissioner of Insurance, Statistics, and History has been an old-time Indian fighter and ranger for many years, which accounts for the happy knack he has of handling a .44.

It is not believed that Mr. Standifer will be put to any inconvenience beyond a necessary formal hearing to-day, as all the witnesses who were present unite in declaring that the deed was done in self-defense.

When Mrs. Sharp appeared at the office of the commissioner, according to appointment, she found that gentleman calmly eating a golden russet apple. He greeted her without embarrassment and without hesitation at approaching the subject that was the topic of the day.

"I had to do it, ma'am," he said, simply, "or get it myself. Mr. Kauffman," he added, turning to the old clerk, "please look up the records of the Security Life Insurance Company and see if they are all right."

"No need to look," grunted Kauffman, who had everything in his head. "It's all O.K. They pay all losses within ten days."

Mrs. Sharp soon rose to depart. She had arranged to remain in town until the policy was paid. The commissioner did not detain her. She was a woman, and he did not know just what to say to her at present. Rest and time would bring her what she needed.

But, as she was leaving, Luke Standifer indulged himself in an official remark:

"The Department of Insurance, Statistics, and History, ma'am, has done the best it could with your case. 'Twas a case hard to cover according to red tape. Statistics failed, and History missed fire, but, if I may be permitted to say it, we came out particularly strong on Insurance."

The Renaissance at Charleroi

Grandemont Charles was a little Creole gentleman, aged thirty-four, with a bald spot on the top of his head and the manners of a prince. By day he was a clerk in a cotton broker's office in one of those cold, rancid mountains of oozy brick, down near the levee in New Orleans. By night, in his three-story-high *chambre garnie* in the old French Quarter he was again the last male descendant of the Charles family, that noble house that had lorded it in France, and had pushed its way smiling, rapiered, and courtly into Louisiana's early and brilliant days. Of late years the Charleses had subsided into the more republican but scarcely less royally carried magnificence and ease of plantation life along the Mississippi. Perhaps Grandemont was even Marquis de Brassé. There was that title in the family. But a marquis on seventy-five dollars per month! *Vraiment!* Still, it has been done on less.

Grandemont had saved out of his salary the sum of six hundred dollars. Enough, you would say, for any man to marry on. So, after a silence of two years on that subject, he reopened that most hazardous question to Mlle. Adèle Fauquier, riding down to Meade d'Or, her father's plantation. Her answer was the same that it had been any time during the last ten years: "First find my brother, Monsieur Charles."

This time he had stood before her, perhaps discouraged by a love so long and hopeless, being dependent upon a contingency so unreasonable, and demanded to be told in simple words whether she loved him or no.

Adèle looked at him steadily out of her gray eyes that betrayed no secrets and answered, a little more softly:

"Grandemont, you have no right to ask that question unless you can do what I ask of you. Either bring back brother Victor to us or the proof that he died."

Somehow, though five times thus rejected, his heart was not so heavy when he left. She had not denied that she loved. Upon what shallow waters can the bark of passion remain afloat! Or, shall we play the doctrinaire, and hint that at thirty-four the tides of life are calmer and cognizant of many sources instead of but one—as at four-and-twenty?

Victor Fauquier would never be found. In those early days of his disappearance there was money to the Charles name, and Grandemont had spent the dollars as if they were picayunes in trying to find the lost youth. Even then he had had small hope of success, for the Mississippi gives up a victim from its oily tangles only at the whim of its malign will.

A thousand times had Grandemont conned in his mind the scene of Victor's disappearance. And, at each time that Adèle had set her stubborn but pitiful alternative against his suit, still clearer it repeated itself in his brain.

The boy had been the family favorite: daring, winning, reckless. His unwise fancy had been captured by a girl on the plantation—the daughter of an overseer. Victor's family was in ignorance of the intrigue, as far as it had gone. To save them the inevitable pain that his course promised, Grandemont strove to prevent it. Omnipotent money smoothed the way. The overseer and his daughter left, between a sunset and dawn, for an undesignated bourne. Grandemont was confident that this stroke would bring the boy to reason. He rode over to Meade d'Or to talk with him. The two strolled out of the house and grounds, crossed the road, and, mounting the levee, walked its broad path while they conversed. A thundercloud was hanging, imminent, above, but, as yet, no rain fell. At Grandemont's disclosure of his interference in the clandestine romance, Victor attacked him, in a wild and sudden fury. Grandemont, though of slight frame, possessed muscles of iron. He caught the wrists amid a shower of blows descending upon him, bent the lad backward and stretched him upon the levee path. In a little while the gust of passion was spent, and he was allowed to rise. Calm now, but a powder mine where he had been but a whiff of the tantrums, Victor extended his hand toward the dwelling house of Meade d'Or.

"You and they," he cried, "have conspired to destroy my happiness. None of you shall ever look upon my face again."

Turning, he ran swiftly down the levee, disappearing in the darkness. Grandemont followed as well as he could, calling to him, but in vain. For longer than an hour he pursued the search. Descending the side of the levee, he penetrated the rank density of weeds and willows that undergrew the trees until the river's edge, shouting Victor's name. There was never an answer, though once he thought he heard a bubbling scream from the dun waters sliding past. Then the storm broke, and he returned to the house drenched and dejected.

There he explained the boy's absence sufficiently, he thought, not speaking of the tangle that had led to it, for he hoped that Victor would return as soon as his anger had cooled. Afterward, when the threat was made good and they saw his face no more, he found it difficult to alter his explanations of that night, and there clung a certain mystery to the boy's reasons for vanishing as well as to the manner of it.

It was on that night that Grandemont first perceived a new and singular expression in Adèle's eyes whenever she looked at him. And through the years following that expression was always there. He could not read it, for it was born of a thought she would never otherwise reveal.

Perhaps, if he had known that Adèle had stood at the gate on that unlucky night, where she had followed, lingering to await the return of her brother and lover, wondering why they had chosen so tempestuous an hour and so black a spot to hold converse—if he had known that a sudden flash of lightning had revealed to her sight that short, sharp struggle as Victor was sinking under his hands, he might have explained everything, and she———

I know not what she would have done. But one thing is clear—there was something besides her brother's disappearance between Grandemont's pleadings for her hand and Adèle's "yes." Ten years had passed, and what she had seen during the space of that lightning flash remained an indelible picture. She had loved her brother, but was she holding out for the solution of that mystery or for the

"Truth"! Women have been known to reverence it, even as an abstract principle. It is said there have been a few who, in the matter of their affections, have considered a life to be a small thing as compared with a lie. That I do not know. But, I wonder, had Grandemont cast himself at her feet crying that his hand had sent Victor to the bottom of that inscrutable river, and that he could no longer sully his love with a lie, I wonder if—I wonder what she would have done!

But, Grandemont Charles, Arcadian little gentleman, never guessed the meaning of that look in Adèle's eyes; and from this last bootless payment of his devoirs he rode away as rich as ever in honor and love, but poor in hope.

That was in September. It was during the first winter month that Grandemont conceived his idea of the *renaissance.* Since Adèle would never be his, and wealth without her were useless trumpery, why need he add to that hoard of slowly harvested dollars? Why should he even retain that hoard?

Hundreds were the cigarettes he consumed over his claret, sitting at the little polished tables in the Royal street cafés while thinking over his plan. By and by he had it perfect. it would cost, beyond doubt, all the money he had, but—*le jeu vaut la chandelle*—for some hours he would be once more a Charles of Charleroi. Once again should the nineteenth of January, that most significant day in the fortunes of the house of Charles, be fittingly observed. On that date the French king had seated a Charles by his side at table; on that date Armand Charles, Marquis de Brassé, landed, like a brilliant meteor, in New Orleans; it was the date of his mother's wedding; of Grandemont's birth. Since Grandemont could remember until the breaking up of the family that anniversary had been the synonym for feasting, hospitality, and proud commemoration.

Charleroi was the old family plantation, lying some twenty miles down the river. Years ago the estate had been sold to discharge the debts of its too-bountiful owners. Once again it had changed hands, and now the must and mildew of litigation had settled upon it. A question of heirship was in the courts, and the dwelling house of Charleroi, unless the tales told of ghostly powdered and laced Charleses haunting its unechoing chambers were true, stood uninhabited.

Grandemont found the solicitor in chancery who held the keys pending the decision. He proved to be an old friend of the family. Grandemont explained briefly that he desired to rent the house for two or three days. He wanted to give a dinner at his old home to a few friends. That was all.

"Take it for a week—a month, if you will," said the solicitor; "but do not speak to me of rental." With a sigh he concluded: "The dinners I have eaten under that roof, *mon fils!*"

There came to many of the old-established dealers in furniture, china, silverware, decorations, and household fittings at their stores on Canal, Chartres, St. Charles and Royal streets, a quiet young man with a little bald spot on the top of his head, distinguished manners, and the eye of a *connoisseur,* who explained what he wanted. To hire the complete and elegant equipment of a dining-room, hall, reception-room, and cloakrooms. The goods were to be packed and sent, by boat, to the Charleroi landing, and would be returned within three or four days. All damage or loss to be promptly paid for.

Many of those old merchants knew Grandemont by sight, and the Charleses of old by association. Some of them were of Creole stock and felt a thrill of responsive sympathy with the magnificently indiscreet design of this impoverished clerk who would revive but for a moment the ancient flame of glory with the fuel of his savings.

"Choose what you want," they said to him. "Handle everything carefully. See that the damage bill is kept low, and the charges for the loan will not oppress you."

To the wine merchants next; and here a doleful slice was lopped from the six hundred. It was an exquisite pleasure to Grandemont once more to pick among the precious vintages. The champagne bins lured him like the abodes of sirens, but these he was forced to pass. With his six hundred he stood before them as a child with a penny stands before a French doll. But he bought with taste and discretion of other wines—Chablis, Moselle, Château d'Or, Hochheimer, and port of right age and pedigree.

The matter of the cuisine gave him some studious hours until he suddenly recollected André—André, their old *chef*—the most sublime master of French Creole cookery in the Mississippi Valley. Perhaps he was yet somewhere about the plantation. The solicitor had told him that the place was still being cultivated, in accordance with a compromise agreement between the litigants.

On the next Sunday after the thought Grandemont rode, horseback, down to Charleroi. The big, square house with its two long ells looked blank and cheerless with its closed shutters and doors.

The shrubbery in the yard was ragged and riotous. Fallen leaves from the grove littered the walks and porches. Turning down the lane at the side of the house, Grandemont rode on to the quarters of the plantation hands. He found the workers streaming back from church, careless, happy, and bedecked in gay yellows, reds, and blues.

Yes, André was still there; his wool a little grayer, his mouth as wide; his laughter as ready as ever. Grandemont told him of his plan, and the old *chef* swayed with pride and delight. With a sigh of relief, knowing that he need have no further concern until the serving of that dinner was announced, he placed in André's hands a liberal sum for the cost of it, giving *carte blanche* for its creation.

Among the blacks were also a number of the old house servants. Absalom, the former major domo, and a half-dozen of the younger men, once waiters and attachés of the kitchen, pantry, and other domestic departments, crowded around to meet *"M'shi Grande."* Absalom guaranteed to marshal, of these, a corps of assistants that would perform with credit the serving of the dinner.

After distributing a liberal largesse among the faithful, Grandemont rode back to town well pleased. There were many other smaller details to think of and provide for, but eventually the scheme was complete, and now there remained only the issuance of the invitations to his guests.

Along the river within the scope of a score of miles dwelt some half-dozen families with whose princely hospitality that of the Charleses had been contemporaneous. They were the proudest and most august of the old régime. Their small circle had been a brilliant one; their social relations close and warm; their houses full of rare welcome and discriminating bounty. Those friends, said Grandemont, should once more, if never again, sit at Charleroi on a nineteenth of January to celebrate the festal day of his house.

Grandemont had his cards of invitation engraved. They were expensive, but beautiful. In one particular their good taste might have been disputed; but the Creole allowed himself that one feather in the cap of his fugacious splendor. Might he not be allowed, for the one day of the *renaissance*, to be "Grandemont du Puy Charles, of Charleroi"? He sent the invitations out early in January so that the guests might not fail to receive due notice.

At eight o'clock in the morning of the nineteenth, the lower coast steamboat *River Belle* gingerly approached the long unused landing at Charleroi. The bridge was lowered, and a swarm of the plantation hands streamed along the rotting pier, bearing ashore a strange assortment of freight. Great shapeless bundles and bales and packets swathed in cloths and bound with ropes; tubs and urns of palms, evergreens, and tropical flowers; tables, mirrors, chairs, couches, carpets, and pictures—all carefully bound and padded against the dangers of transit.

Grandemont was among them, the busiest there. To the safe conveyance of certain large hampers eloquent with printed cautions to delicate handling he gave his superintendence, for they contained the fragile china and glassware. The dropping of one of those hampers would have cost him more than he could have saved in a year.

The last article unloaded, the *River Belle* backed off and continued her course down stream. In less than an hour everything had been conveyed to the house. And came then Absalom's task, directing the placing of the furniture and wares. There was plenty of help, for that day was always a holiday in Charleroi, and the Negroes did not suffer the old traditions to lapse. Almost the entire population of the quarters volunteered their aid. A score of piccaninnies were sweeping at the leaves in the yard.In the big kitchen at the rear André was lording it with his old-time magnificence over his numerous sub-cooks and scullions. Shutters were flung wide; dust spun in clouds; the house echoed to voices and the tread of busy feet. The prince had come again, and Charleroi woke from its long sleep.

The full moon, as she rose across the river that night and peeped above the levee, saw a sight that had been long missing from her orbit. The old plantation house shed a soft and alluring radiance from every window. Of its two-score rooms only four had been refurnished—the large reception chamber, the dining hall, and two smaller rooms for the convenience of the expected guests. But lighted wax candles were set in the windows of every room.

The dining hall was the *chef-d'oeuvre*. The long table, set with twenty-five covers, sparkled like a winter landscape with its snowy napery and china and the icy gleam of crystal. The chaste beauty of the room had required small adornment. The polished floor burned to a glowing ruby with the reflection of candlelight. The rich wainscoting reached halfway to the ceiling. Along and above this had been set the relieving lightness of a few water-color sketches of fruit and flower.

The reception chamber was fitted in a simple but elegant style. Its arrangement suggested nothing of the fact that on the morrow the rooms would again be cleared and abandoned to the dust and the spider. The entrance hall was imposing with palms and ferns and the light of an immense candelabrum.

At seven o'clock Grandemont, in evening dress, with pearls—a family passion—in his spotless linen, emerged from somewhere. The invitations had specified eight as the dining hour. He drew an armchair upon the porch, and sat there, smoking cigarettes and half dreaming.

The moon was an hour high. Fifty yards back from the gate stood the house, under its noble grove. The road ran in front, and then came the grass-grown levee and the insatiate river beyond. Just above the levee top a tiny red light was creeping down and a tiny green one was creeping up. Then the passing steamers saluted, and the hoarse din startled the drowsy silence of the melancholy lowlands. The stillness returned, save for the little voices of the night—the owl's recitative, the capriccio of the crickets, the concerto of the frogs in the grass. The piccaninnies and the dawdlers from the quarters had been dismissed to their confines, and the mêlée of the day was reduced to an orderly and intelligent silence. The six colored waiters, in their white jackets, paced, cat-footed, about the table, pretending to arrange where all was beyond betterment. Absalom, in black and shining pumps, posed superior, here and there where the lights set off his grandeur. And Grandemont rested in his chair, waiting for his guests.

He must have drifted into a dream—and an extravagant one—for he was master of Charleroi and Adèle was his wife. She was coming out to him now; he cold hear her steps; he could feel her hand upon his shoulder—

"Pardon moi, M'shi Grande"—it was Absalom's hand touching him, it was Absalom's voice, speaking the *patois* of the blacks—"but it is eight o'clock."

Eight o'clock. Grandemont sprang up. In the moonlight he could see the row of hitching-posts outside the gate. Long ago the horses of the guests should have stood there. They were vacant.

A chanted roar of indignation, a just, waxing bellow of affront and dishonored genius came from André's kitchen, filling the house with rhythmic protest. The beautiful dinner, the pearl of a dinner, the little excellent superb jewel of a dinner! But one moment more of waiting and not even the thousand thunders of black pigs of the quarters would touch it!

"They are a little late," said Grandemont, calmly. "They will come soon. Tell André to hold back dinner. And ask him if, by some chance, a bull from the pastures has broken, roaring, into the house."

He seated himself again to his cigarettes. Though he had said it, he scarcely believed Charleroi would entertain company that night.

For the first time in history the invitation of a Charles had been ignored. So simple in courtesy and honor was Grandemont and, perhaps, so serenely confident in the prestige of his name, that the most likely reasons for his vacant board did not occur to him.

Charleroi stood by a road traveled daily by people from those plantations whither his invitations had gone. No doubt even on the day before the sudden reanimation of the old house they had driven past and observed the evidences of long desertion and decay. They had looked at the corpse of Charleroi and then at Grandemont's invitations, and, though the puzzle or tasteless hoax or whatever the thing meant left them perplexed, they would not seek its solution by the folly of a visit to that deserted house.

The moon was now above the grove, and the yard was pied with deep shadows save where they lightened in the tender glow of outpouring candlelight. A crisp breeze from the river hinted at the possibility of frost when the night should have become older. The grass at one side of the steps was specked with the white stubs of Grandemont's cigarettes. The cotton-broker's clerk sat in his chair with the smoke spiralling above him. I doubt that he once thought of the little fortune he had so impotently squandered. Perhaps it was compensation enough for him to sit thus at Charleroi for a few retrieved hours. Idly his mind wandered in and out many fanciful paths of memory. He smiled to himself as a paraphrased line of Scripture strayed into his mind: "A certain *poor* man made a feast."

He heard the sound of Absalom coughing a note of summons. Grandemont stirred. This time he had not been asleep—only drowsing.

"Nine o'clock, *M'shi Grande*," said Absalom in the uninflected voice of a good servant who states a fact unqualified by personal opinion.

Grandemont rose to his feet. In their time all the Charleses had been proven, and they were gallant losers.

"Serve dinner," he said, calmly. And then he checked Absalom's movement to obey, for something clicked the gate latch and was coming down the walk towards the house. Something that shuffled its feet and muttered to itself as it came. It stopped in the current of light at the foot of the steps and spake, in the universal whine of the gadding mendicant.

"Kind sir, could you spare a poor, hungry man, out of luck, a little to eat? And to sleep in the corner of a shed? For"—the thing concluded, irrelevantly—"I can sleep now. There are no mountains to dance reels in the night; and the copper kettles are all scoured bright. The iron band is still around my ankle, and a link, if it is your desire I should be chained."

It set a foot upon the step and drew up the rags that hung upon the limb. Above the distorted shoe, caked with dust of a hundred leagues, they saw the link and the iron band. The clothes of the tramp were wrecked to piebald tatters by sun and rain and wear. A mat of brown, tangled hair and beard covered his head and face, out of which his eyes stared distractedly. Grandemont noticed that he carried in one hand a white, square card.

"What is that?" he asked.

"I picked it up, sire, at the side of the road." The vagabond handed the card to Grandemont. "Just a little to eat, sir. A little parched corn, a *tortilla*, or a handful of beans. Goat's meat I cannot eat. When I cut their throats they cry like children."

Grandemont held up the card. It was one of his own invitations to dinner. No doubt someone had cast it away from a passing carriage after comparing it with the tenantless house at Charleroi.

"From the hedges and highways bid them come," he said to himself, softly smiling. And then Absalom: "Send Louis to me."

Louis, once his own body-servant, came promptly, in his white jacket.

"This gentleman," said Grandemont, "will dine with me. Furnish him with bath and clothes. In twenty mintues have him ready and dinner served."

Louis approached the disreputable guest with the suavity due to a visitor to Charleroi, and spirited him away to inner regions.

Promptly, in twenty minutes, Absalom announced dinner, and, a moment later, the guest was ushered into the dining hall where Grandemont waited, standing, at the head of the table. The attentions of Louis had transformed the stranger into something resembling the polite animal. Clean linen and an old evening suit that had been sent down from town to clothe a waiter had worked a miracle with his exterior. Brush and comb had partially subdued the wild disorder of his hair. Now he might have passed for no more extravagant a thing than one of those *poseurs* in art and music who affect such oddity of guise. The man's countenance and demeanor, as he approached the table, exhibited nothing of the awkwardness or confusion to be expected from his Arabian Nights change. He allowed Absalom to seat him at Grandemont's right hand with the manner of one thus accustomed to be waited upon.

"It grieves me," said Grandemont, "to be obliged to exchange names with a guest. My own name is Charles."

"In the mountains," said the wayfarer, "they call me Gringo. Along the roads they call me Jack."

"I prefer the latter," said Grandemont. "A glass of wine with you, Mr. Jack."

Course after course was served by the supernumerous waiters. Grandemont, inspired by the results of André's exquisite skill in cookery and his own in the selection of wines, became the model host, talkative, witty, and genial. The guest was fitful in conversation. His mind seemed to be sustaining a succession of waves of dementia followed by intervals of comparative lucidity. There was the glassy brightness of recent fever in his eyes. A long course of it must have been the cause of his emaciation and weakness, his distracted mind, and the dull pallor that showed even through the tan of wind and sun.

"Charles," he said to Grandemont—for thus he seemed to interpret his name—"you never saw the mountains dance, did you?"

"No, Mr. Jack," answered Grandemont, gravely, "the spectacle has been denied me. But, I assure you, I can understand it must be a diverting sight. The big ones, you know, white with snow on the tops, waltzing—*décolleté*, we may say."

"You first scour the kettles," said Mr. Jack, leaning toward him excitedly, "to cook the beans in the morning, and you lie down on a blanket and keep quite still. Then they come out and dance for you. You would go out and dance with them but you are chained every night to the centre pole of the hut. You believe the mountains dance, don't you, Charlie?"

"I contradict no traveler's tales," said Grandemont, with a smile.

Mr. Jack laughed loudly. He dropped his voice to a confidential whisper.

"You are a fool to believe it," he went on. "They don't really dance. It's the fever in your head. It's the hard work and the bad water that does it. You are sick for weeks and there is no medicine. The fever comes on every evening, and then you are as strong as two men. One night the *compañía* are lying drunk with *mescal*. They have brought back sacks of silver dollars from a ride, and they drink to celebrate. In the night you file the chain in two and go down the mountain. You walk for miles—hundreds of them. By and by the mountains are all gone, and you come to the prairies. They do not dance at night; they are merciful, and you sleep. Then you come to the river, and it says things to you. You follow it down, down, but you can't find what you are looking for."

Mr. Jack leaned back in his chair, and his eyes slowly closed. The food and wine had steeped him in a deep calm. The tense strain had been smoothed from his face. The languor of repletion was claiming him. Drowsily he spoke again.

"It's bad manners—I know—to go to sleep—at table—but—that was—such a good dinner—Grande, old fellow."

Grande! The owner of the name started and set down his glass. How should this wretched tatterdemalion whom he had invited, Caliph-like, to sit at his feast know his name?"

Not at first, but soon, little by little, the suspicion, wild and unreasonable as it was, stole into his brain. He drew out his watch with hands that almost balked him by their trembling, and opened the back case. There was a picture there—a photograph fixed to the inner side.

Rising, Grandemont shook Mr. Jack by the shoulder. The weary guest opened his eyes. Grandemont held the watch.

"Look at this picture, Mr. Jack. Have you ever—"

"*My sister Adèle!*"

The vagrant's voice rang loud and sudden through the room. He started to his feet, but Grandemont's arms were about him, and Grandemont was calling him "Victor!—Victor Fauquier! *Merci, merci, mon Dieu!*"

Too far overcome by sleep and fatigue was the lost one to talk that night. Days afterward, when the tropic *calentura* had cooled in his veins, the disordered fragments he had spoken were completed in shape and sequence. He told the story of his angry flight, of toils and calamities on sea and shore, of his ebbing and flowing fortune in southern lands, and of his latest peril when, held a captive, he served menially in a stronghold of bandits in the Sonora Mountains of Mexico. And of the fever that seized him there and his escape and delirium, during which he strayed, perhaps led by some marvelous instinct, back to the river on whose bank he had been born. And of the proud and stubborn thing in his blood that had kept him silent through all those years, clouding the honor of one, though he knew it not, and keeping apart two loving hearts. "What a thing is love!" you may say. And if I grant it, you shall say, with me: "What a thing is pride!"

On a couch in the reception chamber Victor lay, with a dawning understanding in his heavy eyes and peace in his softened countenance. Absalom was preparing a lounge for the transient master of

Charleroi, who, to-morrow, would be again the clerk of a cotton broker, but also—

"To-morrow," Grandemont was saying, as he stood by the couch of his guest, speaking the words with his face shining as must have shone the face of Elijah's charioteer when he announced the glories of that heavenly journey—"To-morrow I will take you to Her."

Two Renegades

In the Gate City of the South the Confederate Veterans were reuniting; and I stood to see them march, beneath the tangled flags of the great conflict, to the hall of their oratory and commemoration.

While the irregular and halting line was passing I made onslaught upon it and dragged forth from the ranks my friend Barnard O'Keefe, who had no right to be there. For he was a Northerner born and bred; and what should he be doing hallooing for the Stars and Bars among those gray and moribund veterans? And why should he be trudging, with his shining, martial, humorous, broad face, among those warriors of a previous and alien generation?

I say I dragged him forth, and held him till the last hickory leg and waving goatee had stumbled past. And then I hustled him out of the crowd into a cool interior; for the Gate City was stirred that day, and the hand-organs wisely eliminated "Marching Through Georgia" from their repertories.

"Now, what deviltry are you up to?" I asked of O'Keefe when there were a table and things in glasses between us.

O'Keefe wiped his heated face and instigated a commotion among the floating ice in his glass before he chose to answer.

"I am assisting at the wake," said he, "of the only nation on earth that ever did me a good turn. As one gentleman to another, I am ratifying and celebrating the foreign policy of the late Jefferson Davis, as fine a statesman as ever settled the financial question of a country. Equal ratio—that was his platform—a barrel of money for a barrel of flour—a pair of $20 bills for a pair of boots—a hatful of currency for a new hat—say, ain't that simple compared with W.J.B.'s little old oxidized plank?"

"What talk is this?" I asked. "Your financial disgression is merely a subterfuge. Why were you marching in the ranks of the Confederate Veterans?"

"Because, my lad," answered O'Keefe, "the Confederate government in its might and power interposed to protect and defend Barnard O'Keefe against immediate and dangerous assassination at the hands of a blood-thirsty foreign country after the United States of America had overruled his appeal for protection, and had instructed Private Secretary Cortelyou to reduce his estimate of the Republican majority for 1905 by one vote."

"Come, Barney," said I, "the Confederate States of America has been out of existence nearly forty years. You do not look older yourself. When was it that the deceased government exerted its foreign policy in your behalf?"

"Four months ago," said O'Keefe, promptly. "The infamous foreign power I alluded to is still staggering from the official blow dealt it by Mr. Davis's contraband aggregation of states. That's why you see me cake-walking with the ex-rebs to the illegitimate tune about 'simmonseels and cotton. I vote for the Great Father in Washington, but I am not going back on Mars' Jeff. You say the Confederacy has been dead forty years? Well, if it hadn't been for it, I'd have been breathing today with soul so dead I couldn't have whispered a single cussword about my native land. The O'Keefes are not overburdened with ingratitude."

I must have looked bewildered. "The war was over," I said vacantly, "in———"

O'Keefe laughed loudly, scattering my thoughts.

"Ask old Doc Millikin if the war is over!" he shouted, hugely diverted. "Oh, no! Doc hasn't surrendered yet. And the Confederate States! Well, I just told you they bucked officially and solidly and nationally against a foreign government four months ago and kept me from being shot. Old Jeff's country stepped in and brought me off under its wing while Roosevelt was having a gunboat painted and waiting for the National Campaign Committee to look up whether I had ever scratched the ticket."

"Isn't there a story in this, Barney?" I asked.

"No," said O'Keefe; "but I'll give you the facts. You know I went down to Panama when this irritation about a canal began. I thought I'd get in on the ground floor. I did, and had to sleep on it, and drink water with little zoos in it; so, of course, I got the Chagres fever. That was in a little town called San Juan on the coast.

"After I got the fever hard enough to kill a Port-au-Prince nigger, I had a relapse in the shape of Doc Millikin.

"There was a doctor to attend a sick man! If Doc Millikin had your case, he made the terrors of death seem like an invitation to a donkey-party. He had the bedside manners of a Piute medicine-man and the soothing presence of a dray loaded with iron bridge-girders. When he laid his hand on your fevered brow you felt like Cap John Smith just before Pocahontas went his bail.

"Well, this old medical outrage floated down to my shack when I sent for him. He was built like a shad, and his eyebrows was black, and his white whiskers trickled down from his chin like milk coming out of a sprinkling-pot. He had a nigger boy along carrying an old tomato-can full of calomel, and a saw.

"Doc felt my pulse, and then he began to mess up some calomel with an agricultural implement that belonged to the trowel class.

"'I don't want any death-mask made yet, Doc,' I says, 'nor my liver put in a plaster-of-paris cast. I'm sick; and it's medicine I need, not frescoing.'

" 'You're a blame Yankee, ain't you?' asked Doc, going on mixing up his Portland cement.

" 'I'm from the North,' says I, 'but I'm a plain man, and don't care for mural decorations. When you get the Isthmus all asphalted over with that boll-weevil prescription, would you mind giving me a dose of painkiller, or a little strychnine on toast to ease up this feeling of unhealthiness that I have got?'

" 'They was all sassy, just like you,' says old doc, 'but we lowered their temperature considerable. Yes, sir, I reckon we sent a good many of ye over to old *mortuis nisi bonum*. Look at Antietam and Bull Run and Seven Pines and around Nashville! There never was a battle where we didn't lick ye unless you was ten to our one. I knew you were a blame Yankee the minute I laid eyes on you.'

" 'Don't reopen the chasm, Doc,' I begs him. 'Any Yankeeness I may have is geographical; and, as far as I am concerned a Southerner is as good as a Filipino any day. I'm feeling too bad to argue. Let's have secession without misrepresentation, if you say so; but what I need is more laudanum and less Lundy's Lane.If you're mixing that compound gefloxide of gefloxicum for me, please fill my ears with it before you get around to the battle of Gettysburg, for there is a subject full of talk.'

"By this time Doc Millikin had thrown up a line of fortifications on square pieces of paper; and he says to me: 'Yank, take one of these powders every two hours. They won't kill you. I'll be around again about sundown to see if you're alive.'

"Old Doc's powders knocked the chagres. I stayed in San Juan, and got to knowing him better. He was from Mississippi, and the red-hottest Southerner that ever smelled mint. He made Stonewall Jackson and R.E. Lee look like Abolitionists. He had a family somewhere down near Yazoo City; but he stayed away from the States on account of an uncontrollable liking he had for the absence of a Yankee government. Him and me got as thick personally as the Emperor of Russia and the dove of peace, but sectionally we didn't amalgamate.

"'Twas a beautiful system of medical practice introduced by old Doc into that isthmus of land. He'd take that bracket-saw and the mild chloride and his hypodermic, and treat anything from yellow fever to a personal friend.

"Besides his other liabilities Doc could play a flute for a minute or two. He was guilty of two tunes—'Dixie' and another one that was mighty close to the 'Suwanee River'—you might say one of its tributaries. He used to come down and sit with me while I was getting well, and aggrieve his flute and say unreconstructed things about the North. You'd have thought the smoke from the first gun at Fort Sumter was still floating around in the air.

"You know that was about the time they staged them property revolutions down there, that wound up in the fifth act with the thrilling canal scene where Uncle Sam has nine curtain-calls holding Miss Panama by the hand, while the bloodhounds keep Senator Morgan treed up in a cocoanut-palm.

"That's the way it wound up; but at first it seemed as if Colombia was going to make Panama look like one of the $3.98 kind, with dents made in it in the factory, like they wear at North Beach fish fries. For mine, I played the straw-hat crowd to win; and they gave me a colonel's commission over a brigade of twenty-seven men in the left wing and second joint of the insurgent army.

"The Colombian troops were awfully rude to us. One day when I had my brigade in a sandy spot, with its shoes off doing a battalion drill by squads, the Government army rushed from behind a bush at us, acting as noisy and disagreeable as they could.

"My troops enfiladed, left-faced, and left the spot. After enticing the enemy for three miles or so we struck a brier-patch and had to sit down. When we were ordered to throw up our toes and surrender we obeyed. Five of my best staff-officers fell, suffering extremely with stone-bruised heels.

"Then and there those Colombians took your friend Barney, sir, stripped him of the insignia of his rank, consisting of a pair of brass kunckles and a canteen of rum, and dragged him before a military court. The presiding general went through the usual legal formalities that sometimes cause a case to hang on the calendar of a South American military court as long as ten minutes. He asked me my age, and then sentenced me to be shot.

"They woke up the court interpreter, an American named Jenks, who was in the rum business and vice versa, and told him to translate the verdict.

"Jenks stretched himself and took a morphine tablet.

" 'You've got to back up against th' 'dobe, old man,' says he to me. 'Three weeks, I believe, you get. Haven't got a chew of fine-cut on you, have you?'

" 'Translate that again, with footnotes and a glossary,' says I. 'I don't know whether I'm discharged, condemned, or handed over to the Gerry Society.'

" 'Oh,' says Jenks, 'don't you understand? You're to be stood up against a 'dobe wall and shot in two or three weeks—three, I think, they said.'

" 'Would you mind asking 'em which?' says I. 'A week don't amount to much after you are dead, but it sees a real nice long spell while you are alive.'

" 'It's two weeks,' says the interpreter, after inquiring in Spanish of the court. 'Shall I ask 'em again?'

" 'Let be,' says I. 'Let's have a stationary verdict. If I keep on appealing this way they'll have me cut about ten days before I was captured. No, I haven't got any fine-cut.'

"They sends me over to the *calaboza* with a detachment of colored postal-telegraph boys carrying Enfield rifles, and I am locked up in a kind of brick bakery. The temperature in there was just about the kind mentioned in the cooking recipes that call for a quick oven.

"Then I gives a silver dollar to one of the guards to send for the United States consul. He comes around in pajamas with a pair of glasses on his nose and a dozen or two inside of him.

" 'I'm to be shot in two weeks,' says I. 'And although I've made a memorandum of it, I don't seem to get it off my mind. You want to call up Uncle Sam on the cable as quick as you can and get him all worked up about it. Have 'em send the *Kentucky* and the *Kearsarge* and the *Oregon* down right away. That'll be about enough battleships; but it wouldn't hurt to have a couple of cruisers and a torpedo-boat destroyer, too. And—say, if Dewey isn't busy, better have him come along on the fastest one of the fleet.'

" 'Now, see here, O'Keefe,' says the consul, getting the best of a hiccup, 'what do you want to bother the State Department about this matter for?'

" 'Didn't you hear me?' says I; 'I'm to be shot in two weeks. Did you think I said I was going to a lawn-party? And it wouldn't hurt if Roosevelt could get the Japs to send down the *Yellowyamstiskookum* or the *Ogotosingsing* or some other first-class cruiser to help. It would make me feel safer.'

" 'Now, what you want,' says the consul, 'is not to get excited. I'll send you over some chewing tobacco and some banana fritters when I go back. The United States can't interfere in this. You know you were caught insurging against the government, and you're subject to the laws of this country. Tell you the truth, I've had an intimation from the State Department—unofficially, of course—that whenever a soldier of fortune demands a fleet of gunboats in a case of revolutionary *katzenjammer,* I should cut the cable, give him all the tobacco he wants, and after he's shot take his clothes, if they fit me, for part payment of my salary.'

" 'Consul,' says I to him, 'this is a serious question. You are representing Uncle Sam. This ain't any little international tomfoolery, like a universal peace congress or the christening of the *Shamrock IV*. I'm an American citizen and I demand protection. I demand the Mosquito fleet, and Schley, and the Atlantic squadron, and Bob Evans, and General E. Byrd Grubb, and two or three protocols. What are you going to do about it?'

" 'Nothing doing,' says the consul.

" 'Be off with you, then,' says I, out of patience with him, 'and send me Doc Millikin. Ask Doc to come and see me.'

"Doc comes and looks through the bars at me, surrounded by dirty soldiers, with even my shoes and canteen confiscated, and he looks mightily pleased.

" 'Hello, Yank,' says he, 'getting a little taste of Johnson's Island, now, ain't ye?'

" 'Doc,' says I, 'I've just had an interview with the U.S. consul. I gather from his remarks that I might just as well have been caught selling suspenders in Kishineff under the name of Rosenstein as to be in my present condition. It seems that the only maritime aid I am to receive from the United States is some navy-plug to chew. Doc,' says I, 'can't you suspend hostilities on the slavery question long enough to do something for me?'

" 'It ain't been my habit,' Doc Millikin answers, 'to do any painless dentistry when I find a Yank cutting an eyetooth. So the Stars and Stripes ain't landing any marines to shell the huts of the Colombian cannibals, hey? Oh, say, can you see by the dawn's early light the star-spangled banner has fluked in the fight? What's the matter with the War Department, hey? It's a great thing to be a citizen of a gold-standard nation, ain't it?'

" 'Rub it in, Doc, all you want,' says I. 'I guess we're weak on foreign policy.'

" 'For a Yank,' says Doc, putting on his specs and talking more mild, 'you ain't so bad. If you had come from below the line I reckon I would have liked you right smart. Now since your country has gone back on you, you have to come to the old doctor whose cotton you burned and whose mules you stole and whose niggers you freed to help you. Ain't that so, Yank?'

" 'It is,' says I heartily, 'and let's have a diagnosis of the case right away, for in two weeks' time all you can do is to hold an autopsy and I don't want to be amputated if I can help it.'

" 'Now,' says Doc, business-like, 'it's easy enough for you to get out of this scrape. Money'll do it. You've got to pay a long string of 'em from General Pomposo down to this anthropoid ape guarding your door. About $10,000 will do the trick. Have you got the money?'

" 'Me?' says I. 'I've got one Chili dollar, two *real* pieces, and a *medio.*'

" 'Then if you've any last words, utter 'em,' says that old reb. 'The roster of your financial budget sounds quite much to me like the noise of a requiem.'

" 'Change the treatment,' says I. 'I admist that I'm short. Call a consultation or use radium or smuggle me in some saws or something.'

" 'Yank,' says Doc Millikin, 'I've a good notion to help you. There's only one government in the world that can get you out of this difficulty; and that's the Confederate States of America, the grandest nation that ever existed.'

"Just as you said to me I says to Doc; 'Why, the Confederacy ain't a nation. It's been absolved forty years ago.'

" 'That's a campaign lie,' says Doc. 'She's running along as solid as the Roman Empire. She's the only hope you've got. Now, you, being a Yank, have got to go through with some preliminary obsequies before you can get official aid. You've got to take the oath of allegiance to the Confederate Government. Then I'll guarantee she does all she can for you. What do you say, Yank?—it's your last chance.'

" 'If you're fooling with me, Doc,' I answered, 'you're no better than the United States. But as you say it's the last chance, hurry up and swear me. I always did like corn whisky and 'possum anyhow. I believe I'm half Southerner by nature. I'm willing to try the Ku Klux in place of the khaki. Get brisk.'

"Doc Millikin thinks awhile, and then he offers me this oath of allegiance to take without any kind of a chaser:

" 'I, Barnard O'Keefe, Yank, being of sound body but a Republican mind, hereby swear to transfer my fealty, respect, and allegiance to the Confederate States of America, and the Government thereof, in consideration of said government, through its official acts and powers, obtaining my freedom and release from confinement and sentence of death brought about by the exuberance of my Irish proclivities and my general pizenness as a Yank.'

"I repeated these words after doc, but they seemed to me a kind of hocus-pocus; and I don't believe any life-insurance company in the country would have issued me a policy on the strength of 'em.

"Doc went away saying he would communicate with his government immediately.

"Say—you can imagine how I felt—me to be shot in two weeks and my only hope for help being a government that's been dead so long that it isn't even remembered except on Decoration Day and when Joe Wheeler signs the voucher for his pay-check. But it was all there was in sight; and somehow I thought Doc Milliken had something up his old alpaca sleeve that wasn't all foolishness.

"Around to the jail comes old Doc again in about a week. I was fleabitten, a mite sarcastic, and fundamentally hungry.

" 'Any Confederate ironclads in the offing?' I asks. 'Do you notice any sounds resembling the approach of Jeb Stewart's cavalry overland or Stonewall Jackson sneaking up in the rear? If you do, I wish you'd say so.'

" 'It's too soon yet for help to come,' says Doc.

" 'The sooner the better,' says I. 'I don't care if it gets in fully fifteen minutes before I am shot; and if you happen to lay eyes on

Beauregard or Albert Sidney Johnson or any of the relief corps, wig-wag 'em to hike along.'

" 'There's been no answer received yet,' says Doc.

" 'Don't forget,' says I, 'that there's only four days more. I don't know how you propose to work this thing, Doc,' I says to him; 'but it seems to me I'd sleep better if you had got a government that was alive and on the map—like Afghanistan or Great Britain, or old man Kruger's kingdom, to take this matter up. I don't mean any disrespect to your Confederate States, but I can't help feeling that my chances of being pulled out of this scrape was decidedly weakened when General Lee surrendered.'

" 'It's your only chance,' said Doc; 'don't quarrel with it. What did your own country do for you?'

"It was only two days before the morning I was to be shot when Doc Millikin came around again.

" 'All right, Yank,' says he. 'Help's come. The Confederate States of America is going to apply for your release. The representatives of the government arrived on a fruit-steamer last night.'

" 'Bully!' says I—'bully for you, Doc! I suppose it's marines with a Gatling. I'm going to love your country all I can for this.'

" 'Negotiations,' says old Doc, 'will be opened between the two governments at once. You will know later on to-day if they are successful.'

"About four in the afternoon a soldier in red trousers brings a paper round to the jail, and they unlocks the door and I walks out. The guard at the door bows and I bows, and I steps into the grass and wades around to Doc Millikin's shack.

"Doc was sitting in his hammock playing 'Dixie,' soft and low and out of tune, on his flute. I interrupted him at 'Look away! look away!' and shook his hand for five minutes.

" 'I never thought,' says Doc, taking a chew fretfully, 'that I'd ever try to save any blame Yank's life. But, Mr. O'Keefe, I don't see but what you are entitled to be considered part human, anyhow. I never thought Yanks had any of the rudiments of decorum and laudability about them. I reckon I might have been too aggregative in my tabulation. But it ain't me you want to thank—it's the Confederate States of America.'

" 'And I'm much obliged to 'em,' says I. 'It's a poor man that wouldn't be patriotic with a country that's saved his life. I'll drink to the Stars and Bars whenever there's a flag-staff and a glass convenient. But where,' says I , 'are the rescuing troops? If there was a gun fired or a shell burst, I didn't hear it.'

"Doc Millikin raises up and points out the window with his flute at the banana-steamer loading with fruit.

" 'Yank,' says he, 'there's a steamer that's going to sail in the morning. If I was you, I'd sail on it. The Confederate Government's done all it can for you. There wasn't a gun fired. The negotiations was carried on secretly between the two nations by the purser of that steamer. I got him to do it because I didn't want to appear in it. Twelve thousand dollars was paid to the officials in bribes to let you go.'

" 'Man!' says I, sitting down hard—'twelve thousand—how will I ever—who could have—where did the money come from?'

" 'Yazoo City,' says Doc Millikin; 'I've got a little bit saved up there. Two barrels full. It looks good to these Colombians. 'Twas Confederate money, every dollar of it. Now do you see why you'd better leave before they try to pass some of it on an expert?'

" 'I do,' says I.

" 'Now, let's hear you give the password,' says Doc Millikin.

" 'Hurrah for Jeff Davis!' says I.

" 'Correct,' says Doc. 'And let me tell you something. The next tune I learn on my flute is going to be "Yankee Doodle." I reckon there's some Yanks that are not so pizen. Or, if you was me, would you try "The Red, White, and Blue"?' "

"The Rose of Dixie"

When *The Rose of Dixie* magazine was started by a stock company in Toombs City, Georgia, there was never but one candidate for its chief editorial position in the minds of its owners. Col. Aquila Telfair was the man for the place. By all the rights of learning, family, reputation, and Southern traditions, he was its foreordained, fit, and logical editor. So, a committee of the patriotic Georgia citizens who had subscribed the founding fund of $100,000 called upon Colonel Telfair at his residence, Cedar Heights, fearful lest the enterprise and the South should suffer by his possible refusal.

The colonel received them in his great library, where he spent most of his days. The library had descended to him from his father. It contained ten thousand volumes, some of which had been published as late as the year 1861. When the deputation arrived, Colonel Telfair was seated at his massive white-pine centre-table, reading Burton's "Anatomy of Melancholy." He arose and shook hands punctiliously with each member of the committee. If you were familiar with *The Rose of Dixie* you will remember the colonel's portrait, which appeared in it from time to time. You could not forget the long, carefully brushed white hair, the hooked, high-bridged nose, slightly twisted to the left; the keen eyes under the still black eyebrows; the classic mouth beneath the drooping white mustache, slightly frazzled at the ends.

The committee solicitously offered him the position of managing editor, humbly presenting an outline of the field that the publication was designed to cover and mentioning a comfortable salary. The colonel's lands were growing poorer each year and were much cut up by red gullies. Besides, the honor was not one to be refused.

In a forty-minute speech of acceptance, Colonel Telfair gave an outline of English literature from Chaucer to Macaulay, re-fought the battle of Chancellorsville, and said that, God helping him, he would so conduct *The Rose of Dixie* that its fragrance and beauty would permeate the entire world, hurling back into the teeth of the Northern minions their belief that no genius or good could exist in the brains and hearts of the people whose property they had destroyed and whose rights they had curtailed.

Offices for the magazine were partitioned off and furnished in the second floor of the First National Bank building; and it was for the colonel to cause *The Rose of Dixie* to blossom and flourish or to wilt in the balmy air of the land of flowers.

The staff of assistants and contributors that Editor-Colonel Telfair drew about him was a peach. It was a whole crate of Georgia peaches. The first assistant editor, Tolliver Lee Fairfax, had had a father killed during Pickett's charge. The second assistant, Keats Unthank, was the nephew of one of Morgan's Raiders. The book reviewer, Jackson Rockingham, had been the youngest soldier in the Confederate army, having appeared on the field of battle with a sword in one hand and a milk-bottle in the other. The art editor, Roncesvalles Sykes, was a third cousin to a nephew of Jefferson Davis. Miss Lavinia Terhune, the colonel's stenographer and typewriter, had an aunt who had once been kissed by Stonewall Jackson. Tommy Webster, the head office boy, got his job by having recited Father Ryan's poems, complete, at the commencement exercises of the Toombs City High School. The girls who wrapped and addressed the magazine were members of old Southern families in Reduced Circumstances. The cashier was a scrub named Hawkins, from Ann Arbor, Michigan, who had recommendations and a bond from a guarantee company filed with the owners. Even Georgia stock companies sometimes realize that it takes live ones to bury the dead.

Well, sir, if you believe me, *The Rose of Dixie* blossomed five times before anybody heard of it except the people who buy their hooks and eyes in Toombs City. Then Hawkins climbed off his stool and told on 'em to the stock company. Even in Ann Arbor he had been used to having his business propositions heard of at least as far away as Detroit. So an advertising manager was engaged—Beauregard Fitzhugh Banks—a young man in a lavender necktie, whose grandfather had been the Exalted High Pillow-slip of the Kuklux Klan.

In spite of which *The Rose of Dixie* kept coming out every month. Although in every issue it ran photos of either the Taj Mahal or the Luxembourg Gardens, or Carmencita or La Follette, a certain number of people bought it and subscribed for it. As a boom for it, Editor-Colonel Telfair ran three different views of Andrew Jackson's old home, "The Hermitage," a full-page engraving of the seecond battle of Manasses, entitled, "Lee to the Rear!" and a five-thousand-word biography of Belle Boyd in the same number. The subscription list that month advanced 118. Also there were poems in the same issue by Leonina Vashti Haricot (pen-name), related to the Haricots of Charleston, South Carolina, and Bill Thompson, nephew of one of the stockholders. And an article from a special society correspondent describing a tea-party given by the swell Boston and English set, where a lot of tea was spilled overboard by some of the guests masquerading as Indians.

One day a person whose breath would easily cloud a mirror, he was so much alive, entered the office of *The Rose of Dixie*. He was a man about the size of a real-estate agent, with a self-tied tie and a manner that he must have borrowed conjointly from W. J. Bryan, Hackenschmidt, and Hetty Green. He was shown into the editor-colonel's *pons asinorum*. Colonel Telfair rose and began a Prince Albert bow.

"I'm Thacker," said the intruder, taking the editor's chair—"T. T. Thacker, of New York."

He dribbled hastily upon the colonel's desk some cards, a bulk manila envelope, and a letter from the owners of *The Rose of Dixie*.

This letter introduced Mr. Thacker, and politely requested Colonel Telfair to give him a conference and whatever information about the magazine he might desire.

"I've been corresponding with the secretary of the magazine owners for some time," said Thacker, briskly. "I'm a practical magazine man myself, and a circulation booster as good as any, if I do say it. I'll guarantee an increase of anywhere from ten thousand to a hundred thousand a year for any publication that isn't printed in a dead language. I've had my eye on *The Rose of Dixie* ever since it started. I know every end of the business from editing to setting up the classified ads. Now, I've come down here to put a good bunch of money in the magazine, if I can see my way clear. It ought to be made to pay. The secretary tells me it's losing money. I don't see why a magazine in the South, if it's properly handled, shouldn't get a good circulation in the North, too."

Colonel Telfair leaned back in his chair and polished his gold-rimmed glasses.

"Mr. Thacker," said he, courteously but firmly, "*The Rose of Dixie* is a publication devoted to the fostering and the voicing of Southern genius. Its watchword, which you may have seen on the cover, is 'Of, For, and By the South.' "

"But you wouldn't object to a Northern circulation, would you?" asked Thacker.

"I suppose," said the editor-colonel, "that it is customary to open the circulation lists to all. I do not know. I have nothing to do with the business affairs of the magazine. I was called upon to assume editorial control of it, and I have devoted to its conduct such poor literary talents as I may possess and whatever store of erudition I may have acquired."

"Sure," said Thacker. "But a dollar is a dollar anywhere, North, South, or West—whether you're buying codfish, goober peas, or Rocky Ford cantaloupes. Now, I've been looking over your November number. I see one here on your desk. You don't mind running over it with me?

"Well, your leading article is all right. A good write-up of the cotton-belt with plenty of photographs is a winner any time. New York is always interested in the cotton crop. And this sensational account of the Hatfield-McCoy feud, by a schoolmate of a niece of the Governor of Kentucky, isn't such a bad idea. It happened so long ago that most people have forgotten it. Now, here's a poem three pages long called 'The Tyrant's Foot,' by Lorella Lascells. I've pawed around a good deal over manuscripts, but I never saw her name on a rejection slip."

"Miss Lascelles," said the editor, "is one of our most widely recognized Southern poetesses. She is closely related to the Alabama Lascelles family, and made with her own hands the silken Confederate banner that was presented to the governor of that state at his inauguration."

"But why," persisted Thacker, "is the poem illustrated with a view of the M. & O. Railroad depot at Tuscaloosa?"

"The illustration," said the colonel, with dignity, "shows a corner of the fence surrounding the old homestead where Miss Lascelles was born."

"All right," said Thacker. "I read the poem, but I couldn't tell whether it was about the depot or the battle of Bull Run. Now, here's a short story called 'Rosie's Temptation,' by Fosdyke Piggott. It's rotten. What is a Piggott, anyway?"

"Mr. Piggott," said the editor, "is a brother of the principal stockholder of the magazine."

"All's right with the world—Piggott passes," said Thacker. "Well, this article on Arctic exploration and the one on tarpon fishing might go. But how about this write-up of the Atlanta, New Orleans, Nashville, and Savannah breweries? It seems to consist mainly of statistics about their output and the quality of their beer. What's the chip over the bug?"

"If I understand your figurative language," answered Colonel Telfair, "it is this: the article you refer to was handed to me by the owners of the magazine with instructions to publish it. The literary quality of it did not appeal to me. But, in a measure, I feel impelled to conform, in certain matters, to the wishes of the gentlemen who are interested in the financial side of *The Rose*."

"I see," said Thacker. "Next we have two pages of selections from 'Lalla Rookh,' by Thomas Moore. Now, what Federal prison did Moore escape from, or what's the name of the F.F.V. family that he carries as a handicap?"

"Moore was an Irish poet who died in 1852," said Colonel Telfair, pityingly. "He is a classic. I have been thinking of reprinting his translation of Anacreon serially in the magazine."

"Look out for the copyright laws," said Thacker, flippantly. "Who's Bessie Belleclair, who contributes the essay on the newly completed waterworks plants in Milledgeville?"

"The name, sir," said Colonel Telfair, "is the *nom de guerre* of Miss

Elvira Simpkins. I have not the honor of knowing the lady; but her contribution was sent us by Congressman Brower, of her native state. Congressman Brower's mother was related to the Polks of Tennessee."

"Now, see here, Colonel," said Thacker, throwing down the magazine, "this won't do. You can't successfully run a magazine for one particular section of the country. You've got to make a universal appeal. Look how the Northern publications have catered to the South and encouraged the Southern writers. And you've got to go far and wide for your contributors. You've got to buy stuff according to its quality, without any regard to the pedigree of the author. Now, I'll bet a quart of ink that this Southern parlor organ you've been running has never played a note that originated above Mason & Hamlin's line. Am I right?"

"I have carefully and conscientiously rejected all contributions from that section of the country—if I understand your figurative language aright," replied the colonel.

"All right. Now, I'll show you something."

Thacker reached for his thick manila envelope and dumped a mass of typewritten manuscript on the editor's desk.

"Here's some truck," said he, "that I paid cash for, and brought along with me."

One by one he folded back the manuscripts and showed their first pages to the colonel.

"Here are four short stories by four of the highest priced authors in the United States—three of 'em living in New York, and one commuting. There's a special article on Vienna-bred society by Tom Vampson. Here's an Italian serial by Captain Jack—no—it's the other Crawford. Here are three separate exposés of city governments by Sniffings, and here's a dandy entitled 'What Women Carry in Dress-Suit Cases'—a Chicago newspaper woman hired herself out for five years as a lady's maid to get that informtion. And here's a Synopsis of Preceding Chapters of Hall Caine's new serial to appear next June. And here's a couple of pounds of *vers de société* that I got at a rate from the clever magazines. That's the stuff that people everywhere want. And now here's a write-up with photographs at the ages of four, twelve, twenty-two, and thirty of George B. McClellan. It's a prognostication. He's bound to be elected Mayor of New York. It'll make a big hit all over the country. He———"

"I beg your pardon," said Colonel Telfair, stiffening in his chair. "What was the name?"

"Oh, I see," said Thacker, with half a grin. "Yes, he's a son of the General. We'll pass that manuscript up. But, if you'll excuse me, Colonel, it's a magazine we're trying to make go off—not the first gun at Fort Sumter. Now, here's a thing that's bound to get next to you. It's an original poem by James Whitcomb Riley. J.W. himself. You know what that means to a magazine. I won't tell you what I had to pay for that poem; but I'll tell you this—Riley can make more money writing with a fountain-pen than you or I can with one that lets the ink run. I'll read you the last two stanzas:

Pa lays around 'n' loafs all day,
'N' reads and makes us leave him be.
He lets me do just like I please,
'N' when I'm bad he laughs at me,
'N' when I holler loud 'n' say
Bad words 'n' then begin to tease
The cat, 'n' pa just smiles, ma's mad
'N' gives me Jesse crost her knees.
I always wondered why that wuz—
I guess it's cause Pa never does.

'N' after all the lights are out
I'm sorry 'bout it; so I creep
Out of my trundle bed to ma's
'N' say I love her a whole heap,
'N' kiss her, 'n' I hug her tight.
'N' it's too dark to see her eyes,
But every time I do I know
She cries 'n' cries 'n' cries 'n' cries.
I always wondered why that wuz—
I guess it's cause Pa never does.

"That's the stuff," continued Thacker. "What do you think of that?"

"I am not unfamiliar with the works of Mr. Riley," said the colonel deliberately. "I believe he lives in Indiana. For the last ten years I have been somewhat of a literary recluse, and am familiar with nearly all the books in the Cedar Heights library. I am also of the opinon that a magazine should contain a certain amount of poetry. Many of the sweetest singers of the South have already contributed to the pages of *The Rose of Dixie*. I, myself, have thought of translating from the original for publication in its pages the works of the great Italian poet Tasso. Have you ever drunk from the fountain of this immortal poet's lines, Mr. Thacker?"

"Not even a demi-Tasso," said Thacker. "Now, let's come to the point, Colonel Telfair. I've already invested some money in this as a flyer. That bunch of manuscripts cost me $4,000. My object was to try a number of them in the next issue—I believe you make up less than a month ahead—and see what effect it has on the circulation. I believe that by printing the best stuff we can get in the North, South, East, or West we can make the magazine go. You have there the letter from the owning company asking you to coöperate with me in the plan. Let's chuck out some of this slush that you've been publishing just because the writers are related to the Skoopdoodles of Skoopdoodle County. Are you with me?"

"As long as I continue to be the editor of *The Rose*," said Colonel Telfair, with dignity, "I shall be its editor. But I desire also to conform to the wishes of its owners if I can do so conscientiously."

"That's the talk," said Thacker, briskly. "Now, how much of this stuff I've brought can we get into the January number? We want to begin right away."

"There is yet space in the January number," said the editor, "for about eight thousand words, roughly estimated."

"Great!" said Thacker. "It isn't much, but it'll give the readers some change from goobers, governors, and Gettysburg. I'll leave the selection of the stuff I brought to fill the space to you, as it's all good. I've got to run back to New York, and I'll be down again in a couple of weeks."

Colonel Telfair slowly swung his eye-glasses by their broad, black ribbon.

"The space in the January number that I referred to," said he, measuredly, "has been held open purposely, pending a decision that I have not yet made. A short time ago a contribution was submitted to *The Rose of Dixie* that is one of the most remarkable literary efforts that has ever come under my observation. None but a master mind and talent could have produced it. It would about fill the space that I have reserved for its possible use."

Thacker looked anxious.

"What kind of stuff is it?" he asked. "Eight thousand words sounds suspicious. The oldest families must have been collaborating. Is there going to be another secession?"

"The author of the article," continued the colonel, ignoring Thacker's allusions, "is a writer of some reputation. He has also distinguished himself in other ways. I do not feel at liberty to reveal to you his name—at least not until I have decided whether or not to accept his contribution."

"Well," said Thacker, nervously, "is it a continued story, or an account of the unveiling of the new town pump in Whitmire, South Carolina, or a revised list of General Lee's body-servants, or what?"

"You are disposed to be facetious," said Colonel Telfair, calmly. "The article is from the pen of a thinker, a philosopher, a lover of mankind, a student, and a rhetorician of high degree."

"It must have been written by a syndicate," said Thacker. "But, honestly, Colonel, you want to go slow. I don't know of any eight-thousand-word single doses of written matter that are read by anybody these days, except Supreme Court briefs and reports of murder trials. You haven't by any accident gotten hold of a copy of one of Daniel Webster's speeches, have you?"

Colonel Telfair swung a little in his chair and looked steadily from under his bushy eyebrows at the magazine promoter.

"Mr. Thacker," he said, gravely, "I am willing to segregate the somewhat crude expression of your sense of humor from the solicitude that your business investments undoubtedly have conferred upon you. But I must ask you to cease your jibes and derogatory comments upon the South and the Southern people. They, sir, will not be tolerated in the office of *The Rose of Dixie* for one moment. And before you proceed with more of your covert insinuations that I, the editor of this magazine, am not a competent judge of the merits of the matter submitted to its consideration, I beg that you will first present some evidence or proof that you are my superior in any way, shape, or form relative to the question in hand."

"Oh, come, Colonel," said Thacker, good-naturedly. "I didn't do anything like that to you. It sounds like an indictment by the fourth assistant attorney-general. Let's get back to business. What's this 8,000 to 1 shot about?"

"The article," said Colonel Telfair, acknowledging the apology by a slight bow, "covers a wide area of knowledge. It takes up theories and questions that have puzzled the world for centuries, and disposes of them logically and concisely. One by one it holds up to view the evils of the world, points out the way of eradicating them, and then conscientiously and in detail commends the good. There is hardly a phase of human life that it does not discuss wisely, calmly, and equitably. The great policies of governments, the duties of private citizens, the obligations of home life, ehtics, morality—all these important subjects are handled with a calm wisdom and confidence that I must confess has captured my admiration."

"It must be a crackerjack," said Thacker, impressed.

"It is a great contribution to the world's wisdom," said the colonel. "The only doubt remaining in my mind as to the tremendous advantage it would be to us to give it publication in *The Rose of Dixie* is that I have not yet sufficient information about the author to give his work publicity in our magazine."

"I thought you said he is a distinguished man," said Thacker.

"He is," replied the colonel, "both in literary and in other more diversified and extraneous fields. But I am extremely careful about the matter that I accept for publication. My contributors are people of unquestionable repute and connections, which fact can be verified at any time. As I said, I am holding this article until I can acquire more information about its author. I do not know whether I will publish it or not. If I decide against it, I shall be much pleased, Mr. Thacker, to substitute the matter that you are leaving with me in its place."

Thacker was somewhat at sea.

"I don't seem to gather," said he, "much about the gist of this inspired piece of literature. It sounds more like a dark horse than Pegasus to me."

"It is a human document," said the colonel-editor, confidently, "from a man of great accomplishments who, in my opinion, has obtained a stronger grasp on the world and its outcomes than that of any man living to-day."

Thacker rose to his feet excitedly.

"Say!" he said. "It isn't possible that you've cornered John D. Rockefeller's memoirs, is it? Don't tell me that all at once."

"No, sir," said Colonel Telfair. "I am speaking of mentality and literature, not of the less worthy intricacies of trade."

"Well, what's the trouble about running the article," asked Thacker, a little impatiently, "if the man's well known and has got the stuff?"

Colonel Telfair sighed.

"Mr. Thacker," said he, "for once I have been tempted. Nothing has yet appeared in *The Rose of Dixie* that has not been from the pen of one of its sons or daughters. I know little about the author of this article except that he has acquired prominence in a section of the country that has always been inimical to my heart and mind. But I recognize his genius; and, as I have told you, I have instituted an investigation of his personality. Perhaps it will be futile. But I shall pursue the inquiry. Until that is finished, I must leave open the question of filling the vacant space in our January number."

Thacker arose to leave.

"All right, Colonel," he said, as cordially as he could. "You use your own judgment. If you've really got a scoop or something that will make 'em sit up, run it instead of my stuff. I'll drop in again in about two weeks. Good luck!"

Colonel Telfair and the magazine promoter shook hands.

Returning a fortnight later, Thacker dropped off a very rocky Pullman at Toombs City. He found the January number of the magazine made up and the forms closed.

The vacant space that had been yawning for type was filled by an article that was headed thus:

second message to congress
Written for
THE ROSE OF DIXIE
BY
A Member of the Well-Known
BULLOCH FAMILY, OF GEORGIA
T. ROOSEVELT

Schools and Schools

I

Old Jerome Warren lived in a hundred-thousand-dollar house at 35 East Fifty-Soforth Street. He was a downtown broker, so rich that he could afford to walk—for his health—a few blocks in the direction of his office every morning and then call a cab.

He had an adopted son, the son of an old friend named Gilbert—Cyril Scott could play him nicely—who was becoming a successful painter as fast as he could squeeze the paint out of his tubes. Another member of the household was Barbara Ross, a step-niece. Man is born to trouble; so, as old Jerome had no family of his own, he took up the burdens of others.

Gilbert and Barbara got along swimmingly. There was a tacit and tactical understanding all round that the two would stand up under a floral bell some high noon, and promise the minister to keep old Jerome's money in a state of high commotion. But at this point complications must be introduced.

Thirty years before, when old Jerome was young Jerome, there was a brother of his named Dick. Dick went West to seek his or somebody else's fortune. Nothing was heard of him until one day old Jerome had a letter from his brother. It was badly written on ruled paper that smelled of salt bacon and coffee-grounds. The writing was asthmatic and the spelling St. Vitusy.

It appeared that instead of Dick having forced Fortune to stand and deliver, he had been held up himself, and made to give hostages to the enemy. That is, as his letter disclosed, he was on the point of pegging out with a complication of disorders that even whiskey had failed to check. All that his thirty years of prospecting had netted him was one daughter, nineteen years old, as per invoice, whom he was shipping East, charges prepaid, for Jerome to clothe, feed, educate, comfort, and cherish for the rest of her natural life or until matrimony should them part.

Old Jerome was a board-walk. Everybody knows that the world is supported by the shoulders of Atlas; and that Atlas stands on a rail-fence; and that the rail-fence is built on a turtle's back. Now, the turtle has to stand on something; and that is a board-walk made of men like old Jerome.

I do not know whether immortality shall accrue to man; but if not so, I would like to know when men like old Jerome get what is due them?

They met Nevada Warren at the station. She was a little girl, deeply sunburned and wholesomely good-looking, with a manner that was frankly unsophisticated, yet one that not even a cigar-drummer would intrude upon without thinking twice. Looking at her, somehow you would expect to see her in a short skirt and leather leggings, shooting glass balls or taming mustangs. But in her plain white waist and black skirt she sent you guessing again. With an easy exhibition of strength she swung along a heavy valise, which the uniformed porters tried in vain to wrest from her.

"I am sure we shall be the best of friends," said Barbara, pecking at the firm, sunburned cheek.

"I hope so," said Nevada.

"Dear little niece," said old Jerome, "you are as welcome to my house as if it were your father's own."

"Thanks," said Nevada.

"And I am going to call you 'cousin,' " said Gilbert, with his charming smile.

"Thanks," said Nevada.

"Take the valise, please," said Nevada. "It weighs a million pounds. It's got samples from six of dad's old mines in it," she explained to Barbara. "I calculate they'd assay about nine cents to the thousand tons, but I promised him to bring them along."

II

It is a common custom to refer to the usual complications between one man and two ladies, or one lady and two men, or a lady and a man and a nobleman, or—well, any of these problems—as the triangle. But they are never unqualified triangles. They are always isosceles—never equilateral. So, upon the coming of Nevada Warren, she and Gilbert and Barbara Ross lined up into such a figurative triangle; and of that triangle Barbara formed the hypotenuse.

One morning old Jerome was lingering long after breakfast over the dullest morning paper in the city before setting forth to his downtown fly-trap. He had become quite fond of Nevada, finding in her much of his dead brother's quiet independence and unsuspicious frankness.

A maid brought in a note for Miss Nevada Warren.

"A messenger-boy delivered it at the door, please," she said. "He's waiting for an answer."

Nevada, who was whistling a Spanish waltz between her teeth, and watching the carriages and autos roll by in the street, took the envelope. She knew it was from Gilbert, before she opened it, by the little gold palette in the upper left-hand corner.

After tearing it open she pored over the contents for a while, absorbedly. Then, with a serious face, she went and stood at her uncle's elbow.

"Uncle Jerome, Gilbert is a nice boy, isn't he?"

"Why, bless the child!" said old Jerome, crackling his paper loudly; "of course he is. I raised him myself."

"He wouldn't write anything to anybody that wasn't exactly—I mean that everybody couldn't know and read, would he?"

"I'd just like to see him try it," said uncle, tearing a handful from his newspaper. "Why, what———"

"Read this note he just sent me, uncle, and see if you think it's all right and proper. You see, I don't know much about city people and their ways."

Old Jerome threw his paper down and set both his feet upon it. He took Gilbert's note and fiercely perused it twice, and then a third time.

"Why, child," said he, "you had me almost excited, although I was sure of that boy. He's a duplicate of his father, and he was a gilt-edged diamond. He only asks if you and Barbara will be ready at four o'clock this afternoon for an automobile drive over to Long Island. I don't see anything to criticize in it except the stationery. I always did hate that shade of blue."

"Would it be all right to go?" asked Nevada, eagerly.

"Yes, yes, yes, child, or course. Why not? Still, it pleases me to see you so careful and candid. Go, by all means."

"I didn't know," said Nevada, demurely. "I thought I'd ask you. Couldn't you go with us, uncle?"

"I? No, no, no, no! I've ridden once in a car that boy was driving. Never again! But it's entirely proper for you and Barbara to go. Yes, yes. But I will not. No, no, no, no!"

Nevada flew to the door, and said to the maid:

"You bet we'll go. I'll answer for Miss Barbara. Tell the boy to say to Mr. Warren, 'You bet we'll go.' "

"Nevada," called old Jerome, "pardon me, my dear, but wouldn't it be as well to send him a note in reply? Just a line would do."

"No, I won't bother about that," said Nevada, gayly. "Gilbert will understand—he always does. I never rode in an automobile in my life; but I've paddled a canoe down Little Devil River through the Lost Horse Cañon, and if it's any livelier than that I'd like to know!"

III

Two months are supposed to have elapsed.

Barbara sat in the study of the hundred-thousand-dollar house. It was a good place for her. Many places are provided in the world where men and women may repair for the purpose of extricating themselves from divers difficulties. There are cloisters, wailing-places, watering-places, confessionals; hermitages, lawyer's offices, beauty-parlors, airships, and studies; and the greatest of these are studies.

It usually takes a hypotenuse a long time to discover that it is the longest side of a triangle. But it's a long line that has no turning.

Barbara was alone. Uncle Jerome and Nevada had gone to the theatre. Barbara had not cared to go. She wanted to stay at home and study in the study. If you, miss, were a stunning New York girl, and saw every day that a brown, ingenuous Western witch was getting hobbles and a lasso on the young man you wanted for yourself, you, too, would lose taste for the oxidized silver setting of a musical comedy.

Barbara sat by the quartered-oak library table. Her right arm rested upon the table, and her dextral fingers nervously manipulated a sealed letter. The letter was addressed to Nevada Warren; and in the upper lef-hand corner of the envelope was Gilbert's little gold palette. It had been delivered at nine o'clock, after Nevada had left.

Barbara would have given her pearl necklace to know what that letter contained; but she could not open and read it by the aid of steam, or a pen-handle, or a hair-pin, or any of the generally approached methods, because her position in society forbade such an act. She had tried to read some of the lines of the letter by holding the envelope up to a strong light and pressing it hard against the paper, but Gilbert had too good a taste in stationery to make that possible.

At eleven-thirty the theatre-goers returned. It was a delicious winter night. Even so far as from the cab to the door they were powdered thickly with the big flakes downpouring diagonally from the east. Old Jerome growled good-naturedly about villainous cab service and blockaded streets. Nevada, colored like a rose, with sapphire eyes, babbled of the stormy nights in the mountains around dad's cabin. During all these wintry apostrophes, Barbara, cold at heart, sawed wood—the only appropriate thing she could think of to do.

Old Jermone went immediately upstairs to hot-water-bottles and quinine. Nevada fluttered into the study, the only cheerfully lighted room, subsided into an armchair, and, while at the interminable task of unbuttoning her elbow gloves, gave oral testimony as to the demerits of the "show."

"Yes, I think Mr. Fields is really amusing—sometimes," said Barbara. "Here is a letter for you, dear, that came by special delivery just after you had gone."

"Who is it from?" asked Nevada, tugging at a button.

"Well, really," said Barbara, with a smile, "I can only guess. The envelope has that queer little thing in one corner that Gilbert calls a palette, but which looks to me rather like a gilt heart on a schoolgirl's valentine."

"I wonder what he's writing to me about," remarked Nevada, listlessly.

"We're all alike," said Barbara; "all women. We try to find out what is in a letter by studying the postmark. As a last resort we use scissors, and read it from the bottom upward. Here it is."

She made a motion as if to toss the letter across the table to Nevada.

"Great catamounts!" exclaimed Nevada. "These centre-fire buttons are a nuisance. I'd rather wear buckskins. Oh, Barbara, please shuck the hide off that letter and read it. It'll be midnight before I get these gloves off!"

"Why, dear, you don't want me to open Gilbert's letter to you? It's for you, and you wouldn't wish any one else to read it, of course!"

Nevada raised her steady, calm, sapphire eyes from her gloves.

"Nobody writes me anything that everybody mightn't read," she said. "Go on, Barbara. Maybe Gilbert wants us to go out in his car again to-morrow."

Curiosity can do more things than kill a cat; and if emotions, well recognized as feminine, are inimical to feline life, then jealousy would soon leave the whole world catless. Barbara opened the letter, with an indulgent, slightly bored air.

"Well, dear," she said, "I'll read it if you want me to."

She slit the envelope, and read the missive with swift-travelling eyes; read it again, and cast a quick, shrewd glance at Nevada, who, for the time, seemed to consider gloves as the world of her interest, and letters from rising artists as no more than messages from Mars.

For a quarter of a minute Barbara looked at Nevada with a strange steadfastness; and then a smile so small that it widened her mouth only the sixteenth part of an inch, and narrowed her eyes no more than a twentieth flashed like an inspired thought across her face.

Since the beginning no woman has been a mystery to another woman. Swift as light travels, each penetrates the heart and mind of another, sifts her sister's words of their cunningest disguises, reads her most hidden desires, and plucks the sophistry from her wiliest talk like hairs from a comb, twiddling them sardonically between her thumb and fingers before letting them float away on the breezes of fundamental doubt. Long ago Eve's son rang the door-bell of the family residence in Paradise Park, bearing a strange lady on his arm, whom he introduced. Eve took her daughter-in-law aside and lifted a classic eyebrow.

"The Land of Nod," said the bride, languidly flirting the leaf of a palm. "I suppose you've been there, of course?"

"Not lately," said Eve, absolutely unstaggered. "Don't you think the applesauce they serve over there is execrable? I rather like that mulberry-leaf tunic effect, dear; but, of course, the real fig goods are not to be had over there. Come over behind this lilac-bush while the gentlemen split a celery tonic. I think the caterpillar-holes have made your dress open a little in the back."

So, then and there—according to the records—was the alliance formed by the only two who's-who ladies in the world. Then it was agreed that women should forever remain as clear as a pane of glass—though glass was yet to be discovered—to other women, and that she should palm herself off on a man as a mystery.

Barbara seemed to hesitate.

"Really, Nevada," she said, with a little show of embarrassment, "you shouldn't have insisted on my opening this. I—I'm sure it wasn't meant for any one else to know."

Nevada forgot her gloves for a moment.

"Then read it aloud," she said. "Since you've already read it, what's the difference? If Mr. Warren has written to me something that any one else oughtn't to know, that is all the more reason why everybody should know it."

"Well," said Babara, "this is what it says: 'Dearest Nevada—Come to my studio at twelve o'clock to-night. Do not fail.' " Barbara rose and dropped the note in Nevada's lap. "I'm awfully sorry," she said, "that I knew. It isn't like Gilbert. There must be some mistake. Just consider that I am ignorant of it, will you, dear? I must go upstairs now, I have such a headache. I'm sure I don't understand the note. Perhaps Gilbert has been dining too well, and will explain. Good night!"

IV

Nevada tiptoed to the hall, and heard Barbara's door close upstairs. The bronze clock in the study told the hour of twelve was fifteen minutes away. She ran swiftly to the front door, and let herself out into the snowstorm. Gilbert Warren's studio was six squares away.

By aërial ferry the white, silent forces of the storm attacked the city from beyond the sullen East River. Already the snow lay a foot deep on the pavements, the drifts heaping themselves like scaling-ladders against the walls of the besieged town. The Avenue was as quiet as a street in Pompeii. Cabs now and then skimmed past like white-winged gulls over a moonlit ocean; and less frequent motor-cars—sustaining the comparison—hissed through the foaming waves like submarine boats on their jocund, perilous journeys.

Nevada plunged like a wind-driven storm-petrel on her way. She looked up at the ragged sierras of cloud-capped buildings that rose above the streets, shaded by the night lights and the congealed vapors to gray, drab, ashen, lavender, dun, and cerulean tints. They were so like the wintry mountains of her Western home that she felt a satisfaction such as the hundred-thousand-dollar house had seldom brought her.

A policeman caused her to waver on a corner, just by his eye and weight.

"Hello, Mabel!" said he. "Kind of late for you to be out, ain't it?"

"I—I am just going to the drug store," said Nevada, hurrying past him.

The excuse serves as a passport for the most sophisticated. Does it prove that woman never progresses, or that she sprang from Adam's rib, full-fledged in intellect and wiles?

Turning eastward, the direct blast cut down Nevada's speed one half. She made zigzag tracks in the snow; but she was as tough as a piñon sapling, and bowed to it as gracefully. Suddenly the studio-building loomed before her, a familiar landmark, like a cliff above some well-remembered cañon. The haunt of business and its hostile neighbor, art, was darkened and silent. The elevator stopped at ten.

Up eight flights of Stygian stairs Nevada climbed, and rapped firmly at the door numbered "89." She had been there many times before, with Barbara and Uncle Jerome.

Gilbert opened the door. He had a crayon pencil in one hand, a green shade over his eyes, and a pipe in his mouth. The pipe dropped to the floor.

"Am I late?" asked Nevada. "I came as quick as I could. Uncle and me were at the theatre this evening. Here I am, Gilbert!"

Gilbert did a Pygmalion-and-Galatea act. He changed from a statue of stupefaction to a young man with a problem to tackle. He admitted Nevada, got a whiskbroom, and began to brush the snow from her clothes. A great lamp, with a green shade, hung over an easel, where the artist had been sketching in crayon.

"You wanted me," said Nevada, simply, "and I came. You said so in your letter. What did you send for me for?"

"You read my letter?" inquired Gilbert, sparring for wind.

"Barbara read it to me. I saw it afterward. It said: 'Come to my studio at twelve to-night, and do not fail.' I thought you were sick, of course, but you don't seem to be."

"Aha!" said Gilbert, irrelevantly. "I'll tell you why I asked you to come, Nevada. I want you to marry me immediately—to-night. What's a little snowstorm? Will you do it?"

"You might have noticed that I would, long ago," said Nevada. "And I'm rather stuck on the snowstorm idea, myself. I surely would hate one of those flowery church noon-weddings. Gilbert, I didn't know you had grit enough to propose in this way. Let's shock 'em—it's our funeral, ain't it?"

"You bet!" said Gilbert. "Where did I hear that expression?" he added to himself. "Wait a minute, Nevada; I want to do a little 'phoning."

He shut himself up in a little dressing-room, and called upon the lightnings of the heavens—condensed into unromantic numbers and districts.

"That you, Jack? You confounded sleepy-head! Yes, wake up; this is me—or I—oh, bother the difference in grammar! I'm going to be married right away. Yes! Wake up your sister—don't answer me back; bring her along, too—you *must.* Remind Agnes of the time I saved her from drowning in Lake Ronkonkoma—I know it's caddish to refer to it, but she *must* come with you. Yes! Nevada is here, waiting. We've been engaged quite a while. Some opposition among the relatives, you know, and we have to pull it off this way. We're waiting here for you. Don't let Agnes out-talk you—bring her! You will? Good old boy! I'll order a carriage to call for you, double-quick time. Confound you, Jack, you're all right!"

Gilbert returned to the room where Nevada waited.

"My old friend, Jack Peyton, and his sister were to have been here at a quarter to twelve," he explained; "but Jack is so confoundedly slow. I've just 'phoned them to hurry. They'll be here in a few minutes. I'm the happiest man in the world, Nevada! What did you do with the letter I sent you to-day?"

"I've got it cinched here," said Nevada, pulling it out from beneath her opera-cloak.

Gilbert drew the letter from the envelope and looked it over carefully. Then he looked at Nevada thoughtfully.

"Didn't you think it rather queer that I should ask you to come to my studio at midnight?" he asked.

"Why, no," said Nevada, rounding her eyes. "Not if you needed me. Out West, when a pal sends you a hurry call—ain't that what you say here?—we get there first and talk about it after the row is over. And it's usually snowing there, too, when things happen. So I didn't mind."

Gilbert rushed into another room, and came back burdened with overcoats warranted to turn wind, rain, or snow.

"Put this raincoat on," he said, holding it for her. "We have a quarter of a mile to go. Old Jack and his sister will be here in a few minutes." He began to struggle into a heavy coat. "Oh, Nevada," he said, "just look at the headlines on the front page of that evening paper on the table, will you? It's about your section of the West, and I know it will interest you."

He waited a full minute, pretending to find trouble in the getting on of his overcoat, and then turned. Nevada had not moved. She was looking at him with a strange and pensive directness. Her cheeks had a flush on them beyond the color that had been contributed by the wind and snow; but her eyes were steady.

"I was going to tell you," she said, "anyhow, before you—before we—before—well, before anything. Dad never gave me a day of schooling. I never learned to read or write a darned word. Now if—"

Pounding their uncertain way upstairs, the feet of Jack, the somnolent, and Agnes, the grateful, were heard.

V

When Mr. and Mrs. Gilbert Warren were spinning softly homeward in a closed carriage, after the ceremony, Gilbert said:

"Nevada, would you really like to know what I wrote you in the letter that you received to-night?"

"Fire away!" said his bride.

"Word for word," said Gilbert, "it was this: 'My dear Miss Warren—You were right about the flower. It was a hydrangea, and not a lilac.' "

"All right," said Nevada. "But let's forget it. The joke's on Barbara, anyway!"

Thimble, Thimble

These are the directions for finding the office of Carteret & Carteret, Mill Supplies and Leather Belting:

You follow the Broadway trail down until you pass the Crosstown Line, the Bread Line, and the Dead Line, and come to the Big Cañons of the Moneygrubber Tribe. Then you turn to the left, to the right, dodge a push-cart and the tongue of a two-ton four-horse dray, and hop, skip, and jump to a granite ledge on the side of a twenty-one-story synthetic mountain of stone and iron. In the twelfth story is the office of Carteret & Carteret. The factory where they make the mill supplies and leather belting is in Brooklyn. Those commodities—to say nothing of Brooklyn—not being of interest to you, let us hold the incidents within the confines of a one-act, one-scene play, thereby, lessening the toil of the reader and the expenditure of the publisher. So, if you have the courage to face four pages of type and Carteret & Carteret's office boy, Percival, you shall sit on a varnished chair in the inner office and peep at the little comedy of the Old Nigger Man, the Hunting-Case Watch, and the Open-Faced Question—mostly borrowed from the late Mr. Frank Stockton, as you will conclude.

First, biography (but pared to the quick) must intervene. I am for the inverted sugar-coated quinine pill—the bitter on the outside.

The Carterets were, or was (Columbia College professors please rule), an old Virginia family. Long time ago the gentlemen of the family had worn lace ruffles and carried tinless foils and owned plantations and had slaves to burn. But the war had greatly reduced their holdings. (Of course you can perceive at once that this flavor has been shoplifted from Mr. F. Hopkinson Smith, in spite of the "et" after "Carter.") Well, anyhow:

In digging up the Carteret history I shall not take you farther back than the year 1620. The two original American Carterets came over in that year, but by different means of transportation. One brother, named John, came in the *Mayflower* and became a Pilgrim Father. You've seen his pictures on the covers of the Thanksgiving magazines, hunting turkeys in the deep snow with a blunderbuss. Blandford Carteret, the other brother, crossed the pond in his own brigantine, landed on the Virginia coast, and became an F.F.V. John became distinguished for piety and shrewdness in business; Blandford for his pride, juleps, marksmanship, and vast slave-cultivated plantations.

Then came the Civil War. (I must condense this historical interpolation.) Stonewall Jackson was shot; Lee surrendered; Grant toured the world; cotton went to nine cents; Old Crow whiskey and Jim Crow cars were invented; the Seventy-ninth Massachusetts Volunteers returned to the Ninety-seventh Alabama Zouaves the battle flag of Lundy's Lane which they bought at a second-hand store in Chelsea, kept by a man named Skzchnzski; Georgia sent the President a sixty-pound watermelon—and that brings us up to the time when the story begins. My! but that was sparring for an opening! I really must brush up on my Aristotle.

The Yankee Carterets went into business in New York long before the war. Their house, as far as Leather Belting and Mill Supplies was concerned, was as musty and arrogant and solid as one of those old East India tea-importing concerns that you read about in Dickens. There were some rumors of a war behind its counters, but not enough to affect the business.

During and after the war, Blandford Carteret, F.F.V., lost his plantations, juleps, marksmanship, and life. He bequeathed little more than his pride to his surviving family. So it came to pass that Blandford Carteret, the Fifth, aged fifteen, was invited by the leather-and-mill-supplies branch of that name to come North and learn business instead of hunting foxes and boasting of the glory of his fathers on the reduced acres of his impoverished family. The boy jumped at the chance; and at the age of twenty-five, sat in the office of the firm equal partner with John, the fifth, of the blunderbuss-and-turkey branch. Here the story begins again.

The young men were about the same age, smooth of face, alert, easy of manner, and with an air that promised mental and physical quickness. They were razored, blue-serged, straw-hatted, and pearl stick-pinned like other young New Yorkers who might be millionaires or bill clerks.

One afternoon at four o'clock, in the private office of the firm, Blandford Carteret opened a letter that a clerk had just brought to his desk. After reading it, he chuckled audibly for nearly a minute. John looked around from his desk inquiringly.

"It's from mother," said Blandford. "I'll read you the funny part of it. She tells me all the neighborhood news first, of course, and then cautions me against getting my feet wet and musical comedies. After that come vital statistics about calves and pigs and an estimate of the wheat crop. And now I'll quote some:

" 'And what do you think! Old Uncle Jake, who was seventy-six last Wednesday, must go travelling. Nothing would do but he must go to New York and see his "young Marster Blandford." Old as he is, he has a deal of common sense, so I've let him go. I couldn't refuse him—he seemed to have concentrated all his hopes and desires into this one adventure into the wide world. You know he was born on the plantation, and has never been ten miles away from it in his life. And he was your father's body servant during the war, and has been always a faithful vassal and servant of the family. He has often seen the gold watch—the watch that was your father's and your father's father's. I told him it was to be yours, and he begged me to allow him to take it to you and put it into your hands himself.

" 'So he has it, carefully enclosed in a buckskin case, and is bringing it to you with all the pride and importance of a king's messenger. I gave him money for the round trip and for a two weeks' stay in the city. I wish you would see to it that he gets comfortable quarters—Jake won't need much looking after—he's able to take care of himself. But I have read in the papers that African bishops and colored potentates generally have much trouble in obtaining food and lodging in the Yankee metropolis. That may be all right; but I don't see why the best hotel there shouldn't take Jake in. Still, I suppose it's a rule.

" 'I gave him full direction about finding you, and packed his valise myself. You won't have to bother with him; but I do hope you'll see that he is made comfortable. Take the watch that he brings you—it's almost a decoration. It has been worn by true Carterets, and there isn't a stain upon it nor a false movement of the wheels. Bringing it to you is the crowning joy of old Jake's life. I wanted him to have that little outing and that happiness before it is too late. You have often heard us talk about how Jake, pretty badly wounded himself, crawled through the reddened grass at Chancellorsville to where your father lay with the bullet in his dear heart, and took the watch from his pocket to keep it from the "Yanks."

" 'So, my son, when the old man comes consider him as a frail but worthy messenger from the old-time life and home.

" 'You have been so long away from home and so long among the people that we have always regarded as aliens that I'm not sure that Jake will know you when he sees you. But Jake has a keen perception, and I rather believe that he will know a Virginia Carteret at sight. I can't conceive that even ten years in Yankeeland could change a boy of mine. Anyhow, I'm sure you will know Jake. I put eighteen collars in his valise. If he should have to buy others, he wears a number

15½. Please see that he gets the right ones. He will be no trouble to you at all.

" 'If you are not too busy, I'd like for you to find him a place to board where they have white-meal corn-bread, and try to keep him from taking his shoes off in your office or on the street. His right foot swells a little, and he likes to be comfortable.

" 'If you can spare the time, count his handkerchiefs when they come back from the wash. I bought him a dozen new ones before he left. He should be there about the time this letter reaches you. I told him to go straight to your office when he arrives.' "

As soon as Blandford had finished the reading of this, something happened (as there should happen in stories and must happen on the stage).

Percival, the office boy, with his air of despising the world's output of mill supplies and leather belting, came in to announce that a colored gentleman was outside to see Mr. Blandford Carteret.

"Bring him in," said Blandford, rising.

John Carteret swung around in his chair and said to Percival: "Ask him to wait a few minutes outside. We'll let you know when to bring him in."

Then he turned to his cousin with one of those broad, slow smiles that was an inheritance of all the Carterets, and said:

"Bland, I've always had a consuming curiosity to understand the differences that you haughty Southerners believe to exist between 'you all' and the people of the North. Of course, I know that you consider yourselves made out of finer clay and look upon Adam as only a collateral branch of your ancestry; but I don't know why. I never could understand the differences between us."

"Well, John," said Blandford, laughing, "what you don't understand about it is just the difference, of course. I suppose it was the feudal way in which we live that gave us our lordly baronial airs and feeling of superiority."

"But you are not feudal now," went on John. "Since we licked you and stole your cotton and mules you've had to go to work just as we 'damn yankees,' as you call us, have always been doing. And you're just as proud and exclusive and upper-classy as you were before the war. So it wasn't your money that caused it."

"Maybe it was the climate," said Blandford lightly, "or maybe our negroes spoiled us. I'll call old Jake in, now. I'll be glad to see the old villain again."

"Wait just a moment," said John. "I've got a little theory I want to test. You and I are pretty much alike in our general appearance. Old Jake hasn't seen you since you were fifteen. Let's have him in and play fair and see which of us gets the watch. The old darky surely ought to be able to pick out his 'young marster' without any trouble. The alleged aristocratic superiority of a 'reb' ought to be visible to him at once. He couldn't make the mistake of handing over the timepiece to a Yankee, of course. The loser buys the dinner this evening and two dozen 15½ collars for Jake. Is it a go?"

Blandford agreed heartily. Percival was summoned, and told to usher the "colored gentleman" in.

Uncle Jake stepped inside the private office cautiously. He was a little old man, as black as soot, wrinkled and bald except for a fringe of white wool, cut decorously short, that ran over his ears and around his head. There was nothing of the stage "uncle" about him; his black suit nearly fitted him; his shoes shone, and his straw hat was banded with a gaudy ribbon. In his right hand he carried something carefully concealed by his closed fingers.

Uncle Jake stopped a few steps from the door. Two young men sat in their revolving desk-chairs ten feet apart and looked at him in friendly silence. His gaze slowly shifted many times from one to the other. He felt sure that he was in the presence of one, at least, of the revered family among whose fortunes his life had begun and was to end.

One had the pleasing but haughty Carteret air; the other had the unmistakable straight, long family nose. Both had the keen black eyes, horizontal brows, and thin, smiling lips that has distinguished both the Carteret of the *Mayflower* and him of the brigantine. Old Jake had thought that he could have picked out his young master instantly from a thousand Northerners; but he found himself in difficulties. The best he could do was to use strategy.

"Howdy, Marse Blandford—howdy, suh?" he said, looking midway between the young men.

"Howdy, Uncle Jake?" they both answered pleasantly and in unison. "Sit down. Have you brought the watch?"

Uncle Jake chose a hard-bottom chair at a respectful distance, sat on the edge of it, and laid his hat carefully on the floor. The watch in its buckskin case he gripped tightly. He had not risked his life on the battlefield to rescue that watch from his "old marster's" foes to hand it over again to the enemy without a struggle.

"Yes, suh; I got it in my hand, suh. I'm gwine give it to you right away in jus' a minute. Old Missus told me to put it in young Marse Blandford's hand and tell him to wear it for the family pride and honor. It was a mighty lonesome trip for an old nigger man to make—ten thousand miles, it must be, back to old Virginia, suh. You've growed mightily, young marster. I wouldn't have recognized you but for yo' powerful resemblance to the old marster."

With admirable diplomacy the old man kept his eyes roaming in the space between the two men. His words might have been addressed to either. Though neither wicked nor perverse, he was seeking for a sign.

Blandford and John exchanged winks.

"I reckon you done got you ma's letter," went on Uncle Jake. "She said she was gwine to write to you about my comin' along up this er-way."

"Yes, yes, Uncle Jake," said John, briskly. "My cousin and I have just been notified to expect you. We are both Carterets you know."

"Although one of us," said Blandford, "was born and raised in the North."

"So if you will hand over the watch—" said John.

"My cousin and I—" said Blandford.

"We'll then see to it—" said John.

"That comfortable quarters are found for you," said Blandford.

With creditable ingenuity, old Jake set up a cackling, high-pitched, protracted laugh. He beat his knee, picked up his hat and bent the brim in an apparent paroxysm of humorous appreciation. The seizure afforded him a mask behind which he could roll his eye impartially between, above, and beyond his two tormentors.

"I sees what!" he chuckled, after a while. "You gen'lemen is tryin' to have fun with the po' old nigger. But you can't fool ol' Jake. I knowed you, Mars Blandford, the minute I sot eyes on you. You was a po' skimpy little boy no mo' than about fo'teen when you lef' home to come No'th; but I knowed you the minute I sot eyes on you. You is the mawtal image of old marster. The other gen'lemen resembles you mightily, suh; but you can't fool old Jake on a member of the old Vi'ginia family. No, suh."

At exactly the same time both Carterets smiled and extended a hand for the watch.

Uncle Jake's wrinkled black face lost the expression of amusement into which he had vainly twisted it. He knew that he was being teased, and that it made little real difference, as far as its safety went, into which of those outstretched hands he placed the family treasure.

But it seemed to him that not only his own pride and loyalty but much of the Virginia Carterets' was at stake. He had heard down South during the war about that other branch of the family that lived in the North and fought on "the yuther side," and it had always grieved him. He had followed his "old marster's" fortunes from stately luxury through war to almost poverty. And now, with the last relic and reminder of him, blessed by "old missus," and entrusted implicitly to his care, he had come ten thousand miles (as it seemed) to deliver it into the hands of the one who was to wear it and wind it and cherish it and listen to it tick off the unsullied hours that marked the lives of the Carterets—of Virginia.

His experience and conception of the Yankees had been an impression of tyrants—"low-down, common trash"— in blue, laying waste with fire and sword. He had seen the smoke of many burning homesteads almost as grand as Carteret Hall ascending to the drowsy Southern skies. And now he was face to face with one of them—and he could not distinguish him from his "young marster" whom he had come to find and bestow upon him the emblem of his kingship—even as the arm "clothed in white samite, mystic, wonderful" laid Excalibur in the right hand of Arthur. He saw before him two young men, easy, kind, courteous, welcoming, either of whom might have been the one he sought. Troubled, bewildered, sorely grieved at his weakness of judgment, old Jake abandonded his loyal subterfuges. His right hand sweated against the buckskin cover of the watch. He was deeply humiliated and chastened. Seriously, now, his prominent, yellow-white eyes closely scanned the two young men. At the end of his scrutiny he was conscious of but one difference between them. One wore a narrow black tie with a white pearl stickpin. The other's "four-in-hand" was a narrow blue one pinned with a black pearl.

And then, to old Jake's relief, there came a sudden distraction. Drama knocked at the door with imperious knuckles, and forced Comedy to the wings, and Drama peeped with a smiling but set face over the footlights.

Percival, the hater of mill supplies, brought in a card, which he handed with the manner of one bearing a cartel, to Blue-Tie.

"Olivia De Ormond," read Blue-Tie from the card. He looked inquiringly at his cousin.

"Why not have her in," said Black-Tie, "and bring matters to a conclusion?"

"Uncle Jake," said one of the young men, "would you mind taking that chair over there in the corner for a while? A lady is coming in—on some business. We'll take up your case afterward."

The lady whom Percival ushered in was young and petulantly, decidedly, freshly, consciously, and intentionally pretty. She was dressed with such expensive plainness that she made you consider lace and ruffles as mere tatters and rags. But one great ostrich plume that she wore would have marked her anywhere in the army of beauty as the wearer of the merry helmet of Navarre.

Miss De Ormond accepted the swivel chair at Blue-Tie's desk. Then the gentlemen drew leather-upholstered seats conveniently near, and spoke of the weather.

"Yes," said she, "I noticed it was warmer. But I mustn't take up too much of your time during business hours. That is," she continued, "unless we talk business."

She addressed her words to Blue-Tie with a charming smile.

"Very well," said he. "You don't mind my cousin being present, do you? We are generally rather confidential with each other—especially in business matters."

"Oh, no," carolled Miss De Ormond. "I'd rather he did hear. He knows all about it, anyhow. In fact, he's quite a material witness because he was present when you—when it happened. I thought you might want to talk things over before—well, before any action is taken, as I believe the lawyers say."

"Have you anything in the way of a proposition to make?" asked Black-Tie.

Miss De Ormond looked reflectively at the neat toe of one of her dull kid pumps.

"I had a proposal made to me," she said. "If the proposal sticks it cuts out the proposition. Let's have that settled first."

"Well, as far as—" began Blue-Tie.

"Excuse me, cousin," interrupted Black-Tie, "if you don't mind my cutting in." And then he turned, with a good-natured air toward the lady.

"Now, let's recapitulate a bit," he said, cheerfully. "All three of us, besides other mutual acquaintances, have been out on a good many larks together."

"I'm afraid I'll have to call the birds by another name," said Miss De Ormond.

"All right," responded Black-Tie, with unimpaired cheerfulness; "suppose we say 'squabs' when we talk about the 'proposal' and 'larks' when we discuss the 'proposition.' You have a quick mind, Miss De Ormond. Two months ago some half-dozen of us went in a motor-car for a day's run into the country. We stopped at a road-house for dinner. My cousin proposed marriage to you then and there. He was influenced to do so, of course, by the beauty and charm which no one can deny that you possess."

"I wish I had you for a press agent, Mr. Carteret," said the beauty, with a dazzling smile.

"You are on the stage, Miss De Ormond," went on Black-Tie. "You have had, doubtless, many admirers, and perhaps other proposals. You must remember, too, that we were a party of merry-makers on that occassion. There were a good many corks pulled. That the proposal of marriage was made to you by my cousin we cannot deny. But hasn't it been your experience that, by common consent, such things lose their seriousness when viewed in the next day's sunlight? Isn't there something of a 'code' among good 'sports'—I use the word in its best sense—that wipes out each day the follies of the evening previous?"

"Oh, yes," said Miss De Ormond. "I know that very well. And I've always played up to it. But as you seem to be conducting the case—with the silent consent of the defendant—I'll tell you something more. I've got letters from him repeating the proposal. And they're signed too."

"I understand," said Black-Tie, gravely. "What's your price for the letters?"

"I'm not a cheap one," said Miss De Ormond. "But I had decided to make you a rate. You both belong to a swell family. Well, if I *am* on the stage nobody can say a word against me truthfully. And the money is only a secondary consideration It isn't the money I was after. I—I believed him—and—and I liked him."

She cast a soft, entrancing glance at Blue-Tie from under her long eyelashes.

"And the price?" went on Black-Tie, inexorably.

"Ten thousand dollars," said the lady, sweetly.

"Or———"

"Or the fulfilment of the engagement to marry."

"I think it is time," interrupted Blue-Tie, "for me to be allowed to say a word or two. You and I, cousin, belong to a family that has held its head pretty high. You have been brought up in a section of the country very different from the one where our branch of the family lived. Yet both of us are Carterets, even if some of our ways and theories differ. You remember, it is a tradition of the family, that no Carteret ever failed in chivalry to a lady or failed to keep his word when it was given."

Then Blue-Tie, with frank decision showing on his countenance, turned to Miss De Ormond.

"Olivia," said he, "on what date will you marry me?"

Before she could answer, Black-Tie again interposed.

"It is a long journey," said he, "from Plymouth Rock to Norfolk Bay. Between the two points we find the changes that nearly three centuries have brought. In that time the old order has changed. We no longer burn witches or torture slaves. And to-day we neither spread our cloaks on the mud for ladies to walk over nor treat them to the ducking-stool. It is the age of common sense, adjustment, and proportion. All of us—ladies, gentlemen, women, men, Northerners, Southerners, lords, caitiffs, actors, hardware-drummers, senators, hod-carriers and politicians—are coming to a better understanding. Chivalry is one of our words that changes its meaning every day. Family pride is a thing of many constructions—it may show itself by maintaining a moth-eaten arrogance in a cob-webbed Colonial mansion or by the prompt paying of one's debts.

"Now I suppose you've had enough of my monologue. I've learned something of business and a little of life; and I somehow believe, cousin, that our great-great-grandfathers, the original Carterets, would endorse my view of this matter."

Black-Tie wheeled around to his desk, wrote in a checkbook and tore out the check, the sharp rasp of the perforated leaf making the only sound in the room. He laid the check within easy reach of Miss De Ormond's hand.

"Business is business," said he. "We live in a business age. There is my personal check for $10,000. What do you say, Miss De Ormond—will it be orange blossoms or cash?"

Miss De Ormond picked up the check carelessly, folded it indifferently, and stuffed it into her glove.

"Oh, this'll do," she said, calmly. "I just thought I'd call and put it up to you. I guess you people are all right. But a girl has feelings, you know. I've heard one of you was a Southerner—I wonder which one of you it is?"

She arose, smiled sweetly, and walked to the door. There, with a flash of white teeth and a dip of the heavy plume, she disappeared.

Both of the cousins had forgotten Uncle Jake for the time. But now they heard the shuffling of his shoes as he came across the rug toward them from his seat in the corner.

"Young marster," he said, "take yo' watch."

And without hesitation he laid the ancient timepiece in the hand of its rightful owner.

The Moment of Victory

Ben Granger is a war veteran aged twenty-nine—which should enable you to guess the war. He is also principal merchant and postmaster of Cadiz, a little town over which the breezes from the Gulf of Mexico perpetually blow.

Ben helped to hurl the Don from his stronghold in the Greater Antilles; and then, hiking across half the world, he marched as a corporal-usher up and down the blazing tropic aisles of the open-air college in which the Filipino was schooled. Now, with his bayonet beaten into a cheese slicer, he rallies his corporal's guard of cronies in the shade of his well-whittled porch, instead of in the matted jungles of Mindanao. Always have his interest and choice been for deeds rather than for words; but the consideration and digestion of motives is not beyond him, as this story, which is his, will attest.

"What is it," he asked me one moonlit eve, as we sat among his boxes and barrels, "that generally makes men go through danger, and fires, and trouble, and starvation, and battle, and such recourses? What does a man do it for? Why does he try to outdo his fellow-humans, and be braver and stronger and more daring and showy than even his best friends are? What's his game? What does he expect to get out of it? He don't do it just for the fresh air and exercise. What would you say, now, Bill, that an ordinary man expects, generally speaking, for his efforts along the line of ambition and extraordinary bustling in the market-places, forums, shooting-galleries, lyceums, battlefields, links, cinder-paths, and arenas of the civilized and *vice versa* places of the world?"

"Well, Ben," said I, with judicial seriousness, "I think we might safely limit the number of motives of a man who seeks fame to three—to ambition, which is a desire for popular applause; to avarice, which looks to the material side of success; and to love of some woman whom he either possesses or desires to possess."

Ben pondered over my words while a mocking-bird on the top of a mesquite by the porch trilled a dozen bars.

"I reckon," said he, "that your diagnosis about covers the case according to the rules laid down in the copybooks and historical readers. But what I had in my mind was the case of Willie Robbins, a person I used to know. I'll tell you about him before I close up the store, if you don't mind listening.

"Willie was one of our social set up in San Augustine. I was clerking there then for Brady & Murchison, wholesale dry-goods and ranch supplies. Willie and I belonged to the same German club and athletic association and military company. He played the triangle in our serenading and quartet crowd that used to ring the welkin three nights a week somewhere in town.

"Willie jibed with his name considerable. He weighed about as much as a hundred pounds of veal in his summer suitings, and he had a Where-is-Mary? expression on his features so plain that you could almost see the wool growing on him.

"And yet you couldn't fence him away from the girls with barbed wire. You know that kind of young fellows—a kind of a mixture of fools and angels—they rush in and fear to tread at the same time; but they never fail to tread when they get the chance. He was always on hand when 'a joyful occasion was had,' as the morning paper would say, looking as happy as a king full, and at the same time as uncomfortable as a raw oyster served with sweet pickles. He danced like he had hind hobbles on; and he had a vocabulary of about three hundred and fifty words that he made stretch over four germans a week, and plagiarized from to get him through two ice-cream suppers and a Sunday-night call. He seemed to me to be a sort of a mixture of Maltese kitten, sensitive plant, and a member of a stranded 'Two Orphans' company.

"I'll give you an estimate of his physiological and pictorial make-up and then I'll stick spurs into the sides of my narrative.

"Willie inclined to the Caucasian in his coloring and manner of style. His hair was opalescent and his conversation fragmentary. His eyes were the same blue shade as the china dog's in the right-hand corner of your Aunt Ellen's mantlepiece. He took things as they came, and I never felt any hostility against him. I let him live, and so did others.

"But what does this Willie do but coax his heart out of his boots and lose it to Myra Allison, the liveliest, brightest, keenest, smartest, and prettiest girl in San Augustine. I tell you, she had the blackest eyes, the shiniest curls, and the most tantalizing—Oh, no you're off—I wasn't a victim. I might have been, but I knew better. I kept out. Joe Granberry was It from the start. He had everybody else beat a couple of leagues and thence east to a stake and mound. But, anyhow, Myra was a nine-pound, full-merino, fall-clip fleece, sacked and loaded on a four-horse team to San Antone.

"One night there was an ice-cream sociable at Mrs. Colonel Spraggins', in San Augustine. We fellows had a big room upstairs opened up for us to put our hats and things in, and to comb our hair and put on the clean collars we brought along inside the sweat-bands of our hats—in short, a room to fix up in just like they have everywhere at high-toned doings. A little farther down the hall was the girls' room, which they used to powder up in, and so forth. Downstairs we—that is, the San Augustine Social Cotillion and Merrymakers' Club—had a stretcher put down in the parlor where our dance was going on.

"Willie Robbins and me happened to be up in our—cloak-room, I believe we called it—when Myra Allison skipped through the hall on her way downstairs from the girl's room. Willie was standing before the mirror, deeply interested in smoothing down the blond grassplot on his head, which seemed to give him lots of trouble. Myra was always full of life and devilment. She stopped and stuck her head in our door. She certainly was good-looking. But I knew how Joe Granberry stood with her. So did Willie; but he kept on ba-a-a-ing after her and following her around. He had a system of persistence that didn't coincide with pale hair and light eyes.

" 'Hello, Willie!' says Myra. 'What are you doing to yourself in the glass?'

" 'I'm trying to look fly,' says Willie.

" 'Well, you never could *be* fly,' says Myra with her special laugh, which was the provokingest sound I ever heard except the rattle of an empty canteen against my saddle-horn.

"I looked around at Willie after Myra had gone. He had a kind of a lily-white look on him which seemed to show that her remark had, as you might say, disrupted his soul. I never noticed anything in what she said that sounded particularly destructive to a man's ideas of self-consciousness; but he was set back to an extent you could scarcely imagine.

"After we went downstairs with our clean collars on, Willie never went near Myra again that night. After all, he seemed to be a diluted kind of a skim-milk sort of a chap, and I never wondered that Joe Granberry beat him out.

"The next day the battleship *Maine* was blown up, and then pretty soon somebody—I reckon it was Joe Bailey, or Ben Tillman, or maybe the Government—declared war against Spain.

"Well, everybody south of Mason & Hamlin's line knew that the North by itself couldn't whip a whole country the size of Spain. So the Yankees commence to holler for help, and the Johnny Rebs answered the call. 'We're coming, Father William, a hundred thousand strong—and then some,' was the way they sang it. And the old party lines drawn by Sherman's march and the Kuklux and nine-cent cotton and the Jim Crow street-car ordinances faded away. We became one undivided country with no North, very little East, a good-sized chunk of West, and a South that loomed up as big as the first foreign label in a new eight-dollar suitcase.

"Of course the dogs of war weren't a complete pack without a yelp from the San Augustine Rifles, Company D, of the Fourteenth Texas Regiment. Our company was among the first to land in Cuba and strike terror into the hearts of the foe. I'm not going to give you a history of the war; I'm just dragging it in to fill out my story about Willie Robbins, just as the Republican party dragged it in to help out the election in 1898.

"If anybody ever had heroitis, it was that Willie Robbins. From the minute he set foot on the soil of the tyrants of Castile he seemed to engulf danger as a cat laps up cream. He certainly astonished every man in our company, from the captain up. You'd have expectd him to gravitate naturally to the job of an orderly to the colonel, or typewriter in the commissary—but not any. He created the part of the flaxen-haired boy hero who lives and gets back home with the goods, instead of dying with an important despatch in his hands at his colonel's feet.

"Our company got into a section of Cuban scenery where one of the messiest and most unsung portions of the campaign occurred. We were out every day capering around in the bushes, and having little skirmishes with the Spanish troops that looked more like kind of tired-out feuds than anything else. The war was a joke to us, and of no interest to them. We never could see it any other way than as a howling farce-comedy that the San Augustine Rifles were actually fighting to uphold the Stars and Stripes. And the blamed little señors didn't get enough pay to make them care whether they were patriots or traitors. Now and then somebody would get killed. It seemed like a waste of life to me. I was at Coney Island when I went to New York once, and one of them down-hill skidding apparatuses they call 'roller-coasters' flew the track and killed a man in a brown sack-suit. Whenever the Spaniards shot one of our men, it struck me as just about as unnecessary and regrettable as that was.

"But I'm dropping Willie Robbins out of the conversation.

"He was out for bloodshed, laurels, ambitions, medals, recommendations, and all other forms of military glory. And he didn't seem to be afraid of any of the recognized forms of military danger, such as Spaniards, cannon-balls, canned beef, gunpowder, or nepotism. He went forth with his pallid hair and china-blue eyes and ate up Spaniards like you would sardines *à la* canopy. Wars and rumbles of wars never flustered him. He would stand guard-duty, mosquitoes, hard-tack, treat, and fire with equally perfect unanimity. No blondes in history ever come in comparison distance of him except the Jack of Diamonds and Queen Catherine of Russia.

"I remember, one time, a little *caballard* of Spanish men sauntered out from behind a patch of sugar-cane and shot Bob Turner, the first sergeant of our company, while we were eating dinner. As required by the army regulations, we fellows went through the usual tactics of falling into line, saluting the enemy, and loading and firing, kneeling.

"That wasn't the Texas way of scrapping; but, being a very important addendum and annex to the regular army, the San Augustine Rifles had to conform to the red-tape system of getting even.

"By the time we had got out our 'Upton's Tactics,' turned to page fifty-seven, said 'one—two—three—one—two—three' a couple of times, and got black cartridges into our Springfields, the Spanish outfit had smiled repeatedly, rolled and lit cigarettes by squads, and walked away contemptuously.

"I went straight to Captain Floyd, and says to him: 'Sam, I don't think this war is a straight game. You know as well as I do that Bob Turner was one of the whitest fellows that ever threw a leg over a saddle, and now these wire-pullers in Washington have fixed his clock. He's politically and ostensibly dead. It ain't fair. Why should they keep this thing up? If they want Spain licked, why don't they turn the San Augustine Rifles and Joe Seely's ranger company and a carload of West Texas deputy-sheriffs on to these Spaniards, and let us exonerate them from the face of the earth? I never did,' says I, 'care much about fighting by the Lord Chesterfield ring rules. I'm going to hand in my resignation and go home if anybody else I am personally acquainted with gets hurt in this war. If you can get somebody in my place, Sam,' says I, 'I'll quit the first of next week. I don't want to work in any army that don't give its help a chance. Never mind my wages,' says I; 'let the Secretary of the Treasury keep 'em.'

" 'Well, Ben,' says the Captain to me, 'your allegations and estimations of the tactics of war, government, patriotism, guard-mounting, and democracy are all right. But I've looked into the system of international arbitration and the ethics of justifiable slaughter a little closer, maybe, than you have. Now, you can hand in your resignation the first of next week if you are so minded. But if you do,' says Sam, 'I'll order a corporal's guard to take you over by that limestone bluff on the creek and shoot enough lead into you to ballast a submarine airship. I'm captain of this company, and I've swore allegiance to the Amalgamated States regardless of sectional, secessional, and Congressional differences. Have you got any smoking-tobacco?' winds up Sam. 'Mine got wet when I swum the creek this morning.'

"The reason I drag all this *non ex parte* evidence in is because Willie Robbins was standing there listening to us. I was a second sergeant and he was a private then, but among us Texans and Westerners there never was as much tactics and subordination as there was in the regular army. We never called our captain anything but 'Sam' except when there was a lot of major-generals and admirals around, so as to preserve the discipline.

"And says Willie Robbins to me, in a sharp construction of voice much unbecoming to his light hair and previous record:

" 'You ought to be shot, Ben, for emitting any such sentiments. A man that won't fight for his country is worse than a horse-thief. If I was the cap, I'd put you in the guardhouse for thirty days on round steak and tamales. War,' says Willie, 'is great and glorious. I didn't know you were a coward.'

" 'I'm not,' says I. 'If I was, I'd knock some of the pallidness of your marble brow. I'm lenient with you,' I says, 'just as I am with the Spaniards, because you have always reminded me of something with mushrooms on the side. Why, you little Lady of Shalott,' says I, 'you underdone leader of cotillions, you glassy fashion and moulded form, you white-pine soldier made in the Cisalpine Alps in Germany for the late New-Year trade, do you know of whom you are talking to? We've been in the same social circle,' says I, 'and I've put up with you because you seemed so meek and self-unsatisfying. I don't understand why you have so sudden taken a personal interest in chivalrousness and murder. Your nature's undergone a complete revelation. Now, how is it?"

" 'Well, you wouldn't understand, Ben,' says Willie, giving one of his refined smiles and turning away.

" 'Come back here!' says I, catching him by the tail of his khaki coat. 'You've made me kind of mad, in spite of the aloofness in which I have heretofore held you. You are out for making a success in this hero business, and I believe I know what for. You are doing it either because you are crazy or because you expect to catch some girl by it. Now, if it's a girl, I've got something here to show you.'

"I wouldn't have done it, but I was plumb mad. I pulled a San Augustine paper out of my hip-pocket, and showed him an item. It was a half column about the marriage of Myra Allison and Joe Granberry.

"Willie laughed, and I saw I hadn't touched him.

" 'Oh,' says he, 'everybody knew that was going to happen. I heard about that a week ago.' And then he gave me the laugh again.

" 'All right,' says I. 'Then why do you so recklessly chase the bright rainbow of fame? Do you expect to be elected President, or do you belong to a suicide club?'

"And then Captain Sam interferes.

" 'You gentlemen quit jawing and go back to your quarters,' says he, 'or I'll have you escorted to the guardhouse. Now, scat, both of you! Before you go, which one of you has got any chewing-tobacco?'

" 'We're off, Sam,' says I. 'It's supper-time, anyhow. But what do you think of what we was talking about? I've noticed you throwing out a good many grappling-hooks for this here balloon called fame—What's ambition, anyhow? What does a man risk his life day after day for? Do you know of anything he gets in the end that can pay him for the trouble? I want to go back home,' says I. 'I don't care whether Cuba sinks or swims, and I don't give a pipeful of rabbit tobacco whether Queen Sophia Christina or Charlie Culberson rules these fairy isles; and I don't want my name on any list except the list of survivors. But I've noticed you, Sam,' says I, 'seeking the bubble of notoriety in the cannon's larynx a number of times. Now, what do you do it for? Is it ambition, business, or some freckle-faced Phœbe at home that you are heroing for?'

" 'Well, Ben,' says Sam, kind of hefting his sword out from between his knees, 'as your superior officer I could court-martial you for attempted cowardice and desertion. But I won't. And I'll tell you why I'm trying for promotion and the usual honors of war and conquests. A major gets more pay than a captain, and I need the money.'

" 'Correct for you!' says I. 'I can understand that. Your system of fame-seeking is rooted in the deepest soil of patriotism. But I can't comprehend,' says I, 'why Willie Robbins, whose folks at home are well off, and who used to be as meek and undesirous of notice as a cat with cream on his whiskers, should all at once develop into a warrior bold with the most fire-eating kind of proclivities. And the girl in his case seems to have been eliminated by marriage to another fellow. I reckon,' says I, 'it's a plain case of just common ambition. He wants his name, maybe, to go thundering down the corners of time. It must be that.'

"Well, without itemizing his deeds, Willie sure made good as a hero. He simply spent most of his time on his knees begging our captain to send him on forlorn hopes and dangerous scouting expeditions. In every fight he was the first man to mix it at close quarters with the Don Alfonsos. He got three or four bullets planted in various parts of his autonomy. Once he went off with a detail of eight men and captured a whole company of Spanish. He kept Captain Floyd busy writing out recommendations of his bravery to send in to headquarters; and he began to accumulate medals for all kinds of things—heroism and target-shooting and valor and tactics and uninsubordination, and all the little accomplishment that look good to the third assistant secretaries of the War Department.

"Finally, Cap Floyd got promoted to be a major general, or a knight commander of the main herd, or something like that. He pounded around on a white horse, all desecrated up with gold-leaf and hen-feathers and a Good Templar's hat, and wasn't allowed by the regulations to speak to us. And Willie Robbins was made captain of our company.

"And maybe he didn't go after the wreath of fame then! As far as I could see it was him that ended the war. He got eighteen of us boys—friends of his, too—killed in battles that he stirred up himself and that didn't seem to me necessary at all. One night he took twelve of us and waded through a little rill about a hundred and ninety yards wide, and climbed a couple of mountains, and sneaked through a mile of neglected shrubbery and a couple of rock-quarries and into a rye-straw village, and captured a Spanish general named, as they said, Benny Veedus. Benny seemed to me hardly worth the trouble, being a blackish man without shoes or cuffs, and anxious to surrender and throw himself on the commissary of his foe.

"But that job gave Willie the big boost he wanted. The San Augustine *News* and the Galveston, St. Louis, New York, and Kansas City papers printed his picture and columns of stuff about him. Old San Augustine simply went crazy over its 'gallant son.' The *News* had an editorial tearfully begging the government to call off the regular army and the national guard, and let Willie carry on the rest of the war single-handed. It said that a refusal to do so would be regarded as a proof that the Northern jealousy of the South was still as rampant as ever.

"If the war hadn't ended pretty soon, I don't know to what heights of gold braid and encomiums Willie would have climbed; but it did. There was a secession of hostilities just three days after he was appointed a colonel, and got in three more medals by registered mail and shot two Spaniards while they were drinking lemonade in an ambuscade.

"Our company went back to San Augustine when the war was over. There wasn't anywhere else for it to go. And what do you think? The old town notified us in print, by wire cable, special delivery, and a nigger named Saul sent on a gray mule to San Antone, that they was going to give us the biggest blowout, complimentary, alimentary, and elementary, that ever disturbed the kildees on the sand-flats outside of the immediate continguity of the city.

"I say 'we,' but it was all meant for ex-Private, Captain *de facto*, and Colonel-elect Willie Robbins. The town was crazy about him. They notified us that the reception they were going to put up would make the Mardi Gras in New Orleans look like an afternoon tea in Bury St. Edmonds with a curate's aunt.

"Well, the San Augustine Rifles got back home on schedule time. Everybody was at the depot giving forth Roosevelt-Democrat—they used to be called Rebel—yells. There was two brass-bands, and the mayor, and schoolgirls in white frightening the street-car horses by throwing Cherokee roses in the streets, and—well, maybe you've seen a celebration by a town that was inland and out of water.

"They wanted Brevet Colonel Willie to get into a carriage and be drawn by prominent citizens and some of the city aldermen to the armory, but he stuck to his company and marched at the head of it up Sam Houston Avenue. The buildings on both sides was covered with flags and audiences, and everybody hollered 'Robbins!' or 'Hello, Willie!' as we marched up in files of fours. I never saw a illustriouserlooking human in my life than Willie was. He had at least seven or eight medals and diplomas and decorations on the breast of his khaki coat; he was sunburnt the color of saddle, and he certainly done himself proud.

"They told us at the depot that the court-house was to be illuminated at half-past seven, and there would be speeches and chili-concarne at the Palace Hotel. Miss Delphine Thompson was to read an original poem by James Whitcomb Ryan, and Constable Hooker had promised us a salute of nine guns from Chicago that he had arrested that day.

"After we had disbanded in the armory, Willie says to me:

" 'Want to walk out a piece with me?'

" 'Why, yes,' says I, 'if it ain't so far that we can't hear the tumult and the shouting die away. I'm hungry myself,' says I, 'and I'm pining for some home grub, but I'll go with you.'

"Willie steered me down some side streets till we came to a little white cottage in a new lot with a twenty-by-thirty-foot lawn decorated with brickbats and old barrel-staves.

" 'Halt and give the countersign,' says I to Willie. 'Don't you know this dugout? It's the bird's-nest that Joe Granberry built before he married Myra Allison. What you going there for?'

"But Willie already had the gate open. He walked up the brick walk to the steps, and I went with him. Myra was sitting in a rocking chair on the porch, sewing. Her hair was smoothed back kind of hasty and tied in a knot. I never noticed till then that she had freckles. Joe was at one side of the porch, in his shirt-sleeves, with no collar on, and no signs of a shave, trying to scrape out a hole among the brickbats and tin cans to plant a little fruit-tree in. He looked up but never said a word, and neither did Myra.

"Willie was sure dandy-looking in his uniform, with medals strung on his breast and his new gold-handled sword. You'd never have taken him for the little white-headed snipe that the girls used to order about and make fun of. He just stood there for a minute, looking at Myra with a peculiar little smile on his face; and then he says to her, slow, and kind of holding on to his words with his teeth:

" 'Oh, I don't know! Maybe I could if I tried!'

"That was all that was said. Willie raised his hat, and we walked away.

"And, somehow, when he said that, I remembered, all of a sudden, the night of that dance and Willie brushing his hair before the looking-glass, and Myra sticking her head in the door to guy him.

"When we got back to Sam Houston Avenue, Willie says:

" 'Well, so long, Ben. I'm going down home and get off my shoes and take a rest.'

" 'You?' says I. 'What's the matter with you? Ain't the courthouse crammed with everybody in town waiting to honor the hero? And two brass-bands, and recitations and flags and jags, and grub to follow waiting for you?'

"Willie sighs.

" 'All right, Ben,' says he. 'Darned if I didn't forget all about that.'

"And that's why I say," concluded Ben Granger, "that you can't tell where ambition begins any more than you can where it is going to wind up."

No Story

To avoid having this book hurled into a corner of the room by the suspicious reader, I will assert in time that this is not a newspaper story. You will encounter no shirt-sleeved, omniscient city editor, no prodigy "cub" reporter just off the farm, no scoop, no story—no anything.

But if you will concede me the setting of the first scene in the reporters' room of the *Morning Beacon,* I will repay the favor by keeping strictly my promises set forth above.

I was doing space-work on the *Beacon,* hoping to be put on a salary. Some one had cleared with a rake or a shovel a small space for me at the end of a long table piled high with exchanges, *Congressional Records* and old files. There I did my work. I wrote whatever the city whispered or roared or chuckled to me on my diligent wanderings about its streets. My income was not regular.

One day Tripp came in and leaned on my table. Tripp was something in the mechanical department—I think he had something to do with the pictures, for he smelled of photographers' supplies, and his hands were always stained and cut up with acids. He was about twenty-five and looked forty. Half of his face was covered with short, curly red whiskers that looked like a door-mat with the "welcome" left off. He was pale and unhealthy and miserable and fawning, and an assiduous borrower of sums ranging from twenty-five cents to a dollar. One dollar was his limit. He knew the extent of his credit as well as the Chemical National Bank knows the amount of H_2O that collateral will show on analysis. When he sat on my table he held one hand with the other to keep both from shaking. Whiskey. He had a spurious air of lightness and bravado about him that deceived no one, but was useful in his borrowing because it was so pitifully and perceptibly assumed.

This day I had coaxed from the cashier five shining silver dollars as a grumbling advance on a story that the Sunday editor had reluctantly accepted. So if I was not feeling at peace with the world, at least an armistice had been declared; and I was beginning with ardor to write a description of the Brooklyn Bridge by moonlight.

"Well, Tripp," said I, looking up at him rather impatiently, "how goes it?" He was looking to-day more miserable, more cringing and haggard and down-trodden than I had ever seen him. He was at that stage of misery where he drew your pity so fully that you longed to kick him.

"Have you got a dollar?" asked Tripp, with his most fawning look and his dog-like eyes that blinked in the narrow space between his high-growing matted beard and his low-growing matted hair.

"I have," said I; and again I said, "I have," more loudly and inhospitably, "and four besides. And I had hard work corkscrewing them out of old Atkinson, I can tell you. And I drew them," I continued, "to meet a want—a hiatus—a demand—a need—an exigency—a requirement of exactly five dollars."

I was driven to emphasis by the premonition that I was to lose one of the dollars on the spot.

"I don't want to borrow any," said Tripp, and I breathed again. "I thought you'd like to get put onto a good story," he went on. "I've got a rattling fine one for you. You ought to make it run a column at least. It'll make a dandy if you work it up right. It'll probably cost you a dollar or two to get the stuff. I don't want anything out of it myself."

I became placated. The proposition showed that Tripp appreciated past favors, although he did not return them. If he had been wise enough to strike me for a quarter then he would have got it.

"What is the story?" I asked, poising my pencil with a finely calculated editorial air.

"I'll tell you," said Tripp. "It's a girl. A beauty. One of the howlingest Amsden's Junes you ever saw. Rosebuds covered with dew—violets in their mossy bed—and truck like that. She's lived on Long

Island twenty years and never saw New York City before. I ran against her on Thirty-fourth Street. She'd just got in on the East River ferry. I tell you, she's a beauty that would take the hydrogen out of all the peroxides in the world. She stopped me on the street and asked me where she could find George Brown. Asked me where she could find *George Brown in New York City!* What do you think of that?

"I talked to her, and found that she was going to marry a young farmer named Dodd—Hiram Dodd—next week. But it seems that George Brown still holds the championship in her youthful fancy. George had greased his cowhide boots some years ago, and came to the city to make his fortune. But he forgot to remember to show up again at Greenburg, and Hiram got in as second-best choice. But when it comes to the scratch Ada—her name's Ada Lowery—saddles a nag and rides eight miles to the railroad station and catches the 6:45 A.M. train for the city. Looking for George, you know—you understand about women—George wasn't there, so she wanted him.

"Well, you know, I couldn't leave her loose in Wolftown-on-the-Hudson. I suppose she thought the first person she inquired of would say: 'George Brown?—why, yes—lemme see—he's a short man with light-blue eyes, ain't he? Oh, yes—you'll find George on One Hundred and Twenty-fifth Street, right next to the grocery. He's bill-clerk in a saddle-and-harness store.' That's about how innocent and beautiful she is. You know those little Long Island water-front villages like Greenburg—a couple of duck-farms for sport, and clams and about nine summer visitors for industries. That's the kind of a place she comes from. But, say—you ought to see her!

"What could I do? I don't know what money looks like in the morning. And she'd paid her last cent of pocket-money for her railroad ticket except a quarter, which she had squandered on gum-drops. She was eating them out of a paper-bag. I took her to a boarding-house on Thirty-second Street where I used to live, and hocked her. She's in soak for a dollar. That's old Mother McGinnis' price per day. I'll show you the house."

"What words are these, Tripp?" said I. "I thought you said you had a story. Every ferryboat that crosses the East River brings or takes away girls from Long Island."

The premature lines on Tripp's face grew deeper. He frowned seriously from his tangle of hair. He separated his hands and emphasized his answer with one shaking forefinger.

"Can't you see," he said, "what a rattling fine story it would make? You could do it fine. All about the romance, you know, and describe the girl, and put a lot of stuff in it about true love, and sling in a few stickfuls of funny business—joshing the Long Islanders about being green, and, well—you know how to do it. You ought to get fifteen dollars out of it, anyhow. And it'll cost you only about four dollars. You'll make a clear profit of eleven."

"How will it cost me four dollars?" I asked, suspiciously.

"One dollar to Mrs. McGinnis," Tripp answered, promptly, "and two dollars to pay the girl's fare back home."

"And the fourth dimension?" I inquired, making a rapid mental calculation.

"One dollar to me," said Tripp, "for whiskey. Are you on?"

I smiled enigmatically and spread my elbows as if to begin writing again. But this grim, abject, specious, subservient, burr-like wreck of a man would not be shaken off. His forehead suddenly became shiningly moist.

"Don't you see," he said, with a sort of desperate calmness, "that this girl has got to be sent home to-day—not to-night nor to-morrow, but to-day? I can't do anything for her. You know, I'm the janitor and corresponding secretary of the Down-and-Out Club. I thought you could make a newspaper story out of it and win out a piece of money on general results. But, anyhow, don't you see that she's got to get back home before night?"

And then I began to feel that dull, leaden, soul-depressing sensation known as the sense of duty. Why should that sense fall upon one as a weight and a burden? I knew that I was doomed that day to give up the bulk of my store of hard-wrung coin to the relief of this Ada Lowery. But I swore to myself that Tripp's whiskey dollar would not be forthcoming. He might play knight-errant at my expense, but he would indulge in no wassail afterward, commemorating my weakness and guillibility. In a kind of chilly anger I put on my coat and hat.

Tripp, submissive, cringing, vainly endeavoring to please, conducted me *via* the street-cars to the human pawn-shop of Mother McGinnis. I paid the fares. It seemed that the collodion-scented Don Quixote and the smallest minted coin were strangers.

Tripp pulled the bell at the door of the mouldy red-brick boarding-house. At its faint tinkle he paled, and crouched as a rabbit makes ready to spring away at the sound of a hunting-dog. I guessed what a life he had led, terror-haunted by the coming footsteps of landladies.

"Give me one of the dollars—quick!" he said.

The door opened six inches. Mother McGinnis stood there with white eyes—they were white, I say—and a yellow face, holding together at her throat with one hand a dingy pink flannel dressing-sack. Tripp thrust the dollar through the space without a word, and it bought us entry.

"She's in the parlor," said the McGinnis, turning the back of her sack upon us.

In the dim parlor a girl sat at the cracked marble centre-table weeping comfortably and eating gum-drops. She was a flawless beauty. Crying had only made her brilliant eyes brighter. When she crunched a gum-drop you thought only of the poetry of motion and envied the senseless confection. Eve at the age of five minutes must have been a ringer for Miss Ada Lowery at nineteen or twenty. I was introduced, and a gum-drop suffered neglect while she conveyed to me a naïve interest, such as a puppy dog (a prize winner) might bestow upon a crawling beetle or a frog.

Tripp took his stand by the table, with the fingers of one hand spread upon it, as an attorney or a master of ceremonies might have stood. But he looked the master of nothing. His faded coat was buttoned high, as if it sought to be charitable to deficiencies of tie and linen. I thought of a Scotch terrier at the sight of his shifty eyes in the glade between his tangled hair and beard. For one ignoble moment I felt ashamed of having been introduced as his friend in the presence of so much beauty in distress. But evidently Tripp meant to conduct the ceremonies, whatever they might be. I thought I detected in his actions and pose an intention of foisting the situation upon me as material for a newspaper story, in a lingering hope of extracting from me his whiskey dollar.

"My friend" (I shuddered), "Mr. Chalmers," said Tripp, "will tell you, Miss Lowery, the same that I did. He's a reporter, and he can hand out the talk better than I can. That's why I brought him with me." (O Tripp, wasn't it the *silver*-tongued orator you wanted?) "He's wise to a lot of things, and he'll tell you now what's best to do."

I stood on one foot, as it were, as I sat in my rickety chair.

"Why—er—Miss Lowery," I began, secretly enraged at Tripp's awkward opening, "I am at your service, of course, but—er—as I haven't been apprized of the circumstances of the case, I—er———"

"Oh," said Miss Lowery, beaming for a moment, "it ain't as bad as that—there ain't any circumstances. It's the first time I've ever been in New York except once when I was five years old, and I had no idea it was such a big town. And I met Mr.—Mr. Snip on the street and asked him about a friend of mine, and he brought me here and asked me to wait."

"I advise you, Miss Lowery," said Tripp, "to tell Mr. Chalmers all. He's a friend of mine" (I was getting used to it by this time), "and he'll give you the right tip."

"Why, certainly," said Miss Ada, chewing a gum-drop toward me. "There ain't anything to tell except that—well, everything's fixed for me to marry Hiram Dodd next Thursday evening. Hi has got two hundred acres of land with a lot of shore-front, and one of the best truck-farms on the Island. But this morning I had my horse saddled up—he's a white horse named Dancer—and I rode over to the station. I told 'em at home I was going to spend the day with Susie Adams. It was a story, I guess, but I don't care. And I came to New York on the train, and I met Mr.—Mr. Flip on the street and asked him if he knew where I could find G—G———"

"Now, Miss Lowery," broke in Tripp, loudly, and with much bad taste, I thought, as she hesitated with her word, "you like this young man, Hiram Dodd, don't you? He's all right, and good to you, ain't he?"

"Of course I like him," said Miss Lowery, emphatically. "Hi's all right. And of course he's good to me. So is everybody."

I could have sworn it myself. Throughout Miss Ada Lowery's life all men would be good to her. They would strive, contrive, struggle, and compete to hold umbrellas over her hat, check her trunk, pick up her handkerchief, and buy for her soda at the fountain.

"But," went on Miss Lowery, "last night I got to thinking about G—George and I—"

Down went the bright gold head upon her dimpled, clasped hands on the table. Such a beautiful April storm! Unrestrainedly she sobbed. I wished I could have comforted her. But I was not George. And I was glad I was not Hiram—and yet I was sorry, too.

By-and-by the shower passed. She straightened up, brave and half-way smiling. She would have made a splendid wife, for crying only made her eyes more bright and tender. She took a gum-drop and began her story.

"I guess I'm a terrible hayseed," she said, between her little gulps and sighs, "but I can't help it. G—George Brown and I were sweethearts since he was eight and I was five. When he was nineteen—that was four years ago—he left Greenburg and went to the city. He said he was going to be a policeman or a railroad president or something. And then he was coming back for me. But I never heard from him any more. And I—I—liked him."

Another flow of tears seemed imminent, but Tripp hurled himself into the crevasse and dammed it. Confound him, I could see his game. He was trying to make a story of it for his sordid ends and profit.

"Go on, Mr. Chalmers," said he, "and tell the lady what's the proper caper. That's what I told her—you'd hand it to her straight. Spiel up."

I coughed, and tried to feel less wrathful toward Tripp. I saw my duty. Cunningly I had been inveigled, but I was securely trapped. Tripp's first dictum to me had been just and correct. The young lady must be sent back to Greenburg that day. She must be argued with, convinced, assured, instructed, ticketed, and returned without delay. I hated Hiram and despised George; but duty must be done. *Noblesse oblige* and only five silver dollars are not strictly romantic compatibles, but sometimes they can be made to jibe. It was mine to be Sir Oracle, and then pay the freight. So I assumed an air that mingled Solomon's with that of the general passenger agent of the Long Island Railroad.

"Miss Lowery," said I, as impressively as I could, "life is rather a queer proposition, after all." There was a familiar sound to these words after I had spoken them, and I hoped Miss Lowery had never heard Mr. Cohan's song. "Those whom we first love we seldom see. Our earlier romances, tinged with the magic radiance of youth, often fail to materialize." The last three words sounded somewhat trite when they struck the air. "But those fondly cherished dreams," I went on, "may cast a pleasant afterglow on our future lives, however impracticable and vague they may have been. But life is full of realities as well as visions and dreams. One cannot live on memories. May I ask, Miss Lowery, if you think you could pass a happy—that is, a contented and harmonious life with Mr.—er—Dodd—if in other ways than romantic recollections he seems to—er—fill the bill, as I might say?"

"Oh, Hi's all right," answered Miss Lowery. "Yes, I could get along with him fine. He's promised me an automobile and a motor-boat. But somehow, when it got so close to the time I was to marry him, I couldn't help wishing—well, just thinking about George. Something must have happened to him or he'd have written. On the day he left, he and me got a hammer and a chisel and cut a dime into two pieces. I took one piece and he took the other, and we promised to be true to each other and always keep the pieces till we saw each other again. I've got mine at home now in a ring-box in the top drawer of my dresser. I guess I was silly to come up here looking for him. I never realized what a big place it is."

And then Tripp joined in with a little grating laugh that he had, still trying to drag in a little story or drama to earn the miserable dollar that he craved.

"Oh, the boys from the country forget a lot when they come to the city and learn something. I guess George, maybe, in on the bum, or got roped in by some other girl, or maybe gone to the dogs on account of whiskey or the races. You listen to Mr. Chalmers and go back home, and you'll be all right."

But now the time was come for action, for the hands of the clock were moving close to noon. Frowning upon Tripp, I argued gently and philosophically with Miss Lowery, delicately convincing her of the importance of returning home at once. And I impressed upon her the truth that it would not be absolutely necessary to her future happiness that she mention to Hi the wonders or the fact of her visit to the city that had swallowed up the unlucky George.

She said she had left her horse (unfortunate Rosinante) tied to a tree near the railroad station. Tripp and I gave her instructions to mount the patient steed as soon as she arrived and ride home as fast as possible. There she was to recount the exciting adventure of a day spent with Susie Adams. She could "fix" Susie—I was sure of that—and all would be well.

And then, being susceptible to the barbed arrows of beauty, I warmed to the adventure. The three of us hurried to the ferry, and there I found the price of a ticket to Greenburg to be but a dollar and eighty cents. I bought one, and a red, red rose with the twenty cents for Miss Lowery. We saw her aboard her ferry-boat, and stood watching her wave her handkerchief at us until it was the tiniest white patch imaginable. And then Tripp and I faced each other, brought back to earth, left dry and desolate in the shade of the sombre verities of life.

The spell wrought by beauty and romance was dwindling. I looked at Tripp and almost sneered. He looked more careworn, contemptible, and disreputable than ever. I fingered the two silver dollars remaining in my pocket and looked at him with the half-closed eyelids of contempt. He mustered up an imitation of resistance.

"Can't you get a story out of it?" he asked, huskily. "Some sort of a story, even if you have to fake part of it?"

"Not a line," said I. "I can fancy the look on Grimes' face if I should try to put over any slush like this. But we've helped the little lady out, and that'll have to be our only reward."

"I'm sorry," said Tripp, almost inaudibly. "I'm sorry you're out your money. Now, it seemed to me like a find of a big story, you know—that is, a sort of thing that would write up pretty well."

"Let's try to forget it," said I, with a praiseworthy attempt at gayety, "and take the next car 'cross town."

I steeled myself against his unexpressed but palpable desire. He should not coax, cajole, or wring from me the dollar he craved. I had had enough of that wild-goose chase.

Tripp feebly unbuttoned his coat of the faded pattern and glossy seams to reach for something that had once been a handkerchief deep down in some obscure and cavernous pocket. As he did so I caught the shine of a cheap silver-plated watch-chain across his vest, and something dangling from it caused me to stretch forth my hand and seize it curiously. It was the half of a silver dime that had been cut in halves with a chisel.

"What?" I said, looking at him keenly.

"Oh, yes," he responded, dully. "George Brown, alias Tripp. What's the use?"

Barring the W. C. T. U., I'd like to know if anybody disapproves of my having produced promptly from my pocket Tripp's whiskey dollar and unhesitatingly laying it in his hand.

The Gold That Glittered

A story with a moral appended is like the bill of a mosquito. It bores you, and then injects a stinging drop to irritate your conscience. Therefore let us have the moral first and be done with it. All is not gold that glitters, but it is a wise child that keeps the stopper in his bottle of testing acid.

Where Broadway skirts the corner of the square presided over by George the Veracious is the Little Rialto. Here stands the actors of that quarter, and this is their shibboleth: " 'Nit,' says I to Frohman, 'you can't touch me for a kopeck less than two-fifty per,' and out I walks."

Westward and southward from the Thespian glare are one or two streets where a Spanish-American colony had huddled for a little tropical warmth in the nipping North. The centre of life in this precinct is "El Refugio," a café and restaurant that caters to the volatile exiles from the South. Up from Chili, Bolivia, Colombia, the rolling republics of Central America and the ireful islands of the Western Indies flit the cloaked and sombreroed señores, who are scattered like burning lava by the political eruptions of their several countries. Hither they come to lay counterplots, to bide their time, to solicit funds, to enlist filibusterers, to smuggle out arms and ammunitions, to play the game at long taw. In El Refugio they find the atmosphere in which they thrive.

In the restaurant of El Refugio are served compounds delightful to the palate of the man from Capricorn or Cancer. Atruism must halt the story thus long. Oh, diner, weary of the culinary subterfuges of the Gallic chef, hie thee to El Refugio! There only will you find a fish—bluefish, shad or pompano from the Gulf—baked after the Spanish method. Tomatoes give it color, individuality, and soul; chili colorado bestows upon it zest, originality, and fervor; unknown herbs furnish piquancy and mystery, and—but its crowning glory deserves a new sentence. Around it, above it, beneath it, in its vicinity—but never in it—hovers an ethereal aura, an effluvium so rarefied and delicate that only the Society for Physical Research could note its origin. Do not say that garlic is in the fish at El Refugio. It is not otherwise than as if the spirit of Garlic, flitting past, has wafted one kiss that lingers in the parsley-crowned dish as haunting as those kisses in life, "by hopeless fancy feigned on lips that are for others." And then, when Conchito, the waiter, brings you a plate of brown frijoles and a carafe of wine that has never stood still between Oporto and El Refugio—ah, Dios!

One day a Hamburg-American liner deposited upon Pier No. 55 Gen. Perrico Ximenes Villablanca Falcon, a passenger from Cartegena. The General was between a claybank and a bay in complexion, had a 42-inch waist and stood 5 feet 4 with his Du Barry heels. He had the mustache of a shooting-gallery proprietor, he wore the full dress of a Texas congressman, and had the important aspect of an uninstructed delegate.

Gen. Falcon had enough English under his hat to enable him to inquire his way to the street in which El Refugio stood. When he reached that neighborhood he saw a sign before a respectable red-brick house that read, "Hotel Español." In the window was a card in Spanish, "Aqui se habla Español." The General entered, sure of a congenial port.

In the cozy office was Mrs. O'Brien, the proprietress. She had blonde—oh, unimpeachably blonde hair. For the rest she was amiability, and ran largely to inches around. Gen. Falcon brushed the floor with his broad brimmed hat, and emitted a quantity of Spanish, the syllables sounding like firecrackers gently popping their way down the string of a bunch.

"Spanish or Dago?" asked Mrs. O'Brien, pleasantly.

"I am a Colombian, madam," said the General proudly. "I speak the Spanish. The advisement in your window say the Spanish he is spoken here. How is that?"

"Well, you've been speaking it, ain't you?" said the madam. "I'm sure I can't."

At the Hotel Español General Falcon engaged rooms and established himself. At dusk he sauntered out upon the streets to view the wonders of this roaring city of the North. As he walked he thought of the wonderful golden hair of Mme. O'Brien. "It is here," said the General to himself, no doubt in his own language, "that one shall find the most beautiful señoras in the world. I have not in my Colombia viewed among our beauties one so fair. It is not for the General Falcon to think of beauty. It is my country that claims my devotion."

At the corner of Broadway and the Little Rialto the General became involved. The street cars bewildered him, and the fender of one upset him against a pushcart laden with oranges. A cab driver missed him an inch with a hub, and poured barbarous execrations upon his head. He scrambled to the sidewalk and skipped again in terror when the whistle of a peanut-roaster puffed a hot scream into his ear. "Válgame Dios! What devil's city is this?"

As the General fluttered out of the streamers of passers like a wounded snipe he was marked simultaneously as game by two hunters. One was "Bully" McGuire, whose system of sport required the use of a strong arm and the misuse of an eight-inch piece of lead pipe. The other Nimrod of the asphalt was "Spider" Kelley, a sportsman with more refined methods.

In pouncing upon their self-evident prey, Mr. Kelley was a shade the quicker. His elbow fended accurately the onslaught of Mr. McGuire.

"G'wan!" he commanded harshly. "I saw it first." McGuire slunk away, awed by superior intelligence.

"Pardon me," said Mr. Kelley, to the General, "but you got balled up in the shuffle, didn't you? Let me assist you." He picked up the General's hat and brushed the dust from it.

The ways of Mr. Kelley could not but succeed. The General, bewildered and dismayed by the resounding streets, welcomed his deliverer as a caballero with a most disinterested heart.

"I have a desire," said the General, "to return to the hotel of O'Brien, in which I am stop. Caramba! señor, there is a loudness and rapidness of going and coming in the city of this Nueva York."

Mr. Kelley's politeness would not suffer the distinguished Colombian to brave the dangers of the return unaccompanied. At the door of the Hotel Español they paused. A little lower down on the opposite side of the street shone the modest illuminated sign of El Refugio. Mr. Kelley, to whom few streets were unfamiliar, knew the place exteriorly as a "Dago joint." All foreigners Mr. Kelley classed under the two heads of "Dagoes" and Frenchmen. He proposed to the General that they repair thither and substantiate their acquaintance with a liquid foundation.

An hour later found General Falcon and Mr. Kelley seated at a table in the conspirator's corner of El Refugio. Bottles and glasses were between them. For the tenth time the General confided the secret of his mission to the Estados Unidos. He was here, he declared, to purchase arms—2,000 stands of Winchester rifles—for the Colombian revolutionists. He had drafts in his pocket drawn by the Cartegena Bank on its New York correspondent for $25,000. At other tables other revolutionists were shouting their political secrets to their fellow-plotters; but none was as loud as the General. He pounded the table; he halloed for some wine; he roared to his friend that his errand was a secret one, and not to be hinted at to a living soul. Mr. Kelley himself was stirred to sympathetic enthusiasm. He grasped the General's hand across the table.

"Monseer," he said, earnestly, "I don't know where this country of yours is, but I'm for it. I guess it must be a branch of the United States, though, for the poetry guys and the schoolmarms call us Columbia, too, sometimes. It's a lucky thing for you that you butted into me to-night. I'm the only man in New York that can get this gun deal through for you. The Secretary of War of the United States is me best friend. He's in the city now, and I'll see him for you to-morrow. In the meantime, monseer, you keep them drafts tight in your inside pocket. I'll call for you to-morrow, and take you to see him. Say! that ain't the District of Columbia you're talking about, is it?" concluded Mr. Kelley, with a sudden qualm. "You can't capture that with no 2,000 guns—it's been tried with more."

"No, no, no!" exclaimed the General. "It is the republic of Colombia—it is a g-r-reat republic on the top side of America of the South. Yes. Yes."

"All right," said Mr. Kelley, reassured. "Now suppose we trek along home and go by-by. I'll write to the Secretary to-night and make a date with him. It's a ticklish job to get guns out of New York. McClusky himself can't do it."

They parted at the door of the Hotel Español. The General rolled his eyes at the moon and sighed.

"It is a great country, your Nueva York," he said. "Truly the cars in the streets devastate one, and the engine that cooks the nuts terribly makes a squeak in the ear. But, ah, Señor Kelley—the señoras with hair of much goldness, and admirable fatness—they are magnificas! Muy Magnificas!"

Kelley went to the nearest telephone booth and called up McCrary's café, far up on Broadway. He asked for Jimmy Dunn.

"Is this Jimmy Dunn?" asked Kelley.

"Yes," came the answer.

"You're a liar," sang back Kelley, joyfully. "You're the Secretary of War. Wait there till I come up. I've got the finest thing down here in the way of a fish you ever baited for. It's a Colorado-maduro, with a gold band around it and free coupons enough to buy a red hall lamp and a statuette of Psyche rubbering in the brook. I'll be up on the next car."

Jimmy Dunn was an A.M. of Crookdom. He was an artist in the confidence line. He never saw a bludgeon in his life; and he scorned knockout drops. In fact, he would have set nothing before an intended victim but the purest of drinks, if it had been possible to procure such a thing in New York. It was the ambition of "Spider" Kelley to elevate himself into Jimmy's class.

These two gentlemen held a conference that night at McCrary's. Kelley explained.

"He's as easy as a gum shoe. He's from the Island of Colombia, where there's a strike, or a feud, or something going on, and they've sent him up here to buy 2,000 Winchesters to arbitrate the thing with. He showed me two drafts for $10,000 each, and one for $5,000 on a bank here. 'S truth, Jimmy, I felt real mad with him because he didn't have it in thousand-dollar bills, and hand it to me on a silver waiter.

Now, we've got to wait till he goes to the bank and gets the money for us."

The talked it over for two hours, and then Dunn said: "Bring him to No.— Broadway, at four o'clock to-morrow afternoon."

In due time Kelley called at the Hotel Español for the General. He found that wily warrior engaged in delectable conversation with Mrs. O'Brien.

"The Secretary of War is waitin' for us," said Kelley.

The General tore himself away with an effort.

"Ay, Señor," he said, with a sigh, "duty makes a call. But, señor, the señoras of your Estados Unidos—how beauties! For exemplification, take you la Madame O'Brien—que magnifica! She is one goddess—one Juno—what you call one ox-eyed Juno."

Now Mr. Kelley was a wit; and better men have been shriveled by the fire of their own imagination.

"Sure!" he said with a grin; "but you mean a peroxide Juno, don't you?"

Mrs. O'Brien heard, and lifted an auriferous head. Her business-like eye rested for an instant upon the disappearing form of Mr. Kelley. Except in street cars one should never be unnecessarily rude to a lady.

When the gallant Colombian and his escort arrived at the Broadway address, they were held in an anteroom for half an hour, and then admitted into a well-equipped office where a distinguished looking man, with a smooth face, wrote at a desk. General Falcon was presented to the Secretary of War of the United States, and his mission made known by his old friend, Mr. Kelley.

"Ah—Colombia!" said the Secretary, significantly, when he was made to understand; "I'm afraid there will be a little difficulty in that case. The President and I differ in our sympathies there. He prefers the established government, while I—" The Secretary gave the General a mysterious but encouraging smile. "You, of course, know, General Falcon, that since the Tammany war, an act of Congress has been passed requiring all manufactured arms and ammunition exported from this country to pass through the War Department. Now, if I can do anything for you I will be glad to do so to oblige my old friend Mr. Kelley. But it must be in absolute secrecy, as the President, as I have said, does not regard favorably the efforts of your revolutionary party in Colombia. I will have my orderly bring a list of the available arms now in the warehouse."

The Secretary struck a bell, and an orderly with the letters A. D. T. on his cap stepped promptly into the room.

"Bring me Schedule B of the small arms inventory," said the Secretary.

The orderly quickly returned with a printed paper. The Secretary studied it closely.

"I find," he said, "that in Warehouse 9, of Government stores, there is a shipment of 2,000 stands of Winchester rifles that were ordered by the Sultan of Morocco, who forgot to send the cash with his order. Our rule is that legal-tender money must be paid down at the time of purchase. My dear Kelley, your friend, General Falcon, shall have this lot of arms, if he desires it, at the manufacturer's price. And you will forgive me, I am sure, if I curtail our interview. I am expecting the Japanese Minister and Charles Murphy every moment!"

As one result of this interview, the General was deeply grateful to his esteemed friend, Mr. Kelley. As another, the nimble Secretary of War was extremely busy during the next two days buying empty rifle cases and filling them with bricks, which were then stored in a warehouse rented for that purpose. As still another, when the General returned to the Hotel Español, Mrs. O'Brien went up to him, plucked a thread from his lapel, and said:

"Say, señor, I don't want to 'butt in,' but what does that monkey-faced, cat-eyed, rubber-necked tin horn tough want with you?"

"Sangre de mi vida!" exclaimed the General. "Impossible it is that you speak of my good friend, Señor Kelley."

"Come into the summer garden," said Mrs. O'Brien. "I want to have a talk with you."

Let us suppose that an hour has elapsed.

"And you say," said the General, "that for the sum of $18,000 can be purchased the furnishment of the house and the lease of one year with this garden so lovely—so resembling unto the patios of my cara Colombia?"

"And dirt cheap at that," sighed the lady.

"Ah, Dios!" breathed General Falcon. "What to me is war and politics? This spot is one paradise. My country it have other brave heroes to continue the fighting. What to me should be glory and the shooting of mans? Ah! no. It is here I have found one angel. Let us buy the Hotel Español and you shall be mine, and the money shall not be waste on guns."

Mrs. O'Brien rested her blond pompadour against the shoulder of the Colombian patriot.

"Oh, señor," she sighed, happily, "ain't you terrible!"

Two days later was the time appointed for the delivery of the arms to the General. The boxes of supposed rifles were stacked in the rented warehouse, and the Secretary of War sat upon them, waiting for his friend Kelley to fetch the victim.

Mr. Kelley hurried, at the hour, to the Hotel Español. He found the General behind the desk adding up accounts.

"I have decide," said the General, "to buy not guns. I have to-day buy the insides of this hotel, and there shall be marrying of the General Perrico Ximenes Villablanca Falcon with la Madame O'Brien."

Mr. Kelley almost strangled.

"Say, you old bald-headed bottle of shoe polish," he spluttered, "you're a swindler—that's what you are! You've bought a boarding house with money belonging to your infernal country, wherever it is."

"Ah," said the General, footing up a column, "that is what you call politics. War and revolution they are not nice. Yes. It is not best that one shall always follow Minerva. No. It is of quite desirable to keep hotels and be with that Juno—that ox-eyed Juno. Ah! what hair of the gold it is that she have!"

Mr. Kelley choked again.

"Ah, Señor Kelley!" said the General, feelingly and finally, "is that you have never eaten of the corned beef hash that Madame O'Brien she make?"

The Day Resurgent

I can see the artist bite the end of his pencil and frown when it comes to drawing his Easter picture; for his legitimate pictorial conceptions of figures pertinent to the festival are but four in number.

First comes Easter, pagan goddess of spring. Here his fancy may have free play. A beautiful maiden with decorative hair and the proper number of toes will fill the bill. Miss Clarice St. Vavasour, the well-known model, will pose for it in the "Lethergogallagher," or whatever it was that Trilby called it.

Second—the melancholy lady with upturned eyes in a framework of lilies. This is magazine-covery, but reliable.

Third—Miss Manhattan in Fifth Avenue Easter Sunday parade.

Fourth—Maggie Murphy with a new red feather in her old straw hat, happy and self-conscious, in the Grand Street turnout.

Of course, the rabbits do not count. Nor the Easter eggs, since the higher criticism has hard-boiled them.

The limited field of its pictorial possibilities proves that Easter, of all our festival days, is the most vague and shifting in our conception. It belongs to all religions, although the pagans invented it. Going back still further to the first spring, we can see Eve choosing with pride a new green leaf from the tree *ficus carica*.

Now, the object of this critical and learned preamble is to set forth the theorem that Easter is neither a date, a season, a festival, a holiday, nor an occasion. What it is you shall find out if you follow in the footsteps of Danny McCree.

Easter Sunday dawned as it should, bright and early, in its place on the calendar between Saturday and Monday. At 5:24 the sun rose, and at 10:30 Danny followed its example. He went into the kitchen and washed his face at the sink. His mother was frying bacon. She looked at his hard, smooth, knowing countenance as he juggled with the round cake of soap, and thought of his father when she first saw him stopping a hot grounder between second and third twenty-two years before on a vacant lot in Harlem, where the La Paloma apartment house now stands. In the front room of the flat Danny's father sat by an open window smoking his pipe, with his dishevelled gray hair tossed about by the breeze. He still clung to his pipe, although his sight had been taken from him two years before by a precocious blast of giant powder that went off without permission. Very few blind men care for smoking, for the reason that they cannot see the smoke. Now, could you enjoy having the news read to you from an evening paper unless you could see the color of the headlines?

" 'Tis Easter Day," said Mrs. McCree.

"Scramble mine," said Danny.

After breakfast he dressed himself in the Sabbath morning costume of the Canal Street importing house dray chauffeur—frock coat, striped trousers, patent leathers, gilded trace chain across front of vest, and wing collar, rolled-rim derby and butterfly bow from Schonstein's (between Fourteenth Street and Tony's fruit stand) Saturday night sale.

"You'll be goin' out this day, of course, Danny," said old man McCree, a little wistfully. " 'Tis a kind of holiday, they say. Well, it's fine spring weather. I can feel it in the air."

"Why should I not be going out?" demanded Danny in his grumpiest chest tones. "Should I stay in? Am I as good as a horse? One day of rest my team has a week. Who earns the money for the rent and the breakfast you've just eat, I'd like to know? Answer me that!"

"All right, lad," said the old man. "I'm not complainin'. While me two eyes was good there was nothin' better to my mind than a Sunday out. There's a smell of turf and burnin' brush comin' in the windy. I have me tobaccy. A good fine day and rist to ye, lad. Times I wished your mother had larned to read, so I might hear the rest about the hippopotamus—but let that be."

"Now, what is this foolishness he talks of hippopotamuses?" asked Danny of his mother, as he passed through the kitchen. "Have you been taking him to the Zoo? And for what?"

"I have not," said Mrs. McCree. "He sets by the windy all day. 'Tis little recreation a blind man among the poor gets at all. I'm thinkin' they wander in their minds at times. One day he talks of grease without stoppin' for the most of an hour. I looks to see if there's lard burnin' in the fryin' pan. There is not. He says I do not understand. 'Tis weary days, Sundays, and holidays and all, for a blind man, Danny. There was no better nor stronger than him when he had his two eyes. 'Tis a fine day, son. Injoy yerself ag'inst the morning. There will be cold supper at six."

"Have you heard any talk of a hippopotamus?" asked Danny of Mike, the janitor, as he went out of the door downstairs.

"I have not," said Mike, pulling his shirtsleeves higher. "But 'tis the only subject in the animal, natural and illegal lists of outrages that I've not been complained to about these two days. See the landlord. Or else move out if ye like. Have ye hippopotamuses in the lease? No, then?"

"It was the old man who spoke of it," said Danny. "Likely there's nothing in it."

Danny walked up the street to the Avenue and then struck northward into the heart of the district where Easter—modern Easter, in new, bright raiment—leads the pascal march. Out of towering brown churchs came the blithe music of anthems from the living flowers—so it seemed when your eye looked upon the Easter girl.

Gentlemen, frock-coated, silk-hatted, gardeniaed, sustained the background of the tradition. Children carried lilies in their hands. The windows of the brownstone mansions were packed with the most opulent creations of Flora, the sister of the Lady of the Lilies.

Around a corner, white-gloved, pink-gilled, and tightly buttoned, walked Corrigan, the cop, shield to the curb. Danny knew him.

"Why, Corrigan," he asked, "is Easter? I know it comes the first time you're full after the moon rises on the seventeenth of March—but why? Is it a proper and religious ceremony, or does the Government appoint it out of politics?"

" 'Tis an annual celebration," said Corrigan, with the judicial air of the Third Deputy Police Commissioner, "peculiar to New York. It extends up to Harlem. Sometimes they has the reserves out at One Hundred and Twenty-fifth Street. In my opinion 'tis not political."

"Thanks," said Danny. "And say—did you ever hear a man complain of hippopotamuses? When not specially in drink, I mean."

"Nothing larger than sea turtles," said Corrigan, reflecting, "and there was wood alcohol in that."

Danny wandered. The double, heavy incumbency of enjoying simultaneously a Sunday and a festival day was his.

The sorrows of the hand-toiler fit him easily. They are worn so often that they hang with the picturesque lines of the best tailor-made garments. That is why well-fed artists of pencil and pen find in the griefs of the common people their most striking models. But when the Philistine would disport himself, the grimness of Melpomene, herself, attends upon his capers. Therefore, Danny set his jaw hard at Easter, and took his pleasure sadly.

The family entrance of Dugan's café was feasible; so Danny yielded to the vernal season as for as a glass of bock. Seated in a dark linoleumed, humid back room, his heart and mind still groped after the mysterious meaning of the springtime jubilee.

"Say, Tim," he said to the waiter, "why do they have Easter?"

"Skiddoo!" said Tim, closing a sophisticated eye. "Is that a new one? All right. Tony Pastor's for you last night, I guess. I give it up. What's the answer—two apples or a yard and a half?"

From Dugan's Danny turned back eastward. The April sun seemed to stir in him a vague feeling that he could not construe. He made a wrong diagnosis and decided that it was Katy Conlon.

A block from her house on Avenue A he met her going to church. They pumped hands on the corner.

"Gee! but you look dumpish and dressed up," said Katy. "What's wrong? Come away with me to church and be cheerful."

"What's doing at church?" asked Danny.

"Why, it's Easter Sunday. Silly! I waited till after eleven expectin' you might come around to go."

"What does this Easter stand for, Katy?" asked Danny gloomily. "Nobody seems to know."

"Nobody as blind as you," said Katy with spirit. "You haven't even looked at my new hat. And skirt. Why, it's when all the girls put on new spring clothes. Silly! Are you coming to church with me?"

"I will," said Danny. "If this Easter is pulled off there, they ought to be able to give some excuse for it. Not that the hat ain't a beauty. The green roses are great."

At church the preacher did some expounding with no pounding. He spoke rapidly, for he was in a hurry to get home to his early Sabbath dinner; but he knew his business. There was one word that controlled his theme—resurrection. Not a new creation; but a new life arising out of the old. The congregation had heard it often before. But there was a wonderful hat, a combination of sweet peas and lavender, in the sixth pew from the pulpit. It attracted much attention.

After church Danny lingered on a corner while Katy waited, with pique in her sky-blue eyes.

"Are you coming along to the house?" she asked. "But don't mind me. I'll get there all right. You seem to be studyin' a lot about something. All right. Will I see you at any time specially, Mr. McCree?"

"I'll be around Wednesday night as usual," said Danny, turning and crossing the street.

Katy walked away with the green roses dangling indignantly. Danny stopped two blocks away. He stood still with his hands in his pockets, at the curb on the corner. His face was that of a graven image. Deep in his soul something stirred so small, so fine, so keen and leavening that his hard fibres did not recognize it. It was something more tender than the April day, more subtle than the call of the senses, purer and deeper-rooted than the love of woman—for had he not turned away from green roses and eyes that had kept him chained for a year? And Danny did not know what it was. The preacher, who was in a hurry to go to his dinner, had told him, but Danny had had no libretto with which to follow the drowsy intonation. But the preacher spoke the truth.

Suddenly Danny slapped his leg and gave forth a hoarse yell of delight.

"Hippopotamus!" he shouted to an elevated road pillar. "Well, how is that for a bum guess? Why, blast my skylights! I know what he was driving at now.

"Hippopotamus! Wouldn't that send you to the Bronx! It's been a year since he heard it; and he didn't miss it so very far. We quit at 469 B.C. and this comes next. Well, a wooden man wouldn't have guessed what he was trying to get out of him."

Danny caught a crosstown car and went up to the rear flat that his labor supported.

Old man McCree was still sitting by the window. His extinct pipe lay on the sill.

"Will that be you, lad?" he asked.

Danny flared into the rage of a strong man who is surprised at the outset of committing a good deed.

"Who pays the rent and buys the food that is eaten in this house?" he snapped, viciously. "Have I no right to come in?"

"Ye're a faithful lad," said old man McCree, with a sigh. "Is it evening yet?"

Danny reached up on a shelf and took down a thick book labeled in gilt letters, "The History of Greece." Dust was on it half an inch thick. He laid it on the table and found a place in it marked by a strip of paper. And then he gave a short roar at the top of his voice, and said:

"Was it the hippopotamus you wanted to be read to about then?"

"Did I hear ye open the book?" said old man McCree. "Many and weary be the months since my lad has read it to me. I dinno; but I took a great likings to them Greeks. Ye left off at a place. 'Tis a fine day outside, lad. Be out and take rest from your work. I have gotten used to me chair by the windy and me pipe."

"Pel-Peloponnesus was the place where we left off, and not hippopotamus," said Danny. "The war began there. It kept something doing for thirty years. The headlines say that a guy named Philip of Macedon, in 338 B.C., got to be boss of Greece by getting the decision at the battle of Cher-Cheronoea. I'll read it."

With his hand to his ear, rapt in the Peloponnesian War, old man McCree sat for an hour, listening.

Then he got up and felt his way to the door of the kitchen. Mrs. McCree was slicing cold meat. She looked up. Tears were running from old man McCree's eyes.

"Do ye hear our lad readin' to me?" he said. "There is none finer in the land. My two eyes have come back to me again."

After supper he said to Danny: " 'Tis a happy day, this Easter. And now ye will be off to see Katy in the evening. Well enough."

"Who pays the rent and buys the food that is eaten in this house?" said Danny, angrily. "Have I no right to stay in it? After supper there is yet to come the reading of the battle of Corinth, 146 B.C., when the kingdom, as they say, became an in-integral portion of the Roman Empire. Am I nothing in this house?"

The Thing's the Play

Being acquainted with a newspaper reporter who had a couple of free passes, I got to see the performance a few nights ago at one of the popular vaudeville houses.

One of the numbers was a violin solo by a striking-looking man not much past forty, but with very gray thick hair. Not being afflicted with a taste for music, I let the system of noises drift past my ears while I regarded the man.

"There was a story about that chap a month or two ago," said the reporter. "They gave me the assignment. It was to run a column and was to be on the extremely light and joking order. The old man seems to like the funny touch I give to local happenings. Oh, yes, I'm working on a farce comedy now. Well, I went down to the house and got all the details; but I certainly fell down on that job. I went back and turned in a comic write-up of an east side funeral instead. Why? Oh, I couldn't seem to get hold of it with my funny hooks, somehow. Maybe you could make a one-act tragedy out of it for a curtain-raiser. I'll give you the details."

After the performance my friend, the reporter, recited to me the facts over the Würzburger.

"I see no reason," said I, when he had concluded, "why that shouldn't make a rattling good funny story. Those three people couldn't have acted in a more absurd and preposterous manner if they had been real actors in a real theatre. I'm really afraid that all the stage is a world, anyhow, and all the players merely men and women. 'The thing's the play,' is the way I quote Mr. Shakespeare."

"Try it," said the reporter.

"I will," said I; and I did, to show him how he could have made a humorous column of it for his paper.

There stands a house near Abingdon Square. On the ground floor there has been for twenty-five years a little store where toys and notions and stationery are sold.

One night twenty years ago there was a wedding in the rooms above the store. The Widow Mayo owned the house and store. Her daughter Helen was married to Frank Barry. John Delaney was best man. Helen was eighteen, and her picture had been printed in a morning paper next to the headlines of a "Wholesale Female Murderess" story from Butte, Mont. But after your eye and intelligence had rejected the connection, you seized your magnifying glass and read beneath the portrait her description as one of a series of Prominent Beauties and Belles of the lower west side.

Frank Barry and John Delaney were "prominent" young beaux of the same side, and bosom friends, whom you expected to turn upon each other every time the curtain went up. One who pays his money for orchestra seats and fiction expects this. That is the first funny idea that has turned up in the story yet. Both had made a great race for Helen's hand. When Frank won, John shook his hand and congratulated him—honestly, he did.

After the ceremony Helen ran upstairs to put on her hat. She was getting married in a traveling dress. She and Frank were going to Old Point Comfort for a week. Downstairs the usual horde of gibbering cave-dwellers were waiting with their hands full of old Congress gaiters and paper bags of hominy.

Then there was a rattle of the fire-escape, and into her room jumps the mad and infatuated John Delaney, with a damp curl drooping upon his forehead, and made violent and reprehensive love to his lost one, entreating her to flee or fly with him to the Riviera, or the Bronx, or any old place where there are Italian skies and *dolce far niente*.

It would have carried Blaney off his feet to see Helen repulse him. With blazing and scornful eyes she fairly withered him by demanding whatever he meant by speaking to respectable people that way.

In a few moments she had him going. The manliness that had possessed him departed. He bowed low, and said something about "irresistible impulse" and "forever carry in his heart the memory of"—and she suggested that he catch the first fire-escape going down.

"I will away," said John Delaney, "to the furthermost parts of the earth. I cannot remain near you and know that you are another's. I will to Africa, and there amid other scenes strive to for—"

"For goodness sake, get out," said Helen. "Somebody might come in."

He knelt upon one knee, and she extended him one white hand that he might give it a farewell kiss.

Girls, was this choice boon of the great little god Cupid ever vouchsafed you—to have the fellow you want hard and fast, and have the one you don't want come with a damp curl on his forehead and kneel to you and babble of Africa and love which, in spite of everything, shall forever bloom, an amaranth, in his heart? To know your power, and to feel the sweet security of your own happy state; to send the unlucky one, broken-hearted, to foreign climes, while you congratulate yourself as he presses his last kiss upon your knuckles, that your nails are well manicured—say, girls, it's galluptious—don't ever let it get by you.

And then, of course—how did you guess?—the door opened and in stalked the bridegroom, jealous of slow-tying bonnet strings.

The farewell kiss was imprinted upon Helen's hand, and out of the window and down the fire-escape sprang John Delaney, Africa bound.

A little slow music, if you please—faint violin, just a breath in the clarinet and a touch of the 'cello. Imagine the scene. Frank, white-hot, with the cry of a man wounded to death bursting from him. Helen, rushing and clinging to him, trying to explain. He catches her wrists and tears them from his shoulders—once, twice, thrice he sways her this way and that—the stage manager will show you how—and throws her from him to the floor a huddled, crushed, moaning thing. Never, he cries, will he look upon her face again, and rushes from the house through the staring groups of astonished guests.

And now, because it is the Thing instead of the Play, the audience must stroll out into the real lobby of the world and marry, die, grow gray, rich, poor, happy, or sad during the intermission of twenty years which must precede the rising of the curtain again.

Mrs. Barry inherited the shop and the house. At thirty-eight she could have bested many an eighteen-year-old at a beauty show on points and general results. Only a few people remembered her wedding comedy but she made of it no secret. She did not pack it in lavender or moth balls, nor did she sell it to a magazine.

One day a middle-aged, money-making lawyer who bought his legal cap and ink of her, asked her across the counter to marry him.

"I'm really much obliged to you," said Helen, cheerfully, "but I married another man twenty years ago. He was more goose than a man, but I think I love him yet. I have never seen him since about half an hour after the ceremony. Was it copying ink that you wanted or just writing fluid?"

The lawyer bowed over the counter with oldtime grace and left a respectful kiss on the back of her hand. Helen sighed. Parting salutes, however romantic, may be overdone. Here she was at thirty-eight, beautiful and admired; and all that she seemed to have got from her lovers were reproaches and adieus. Worse still, in the last one she had lost a customer, too.

Business languished, and she hung out a Room to Let card. Two large rooms on the third floor were prepared for desirable tenants. Roomers came, and went regretfully, for the house of Mrs. Barry was the abode of neatness, comfort, and taste.

One day came Ramonti, the violinist, and engaged the front room above. The discord and clatter uptown offended his nice ear; so a friend had sent him to this oasis in the desert of noise.

Ramonti, with his still youthful face, his dark eyebrows, his short, pointed, foreign, brown beard, his distinguished head of gray hair and his artist's temperament—revealed in his light, gay, and sympathetic manner—was a welcome tenant in the old house near Abingdon Square.

Helen lived on the floor above the store. The architecture of it was singular and quaint. The hall was large and almost square. Up one side of it and then across the end of it ascended an open stairway to the floor above. This hall space she had furnished as a sitting room and office combined. There she kept her desk and wrote her business letters; and there she sat of evenings by a warm fire and a bright red light and sewed or read. Ramonti found the atmosphere so agreeable that he spent much time there, describing to Mrs. Barry the wonders of Paris, where he had studied with a particularly notorious and noisy fiddler.

Next comes lodger No. 2, a handsome, melancholy man in the early 40's, with a brown, mysterious beard, and strangely pleading, haunting eyes. He, too, found the society of Helen a desirable thing. With the eyes of Romeo and Othello's tongue, he charmed her with tales of distant climes and wooed her by respectful innuendo.

From the first Helen felt a marvelous and compelling thrill in the presence of this man. His voice somehow took her swiftly back to the days of her youth's romance. This feeling grew, and she gave way to it, and led her to an instinctive belief that he had been a factor in that romance. And then with a woman's reasoning (oh, yes, they do, sometimes) she leaped over common syllogisms and theory, and logic, and was sure that her husband had come back to her. For she saw in his eyes love, which no woman can mistake, and a thousand tons of regret and remorse, which aroused pity which is perilously near to love requited, which is the *sine qua non* in the house that Jack built.

But she made no sign. A husband who steps around the corner for twenty years and then drops in again should not expect to find his slippers laid out too conveniently near nor a match ready lighted for his cigar. There must be expiation, explanation, and possibly execration. A little purgatory, and then, maybe, if he were properly humble, he might be trusted with a harp and crown. And so she made no sign that she knew or suspected.

And my friend, the reporter, could see nothing funny in this! Sent out on an assignment to write up a roaring, hilarious, brilliant joshing story of—but I will not knock a brother—let us go on with the story.

One evening Ramonti stopped in Helen's hall-office-reception-room and told his love with the tenderness and ardor of the enraptured artist. His words were a bright flame of the divine fire that glows in the heart of a man who is a dreamer and a doer combined.

"But before you give me an answer," he went on, before she could accuse him of suddenness, "I must tell you that 'Ramonti' is the only name I have to offer you. My manager gave me that. I do not know who I am or where I came from. My first recollection is of opening my eyes in a hospital. I was a young man, and I had been there for weeks. My life before that is a blank to me. They told me that I was found lying in the street with a wound on my head and was brought there in an ambulance. They thought I must have fallen and struck my head upon the stones. There was nothing to show who I was. I have never been able to remember. After I was discharged from the hospital, I took up the violin. I have had success. Mrs. Barry—I do not know your name except that—I love you; the first time I saw you I realized that you were the one woman in the world for me—and"—oh, a lot of stuff like that.

Helen felt young again. First a wave of pride and a sweet little thrill of vanity went all over her; and then she looked Ramonti in the eyes, and a tremendous throb went through her heart. She hadn't expected that throb. It took her by surprise. The musician had become a big factor in her life, and she hadn't been aware of it.

"Mr. Ramonti," she said sorrowfully (this was not on the stage, remember; it was in the old home near Abingdon Square), "I'm awfully sorry, but I'm a married woman."

And then she told him the sad story of her life, as a heroine must do, sooner or later, either to a theatrical manager or to a reporter.

Ramonti took her hand, bowed low and kissed it, and went up to his room.

Helen sat down and looked mournfully at her hand. Well she might. Three suitors had kissed it, mounted their red roan steeds and ridden away.

In an hour entered the mysterious stranger with the haunting eyes. Helen was in the willow rocker, knitting a useless thing in cotton-wool. He ricocheted from the stairs and stopped for a chat. Sitting across the table from her, he also poured out his narrative of love. And then he said: "Helen, do you not remember me? I think I have seen it in your eyes. Can you forgive the past and remember the love that has lasted for twenty years? I wronged you deeply—I was afraid to come back to you—but my love overpowered my reason. Can you, will you, forgive me?"

Helen stood up. The mysterious stranger held one of her hands in a strong and trembling clasp.

There she stood, and I pity the stage that it has not acquired a scene like that and her emotions to portray.

For she stood with a divided heart. The fresh, unforgettable, virginal love for her bridegroom was hers; the treasured, sacred, honored memory of her first choice filled half her soul. She leaned to that pure feeling. Honor and faith and sweet, abiding romance bound her to it. But the other half of her heart and soul was filled with something else—a later, fuller, nearer influence. And so the old fought against the new.

And while she hesitated, from the room above came the soft, racking, petitionary music of a violin. The hag, music, bewitches some of the noblest. The daws may peck upon one's sleeve without injury but whoever wears his heart upon his typanum gets it not far from the neck.

The music and the musician called her, and at her side honor and the old love held her back.

"Forgive me," he pleaded.

"Twenty years is a long time to remain away from the one you say you love," she declared, with a purgatorial touch.

"How could I tell?" he begged. "I will conceal nothing from you. That night when he left I followed him. I was mad with jealousy. On a dark street I struck him down. He did not rise. I examined him. His head had struck a stone. I did not intend to kill him. I was mad with love and jealousy. I hid near by and saw an ambulance take him away. Although you married him, Helen—"

"Who Are You?" cried the woman, with wide-open eyes, snatching her hand away.

"Don't you remember me, Helen—the one who has always loved you the best? I am John Delaney. If you can forgive—"

But she was gone, leaping, stumbling, hurrying, flying up the stairs toward the music and him who had forgotten, but who had known her for his in each of his two existences, and as she climbed up she sobbed, cried, and sang: "Frank! Frank! Frank!"

Three mortals thus juggling with years as though they were billiard balls, and my friend, the reporter, couldn't see anything funny in it!

A Municipal Report

The cities are full of pride,
Challenging each to each—
This from her mountainside,
That from her burthened beach.
R. KIPLING

Fancy a novel about Chicago or Buffalo, let us say, of Nashville, Tennessee! There are just three big cities in the United States that are "story cities"—New York, of course, New Orleans, and, best of the lot, San Francisco.

—FRANK NORRIS.

East is East, and West is San Francisco, according to Californians. Californians are a race of people; they are not merely inhabitants of a State. They are the Southerners of the West. Now, Chicagoans are no less loyal to their city; but when you ask them why, they stammer and speak of lake fish and the new Odd Fellows Building. But Californians go into detail.

Of course they have, in the climate, an argument that is good for half an hour while you are thinking of your coal bills and heavy underwear. But as soon as they come to mistake your silence for conviction, madness comes upon them, and they picture the city of the Golden Gate as the Bagdad of the New World. So far, as a matter of opinion, no refutation is necessary. But dear cousins all (from Adam and Eve descended), it is a rash one who will lay his finger on the map and say: "In this town there can be no romance—what could happen here?" Yes, it is a bold and a rash deed to challenge in one sentence history, romance, and Rand and McNally.

NASHVILLE.—A city, port of delivery, and the capital of the State of Tennessee, is on the Cumberland River and on the N. C. $ St. L. and the L. & N. railroads. The city is regarded as the most important educational centre in the South.

I stepped off the train at 8 P.M. Having searched thesaurus in vain for adjectives, I must, as a substitution, hie me to comparison in the form of a recipe.

Take of London fog 30 parts; malaria 10 parts; gas leaks 20 parts; dewdrops gathered in a brick yard at sunrise, 25 parts; odor of honeysuckle 15 parts. Mix.

The mixture will give you an approximate conception of a Nashville drizzle. It is not so fragrant as a moth-ball nor as thick as pea-soup; but 'tis enough—'twill serve.

I went to a hotel in a tumbril. It required strong self-suppression for me to keep from climbing to the top of it and giving an imitation of Sidney Carton. The vehicle was drawn by beasts of a bygone era and driven by something dark and emancipated.

I was sleepy and tired, so when I got to the hotel I hurriedly paid it the fifty cents it demanded (with approximate lagniappe, I assure you). I knew its habits; and I did not want to hear it prate about its old "marster" or anything that happened "befo' de wah."

The hotel was one of the kind described as "renovated." That means $20,000 worth of new marble pillars, tiling, electric lights and brass cuspidors in the lobby, and a new L. & N. time table and a lithograph of Lookout Mountain in each one of the great rooms above. The management was without reproach, the attention full of exquisite Southern courtesy, the service as slow as the progress of a snail and as good-humored as Rip Van Winkle. The food was worth traveling a thousand miles for. There is no other hotel in the world where you can get such chicken livers *en brochette*.

At dinner I asked a Negro waiter if there was anything doing in town. He pondered gravely for a minute, and then replied: "Well, boss, I don't really reckon there's anything at all doin' after sundown."

Sundown had been accomplished; it had been drowned in the drizzle long before. So that spectacle was denied me. But I went forth upon the streets in the drizzle to see what might be there.

It is built on undulating grounds; and the streets are lighted by electricity at a cost of $32,470 per annum.

As I left the hotel there was a race riot. Down upon me charged a company of freedmen, or Arabs, or Zulus, armed with—no, I saw with relief that they were not rifles, but whips. And I saw dimly a caravan of black, clumsy vehicles; and at the reassuring shouts, "Kyar you anywhere in the town, boss, fuh fifty cents," I reasoned that I was merely a "fare" instead of a victim.

I walked through long streets, all leading uphill. I wondered how those streets ever came down again. Perhaps they didn't until they were "graded." On a few of the "main streets" I saw lights in stores here and there; saw street cars go by conveying worthy burghers hither and yon; saw people pass engaged in the art of conversation, and heard a bust of semi-lively laughter issuing from a soda-water and ice-cream parlor. The streets other than "main" seemed to have enticed upon their borders houses consecrated to peace and domesticity. In many of them lights shone behind discreetly drawn window shades, in a few pianos tinkled orderly and irreproachable music. There was, indeed, little "doing." I wished I had come before sundown. So I returned to my hotel.

In November, 1864, the Confederate General Hood advanced against Nashville, where he shut up a National force under General Thomas. The latter then sallied forth and defeated the Confederates in a terrible conflict.

All my life I have heard of, admired, and witnessed the fine marksmanship of the south in its peaceful conflicts in the tobacco-chewing regions. But in my hotel a surprise awaited me. There were twelve bright, new, imposing, capacious brass cuspidors in the great lobby, tall enough to be called urns and so wide-mouthed that the crack pitcher of a lady basebell team should have been able to throw a ball into one of them at five paces distant. But, although a terrible battle had raged and was still raging, the enemy had not suffered. Bright, new, imposing, capacious, untouched, they stood. But, shades of Jefferson Brick! the tile floor—the beautiful tile floor! I could not avoid thinking of the battle of Nashville and trying to draw, as is my foolish habit, some deductions about hereditary marksmanship.

Here I first saw Major (by misplaced courtesy) Wentworth Caswell. I knew him for a type the moment my eyes suffered from the sight of him. A rat has no geographical habitat. My old friend, A. Tennyson, said, as he so well said almost everything:

Prophet, curse me the blabbing lip,
And curse me the British vermin, the rat.

Let us regard the word "British" as interchangeable *ad lib.* A rat is a rat.

This man was hunting about the hotel lobby like a starved dog that had forgotten where he had buried a bone. He had a face of great acreage, red, pulpy, and with a kind of sleepy massiveness like that of Buddha. He possessed one single virtue—he was very smoothly shaven. The mark of the beast is not indelible upon a man until he goes about with a stubble. I think that if he had not used his razor that day I would have repulsed his advances, and the criminal calendar of the world would have been spared the addition of one murder.

I happened to be standing within five feet of a cuspidor when Major Caswell opened fire upon it. I had been observant enough to perceive that the attacking force was using Gatlings instead of squirrel rifles, so I sidestepped so promptly that the major seized the opportunity to apologize to a noncombatant. He had the blabbing lip. In four minutes he had become my friend and had dragged me to the bar.

I desire to interpolate here that I am a Southerner. But I am not one by profession or trade. I eschew the string tie, the slouch hat, the Prince Albert, the number of bales of cotton destroyed by Sherman, and plug chewing. When the orchestra plays "Dixie" I do not cheer. I slide a little lower on the leather-cornered seat and, well, order another Würzburger and wish that Longstreet had—but what's the use?

Major Caswell banged the bar with his fist, and the first gun at Fort Sumter re-echoed. When he fired the last one at Appomattox I began to hope. But then he began on family trees, and demonstrated that Adam was only a third cousin of a collateral branch of the Caswell family. Genealogy disposed of, he took up, to my distaste, his private family matters. He spoke of his wife, traced her descent back to Eve, and profanely denied any possible rumor that she may have had relations in the land of Nod.

By this time I began to suspect that he was trying to obscure by noise the fact that he had ordered the drinks, on the chance that I would be bewildered into paying for them. But when they were down he crashed a silver dollar loudly upon the bar. Then, of course, another serving was obligatory. And when I had paid for that I took leave of him brusquely; for I wanted no more of him. But before I had obtained my release he had prated loudly of an income that his wife received, and showed a handful of silver money.

When I got my key at the desk the clerk said to me courteously: "If that man Caswell has annoyed you, and if you would like to make a complaint, we will have him ejected. He is a nuisance, a loafer, and without any known means of support, although he seems to have some money most the time. But we don't seem to be able to hit upon any means of throwing him out legally."

"Why, no," said I, after some reflection; "I don't see my way clear to making a complaint. But I would like to place myself on record as asserting that I do not care for his company. Your town," I continued, "seems to be a quiet one. What manner of entertainment, adventure, or excitement, have you to offer to the stranger within your gates?"

"Well, sir," said the clerk, "there will be a show here next Thursday. It is—I'll look it up and have the announcement sent up to your room with the ice water. Good-night."

After I went up to my room I looked out the window. It was only about ten o'clock, but I looked upon a silent town. The drizzle continued, spangled with dim lights, as far apart as currants in a cake sold at the Ladies' Exchange.

"A quiet place," I said to myself, as my first shoe struck the ceiling of the occupant of the room beneath mine. "Nothing of the life here that gives color and good variety to the cities in the East and West. Just a good, ordinary, hum-drum business town."

Nashville occupies a foremost place among the manufacturing centres of the country. It is the fifth boot and shoe market in the United States, the largest candy and cracker manufacturing city in the South, and does an enormous wholesale drygoods, grocery, and drug business.

I must tell you how I came to be in Nashville, and I assure you the digression brings as much tedium to me as it does to you. I was traveling elsewhere on my own business, but I had a commission from a Northern literary magazine to stop over there and establish a personal connection between the publication and one of its contributors, Azalea Adair.

Adair (there was no clue to the personality except the handwriting) had sent in some essays (lost art!) and poems that had made the editors swear approvingly over their one o'clock luncheon. So they had commissioned me to round up said Adair and corner by contract his or her output at two cents a word before some other publisher offered her ten or twenty.

At nine o'clock the next morning, after my chicken livers *en brochette* (try them if you can find that hotel), I strayed out into the drizzle, which was still on for an unlimited run. At the first corner I came upon Uncle Cæsar. He was a stalwart Negro, older than the pyramids, with gray wool and a face that reminded me of Brutus, and a second afterwards of the late King Cettiwayo. He wore the most remarkable coat that I ever had seen or expect to see. It reached to his ankles and had once been a Confederate gray in color. But rain and sun and age had so variegated it that Joseph's coat, beside it, would have faded to a pale monochrome. I must linger with that coat, for it has to do with the story—the story that is so long in coming, because you can hardly expect anything to happen in Nashville.

Once it must have been the military coat of an officer. The cape of it had vanished, but all adown its front it had been frogged and tasseled magnificently. But now the frogs and tassels were gone. In their stead had been patiently stitched (I surmised by some surviving "black mammy") new frogs made of cunningly twisted common hempen twine. This twine was frayed and disheveled. It must have been added to the coat as a substitute for vanished splendors, with tasteless but painstaking devotion, for it followed faithfully the curves of the long-missing frogs. And, to complete the comedy and pathos of the garment, all its buttons were gone save one. The second button from the top alone remained. The coat was fastened by other twine strings tied through the buttonholes and other holes rudely pierced in the opposite side. There was never such a weird garment so fantastically bedecked and of so many mottled hues. The lone button was the size of a half-dollar, made of yellow horn and sewed on with coarse twine.

This Negro stood by a carriage so old that Ham himself might have started a hack line with it after he left the ark with the two animals hitched to it. As I approached he threw open the door, drew out a feather duster, waved it without using it, and said in deep, rumbling tones:

"Step right in, suh; ain't a speck of dust in it—jus' got back from a funeral, suh."

I inferred that on such gala occasions carriages were given an extra cleaning. I looked up and down the street and perceived that there was little choice among the vehicles for hire that lined the curb. I looked in my memorandum book for the address of Azalea Adair.

"I want to go to 861 Jessamine Street," I said, and was about to step into the hack. But for an instant the thick, long, gorilla-like arm of the Negro barred me. On his massive and saturnine face a look of sudden suspicion and enmity flashed for a moment. Then, with quickly returning conviction, he asked, blandishingly: "What are you gwine there for, boss?"

"What is that to you?" I asked, a little sharply.

"Nothin', suh, jus' nothin'. Only it's a lonesome kind of part of town and few folks ever has business out there. Step right in. The seats is clean—jes' got back from a funeral, suh."

A mile and a half it must have been to our journey's end. I could hear nothing but the fearful rattle of the ancient hack over the uneven brick paving; I could smell nothing but the drizzle, now further flavored with coal smoke and something like a mixture of tar and oleander blossoms. All I could see through the streaming windows were two rows of dim houses.

The city has an area of 10 square miles; 181 miles of streets, of which 137 miles are paved; a system of waterworks that cost $2,000,000 with 77 miles of mains.

Eight-sixty-one Jessamine Street was a decayed mansion. Thirty yards back from the street it stood, outmerged in a splendid grove of trees and untrimmed shrubbery. A row of box bushes overflowed and almost hid the paling fence from sight; the gate was kept closed by a rope noose that encircled the gate post and the first paling of the gate. But when you got inside you saw that 861 was a shell, a shadow, a ghost of former grandeur and excellence. But in the story, I have not yet got inside.

When the hack had ceased from rattling and the weary quadrupeds came to a rest I handed my jehu his fifty cents with an additional quarter, feeling a glow of conscious generosity as I did so. He refused it.

"It's two dollars, suh," he said.

"How's that?" I asked. "I plainly heard you call out at the hotel. 'Fifty cents to any part of the town.' "

"It's two dollars, suh," he repeated obstinately. "It's a long ways from the hotel."

"It is within the city limits and well within them," I argued. "Don't think that you have picked up a greenhorn Yankee. Do you see those hills over there?" I went on, pointing toward the east (I could not see them, myself, for the drizzle); "well, I was born and raised on their other side. You old fool nigger, can't you tell people from other people when you see 'em?"

The grim face of King Cettiwayo softened. "Is you from the South, suh? I reckon it was them shoes of yourn fooled me. They is somethin' sharp in the toes for a Southern gen'l'man to wear."

"Then the charge is fifty cents, I suppose?" said I, inexorably.

His former expression, a mingling of cupidity and hostility, returned, remained ten seconds, and vanished.

"Boss," he said, "fifty cents is right; but I *needs* two dollars, suh; I'm *obleeged* to have two dollars. I ain't *demandin'* it now, suh; after I knows whar you's from; I'm jus sayin' that I *has* to have two dollars to-night and business is mighty po'."

Peace and confidence settled upon his heavy features. He had been luckier than he had hoped. Instead of having picked up a greenhorn, ignorant of rates, he had come upon an inheritance.

"You confounded old rascal," I said, reaching down to my pocket, "you ought to be turned over to the police."

For the first time I saw him smile. He knew; *he knew;* HE KNEW.

I gave him two one-dollar bills. As I handed them over I noticed that one of them had seen parlous times. Its upper right-hand corner was missing, and it had been torn through in the middle, but joined again. A strip of blue tissue paper, pasted over the split, preserved its negotiability.

Enough of the African bandit for the present: I left him happy, lifted the rope, and opened the creaky gate.

The house, as I said, was a shell. A paint brush had not touched it in twenty years. I could not see why a strong wind should not have bowled it over like a house of cards until I looked again at the trees that hugged it close—the trees that saw the battle of Nashville and still drew their protecting branches around it against storm and enemy and cold.

Azalea Adair, fifty years old, white-haired, a descendant of the cavaliers, as thin and frail as the house she lived in, robed in the cheapest and cleanest dress I ever saw, with an air as simple as a queen's, received me.

The reception room seemed a mile square, because there was nothing in it except some rows of books, on unpainted white-pine bookshelves, a cracked marble-topped table, a rag rug, a hairless horsehair sofa, and two or three chairs. Yes, there was a picture on the wall, a colored crayon drawing of a cluster of pansies. I looked around for the portrait of Andrew Jackson and the pine-cone hanging basket but they were not there.

Azalea Adair and I had conversation, a little of which will be repeated to you. She was a product of the old South, gently nurtured in the sheltered life. Her learning was not broad, but was deep and of splendid originality in its somewhat narrow scope. She had been educated at home, and her knowledge of the world was derived from inference and by inspiration. Of such is the precious, small group of essayists made. While she talked to me I kept brushing my fingers, trying, unconsciously, to rid them guiltily of the absent dust from the half-calf backs of Lamb, Chaucer, Hazlitt, Marcus Aurelius, Montaigne, and Hood. She was exquisite, she was a valuable discovery. Nearly everybody nowadays knows too much—oh, so much too much—of real life.

I could perceive clearly that Azalea Adair was very poor. A house and a dress she had, not much else, I fancied. So, divided between my duty to the magazine and my loyalty to the poets and essayists who fought Thomas in the valley of the Cumberland, I listened to her voice which was like a harpsichord's, and found that I could not speak of contracts. In the presence of the nine Muses and the three Graces one hesitated to lower the topic to two cents. There would have to be another colloquy after I had regained my commercialism. But I spoke of my mission, and three o'clock of the next afternoon was set for the discussion of the business proposition.

"Your town," I said, as I began to make ready to depart (which is the time for smooth generalities) "seems to be a quiet, sedate place. A home town, I should say, where few things out of the ordinary ever happen."

It carries on an extensive trade in stoves and hollow ware with the West and South, and its flouring mills have a daily capacity of more than 2,000 barrels.

Azalea Adair seemed to reflect.

"I have never thought of it that way," she said, with a kind of sincere intensity that seemed to belong to her. "Isn't it in the still, quiet places that things do happen? I fancy that when God began to create the earth on the first Monday morning one could have leaned out one's window and heard the drops of mud splashing from His trowel as He built up the everlasting hills. What did the noisiest project in the world—I mean the building of the tower of Babel—result in finally? A page and a half of Esperanto in the *North American Review*."

"Of course," said I, platitudinously, "human nature is the same everywhere; but there is more color—er—more drama and movement and—er—romance in some cities than in others."

"On the surface," said Azalea Adair. "I have traveled many times around the world in a golden airship wafted on two wings—print and dreams. I have seen (on one of my imaginary tours) the Sultan of Turkey bowstring with his own hands one of his wives who had uncovered her face in public. I have seen a man in Nashville tear up his theatre tickets because his wife was going out with her face covered—with rice powder. In San Francisco's Chinatown I saw the slave girl Sing Yee dipped slowly, inch by inch, in boiling almond oil to make her swear she would never see her American lover again. She gave in when the boiling oil had reached three inches above her knee. At a euchre party in East Nashville the other night I saw Kitty Morgan cut dead by seven of her schoolmates and lifelong friends because she had married a house painter. The boiling oil was sizzling as high as her heart; but I wish you could have seen the fine little smile that she carried from table to table. Oh, yes, it is a humdrum town. Just a few miles of red brick houses and mud and stores and lumber yards."

Some one had knocked hollowly at the back of the house. Azalea Adair breathed a soft apology and went to investigate the sound. She came back in three minutes with brightened eyes, a faint flush on her cheeks, and ten years lifted from her shoulders.

"You must have a cup of tea before you go," she said, "and a sugar cake."

She reached and shook a little iron bell. In shuffled a small Negro girl about twelve, barefoot, not very tidy, glowering at me with thumb in mouth and bulging eyes.

Azalea Adair opened a tiny, worn purse and drew out a dollar bill, a dollar bill with the upper right-hand corner missing, torn in two pieces and pasted together again with a strip of blue tissue paper. It was one of those bills I had given the piratical Negro—there was no doubt of it.

"Go up to Mr. Baker's store on the corner, Impy," she said, handing the girl the dollar bill, "and get a quarter of a pound of tea—the kind he always sends me—and ten cents' worth of sugar cakes. Now, hurry. The supply of tea in the house happens to be exhausted," she explained to me.

Impy left by the back way. Before the scrape of her hard, bare feet had died away on the back porch, a wild shriek—I was sure it was hers—filled the hollow house. Then the deep, gruff tones of an angry man's voice mingled with the girl's further squeals and unintelligible words.

Azalea Adair rose without surprise or emotion and disappeared. For two minutes I heard the hoarse rumble of the man's voice; then something like an oath and a slight scuffle, and she returned calmly to her chair.

"This is a roomy house," she said, "and I have a tenant for part of it. I am sorry to have to rescind my invitation to tea. It is impossible to get the kind I always use at the store. Perhaps to-morrow Mr. Baker will be able to supply me."

I was sure that Impy had not had time to leave the house. I inquired concerning street-car lines and took my leave. After I was well on my way I remembered that I had not learned Azalea Adair's name. But to-morrow would do.

That same day I started in on the course of iniquity that this uneventful city forced upon me. I was in the town only two days, but in that time I managed to lie shamelessly by telegraph, and to be an accomplice—after the fact, if that is the correct legal term—to a murder.

As I rounded the corner nearest my hotel the Afrite coachman of the polychromatic, nonpareil coat seized me, swung open the dungeony door of his peripatetic sarcophagus, flirted his feather duster and began his ritual: "Step right in, boss. Carriage is clean—jus' got back from a funeral. Fifty cents to any—"

And then he knew me and grinned broadly. " 'Scuse me, boss; you is de gen'l'man what rid out with me dis mawnin'. Thank you kindly, suh."

"I am going out to 861 again to-morrow afternoon at three," said I, "and if you will be here, I'll let you drive me. So you know Miss Adair?" I concluded, thinking of my dollar bill.

"I belonged to her father, Judge Adair, suh," he replied.

"I judge that she is pretty poor," I said. "She hasn't much money to speak of, has she?"

For an instant I looked again at the fierce countenance of King Cettiwayo, and then he changed back to an extortionate old Negro hack driver.

"She ain't gwine to starve, suh," he said, slowly. "She has reso'ces, suh; she has reso'ces."

"I shall pay you fifty cents for the trip," said I

"Dat is puffeckly correct, suh," he answered, humbly. "I jus' *had* to have dat two dollars dis mawnin', boss."

I went to the hotel and lied by electricity. I wired the magazine: "A. Adair holds out for eight cents a word."

The answer that came back was: "Give it to her quick, you duffer."

Just before dinner "Major" Wentworth Caswell bore down upon me with the greetings of a long-lost friend. I have seen few men whom I have so instantaneously hated, and of whom it was so difficult to be rid. I was standing at the bar when he invaded me; therefore I could not wave the white ribbon in his face. I would have paid gladly for the drinks, hoping thereby, to escape another; but he was one of those despicable, roaring, advertising bibbers who must have brass bands and fireworks attend upon every cent that they waste in their follies.

With an air of producing millions he drew two one-dollar bills from a pocket and dashed one of them upon the bar. I looked once more at the dollar bill with the upper right-hand corner missing, torn through the middle, and patched with a strip of blue tissue paper. It was my dollar again. It could have been no other.

I went up to my room. The drizzle and the monotony of a dreary, eventless Southern town had made me tired and listless. I remember that just before I went to bed I mentally disposed of the mysterious dollar bill (which might have formed the clue to a tremendously fine detective story of San Francisco) by saying to myself sleepily: "Seems as if a lot of people here own stock in the Hack-Drivers' Trust. Pays dividends promptly, too. Wonder if—" Then I fell asleep.

King Cettiwayo was at his post the next day, and rattled my bones over the stones out to 861. He was to wait and rattle me back again when I was ready.

Azalea Adair looked paler and cleaner and frailer than she had looked on the day before. After she had signed the contract at eight cents per word she grew still paler and began to slip out of her chair.

Without much trouble I managed to get her up on the antediluvian horsehair sofa and then I ran out to the sidewalk and yelled to the coffee-colored Pirate to bring a doctor. With a wisdom that I had not suspected in him, he abandoned his team and struck off up the street afoot, realizing the value of speed. In ten minutes he returned with a grave, gray-haired, and capable man of medicine. In a few words (worth much less than eight cents each) I explained to him my presence in the hollow house of mystery. He bowed with stately understanding, and turned to the old Negro.

"Uncle Cæsar," he said, calmly, "run up to my house and ask Miss Lucy to give you a cream pitcher full of fresh milk and half a tumbler of port wine. And hurry back. Don't drive—run. I want you to get back sometime this week."

It occurred to me that Mr. Merriman also felt a distrust as to the speeding powers of the land-pirate's steeds. After Uncle Cæsar was gone, lumberingly, but swiftly, up the street, the doctor looked me over with great politeness and as much careful calculation until he had decided that I might do.

"It is only a case of insufficient nutrition," he said. "In other words, the result of poverty, pride, and starvation. Mrs. Caswell has many devoted friends who would be glad to aid her, but she will accept nothing except from that old Negro, Uncle Cæsar, who was once owned by her family."

"Mrs. Caswell!" said I, in surprise. And then I looked at the contract and saw that she had signed it "Azalea Adair Caswell."

"I thought she was Miss Adair," I said.

"Married to a drunken, worthless loafer, sir," said the doctor. "It is said that he robs her even of the small sums that her old servant contributes toward her support."

When the milk and wine had been brought the doctor soon revived Azalea Adair. She sat up and talked of the beauty of the autumn leaves that were then in season and their height of color. She referred lightly to her fainting seizure as the outcome of an old palpitation of the heart. Impy fanned her as she lay on the sofa. The doctor was due elsewhere, and I followed him to the door. I told him that it was within my power and intentions to make a reasonable advance of money to Azalea Adair on future contributions to the magazine, and he seemed pleased.

"By the way," he said, "perhaps you would like to know that you have had royalty for a coachman. Old Cæsar's grandfather was a king in Congo. Cæsar himself has royal ways, as you may have observed."

As the doctor was moving off I heard Uncle Cæsar's voice inside: "Did he git bofe of dem two dollars from you, Mis' Zalea?"

"Yes, Cæsar," I heard Azalea Adair answer, weakly. And then I went in and concluded my business negotiations with our contributor. I assumed the responsibility of advancing fifty dollars, putting it as a necessary formality in binding our bargain. And then Uncle Cæsar drove me back to the hotel.

Here ends all of the story as far as I can testify as a witness. The rest must be only bare statements of facts.

At about six o'clock I went out for a stroll. Uncle Cæsar was at his corner. He threw open the door of his carriage, flourished his duster, and began his depressing formula: "Step right in, suh. Fifty cents to anywhere in the city—hack's puffickly clean, suh—jus' got back from a funeral—"

And then he recognized me. I think his eyesight was getting bad. His coat had taken on a few more faded shades of color, the twine strings were more frayed and ragged, the last remaining button—the button of yellow horn—was gone. A motley descendant of kings was Uncle Cæsar!

About two hours later I saw an excited crowd besieging the front of the drug store. In a desert where nothing happens this was manna; so I wedged my way inside. On an extemporized couch of empty boxes and chairs was stretched the mortal corporeality of Major Wentworth Caswell. A doctor was testing him for the mortal ingredient. His decision was that it was conspicuous by its absence.

The erstwhile Major had been found dead on a dark street and brought by curious and ennuied citizens to the drug store. The late human being had been engaged in terrific battle—the details showed that. Loafer and reprobate though he had been, he had been also a warrior. But he had lost. His hands were yet clinched so tightly that his fingers would not be opened. The gentle citizens who had known him stood about and searched their vocabularies to find some good words, if it were possible, to speak of him. One kind-looking man said, after much thought: "When 'Cas' was about fo'teen he was one of the best spellers in the school."

While I stood there the fingers of the right hand of "the man that was," which hung down the side of a white pine box, relaxed, and dropped something at my feet. I covered it with one foot quietly, and a little later on I picked it up and pocketed it. I reasoned that in his last struggle his hand must have seized that object unwittingly and held it in a death grip.

At the hotel that night the main topic of conversation, with the possible exceptions of politics and prohibition, was the demise of Major Caswell. I heard one man say to a group of listeners:

"In my opinion, gentlemen, Caswell was murdered by some of these no-account niggars for his money. He had fifty dollars this afternoon which he showed to several gentlemen in the hotel. When he was found the money was not on his person."

I left the city the next morning at nine, and as the train was crossing the bridge over the Cumberland River I took out of my pocket a yellow horn overcoat button the size of a fifty-cent piece, with frayed ends of coarse twine hanging from it, and cast it out of the window into the slow, muddy waters below.

I wonder what's doing in Buffalo!

Proof of the Pudding

Spring winked a vitreous optic at Editor Westbrook of the *Minerva Magazine,* and deflected him from his course. He had lunched in his favorite corner of a Broadway hotel, and was returning to his office when his feet became entangled in the lure of the vernal coquette. Which is by way of saying that he turned eastward in Twenty-sixth Street, safely forded the spring freshet of vehicles in Fifth Avenue, and meandered along the walks of budding Madison Square.

The lenient air and the settings of the little park almost formed a pastorale, the color motif was green—the presiding shade at the creation of man and vegetation.

The callow grass between the walks was the color of verdigris, a poisonous green, reminiscent of the horde of derelict humans that had breathed upon the soil during the summer and autumn. The bursting tree buds looked strangely familiar to those who had botanized among the garnishings of the first course of a forty-cent dinner. The sky above was of that pale aquamarine tint that hall-room poets rhyme with "true" and "Sue" and "coo." The one natural and frank color visible was the ostensible green of the newly painted benches—a shade between the color of a pickled cucumber and that of a last year's fast-black cravenette raincoat. But, to the city-bred eye of Editor Westbrook, the landscape appeared a masterpiece.

And now, whether you are of those who rush in, or of the gentle concourse that fears to tread, you must follow in a brief invasion of the editor's mind.

Editor Westbrook's spirit was contented and serene. The April number of the *Minerva* had sold its entire edition before the tenth day of the month—a newsdealer in Keokuk had written that he could have sold fifty copies more if he had had 'em. The owners of the magazine had raised his (the editor's) salary; he had just installed in his home a jewel of a recently imported cook who was afraid of policemen; and the morning papers had published in full a speech he had made at a publishers' banquet. Also there were echoing in his mind the jubilant notes of a splendid song that his charming young wife had sung to him before he left his up-town apartment that morning. She was taking enthusiastic interest in her music of late, practising early and diligently. When he had complimented her for the improvement in her voice she had fairly hugged him for joy at his praise. He felt, too, the benign, tonic medicament of the trained nurse, Spring, tripping softly adown the wards of the convalescent city.

While Editor Westbrook was sauntering between the rows of park benches (already filling with vagrants and the guardians of lawless childhood) he felt his sleeve grasped and held. Suspecting that he was about to be panhandled, he turned a cold and unprofitable face, and saw that his captor was—Dawe—Shackleford Dawe, dingy, almost ragged, the genteel scarcely visible in him through the deeper lines of the shabby.

While the editor is pulling himself out of his surprise a flashlight biography of Dawe is offered.

He was a fiction writer and one of Westbrook's old acquaintances. At one time they might have called each other old friends. Dawe had some money in those days, and lived in a decent apartment house near Westbrook's. The two families often went to theatres and dinners together. Mrs. Dawe and Mrs. Westbrook became "dearest" friends. Then one day a little tentacle of the octopus, just to amuse itself, ingurgitated Dawe's capital, and he moved to the Gramercy Park neighborhood where one, for a few groats per week, may sit upon one's trunk under eight-branched chandeliers and opposite Carrara marble mantels and watch the mice play upon the floor. Dawe thought to live by writing fiction. Now and then he sold a story. He submitted many to Westbrook. The *Minerva* printed one or two of them; the rest were returned. Westbrook sent a careful and conscientious personal letter with each rejected manuscript, pointing out in detail his reasons for considering it unavailable. Editor Westbrook had his own clear conception of what constituted good fiction. So had Dawe. Mrs. Dawe was mainly concerned about the constituents of the scanty dishes of food that she managed to scrape together. One day Dawe had been spouting to her about the excellencies of certain French writers. At dinner they sat down to a dish that a hungry schoolboy could have encompassed at a gulp. Dawe commented.

"It's Maupassant hash," said Mrs. Dawe. "It may not be art, but I do wish you would do a five-course Marion Crawford serial with an Ella Wheeler Wilcox sonnet for dessert. I'm hungry."

As far as this from success was Shackleford Dawe when he plucked Editor Westbrook's sleeve in Madison Square. That was the first time the editor had seen Dawe in several months.

"Why, Shack, is this you?" said Westbrook, somewhat awkwardly, for the form of his phrase seemed to touch upon the other's changed appearance.

"Sit down for a minute," said Dawe, tugging at his sleeve. "This is my office. I can't come to yours, looking as I do. Oh, sit down—you won't be disgraced. Those half-plucked birds on the other benches will take you for a swell porch-climber. They won't know you are only an editor."

"Smoke, Shack?" said Editor Westbrook, sinking cautiously upon the virulent green bench. He always yielded gracefully when he did yield.

Dawe snapped at the cigar as a kingfisher darts at a sunperch, or a girl pecks at a chocolate cream.

"I have just———" began the editor.

"Oh, I know; don't finish," said Dawe. "Give me a match. You have just ten minutes to spare. How did you manage to get past my office-boy and invade my sanctum? There he goes now, throwing his club at a dog that couldn't read the 'Keep off the Grass' signs."

"How goes the writing?" asked the editor.

"Look at me," said Dawe, "for your answer. Now don't put on that embarrassed, friendly-but-honest look and ask me why I don't get a job as a wine agent or a cab driver. I'm in the fight to a finish.

I know I can write good fiction and I'll force you fellows to admit it yet. I'll make you change the spelling of 'regrets' to 'c-h-e-q-u-e' before I'm done with you."

Editor Westbrook gazed through his noseglasses with a sweetly sorrowful, omniscient, sympathetic, skeptical expression—the copyrighted expression of the editor beleaguered by the unavailable contributor.

"Have you read the last story I sent you—'The Alarum of the Soul'?" asked Dawe.

"Carefully. I hesitated over that story, Shack, really I did. It had some good points. I was writing you a letter to send with it when it goes back to you. I regret———"

"Never mind the regrets," said Dawe, grimly. "There's neither salve nor sting in 'em any more. What I want to know is *why*. Come, now; out with the good points first."

"The story," said Westbrook, deliberately, after a suppressed sigh, "is written around an almost original plot. Characterization—the best you have done. Construction—almost as good, except for a few weak joints which might be strengthened by a few changes and touches. It was a good story, except———"

"I can write English, can't I?" interrupted Dawe.

"I have always told you," said the editor, "that you had a style."

"Then the trouble is the———"

"Same old thing," said Editor Westbrook. "You work up to your climax like an artist. And then you turn yourself into a photographer. I don't know what form of obstinate madness possesses you, Shack, but that is what you do with everything that you write. No. I will retract the comparison with the photographer. Now and then photography, in spite of its impossible perspective, manages to record a fleeting glimpse of truth. But you spoil every dénouement by those flat, drab, obliterating strokes of your brush that I have so often complained of. If you would rise to the literary pinnacle of your dramatic scenes, and paint them in the high colors that art requires, the postman would leave fewer bulky, self-addressed envelopes at your door."

"Oh, fiddles and footlights!" cried Dawe, derisively. "You've got that old sawmill drama king in your brain yet. When the man with the black mustache kidnaps golden-haired Bessie you are bound to have the mother kneel and raise her hands in the spotlight and say: 'May high heaven witness that I will rest neither night nor day till the heartless villain that has stolen me child feels the weight of a mother's vengeance!' "

Editor Westbrook conceded a smile of impervious complacency.

"I think," said he, "that in real life the woman would express herself in those words or in very similar ones."

"Not in a six hundred nights' run anywhere but on the stage," said Dawe, hotly. "I'll tell you what she'd say in real life. She'd say: 'What! Bessie led away by a strange man? Good Lord! It's one trouble after another! Get my other hat, I must hurry around to the police-station. Why wasn't somebody looking after her, I'd like to know? For God's sake, get out of my way or I'll never get ready. Not that hat—the brown one with the velvet bows. Bessie must have been crazy; she's usually shy of strangers. Is that too much powder? Lordy! How I'm upset!'

"That's the way she'd talk," continued Dawe. "People in real life don't fly into heroics and blank verse at emotional crises. They simply can't do it. If they talk at all on such occasions they draw from the same vocabulary that they use every day, and muddle up their words and ideas a little more, that's all."

"Shack," said Editor Westbook, impressively, "did you ever pick up the mangled and lifeless form of a child from under the fender of a street car, and carry it in your arms and lay it down before the distracted mother? Did you ever do that and listen to the words of grief and despair as they flowed spontaneously from her lips?"

"I never did," said Dawe. "Did you?"

"Well, no," said Editor Westbrook, with a slight frown. "But I can well imagine what she would say."

"So can I," said Dawe.

And now the fitting time had come for Editor Westbrook to play the oracle and silence his opinionated contributor. It was not for an unarrived fictionist to dictate words to be uttered by the heroes and heroines of the *Minerva Magazine,* contrary to the theories of the editor thereof.

"My dear Shack," said he, "if I know anything of life I know that every sudden, deep, and tragic emotion in the human heart calls forth an opposite, concordant, conformable, and proportionate expression of feeling. How much of this inevitable accord between expression and feeling should be attributed to nature, and how much to the influence of art, it would be difficult to say. The sublimely terrible roar of the lioness that has been deprived of her cubs is dramatically as far above her customary whine and purr as the kingly and transcendent utterances of Lear are above the level of his senile vaporings. But it is also true that all men and women have what may be called a sub-conscious dramatic sense that is awakened by a sufficiently deep and powerful emotion—a sense unconsciously acquired from literature and the stage that prompts them to express those emotions in language befitting their importance and histrionic value."

"And in the name of the seven sacred saddle-blankets of Sagittarius, where did the stage and literature get the stunt?" asked Dawe.

"From life," answered the editor, triumphantly.

The story writer rose from the bench and gesticulated eloquently but dumbly. He was beggared for words with which to formulate adequately his dissent.

On a bench near by a frowzy loafer opened his red eyes and perceived that his moral support was due a downtrodden brother.

"Punch him one, Jack," he called hoarsely to Dawe. "W'at's he come makin' a noise like a penny arcade for amongst gen'lemen that comes in the Square to set and think?"

Editor Westbrook looked at his watch with an affected show of leisure.

"Tell me," asked Dawe, with truculent anxiety, "what especial faults in 'The Alarum of the Soul' caused you to throw it down?"

"When Gabriel Murray," said Westbrook, "goes to his telephone and is told that his financée has been shot by a burglar, he says—I do not recall the exact words, but———"

"I do," said Dawe. "He says: 'Damn Central; she always cuts me off.' (And then to his friend) 'Say, Tommy, does a thirty-two bullet make a big hole? It's kind of hard luck, ain't it? Could you get me a drink from the sideboard, Tommy? No; straight; nothing on the side.' "

"And again," continued the editor, without pausing for argument, "when Berenice opens the letter from her husband informing her that he has fled with the manicure girl, her words are—let me see———"

"She says," interposed the author: " 'Well, what do you think of that!' "

"Absurdly inappropriate words," said Westbrook, "presenting an anticlimax—plunging the story into hopeless bathos. Worse yet; they mirror life falsely. No human being ever uttered banal colloquialisms when confronted by sudden tragedy."

"Wrong," said Dawe, closing his unshaven jaws doggedly. "I say no man or woman ever spouts 'high-falutin' talk when they go up against a real climax. They talk naturally and a little worse."

The editor rose from the bench with his air of indulgence and inside information.

"Say, Westbrook," said Dawe, pinning him by the lapel, "would you have accepted 'The Alarum of the Soul' if you had believed that the actions and words of the characters were true to life in the parts of the story that we discussed?"

"It is very likely that I would, if I believed that way," said the editor. "But I have explained to you that I do not."

"If I could prove to you that I am right?"

"I'm sorry, Shack, but I'm afraid I haven't time to argue any further just now."

"I don't want to argue," said Dawe. "I want to demonstrate to you from life itself that my view is the correct one."

"How could you do that?" asked Westbrook, in a surprised tone.

"Listen," said the writer, seriously, "I have thought of a way. It is important to me that my theory of true-to-life fiction be recognized as correct by the magazines. I've fought for it for three years, and I'm down to my last dollar, with two months' rent due."

"I have applied the opposite of your theory," said the editor, "in selecting the fiction for the *Minerva Magazine*. The circulation has gone up from ninety thousand to——"

"Four hundred thousand," said Dawe. "Whereas it should have been boosted to a million."

"You said something to me just now about demonstrating your pet theory."

"I will. If you'll give me about half an hour of your time I'll prove to you that I am right. I'll prove it by Louise."

"Your wife!" exclaimed Westbrook. "How?"

"Well, not exactly by her, but *with* her," said Dawe. "Now, you know how devoted and loving Louise has always been. She thinks I'm the only genuine preparation on the market that bears the old doctor's signature. She's been fonder and more faithful than ever, since I've been cast for the neglected genius part."

"Indeed, she is a charming and admirable life companion," agreed the editor. "I remember what inseparable friends she and Mrs. Westbrook once were. We are both lucky chaps, Shack, to have such wives. You must bring Mrs. Dawe up some evening soon, and we'll have one of those informal chafing-dish suppers that we used to enjoy so much."

"Later," said Dawe. "When I get another shirt. And now I'll tell you my scheme. When I was about to leave home after breakfast—if you can call tea and oatmeal breakfast—Louise told me she was going to visit her aunt in Eighty-ninth Street. She said she would return home at three o'clock. She is always on time to a minute. It is now———"

Dawe glanced toward the editor's watch pocket.

"Twenty-seven minutes to three," said Westbrook, scanning his timepiece.

"We have just enough time," said Dawe. "We will go to my flat at once. I will write a note, address it to her and leave it on the table where she will see it as she enters the door. You and I will be in the dining room concealed by the portières. In that note I'll say that I have fled from her forever with an affinity who understands the needs of my artistic soul as she never did. When she reads it we will observe her actions and hear her words. Then we will know which theory is the correct one—yours or mine."

"Oh, never!" exclaimed the editor, shaking his head. "That would be inexcusably cruel. I could not consent to have Mrs. Dawe's feelings played upon in such a manner."

"Brace up," said the writer, "I guess I think as much of her as you do. It's for her benefit as well as mine. I've got to get market for my stories in some way. It won't hurt Louise. She's healthy and sound. Her heart goes as strong as a ninety-eight-cent watch. It'll last for only a minute, and then I'll step out and explain to her. You really owe it to me to give me the chance, Westbrook."

Editor Westbrook at length yielded, though but half willingly. And in the half of him that consented lurked the vivisectionist that is in all of us. Let him who has not used the scalpel rise and stand in his place. Pity 'tis that there are not enough rabbits and guinea-pigs to go around.

The two experimenters in Art left the Square and hurried eastward and then to the south until they arrived in the Gramercy neighborhood. Within its high iron railings the little park had put on its smart coat of vernal green, and was admiring itself in its fountain mirror. Outside the railings the hollow square of crumbling houses, shells of a bygone gentry, leaned as if in ghostly gossip over the forgotten doings of the vanished quality. *Sic transit gloria urbis.*

A block or two north of the Park, Dawe steered the editor again eastward, then, after covering a short distance, into a lofty but narrow flathouse burdened with a floridly over-decorated façade. To the fifth story they toiled, and Dawe, panting, pushed his latch-key into the door of one of the front flats.

When the door opened Editor Westbrook saw, with feelings of pity, how meanly and meagrely the rooms were furnished.

"Get a chair, if you can find one," said Dawe, "while I hunt up pen and ink. Hello, what's this? Here's a note from Louise. She must have left it there when she went out this morning."

He picked up an envelope that lay on the centre-table and tore it open. He began to read the letter that he drew out of it; and once having begun it aloud he so read it through to the end. These are the words that Editor Westbrook heard:

"Dear Shackleford:

"By the time you get this I will be about a hundred miles away and still a-going. I've got a place in the chorus of the Occidental Opera Co., and we start on the road to-day at twelve o'clock. I didn't want to starve to death, and so I decided to make my own living. I'm not coming back. Mrs. Westbrook is going with me. She said she was tired of living with a combination phonograph, iceberg, and dictionary, and she's not coming back, either. We've been practicing the songs and dances for two months on the quiet. I hope you will be successful, and get along all right! Good-bye.

"Louise"

Dawe dropped the letter, covered his face with his trembling hands, and cried out in a deep, vibrating voice:

"My God, why hast thou given me this cup to drink? Since she is false, then let Thy Heaven's fairest gifts, faith and love, become the jesting by-words of traitors and fiends!"

Editor Westbrook's glasses fell to the floor. The fingers of one hand fumbled with a button on his coat as he blurted between his pale lips:

"Say, Shack, ain't that a hell of a note? Wouldn't that knock you off your perch, Shack? Ain't it hell, now, Shack—ain't it?"

The Venturers

Let the story wreck itself on the spreading rails of the *Non Sequitur* Limited, if it will; first you must take your seat in the observation car *"Raison d'être"* for one moment. It is for no longer than to consider a brief essay on the subject—let us call it: "What's Around the Corner."

Omne mundus in duas partes divisum est—men who wear rubbers and pay poll-taxes, and men who discover new continents. There are no more continents to discover; but by the time overshoes are out of date and the poll has developed into an income tax, the other half will be paralleling the canals of Mars with radium railways.

Fortune, Chance, and Adventure are given as synonyms in the dictionaries. To the knowing each has a different meaning. Fortune is a prize to be won. Adventure is the road to it. Chance is what may lurk in the shadows at the roadside. The face of Fortune is radiant and alluring; that of Adventure flushed and heroic. The face of Chance is the beautiful countenance—perfect because vague and dream-born—that we see in our tea-cups at breakfast while we growl over our chops and toast.

The VENTURER is one who keeps his eye on the hedgerows and wayside groves and meadows while he travels the road to Fortune. That is the difference between him and the Adventurer. Eating the forbidden fruit was the best record ever made by a Venturer. Trying to prove that it happened is the highest work of the Adventuresome. To be either is disturbing to the cosmogony of creation. So, as bracket-sawed and city-directoried citizens, let us light our pipes, chide the chicken and the cat, arrange ourselves in the willow rocker under the flickering gas jet at the coolest window and scan this little tale of two modern followers of Chance.

"Did you ever hear that story about the man from the West?" asked Billinger, in the little dark-oak room to your left as you penetrate the interior of the Powhatan Club.

"Doubtless," said John Reginald Forster, rising and leaving the room.

Forster got his straw hat (straws will be in and maybe out again long before this is printed) from the check-room boy, and walked out of the air (as Hamlet says). Billinger was used to having his stories insulted and would not mind. Forster was in his favorite mood and wanted to go away from anywhere. A man, in order to get on good terms with himself, must have his opinions corroborated and his moods matched by some one else. (I had written that "somebody"; but an A. D. T. boy who once took a telegram from me pointed out that I could save money by using the compound word. This is a vice versa case.)

Forster's favorite mood was that of greatly desiring to be a follower of Chance. He was a Venturer by nature, but convention, birth, tradition, and the narrowing influences of the tribe of Manhattan had denied him full privilege. He had trodden all the main-traveled thoroughfares and many of the side roads that are supposed to relieve the tedium of life. But none had sufficed. The reason was that he knew what was to be found at the end of every street. He knew from experience and logic almost precisely to what end each digression from routine must lead. He found a depressing monotony in all the variations that the music of his sphere had grafted upon the tune of life. He had not learned that, although the world was made round, the cirle had been squared, and that its true interest is to be found in "What's Around the Corner."

Forster walked abroad aimlessly from the Powhatan, trying not to tax either his judgment or his desire as to what streets he traveled. He would have been glad to lose his way if it were possible; but he had no hope of that. Adventure and Fortune move at your beck and call in the Greater City; but Chance is oriental. She is a veiled lady in a sedan chair, protected by a special traffic squad of dragomans. Crosstown, uptown, and downtown you may move without seeing her.

At the end of an hour's stroll, Forster stood on a corner of a broad, smooth avenue, looking disconsolately across it at a picturesque old hotel softly but brilliantly lit. Disconsolately, because he knew that he must dine; and dining in that hotel was no venture. It was one of his favorite caravansaries, and so silent and swift would be the service and so delicately choice the food, that he regretted the hunger that must be appeased by the "dead perfection" of the place's cuisine. Even the music there seemed to be always playing *da capo*.

Fancy came to him that he would dine at some cheap, even dubious, restaurant lower down in the city, where the erratic chefs from all countries of the world spread their national cookery for the omnivorous American. Something might happen there out of the routine—he might come upon a subject without a predicate, a road without an end, a question without an answer, a cause without an effect, a gulf stream in life's salt ocean. He had not dressed for evening; he wore a dark business suit that would not be questioned even where the waiters served the spaghetti in their shirt sleeves.

So John Reginald Forster began to search his clothes for money; because the more cheaply you dine, the more surely must you pay. All of the thirteen pockets, large and small, of his business suit he explored carefully and found not a penny. His bank book showed a balance of five figures to his credit in the Old Ironsides Trust Company, but———

Forster became aware of a man near by at his left hand who was really regarding him with some amusement. He looked like any business man of thirty or so, neatly dressed and standing in the attitude of one waiting for a street car. But there was no car line on that avenue. So his proximity and unconcealed curiosity seemed to Forster to partake of the nature of a personal intrusion. But, as he was a consistent seeker after "What's Around the Corner," instead of manifesting resentment he only turned a half-embarrassed smile upon the other's grin of amusement.

"All in?" asked the intruder, drawing nearer.

"Seems so," said Forster. "Now, I thought there was a dollar in—"

"Oh, I know," said the other man, with a laugh. "But there wasn't. I've just been through the same process myself, as I was around the corner. I found in an upper vest pocket—I don't know how they got there—exactly two pennies. You know what kind of a dinner exactly two pennies will buy!"

"You haven't dined, then?" asked Forster.

"I have not. But I would like to. Now, I'll make you a proposition. You look like a man who would take up one. Your clothes look neat and respectable. Excuse personalities. I think mine will pass the scrutiny of a head waiter, also. Suppose we go over to that hotel and dine together. We will choose from the menu like millionaires—or, if you prefer, like gentlemen in moderate circumstances dining extravagantly for once. When we have finished we will match with my two pennies to see which of us will stand the brunt of the house's displeasure and vengeance. My name is Ives. I think we have lived in the same station of life—before our money took wings."

"You're on," said Forster, joyfully.

Here was a venture at least within the borders of the mysterious country of Chance—anyhow, it promised something better than the stale infestivity of a table d'hôte.

The two were soon seated at a corner table in the hotel dining room. Ives chucked one of his pennies across the table to Forster.

"Match for which of us gives the order," he said.

Forster lost.

Ives laughed and began to name liquids and viands to the waiter with the absorbed but calm deliberation of one who was to the menu born. Forster, listening, gave his admiring approval of the order.

"I am a man," said Ives, during the oysters, "who has made a lifetime search after the to-be-continued-in-our-next. I am not like the ordinary adventurer who strikes for a coveted prize. Nor yet am I like a gambler who knows he is either to win or lose a certain set stake. What I want is to encounter an adventure to which I can predict no conclusion. It is the breath of existence to me to dare Fate in its blindest manifestations. The world had come to run so much by rote and gravitation that you can enter upon hardly any foot-path of chance in which you do not find signboards informing you of what you may expect at its end. I am like the clerk in the Circumlocution Office who always complained bitterly when any one came in to ask information. 'He wanted to *know!*' was the kick he made to his fellow-clerks. Well, I don't want to know, I don't want to reason, I don't want to guess—I want to bet my hand without seeing it."

"I understand," said Forster, delightedly. "I've often wanted the way I feel put into words. You've done it. I want to take chances on what's coming. Suppose we have a bottle of Moselle with the next course."

"Agreed," said Ives. "I'm glad you catch my idea. It will increase the animosity of the house toward the loser. If it does not weary you, we will pursue the theme. Only a few times have I met a true venturer—one who does not ask a schedule and map from Fate when he begins a journey. But, as the world becomes more civilized and wiser, the more difficult it is to come upon an adventure the end of which you cannot foresee. In the Elizabethan days you could assault the watch, wring knockers from doors, and have a jolly set-to with the blades in any convenient angle of a wall and 'get away with it.' Nowadays, if you speak disrespectfully to a policeman, all that is left to the most romantic fancy is to conjecture in what particular police station he will land you."

"I know—I know," said Forster, nodding approval.

"I returned to New York to-day," continued Ives, "from a three years' ramble around the globe. Things are not much better abroad than they are at home. The whole world seems to be overrun by conclusions. The only thing that interests me greatly is a premise. I've tried shooting big game in Africa. I know what an express rifle will do at so many yards; and when an elephant or a rhinoceros falls to the bullet, I enjoy it about as much as I did when I was kept in after school to do a sum in long division on the blackboard."

"I know—I know," said Forster.

"There might be something in aeroplanes," went on Ives, reflectively. "I've tried ballooning; but it seems to be merely a cut-and-dried affair of wind and ballast."

"Women," suggested Forster, with a smile.

"Three months ago," said Ives, "I was pottering around in one of the bazaars in Constantinople. I noticed a lady, veiled, of course, but with a pair of especially fine eyes visible, who was examining some amber and pearl ornaments at one of the booths. With her was an attendant—a big Nubian, as black as coal. After a while the attendant drew nearer to me by degrees and slipped a scrap of paper into my hand. I looked at it when I got a chance. On it was scrawled hastily in pencil: 'The arched gate of the Nightingale Garden at nine to-night.' Does that appear to you to be an interesting premise, Mr. Forster?"

"Go on," said Forster eagerly.

"I made inquiries and learned that the Nightingale Garden was the property of an old Turk—a grand vizier, or something of the sort. Of course I prospected for the arched gate and was there at nine. The same Nubian attendant opened the gate promptly on time, and I went inside and sat on a bench by a perfumed fountain with the veiled lady. We had quite an extended chat. She was Myrtle Thompson, a lady journalist, who was writing up the Turkish harems for a Chicago newspaper. She said she noticed the New York cut of my clothes in the bazaar and wondered if I couldn't work something into the metropolitan papers about it."

"I see," said Forster. "I see."

"I've canoed through Canada," said Ives, "down many rapids and over many falls. But I didn't seem to get what I wanted out of it because I knew there were only two possible outcomes—I would either go to the bottom or arrive at the sea level. I've played all games at cards; but the mathematicians have spoiled that sport by computing the percentages. I've made acquaintances on trains, I've answered advertisements, I've rung strange door-bells, I've taken every chance that presented itself; but there has always been the conventional ending—the logical conclusion to the premise."

"I know," repeated Forster. "I've felt it all. But I've had few chances to take my chance at chances. Is there any life so devoid of impossibilities as life in this city? There seems to be a myriad of opportunities for testing the undeterminable; but not one in a thousand fails to land you where you expected it to stop. I wish the subways and street cars disappointed one as seldom."

"The sun has risen," said Ives, "on the Arabian nights. There are no more caliphs. The fisherman's vase is turned to a vacuum bottle, warranted to keep any genie boiling or frozen for forty-eight hours. Life moves by rote. Science has killed adventure. There are no more opportunities such as Columbus and the man who ate the first oyster had. The only certain thing is that there is nothing uncertain."

"Well," said Forster, "my experience has been the limited one of a city man. I haven't seen the world as you have; but it seems that we view it with the same opinion. But, I tell you I am grateful for even this little venture of ours into the borders of the haphazard. There may be at least one breathless moment when the bill for the dinner is presented. Perhaps, after all, the pilgrims who traveled without scrip or purse found a keener taste to life than did the knights of the Round Table who rode abroad with a retinue and King Arthur's certified checks in the lining of their helmets. And now, if you've finished your coffee, suppose we match one of your insufficient coins for the impending blow of Fate. What have I up?"

"Heads," called Ives.

"Heads it is," said Forster, lifting his hand. "I lose. We forgot to agree upon a plan for the winner to escape. I suggest that when the waiter comes you make a remark about telephoning to a friend. I will hold the fort and the dinner check long enough for you to get your hat and be off. I thank you for an evening out of the ordinary, Mr. Ives, and wish we might have others."

"If my memory is not at fault," said Ives, laughing, "the nearest police station is in MacDougal Street. I have enjoyed the dinner, too, let me assure you."

Forster crooked his finger for the waiter. Victor, with a locomotive effort that seemd to owe more to pneumatics than to pedestrianism, glided to the table and laid the card, face downward, by the loser's cup. Forster took it up and added the figures with deliberate care. Ives leaned back comfortably in his chair.

"Excuse me," said Forster; "but I thought you were going to ring up Grimes about that theatre party for Thursday night. Had you forgotten about it?"

"Oh," said Ives, settling himself more comfortably, "I can do that later on. Get me a glass of water, waiter."

"Want to be in at the death, do you?" asked Forster.

"I hope you don't object," said Ives, pleadingly. "Never in my life have I seen a gentleman arrested in a public restaurant for swindling it out of a dinner."

"All right," said Forster, calmly. "You are entitled to see a Christian die in the arena as your *pousse-café*."

Victor came with the glass of water and remained, with the disengaged air of an inexorable collector.

Forster hesitated for fifteen seconds, and then took a pencil from his pocket and scribbled his name on the dinner check. The waiter bowed and took it away.

"The fact is," said Forster, with a little embarrassed laugh, "I doubt whether I'm what they call a 'game sport,' which means the same as a 'soldier of Fortune.' I'll have to make confession. I've been dining at this hotel two or three times a week for more than a year. I always sign my checks." And then, with a note of appreciation in his voice: "It was first-rate of you to stay to see me through with it when you know I had no money, and that you might be scooped in, too."

"I guess I'll confess, too," said Ives, with a grin. "I own the hotel. I do run it, of course, but I always keep a suite on the third floor for my use when I happen to stray into town."

He called a waiter and said: "Is Mr. Gilmore still behind the desk? All right. Tell him that Mr. Ives is here, and ask him to have my rooms made ready and aired."

"Another venture cut short by the inevitable," said Forster. "Is there a conundrum without an answer in the next number? But let's hold to our subject just for a minute or two, if you will. It isn't often that I meet a man who understands the flaws I pick in existence. I am engaged to be married a month from to-day."

"I reserve comment," said Ives.

"Right; I am going to add to the assertion. I am devotedly fond of the lady; but I can't decide whether to show up at the church or make a sneak for Alaska. It's the same idea, you know, that we were discussing—it does for a fellow as far as possibilities are concerned. Everybody knows the routine—you get a kiss flavored with Ceylon tea after breakfast; you go to the office; you come back home and dress for dinner—theatre twice a week—bills—

moping around most evenings trying to make conversation— a little quarrel occasionally—maybe sometimes a big one, and a separation—or else a settling down into a middle-aged contentment, which is worst of all."

"I know," said Ives, nodding wisely.

"It's the dead certainty of the thing," went on Forster, "that keeps me in doubt. There'll nevermore be anything around the corner."

"Nothing after the 'Little Church,' " said Ives, "I know."

"Understand," said Forster, "that I am in no doubt as to my feelings toward the lady. I may say that I love her truly and deeply. But there is something in the current that runs through my veins that cries out against any form of the calculable. I do not know what I want; but I know that I want it. I'm talking like an idiot, I suppose, but I'm sure of what I mean."

"I understand you," said Ives, with a slow smile. "Well I think I will be going up to my rooms now. If you would dine with me here one evening soon, Mr. Forster, I'd be glad."

"Thursday?" suggested Forster.

"At seven, if it's convenient," answered Ives.

"Seven goes," assented Forster.

At half-past eight Ives got into a cab and was driven to a number in one of the correct West Seventies. His card admitted him to the reception room of an old-fashioned house into which the spirits of Forture, Chance, and Adventure had never dared to enter. On the walls were the Whistler etchings, the steel engravings by Oh-what's-his-name?, the still-life paintings of the grapes and garden truck with the watermelon seeds spilled on the table as natural as life, and the Greuze head. It was a household. There were even brass andirons. On a table was an album, half-morocco, with oxidized-silver protections on the corners of the lids. A clock on the mantel ticked loudly, with a warning click at five minutes to nine. Ives looked at it curiously, remembering a time-piece in his grandmother's home that gave such a warning.

And then down the stairs into the room came Mary Marsden. She was twenty-four, and I leave her to your imagination. But I must say this much—youth and health and simplicity and courage and greenish-violet eyes are beautiful, and she had all these. She gave Ives her hand with the sweet cordiality of an old friendship.

"You can't think what a pleasure it is," she said, "to have you drop in once every three years or so."

For half an hour they talked. I confess that I cannot repeat the conversation. You will find it in books in the circulating library. When that part of it was over, Mary said:

"And did you find what you wanted while you were abroad?"

"What I wanted?" said Ives.

"Yes. You know you were always queer. Even as a boy you wouldn't play marbles or baseball or any games with rules. You wanted to dive in water where you didn't know whether it was ten inches or ten feet deep. And when you grew up you were just the same. We've often talked about your peculiar ways."

"I suppose I am an incorrigible," said Ives. "I am opposed to the doctrine of predestination to the rule of three, gravitation, taxes, and everything of the kind. Life has always seemed to me something like a serial story would be if they printed above each installment a synopsis of *succeeding* chapters."

Mary laughed merrily.

"Bob Ames told us once," she said, "of a funny thing you did. It was when you and he were on a train in the South, and you got off at a town where you hadn't intended to stop just because the brakeman hung up a sign in the end of the car with the name of the next station on it."

"I remember," said Ives. "That 'next station' has been the thing I've always tried to get away from."

"I know it," said Mary. "And you've been very foolish. I hope you didn't find what you wanted not to find, or get off at the station where there wasn't any, or whatever it was you expected wouldn't happen to you during the three years you've been away."

"There was something I wanted before I went away," said Ives.

Mary looked in his eyes clearly, with a slight but perfectly sweet smile.

"There was," she said. "You wanted me. And you could have had me as you very well know."

Without replying, Ives let his gaze wander slowly about the room. There had been no change in it since last he had been in it, three years before. He vividly recalled the thoughts that had been in his mind then. The contents of that room were as fixed, in their way, as the everlasting hills. No change would ever come there except the inevitable ones wrought by time and decay. That silver-mounted album would occupy the corner of that table, those pictures would hang on the walls, those chairs be found in their same places every morn and noon and night while the houehold hung together. The brass andirons were monuments to order and stability. Here and there were relics of a hundred years ago which were still living mementos and would be for many years to come. One going from and coming back to that house would never need to forecast or doubt. He would find what he left, and leave what he found. The veiled lady, Chance, would never lift her hand to the knocker on the outer door.

And before him sat the lady who belonged in the room. Cool and sweet and unchangeable she was. She offered no surprises. If one should pass his life with her, though she might grow white-haired and wrinkled, he would never perceive the change. Three years he had been away from her, and she was still waiting for him as established and constant as the house itself. He was sure that she had once cared for him. It was the knowledge that she would always do so that had driven him away. Thus his thoughts ran.

"I am going to be married soon," said Mary.

On the next Thursday afternoon Forster came hurriedly to Ives's hotel.

"Old man," said he, "we'll have to put that dinner off for a year or so; I'm going abroad. The steamer sails at four. That was a great talk we had the other night, and it decided me. I'm going to knock around the world and get rid to that incubus that has been weighing on both you and me—the terrible dread of knowing what's going to happen. I've done one thing that hurts my conscience a little; but I know it's best for both of us. I've written to the lady to whom I was engaged and explained everything—told her plainly why I was leaving—that the monotony of matrimony would never do for me. Don't you think I was right?"

"It is not for me to say," answered Ives. "Go ahead and shoot elephants if you think it will bring the element of chance into your life. We've got to decide these things for ourselves. But I tell you one thing, Forster, I've found the way. I've found out the biggest hazard in the world—a game of chance that never is concluded, a venture that may end in the highest heaven or the blackest pit. It will keep a man on edge until the clods fall on his coffin, because he will never know—not until his last day, and not then will he know. It is a voyage without a rudder or compass, and you must be captain and crew and keep watch, every day and night, yourself, with no one to relieve you. I have found the VENTURE. Don't bother yourself about leaving Mary Marsden, Forster. I married her yesterday at noon."

The Theory and the Hound

Not many days ago my old friend from the tropics, J. P. Bridger, United States consul on the island of Ratona, was in the city. We had wassail and jubilee and saw the Flatiron building, and missed seeing the Bronxless menagerie by about a couple of nights. And then, at the ebb tide, we were walking up a street that parallels and parodies Broadway.

A woman with a comely and mundane countenance passed us, holding in leash a wheezing, vicious, waddling brute of a yellow pug. The dog entangled himself with Bridger's legs and mumbled his ankles in a snarling, peevish, sulky bite. Bridger, with a happy smile kicked the breath out of the brute; the woman showered us with a quick rain of well-conceived adjectives that left us in no doubt as to our place in her opinion, and we passed on. Ten yards farther an old woman with disordered white hair and her bankbook tucked well hidden beneath her tattered shawl begged. Bridger stopped and disinterred for her a quarter from his holiday waistcoat.

On the next corner a quarter of a ton of well-clothed man with a rice-powdered, fat, white jowl, stood holding the chain of a devil-born bulldog whose forelegs were strangers by the length of a dachshund. A little woman in a last-season's hat confronted him and wept, which was plainly all she could do, while he cursed her in low, sweet, practised tones.

Bridger smiled again—strictly to himself—and this time he took out a little memorandum book and made a note of it. This he had no right to do without due explanation, and I said so.

"It's a new theory," said Bridger, "that I picked up down in Ratona. I've been gathering support for it as I knock about. The world isn't ripe for it yet, but—well, I'll tell you; and then you run your mind back along the people you've known and see what you make of it."

And so I cornered Bridger in a place where they have artificial palms and wine; and he told me the story which is here in my words and on his responsibility.

One afternon at three o'clock, on the island of Ratona, a boy raced along the beach screaming, "*Pájaro,* ahoy!"

Thus he made known the keenness of his hearing and the justice of his discrimination in pitch.

He who first heard and made oral proclamation concerning the toot of an approaching steamer's whistle, and correctly named the steamer, was a small hero in Ratona—until the next steamer came. Wherefore, there was rivalry among the barefoot youth of Ratona, and many fell victims to the softly blown conch shells of sloops which, as they enter harbor, sound surprisingly like a distant steamer's signal. And some could name you the vessel when its call, in your duller ears, sounded no louder than the sigh of the wind through the branches of the cocoanut palms.

But to-day he who proclaimed the *Pájaro* gained his honors. Ratona bent its ear to listen; and soon the deep-tongued blast grew louder and nearer, and at length Ratona saw above the line of palms on the low "point" the two black funnels of the fruiter slowly creeping toward the mouth of the harbor.

You must know that Ratona is an island twenty miles off the south of a South American republic. It is a port of that republic; and it sleeps sweetly in a smiling sea, toiling not nor spinning; fed by the abundant tropics where all things "ripen, cease and fall toward the grave."

Eight hundred people dream life away in a green-embowered village that follows the horseshoe curve of its bijou harbor. They are mostly Spanish and Indian mestizos, with a shading of San Domingo Negroes, a lightening of pure-blood Spanish officials, and a slight leavening of the froth of three or four pioneering white races. No steamers touch at Ratona save the fruit steamers which take on their banana inspectors there on their way to the coast. They leave Sunday newspapers, ice, quinine, bacon, watermelons, and vaccine matter at the island and that is about all the touch Ratona gets with the world.

The *Pájaro* paused at the mouth of the harbor, rolling heavily in the swell that sent the whitecaps racing beyond the smooth water inside. Already two dories from the village—one conveying fruit inspectors, the other going for what it could get—were halfway out to the steamer.

The inspector's dory was taken on board with them, and the *Pájaro* steamed away for the mainland for its load of fruit.

The other boat returned to Ratona bearing a contribution from the *Pájaro*'s store of ice, the usual roll of newspapers, and one passenger—Taylor Plunkett, sheriff of Chatham County, Kentucky.

Bridger, the United States consul at Ratona, was cleaning his rifle in the official shanty under a bread-fruit tree twenty yards from the water of the harbor. The consul occupied a place somewhat near the tail of his political party's procession. The music of the band wagon sounded very faintly to him in the distance. The plums of office went to others. Bridger's share of the spoils—the consulship at Ratona—was little more than a prune—a dried prune from the boarding-house department of the public crib. But $900 yearly was opulence in Ratona. Besides, Bridger had contracted a passion for shooting alligators in the lagoons near his consulate, and he was not unhappy.

He looked up from a careful inspection of his rifle lock and saw a broad man filling his doorway. A broad, noiseless, slow-moving man sunburned almost to the brown of Vandyke. A man of forty-five, neatly clothed in homespun, with scanty light hair, a close-clipped brown-and-gray beard and pale-blue eyes expressing mildness and simplicity.

"You are Mr. Bridger, the consul," said the broad man. "They directed me here. Can you tell me what those big bunches of things like gourds are in those trees that look like feather dusters along the edge of the water?"

"Take that chair," said the consul, reoiling his cleaning rag. "No, the other one—that bamboo thing won't hold you. Why, they're cocoanuts—green cocoanuts. The shell of 'em is always a light green before they're ripe."

"Much obliged," said the other man, sitting down carefully. "I didn't quite like to tell the folks at home they were olives unless I was sure about it. My name is Plunkett. I'm sheriff of Chatham County, Kentucky. I've got extradition papers in my pocket authorizing the arrest of a man on this island. They've been signed by the President of this country, and they're in correct shape. The man's name is Wade Williams. He's in the cocoanut raising business. What he's wanted for is the murder of his wife two years ago. Where can I find him?"

The consul squinted an eye and looked through his rifle barrel.

"There's nobody on the island who calls himself 'Williams,' " he remarked.

"Didn't suppose there was," said Plunkett mildly. "He'll do by any other name."

"Besides myself," said Bridger, "there are only two Americans on Ratona—Bob Reeves and Henry Morgan."

"The man I want sells cocoanuts," suggested Plunkett.

"You see the cocoanut walk extending up to the point?" said the consul, waving his hand toward the open door. "That belongs to Bob Reeves. Henry Morgan owns half the trees to loo'ard on the island."

"One month ago," said the sheriff, "Wade Williams wrote a confidential letter to a man in Chatham County, telling him where he was and how he was getting along. The letter was lost; and the person that found it gave it away. They sent me after him, and I've got the papers. I reckon he's one of your cocoanut men for certain."

"You've got his picture, of course," said Bridger. "It might be Reeves or Morgan, but I'd hate to think it. They're both as fine fellows as you'd meet in an all-day auto ride."

"No," doubtfully answered Plunkett; "there wasn't any picture of Williams to be had. And I never saw him myself. I've been sheriff only a year. But I've got a pretty accurate description of him. About 5 feet 11; dark hair and eyes; nose inclined to be Roman; heavy about the shoulders; strong, white teeth, with none missing; laughs a good deal, talkative; drinks considerably but never to intoxication; looks you square in the eye when talking; age thirty-five. Which one of your men does that description fit?"

The consul grinned broadly.

"I'll tell you what you do," he said, laying down his rifle and slipping on his dingy black alpaca coat. "You come along, Mr. Plunkett, and I'll take you up to see the boys. If you can tell which one of 'em your descripton fits better than it does the other you have the advantage of me."

Bridger conducted the sheriff out and along the hard beach close to which the tiny houses of the village were distributed. Immediately back of the town rose sudden, small, thickly wooded hills. Up one of these, by means of steps cut in the hard clay, the consul led Plunkett. On the very verge of an eminence was perched a two-room wooden cottage with a thatched roof. A Carib woman was washing clothes outside. The consul ushered the sheriff to the door of the room that overlooked the harbor.

Two men were in the room, about to sit down, in their shirt sleeves, to a table spread for dinner. They bore little resemblance one to the other in detail; but the general description given by Plunkett could have been justly applied to either. In height, color of hair, shape of nose, build, and manners each of them tallied with it. They were fair types of jovial, ready-witted, broad-gauged Americans who had gravitated together for companionship in an alien land.

"Hello, Bridger!" they called in unison at sight of the consul. "Come and have dinner with us!" And then they noticed Plunkett at his heels, and came forward with hospitable curiosity.

"Gentlemen," said the consul, his voice taking an unaccustomed formality, "this is Mr. Plunkett. Mr. Plunkett—Mr. Reeves and Mr. Morgan."

The cocoanut barons greeted the newcomer joyously. Reeves seemed about an inch taller than Morgan, but his laugh was not quite as loud. Morgan's eyes were deep brown; Reeves's were black. Reeves was the host and busied himself with fetching other chairs and calling to the Carib woman for supplemental table ware. It was explained that Morgan lived in a bamboo shack to "loo'ard," but that every day the two friends dined together. Plunkett stood still during the preparations, looking about mildly with his pale-blue eyes. Bridger looked apologetic and uneasy.

At length two other covers were laid and the company was assigned to places. Reeves and Morgan stood side by side across the table from the visitors. Reeves nodded genially as a signal for all to seat themselves. And then suddenly Plunkett raised his hand with a gesture of authority. He was looking straight between Reeves and Morgan.

"Wade Williams," he said quietly, "you are under arrest for murder."

Reeves and Morgan instantly exchanged a quick, bright glance, the quality of which was interrogation, with a seasoning of surprise. Then, simultaneously they turned to the speaker with a puzzled and frank deprecation in their gaze.

"Can't say we understand you, Mr. Plunkett," said Morgan, cheerfully. "Did you say 'Williams'?"

"What's the joke, Bridgy?" asked Reeves, turning to the consul with a smile.

Before Bridger could answer, Plunkett spoke again.

"I'll explain," he said, quietly. "One of you don't need any explanation, but this is for the other one. One of you is Wade Williams of Chatham County, Kentucky. You murdered your wife on May 5, two years ago, after ill-treating and abusing her continually for five years. I have the proper papers in my pocket for taking you back with me, and you are going. We will return on the fruit steamer that comes back by this island to-morrow to leave its inspectors. I acknowledge, gentlemen, that I'm not quite sure which one of you is Williams. But Wade Williams goes back to Chatham County tomorrow. I want you to understand that."

A great sound of merry laughter from Morgan and Reeves went out over the still harbor. Two or three fishermen in the fleet of sloops anchored there looked up at the house of the *diablos Americanos* on the hill and wondered.

"My dear Mr. Plunkett," cried Morgan, conquering his mirth, "the dinner is getting cold. Let us sit down and eat. I am anxious to get my spoon into the shark-fin soup. Business afterward."

"Sit down, gentlemen, if you please," added Reeves, pleasantly. "I am sure Mr. Plunkett will not object. Perhaps a little time may be of advantage to him in identifying—the gentleman he wishes to arrest."

"No objections, I'm sure," said Plunkett, dropping into his chair heavily. "I'm hungry myself. I didn't want to accept the hospitality of you folks without giving you notice; that's all."

Reeves set bottles and glasses on the table.

"There's cognac," he said, "and anisada, and Scotch 'smoke,' and rye. Take your choice."

Bridger chose rye, Reeves poured three fingers of Scotch for himself, Morgan took the same. The sheriff, against much protestation, filled his glass from the water bottle.

"Here's to the appetite," said Reeves, raising his glass, "of Mr. Williams!" Morgan's laugh and his drink encountering sent him into a choking-splutter. All began to pay attention to the dinner, which was well cooked and palatable.

"Williams!" called Plunkett, suddenly and sharply.

All looked up wonderingly. Reeves found the sheriff's mild eye resting upon him. He flushed a little.

"See here," he said, with some asperity, "my names's Reeves, and I don't want you to—" But the comedy of the thing came to his rescue and he ended with a laugh.

"I suppose, Mr. Plunkett," said Morgan, carefully seasoning an alligator pear, "that you are aware of the fact that you will import a good deal of trouble for yourself into Kentucky if you take back the wrong man—that is, of course, if you take anybody back?"

"Thank you for the salt," said the sheriff. "Oh, I'll take somebody back. It'll be one of you two gentlemen. Yes, I know I'll get stuck for damages if I make a mistake. But I'm going to try to get the right man."

"I'll tell you what you do," said Morgan, leaning forward with a jolly twinkle in his eyes. "You take me. I'll go without any trouble. The cocoanut business hasn't panned out well this year, and I'd like to make some extra money out of your bondsmen."

"That's not fair," chimed in Reeves. "I got only $16 a thousand for my last shipment. Take me, Mr. Plunkett."

"I'll take Wade Williams," said the sheriff, patiently, "or I'll come pretty close to it."

"It's like dining with a ghost," remarked Morgan, with a pretended shiver. "The ghost of a murderer, too! Will somebody pass the toothpicks to the shade of the naughty Mr. Williams?"

Plunkett seemed as unconcerned as if he were dining at his own table in Chatham County. He was a gallant trencherman, and the strange tropic viands tickled his palate. Heavy, commonplace, almost slothful in his movements, he appeared to be devoid of all the cunning and watchfulness of the sleuth. He even ceased to observe, with any sharpness or attempted discrimination, the two men, one of whom he had undertaken with surprising self-confidence to drag away upon the serious charge of wife-murder. Here, indeed, was a problem set before him that if wrongly solved would have amounted to his serious discomfiture, yet there he sat puzzling his soul (to all appearances) over the novel flavor of a broiled iguana cutlet.

The consul felt a decided discomfort. Reeves and Morgan were his friends and pals; yet the sheriff from Kentucky had a certain right to his official aid and moral support. So Bridger sat the silentest around the board and tried to estimate the peculiar situation. His conclusion was that both Reeves and Morgan, quickwitted, as he knew them to be, had conceived at the moment of Plunkett's disclosure of his mission—and in the brief space of a lightning flash—the idea that the other might be the guilty Williams; and that each of them had decided in that moment loyally to protect his comrade against the doom that threatened him. This was the consul's theory, and if he had been a bookmaker at a race of wits for life and liberty he would have offered heavy odds against the plodding sheriff from Chatham County, Kentucky.

When the meal was concluded the Carib woman came and removed the dishes and cloth. Reeves strewed the table with excellent cigars, and Plunkett, with the others, lighted one of these with evident gratification.

"I may be dull," said Morgan, with a grin and a wink at Bridger; "but I want to know if I am. Now, I say this is all a joke of Mr. Plunkett's concocted to frighten two babes-in-the-woods. Is this Williamson to be taken seriously or not?"

" 'Williams,' " corrected Plunkett, gravely. "I never got off any jokes in my life. I know I wouldn't travel 2,000 miles to get off a poor one as this would be if I didn't take Wade Williams back with me. Gentlemen!" continued the sheriff, now letting his mild eyes travel impartially from one of the company to another, "see if you can find any joke in this case. Wade Williams is listening to the words I utter now; but out of politeness I will speak of him as a third person. For five years he made his wife lead the life of a dog—No; I'll take that back. No dog in Kentucky was ever treated as she was. He spent the money that she brought him—spent it at races, at the card table, and on horses and hunting. He was a good fellow to his friends, but a cold, sullen demon at home. He wound up the five years of neglect by striking her with his closed hand—a hand as hard as a stone—when she was ill and weak from suffering. She died the next day; and he skipped. That's all there is to it. It's enough. I never saw Williams; but I knew his wife. I'm not a man to tell half. She and I were keeping company when she met him. She went to Louisville on a visit and saw him there. I'll admit that he spoilt my chances in no time. I lived then on the edge of the Cumberland Mountains. I was elected sheriff of Chatham County a year after Wade Williams killed his wife. My official duty sends me out here after him; but I'll admit that there's personal feeling, too. And he's going back with me. Mr.—er—Reeves, will you pass me a match?"

"Awfully imprudent of Williams," said Morgan, putting his feet up against the wall, "to strike a Kentucky lady. Seems to me I've heard they were scrappers."

"Bad, bad Williams," said Reeves, pouring out more "Scotch."

The two men spoke lightly, but the consul saw and felt the tension and the carefulness in their actions and words. "Good old fellows," he said to himself; "they're both all right. Each of 'em is standing by the other like a little brick church."

And then a dog walked into the room where they sat—a black-and-tan hound, long-eared, lazy, confident of welcome.

Plunkett turned his head and looked at the animal, which halted, confidently, within a few feet of his chair.

Suddenly the sheriff, with a deep-mouthed oath, left his seat and bestowed upon the dog a vicious and heavy kick, with his ponderous shoe.

The hound, heart-broken, astonished, with flapping ears and in-curved tail, uttered a piercing yelp of pain and surprise.

Reeves and the consul remained in their chairs, saying nothing, but astonished at the unexpected show of intolerance from the easy-going man from Chatham County.

But Morgan, with a suddenly purpling face, leaped to his feet and raised a threatening arm above the guest.

"You—brute!" he shouted, passionately; "why did you do that?"

Quickly the amenities returned, Plunkett muttered some indistinct apology and regained his seat. Morgan with a decided effort controlled his indignation and also returned to his chair.

And then Plunkett, with the spring of a tiger, leaped around the corner of the table and snapped handcuffs on the paralyzed Morgan's wrists.

"Hound-lover and woman-killer!" he cried; "get ready to meet your God."

When Bridger had finished I asked him:

"Did he get the right man?"

"He did," said the consul.

"And how did he know?" I inquired, being in a kind of bewilderment.

"When he put Morgan in the dory," answered Bridger, "the next day to take him aboard the *Pájaro,* this man Plunkett stopped to shake hands with me and I asked him the same question.

" 'Mr. Bridger,' said he. 'I'm a Kentuckian, and I've seen a great deal of both men and animals. And I never yet saw a man that was overfond of horses and dogs but what was cruel to women.' "

The Ransom of Red Chief

It looked like a good thing: but wait till I tell you. We were down South, in Alabama—Bill Driscoll and myself—when this kidnapping idea struck us. It was, as Bill afterward expressed it, "during a moment of temporary mental apparition"; but we didn't find that out till later.

There was a town down there, as flat as a flannel-cake, and called Summit, of course. It contained inhabitants of as undeleterious and self-satisfied a class of peasantry as ever clustered around a Maypole.

Bill and me had a joint capital of about six hundred dollars, and we needed just two thousand dollars more to pull off a fraudulent town-lot scheme in Western Illinois with. We talked it over on the front steps of the hotel. Philoprogenitoveness, says we, is strong in semi-rural communities; therefore, and for other reasons, a kidnapping project ought to do better there than in the radius of newspapers that send reporters out in plain clothes to stir up talk about such things. We knew that Summit couldn't get after us with anything stronger than constables and, maybe, some lackadaisical bloodhounds and a diatribe or two in the *Weekly Farmers' Budget*. So, it looked good.

We selected for our victim the only child of a prominent citizen named Ebenezer Dorset. The father was respectable and tight, a mortgage fancier and a stern, upright collection-plate passer and forecloser. The kid was a boy of ten, with bas-relief freckles, and hair the color of the cover of the magazine you buy at the news-stand when you want to catch a train. Bill and me figured that Ebenezer would melt down for a ransom of two thousand dollars to a cent. But wait till I tell you.

About two miles from Summit was a little mountain, covered with a dense cedar brake. On the rear elevation of this mountain was a cave. There we stored provisions.

One evening after sundown, we drove in a buggy past old Dorset's house. The kid was in the street, throwing rocks at a kitten on the opposite fence.

"Hey, little boy!" says Bill, "would you like to have a bag of candy and a nice ride?"

The boy catches Bill neatly in the eye with a piece of brick.

"That will cost the old man an extra five hundred dollars," says Bill, climbing over the wheel.

That boy put up a fight like a welter-weight cinnamon bear; but, at last, we got him down in the bottom of the buggy and drove away. We took him up to the cave, and I hitched the horse in the cedar brake. After dark I drove the buggy to the little village, three miles away, where we had hired it, and walked back to the mountain.

Bill was pasting court-plaster over the scratches and bruises on his features. There was a fire burning behind the big rock at the entrance of the cave, and the boy was watching a pot of boiling coffee, with two buzzard tail-feathers stuck in his red hair. He points a stick at me when I come up, and says:

"Ha! cursed paleface, do you dare to enter the camp of Red Chief, the terror of the plains?"

"He's all right now," says Bill, rolling up his trousers and examining some bruises on his shins. "We're playing Indian. We're making Buffalo Bill's show look like magic-lantern views of Palestine in the town hall. I'm Old Hank, the Trapper, Red Chief's captive, and I'm to be scalped at daybreak. By Geronimo! that kid can kick hard."

Yes, sir, that boy seemed to be having the time of his life. The fun of camping out in a cave had made him forget that he was a captive himself. He immediately christened me Snake-eye, the Spy, and announced that, when his braves returned from the warpath, I was to be broiled at the stake at the rising of the sun.

Then we had supper; and he filled his mouth full of bacon and bread and gravy, and began to talk. He made a during-dinner speech something like this:

"I like this fine. I never camped out before; but I had a pet 'possum once, and I was nine last birthday. I hate to go to school. Rats ate up sixteen of Jimmy Talbot's aunt's speckled hen's eggs. Are there any real Indians in these woods? I want some more gravy. Does the trees moving make the wind blow? We had five puppies. What makes your nose so red, Hank? My father has lots of money. Are the stars hot? I whipped Ed Walker twice, Saturday. I don't like girls. You dassent catch toads unless with a string. Do oxen make any noise? Why are oranges round? Have you got beds to sleep on in this cave? Amos Murray has got six toes. A parrot can talk, but a monkey or a fish can't. How many does it take to make twelve?"

Every few minutes he would remember that he was a pesky redskin, and pick up his stick rifle and tiptoe to the mouth of the cave to rubber for the scouts of the hated paleface. Now and then he would let out a war-whoop that made Old Hank the Trapper shiver. That boy had Bill terrorized from the start.

"Red Chief," says I to the kid, "would you like to go home?"

"Aw, what for?" says he. "I don't have any fun at home. I hate to go to school. I like to camp out. You won't take me back home again, Snake-eye, will you?"

"Not right away," says I. "We'll stay here in the cave awhile."

"All right!" says he. "That'll be fine. I never had such fun in all my life."

We went to bed about eleven o'clock. We spread down some wide blankets and quilts and put Red Chief between us. We weren't afraid he'd run away. He kept us awake for three hours, jumping up and reaching for his rifle and screeching: "Hist! pard," in mine and Bill's ears, as the fancied crackle of a twig or the rustle of a leaf revealed to his young imagination the stealthy approach of the outlaw band. At last, I fell into a troubled sleep, and dreamed that I had been kidnapped and chained to a tree by a ferocious pirate with red hair.

Just at daybreak, I was awakened by a series of awful screams from Bill. They weren't yells, or howls, or shouts, or whoops, or yawps, such as you'd expect from a manly set of vocal organs—they were simply indecent, terrifying, humiliating screams, such as women emit when they see ghosts or caterpillars. It's an awful thing to hear a strong, desperate, fat man scream incontinently in a cave at daybreak.

I jumped up to see what the matter was. Red Chief was sitting on Bill's chest, with one hand twined in Bill's hair. In the other he had the sharp case-knife we used for slicing bacon; and he was industriously and realistically trying to take Bill's scalp, according to the sentence that had been pronounced upon him the evening before.

I got the knife away from the kid and made him lie down again. But, from that moment, Bill's spirit was broken. He laid down on his side of the bed, but he never closed an eye again in sleep as long as that boy was with us. I dozed off for a while, but along toward sun-up I remembered that Red Chief had said I was to be burned at the stake at the rising of the sun I wasn't nervous or afraid; but I sat up and lit my pipe and leaned against a rock.

"What you getting up so soon for, Sam?" asked Bill.

"Me?" says I. "Oh, I got a kind of pain in my shoulder. I thought sitting up would rest it."

"You're a liar!" says Bill. "You're afraid. You was to be burned at sunrise, and you was afraid he'd do it. And he would, too, if he could find a match. Ain't it awful, Sam? Do you think anybody will pay out money to get a little imp like that back home?"

"Sure," said I. "A rowdy kid like that is just the kind that parents dote on. Now, you and the Chief get up and cook breakfast, while I go up on the top of this mountain and reconnoitre."

I went up on the peak of the little mountain and ran my eye over the contiguous vicinty. Over towards Summit I expected to see the sturdy yeomanry of the village armed with scythes and pitchforks beating the countryside for the dastardly kidnappers. But what I saw was a peaceful landscape dotted with one man ploughing with a dun mule. Nobody was dragging the creek; no couriers dashed hither and yon, bringing tidings of no news to the distracted parents. There was a slyvan attitude of somnolent sleepiness pervading that section of the external outward surface of Alabama that lay exposed to my view. "Perhaps," says I to myself, "it has not yet been discovered that the wolves have borne away the tender lambkin from the fold. Heaven help the wolves!" says I, and I went down the mountain to breakfast.

When I got to the cave I found Bill backed up against the side of it, breathing hard, and the boy threatening to smash him with a rock half as big as a cocoanut.

"He put a red-hot boiled potato down my back," explained Bill, "and then mashed it with his foot; and I boxed his ears. Have you got a gun about you, Sam?"

I took the rock away from the boy and kind of patched up the argument. "I'll fix you," says the kid to Bill. "No man ever yet struck the Red Chief but he got paid for it. You better beware!"

After breakfast the kid takes a piece of leather with strings wrapped around it out of his pocket and goes outside the cave unwinding it.

"What's he up to now?" says Bill, anxiously. "You don't think he'll run away, do you, Sam?"

"No fear of it," says I. "He don't seem to be much of a home body. But we've got to fix up some plan about the ransom. There don't seem to be much excitement around Summit on account of his disappearance; but maybe they haven't realized yet that he's gone. His folks may think he's spending the night with Aunt Jane or one of the neighbors. Anyhow, he'll be missed to-day. To-night we must get a message to his father demanding the two thousand dollars for his return."

Just then we heard a kind of war-whoop, such as David might have emitted when he knocked out the champion Goliath. It was a sling that Red Chief had pulled out of his pocket, and he was whirling it around his head.

I dodged, and heard a heavy thud and a kind of a sigh from Bill, like a horse gives out when you take his saddle off. A niggerhead rock the size of an egg had caught Bill just behind his left ear. He loosened himself all over and fell in the fire across the frying pan of hot water for washing the dishes. I dragged him out and poured cold water on his head for half an hour.

By and by, Bill sits up and feels behind his ear and says: "Sam, do you know who my favorite Biblical character is?"

"Take it easy," said I. "You'll come to your senses presently."

"King Herod," says he. "You won't go away and leave me here alone, will you, Sam?"

I went out and caught that boy and shook him until his freckles rattled.

"If you don't behave," says I, "I'll take you straight home. Now, are you going to be good, or not?"

"I was only funning," says he, sullenly. "I didn't mean to hurt Old Hank. But what did he hit me for? I'll behave, Snake-eye, if you won't send me home, and if you'll let me play the Black Scout to-day."

"I don't know the game," says I. "That's for you and Mr. Bill to decide. He's your playmate for the day. I'm going away for a while, on business. Now, you come in and make friends with him and say you are sorry for hurting him, or home you go, at once."

I made him and Bill shake hands, and then I took Bill aside and told him I was going to Poplar Grove, a little village three miles from the cave, and find out what I could about how the kidnapping had been regarded in Summit. Also, I thought it best to send a peremptory letter to old man Dorset that day, demanding the ransom and dictating how it should be paid.

"You know, Sam." says Bill, "I've stood by you without batting an eye in earthquakes, fire and flood—in poker games, dynamite outrages, police raids, train robberies, and cyclones. I never lost my nerve yet till we kidnapped that two-legged skyrocket of a kid. He's got me going. You won't leave me long with him, will you, Sam?"

"I'll be back some time this afternoon," says I. "You must keep the boy amused and quiet till I return. And now we'll write the letter to old Dorset."

Bill and I got paper and pencil and worked on the letter while Red Chief, with a blanket wrapped around him, strutted up and down, guarding the mouth of the cave. Bill begged me tearfully to make the ransom fifteen hundred dollars instead of two thousand. "I ain't attempting," says he, "to decry the celebrated moral aspect of parental affection, but we're dealing with humans, and it ain't human for anybody to give up two thousand dollars for that forty-pound chunk of freckled wildcat. I'm willing to take a chance at fifteen hundred dollars. You can charge the difference up to me."

So, to relieve Bill, I acceded, and we collaborated a letter that ran this way:

Ebenezer Dorset, Esq.:

We have your boy concealed in a place far from Summit. It is useless for you or the most skilful detectives to attempt to find him. Absolutely, the only terms on which you can have him restored to you are these: We demand fifteen hundred dollars in large bills for his return; the money to be left at midnight to-night at the same spot and in the same box as your reply—as hereinafter described. If you agree to these terms, send your answer in writing by a solitary messenger to-night at half-past eight o'clock. After crossing Owl Creek on the road to Poplar Grove, there are three large trees about a hundred yards apart, close to the fence of the wheat field on the right-hand side. At the bottom of the fence-post, opposite the third tree, will be found a small pasteboard box.

The messenger will place the answer in this box and return immediately to Summit.

If you attempt any treachery or fail to comply with our demand as stated, you will never see your boy again.

If you pay the money as demanded, he will be returned to you safe and well within three hours. These terms are final, and if you do not accede to them no further communication will be attempted.

Two Desperate Men

I addressed this letter to Dorset, and put it in my pocket. As I was about to start, the kid comes up to me and says:

"Aw, Snake-eye, you said I could play the Black Scout while you was gone."

"Play it, of course," says I. "Mr. Bill will play with you. What kind of a game is it?"

"I'm the Black Scout," says Red Chief, "and I have to ride to the stockade to warn the settlers that the Indians are coming. I'm tired of playing Indian myself. I want to be the Black Scout."

"All right," says I. "It sounds harmless to me. I guess Mr. Bill will help you foil the pesky savages."

"What am I to do?" asks Bill, looking at the kid suspiciously.

"You are the hoss," says Black Scout. "Get down on your hands and knees. How can I ride to the stockade without a hoss?"

"You'd better keep him interested," said I, "till we get the scheme going. Loosen up."

Bill gets down on his all fours, and a look comes in his eye like a rabbit's when you catch it in a trap.

"How far is it to the stockade, kid?" he asks, in a husky manner of voice.

"Ninety miles," says the Black Scout. "And you have to hump yourself to get there on time. Whoa, now!"

The Black Scout jumps on Bill's back and digs his heels in his side.

"For Heaven's sake," says Bill, "hurry back, Sam, as soon as you can. I wish we hadn't made the ransom more than a thousand. Say, you quit kicking me or I'll get up and warm you good."

I walked over to Poplar Grove and sat around the post-office and store, talking with the chaw-bacons that came in to trade. One whiskerando says that he hears Summit is all upset on account of Elder Ebenezer Dorset's boy having been lost or stolen. That was all I wanted to know. I bought some smoking tobacco, referred casually to the price of black-eyed peas, posted my letter surreptitiously, and came away. The postmaster said the mail-carrier would come by in an hour to take the mail to Summit.

When I got back to the cave Bill and the boy were not to be found. I explored the vicinity of the cave, and risked a yodel or two, but there was no response.

So I lighted my pipe and sat down on a mossy bank to await developments.

In about half an hour I heard the bushes rustle, and Bill wabbled out into the little glade in front of the cave. Behind him was the kid, stepping softly like a scout, with a broad grin on his face. Bill stopped, took off his hat, and wiped his face with a red handkerchief. The kid stopped about eight feet behind him.

"Sam," says Bill, "I suppose you'll think I'm a renegade, but I couldn't help it. I'm a grown person with masculine proclivities and habits of self-defense, but there is a time when all systems of egotism and predominance fail. The boy is gone. I sent him home. All is off. There was martyrs in old times," goes on Bill, "that suffered death rather than give up the particular graft they enjoyed. None of 'em ever was subjugated to such supernatural tortures as I have been. I tried to be faithful to our articles of depredation; but there came a limit."

"What's the trouble, Bill?" I asks him.

"I was rode," says Bill, "the ninety miles to the stockade, not barring an inch. Then, when the settlers was rescued, I was given oats. Sand ain't a palatable substitute. And then, for an hour I had to try to explain to him why there was nothin' in holes, how a road can run both ways, and what makes the grass green. I tell you, Sam, a human can only stand so much. I takes him by the neck of his clothes and drags him down the mountain. On the way he kicks my legs black and blue from the knees down; and I've got to have two or three bites on my thumb and hand cauterized.

"But he's gone"—continues Bill—"gone home. I showed him the road to Summit and kicked him about eight feet nearer there at one kick. I'm sorry we lose the ransom; but it was either that or Bill Driscoll to the madhouse."

Bill is puffing and blowing, but there is a look of ineffable peace and growing content on his rose-pink features.

"Bill," says I, "there isn't any heart disease in your family, is there?"

"No," says Bill, "nothing chronic except malaria and accidents. Why?"

"Then you might turn around," says I, "and have a look behind you."

Bill turns and see the boy, and loses his complexion and sits down plump on the ground and begins to pluck aimlessly at grass and little sticks. For an hour I was afraid of his mind. And then I told him that my scheme was to put the whole job through immediately and that we would get the ransom and be off with it by midnight if old Dorset fell in with our proposition. So Bill braced up enough to give the kid a weak sort of a smile and a promise to play the Russian in a Japanese war with him as soon as he felt a little better.

I had a scheme for collecting that ransom without danger of being caught by counterplots that ought to commend itself to professional kidnappers. The tree under which the answer was to be left—and the money later on—was close to the road fence with big, bare fields on all sides. If a gang of constables should be watching for any one to come for the note, they could see him a long way off crossing the fields or in the road. But no, sirree! At half-past eight I was up in that tree as well hidden as a tree toad, waiting for the messenger to arrive.

Exactly on time, a half-grown boy rides up the road on a bicycle, locates the pasteboard box at the foot of the fence-post, slips a folded piece of paper into it, and pedals away again back toward Summit.

I waited an hour and then concluded the thing was square. I slid down the tree, got the note, slipped along the fence till I struck the woods, and was back at the cave in another half an hour. I opened the note, got near the lantern, and read it to Bill. It was written with a pen in a crabbed hand, and the sum and substance of it was this:

Two Desperate Men.

Gentlemen: I received your letter to-day by post, in regard to the ransom you ask for the return of my son. I think you are a little high in your demands, and I hereby make you a counter-proposition, which I am inclined to believe you will accept. You bring Johnny home and pay me two hundred and fifty dollars in cash, and I agree to take him off your hands. You had better come at night, for the neighbors believe he is lost, and I couldn't be responsible for what they would do to anybody they saw bringing him back. Very respectfully,

Ebenezer Dorset

"Great pirates of Penzance," says I; "of all the impudent—"

But I glanced at Bill, and hesitated. He had the most appealing look in his eyes I ever saw on the face of a dumb or a talking brute.

"Sam," says he, "what's two hundred and fifty dollars, after all? We've got the money. One more night of this kid will send me to a bed in Bedlam. Besides being a thorough gentleman, I think Mr. Dorset is a spend-thrift for making us such a liberal offer. You ain't going to let the chance go, are you?"

"Tell you the truth, Bill," says I, "this little he ewe lamb has somewhat got on my nerves too. We'll take him home, pay the ransom, and make our getaway."

We took him home that night. We got him to go by telling him that his father had bought a silver-mounted rifle and a pair of moccasins for him, and we were to hunt bear the next day.

It was just twelve o'clock when we knocked at Ebenezer's front door. Just at the moment when I should have been abstracting the fifteen hundred dollars from the box under the tree, according to the original proposition, Bill was counting out two hundred and fifty dollars into Dorset's hand.

When the kid found out we were going to leave him at home he started up a howl like a calliope and fastened himself as tight as a leech to Bill's leg. His father peeled him away gradually, like a porous plaster.

"How long can you hold him?" asks Bill.

"I'm not as strong as I used to be," says old Dorset, "but I think I can promise you ten minutes."

"Enough," says Bill. "In ten minutes I shall cross the Central, Southern, and Middle Western States, and be legging it trippingly for the Canadian border."

And, as dark as it was, and as fat as Bill was, and as good a runner as I am, he was a good mile and a half out of Summit before I could catch up with him.

The Whirligig of Life

Justice-of-the-peace Benaja Widdup sat in the door of his office smoking his elder-stem pipe. Halfway to the Zenith the Cumberland range rose blue-gray in the afternoon haze. A speckled hen swaggered down the main street of the "settlement," cackling foolishly.

Up the road came a sound of creaking axles, and then a slow cloud of dust, and then a bull-cart bearing Ransie Bilbro and his wife. The cart stopped at the Justice's door, and the two climbed down. Ransie was a narrow six feet of sallow brown skin and yellow hair. The imperturbability of the mountains hung upon him like a suit of armor. The woman was calicoed, angled, snuff-brushed, and weary with unknown desires. Through it all gleamed a faint protest of cheated youth unconscious of its loss.

The Justice of the Peace slipped his feet into his shoes, for the sake of dignity, and moved to let them enter.

"We-all, "said the woman, in a voice like the wind blowing through pine boughs, "wants a divo'ce." She looked at Ransie to see if he noted any flaw or ambiguity or evasion or partiality or self-partisanship in her statement of their business.

"A divo'ce," repeated Ransie, with a solemn nod. "We-all can't git along together nohow. It's lonesome enough fur to live in the mount'ins when a man and a woman keers fur one another. But when she's a-spittin' like a wildcat or a-sullenin' like a hoot-owl in the cabin, a man ain't got no call to live with her."

"When he's a no-'count varmint," said the woman, without any special warmth, "a-traipsin' along of scalawags and moonshiners and a-layin' on his back pizen 'ith co'n whiskey, and a-pesterin' folks with a pack o' hungry, triflin' houn's to feed!"

"When she keeps a-throwin skillet lids," came Ransie's antiphony, "and slings b'ilin' water on the best coon-dog in the Cumberlands, and sets herself again' cookin' a man's victuals, and keeps him awake o' nights accusin' him of a sight of doin's!"

"When he's al'ays a-fightin' the revenues, and git a hard name in the mount'ins fur a mean man, who' gwine to be able fur to sleep o' nights?"

The Justice of the Peace stirred deliberately to his duties. He placed his one chair and a wooden stool for his petitioners. He opened his book of statutes on the table and scanned the index. Presently he wiped his spectacles and shifted his inkstand.

"The law and the statutes," said he, "air silent on the subjeck of divo'ce as fur as the jurisdiction of this co't air concerned. But, accordin' to equity and the Constitution and the golden rule, it's a bad barg'in that can't run both ways. If a justice of the peace can marry a couple, it's plain that he is bound to be able to divo'ce 'em. This here office will issue a decree of divo'ce and abide by the decision of the Supreme Co't to hold it good."

Ransie Bilbro drew a small tobacco-bag from his trousers pocket. Out of this he shook upon the table a five-dollar note. "Sold a b'arskin and two foxes fur that," he remarked. "It's all the money we got."

"The regular price of a divo'ce in this co't," said the Justice, "air five dollars." He stuffed the bill into the pocket of his homespun vest with a deceptive air of indifference. With much bodily toil and mental travail he wrote the decree upon half a sheet of foolscap, and then copied it upon the other. Ransie Bilbro and his wife listened to his reading of the document that was to give them freedom:

Know all men by these presents that Ransie Bilbro and his wife, Ariela Bilbro, this day personally appeared before me and promises that hereinafter they will neither love, honor, nor obey each other, neither for better nor worse, being of sound mind and body, and accept summons for divorce according to the peace and dignity of the State. Herein fail not, so help you God. Benaja Widdup, justice of the peace in and for the county of Piedmont, State of Tennessee.

The Justice was about to hand one of the documents to Ransie. The voice of Ariela delayed the transfer. Both men looked at her. Their dull masculinity was confronted by something sudden and unexpected in the woman.

"Judge, don't you give him that air paper yit. 'Tain't all settled, nohow. I got to have my rights first. I got to have my ali-money. 'Tain't no kind of a way to do fur a man to divo'ce his wife 'thout her havin' a cent fur to do with. I'm a-layin' off to be a-goin' up to brother Ed's up on Hogback Mount'in. I'm bound fur to hev a pa'r of shoes and some snuff and things besides. Ef Rance kin affo'd a divo'ce, let him pay me ali-money."

Ransie Bilbro was stricken to dumb perplexity. There had been no previous hint of alimony. Women were always bringing up startling and unlooked-for issues.

Justice Benaja Widdup felt that the point demanded judicial decision. The authorities were also silent on the subject of alimony. But the woman's feet were bare. The trail to Hogback Mountain was steep and flinty.

"Ariela Bilbro," he asked, in official tones, "how much did you 'low would be good and sufficient ali-money in the case befo' the co't?"

"I 'lowed," she answered, "fur the shoes and all, to say five dollars. That ain't much fur ali-money, but I reckon that'll git me up to brother Ed's."

"The amount," said the Justice, "air not onreasonable. Ransie Bilbro, you air ordered by the co't to pay the plaintiff the sum of five dollars befo' the decree of divo'ce air issued."

"I hain't no mo' money," breathed Ransie, heavily. "I done paid you all I had."

"Otherwise," said the Justice, looking severely over his spectacles, "you air in contempt of co't."

"I reckon if you gimme till to-morrow," pleaded the husband, "I mout be able to rake or scrape it up somewhars. I never looked for to be a-payin' no ali-money."

"The case air adjourned," said Benaja Widdup, "till to-morrow, when you-all will present yo'selves and obey the order of the co't. Followin' of which the decrees of divo'ce will be delivered." He sat down in the door and began to loosen a shoestring.

"We mout as well go down to Uncle Ziah's," decided Ransie, "and spend the night." He climbed into the cart on one side, and Ariela climbed in on the other. Obeying the flat of his rope, the little red bull slowly came around on a tack, and the cart crawled away in the nimbus arising from its wheels.

Justice-of-the-peace Benaja Widdup smoked his elder-stem pipe. Late in the afternoon he got his weekly paper, and read it until the twilight dimmed its lines. Then he lit the tallow candle on his table, and read until the moon rose, marking the time for supper. He lived in the double log cabin on the slope near the girdled poplar. Going home to supper he crossed a little branch darkened by a laurel thicket. The dark figure of a man stepped from the laurels and pointed a rifle at his breast. His hat was pulled down low, and something covered most of his face.

"I want yo' money," said the figure, " 'thout any talk. I'm gettin' nervous, and my finger's a-wabblin on this here trigger."

"I've only got f-f-five dollars," said the Justice, producing it from his vest pocket.

"Roll it up," came the order, "and stick it in the end of this here gunbar'l."

The bill was crisp and new. Even fingers that were clumsy and trembling found little difficulty in making a spill of it and inserting it (this with less ease) into the muzzle of the rifle.

"Now I reckon you kin be goin' along," said the robber.

The Justice lingered not on his way.

The next day came the little red bull, drawing the cart to the office door. Justice Benaja Widdup had his shoes on, for he was expecting the visit. In his presence Ransie Bilbro handed to his wife a five-dollar bill. The official's eye sharply viewed it. It seemed to curl up as though it had been rolled and inserted into the end of a gun-barrel. But the Justice refrained from comment. It is true that other bills might be inclined to curl. He handed each one a decree of divorce. Each stood awkwardly silent, slowly folding the guarantee of freedom. The woman cast a shy glance full of constraint at Ransie.

"I reckon you'll be goin' back up to the cabin," she said, "along 'ith the bull-cart. There's bread in the tin box settin' on the shelf. I put the bacon in the bilin'-pot to keep the hounds from gettin' it. Don't forget to wind the clock to-night."

"You air a-goin' to your brother Ed's?" asked Ransie, with fine unconcern.

"I was 'lowin' to get along up thar afore night. I ain't sayin' as they'll pester theyselves any to make me welcome, but I hain't nowhar else fur to go. It's a right smart ways, and I reckon I better be goin'. I'll be a-sayin' good-bye, Ranse—that is, if you keer fur to say so."

"I don't know as anybody's a hound dog," said Ransie, in a martyr's voice, "fur to not want to say good-bye—'less you air so anxious to git away that you don't want me to say it."

Ariela was silent. She folded the five-dollar bill and her decree carefully, and placed them in the bosom of her dress. Benaja Widdup watched the money disappear with mournful eyes behind his spectacles.

And then with his next words he achieved rank (as his thoughts ran) with either the great crowd of the world's sympathizers or the little crowd of its great financiers.

"Be kind o' lonesome in the old cabin to-night, Ransie," he said.

Ransie Bilbro stared out at the Cumberlands, clear blue now in the sunlight. He did not look at Ariela.

"I 'low it might be lonesome," he said; "but when folks gits mad and wants a divo'ce, you can't make folks stay."

"There's others wanted a divo'ce," said Ariela, speaking to the wooden stool. "Besides, nobody don't want nobody to stay."

"Nobody never said they didn't."

"Nobody never said they did. I reckon I better start on now to brother Ed's"

"Nobody can't wind that old clock."

"Want me to go along 'ith you in the cart and wind it fur you, Ranse?"

The mountaineer's countenance was proof against emotion. But he reached out a big hand and enclosed Ariela's thin brown one. Her soul peeped out once through her impassive face, hallowing it.

"Them hounds sha'n't pester you no more," said Ransie. "I reckon I been mean and low down. You wind that clock, Ariela."

"My heart hit's in that cabin, Ranse," she whispered, "along 'ith you. I ain't a-goin' to git mad no more. Let's be startin', Ranse, so's we kin git home by sundown."

Justice-of-the-peace Benaja Widdup interposed as they started for the door, forgetting his presence.

"In the name of the State of Tennessee," he said, "I forbid you-all to be a-defyin' of its laws and statutes. This co't is mo' than willin' and full of joy to see the clouds of discord and misunderstandin' rollin' away from two lovin' hearts, but it air the duty of the co't to p'eserve the morals and integrity of the State. The co't reminds you that you air no longer man and wife, but air divo'ced by regular decree, and as such air not entitled to the benefits and 'purtenances of the mattermonal estate."

Ariela caught Ransie's arm. Did those words mean that she must lose him now when they had just learned the lesson of life?

"But the co't air prepared," went on the Justice, "fur to remove the disabilities set up by the decree of divo'ce. The co't air on hand to perform the solemn ceremony of marri'ge, thus fixin' things up and enablin' the parties in the case to resume the honor'ble and elevatin' state of mattermony which they desires. The fee fur performin' said ceremony will be, in this case, to wit, five dollars."

Ariela caught the gleam of promise in his words. Swiftly her hand went to her bosom. Freely as an alighting dove the bill fluttered to the Justice's table. Her sallow cheek colored as she stood hand in hand with Ransie and listened to the reuniting words.

Ransie helped her into the cart, and climbed in beside her. The little red bull turned once more, and they set out, hand-clasped, for the mountains.

Justice-of-the-peace Benaja Widdup sat in his door and took off his shoes. Once again he fingered the bill tucked down in his vest pocket. Once again he smoked his elder-stem pipe. Once again the speckled hen swaggered down the main street of the "settlement," cackling foolishly.

The Roads We Take

Twenty miles west of Tucson the "Sunset Express" stopped at a tank to take on water. Beside the aqueous addition the engine of that famous flyer acquired some other things that were not good for it.

While the fireman was lowering the feeding hose, Bob Tidball, "Shark" Dodson, and a quarter-bred Creek Indian called John Big Dog climbed on the engine and showed the engineer three round orifices in pieces of ordnance that they carried. These orifices so impressed the engineer with their possibilities that he raised both hands in a gesture such as accompanies the ejaculation "Do tell!"

At the crisp command of Shark Dodson, who was leader of the attacking force, the engineer descended to the ground and uncoupled the engine and tender. Then John Big Dog, perched upon the coal, sportively held two guns upon the engine driver and the fireman, and suggested that they run the engine fifty yards away and there await further orders.

Shark Dodson and Bob Tidball, scorning to put such low-grade ore as the passengers through the mill, struck out for the rich pocket of the express car. They found the messenger serene in the belief that the "Sunset Express" was taking on nothing more stimulating and dangerous than aqua pura. While Bob was knocking this idea out of his head with the butt-end of his six-shooter Shark Dodson was already dosing the express-car safe with dynamite.

The safe exploded to the tune of $30,000, all gold and currency. The passengers thrust their heads casually out of the windows to look for the thunder-cloud. The conductor jerked at the bell rope, which sagged down loose and unresisting, at his tug. Shark Dodson and Bob Tidball, with their booty in a stout canvas bag, tumbled out of the express car and ran awkwardly in their high-heeled boots to the engine.

The engineer, sullenly angry but wise, ran the engine, according to orders, rapidly away from the inert train. But before this was accomplished the express messenger, recovered from Bob Tidball's persuader to neutrality, jumped out of his car with a Winchester rifle and took a trick in the game. Mr. John Big Dog, sitting on the coal tender, unwittingly made a wrong lead by giving an imitation of a target, and the messenger trumped him. With a ball exactly between his shoulder blades the Creek chevalier of industry rolled off to the ground, thus increasing the share of his comrades in the loot by one-sixth each.

Two miles from the tank the engineer was ordered to stop.

The robbers waved a defiant adieu and plunged down the steep slope into the thick woods that lined the track. Five minutes of crashing through a thicket of chaparral brought them to open woods, where the three horses were tied to low-hanging branches. One was waiting for John Big Dog, who would never ride by night or day again. This animal the robbers divested of saddle and bridle and set free. They mounted the other two with the bag across one pommel, and rode fast and with discretion through the forest and up a primeval, lonely gorge. Here the animal that bore Bob Tidball slipped on a mossy boulder and broke a foreleg. They shot him through the head at once and sat down to hold a council of flight. Made secure for the present by the tortuous trail they had traveled, the question of time was no longer so big. Many miles and hours lay between them and the spryest posse that could follow. Shark Dodson's horse, with trailing rope and dropped bridle, panted and cropped thankfully of the grass along the stream in the gorge. Bob Tidball opened the sack, and drew out double handfuls of the neat packages of currency and the one sack of gold and chuckled with the glee of a child.

"Say, you old double-decked pirate," he called joyfully to Dodson, "you said we could do it—you got a head for financing that knocks the horns off of anything in Arizona."

"What are we going to do about a hoss for you, Bob? We ain't got long to wait here. They'll be on our trail before daylight in the mornin'."

"Oh, I guess that cayuse of yourn'll carry double for a while," answered the sanguine Bob. "We'll annex the first animal we come across. By jingoes, we made a haul, didn't we? Accordin' to marks on this money there's $30,000—$15,000 apiece!"

"It's short of what I expected,"said Shark Dodson, kicking softly at the packages with the toe of his boot. And then he looked pensively at the wet sides of his tired horse.

"Old Bolivar's mighty nigh played out," he said, slowly. "I wish that sorrel of yours hadn't got hurt."

"So do I," said Bob, heartily, "but it can't be helped. Bolivar's got plenty of bottom—he'll get us both far enough to get fresh mounts. Dang it, Shark, I can't help thinkin' how funny it is that an Easterner like you can come out here and give us Western fellows cards and spades in the desperado business. What part of the East was you from, anyway?"

"New York State," said Shark Dodson, sitting down on a boulder and chewing a twig. "I was born on a farm in Ulster County. I ran away from home when I was seventeen. It was an accident my comin' West. I was walkin' along the road with my clothes in a bundle, makin' for New York City. I had an idea of goin' there and makin' lots of money. I always felt like I could do it. I came to a place one evenin' where the road forked and I didn't know which fork to take. I studied about it for half an hour and then I took the left-hand. That night I run into the camp of a Wild West show that was travelin' among the little towns, and I went West with it. I've often wondered if I wouldn't have turned out different if I'd took the other road."

"Oh, I reckon you'd have ended up about the same," said Bob Tidball, cheerfully philosophical. "It ain't the roads we take; it's what's inside of us that makes us turn out the way we do."

Shark Dodson got up and leaned against a tree.

"I'd a good deal rather that sorrel of yourn hadn't hurt himself, Bob," he said again, almost pathetically.

"Same here," agreed Bob; "he sure was a first-rate kind of a crow-bait. But Bolivar, he'll pull us through all right. Reckon we'd better be movin' on, hadn't we, Shark? I'll bag the boodle ag'in and we'll hit the trail for higher timber."

Bob Tidball replaced the spoil in the bag and tied the mouth of it tightly with a cord. When he looked up the most prominent object that he saw was the muzzle of Shark Dodson's .45 held upon him without a waver.

"Stop your funnin'," said Bob, with a grin. "We got to be hittin' the breeze."

"Set still," said Shark. "You ain't goin' to hit no breeze, Bob. I hate to tell you, but there ain't any chance for but one of us. Bolivar, he's plenty tired, and he can't carry double."

"We been pards, me and you, Shark Dodson, for three years," Bob said quietly. "We've risked our lives together time and again. I've always give you a square deal, and I thought you was a man. I've heard some queer stories about you shootin' one or two men in a peculiar way, but I never believed 'em. Now if you're just havin' a little fun with me, Shark, put your gun up, and we'll get on Bolivar and vamoose. If you mean to shoot—shoot, you blackhearted son of a tarantula!"

Shark Dodson's face bore a deeply sorrowful look.

"You don't know how bad I feel," he sighed, "about that sorrel of yourn breakin' his leg, Bob."

The expression on Dodson's face changed in an instant to one of cold ferocity mingled with inexorable cupidity. The soul of the man showed itself for a moment like an evil face in the window of a reputable house.

Truly Bob Tidball was never to "hit the breeze" again. The deadly .45 of the false friend cracked and filled the gorge with a roar that the walls hurled back with indignant echoes. And Bolivar, unconscious accomplice, swiftly bore away the last of the holders-up of the "Sunset Express," not put to the stress of "carrying double."

But as Shark Dodson galloped away the woods seemed to fade from his view; the revolver in his right hand turned to the curved arm of a mahogany chair; his saddle was strangely upholstered, and he opened his eyes and saw his feet, not in stirrups, but resting quietly on the edge of a quartered-oak desk.

I am telling you that Dodson, of the firm of Dodson & Decker, Wall Street brokers, opened his eyes. Peabody, the confidential clerk, was standing by his chair, hesitating to speak. There was a confused hum of wheels below, and the sedative buzz of an electric fan.

"Ahem! Peabody," said Dodson, blinking. "I must have fallen asleep. I had a most remarkable dream. What is it, Peabody?"

"Mr. Williams, sir, of Tracy & Williams, is outside. He has come to settle his deal in X. Y. Z. The market caught him short, sir, if you remember."

"Yes, I remember. What is X. Y. Z. quoted at to-day, Peabody?"

"One eight-five, sir."

"Then that's his price."

"Excuse me," said Peabody, rather nervously, "for speaking of it, but I've been talking to Williams. He's an old friend of yours, Mr. Dodson, and you practically have a corner in X. Y. Z. I thought you might—that is, I thought you might not remember that he sold you the stock at 98. If he settles at the market price it will take every cent he has in the world and his home too to deliver the shares."

The expression on Dodson's face changed in an instant to one of cold ferocity mingled with inexorable cupidity. The soul of the man showed itself for a moment like an evil face in the window of a reputable house.

"He will settle at one eighty-five," said Dodson. "Bolivar cannot carry double."

A Blackjack Bargainer

The most disreputable thing in Yancey Goree's law office was Goree himself, sprawled in his creaky old arm chair. The rickety little office, built of red brick, was set flush with the street—the main street of the town of Bethel.

Bethel rested upon the foot-hills of the Blue Ridge. Above it the mountains were piled to the sky. Far below it the turbid Catawba gleamed yellow along its disconsolate valley.

The June day was at it sultriest hour. Bethel dozed in the tepid shade. Trade was not. It was so still that Goree, reclining in his chair, distinctly heard the clicking of the chips in the grand-jury room, where the "court-house gang" was playing poker. From the open back door of the office a well-worn path meandered across the grassy lot to the court-house. The treading out of that path had cost Goree all he ever had—first inheritance of a few thousand dollars, next the old family home, and, latterly, the last shreds of his self-respect and manhood. The "gang" had cleaned him out. The broken gambler had turned drunkard and parasite; he had lived to see this day come when the men who had stripped him denied him a seat at the game. His word was no longer to be taken. The daily bout at cards had arranged itself accordingly, and to him was assigned the ignoble part of the onlooker. The sheriff, the county clerk, a sportive deputy, a gay attorney, and a chalk-faced man hailing "from the valley," sat at table, and the sheared one was thus tacitly advised to go and grow more wool.

Soon wearying of his ostracism, Goree had departed for his office, muttering to himself as he unsteadily traversed the unlucky pathway.

After a drink of corn whiskey from a demijohn under the table he had flung himself into the chair, staring, in a sort of maudlin apathy, out at the mountains immersed in the summer haze. The little white patch he saw away up on the side of Blackjack was Laurel, the village near which he had been born and bred. There, also, was the birthplace of the feud between the Gorees and the Coltranes. Now no direct heir of the Gorees survived except this plucked and singed bird of misfortune. To the Coltranes, also, but one male supporter was left—Colonel Abner Coltrane, a man of substance and standing, a member of the State Legislature, and a contemporary with Goree's father. The feud had been a typical one of the region; it had left a red record of hate, wrong, and slaughter.

But Yancey Goree was not thinking of feuds. His befuddled brain was hopelessly attacking the problem of the future maintenance of himself and his favorite follies. Of late, old friends of the family had seen to it that he had whereof to eat and a place to sleep, but whiskey they would not buy for him, and he must have whiskey. His law business was extinct; no case had been intrusted to him in two years. He had been a borrower and a sponge, and it seemed that if he fell no lower it would be from lack of opportunity. One more chance—he was saying to himself—if he had one more stake at the game, he thought he could win; but he had nothing left to sell, and his credit was more than exhausted.

He could not help smiling, even in his misery, as he thought of the man to whom, six months before, he had sold the old Goree homestead. There had come from "back yan' " in the mountains two of the strangest creatures, a man named Pike Garvey and his wife. "Back yan'," with a wave of the hand toward the hills, was understood among the mountaineers to designate the remotest fastnesses, the unplumbed gorges, the haunts of lawbreakers, the wolf's den, and the boudoir of the bear. In the cabin far up on Blackjack's shoulder, in the wildest part of these retreats, this odd couple had lived for twenty years. They had neither dog nor children to mitigate the heavy silence of the hills. Pike Garvey was little known in the settlements, but all who had dealt with him pronounced him "crazy as a loon." He acknowledged no occupation save that of a squirrel hunter, but he "moonshined" occasionally by way of diversion. Once the "revenues" had dragged him from his lair, fighting silently and desperately like a terrier, and he had been sent to state's prison for two years. Released, he popped back into his hole like an angry weasel.

Fortune, passing over many anxious wooers, made a freakish flight into Blackjack's bosky pockets to smile upon Pike and his faithful partner.

One day a party of spectacled, knickerbockered, and altogether absurd prospectors invaded the vicinity of the Garveys' cabin. Pike lifted his squirrel rifle off the hook and took a shot at them at long range on the chance of their being revenues. Happily he missed, and the unconscious agents of good luck drew nearer, disclosing their innocence of anything resembling law or justice. Later on, they offered the Garveys an enormous quantity of ready, green, crisp money for their thirty-acre patch of cleared land, mentioning, as an excuse for such a mad action, some irrelevant and inadequate nonsense about a bed of mica underlying the said property.

When the Garveys became possessed of so many dollars that they faltered in computing them, the deficiencies of life on Blackjack began to grow prominent. Pike began to talk of new shoes, a hogshead of tobacco to set in the corner, a new lock to his rifle; and, leading Martella to a cerain spot on the mountainside, he pointed out to her how a small cannon—doubtless a thing not beyond the scope of their fortune in price—might be planted so as to command and defend the sole accessible trail to the cabin, to the confusion of revenues and meddling strangers forever.

But Adam reckoned without his Eve. These things represented to him the applied power of wealth, but there slumbered in his dingy cabin an ambition that soared far above his primitive wants. Somewhere in Mrs. Garvey's bosom still survived a spot of femininity unstarved by twenty years of Blackjack. For so long a time the sounds in her ears had been the scaly-barks dropping in the woods at noon, and the wolves singing among the rocks at night, and it was enough to have purged her vanities. She had grown fat and sad and yellow and dull. But when the means came, she felt a rekindled desire to assume the perquisites of her sex—to sit at tea tables; to buy inutile things; to whitewash the hideous veracity of life with a little form and ceremony. So she coldly vetoed Pike's proposed system of fortifications, and announced that they would descend upon the world, and gyrate socially.

And thus, at length, it was decided, and the thing done. The village of Laurel was their compromise between Mrs. Garvey's preference for one of the large valley towns and Pike's hankering for primeval solitudes. Laurel yielded a halting round of feeble social distractions comportable with Martella's ambitions, and was not entirely without recommendation to Pike, its contiguity to the mountains presenting advantages for sudden retreat in case fashionable society should make it advisable.

Their descent upon Laurel had been coincident with Yancey Goree's feverish desire to convert property into cash, and they bought the old Goree homestead, paying four thousand dollars ready money into the spendthrift's shaking hand.

Thus it happened that while the disreputable last of the Gorees sprawled in his disreputable office, at the end of his row, spurned by the cronies whom he had gorged, strangers dwelt in the halls of his fathers.

A cloud of dust was rolling slowly up the parched street, with something traveling in the midst of it. A little breeze wafted the cloud to one side and a new, brightly painted carryall, drawn by a slothful gray horse, became visible. The vehicle deflected from the middle of the street as it neared Goree's office, and stopped in the gutter directly in front of his door.

On the front seat sat a gaunt, tall man, dressed in black broadcloth, his rigid hands incarcerated in yellow kid gloves. On the back seat was a lady who triumphed over the June heat. Her stout form was armored in a skintight silk dress of the description known as "changeable," being a gorgeous combination of shifting hues. She sat erect, waving a much-ornamented fan, with her eyes fixed stonily far down the street. However Martella Garvey's heart might be rejoicing at the pleasures of her new life, Blackjack had done his work with her exterior. He had carved her countenance to the image of emptiness and inanity; had imbued her with the stolidity of his crags and the reserve of his hushed interiors. She always seemed to hear, whatever her surroundings were, the scaly-barks falling and pattering down the mountainside. She could always hear the awful silence of Blackjack sounding through the stillest of nights.

Goree watched this solemn equipage, as it drove to his door, with only faint interest but when the lank driver wrapped the reins about his whip, and awkwardly descended, and stepped into the office, he rose unsteadily to receive him, recognizing Pike Garvey, the new, the transformed, the recently civilized.

The mountaineer took the chair Goree offered him. They who cast doubts upon Garvey's soundness of mind had a strong witness in the man's countenance. His face was too long, a dull saffron in hue, and immobile as a statue's. Pale-blue, unwinking round eyes without lashes added to the singularity of his gruesome visage. Goree was at a loss to account for the visit.

"Everything all right at Laurel, Mr. Garvey?" he inquired.

"Everything all right, sir, and mighty pleased is Missis Garvey and me with the property. Missis Garvey likes yo' old place, and she likes the neighborhood. Society is what she 'lows she wants, and she is gettin' of it. The Rogerses, the Hapgoods, the Pratts, and the Torys hev been to see Missis Garvey, and she hev et meals to most of thar houses. The best folks hev axed her to differ'nt of doin's. I cyan't say, Mr. Goree, that sech things suits me—fur me, give me them thar." Garvey's huge yellow-gloved hand flourished in the direction of the mountains. "That's whar I b'long 'mongst the wild honey bees and the b'ars. But that ain't what I come fur to say, Mr. Goree. Thar's somethin' you got what me and Missis Garvey wants to buy."

"Buy!" echoed Gore. "From me?" Then he laughed harshly. "I reckon you are mistaken about that. I sold out to you, as you yourself expressed it, 'lock, stock, and barrel.' There isn't even a ramrod left to sell."

"You've got it; and we 'uns want it. 'Take the money,' says Missis Garvey, 'and buy it fa'r and squar'.' "

Goree shook his head. "The cupboard's bare," he said.

"We've riz," pursued the mountaineer, undeflected from his object, "a heap. We was pore as possums, and now we could hev folks to dinner every day. We been reco'nized, Missis Garvey says, by the best society. But there's somethin' we need we ain't got. She says it ought to been put in the 'ventory ov the sale, but it 'tain't thar. 'Take the money, then,' she says, 'and buy it fa'r and squar'.' "

"Out with it," said Goree, his racked nerves growing impatient.

Garvey threw his slouch hat upon the table, and leaned forward, fixing his unblinking eyes upon Goree's.

"There's a old feud," he said, distinctly and slowly, " 'tween you 'uns and the Coltranes."

Goree frowned ominously. To speak of his feud to a feudist is a serious breach of the mountain etiquette. The man from "back yan' " knew it as well as the lawyer did.

"Na offense," he went on, "but purely in the way of business. Missis Garvey hev studied all about feuds. Most of the quality folks in the mountains hev 'em. The Settles and the Goforths, the Rankins and the Boyds, the Silers and the Galloways, hev all been cyarin' on feuds f'om twenty to a hundred year. The last man to drap was when yo' uncle, Jedge Paisley Goree, 'journed co't and shot Len Coltrane f'om the bench. Missis Garvey and me, we come f'om the po' white trash. Nobody wouldn't pick a feud with we'uns, no mo'n with a fam'ly of treetoads. Quality people everywhar, says Missis Garvey, has feuds. We 'uns ain't quality, but we're buyin' into it as fur as we can. 'Take the money, then,' says Missis Garvey, 'and buy Mr. Goree's feud, fa'r and squar'.' "

The squirrel hunter straightened a leg half across the room, drew a roll of bills from his pocket, and threw them on the table.

"Thar's two hundred dollars, Mr. Goree, what you would call a fa'r price for a feud that's been 'lowed to run down like yourn hev. Thar's only you left to cyar' on yo' side of it, and you'd make mighty po' killin'. I'll take it off yo' hands, and it'll set me and Missis Garvey up among the quality. Thar's the money."

The little roll of currency on the table slowly untwisted itself, writhing and jumping as its folds relaxed. In the silence that followed Garvey's last speech the rattling of the poker chips in the court-house could be plainly heard. Goree knew that the sheriff had just won a pot, for the subdued whoop with which he always greeted a victory floated across the square upon the crinkly heat waves. Beads of moisture stood on Goree's brow. Stooping, he drew the wicker-covered demijohn from under the table, and filled a tumbler from it.

"A little corn liquor, Mr. Garvey? Of course you are joking about—what you spoke of? Opens quite a new market, doesn't it? Feuds, prime, two-fifty to three. Feuds, slightly damaged—two hundred, I believe you said, Mr. Garvey."

The mountaineer took the glass Goree handed him, and drank the whiskey without a tremor of the lids of his staring eyes. The lawyer applauded the feat by a look of envious admiration. He poured his own drink, and took it like a drunkard, by gulps, and with shudders at the smell and taste.

"Two hundred," repeated Garvey. "Thar's the money."

A sudden passion flared up in Goree's brain. He struck the table with his fist. One of the bills flipped over and touched his hand. He flinched as if something had stung him.

"Do you come to me," he shouted, "seriously with such a ridiculous, insulting, darn-fool proposition?"

"It's fa'r and squar'," said the squirrel hunter, but he reached out his hand as if to take back the money; and then Goree knew that his own flurry of rage had not been from pride or resentment, but from anger at himself, knowing that he would set foot in the deeper depths that were being opened to him. He turned in an instant from an outraged gentleman to an anxious chafferer recommending his goods.

"Don't be in a hurry, Garvey," he said, his face crimson and his speech thick. "I accept your p-p-proposition, though it's dirt cheap at two hundred. A t-trade's all right when both p-purchaser and b-buyer are s-satisfied. Shall I w-wrap it up for you, Mr Garvey?"

Garvey rose, and shook out his broadcloth. "Missis Garvey will be pleased. You air out of it, and it stands Coltrane and Garvey. Just a scrap ov writin', Mr. Goree, you bein' a lawyer, to show we traded."

Goree seized a sheet of paper and a pen. The money was clutched in his moist hand. Everything else suddenly seemed to grow trivial and light.

"Bill of sale, by all means. 'Right, title, and interest in and to' . . .'forever warrant and —' No, Garvey, we'll have to leave out that 'defend,' " said Goree with a loud laugh. "You'll have to defend this title yourself."

The mountaineer received the amazing screed that the lawyer handed him, folded it with immense labor, and placed it carefully in his pocket.

Goree was standing near the window. "Step here," he said, raising his finger, "and I'll show you your recently purchased enemy. There he goes, down the other side of the street."

The mountaineer crooked his long frame to look through the window in the direction indicated by the other. Colonel Abner Coltrane, an erect, portly gentleman of about fifty wearing the inevitable long, double-breasted frock coat of the Southern lawmaker, and an old high silk hat, was passing on the opposite sidewalk. As Garvey looked, Goree glanced at his face. If there be such a thing as a yellow wolf, here was its counterpart. Garvey snarled as his unhuman eyes followed the moving figure, disclosing long amber-colored fangs.

"Is that him? Why, that's the man who sent me to the pen'tentiary once!"

"He used to be district attorney," said Goree, carelessly. "And by the way, he's a first-class shot."

"I kin hit a squirrel's eye at a hundred yard," said Garvey. "So that thar's Coltrane! I made a better trade than I was thinkin'. I'll take keer of this feud, Mr. Goree, better'n you ever did!"

He moved toward the door, but lingered there, betraying a slight perplexity.

"Anything else to-day?" inquired Goree with frothy sarcasm. "Any family traditions, ancestral ghosts, or skeletons in the closet? Prices as low as the lowest."

"Thar was another thing," replied the unmoved squirrrel hunter, "that Missis Garvey was thinkin' of. 'Tain't so much in my line as t'other, but she wanted partic'lar that I should inquire, and ef you was willin', 'pay fur it,' she says, 'fa'r and squar'.' Thar's a buryin' groun', as you know, Mr. Goree, in the yard of yo' old place, under the cedars. Them that lies thar is yo' folks what was killed by the Coltranes. The monyments has the names on 'em. Missis Garvey says a fam'ly buryin' groun' is a sho' sign of quality. She says ef we git the feud, that's somethin' else ought to go with it. The names on them monyments is 'Goree,' but they can be changed to ourn by—"

"Go! Go!" screamed Goree, his face turning purple. He stretched out both hands toward the mountaineer, his fingers hooked and shaking. "Go, you ghoul! Even a Ch-Chinaman protects the g-graves of his ancestors—go!"

The squirrel hunter slouched out of the door to his carryall. While he was climbing over the wheel Goree was collecting, with feverish celerity, the money that had fallen from his hand to the floor. As the vehicle slowly turned about, the sheep with a coat of newly grown wool was hurrying, in indecent haste, along the path to the courthouse.

At three o'clock in the morning they brought him back to his office, shorn and unconscious. The sheriff, the sportive deputy, the county clerk, and the gay attorney carried him, the chalk-faced man "from the valley" acting as escort.

"On the table," said one of them and they deposited him there among the litter of his unprofitable books and papers.

"Yance thinks a lot of a pair of deuces when he's liquored up," sighed the sheriff, reflectively.

"Too much," said the gay attorney. "A man has no business to play poker who drinks as much as he does. I wonder how much he dropped to-night."

"Close to two hundred. What I wonder is whar he got it. Yance ain't had a cent fur over a month, I know."

"Struck a client, maybe. Well, let's get home before daylight. He'll be all right when he wakes up, except for a sort of beehive about the cranium."

The gang slipped away through the early morning twilight. The next eye to gaze upon the miserable Goree was the orb of day. He peered through the uncurtained window, first deluging the sleeper in a flood of faint gold, but soon pouring upon the mottled red of his flesh a searching, white, summer heat. Goree stirred, half unconsciously, among the table's débris, and turned his face from the window. His movement dislodged a heavy law book, which crashed upon the floor. Opening his eyes, he saw, bending over him, a man in a black frock coat. Looking higher, he discovered a well-worn silk hat, and beneath it the kindly, smooth face of Colonel Abner Coltrane.

A little uncertain of the outcome, the colonel waited for the other to make some sign of recognition. Not in twenty years had male members of these two families faced each other in peace. Goree's eyelids puckered as he strained his blurred sight toward this visitor, and then he smiled serenely.

"Have you brought Stella and Lucy over to play?" he said, calmly.

"Do you know me, Yancey?" asked Coltrane.

"Of course I do. You brought me a whip with a whistle in the end."

So he had—twenty-four years ago; when Yancey's father was his best friend.

Goree's eyes wandered about the room. The colonel understood. "Lie still, and I'll bring you some," said he. There was a pump in the yard at the rear, and Goree closed his eyes, listening with rapture to the click of its handle and the bubbling of the falling stream. Coltrane brought a pitcher of the cool water, and held it for him to drink. Presently Goree sat up—a most forlorn object, his summer suit of flax soiled and crumpled, his discreditable head tousled and unsteady. He tried to wave one of his hands toward the colonel.

"Ex-excuse—everything, will you?" he said. "I must have drunk too much whiskey last night, and gone to bed on the table." His brows knitted into a puzzled frown.

"Out with the boys a while?" asked Coltrane, kindly.

"No, I went nowhere. I haven't had a dollar to spend in the last two months. Struck the demijohn too often, I reckon, as usual."

Colonel Coltrane touched him on the shoulder.

"A little while ago, Yancey," he began, "you asked me if I had brought Stella and Lucy over to play. You weren't quite awake then, and must have been dreaming you were a boy again. You are awake now, and I want you to listen to me. I have come from Stella and Lucy to their old playmate, and to my old friend's son. They know that I am going to bring you home with me, and you will find them as ready with a welcome as they were in the old days. I want you to come to my house and stay until you are yourself again, and as much longer as you will. We heard of your being down in the world, and in the midst of temptation, and we agreed that you should come over and play at our house once more. Will you come, my boy? Will you drop our old family trouble and come with me?"

"Trouble!" said Goree, opening his eyes wide. "There was never any trouble between us that I know of. I'm sure we've always been the best of friends. But, good Lord, Colonel, how could I go to your home as I am—a drunken wretch, a miserable, degraded spendthrift and gambler—"

He lurched from the table to his armchair, and began to weep maudlin tears, mingled with genuine drops of remorse and shame. Coltrane talked to him persistently and reasonably, reminding him of the simple mountain pleasures of which he had once been so fond, and insisting upon the genuineness of the invitation.

Finally he landed Goree by telling him he was counting upon his help in the engineering and transportation of a large amount of felled timber from a high mountainside to a waterway. He knew that Goree had once invented a device for this purpose—a series of slides and chutes—upon which he had justly prided himself. In an instant the poor fellow, delighted at the idea of his being of use to any one, had paper spread upon the table, and was drawing rapid but pitifully shaky lines in demonstration of what he could and would do.

The man was sickened of the husks; his prodigal heart was turning again toward the mountains. His mind was yet strangely clogged, and his thoughts and memories were returning to his brain one by one, like carrier pigeons over a stormy sea. But Coltrane was satisfied with the progress he had made.

Bethel received the surprise of its existence that afternoon when a Coltrane and a Goree rode amicably together through the town. Side by side they rode, out from the dusty streets and gaping townspeople, down across the creek bridge, and up toward the mountain. The prodigal had brushed and washed and combed himself to a more decent figure, but he was unsteady in the saddle, and he seemed to be deep in the contemplation of some vexing problem. Coltrane left him in his mood, relying upon the influence of changed surroundings to restore his equilibrium.

Once Goree was seized with a shaking fit, and almost came to a collapse. He had to dismount and rest at the side of the road. The colonel, foreseeing such a condition, had provided a small flask of whiskey for the journey but when it was offered to him Goree refused it almost with violence, declaring he would never touch it again. By and by he was recovered, and went quietly enough for a mile or two. Then he pulled up his horse suddenly, and said:

"I lost two hundred dollars last night, playing poker. Now, where did I get that money?"

"Take it easy, Yancey. The mountain air will soon clear it up. We'll go fishing, first thing, at the Pinnacle Falls. The trout are jumping there like bullfrogs. We'll take Stella and Lucy along, and have a picnic on Eagle Rock. Have you forgotten how a hickory-cured-ham sandwich tastes, Yancey, to a hungry fisherman?"

Evidently the colonel did not believe the story of his lost wealth; so Goree retired again into brooding silence.

By late afternoon they had traveled ten of the twelve miles between Bethel and Laurel. Half a mile this side of Laurel lay the old Goree place; a mile or two beyond the village lived the Coltranes. The road was now steep and laborious, but the compensations were many. The tilted aisles of the forest were opulent with leaf and bird and bloom. The tonic air put to shame the pharmacopia. The glades were dark with mossy shade, and bright with shy rivulets winking from the ferns and laurels. On the lower side they viewed, framed in the near foliage, exquisite sketches of the far valley swooning in its opal haze.

Coltrane was pleased to see that his companion was yielding to the spell of the hills and woods. For now they had but to skirt the base of Painter's Cliff; to cross Elder Branch and mount the hill beyond, and Goree would have to face the squandered home of his fathers. Every rock he passed, every tree, every foot of the roadway, was familiar to him. Though he had forgotten the woods, they thrilled him like the music of "*Home, Sweet Home*."

They rounded the cliff, descended into Elder Branch, and paused there to let the horses drink and splash in the swift water. On the right was a rail fence that cornered there, and followed the road and stream. Inclosed by it was the old apple orchard of the home place; the house was yet concealed by the brow of the steep hill. Inside and along the fence, pokeberries, elders, sassafras, and sumac grew high and dense. At a rustle of their branches, both Goree and Coltrane glanced up, and saw a long, yellow, wolfish face above the fence, staring at them with pale, unwinking eyes. The head quickly disappeared; there was a violent swaying of the bushes, and an ungainly figure ran up through the apple orchard in the direction of the house zigzagging among the trees.

"That's Garvey," said Coltrane; "the man you sold out to. There's no doubt but he's considerably cracked. I had to send him up for moonshining once, several years ago, in spite of the fact that I believed him irresponsible. Why, what's the matter, Yancey?"

Goree was wiping his forehead, and his face had lost its color. "Do I look queer, too?" he asked, trying to smile. "I'm just remembering a few more things." Some of the alcohol had evaporated from his brain. "I recollect now where I got that two hundred dollars."

"Don't think of it," said Coltrane, cheerfully. "Later on we'll figure it all out together."

They rode out of the branch, and when they reached the foot of the hill Goree stopped again.

"Did you ever suspect I was a very vain kind of fellow, Colonel?" he asked. "Sort of foolish proud about appearances?"

The colonel's eyes refused to wander to the soiled, sagging suit of flax and the faded slouch hat.

"It seems to me," he replied, mystified, but humoring him, "I remember a young buck about twenty, with the tightest coat, the sleekest hair, and the prancingest saddle horse in the Blue Ridge."

"Right you are," said Goree, eagerly. "And it's in me yet, though it don't show. Oh, I'm as vain as a turkey gobbler, and as proud as Lucifer. I'm going to ask you to indulge this weakness of mine in a little matter."

"Speak out, Yancey. We'll create you Duke of Laurel and Baron of Blue Ridge, if you choose; and you shall have a feather out of Stella's peacock's tail to wear in your hat."

"I'm in earnest. In a few minutes we'll pass the house up there on the hill where I was born, and where my people have lived for nearly a century. Strangers live there now—and look at me! I am about to show myself to them ragged and poverty-stricken, a wastrel and a beggar. Colonel Coltrane, I'm ashamed to do it. I want you to let me wear your coat and hat until we are out of sight beyond. I know you think it a foolish pride, but I want to make as good a showing as I can when I pass the old place."

"Now, what does this mean?" said Coltrane to himself, as he compared his companion's sane looks and quiet demeanor with his strange request. But he was already unbuttoning the coat, assenting readily, as if the fancy were in no wise to be considered strange.

The coat and hat fitted Goree well. He buttoned the former about him with a look of satisfaction and dignity. He and Coltrane were nearly the same size—rather tall, portly and erect. Twenty-five years were between them, but in appearance they might have been brothers. Goree looked older than his age; his face was puffy and lined; the colonel had the smooth, fresh complexion of a temperate liver. He put on Goree's disreputable old flax coat and faded slouch hat.

"Now," said Goree, taking up the reins, "I'm all right. I want you to ride about ten feet in the rear as we go by, Colonel, so that they can get a good look at me. They'll see I'm no back number yet, by any means. I guess I'll show up pretty well to them once more, anyhow. Let's ride on."

He set out up the hill at a smart trot, the colonel following, as he had been requested.

Goree sat straight in the saddle, with head erect, but his eyes were turned to the right, sharply scanning every shrub and fence and hiding-place in the old homestead yard. Once he muttered to himself, "Will the crazy fool try it, or did I dream half of it?"

It was when he came opposite the little family burying ground that he saw what he had been looking for—a puff of white smoke, coming from the thick cedars in one corner. He toppled so slowly to the left that Coltrane had time to urge his horse to that side, and catch him with one arm.

The squirrel hunter had not overpraised his arm. He had sent the bullet where he intended, and where Goree had expected that it would pass through the breast of Colonel Abner Coltrane's black frock coat.

Goree leaned heavily against Coltrane, but he did not fall. The horses kept pace, side by side, and the colonel's arm kept him steady. The little white houses of Laurel shone through the trees, half a mile away. Goree reached out one hand and groped until it rested upon Coltrane's fingers, which held his bridle.

"Good friend," he said, and that was all.

Thus did Yancey Goree, as he rode past his old home, make, considering all things, the best showing that was in his power.

One Dollar's Worth

The judge of the United States court of the district lying along the Rio Grande border found the following letter one morning in his mail:

Judge:

When you sent me up for four years you made a talk. Among other hard things, you called me a rattlesnake. Maybe I am one—anyhow, you hear me rattling now. One year after I got to the pen, my daughter died of—well, they said it was poverty and the disgrace together. You've got a daughter, Judge, and I'm going to make you know how it feels to lose one. And I'm going to bite that district attorney that spoke against me. I'm free now, and I guess I've turned to rattlesnake all right. I feel like one. I don't say much, but this is my rattle. Look out what I strike.

Yours respectfully,

Rattlesnake

Judge Derwent threw the letter carelessly aside. It was nothing new to receive such epistles from desperate men whom he had been called up to judge. He felt no alarm. Later on he showed the letter to Littlefield, the young district attorney, for Littlefield's name was included in the threat, and the judge was punctilious in matters between himself and his fellow men.

Littlefield honored the rattle of the writer, as far as it concerned himself, with a smile of contempt; but he frowned a little over the reference to the Judge's daughter, for he and Nancy Derwent were to be married in the fall.

Littlefield went to the clerk of the court and looked over the records with him. They decided that the letter might have been sent by Mexico Sam, a half-breed border desperado who had been imprisoned for manslaughter four years before. Then official duties crowded the matter from his mind, and the rattle of the revengeful serpent was forgotten.

Court was in session in Brownsville. Most of the cases to be tried were charges of smuggling, counterfeiting, post-office robberies, and violations of Federal laws along the border. One case was that of a young Mexican, Rafael Ortiz, who had been rounded up by a clever deputy marshal in the act of passing a counterfeit silver dollar. He had been suspected of many such deviations from rectitude, but this was the first time that anything provable had been fixed upon him. Ortiz languished cozily in jail, smoking brown cigarettes and waiting for trial. Kilpatrick, the deputy, brought the counterfeit dollar and handed it to the district attorney in his office in the court-house. The deputy and a reputable druggist were prepared to swear that Ortiz paid for a bottle of medicine with it. The coin was a poor counterfeit, soft, dull-looking, and made principally of lead. It was the day before the morning on which the docket would reach the case of Ortiz, and the district attorney was preparing himself for the trial.

"Not much need of having in high-priced experts to prove the coin's queer, is there, Kil?" smiled Littlefield, as he thumped the dollar down upon the table, where it fell with no more ring than would have come from a lump of putty.

"I guess the Greaser's as good as behind the bars," said the deputy, easing up his holsters. "You've got him dead. If it had been just one time, these Mexicans can't tell good money from bad; but this little yaller rascal belongs to a gang of counterfeiters, I know. This is the first time I've been able to catch him doing the trick. He's got a girl down there in them Mexican jacals on the river bank. I seen her one day when I was watching him. She's as pretty as a red heifer in a flower bed."

Littlefield shoved the counterfiet dollar into his pocket, and slipped his memoranda of the case into an envelope. Just then a bright, winsome face, as frank and jolly as a boy's, appeared in the doorway, and in walked Nancy Derwent.

"Oh, Bob, didn't court adjourn at twelve to-day until to-morrow?" she asked of Littlefield.

"It did," said the district attorney, "and I'm very glad of it. I've got a lot of rulings to look up, and—"

"Now, that's just like you. I wonder you and Father don't turn to law books or rulings or something! I want you to take me out plover-shooting this afternoon. Long Prairie is just alive with them. Don't say no, please! I want to try my new twelve-bore hammerless. I've sent to the livery stable to engage Fly and Bess for the buckboard; they stand fire so nicely. I was sure you would go."

They were to be married in the fall. The glamour was at its height. The plovers won the day—or, rather, the afternoon—over the calf-bound authorities. Littlefield began to put his papers away.

There was a knock at the door. Kilpatrick answered it. A beautiful, dark-eyed girl with a skin tinged with the faintest lemon color walked into the room. A black shawl was thrown over her head and wound once around her neck.

She began to talk in Spanish, a voluble, mournful stream of melancholy music. Littlefield did not understand Spanish. The deputy did, and he translated her talk by portions, at intervals holding up his hands to check the flow of her words.

"She came to see you, Mr. Littlefield. Her name's Joya Treviñas.

She wants to see you about—well, she's mixed up with that Rafael Ortiz. She's his—she's his girl. She says he's innocent. She says she made the money and got him to pass it. Don't you believe her, Mr. Littlefield. That's the way with these Mexican girls; they'll lie, steal, or kill for a fellow when they get stuck on him. Never trust a woman that's in love!"

"Mr. Kilpatrick!"

Nancy Derwent's indignant exclamation caused the deputy to flounder for a moment in attempting to explain that he had misquoted his own sentiments, and then he went on with the translation:

"She says she's willing to take his place in the jail if you'll let him out. She says she was down sick with the fever, and the doctor said she'd die if she didn't have medicine. That's why he passed the lead dollar on the drug store. She says it saved her life. This Rafael seems to be her honey, all right; there's a lot of stuff in her talk about love and such things that you don't want to hear."

It was an old story to the district attorney.

"Tell her," said he, "that I can do nothing. The case comes up in the morning, and he will have to make his fight before the court."

Nancy Derwent was not so hardened. She was looking with sympathetic interest at Joya Treviñas and at Littlefield alternately. The deputy repeated the district attorney's words to the girl. She spoke a sentence or two in a low voice, pulled her shawl closely about her face, and left the room.

"What did she say then?" asked the district attorney.

"Nothing special," said the deputy. "She said: 'If the life of the one'—let's see how it went—'*Si la vida de ella a quien tu amas*—if the life of the girl you love is ever in danger, remember Rafael Ortiz.' "

Kilpatrick strolled out through the corridor in the direction of the marshal's office.

"Can't you do anything for them, Bob?" asked Nancy. "It's such a little thing—just one counterfeit dollar—to ruin the happiness of two lives! She was in danger of death, and he did it to save her. Doesn't the law know the feeling of pity?"

"It hasn't a place in jurisprudence, Nan," said Littlefield, "especially *in re* the district attorney's duty. I'll promise you that the prosecution will not be vindictive; but the man is as good as convicted when the case is called. Witnesses will swear to his passing the bad dollar which I have in my pocket at this moment as 'Exhibit A.' There are no Mexicans on the jury, and it will vote Mr. Greaser guilty without leaving the box."

The plover-shooting was fine that afternoon, and in the excitement of the sport the case of Rafael and the grief of Joya Treviñas was forgotten. The district attorney and Nancy Derwent drove out from the town three miles along a smooth, grassy road, and then struck across a rolling prairie toward a heavy line of timber on Piedra Creek. Beyond this creek lay Long Prairie, the favorite haunt of the plover. As they were nearing the creek they heard the galloping of a horse to their right, and saw a man with black hair and a swarthy face riding toward the woods at a tangent, as if he had come up behind them.

"I've seen that fellow somewhere," said Littlefield, who had a memory for faces, "but I can't exactly place him. Some ranchman, I suppose, taking a short cut home."

They spent an hour on Long Prairie, shooting from the buckboard. Nancy Derwent, an active, outdoor Western girl, was pleased with her twelve-bore. She had bagged within two brace of her companion's score.

They started homeward at a gentle trot. When within a hundred yards of Piedra Creek a man rode out of the timber directly toward them.

"It looks like the man we saw coming over," remarked Miss Derwent.

As the distance between them lessened, the district attorney suddenly pulled up his team sharply, with his eyes fixed upon the advancing horseman. That individual had drawn a Winchester from its scabbard on his saddle and thrown it over his arm.

"Now I know you, Mexico Sam!" muttered Littlefield to himself. "It *was* you who shook your rattles in that gentle epistle."

Mexico Sam did not leave things long in doubt. He had a nice eye in matters relating to firearms, so when he was within good rifle range, but outside of danger from No. 8 shot, he threw up his Winchester and opened fire upon the occupants of the buckboard.

The first shot cracked the back of the seat within the two-inch space between the shoulders of Littlefield and Miss Derwent. The next went through the dashboard and Littlefield's trouser leg.

The district attorney hustled Nancy out of the buckboard to the ground. She was a little pale, but asked no questions. She had the frontier instinct that accepts conditions in an emergency without superfluous argument. They kept their guns in hand, and Littlefield hastily gathered some handfuls of cartridges from the pasteboard box on the seat and crowded them into his pockets.

"Keep behind the horses, Nan," he commanded. "That fellow is a ruffian I sent to prison once. He's trying to get even. He knows our shot won't hurt him at that distance."

"All right, Bob," said Nancy, steadily. "I'm not afraid. But you come close, too. Whoa, Bess; stand still, now!"

She stroked Bess's mane. Littlefield stood with his gun ready, praying that the desperado would come within range.

But Mexico Sam was playing his vendetta along safe lines. He was a bird of different feather from the plover. His accurate eye drew an imaginary line of circumference around the area of danger from birdshot, and upon this line he rode. His horse wheeled to the right, and as his victims rounded to the safe side of their equine breastwork he sent a ball through the district attorney's hat. Once he miscalculated in making a detour, and overstepped his margin. Littlefield's gun flashed, and Mexico Sam ducked his head to the harmless patter of the shot. A few of them stung his horse, which pranced promptly back to the safety line.

The desperado fired again. A little cry came from Nancy Derwent. Littlefield whirled, with blazing eyes, and saw the blood trickling down her cheek.

"I'm not hurt, Bob—only a splinter struck me, I think he hit one of the wheel-spokes."

"Lord!" groaned Littlefield. "If I only had a charge of buckshot!"

The ruffian got his horse still, and took careful aim. Fly gave a snort and fell in the harness, struck in the neck. Bess, now disabused of the idea that plover were being fired at, broke her traces and galloped wildly away. Mexico Sam sent a ball neatly through the fullness of Nancy Derwent's shooting jacket.

"Lie down—lie down!" snapped Littlefield. "Close to the horse—flat on the ground—so." He almost threw her upon the grass against the back of the recumbent Fly. Oddly enough, at that moment the words of the Mexican girl returned to his mind:

"If the life of the girl you love is ever in danger, remember Rafael Ortiz."

Littlefield uttered an exclamation.

"Open fire on him, Nan, across the horse's back! Fire as fast as you can! You can't hurt him, but keep him dodging shot for one minute while I try to work a little scheme."

Nancy gave a quick glance at Littlefield and saw him take out his pocket-knife and open it. Then she turned her face to obey orders, keeping up a rapid fire at the enemy.

Mexico Sam waited patiently until this innocuous fusillade ceased. He had plenty of time, and he did not care to risk the chance of a bird-shot in his eye if it could be avoided by a little caution. He pulled his heavy Stetson low down over his face until the shots ceased. Then he drew a little nearer, and fired with careful aim at what he could see of his victims above the fallen horse.

Neither of them moved. He urged his horse a few steps nearer. He saw the district attorney rise to one knee, and deliberately level his shotgun. He pulled his hat down and awaited the harmless rattle of the tiny pellets.

The shotgun blazed with a heavy report. Mexico Sam sighed, turned limp all over, and slowly fell from his horse—a dead rattlesnake.

At ten o'clock the next morning court opened, and the case of the United States *versus* Rafael Ortiz was called. The district attorney, with his arm in a sling, rose and addressed the court.

"May it please your honor," he said, "I desire to enter a *nolle pros.* in this case. Even though the defendant should be guilty, there is not sufficient evidence in the hands of the government to secure a conviction. The piece of counterfeit coin upon the identity of which the case was built is not now available as evidence. I ask, therefore, that the case be stricken off."

At the noon recess, Kilpatrick strolled into the district attorney's office.

"I've just been down to take a squint at old Mexico Sam," said the deputy. "They've got him laid out. Old Mexico was a tough outfit, I reckon. The boys was wonderin' down there what you shot him with. Some said it must have been nails. I never see a gun carry anything to make holes like he had."

"I shot him," said the district attorney, "with Exhibit A of your counterfeiting case. Lucky thing for me—and somebody else—that it was as bad money as it was! It sliced up into slugs very nicely. Say, Kil, can't you go down to the jacals and find where that Mexican girl lives? Miss Derwent wants to know."

Madame Bo-Peep, of the Ranches

"Aunt Ellen," said Octavia, cheerfully, as she threw her black kid gloves carefully at the dignified Persian cat on the window-seat, "I'm a pauper."

"You are so extreme in your statements, Octavia, dear," said Aunt Ellen, mildly, looking up from her paper. "If you find yourself temporarily in need of some small change for bonbons, you will find my purse in the drawer of the writing desk."

Octavia Beaupree removed her hat and seated herself on a footstool near her aunt's chair, clasping her hands about her knees. Her slim and flexible figure, clad in a modish mourning costume, accommodated itself easily and gracefully to the trying position. Her bright and youthful face, with its pair of sparkling, life-enamored eyes, tried to compose itself to the seriousness that the occasion seemed to demand.

"You good auntie, it isn't a case of bonbons, it is abject, staring, unpicturesque poverty, with ready-made clothes, gasolined gloves, and probably one-o'clock dinners all waiting with the traditional wolf at the door. I've just come from my lawyer, Auntie, and, 'Please, ma'am, I ain't got nothink 't all. Flowers, lady? Buttonhole, gentleman? Pencils, sir, three for five, to help a poor widow?' Do I do it nicely, Auntie, or, as a bread-winner accomplishment, were my lessons in elocution entirely wasted?"

"Do be serious, my dear," said Aunt Ellen, letting her paper fall to the floor, "long enough to tell me what you mean. Colonel Beaupree's estate—"

"Colonel Beaupree's estate," interrupted Octavia, emphasizing her words with appropriate dramatic gestures, "is of Spanish castellar architecture. Colonel Beaupree's resources are—wind. Colonel Beaupree's stocks are—water. Colonel Beaupree's income is—all in. The statement lacks the legal technicalities to which I have been listening for an hour, but that is what it means when translated."

"Octavia!" Aunt Ellen was now visibly possessed by consternation. "I can hardly believe it. And it was the impression that he was worth a million. And the De Peysters themselves introduced him!"

Octavia rippled out a laugh, and then became properly grave.

"*De mortuis nil,* Auntie—not even the rest of it. The dear old colonel—what a gold brick he was, after all! I paid for my bargain fairly—I'm all here, am I not?—items: eyes, fingers, toes, youth, old family, unquestionable position in society as called for in the contract—no wild-cat stock here." Octavia picked up the morning paper from the floor. "But I'm not going to 'squeal'—isn't that what they call it when you rail at Fortune because you've lost the game?" She turned the pages of the paper calmly. " 'Stock market'—no use for that. 'Society's doings'—that's done. Here is my page—the wish column. A Van Dresser could not be said to 'want' for anything, of course. Chambermaids, cooks, canvassers, stenographers—"

"Dear," said Aunt Ellen, with a little tremor in her voice, "please do not talk in that way. Even if your affairs are in so unfortunate a condition, there is my three thousand—"

Octavia sprang up lithely, and deposited a smart kiss on the delicate cheek of the prim little elderly maid.

"Blessed auntie, your three thousand is just sufficient to insure your Hyson to be free from willow leaves and keep the Persian in sterilized cream. I know I'd be welcome, but I prefer to strike bottom like Beelzebub rather than hang around like the Peri listening to the music from the side entrance. I'm going to earn my own living. There's nothing else to do. I'm a—Oh, oh, oh!—I had forgotten. There's one thing saved from the wreck. It's a corral—no, a ranch in—let me see—Texas; an asset, dear old Mr. Bannister called it. How pleased he was to show me something he could describe as unencumbered! I've a description of it among those stupid papers he made me bring away with me from his office. I'll try to find it."

Octavia found her shopping-bag, and drew from it a long envelope filled with typewritten documents.

"A ranch in Texas," sighed Aunt Ellen. "It sounds to me more like a liability than an asset. Those are the places where the centipedes are found, and cowboys, and fandangos."

" 'The Rancho de las Sombras,' " read Octavia from a sheet of violently purple typewriting, "is situated one hundred and ten miles southeast of San Antonio, and thirty-eight miles from its nearest railroad station, Nopal, on the I. and G. N. Ranch consists of 7,680 acres of well-watered land, with title conferred by State patents, and twenty-two sections, or 14,080 acres, partly under yearly running lease and partly bought under State's twenty-year-purchase act. Eight thousand graded merino sheep, with the necessary equipment of horses, vehicles, and general ranch paraphernalia. Ranch-house built of brick, with six rooms comfortably furnished according to the requirements of the climate. All within a strong barbed-wire fence.

" 'The present ranch manager seems to be competent and reliable, and is rapidly placing upon a paying basis a business that, in other hands, had been allowed to suffer from neglect and misconduct.

" 'This property was secured by Colonel Beaupree in a deal with a Western irrigation syndicate, and the title to it seems to be perfect. With careful management and the natural increase of land values, it ought to be made the foundation for a comfortable fortune for its owner.' "

When Octavia ceased reading, Aunt Ellen uttered something as near a sniff as her breeding permitted.

"The prospectus," she said, with uncompromising metropolitan suspicion, "doesn't mention the centipedes, or the Indians. And you never did like mutton, Octavia. I don't see what advantage you can derive from this—desert."

But Octavia was in a trance. Her eyes were steadily regarding something quite beyond their focus. Her lips were parted, and her face was lighted by the kindling furor of the explorer, the ardent, stirring disquiet of the adventurer. Suddenly she clasped her hands together exultantly.

"The problem solves itself, auntie," she cried. "I'm going to that ranch. I'm going to live on it. I'm going to learn to like mutton, and even concede the good qualities of centipedes—at a respectful distance. It's just what I need. It's a new life that comes when my old one is just ending. It's a release, auntie; it isn't a narrowing. Think of the gallops over those leagues of prairies, with the wind tugging at the roots of your hair, the coming close to the earth and learning over again the stories of the growing grass and the little wild flowers without names! Glorious is what it will be. Shall I be a sheperdess with a Watteau hat, and a crook to keep the bad wolves from the lambs, or a typical Western ranch girl, with short hair, like the pictures of her in the Sunday papers? I think the latter. And they'll have my picture, too, with the wild-cats I've slain, single-handed, hanging from my saddle horn. 'From the Four Hundred to the Flocks' is the way they'll headline it, and they'll print photographs of the old Van Dresser mansion and the church where I was married. They won't have my picture, but they'll get an artist to draw it. I'll be wild and woolly, and I'll grow my own wool."

"Octavia!" Aunt Ellen condensed into the one word all the protests she was unable to utter.

"Don't say a word, auntie. I'm going. I'll see the sky at night fit down on the world like a big butter-dish cover, and I'll make friends again with the stars that I haven't had a chat with since I was a wee child. I wish to go. I'm tired of all this. I'm glad I haven't any money. I could bless Colonel Beaupree for that ranch, and forgive him for all his bubbles. What if the life will be rough and lonely! I—I deserve it. I shut my heart to everything except that miserable ambition. I—oh, I wish to go away, and forget—forget!"

Octavia swerved suddenly to her knees, laid her flushed face in her aunt's lap, and shook with turbulent sobs.

Aunt Ellen bent over her, and smoothed the coppery-brown hair.

"I didn't know," she said, gently; "I didn't know—that. Who was it, dear?"

When Mrs. Octavia Beaupree, née Van Dresser, stepped from the train at Nopal, her manner lost, for the moment, some of that easy certitude which had always marked her movements. The town was of recent establishment, and seemed to have been hastily constructed of undressed lumber and flapping canvas. The element that had congregated about the station, though not offensively demonstrative, was clearly composed of citizens accustomed to and prepared for rude alarms.

Octavia stood on the platform, against the telegraph office, and attempted to choose by intuition from the swaggering, straggling string of loungers, the manager of the Rancho de las Sombras, who had been instructed by Mr. Bannister to meet her there. That tall, serious-looking, elderly man in the blue flannel shirt and white tie she thought must be he. But no, he passed by, removing his gaze from the lady as hers rested on him, according to the Southern custom. The manager, she thought, with some impatience at being kept waiting, should have no difficulty in selecting her. Young women wearing the most recent thing in ash-colored traveling suits were not so plentiful in Nopal!

Thus keeping a speculative watch on all persons of possible managerial aspect, Octavia, with a catching breath and a start of surprise, suddenly became aware of Teddy Westlake hurrying along the platform in the direction of the train—of Teddy Westlake or his sun-browned ghost in cheviot, boots and leather-girdled hat—Theodore Westlake, Jr., amateur polo (almost) champion, all-round butterfly and cucumber of the soil; but a broader, surer, more emphasized and determined Teddy than the one she had known a year ago when last she saw him.

He perceived Octavia at almost the same time, deflected his course, and steered for her in his old, straightforward way. Something like awe came upon her as the strangeness of his metamorphosis was brought into closer range; the rich, red-brown of his complexion brought out so vividly his straw-colored mustache and steel-gray eyes. He seemed more grown-up, and, somehow, farther away. But, when he spoke, the old, boyish Teddy came back again. They had been friends from childhood.

"Why, 'Tave!" he exclaimed, unable to reduce his perplexity to coherence. "How—what—when—where?"

"Train," said Octavia; "necessity; ten minutes ago; home. Your complexion's gone, Teddy. Now, how—what—when—where?"

"I'm working down here," said Teddy. He cast side glances about the station as one does who tries to combine politeness with duty.

"You didn't notice on the train," he asked, "an old lady with gray curls and a poodle, who occupied two seats with her bundles and quarrelled with the conductor, did you?"

"I think not," answered Octavia, reflecting. "And you haven't, by any chance, noticed a big, gray-mustached man in a blue shirt and six-shooters, with little flakes of merino wool sticking in his hair, have you?"

"Lots of 'em," said Teddy, with symptoms of mental delirium under the strain. "Do you happen to know any such individual?"

"No; the description is imaginary. Is your interest in the old lady whom you describe a personal one?"

"Never saw her in my life. She's painted entirely from fancy. She owns the little piece of property where I earn my bread and butter—the Rancho de las Sombras. I drove up to meet her according to arrangements with her lawyer."

Octavia leaned against the wall of the telegraph office. Was this possible? And didn't he know?

"Are you the manager of that ranch?" she asked, weakly.

"I am," said Teddy, with pride.

"I am Mrs. Beaupree," said Octavia, faintly; "but my hair never would curl, and I was polite to the conductor."

For a moment that strange, grown-up look came back, and removed Teddy miles away from her.

"I hope you'll excuse me," he said, rather awkwardly. "You see, I've been down here in the chaparral a year. I hadn't heard. Give me your checks, please, and I'll have your traps loaded into the wagon. José will follow with them. We travel ahead in the buckboard."

Seated by Teddy in a feather-weight buckboard, behind a pair of wild, cream-colored Spanish ponies, Octavia abandoned all thought for the exhilaration of the present. They swept out of the little town and down the level road toward the south. Soon the road dwindled and disappeared, and they struck across a world carpeted with an endless reach of curly mesquite grass. The wheels made no sound. The tireless ponies bounded ahead at an unbroken gallop. The temperate wind, made fragrant by thousands of acres of blue and yellow wild flowers, roared gloriously in their ears. The motion was aërial, ecstatic, with a thrilling sense of perpetuity in its effect. Octavia sat silent, possessed by a feeling of elemental, sensual bliss. Teddy seemed to be wrestling with some internal problem.

"I'm going to call you madama," he announced as the result of his labors. "That is what the Mexicans will call you—they're nearly all Mexicans on the ranch, you know. That seems to me about the proper thing."

"Very well, Mr. Westlake," said Octavia, primly.

"Oh, now," said Teddy, in some consternation, "that's carrying the thing too far, isn't it?"

"Don't worry me with your beastly etiquette. I'm just beginning to live. Don't remind me of anything artificial. If only this air could be bottled! This much alone is worth coming for. Oh, look! there goes a deer!"

"Jack-rabbit," said Teddy, without turning his head.

"Could I—might I drive?" suggested Octavia, panting, with rose-tinted cheeks and the eye of an eager child.

"On one condition. Could I—might I smoke?"

"Forever!" cried Octavia, taking the lines with solemn joy. "How shall I know which way to drive?"

"Keep her sou' by sou'east, and all sail set. You see that black speck on the horizon under that lowermost Gulf cloud? That's a group of live-oaks and a landmark. Steer halfway between that and the little hill to the left. I'll recite you the whole code of driving rules for the Texas prairies: keep the reins from under the horses' feet, and swear at 'em frequent."

"I'm too happy to swear, Ted. Oh, why do people buy yachts or travel in palace-cars, when a buckboard and a pair of plugs and a spring morning like this can satisfy all desire?"

"Now, I'll ask you," protested Teddy, who was futilely striking match after match on the dashboard, "not to call those denizens of the air plugs. They can kick out a hundred miles between daylight and dark." At last he succeeded in snatching a light for his cigar from the flame held in the hollow of his hands.

"Room!" said Octavia, intensely. "That's what produces the effect. I know now what I've wanted—scope—range—room!"

"Smoking-room," said Teddy, unsentimentally. "I love to smoke in a buckboard. The wind blows the smoke into you and out again. It saves exertion."

The two fell so naturally into their old-time goodfellowship that it was only by degrees that a sense of the strangeness of the new relations between them came to be felt.

"Madama," said Teddy, wonderingly, "however did you get it into your head to cut the crowd and come down here? Is it a fad now among the upper classes to trot off to sheep ranches instead of to Newport?"

"I was broke, Teddy," said Octavia, sweetly, with her interest centred upon steering safely between a Spanish dagger plant and a clump of chaparral; "I haven't a thing in the world but this ranch—not even any other home to go to."

"Come, now," said Teddy, anxiously but incredulously, "you don't mean it?"

"When my husband," said Octavia, with a shy slurring of the word, "died three months ago I thought I had a reasonable amount of the world's goods. His lawyer exploded that theory in a sixty-minute fully illustrated lecture. I took to the sheep as a last resort. Do you happen to know of any fashionable caprice among the gilded youth of Manhattan that induces them to abandon polo and club windows to become managers of sheep ranches?"

"It's easily explained in my case," responded Teddy, promptly. "I had to go to work. I couldn't have earned my board in New York, so I chummed a while with old Sandford, one of the syndicate that owned the ranch before Colonel Beaupree bought it, and got a place down here. I wasn't manager at first. I jogged around on ponies and studied the business in detail, until I got all the points in my head. I saw where it was losing and what the remedies were, and then Sandford put me in charge. I get a hundred dollars a month, and I earn it."

"Poor Teddy!" said Octavia, with a smile.

"You needn't. I like it. I save half my wages, and I'm as hard as a water plug. It beats polo."

"Will it furnish bread and tea and jam for another outcast from civilization?"

"The spring shearing," said the manager, "just cleaned up a deficit in last year's business. Wastefulness and inattention have been the rule heretofore. The autumn clip will leave a small profit over all expenses. Next year there will be jam."

When, about four o'clock in the afternoon, the ponies rounded a gentle, brush-covered hill, and then swooped, like a double cream-colored cyclone, upon the Rancho de las Sombras, Octavia gave a little cry of delight. A lordly grove of magnificent live-oaks cast an area of grateful, cool shade, whence the ranch had drawn its name, "de las Sombras"—of the shadows. The house, of red brick, one story, ran low and long beneath the trees. Through its middle, dividing its six rooms in half, extended a broad, arched passageway, picturesque with flowering cactus and hanging red earthen jars. A "gallery," low and broad, encircled the building. Vines climbed about it, and the adjacent ground was, for space, covered with transplanted grass and shrubs. A little lake, long and narrow, glimmered in the sun at the rear. Farther away stood the shacks of the Mexican workers, the corrals, wool sheds and shearing pens. To the right lay the low hills, splattered with dark patches of chaparral; to the left the unbounded green prairie blending against the blue heavens.

"It's a home, Teddy," said Octavia, breathlessly; "that's what it is—it's a home."

"Not so bad for a sheep ranch," admitted Teddy, with excusable pride. "I've been tinkering on it at odd times."

A Mexican youth sprang from somewhere in the grass, and took charge of the creams. The mistress and the manager entered the house.

"Here's Mrs. MacIntyre," said Teddy, as a placid, neat, elderly lady come out upon the gallery to meet them. "Mrs. Mac, here's the boss. Very likely she will be wanting a hunk of bacon and a dish of beans after her drive."

Mrs. MacIntyre, the housekeeper, as much a fixture on the place as the lake or the live-oaks, received the imputation of the ranch's resources of refreshment with mild indignation, and was about to give it utterance when Octavia spoke.

"Oh, Mrs. MacIntyre, don't apologize for Teddy. Yes, I call him Teddy. So does every one whom he hasn't duped into taking him seriously. You see, we used to cut paper dolls and play jackstraws together ages ago. No one minds what he says."

"No," said Teddy, "no one minds what he says, just so he doesn't do it again."

Octavia cast one of those subtle, sidelong glances toward him from beneath her lowered eyelids—a glance that Teddy used to describe as an upper-cut. But there was nothing in his ingenuous, weather-tanned face to warrant a suspicion that he was making an allusion—nothing. Beyond a doubt, thought Octavia, he had forgotten.

"Mr. Westlake likes his fun," said Mrs. MacIntyre, as she conducted Octavia to her rooms. "But," she added, loyally, "people around here usually pay attention to what he says when he talks in earnest. I don't know what would have become of this place without him."

Two rooms at the east end of the house had been arranged for the occupancy of the ranch's mistress. When she entered them a slight dismay seized her at their bare appearance and the scantiness of their furniture; but she quickly reflected that the climate was a semi-tropical one, and was moved to appreciation of the well-conceived efforts to conform to it. The sashes had already been removed from the big windows, and white curtains waved in the Gulf breeze that streamed through the wide jalousies. The bare floor was amply strewn with cool rugs; the chairs were inviting, deep, dreamy willows; the walls were papered with a light, cheerful olive. One whole side of her sitting room was covered with books on smooth, unpainted pine shelves. She flew to these at once. Before her was a well-selected library. She caught glimpses of titles of volumes of fiction and travel not yet seasoned from the dampness of the press.

Presently, recollecting that she was now in a wilderness given over to mutton, centipedes, and privations, the incongruity of these luxuries struck her, and, with intuitive feminine suspicion, she began turning to the fly-leaves of volume after volume. Upon each one was inscribed in fluent characters the name of Theodore Westlake, Jr.

Octavia, fatigued by her long journey, retired early that night. Lying upon her white, cool bed, she rested deliciously, but sleep coquetted long with her. She listened to faint noises whose strangeness kept her faculties on the alert—the fractious yelping of the coyotes, the ceaseless, low symphony of the wind, the distant booming of the frogs about the lake, the lamentation of a concertina in the Mexicans' quarters. There were many conflicting feelings in her heart—thankfulness and rebellion, peace and disquietude, loneliness and a sense of protecting care, happiness and an old, haunting pain.

She did what any other woman would have done—sought relief in a wholesome tide of unreasonable tears, and her last words, murmured to herself before slumber, capitulating, come softly to woo her, were, "He has forgotten."

The manager of the Rancho de las Sombras was no dilettante. He was a "hustler." He was generally up, mounted, and away of mornings before the rest of the household were awake, making the rounds of the flocks and camps. This was the duty of the major-domo, a stately old Mexican with a princely air and manner, but Teddy seemed to have a great deal of confidence in his own eyesight. Except in the busy seasons, he nearly always returned to the ranch to breakfast at eight o'clock, with Octavia and Mrs. MacIntyre, at the little table set in the central hallway, bringing with him a tonic and breezy cheerfulness full of the health and flavor of the prairies.

A few days after Octavia's arrival he made her get out one of her riding skirts, and curtail it to a shortness demanded by the chaparral brakes.

With some misgivings she donned this and the pair of buckskin leggings he prescribed in addition, and mounted upon a dancing pony, rode with him to view her possessions. He showed her everything—the flocks of ewes, muttons and grazing lambs, the dipping vats, the shearing pens, the uncouth merino rams in their little pasture, the water-tanks prepared against the summer drought—giving account of his stewardship with a boyish enthusiasm that never flagged.

Where was the old Teddy that she knew so well? This side of him was the same, and it was a side that pleased her; but this was all she ever saw of him now. Where was his sentimentality—those old, varying moods of impetuous love-making, of fanciful, quixotic devotion, of heart-breaking gloom, of alternating, absurd tenderness and haughty dignity? His nature had been a sensitive one, his temperament bordering closely on the artistic. She knew that, besides being a follower of fashion and its fads and sports, he had cultivated tastes of a finer nature. He had written things, he had tampered with colors, he was something of a student in certain branches of art, and once she had been admitted to all his aspirations and thoughts. But now—and she could not avoid the conclusion—Teddy had barricaded against her every side of himself except one—the side that showed the manager of the Rancho de las Sombras and a jolly chum who had forgiven and forgotten. Queerly enough the words of Mr. Bannister's description of her property came into her mind—"all inclosed within a strong barbed-wire fence."

"Teddy's fenced, too," said Octavia to herself.

It was not difficult for her to reason out the cause of his fortifications. It had originated one night at the Hammersmiths' ball. It occurred at a time soon after she had decided to accept Colonel Beaupree and his millions, which was no more than her looks and the entrée she held to the inner circles were worth. Teddy had proposed with all his impetuosity and fire, and she looked him straight in the eyes, and said, coldly and finally: "Never let me hear any such silly nonsense from you again." "You won't," said Teddy, with a new expression around his mouth, and—now Teddy was inclosed within a strong barbed-wire fence.

It was on this first ride of inspection that Teddy was seized by the inspiration that suggested the name of Mother Goose's heroine, and he at once bestowed it upon Octavia. The idea, supported by both a similarity of names and identity of occupations, seemed to strike him as a peculiarly happy one, and he never tired of using it. The Mexicans on the ranch also took up the name, adding another syllable to accommodate their lingual incapacity for the final "p," gravely referring to her as "La Madama Bo-Peepy." Eventually it spread, and "Madame Bo-Peep's ranch" was as often mentioned as the "Rancho de las Sombras."

Came the long, hot season from May to September, when work is scarce on the ranches. Octavia passed the days in a kind of lotus-eater's dream. Books, hammocks, correspondence with a few intimate friends, a renewed interest in her old water-color box and easel—these disposed of the sultry hours of daylight. The evenings were always sure to bring enjoyment. Best of all were the rapturous horseback rides with Teddy, when the moon gave light over the wind-swept leagues, chaperoned by the wheeling night-hawk and the startled owl. Often the Mexicans would come up from their shacks with their guitars and sing the weirdest of heart-breaking songs. There were long, cosy chats on the breezy gallery, and an interminable warfare of wits between Teddy and Mrs. MacIntyre, whose abundant Scotch shrewdness often more than overmatched the lighter humor in which she was lacking.

And the nights came, one after another, and were filed away by weeks and months—nights soft and languorous and fragrant, that should have driven Strephon to Chloe over wires however barbed, that might have drawn Cupid himself to hunt, lasso in hand, among those amorous pastures—but Teddy kept his fences up.

One July night Madame Bo-Peep and her ranch manager were sitting on the east gallery. Teddy had been exhausting the science of prognostication as to the probabilities of a price of twenty-four cents for the autumn clip, and had then subsided into an anaesthetic cloud of Havana smoke. Only as incompetent a judge as a woman would have failed to note long ago that at least a third of his salary must have gone up in the fumes of those imported Regalias.

"Teddy," said Octavia, suddenly, and rather sharply, "what are you working down here on a ranch for?"

"One hundred per," said Teddy, glibly, "and found."

"I've a good mind to discharge you."

"Can't do it," said Teddy, with a grin.

"Why not?" demanded Octavia, with argumentative heat.

"Under contract. Terms of sale respect all unexpired contracts. Mine runs until 12 P.M., December thirty-first. You might get up at midnight on that date and fire me. If you try it sooner I'll be in a position to bring legal proceedings."

Octavia seemed to be considering the prospects of litigation.

"But," continued Teddy, cheerfully, "I've been thinking of resigning anyway."

Octavia's rocking-chair ceased its motion. There were centipedes in this country, she felt sure; and Indians; and vast, lonely, desolate, empty wastes; all within strong barbed-wire fence. There was a Van Dresser pride, but there was also a Van Dresser heart. She must know for certain whether or not he had forgotten.

"Ah, well, Teddy," she said, with a fine assumption of polite interest, "it's lonely down here; you're longing to get back to the old life—to polo and lobsters and theatres and balls."

"Never cared much for balls," said Teddy, virtuously.

"You're getting old, Teddy. Your memory is failing. Nobody ever knew you to miss a dance, unless it occurred on the same night with another one which you attended. And you showed such shocking bad taste, too, in dancing too often with the same partner. Let me see, what was that Forbes girl's name—the one with wall eyes—Mabel, wasn't it?"

"No; Adèle. Mabel was the one with the bony elbows. That wasn't wall in Adèle's eyes. It was soul. We used to talk sonnets together, and Verlaine. Just then I was trying to run a pipe from the Pierian spring."

"You were on the floor with her," said Octavia, undeflected, "five times at the Hammersmiths'."

"Hammersmiths' what?" questioned Teddy, vacuously.

"Ball—ball," said Octavia, viciously. "What were we talking of?"

"Eyes, I thought," said Teddy, after some reflection; "and elbows."

"Those Hammersmiths," went on Octavia, in her sweetest society prattle, after subduing an intense desire to yank a handful of sunburnt, sandy hair from the head lying back contentedly against the canvas of the steamer chair, "had too much money. Mines, wasn't it? It was something that paid something to the ton. You couldn't get a glass of plain water in their house. Everything at that ball was dreadfully overdone."

"It was," said Teddy.

"Such a crowd there was!" Octavia continued conscious that she was talking the rapid drivel of a school-girl describing her first dance. "The balconies were as warm as the rooms. I—lost—something at that ball." The last sentence was uttered in a tone calculated to remove the barbs from miles of wire.

"So did I," confessed Teddy, in a lower voice.

"A glove," said Octavia, falling back as the enemy approached her ditches.

"Caste," said Teddy, halting his firing line without loss. "I hob-nobbed, half evening, with one of Hammersmith's miners, a fellow who kept his hands in his pockets, and talked like an archangel about reduction plants and drifts and levels and sluice-boxes."

"A pearl-gray glove, nearly new," sighed Octavia, mournfully.

"A bang-up chap, that McArdle," maintained Teddy, approvingly. "A man who hated olives and elevators; a man who handled mountains as coquettes, and built tunnels in the air; a man who never uttered a word of silly nonsense in his life. Did you sign those lease-renewal applications yet, madama? They've got to be on file in the land office by the thirty-first."

Teddy turned his head lazily. Octavia's chair was vacant.

A certain centipede, crawling along the lines marked out by fate, expounded the situation. It was early one morning while Octavia and Mrs. MacIntyre were trimming the honeysuckle on the west gallery. Teddy had risen and departed hastily before daylight in response to a word that a flock of ewes had been scattered from their bedding ground during the night by a thunder-storm.

The centipede, driven by destiny, showed himself on the floor of the gallery, and then, the screeches of the two women giving him his cue, he scuttled with all his yellow legs through the open door into the furthermost west room, which was Teddy's. Arming themselves with domestic utensils selected with regard to their length, Octavia and Mrs. MacIntyre, with much clutching of skirts and skirmishing for the position of rear guard in the attacking force, followed.

Once inside, the centipede seemed to have disappeared, and his prospective murderers began a thorough but cautious search for their victim.

Even in the midst of such a dangerous and absorbing adventure Octavia was conscious of an awed curiosity on finding herself in Teddy's sanctum. In that room he sat alone, silently communing with those secret thoughts that he now shared with no one, dreamed there whatever dreams he now called on no one to interpret.

It was the room of a Spartan or a soldier. In one corner stood a wide, canvas-covered cot; in another, a small bookcase; in another, a grim stand of Winchesters and shotguns. An immense table, strewn with letters, papers, and documents and surmounted by a set of pigeon-holes, occupied one side.

The centipede showed genius in concealing himself in such bare quarters. Mrs. MacIntyre was poking a broom-handle behind the bookcase. Octavia approached Teddy's cot. The room was just as the manager had left it in his hurry. The Mexican maid had not yet given it her attention. There was his big pillow with the imprint of his head still in the centre. She thought the horrid beast might have climbed the cot and hidden itself to bite Teddy. Centipedes were thus cruel and vindictive toward managers.

She catiously overturned the pillow, and then parted her lips to give the signal for reinforcements at sight of a long, slender, dark object lying there. But, repressing it in time, she caught up a glove, a pearl-gray glove, flattened—it might be conceived—by many, many months of nightly pressure beneath the pillow of the man who had forgotten the Hammersmiths' ball. Teddy must have left so hurriedly that morning that he had, for once, forgotten to transfer it to its resting-place by day. Even managers, who are notoriously wily and cunning, are sometimes caught up with.

Octavia slid the gray glove into the bosom of her summery morning gown. It was hers. Men who put themselves within a strong barbed-wire fence, and remember Hammersmith balls only by the talk of miners about sluice boxes, should not be allowed to possess such articles.

After all, what a paradise this prairie country was! How it blossomed like the rose when you found things that were thought to be lost! How delicious was that morning breeze coming in the windows, fresh and sweet with the breath of the yellow ratama blooms! Might one not stand, for a minute, with shining, far-gazing eyes, and dream that mistakes might be corrected?

Why was Mrs. MacIntyre poking about so absurdly with a broom?

"I've found it," said Mrs. MacIntyre, banging the door. "Here it is."

"Did you lose something?" asked Octavia, with sweetly polite non-interest.

"The little devil!" said Mrs. MacIntyre, driven to violence. "Ye've no forgotten him alretty?"

Between them they slew the centipede. Thus was he rewarded for his agency toward the recovery of things lost at the Hammersmiths' ball.

It seems that Teddy, in due course, remembered the glove, and when he returned to the house at sunset made a secret but exhaustive search for it. Not until evening, upon the moonlit eastern gallery, did he find it. It was upon the hand that he had thought lost to him forever, and so he was moved to repeat certain nonsense that he had been commanded never, never to utter again. Teddy's fences were down.

This time there was no ambition to stand in the way, and the wooing was as natural and successful as should be between ardent shepherd and gentle shepherdess.

The prairies changed to a garden. The Rancho de las Sombras became the Ranch of Light.

A few days later Octavia received a letter from Mr. Bannister, in reply to one she had written to him asking some questions about her business. A portion of the letter ran as follows:

> I am at a loss to account for your references to the sheep ranch. Two months after your departure to take up your residence upon it, it was discovered that Colonel Beaupree's title was worthless. A deed came to light showing that he disposed of the property before his death. The matter was reported to your manager, Mr. Westlake, who at once repurchased the property. It is entirely beyond my powers of conjecture to imagine how you have remained in ignorance of this fact. I beg that you will at once confer with that gentleman, who will, at least, corroborate my statement.

Octavia sought Teddy, with battle in her eye.

"What are you working on this ranch for?" she asked once more.

"One hundred—" he began to repeat, but saw in her face that she knew. She held Mr. Bannister's letter in her hand. He knew that the game was up.

"It's my ranch," said Teddy, like a schoolboy detected in evil. "It's a mighty poor manager that isn't able to absorb the boss's business if you give him time."

"Why were you working down here?" pursued Octavia, still struggling after the key to the riddle of Teddy.

"To tell the truth, 'Tave," said Teddy, with quiet candor, "it wasn't for the salary. That about kept me in cigars and sunburn lotions. I was sent south by my doctor. 'Twas that right lung that was going to the bad on account of over-exercise and strain at polo and gymnastics. I needed climate and ozone and rest and things of that sort."

In an instant Octavia was close against the vicinity of the affected organ. Mr. Bannister's letter fluttered to the floor.

"It's—it's well now, isn't it, Teddy?"

"Sound as a mesquite chunk. I deceived you in one thing. I paid fifty thousand for your ranch as soon as I found you had no title. I had just about that much income accumulated at my banker's while I've been herding sheep down here, so it was almost like picking the thing up on a bargain-counter for a penny. There's another little surplus of unearned increment piling up there, 'Tave. I've been thinking of a wedding trip in a yacht with white ribbons tied to the mast, through the Mediterranean, and then up among the Hebrides and down Norway to the Zuyder Zee."

"And I was thinking," said Octavia, softly, "of a wedding gallop with my manager among the flocks of sheep and back to a wedding breakfast with Mrs. MacIntyre on the gallery, with, maybe, a sprig of orange blossom fastened to the red jar above the table."

Teddy laughed, and began to chant:

"Little Bo-Peep has lost her sheep,
And doesn't know where to find 'em.
Let 'em alone, and they'll come home,
And—"

Octavia drew his head down, and whispered in his ear.

But that is one of the tales they brought behind them.

Witches' Loaves

Miss Martha Meacham kept the little bakery on the corner (the one where you go up three steps, and the bell tinkles when you open the door).

Miss Martha was forty, her bank-book showed a credit of two thousand dollars, and she possessed two false teeth and a sympathetic heart. Many people have married whose chances to do so were much inferior to Miss Martha's.

Two or three times a week a customer came in in whom she began to take an interest. He was a middle-aged man, wearing spectacles and a brown beard trimmed to a careful point.

He spoke English with a strong German accent. His clothes were worn and darned in places, and wrinkled and baggy in others. But he looked neat, and had very good manners.

He always bought two loaves of stale bread. Fresh bread was five cents a loaf. Stale ones were two for five. Never did he call for anything but stale bread.

Once Miss Martha saw a red and brown stain on his fingers. She was sure then that he was an artist and very poor. No doubt he lived in a garret, where he painted pictures and ate stale bread and thought of the good things to eat in Miss Martha's bakery.

Often when Miss Martha sat down to her chops and light rolls and jam and tea she would sigh, and wish that the gentle-mannered artist might share her tasty meal instead of eating his dry crust in that draughty attic. Miss Martha's heart, as you have been told, was a sympathetic one.

In order to test her theory as to his occupation, she brought from her room one day a painting that she had bought at a sale, and set it against the shelves behind the bread counter.

It was a Venetian scene. A splendid marble palazzio (so it said on the picture) stood in the foreground—or rather forewater. For the rest there were gondolas (with the lady trailing her hand in the water), clouds, sky, and chiaro-oscuro in plenty. No artist could fail to notice it.

Two days afterward the customer came in.

"Two loafs of stale bread, if you blease.

"You haf here a fine bicture, madame," he said while she was wrapping up the bread.

"Yes?" says Miss Martha, revelling in her own cunning. "I do so admire art and" (no, it would not do to say "artists" thus early) "and paintings," she substituted. "You think it is a good picture?"

"Der balace," said the customer, "is not in good drawing. Der bairspective of it is not true. Goot morning, madame."

He took his bread, bowed, and hurried out.

Yes, he must be an artist. Miss Martha took the picture back to her room.

How gentle and kindly his eyes shone behind his spectacles! What a broad brow he had! To be able to judge perspective at a glance—and to live on stale bread! But genius often has a struggle before it is recognized.

What a thing it would be for art and perspective if genius were backed by two thousand dollars in bank, a bakery, and a sympathetic heart to—But these were day-dreams, Miss Martha.

Often now when he came he would chat for a while across the showcase. He seemed to crave Miss Martha's cheerful words.

He kept on buying stale bread. Never a cake, never a pie, never one of her delicious Sally Lunns.

She thought he began to look thinner and discouraged. Her heart ached to add something good to eat to his meagre purchase, but her courage failed at the act. She did not dare affront him. She knew the pride of artists.

Miss Martha took to wearing her blue-dotted silk waist behind the counter. In the back room she cooked a mysterious compound of quince seeds and borax. Ever so many people use it for the complexion.

One day the customer came in as usual, laid his nickel on the showcase, and called for his stale loaves. While Miss Martha was reaching for them there was a great tooting and clanging, and a fire-engine came lumbering past.

The customer hurried to the door to look, as any one will. Suddenly inspired, Miss Martha seized the opportunity.

On the bottom shelf behind the counter was a pound of fresh butter that the dairyman had left ten minutes before. With a bread knife Miss Martha made a deep slash in each of the stale loaves, inserted a generous quantity of butter, and pressed the loaves tight again.

When the customer turned once more she was tying the paper around them.

When he had gone, after an unusually pleasant little chat, Miss Martha smiled to herself, but not without a slight fluttering of the heart.

Had she been too bold? Would he take offense? But surely not. There was no language of edibles. Butter was no emblem of unmaidenly forwardness.

For a long time that day her mind dwelt on the subject. She imagined the scene when he should discover her little deception.

He would lay down his brushes and palette. There would stand his easel with the picture he was painting in which the perspective was behond criticism.

He would prepare for his luncheon of dry bread and water. He would slice into a loaf—ah!

Miss Martha blushed. Would he think of the hand that placed it there as he ate? Would he—

The front door bell jangled viciously. Somebody was coming in, making a great deal of noise

Miss Martha hurried to the front. Two men were there. One was a young man smoking a pipe—a man she had never seen before. The other was her artist.

His face was very red, his hat was on the back of his head, his hair was wildly rumpled. He clinched his two fists and shook them ferociously at Miss Martha. *At Miss Martha.*

"Dummkopf!" he shouted with extreme loudness; and then *"Tausendonfer!"* or something like it in German.

The young man tried to draw him away.

"I vill not go," he said angrily, "else I shall told her."

He made a bass drum of Miss Martha's counter.

"You haf shpoilt me," he cried, his blue eyes blazing behind his spectacles. "I vill tell you. You vas von *meddingsome old cat!*"

Miss Martha leaned weakly against the shelves and laid one hand on her blue-dotted silk waist. The younger man took the other by the collar.

"Come on," he said, "you've said enough." He dragged the angry one out at the door to the sidewalk, and then came back.

"Guess you ought to be told, ma'am," he said, "what the row is about. That's Blumberger. He's an architectural draftsman. I work in the same office with him.

"He's been working hard for three months drawing a plan for a new city hall. It was a prize competition. He finished inking the lines yesterday. You know, a draftsman always makes his drawing in pencil first. When it's done he rubs out the pencil lines with handfuls of stale bread crumbs. That's better than India rubber.

"Blumberger's been buying the bread here. Well, to-day—well, you know, ma'am, that butter isn't—well, Blumberger's plan isn't good for anything now except to cut up into railroad sandwiches."

Miss Martha went into the back room. She took off the blue-dotted silk waist and put on the old brown serge she used to wear. Then she poured the quince seed and borax mixture out of the window into the ash can.

The Duplicity of Hargraves

When Major Pendleton Talbot, of Mobile, sir, and his daughter, Miss Lydia Talbot, came to Washington to reside, they selected for a boarding place a house that stood fifty yards back from one of the quietest avenues. It was an old-fashioned brick building, with a portico upheld by tall white pillars. The yard was shaded by stately locusts and elms, and a catalpa tree in season rained its pink and white blossoms upon the grass. Rows of high box bushes lined the fence and walks. It was the Southern style and aspect of the place that pleased the eyes of the Talbots.

In this pleasant, private boarding house they engaged rooms, including a study for Major Talbot, who was adding the finishing chapters to his book, "Anecdotes and Reminiscences of the Alabama Army, Bench, and Bar."

Major Talbot was of the old, old South. The present day had little interest or excellence in his eyes. His mind lived in that period before the Civil War, when the Talbots owned thousands of acres of fine cotton land and the slaves to till them; when the family mansion was the scene of princely hospitality, and drew its guests from the aristocracy of the South. Out of that period he had brought all of its old pride and scruples of honor, and antiquated and punctilious politeness, and (you would think) its wardrobe.

Such clothes were surely never made within fifty years. The major was tall, but whenever he made that wonderful, archaic genuflexion he called a bow, the corners of his frock coat swept the floor. That garment was a surprise even to Washington, which has long ago ceased to shy at the frocks and broad-brimmed hats of Southern congressmen. One of the boarders christened it a "Father Hubbard," and it certainly was high in the waist and full in the skirt.

But the major, with all his queer clothes, his immense area of plaited, ravelling shirt bosom, and the little black string tie with the bow always slipping on one side, both was smiled at and liked in Mrs. Vardeman's select boarding house. Some of the young department clerks would often "string him," as they called it, getting him started upon the subject dearest to him—the traditions and history of his beloved Southland. During his talks he would quote freely from the "Anecdotes and Reminiscences." But they were very careful not to let him see their designs, for in spite of his sixty-eight years, he could make the boldest of them uncomfortable under the steady regard of his piercing gray eyes.

Miss Lydia was a plump, little old maid of thirty-five, with smoothly drawn, tightly twisted hair that made her look still older. Old fashioned, too, she was; but ante-bellum glory did not radiate from her as it did from the major. She possessed a thrifty common sense; and it was she who handled the finances of the family, and met all comers when there were bills to pay. The major regarded board bills and wash bills as contemptible nuisances. They kept coming in so persistently and so often. Why, the major wanted to know, could they not be filed and paid in a lump sum at some convenient period—say when the "Anecdotes and Reminiscences" had been published and paid for? Miss Lydia would calmly go on with her sewing, and say, "We'll pay as we go as long as the money lasts, and then perhaps they'll have to lump it."

Most of Mrs. Vandeman's boarders were away during the day, being nearly all department clerks and business men; but there was one of them who was about the house a great deal from morning to night. This was a young man named Henry Hopkins Hargraves—every one in the house addressed him by his full name—who was engaged at one of the popular vaudeville theatres. Vaudeville has risen to such a respectable plane in the last few years, and Mr. Hargraves was such a modest and well-mannered person, that Mrs. Vardeman could find no objection to enrolling him upon her list of boarders.

At the theatre Hargraves was known as an all-round dialect comedian, having a large repertoire of German, Irish, Swede, and black-face specialties. But Mr. Hargraves was ambitious, and often spoke of his great desire to succeed in legitimate comedy.

This young man appeared to conceive a strong fancy for Major

Talbot. Whenever that gentleman would begin his Southern reminiscences, or repeat some of the liveliest of the ancedotes, Hargraves could always be found, the most attentive among his listeners.

For a time the major showed an inclination to discourage the advances of the "play actor," as he privately termed him; but soon the young man's agreeable manner and indubitable appreciation of the old gentleman's stories completely won him over.

It was not long before the two were like old chums. The major set apart each afternoon to read to him the manuscript of his book. During the anecdotes Hargraves never failed to laugh at exactly the right point. The major was moved to declare to Miss Lydia one day that young Hargraves possessed remarkable perception and a gratifying respect for the old regime. And when it came to talking of those old days—if Major Talbot liked to talk, Mr. Hargraves was entranced to listen.

Like almost all old people who talk of the past, the major loved to linger over details. In describing the splendid, almost royal, days of the old planters, he would hesitate until he had recalled the name of the Negro who held his horse, or the exact date of certain minor happenings, or the number of bales of cotton raised in such a year; but Hargraves never grew impatient or lost interest. On the contrary, he would advance questions on a variety of subjects connected with the life of that time, and he never failed to extract ready replies.

The fox hunts, the 'possum suppers, the hoe downs and jubilees in the Negro quarters, the banquets in the plantation-house hall, when invitations went to fifty miles around; the occasional feuds with the neighboring gentry; the major's duel with Rathbone Culbertson about Kitty Chalmers, who afterward married a Thwaite of South Carolina; and private yacht races for fabulous sums on Mobile Bay; the quaint beliefs, improvident habits, and loyal virtues of the old slaves—all these were subjects that held both the major and Hargraves absorbed for hours at a time.

Sometimes, at night, when the young man would be coming upstairs to his room after his turn at the theatre was over, the major would appear at the door of his study and beckon archly to him. Going in, Hargraves would find a little table set with a decanter, sugar bowl, fruit, and a big bunch of fresh green mint.

"It occurred to me," the major would begin—he was always ceremonious—"that perhaps you might have found your duties at the—at your place of occupation—sufficiently arduous to enable you, Mr.

Hargraves, to appreciate what the poet might well have had in his mind when he wrote, 'tired Nature's sweet restorer,'—one of our Southern juleps."

It was a fascination to Hargraves to watch him make it. He took rank among artists when he began, and he never varied the process. With what delicacy he bruised the mint; with what exquisite nicety he estimated the ingredients; with what solicitous care he capped the compound with the scarlet fruit glowing against the dark green fringe! And then the hospitality and grace with which he offered it, after the selected oat straws had been plunged into its tinkling depths!

After about four months in Washington, Miss Lydia discovered one morning that they were almost without money. The "Anecdotes and Reminiscences" was completed, but publishers had not jumped at the collected gems of Alabama sense and wit. The rental of a small house which they still owned in Mobile was two months in arrears. Their board money for the month would be due in three days. Miss Lydia called her father to a consultation.

"No money?" said he with a surprised look. "It is quite annoying to be called on so frequently for these petty sums. Really, I—"

The major searched his pockets. He found only a two-dollar bill, which he returned to his vest pocket.

"I must attend to this at once, Lydia," he said. "Kindly get me my umbrella and I will go down town immediately. The congressman from our district, General Fulghum, assured me some days ago that he would use his influence to get my book published at an early date. I will go to his hotel at once and see what arrangement has been made."

With a sad little smile Miss Lydia watched him button his "Father Hubbard" and depart, pausing at the door, as he always did, to bow profoundly.

That evening, at dark, he returned. It seemed that Congressman Fulghum had seen the publisher who had the major's manuscript for reading. That person had said that if the anecdotes, etc., were carefully pruned down about one half, in order to eliminate the sectional and class prejudice with which the book was dyed from end to end, he might consider its publication.

The major was in a white heat of anger, but regained his equanimity, according to his code of manners, as soon as he was in Miss Lydia's presence.

"We must have money," said Miss Lydia, with a little wrinkle above her nose. "Give me the two dollars, and I will telegraph to Uncle Ralph for some to-night."

The major drew a small envelope from his upper vest pocket and tossed it on the table.

"Perhaps it was injudicious," he said mildly, "but the sum was so merely nominal that I bought tickets to the theatre to-night. It's new war drama, Lydia. I thought you would be pleased to witness its first production in Washington. I am told that the South has very fair treatment in the play. I confess I should like to see the performance myself."

Miss Lydia threw up her hands in silent despair.

Still, as the tickets were bought, they might as well be used. So that evening, as they sat in the theatre listening to the lively overture, even Miss Lydia was minded to relegate their troubles, for the hour, to second place. The major, in spotless linen, with his extraordinary coat showing only where it was closely buttoned, and his white hair smoothly roached, looked really fine and distinguished. The curtain went up on the first act of "A Magnolia Flower," revealing a typical Southern plantation scene. Major Talbot betrayed some interest.

"Oh, see!" exclaimed Miss Lydia, nudging his arm, and pointing to his programme.

The major put on his glasses and read the line in the cast of characters that her finger indicated.

Col. Webster Calhoun. . . . H. Hopkins Hargraves.

"It's our Mr. Hargraves," said Miss Lydia. "It must be his first appearance in what he calls 'the legitimate.' I'm so glad for him."

Not until the second act did Col. Webster Calhoun appear upon the stage. When he made his entry Major Talbot gave an audible sniff, glared at him, and seemed to freeze solid. Miss Lydia uttered a little ambiguous squeak and crumpled her programme in her hand. For Colonel Calhoun was made up as nearly resembling Major Talbot as one pea does another. The long, thin, white hair, curly at the ends, the aristocratic beak of a nose, the crumpled, wide, ravelling shirt front, the string tie, with the bow nearly under one ear, were almost exactly duplicated. And then, to clinch the imitation, he wore the twin to the major's supposed to be unparalleled coat. High-collared, baggy, empire-waisted, ample-skirted, hanging a foot lower in front than behind, the garment could have been designed from no other pattern. From then on, the major and Miss Lydia sat bewitched, and saw the counterfeit presentment of a haughty Talbot "dragged," as the major afterward expressed it, "through the slanderous mire of a corrupt stage."

Mr. Hargraves had used his opportunities well. He had caught the major's little idiosyncrasies of speech, accent, and intonation and his pompous courtliness to perfection—exaggerating all to the purpose of the stage. When he performed that marvelous bow that the major fondly imagined to be the pink of all salutations, the audience sent forth a sudden round of hearty applause.

Miss Lydia sat immovable, not daring to glance toward her father. Sometimes her hand next to him would be laid against her cheek, as if to conceal the smile which, in spite of her disapproval, she could not entirely suppress.

The culmination of Hargrave's audacious imitation took place in the third act. The scene is where Colonel Calhoun entertains a few of the neighboring planters in his "den."

Standing at a table in the centre of the stage, with his friends grouped about him, he delivers that inimitable, rambling, character monologue so famous in "A Magnolia Flower," at the same time that he deftly makes juleps for the party.

Major Talbot, sitting quietly, but white with indignation, heard his best stories retold, his pet theories and hobbies advanced and expanded, and the dream of the "Anecdotes and Reminiscences" served, exaggerated and garbled. His favorite narrative—that of his duel with Rathbone Culbertson—was not omitted, and it was delivered with more fire, egotism, and gusto than the major himself put into it.

The monologue concluded with a quaint, delicious, witty little lecture on the art of concocting a julep, illustrated by the act. Here Major Talbot's delicate but showy science was reproduced to a hair's breadth—from his dainty handling of the fragrant weed—"the one-thousandth part of a grain too much pressure, gentlemen, and you extract the bitterness, instead of the aroma, of this heaven-bestowed plant"—to his solicitous selection of the oaten straws.

At the close of the scene the audience raised a tumultuous roar of appreciation. The portrayal of the type was so exact, so sure and thorough, that the leading characters in the play were forgotten. After repeated calls, Hargraves came before the curtain and bowed, his rather boyish face bright and flushed with the knowledge of success.

At last Miss Lydia turned and looked at the major. His thin nostrils were working like the gills of a fish. He laid both shaking hands upon the arms of his chair to rise.

"We will go, Lydia," he said, chokingly. "This is an abominable—desecration."

Before he could rise, she pulled him back into his seat.

"We will stay it out," she declared. "Do you want to advertise the copy by exhibiting the original coat?" So they remained to the end.

Hargraves's success must have kept him up late that night, for neither at the breakfast nor at the dinner table did he appear.

About three in the afternoon he tapped at the door of Major Talbot's study. The major opened it, and Hargraves walked in with his hands full of the morning papers—too full of his triumph to notice anything unusual in the major's demeanor.

"I put it all over 'em last night, major," he began, exultantly. "I had my inning, and, I think, scored. Here's what the *Post* says:

> "His conception and portrayal of the old-time Southern colonel, with his absurd grandiloquence, his eccentric garb, his quaint idioms and phrases, his moth-eaten pride of family, and his really kind heart, fastidious sense of honor, and lovable simplicity, is the best delineation of a character rôle on the boards to-day. The coat worn by Colonel Calhoun is itself nothing less than an evolution of genius. Mr. Hargraves has captured his public.

"How does that sound, major, for a first nighter?"

"I had the honor"—the major's voice sounded ominously frigid—"of witnessing your very remarkable performance, sir, last night."

Hargraves looked disconcerted.

"You were there? I didn't know you ever—I didn't know you cared for the theatre. Oh, I say, Major Talbot," he exclaimed, frankly, "don't you be offended. I admit I did get a lot of pointers from you that helped me out wonderfully in the part. But it's a type, you know—not individual. The way the audience caught on shows that. Half the patrons of that theatre are Southerners. They recognized it."

"Mr. Hargraves," said the major, who had remained standing, "you have put upon me an unpardonable insult. You have burlesqued my person, grossly betrayed my confidence, and misused my hospitality. If I thought you possessed the faintest conception of what is the sign manual of a gentleman, or what is due one, I would call you out, sir, old as I am. I will ask you to leave the room, sir."

The actor appeared to be slightly bewildered, and seemed hardly to take in the full meaning of the old gentleman's words.

"I am truly sorry you took offence," he said, regretfully. "Up here we don't look at things just as you people do. I know men who would buy out half the house to have their personality put on the stage so the public would recognize it."

"They are not from Alabama, sir," said the major, haughtily.

"Perhaps not. I have a pretty good memory, major; let me quote a few lines from your book. In response to a toast at a banquet given in Milledgeville, I believe—you uttered, and intend to have printed these words:

> "The Northern man is utterly without sentiment or warmth except in so far as the feelings may be turned to his own commercial profit. He will suffer without resentment any imputation cast upon the honor of himself or his loved ones that does not bear with it the consequence of pecuniary loss. In his charity, he gives with a liberal hand; but it must be heralded with the trumpet and chronicled in brass.

"Do you think that picture is fairer than the one you saw of Colonel Calhoun last night?"

"The description," said the major frowning, "is—not without grounds. Some exag—latitude must be allowed in public speaking."

"And in public acting," replied Hargraves.

"That is not the point," persisted the major, unrelenting. "It was a personal caricature. I positively decline to overlook it, sir."

"Major Talbot," said Hargraves, with a winning smile, "I wish you would understand me. I want you to know that I never dreamed of insulting you. In my profession, all life belongs to me. I take what I want, and what I can, and return it over the footlights. Now, if you will, let's let it go at that. I came in to see you about something else. We've been pretty good friends for some months, and I'm going to take the risk of offending you again. I know you are hard up for money—never mind how I found out; a boarding house is no place to keep such matters secret—and I want you to let me help you out of the pinch. I've been there often enough myself. I've been getting a fair salary all the season, and I've saved some money. You're welcome to a couple hundred—or even more—until you get—"

"Stop!" commanded the major, with his arm outstretched. "It seems that my book didn't lie, after all. You think your money salve will heal all the hurts of honor. Under no circumstances would I accept a loan from a casual acquaintance; and as to you, sir, I would starve before I would consider your insulting offer of a financial adjustment of the circumstances we have discussed. I beg to repeat my request relative to your quitting the apartment."

Hargraves took his departure without another word. He also left the house the same day, moving, as Mrs. Vardeman explained at the supper table, nearer the vicinity of the down-town theatre, where "A Magnolia Flower" was booked for a week's run.

Critical was the situation with Major Talbot and Miss Lydia. There was no one in Washington to whom the major's scruples allowed him to apply for a loan. Miss Lydia wrote a letter to Uncle Ralph, but it was doubtful whether that relative's constricted affairs would permit him to furnish help. The major was forced to make an apologetic address to Mrs. Vardeman regarding the delayed payment for board, referring to "delinquent rentals" and "delayed remittances" in a rather confused strain.

Deliverance came from an entirely unexpected source.

Late one afternoon the door maid came up and announced an old colored man who wanted to see Major Talbot. The major asked that he be sent up to his study. Soon an old darkey appeared in the doorway, with his hat in hand, bowing, and scraping with one clumsy foot. He was quite decently dressed in a baggy suit of black. His big, coarse shoes shone with a metallic lustre suggestive of stove polish. His bushy wool was gray—almost white. After middle life, it is difficult to estimate the age of a Negro. This one might have seen as many years as had Major Talbot.

"I be bound you don't know me, Mars' Pendleton," were his first words.

The major rose and came forward at the old, familiar style of address. It was one of the old plantation darkeys without a doubt; but they had been widely scattered, and he could not recall the voice or face.

"I don't believe I do," he said, kindly—"unless you will assist my memory."

"Don't you 'member Cindy's Mose, Mars' Pendleton, what 'migrated 'mediately after de war?"

"Wait a moment," said the major, rubbing his forehead with the tips of his fingers. He loved to recall everything connected with those beloved days. "Cindy's Mose," he reflected. "You worked among the horses—breaking the colts. Yes, I remember now. After the surrender, you took the name of—don't prompt me—Mitchell, and went to the West—to Nebraska."

"Yassir, yassir,"—the old man's face stretched with a delighted grin—"dat's him, dat's it. Newbraska. Dat's me—Mose Mitchell. Old Uncle Mose Mitchell, dey calls me now. Old mars', your pa, gimme a pah of dem mule colts when I lef' fur to staht me goin' with. You 'member dem colts, Mars' Pendleton?"

"I don't seem to recall the colts," said the major. "You know I was married the first year of the war and living at the old Follinsbee place. But sit down, sit down, Uncle Mose. I'm glad to see you. I hope you have prospered."

Uncle Mose took a chair and laid his hat carefully on the floor beside it.

"Yassir; of late I done mouty famous. When I first got to Newbraska, dey folks come all roun' me to see dem mule colts. Dey ain't see no mules like dem in Newbraska. I sold dem mules for three hundred dollars. Yassir—three hundred.

"Den I open a blacksmith shop, suh, and made some money and bought some lan'. Me and my old 'oman done raised up seb'm chillun, and all doin' well 'cept two of 'em what died. Fo' year ago a railroad come along and staht a town slam ag'inst my lan', and, suh, Mars' Pendleton, Uncle Mose am worth lem'm thousand dollars in money, property, and lan'."

"I'm glad to hear it," said the major heartily. "Glad to hear it."

"And dat little baby of yo'n, Mars' Pendleton—one what you name Miss Lyddy—I be bound dat little tad done growed up tell nobody wouldn't know her."

The major stepped to the door and called: "Lydia, dear, will you come?"

Miss Lydia, looking quite grown up and a little worried, came in from her room.

"Dar, now! What'd I tell you? I knowed dat baby be plum growed up. You don't 'member Uncle Mose, child?"

"This is Aunt Cindy's Mose, Lydia," explained the major. "He left Sunnymead for the West when you were two years old."

"Well," said Miss Lydia, "I can hardly be expected to remember you, Uncle Mose, at that age. And, as you say, I'm 'plum growed up,' and was a blessed long time ago. But I'm glad to see you, even if I can't remember you."

And she was. And so was the major. Something alive and tangible had come to link them with the happy past. The three sat and talked over the olden times, the major and Uncle Mose, correcting or prompting each other as they reviewed the plantation scenes and days.

The major inquired what the old man was doing so far from his home.

"Uncle Mose am a delicate," he explained, "to de grand Baptis' convention in dis city. I never preached none, but bein' a residin' elder in de church, and able fur to pay my own expenses, dey sent me along."

"And how did you know we were in Washington?" inquired Miss Lydia.

"Dey's a culluld man works in de hotel whar I stops, what comes from Mobile. He told me he seen Mars' Pendelton comin' outen dish here house one mawnin'.

"What I come fur," continued Uncle Mose, reaching into his pocket—"besides de sight of home folks—was to pay Mars' Pendleton what I owes him."

"Owe me?" said the major, in surprise.

"Yassir—three hundred dollars." He handed the major a roll of bills. "When I lef' old mars' says: 'Take dem mule colts, Mose, and, if it be so you gits able, pay fur 'em.' Yas sir—dem was his words. De war had done lef' old mars po' hisself. Old mars' bein' 'long ago dead, de debt descends to Mars' Pendleton. Three hundred dollars. Uncle Mose is plenty able to pay now. When dat railroad buy my lan' I laid off to pay for dem mules. Count de money, Mars' Pendleton. Dat's what I sold dem mules fur. Yassir."

Tears were in Major Talbot's eyes. He took Uncle Mose's hand and laid his other upon his shoulder.

"Dear, faithful old servitor," he said in an unsteady voice, "I don't mind saying to you that 'Mars' Pendleton' spent his last dollar in the world a week ago. We will accept this money, Uncle Mose, since, in a way, it is a sort of payment, as well as a token of the loyalty and devotion of the old régime. Lydia, my dear, take the money. You are better fitted than I to manage its expenditure."

"Take it, honey," said Uncle Mose. "Hit belongs to you. Hit's Talbot money."

After Uncle Mose had gone, Miss Lydia had a good cry—for joy; and the major turned his face to a corner, and smoked his clay pipe volcanically.

The succeeding days saw the Talbots restored to peace and ease. Miss Lydia's face lost its worried look. The major appeared in a new frock coat, in which he looked like a wax figure personifying the memory of his golden age. Another publisher who read the manuscript of the "Anecdotes and Reminiscences" thought that, with a little retouching and toning down of the high lights, he could make a really bright and salable volume of it. Altogether, the situation was comfortable, and not without the touch of hope that is often sweeter than arrived blessings.

One day, about a week after their piece of good luck, a maid brought a letter for Miss Lydia to her room. The postmark showed that it was from New York. Not knowing any one there, Miss Lydia, in a mild flutter of wonder, sat down by her table and opened the letter with her scissors. This was what she read:

Dear Miss Talbot:

I thought you might be glad to learn of my good fortune. I have received and accepted an offer of two hundred dollars per week by a New York stock company to play Colonel Calhoun in "A Magnolia Flower."

There is something else I wanted you to know. I guess you'd better not tell Major Talbot. I was anxious to make him some amends for the great help he was to me in studying the part, and for the bad humor he was in about it. He refused to let me, so I did it anyhow. I could easily spare the three hundred.

Sincerely yours,
H. Hopkins Hargraves

P.S. How did I play Uncle Mose?

Major Talbot, passing through the hall, saw Miss Lydia's door open and stopped.

"Any mail for us this morning, Lydia dear?" he asked.

Miss Lydia slid the letter beneath a fold of her dress.

"The *Mobile Chronicle* came," she said, promptly. "It's on the table in your study."

October and June

The Captain gazed gloomily at his sword that hung upon the wall. In the closet near by was stored his faded uniform, stained and worn by weather and service. What a long, long time it seemed since those old days of war's alarms!

And now, veteran that he was of his country's strenuous times, he had been reduced to abject surrender by a woman's soft eyes and smiling lips. As he sat in his quiet room he held in his hand the letter he had just received from her—the letter that had caused him to wear that look of gloom. He re-read the fatal paragraph that had destroyed his hope.

> In declining the honor you have done me in asking me to be your wife, I feel that I ought to speak frankly. The reason I have for so doing is the great difference between our ages. I like you very, very much, but I am sure that our marriage would not be a happy one. I am sorry to have to refer to this, but I believe that you will appreciate my honesty in giving you the true reason.

The Captain sighed, and leaned his head upon his hand. Yes, there were many years between their ages. But he was strong and rugged, he had position and wealth. Would not his love, his tender care, and the advantages he could bestow upon her make her forget the question of age? Besides, he was almost sure that she cared for him.

The Captain was a man of prompt action. In the field he had been distinguished for his decisiveness and energy. He would see her and plead his cause again in person. Age!—what was it to come between him and the one he loved?

In two hours he stood ready, in light marching order, for his greatest battle. He took the train for the old Southern town in Tennessee where she lived.

Theodora Deming was on the steps of the handsome, porticoed old mansion, enjoying the summer twilight, when the Captain entered the gate and came up the gravelled walk. She met him with a smile that was free from embarrassment. As the Captain stood on the step below her, the difference in their ages did not appear so great. He was tall and straight and clear-eyed and browned. She was in the bloom of lovely womanhood.

"I wasn't expecting you," said Theodora; "but now that you've come you may sit on the step. Didn't you get my letter?"

"I did," said the Captain, "and that's why I came. I say, now, Theo, reconsider your answer, won't you?"

Theodora smiled softly upon him. He carried his years well. She was really fond of his strength, his wholesome looks, his manliness—perhaps, if—

"No, no," she said, shaking her head, positively; "it's out of the question. I like you a whole lot, but marrying won't do. My age and yours are—but don't make me say it again—I told you in my letter."

The Captain flushed a little through the bronze on his face. He was silent for a while, gazing sadly into the twilight. Beyond a line of woods that he could see was a field where the boys in blue had once bivouacked on their march toward the sea. How long ago it seemed now! Truly, Fate and Father Time had tricked him sorely. Just a few years interposed between himself and happiness!

Theodora's hand crept down and rested in the clasp of his firm brown one. She felt, at least, that sentiment that is akin to love.

"Don't take it so hard, please," she said, gently. "It's all for the best. I've reasoned it out very wisely all by myself. Some day you'll be glad I didn't marry you. It would be very nice and lovely for a while—but, just think! In only a few short years what different tastes we would have. One of us would want to sit by the fireside and read, and maybe nurse neuralgia and rheumatism of evenings, while the other would be crazy for balls and theatres and late suppers. No, my dear friend. While it isn't exactly January and May, it's a clear case of October and pretty early in June."

"I'd always do what you wanted me to do, Theo. If you wanted to—"

"No, you wouldn't. You think now that you would, but you wouldn't. Please don't ask me any more."

The Captain had lost his battle. But he was a gallant warrior, and when he rose to make his final adieu his mouth was grimly set and his shoulders were squared.

He took the train for the North that night. On the next evening he was back in his room, where his sword was hanging against the wall. He was dressing for dinner, tying his white tie into a very careful bow. And at the same time he was indulging in a pensive soliloquy.

" 'Pon my honor, I believe Theo was right, after all. Nobody can deny that she's a peach, but she must be twenty-eight, at the very kindest calculation."

For you see, the Captain was only nineteen, and his sword had never been drawn except on the parade ground at Chattanooga, which was as near as he ever got to the Spanish-American War.

The Church with an Overshot-Wheel

Lakelands is not to be found in the catalogues of fashionable summer resorts. It lies on a low spur of the Cumberland range of mountains on a little tributary of the Clinch River. Lakelands proper is a contented village of two dozen houses situated on a forlorn, narrow-gauge railroad line. You wonder whether the railroad lost itself in the pine woods and ran into Lakelands from fright and lineliness, or whether Lakelands got lost and huddled itself along the railroad to wait for the cars to carry it home.

You wonder again why it was named Lakelands. There are no lakes, and the lands about are too poor to be worth mentioning.

Half a mile from the village stands the Eagle House, a big, roomy old mansion run by Josiah Rankin for the accommodation of visitors who desire the mountain air at inexpensive rates. The Eagle House is delightfully mismanaged. It is full of ancient instead of modern improvements, and it is altogether as comfortably neglected and pleasingly disarranged as your own home. But you are furnished with clean rooms and good and abundant fare: yourself and the piny woods must do the rest. Nature has provided a mineral spring, grape-vine swings, and croquet—even the wickets are wooden. You have Art to thank only for the fiddle-and-guitar music twice a week at the hop in the rustic pavilion.

The patrons of the Eagle House are those who seek recreation as a necessity, as well as a pleasure. They are busy people, who may be likened to clocks that need a fortnight's winding to insure a year's running their wheels. You will find students there from the lower towns, now and then an artist, or a geologist absorbed in construing the ancient strata of the hills. A few quiet families spend the summers there; and often one or two tired members of that patient sisterhood known to Lakelands as "schoolmarms."

A quarter of a mile from the Eagle House was what would have been described to its guests as "an object of interest" in a catalogue, had the Eagle House issued a catalogue. This was an old, old mill that was no longer a mill. In the words of Josiah Rankin, it was "the only church in the United States, sah, with a overshot-wheel; and the only mill in the world, sah, with pews and a pipe-organ." The guests of the Eagle House attended the old mill church each Sabbath, and heard the preacher liken the purified Christian to bolted flour ground to usefulness between the millstones of experience and suffering.

Every year about the beginning of autumn there came to the Eagle House one Abram Strong, who remained for a time an honored and beloved guest. In Lakelands he was called "Father Abram," because his hair was so white, his face so strong and kind and florid, his laugh so merry, and his black clothes and broad hat so priestly in appearance. Even new guests, after three or four days' acquaintance gave him this familiar title.

Father Abram came a long way to Lakelands. He lived in a big, roaring town in the northwest where he owned mills, not little mills with pews and an organ in them, but great, ugly, mountain-like mills that the freight trains crawled around all day like ants round an ant-heap. And now you must be told about Father Abram and the mill that was a church, for their stories run together.

In days when the church was a mill, Mr. Strong was the miller. There was no jollier, dustier, busier, happier miller in all the land than he. He lived in a little cottage across the road from the mill. His hand was heavy, but his toll was light, and the mountaineers brought their grain to him across many weary miles of rocky roads.

The delight of the miller's life was his little daughter, Aglaia. That was a brave name, truly, for a flaxen-haired toddler; but the mountaineers love sonorous and stately names. The mother had encountered it somewhere in a book, and the deed was done. In her babyhood Aglaia herself repudiated the name, as far as common use went, and persisted in calling herself "Dums." The miller and his wife often tried to coax from Aglaia the source of this mysterious name, but without results. At last they arrived at a theory. In the little garden behind the cottage was a bed for rhododendrons in which the child took a peculiar delight and interest. It may have been that she perceived in "Dums" a kinship to the formidable name of her favorite flowers.

When Aglaia was four years old she and her father used to go through a little performance in the mill every afternoon, that never failed to come off, the weather permitting. When supper was ready her mother would brush her hair and put on a clean apron and send her across to the mill to bring her father home. When the miller saw her coming in the mill door he would come forward, all white with the flour dust, and wave his hand and sing an old miller's song that was familiar in those parts and ran something like this:

"The wheel goes round,
The grist is ground,
The dusty miller's merry.
He sings all day,
His work is play,
While thinking of his dearie."

Then Aglaia would run to him laughing, and call: "Da-da, come take Dums home"; and the miller would swing her to his shoulder and march over to supper, singing the miller's song. Every evening this would take place.

One day, only a week after her fourth birthday, Aglaia disappeared. When last seen she was plucking wild flowers by the side of the road in front of the cottage. A little while later her mother went out to see that she did not stray too far away, and she was already gone.

Of course every effort was made to find her. The neighbors gathered and searched the woods and the mountains for miles around. They dragged every foot of the mill race and the creek for a long distance below the dam. Never a trace of her did they find. A night or two before there had been a family of wanderers camped in a grove near by. It was conjectured that they might have stolen the child; but when their wagon was overtaken and searched she could not be found.

The miller remained at the mill for nearly two years; and then his hope of finding her died out. He and his wife moved to the Northwest. In a few years he was the owner of a modern mill in one of the important milling cities in that region. Mrs. Strong never recovered from the shock caused by the loss of Aglaia, and two years after they moved away the miller was left to bear his sorrow alone.

When Abram Strong became prosperous he paid a visit to Lakelands and the old mill. The scene was a sad one for him, but he was a strong man, and always appeared cheery and kindly. It was then that he was inspired to convert the old mill into a church. Lakelands was too poor to build one; and the still poorer mountaineers could not assist. There was no place of worship nearer than twenty miles.

The miller altered the appearance of the mill as little as possible. The big overshot-wheel was left in its place. The young people who came to the church used to cut their initials in its soft and slowly decaying wood. The dam was partly destroyed, and the clear mountain stream rippled unchecked down its rocky bed. Inside the mill the changes were greater. The shafts and millstones and belt and pulleys were, of course, all removed. There were two rows of benches with aisles between, and a little raised platform and pulpit at one end. On three sides overhead was a gallery containing seats, and reached by a stairway inside. There was also an organ—a real pipe organ—in the gallery, that was the pride of the congregation of the Old Mill Church. Miss Phoebe Summers was the organist. The Lakelands boys proudly took turns at pumping it for her at each Sunday's service. The Rev. Mr. Bainbridge was the preacher, and rode down from Squirrel Gap on his old white horse without ever missing a service. And Abram Strong paid for everything. He paid the preacher five hundred dollars a year; and Miss Phoebe two hundred dollars.

Thus, in memory of Aglaia, the old mill was converted into a blessing for the community in which she had once lived. It seemed that the brief life of the child had brought about more good than the three score years and ten of many. But Abram Strong set up yet another monument to her memory.

Out from his mills in the Northwest came the "Aglaia" flour, made from the hardest and finest wheat that could be raised. The country soon found out that the "Aglaia" flour had two prices. One was the highest market price, and the other was—nothing.

Wherever there happened a calamity that left people destitute—a fire, a flood, a tornado, a strike, or a famine, there would go hurrying a generous consignment of the "Aglaia" at its "nothing" price. It was given away cautiously and judiciously, but it was freely given, and not a penny could the hungry ones pay for it. There got to be a saying that whenever there was a disastrous fire in the poor districts of a city the fire chief's buggy reached the scene first, next the "Aglaia" flour wagon, and then the fire engines.

So this was Abram Strong's other monument to Aglaia. Perhaps to a poet the theme may seem too utilitarian for beauty; but to some the fancy will seem sweet and fine that the pure, white, virgin flour, flying on its mission of love and charity, might be likened to the spirit of the lost child whose memory it signalized.

There came a year that brought hard times to the Cumberlands. Grain crops everywhere were light, and there were no local crops at all. Mountain floods had done much damage to property. Even game in the woods was so scarce that the hunters brought hardly enough home to keep their folks alive. Especially about Lakelands was the rigor felt.

As soon as Abram Strong heard of this his messages flew; and the little narrow-gauge cars began to unload "Aglaia" flour there. The miller's orders were to store the flour in the gallery of the Old Mill Church; and that every one who attended the Church was to carry home a sack of it.

Two weeks after that Abram Strong came for his yearly visit to the Eagle House, and became "Father Abram" again.

That season the Eagle House had fewer guests than usual. Among them was Rose Chester. Miss Chester came to Lakelands from Atlanta, where she worked in a department store. This was the first vacation outing of her life. The wife of the store manager had once spent a summer at the Eagle House. She had taken a fancy to Rose, and had persuaded her to go there for her three weeks' holiday. The manager's wife gave her a letter to Mrs. Rankin, who gladly received her in her own charge and care.

Miss Chester was not very strong. She was about twenty, and pale and delicate from an indoor life. But one week of Lakelands gave her a brightness and spirit that changed her wonderfully. The time was early September when the Cumberlands are at their greatest beauty. The mountain foliage was growing brilliant with autumnal colors; one breathed aerial champagne, the nights were deliciously cool, causing one to snuggle cosily under the warm blankets of the Eagle House.

Father Abram and Miss Chester became great friends. The old miller learned her story from Mrs. Rankin, and his interest went out quickly to the slender, lonely girl who was making her own way in the world.

The mountain country was new to Miss Chester. She had lived many years in the warm, flat town of Atlanta; and the grandeur and variety of the Cumberlands delighted her. She was determined to enjoy every moment of her stay. Her little hoard of savings had been estimated so carefully in connection with her expenses that she knew almost to a penny what her very small surplus would be when she returned to work.

Miss Chester was fortunate in gaining Father Abram for a friend and companion. He knew every road and peak and slope of the mountains near Lakelands. Through him she became acquainted with the solemn delight of the shadowy, tilted aisles of the pine forests, the dignity of the bare crags, the crystal, tonic mornings, the dreamy, golden afternoons full of mysterious sadness. So her health improved and her spirits grew light. She had a laugh as genial and hearty in its feminine way as the famous laugh of Father Abram. Both of them were natural optimists; and both knew how to present a serene and cheerful face to the world.

One day Miss Chester learned from one of the guests the history of Father Abram's lost child. Quickly she hurried away and found the miller seated on his favorite rustic bench near the chalybeate spring. He was surprised when his little friend slipped her hand into his, and looked at him with tears in her eyes.

"Oh, Father Abram," she said. "I'm so sorry! I didn't know until to-day about your little daughter. You will find her yet some day—Oh, I hope you will."

The miller looked down at her with his strong, ready smile.

"Thank you, Miss Rose," he said, in his usual cheery tones. "But I do not expect to find Aglaia. For a few years I hoped that she had been stolen by vagrants, and that she still lived; but I have lost that hope. I believe that she was drowned."

"I can understand," said Miss Chester, "how the doubt must have made it so hard to bear. And yet you are so cheerful and so ready to make other people's burden light. Good Father Abram!"

"Good Miss Rose!" mimicked the miller, smiling. "Who thinks of others more than you do?"

A whimsical mood seemed to strike Miss Chester.

"Oh, Father Abram," she cried, "wouldn't it be grand if I should prove to be your daughter? Wouldn't it be romantic? And wouldn't you like to have me for a daughter?"

"Indeed, I would," said the miller, heartily. "If Aglaia had lived I could wish for nothing better than for her to have grown up to be just such a little woman as you are. Maybe you are Aglaia," he continued, falling in with her playful mood; "can't you remember when we lived at the mill?"

Miss Chester fell swiftly into serious meditation. Her large eyes were fixed vaguely upon something in the distance. Father Abram was amused at her quick return to seriousness. She sat thus for a long time before she spoke.

"No," she said at length, with a long sigh, "I can't remember anything at all about a mill. I don't think that I ever saw a flour mill in my life until I saw your funny little church. And if I were your little girl I would remember it, wouldn't I? I'm so sorry, Father Abram."

"So am I," said Father Abram, humoring her. "But if you cannot remember that you are my little girl, Miss Rose, surely you can recollect being some one else's. You remember your own parents, of course."

"Oh, yes; I remember them very well—especially my father. He wasn't a bit like you, Father Abram. Oh, I was only making believe. Come, now, you've rested long enough. You promised to show me the pool where you can see the trout playing, this afternoon. I never saw a trout."

Late one afternoon Father Abram set out for the old mill alone. He often went to sit and think of the old days when he lived in the cottage across the road. Time had smoothed away the sharpness of his grief until he no longer found the memory of those times painful. But whenever Abram Strong sat in the melancholy September afternoons on the spot where "Dums" used to run in every day with her yellow curls flying, the smile that Lakelands always saw upon his face was not there.

The miller made his way slowly up the winding, steep road. The trees crowded so close to the edge of it that he walked in their shade, with his hat in his hand. Squirrels ran playfully upon the old rail fence at his right. Quails were calling to their young broods in the wheat stubble. The low sun sent a torrent of pale gold up the ravine that opened to the west. Early September!—it was within a few days only of the anniversary of Aglaia's disappearance.

The old overshot-wheel, half covered with mountain ivy, caught patches of the warm sunlight filtering through the trees. The cottage across the road was still standing, but it would doubtless go down before the next winter's mountain blasts. It was overrun with morning glory and wild gourd vines, and the door hung by one hinge.

Father Abram pushed open the mill door, and entered softly. And then he stood still, wondering. He heard the sound of some one within, weeping inconsolably. He looked, and saw Miss Chester sitting in a dim pew, with her head bowed upon an open letter that her hands held.

Father Abram went to her, and laid one of his strong hands firmly upon hers. She looked up, breathed his name and tried to speak further.

"Not yet, Miss Rose," said the miller kindly. "Don't try to talk yet. There's nothing as good for you as a nice, quiet little cry when you are feeling blue."

It seemed that the old miller, who had known so much sorrow himself, was a magician in driving it away from others. Miss Chester's sobs grew easier. Presently she took her little plain-bordered handkerchief and wiped away a drop or two that had fallen from her eyes upon Father Abram's big hand. Then she looked up and smiled through her tears. Miss Chester could always smile before her tears had dried, just as Father Abram could smile through his own grief. In that way the two were very much alike.

The miller asked her no questions; but by and by Miss Chester began to tell him.

It was the old story that always seems so big and important to the young, and that brings reminiscent smiles to their elders. Love was the theme, as may be supposed. There was a young man in Atlanta, full of all goodness and the graces, who had discovered that Miss Chester also possessed these qualities above all other people in Atlanta or anywhere else from Greenland to Patagonia. She showed Father Abram the letter over which she had been weeping. It was a manly, tender letter, a little superlative and urgent, after the style of love letters written by young men full of goodness and the graces. He proposed for Miss Chester's hand in marriage at once. Life, he said, since her departure for a three weeks' visit, was not to be endured. He begged for an immediate answer; and if it were favorable he promised to fly, ignoring the narrow-gauge railroad, at once to Lakelands.

"And now where does the trouble come in?" asked the miller when he had read the letter.

"I cannot marry him," said Miss Chester.

"Do you want to marry him?" asked Father Abram.

"Oh, I love him," she answered, "but—" Down went her head and she sobbed again.

"Come, Miss Rose," said the miller; "you can give me your confidence. I do not question you, but I think you can trust me."

"I do trust you," said the girl. "I will tell you why I must refuse Ralph. I am nobody; I haven't even a name; the name I call myself is a lie. Ralph is a noble man. I love him with all my heart, but I can never be his."

"What talk is this?" said Father Abram. "You said that you remember your parents. Why do you say that you have no name? I do not understand."

"I do remember them," said Miss Chester. "I remember them too well. My first recollections are of our life somewhere in the far South. We moved many times to different towns and states. I have picked cotton, and worked in factories, and have often gone without enough food and clothes. My mother was sometimes good to me; my father was always cruel, and beat me. I think they were both idle and unsettled.

"One night when we were living in a little town on a river near

Atlanta they had a great quarrel. It was while they were abusing and taunting each other that I learned—oh, Father Abram, I learned that I didn't even have the right to be—don't you understand? I had no right even to a name; I was nobody.

"I ran away that night. I walked to Atlanta and found work. I gave myself the name of Rose Chester, and have earned my own living ever since. Now you know why I cannot marry Ralph—and, oh, I can never tell him why."

Better than any sympathy, more helpful than pity, was Father Abram's depreciation of her woes.

"Why, dear! is that all?" he said. "Fie, fie! I thought something was in the way. If this perfect young man is a man at all he will not care a pinch of bran for your family tree. Dear Miss Rose, take my word for it, it is yourself he cares for. Tell him frankly, just as you have told me and I'll warrant that he will laugh at your story, and think all the more of you for it."

"I shall never tell him," said Miss Chester, sadly, "and I shall never marry him nor any one else. I have not the right."

But they saw a long shadow come bobbing up the sunlit road. And then came a shorter one bobbing by its side; and presently two strange figures approached the church. The long shadow was made by Miss Phoebe Summers, the organist, come to practice. Tommy Teague, aged twelve, was responsible for the shorter shadow. It was Tommy's day to pump the organ for Miss Phoebe, and his bare toes proudly spurned the dust of the road.

Miss Phoebe, in her lilac-spray chintz dress; with her accurate little curls hanging over each ear, courtsied low to Father Abram, and shook her curls ceremoniously at Miss Chester. Then she and her assistant climbed the steep stairway to the organ loft.

In the gathering shadows below, Father Abram and Miss Chester lingered. They were silent; and it is likely that they were busy with their memories. Miss Chester sat, leaning her head on her hand, with her eyes fixed far away. Father Abram stood in the next pew, looking thoughtfully out of the door at the road and the ruined cottage.

Suddenly the scene was transformed for him back almost a score of years into the past. For, as Tommy pumped away, Miss Phoebe struck a low bass note on the organ and held it to test the volume of air that it contained. The church ceased to exist, so far as Father Abram was concerned. The deep, booming vibration that shook the little frame building was no note from an organ, but the humming of the mill machinery. He felt sure that the old overshot-wheel was turning;

that he was back again, a dusty, merry miller in the old mountain mill. And now evening was come, and soon would come Aglaia with flying colors, toddling across the road to take him home to supper. Father Abram's eyes were fixed upon the broken door of the cottage.

And then came another wonder. In the gallery overhead the sacks of flour were stacked in long rows. Perhaps a mouse had been at one of them; anyway, the jar of the deep organ note shook down between the cracks of the gallery floor a stream of flour, covering Father Abram from head to foot with the white dust. And then the old miller stepped into the aisle, and waved his arms and began to sing the miller's song:

"The wheel goes round,
The grist is ground,
The dusty miller's merry."

—and then the rest of the miracle happened. Miss Chester was leaning forward from her pew, as pale as the flour itself, her wide-open eyes staring at Father Abram like one in a waking dream. When he began the song she stretched out her arms to him; her lips moved; she called to him in dreamy tones: "Da-da, come take Dums home!"

Miss Phoebe released the low key of the organ. But her work had been well done. The note that she struck had beaten down the doors of a closed memory; and Father Abram held his lost Aglaia close in his arms.

When you visit Lakelands they will tell you more of this story. They will tell you how the lines of it were afterward traced, and the history of the miller's daughter revealed after the gipsy wanderers had stolen her on that September day, attracted by her childish beauty. But you should wait until you sit comfortably on the shaded porch of the Eagle House, and then you can have the story at your ease. It seems best that our part of it should close while Miss Phoebe's deep bass note was yet reverberating softly.

And yet, to my mind, the finest thing of it all happened while Father Abram and his daughter were walking back to the Eagle House in the long twilight, almost too glad to speak.

"Father," she said, somewhat timidly and doubtfully, "have you a great deal of money?"

"A great deal?" said the miller. "Well, that depends. There is plenty unless you want to buy the moon or something equally expensive."

"Would it cost very, very much," asked Aglaia, who had always counted her dimes so carefully, "to send a telegram to Atlanta?"

"Ah," said Father Abram, with a little sigh, "I see. You want to ask Ralph to come."

"I want to ask him to wait," she said. "I have just found my father, and I want it to be just two for a while. I want to tell him he will have to wait."

The Atavism of John Tom Little Bear

I saw a light in Jeff Peters's room over the Red Front Drug Store. I hastened toward it, for I had not known that Jeff was in town. He is a man of the Hadji breed, of a hundred occupations, with a story to tell (when he will) of each one.

I found Jeff repacking his grip for a run down to Florida to look at an orange grove for which he had traded, a month before, his mining claim on the Yukon. He kicked me a chair, with the same old humorous, profound smile on his seasoned countenance. It had been eight months since we had met, but his greeting was such as men pass from day to day. Time is Jeff's servant, and the continent is a big lot across which he cuts to his many roads.

For a while we skirmished along the edges of unprofitable talk which culminated in that unquiet problem of the Philippines.

"All them tropical races," said Jeff, "could be run out better with their own jockeys up. The tropical man knows what he wants. All he wants is a season ticket to the cock-fights and a pair of Western Union climbers to go up the bread-fruit tree. The Anglo-Saxon man wants him to learn to conjugate and wear suspenders. He'll be happiest in his own way."

I was shocked.

"Education, man," I said, "is the watchword. In time they will rise to our standard of civilization. Look at what education has done for the Indian."

"O-ho!" sang Jeff, lighting his pipe (which was a good sign). "Yes, the Indian! I'm looking. I hasten to contemplate the redman as a standard bearer of progress. He's the same as the other brown boys. You can't make an Anglo-Saxon of him. Did I ever tell you about the time my friend John Tom Little Bear bit off the right ear of the arts of culture and education and spun the teetotum back round to where it was when Columbus was a little boy? I did not?

"John Tom Little Bear was an educated Cherokee Indian and an old friend of mine when I was in the Territories. He was a graduate of one of them Eastern football colleges that have been so successful in teaching the Indian to use the gridiron instead of burning his victims at the stake. As an Anglo-Saxon, John Tom was copper-colored in spots. As an Indian, he was one of the whitest men I ever knew. As a Cherokee, he was a gentleman on the first ballot. As a ward of the nation, he was mighty hard to carry at the primaries.

"John Tom and me got together and began to make medicine—how to get up some lawful, genteel swindle which we might work in a quiet way so as not to excite the stupidity of the police or the cupidity of the larger corporations. We had close upon $500 between us, and we pined to make it grow, as all respectable capitalists do.

"So we figured out a proposition which seems to be as honorable as a gold mine prospectus and as profitable as a church raffle. And inside of thirty days you find us swarming into Kansas with a pair of fluent horses and a red camping wagon on the European plan. John Tom is Chief Wish-Heap-Dough, the famous Indian medicine man and Samaritan Sachem of the Seven Tribes. Mr. Peters is business manager and half owner. We needed a third man, so we looked around and found J. Conyngham Binkly leaning against the want column of a newspaper. This Binkly has a disease for Shakespearian rôles, and an hallucination about a 200 nights' run on the New York stage. But he confesses that he never could earn the butter to spread on his William S. rôles, so he is willing to drop to the ordinary baker's kind, and be satisfied with a 200-mile run behind the medicine ponies. Besides Richard III, he could do twenty-seven coon songs and banjo specialties, and was willing to cook, and curry the horses. We carried a fine line of excuses for taking money. One was a magic soap for removing grease spots and quarters from clothes. One was a Sum-wah-tah, the great Indian Remedy made from a prairie herb revealed by the Great Spirit in a dream to his favorite medicine men, the great chiefs McGarrity and Siberstein, bottlers, Chicago. And the other was a frivolous system of pick-pocketing the Kansasters that had the department stores reduced to a decimal fraction. Look ye! A pair of silk garters, a dream book, one dozen clothespins, a gold tooth, and 'When Knighthood Was in Flower' all wrapped up in a genuine Japanese silkarina handkerchief and handed to the handsome lady by

Mr. Peters for the trivial sum of fifty cents, while Professor Binkly entertains us in a three-minute round with the banjo.

" 'Twas an eminent graft we had. We ravaged peacefully through the State, determined to remove all doubt as to why 'twas called bleeding Kansas. John Tom Little Bear, in full Indian chief's costume, drew crowds away from the parchesi sociables and government ownership conversaziones. While at the football college in the East he had acquired quantities of rhetoric and the art of calisthenics and sophistry in his classes, and when he stood up in the red wagon and explained to the farmers, eloquent, about chilblains and hyperaesthesia of the cranium, Jeff couldn't hand out the Indian Remedy fast enough for 'em.

"One night we was camped on the edge of a little town out west of Salina. We always camped near a stream, and put up a little tent. Sometimes we sold out of the Remedy unexpected, and then Chief Wish-Heap-Dough would have a dream in which the Manitou commanded him to fill up a few bottles of Sum-wah-tah at the most convenient place. 'Twas about ten o'clock, and we'd just got in from a street performance. I was in the tent with a lantern, figuring up the day's profits. John Tom hadn't taken off his Indian make-up, and was sitting by the campfire minding a fine sirloin steak in the pan for the Professor till he finished his hair-raising scene with the trained horses.

"All at once out of dark bushes comes a pop like a fire-cracker, and John Tom gives a grunt and digs out of his bosom a little bullet that has dented itself against his collar-bone. John Tom makes a dive in the direction of the fireworks, and comes back dragging by the collar a kid about nine or ten years young, in a velveteen suit, with a little nickel-mounted rifle in his hand about as big as a fountain-pen.

" 'Here, you papoose,' says John Tom, 'what are you gunning for with that howitzer? You might hit somebody in the eye. Come out, Jeff, and mind the steak. Don't let it burn, while I investigate this demon with the pea shooter.'

" 'Cowardly redskin,' says the kid like he was quoting from a favorite author. 'Dare to burn me at the stake and the paleface will sweep you from the prairies like—like everything. Now, you lemme go, or I'll tell mamma.'

"John Tom plants the kid on a camp-stool, and sits down by him. 'Now, tell the big chief,' he says, 'why you try to shoot pellets into your Uncle John's system. Didn't you know it was loaded?'

" 'Are you a Indian?' asks the kid, looking up cute as you please at John Tom's buckskin and eagle feathers. 'I am,' says John Tom. 'Well, then, that's why,' answered the boy, swinging his feet. I nearly let the steak burn watching the nerve of the youngster.

" 'Oh-ho!' says John Tom, 'I see. You're the Boy Avenger. And you've sworn to rid the continent of the savage redman. Is that about the way of it, son?'

"The kid halfway nodded his head. And then he looked glum. 'Twas indecent to wring his secret from his bosom before a single brave had fallen before his parlor-rifle.

" 'Now, tell us where your wigwam is, papoose,' says John Tom— 'where you live? Your mamma will be worrying about your being out so late. Tell me, and I'll take you home.'

"The kid grins. 'I guess not,' he says, 'I live thousands and thousands of miles over there.' He gyrated his hand toward the horizon. 'I come on the train,' he says, 'by myself. I got off here because the conductor said my ticket had ex-pirated.' He looks at John Tom with a sudden suspicion. 'I bet you ain't a Indian,' he says. 'You don't talk like a Indian. You look like one, but all a Indian can say is "heap good" and "paleface die." Say, I bet you are one of them make-believe Indians that sell medicine on the streets. I saw one once in Quincy.'

" 'You never mind,' says John Tom, 'whether a cigar-sign or a Tammany cartoon. The question before the council is what's to be done with you. You've run away from home. You've been reading Howells. You've disgraced the profession of boy avengers by trying to shoot a tame Indian, and never saying: "Die, dog of a redskin! You have crossed the path of the Boy Avenger nineteen times too often." What do you mean by it?'

"The kid thought for a minute. 'I guess I made a mistake,' he says. 'I ought to have gone farther west. They find 'em wild out there in the cañons.' He holds out his hand to John Tom, the little rascal. 'Please excuse me, sir,' says he, 'for shooting at you. I hope it didn't hurt you. But you ought to be more careful. When a scout sees a Indian in his war-dress, his rifle must speak.' Little Bear gave a big laugh with a whoop at the end of it, and swings the kid ten feet high and sets him on his shoulder, and the runaway fingers the fringe and the eagle feathers and is full of the joy the white man knows when he dangles his heels against an inferior race. It is plain that Little Bear and that kid are chums from that on. The little renegade has already smoked the pipe of peace with the savage; and you can see in his eye that he is figuring on a tomahawk and a pair of moccasins, children's size.

"We have supper in the tent. The youngster looks upon me and the Professor as ordinary braves, only intended as background to the camp scene. When he is seated on a box of Sum-wah-tah, with the edge of the table sawing his neck, and his mouth full of beefsteak, Little Bear calls for his name, 'Roy,' says the kid, with a sirloiny sound to it. But when the rest of it, and his post-office address is referred to, he shakes his head. 'I guess not,' he says. 'You'll send me back. I want to stay with you. I like this camping out. At home, we fellows had a camp in our back yard. They called me Roy, the Red Wolf! I guess that'll do for a name. Gimme another piece of beefsteak, please.'

"We had to keep that kid. We knew there was a hullabaloo about him somewheres, and that Mamma, and Uncle Harry, and Aunt Jane, and the Chief of Police were hot after finding his trail, but not another word would he tell us. In two days he was the mascot of the Big Medicine outfit, and all of us had a sneaking hope that his owners wouldn't turn up. When the red wagon was doing business he was in it, and passed up the bottles to Mr. Peters as proud and satisfied as a prince that's abjured a two-hundred-dollar crown for a million-dollar parvenuess. Once John Tom asked him something about his papa. 'I ain't got any papa,' he says. 'He runned away and left us. He made my mamma cry. Aunt Lucy says he's a shape.' 'A what?' somebody asks him. 'A shape,' says the kid; 'some kind of a shape—lemme see—oh, yes, a feendenuman shape. I don't know what it means.' John Tom was for putting our brand on him, and dressing him up like a little chief, with wampum and beads, but I vetoes it. 'Somebody's lost that kid, is my view of it, and they may want him. You let me try him with a few stratagems, and see if I can't get a look at his visiting-card.'

"So that night I goes up to Mr. Roy Blank by the camp-fire, and looks at him contemptuous and scornful. 'Snickenwitzel!' says I, like the word made me sick; 'Snickenwitzel! Bah! Before I'd be named Snickenwitzel!'

" 'What's the matter with you, Jeff?' says the kid, opening his eyes wide.

" 'Snickenwitzel!' I repeats, and I spat the word out. 'I saw a man today from your town and he told me your name. I'm not surprised you was ashamed to tell it. Snickenwitzel! Whew!'

" 'Ah, here, now,' says the boy, indignant and wriggling all over, 'what's the matter with you? That ain't my name. It's Conyers. What's the matter with you?'

" 'And that's not the worst of it,' I went on quick, keeping him hot and not giving him time to think. 'We thought you was from a nice, well-to-do family. Here's Mr. Little Bear, a chief of the Cherokee, entitled to wear nine otter tails on his Sunday blanket, and Professor Binkly, who plays Shakespeare and the banjo, and me, that's got hundreds of dollars in that black tin box in the wagon, and we've got to be careful about the company we keep. That man tells me your folks live 'way down in little old Hencoop Alley, where there are no sidewalks, and the goats eat off the table with you.'

"That kid was almost crying now. ' 'Tain't so,' he splutters. 'He—he don't know what he's talking about. We live on Poplar Av'noo. I don't 'sociate with goats. What's the matter with you?'

" 'Poplar Avenue,' says I, sarcastic. 'Poplar Avenue! That's a street to live on! It only runs two blocks and then falls off a bluff. You can throw a keg of nails the whole length of it. Don't talk to me about Poplar Avenue.'

" 'It's—it's miles long,' says the kid. 'Our number's 862 and there are lots of houses after that. What's the matter with—aw, you make me tired, Jeff.'

" 'Well, well, now' says I. 'I guess that man made a mistake. Maybe it was some other boy he was talking about. If I catch him I'll teach him to go around slandering people.' And after supper I goes up town and telegraphs to Mrs. Conyers, 862 Poplar Avenue, Quincy, Ill., that the kid is safe and sassy with us, and will be held for further orders. In two hours an answer comes to hold him tight, and she'll start for him by next train.

"The next train was due at 6 P.M. the next day, and me and John Tom was at the depot with the kid. You might scour the plains in vain for the big Chief Wish-Heap-Dough. In his place is Mr. Little Bear, in the human habiliments of the Anglo-Saxon sect; and the leather of his shoes is patented and the loop of his necktie is copyrighted. For these things John Tom had grafted on him at college along with metaphysics and the knockout guard for the low tackle. But for his complexion, which is some yellowish, and the black mop of his straight hair, you might have thought here was an ordinary man out of the city directory that subscribes for magazines and pushes the lawn-mower in his shirt-sleeves of evenings.

"Then the train rolled in, and a little woman in a gray dress, with sort of illuminating hair, slides off and looks around quick. And the

Boy Avenger sees her, and yells 'Mamma,' and she cries 'O!' and they meet in a clinch, and now the pesky redskin can come forth from their caves on the plains without fear any more of the rifle of Roy, the Red Wolf. Mrs. Conyers comes up and thanks me an' John Tom without the usual extremities you always look for in a woman. She says just enough, in a way to convince, and there is no incidental music by the orchestra. I made a few illiterate requisitions upon the art of conversation, at which the lady smiles friendly, as if she had known me a week. And then Mr. Little Bear adorns the atmosphere with the various idioms into which education can fracture the wind of speech. I could see the kid's mother didn't quite place John Tom; but it seemed she was apprised of his dialects, and she played up to his lead in the science of making three words do the work of one.

"That kid introduced us, with some footnotes and explanations that made things plainer than a week of rhetoric. He danced around, and punched us in the back, and tried to climb John Tom's leg. 'This is John Tom, mamma,' says he. 'He's an Indian. He sells medicine in a red wagon. I shot him, but he wasn't wild. The other one's Jeff. He's a fakir, too. Come on and see the camp where we live, won't you, mamma?'

"It is plain to see that the life of the woman is in that boy. She has got him again where her arms can gather him, and that's enough. She's ready to do anything to please him. She hesitates the eighth of a second and takes another look at these men. I imagine she says to herself about John Tom, 'Seems to be a gentleman, if his hair don't curl.' And Mr. Peters she disposes of as follows: 'No ladies' man, but a man who knows a lady.'

"So we all rambled down to the camp as neighborly as coming from a wake. And there she inspects the wagon and pats the place with her hand where the kid used to sleep, and dabs around her eyewinkers with her handkerchief. And Professor Binkly gives us 'Trovatore' on one string of the banjo, and is about to slide off into Hamlet's monologue when one of the horses gets tangled in his rope and he must go look after him, and says something about 'foiled again.'

"When it got dark me and John Tom walked back to the Corn Exchange Hotel, and the four of us had supper there. I think the trouble started at that supper, for then was when Mr. Little Bear made an intellectual balloon ascension. I held on to the tablecloth, and listened to him soar. That redman, if I could judge, had the gift of information. He took languages, and did with it all a Roman can do with macaroni. His vocal remarks was all embroidered over with the most scholarly verbs and prefixes. And his syllables was smooth, and fitted nicely to the joints of his idea. I thought I'd heard him talk before, but I hadn't. And it wasn't the size of his words, but the way they come; and 'twasn't his subjects, for he spoke of common things like cathedrals and football and poems and catarrh and souls and freight rates and sculpture. Mrs. Conyers understood his accents, and the elegant sounds went back and forth between 'em. And now and then Jefferson D. Peters would intervene a few shopworn, senseless words to have the butter passed or another leg of the chicken.

"Yes, John Tom Little Bear appeared to be inveigled some in his bosom about that Mrs. Conyers. She was the kind that pleases. She had the good looks and more, I'll tell you. You take one of those cloak models in a big store. They strike you as being on the impersonal system. They are adapted for the eye. What they run to is inches around and complexion, and the art of fanning the delusion that the sealskin would look just as well on the lady with the warts and the pocket-book. Now, if one of them models was off duty, and you took it, and it would say 'Charlie' when you pressed it, and sit up at the table, why, then you would have something similar to Mrs. Conyers. I could see how John Tom could resist any inclination to hate that white squaw.

"The lady and the kid stayed at the hotel. In the morning, they say, they will start for home. Me and Little Bear left at eight o'clock, and sold Indian Remedy on the courthouse square till nine. He leaves me and the Professor to drive down to camp, while he stays up town. I am not enamored with that plan, for it shows John Tom is uneasy in his composures, and that leads to fire-water, and sometimes to the green-corn dance and costs. Not often does Chief Wish-Heap-Dough get busy with the firewater, but whenever he does there is heap much doing in the lodges of the palefaces who wear blue and carry the club.

"At half-past nine Professor Binkly is rolled in his quilt snoring in blank verse, and I am sitting by the fire listening to the frogs. Mr. Little Bear slides into camp and sits down against a tree. There is no symptoms of firewater.

" 'Jeff,' says he, after a long time, 'a little boy came West to hunt Indians.'

" 'Well, then?' says I, for I wasn't thinking as he was.

" 'And he bagged one,' says John Tom, 'and 'twas not with a gun, and he never had on a velveteen suit of clothes in his life.' And then I began to catch his smoke.

" 'I know it,' says I. 'And I'll bet you his pictures are on valentines, and fool men are his game, red and white.'

" 'You win on the red,' says John Tom, calm. 'Jeff, for how many ponies do you think I could buy Mrs. Conyers?'

" 'Scandalous talk!' I replies. ' 'Tis not a paleface custom.' John Tom laughs loud and bites into his cigar. 'No,' he answers; ' 'tis the savage equivalent for the dollars of the white man's marriage settlement. Oh, I know. There's an eternal wall between the races. If I could do it, Jeff, I'd put a torch to every white college that a redman has ever set foot inside. Why don't you leave us alone,' he says, 'to our own ghost-dances and dog-feasts and our dingy squaws to cook our grass-hopper soup and darn our moccasins?'

" 'Now, you don't mean disrespect to the perennial blossom entitled education?' says I, scandalized, 'because I wear it in the bosom of my own intellectual shirtwaist. I've had education,' says I, 'and never took any harm from it.'

" 'You lasso us,' goes on Little Bear, not noticing my prose insertions, 'and teach us what is beautiful in literature and life, and how to appreciate what is fine in men and women. What have you done to me?' says he. 'You've made me a Cherokee Moses. You've taught me to hate the wigwams and love the white man's ways. I can look over into the promised land and see Mrs. Conyers, but my place is—on the reservation.'

"Little Bear stands up in his chief's dress, and laughs again. 'But, white man Jeff,' he goes on, 'the paleface provides a recourse. 'Tis a temporary one, but it gives a respite and the name of it is whiskey.' And straight off he walks up the path to town again. 'Now,' says I in my mind, 'may the Manitou move him to do only bailable things this night!' For I perceive that John Tom is about to avail himself of the white man's solace.

"Maybe it was 10:30, as I sat smoking, when I hear pit-a-pats on the path, and here comes Mrs. Conyers running, her hair twisted up any way, and a look on her face that says burglars and mice and the flour's-all-out rolled in one. 'Oh, Mr. Peters,' she calls out, as they will, 'oh, oh!' I made a quick think, and I spoke the gist of it out loud. 'Now,' says I, 'we've been brothers, me and that Indian, but I'll make a good one of him in two minutes if—'

" 'No, no,' she says, wild and cracking her knuckles. 'I haven't seen Mr. Little Bear. 'Tis my—husband. He's stolen my boy. Oh,' she says, 'just when I had him back in my arms again! That heartless villain! Every bitterness life knows,' she says, 'he's made me drink.

My poor little lamb, that ought to be warm in his bed, carried off by that fiend!'

" 'How did all this happen?' I ask. 'Let's have the facts.'

" 'I was fixing his bed,' she explains, 'and Roy was playing on the hotel porch and he drives up to the steps. I heard Roy scream, and ran out. My husband had him in the buggy then. I begged him for my child. This is what he gave me.' She turns her face to the light. There is a crimson streak running across her cheek and mouth. 'He did that with his whip,' she says.

" 'Come back to the hotel,' says I, 'and we'll see what can be done.'

"On the way she tells me some of the wherefores. When he slashed her with the whip he told her he found out she was coming for the kid, and he was on the same train. Mrs. Conyers had been living with her brother, and they'd watched the boy always, as her husband had tried to steal him before. I judge that man was worse than a street railway promoter. It seems he had spent her money and slugged her and killed her canary bird, and told it around that she had cold feet.

"At the hotel we found a mass meeting of five infuriated citizens chewing tobacco and denouncing the outrage. Most of the town was asleep by ten o'clock. I talks to the lady some quiet, and tells her I will take the one o'clock train for the next town, forty miles east, for it is likely that the esteemed Mr. Conyers will drive there to take the cars. 'I don't know,' I tells her, 'but what he has legal rights; but if I find him I can give him an illegal left in the eye, and tie him up for a day or two, anyhow, on a disturbal of the peace proposition.'

"Mrs. Conyers goes inside and cries with the landlord's wife, who is fixing some catnip tea that will make everything all right for the poor dear. The landlord comes out on the porch, thumbing his one suspender, and says to me:

" 'Ain't had so much excitement in town since Bedford Steegall's wife swallowed a spring lizard. I seen him through the winder hit her with the buggy whip, and everything. What's that suit of clothes cost you you got on? 'Pears like we'd have some rain, don't it? Say, doc, that Indian of yorn's on a kind of a whizz to-night, ain't he? He comes along just before you did, and I told him about this here occurrence. He gives a cur'us kind of a hoot, and trotted off. I guess our constable'll have him in the lock-up 'fore morning.'

"I thought I'd sit on the porch and wait for the one o'clock train. I wasn't feeling saturated with mirth. Here was John Tom on one of his sprees, and this kidnapping business losing sleep for me. But then, I'm always having trouble with other people's trouble. Every few minutes Mrs. Conyers would come out on the porch and look down the road the way the buggy went, like she expected to see that kid coming back on a white pony with a red apple in his hand. Now, wasn't that like a woman? And that brings up cats. 'I saw a mouse go in this hole,' says Mrs. Cat; 'you can go prize up a plant over there if you like; I'll watch this hole.'

"About a quarter to one o'clock the lady comes out again, restless, crying easy, as females do for their own amusement, and she looks down that road again and listens. 'Now, ma'am,' says I, 'there's no use watching cold wheel-tracks. By this time they're halfway to—' 'Hush,' she says, holding up her hand. And I do hear something coming 'flip-flap' in the dark; and then there is the awfullest war-whoop ever heard outside of Madison Square Garden at a Buffalo Bill matinée. And up the steps and on to the porch jumps the disrespectable Indian. The lamp in the hall shines on him, and I fail to recognize Mr. J. T. Little Bear, alumnus of the class of '91. What I see is a Cherokee brave, and the warpath is what he has been traveling. Firewater and other things have got him going. His buckskin is hanging in strings, and his feathers are mixed up like a frizzly hen's. The dust of miles is on his moccasins, and the light in his eye is the kind the aborigines wear. But in his arms he brings that kid, his eyes half closed, with his little shoes dangling and one hand fast around the Indian's collar.

" 'Papoose!' says John Tom, and I notice that the flowers of the white man's syntax have left his tongue. He is the original proposition in bear's claws and copper color. 'Me bring,' says he, and he lays the kid in his mother's arms. 'Run fifteen mile,' says John Tom—'Ugh! Catch white man. Bring papoose.'

"The little woman is in extremities of gladness. She must wake up that stir-up trouble youngster and hug him and make proclamation that he is his mamma's own precious treasure. I was about to ask questions, but I looked at Mr. Little Bear, and my eye caught the sight of something in his belt. 'Now go to bed, ma'am,' says I, 'and this gadabout youngster likewise, for there's no more danger, and the kidnapping business is not what it was earlier in the night.'

"I inveigled John Tom down to camp quick, and when he tumbled over asleep I got that thing out of his belt and disposed of it where the eye of education can't see it. For even the football colleges disapprove of the art of scalp-taking in their curriculums.

"It is ten o'clock next day when John Tom wakes up and looks around. I am glad to see the nineteenth century in his eyes again.

" 'What was it, Jeff?' he asks.

" 'Heap firewater,' says I.

"John Tom frowns, and thinks a little. 'Combined,' says he directly, 'with the interesting little physiological shake-up known as reversion to type. I remember now. Have they gone yet?'

" 'On the 7:30 train,' I answers.

" 'Ugh!' says John Tom; 'better so. Paleface, bring big Chief Wish-Heap-Dough a little bromo-seltzer, and then he'll take up the red man's burden again.' "

The Marquis and Miss Sally

Without knowing it, Old Bill Bascom had the honor of being overtaken by fate the same day with the Marquis of Borodale.

The Marquis lived in Regent Square, London. Old Bill lived on Limping Doe Creek, Hardeman County, Texas. The cataclysm that engulfed the Marquis took the form of a bursting bubble known as the Central and South American Mahogany and Caoutchouc Monopoly. Old Bill's Nemesis was in the no less perilous shape of a band of civilized Indian cattle thieves from the Territory who ran off his entire herd of four hundred head, and shot old Bill dead as he trailed after them. To even up the consequences of the two catastrophes, the Marquis, as soon as he found that all he possessed would pay only fifteen shillings on the pound of his indebtedness, shot himself.

Old Bill left a family of six motherless sons and daughters, who found themselves without even a red steer left to eat or a red cent to buy one with.

The Marquis left one son, a young man, who had come to the States and established a large and well-stocked ranch in the Panhandle of Texas. When this young man learned the news he mounted his pony and rode to town. There he placed everything he owned except his horse, saddle, Winchester, and fifteen dollars in his pockets, in the hands of his lawyers, with instructions to sell and forward the proceeds to London to be applied upon the payment of his father's debts. Then he mounted his pony and rode southward.

One day, arriving about the same time, but by different trails, two young chaps rode up to the Diamond-cross ranch, on the Little Piedra, and asked for work. Both were dressed neatly and sprucely in cowboy costume. One was a straight-set fellow, with delicate, handsome features, short brown hair, and smooth face, sunburned to a golden brown. The other applicant was stouter and broad-shouldered, with fresh red complexion, somewhat freckled, reddish, curling hair, and a rather plain face, made attractive by laughing eyes and a pleasant mouth.

The superintendent of the Diamond-Cross was of the opinion that he could give them work. In fact, word had reached him that morning that the camp cook—a most important member of the outfit—had straddled his bronco and departed, being unable to withstand the fire of fun and practical jokes of which he was, ex-officio, the legitimate target.

"Can either of you cook?" asked the superintendent.

"I can," said the reddish-haired fellow, promptly. "I've cooked in camp quite a lot. I'm willing to take the job until you've got something else to offer."

"Now, that's the way I like to hear a man talk," said the superintendent, approvingly. "I'll give you a note to Saunders, and he'll put you to work."

Thus the names of John Bascom and Charles Norwood were added to the pay-roll of the Diamond-Cross. The two left for the round-up camp immediately after dinner. Their directions were simple, but sufficient: "Keep down the arroyo for fifteen miles till you get there." Both being strangers from afar, young, spirited, and thus thrown together by chance for a long ride, it is likely that the comradeship that afterward existed so strongly between them began that afternoon as they meandered along the little valley of the Candad Verda.

They reached their destination just after sunset. The main camp of the round-up was comfortably located on the bank of a long water-hole, under a fine mott of timber. A number of small A tents pitched upon grassy spots and the big wall tent for provisions showed that the camp was intended to be occupied for a considerable length of time.

The round-up had ridden in but a few moments before, hungry and tired, to a supperless camp. The boys were engaged in an emulous display of anathemas supposed to fit the case of the absconding cook. While they were unsaddling and hobbling their ponies, the newcomers rode in and inquired for Pink Saunders. The boss of the round-up came forth and was given the superintendent's note.

Pink Saunders, though a boss during working hours, was a humorist in camp, where everybody, from cook to superintendent, is equal. After reading the note he waved his hand toward the camp and shouted, ceremoniously, at the top of his voice, "Gentlemen, allow me to present to you the Marquis and Miss Sally."

At the words both the new arrivals betrayed confusion. The newly employed cook started, with a surprised look on his face, but, immediately recollecting that "Miss Sally" is the generic name for the male cook in every west Texas cow camp, he recovered his composure with a grin at his own expense.

His companion showed little less discomposure, even turning angrily, with a bitten lip, and reaching for his saddle pommel, as if to remount his pony; but "Miss Sally" touched his arm and said, laughingly, "Come now, Marquis; that was quite a compliment from Saunders. It's that distinguished air of yours and aristocratic nose that made him call you that."

He began to unsaddle, and the Marquis, restored to equanimity, followed his example. Rolling up his sleeves, Miss Sally sprang for the grub wagon, shouting:

"I'm the new cook b'thunder! Some of you chaps rustle a little wood for a fire, and I'll guarantee you a hot square meal inside of thirty minutes." Miss Sally's energy and good-humor as he ransacked the grub wagon for coffee, flour, and bacon, won the good opinion of the camp instantly.

And also, in days following, the Marquis, after becoming better acquainted, proved to be a cheerful, pleasant fellow, always a little reserved, and taking no part in the rough camp frolics; but the boys gradually came to respect this reserve—which fitted the title Saunders had given him—and even to like him for it. Saunders had assigned him to a place holding the herd during the cuttings. He proved to be a skilful rider and as good with the lariat or in the branding pen as most of them.

The Marquis and Miss Sally grew to be quite close comrades. After supper was over, and everything cleaned up, you would generally find them together, Miss Sally smoking his brier-root pipe, and the Marquis plaiting a quirt or scraping rawhide for a new pair of hobbles.

The superintendent did not forget his promise to keep an eye on the cook. Several times, when visiting the camp, he held long talks with him. He seemed to have taken a fancy to Miss Sally. One afternoon he rode up, on his way back to the ranch from a tour of the camps and said to him:

"There'll be a man here in the morning to take your place. As soon as he shows up you come to the ranch. I want you to take charge of the ranch accounts and correspondence. I want somebody that I can depend upon to keep things straight when I'm away. The wages'll be all right. The Diamond-Cross'll hold its end up with a man who'll look after its interests."

"All right," said Miss Sally, as quietly as if he had expected the notice all along. "Any objections to my bringing my wife down to the ranch?"

"You married?" said the superintendent, frowning a little. "You didn't mention it when we were talking."

"Because I'm not," said the cook. "But I'd like to be. Thought I'd wait til I got a job under roof. I couldn't ask her to live in a cow camp."

"Right," agreed the superintendent. "A camp isn't quite the place for a married man—but—well, there's plenty of room at the house, and if you suit us as well as I think you will you can afford it. You write to her to come on."

"All right," said Miss Sally again, "I'll ride in as soon as I am relieved to-morrow."

It was a rather chilly night, and after supper the cow-punchers were lounging about a big fire of dried mesquite chunks.

Their usual exchange of jokes and repartee had dwindled almost to silence, but silence in a cow camp generally betokens the brewing of mischief.

Miss Sally and the Marquis were seated upon a log, discussing the relative merits of the lenthened or shortened stirrup in long-distance riding. The Marquis arose presently and went to a tree near by to examine some strips of rawhide he was seasoning for making a lariat. Just as he left a little puff of wind blew some scraps of tobacco from a cigarette that Dry-Creek Smithers was rolling, into Miss Sally's eyes. While the cook was rubbing at them, with tears flowing, "Phonograph" Davis—so called on account of his strident voice—arose and began a speech.

"Fellers and citizens! I desire to perpound a interrogatory. What is the most grievous spectacle what the human mind can contemplate?"

A volley of answers responded to his question.

"A busted flush!"

"A Maverick when you ain't got your branding iron!"

"Yourself!"

"The hole in the end of some other feller's gun!"

"Shet up, you ignoramuses," said Old Taller, the fat cow-puncher. "Phony knows what it is. He's waitin' for to tell us."

"No, fellers and citizens," continued Phonograph. "Them spectacles you've e-numerated air shore grievious, and way up yonder close to the so-lution, but they ain't it. The most grievious spectacle air that"—he pointed to Miss Sally, who was still rubbing his streaming eyes—"a trustin' and a in-veegled female a-weepin' tears on account ofher heart bein' busted by a false deceiver. Air we men or air we catamounts to gaze upon the blightin' of our Miss Sally's affections by a a-risto-crat, which has come among us with his superior beauty and his glitterin' title to give the weeps to the lovely critter we air bound to pertect? Air we goin' to act like men, or air we goin' to keep on eatin' soggy chuck from her cryin' so plentiful over the bread-pan?"

"It's a gallopin' shame," said Dry-Creek, with a sniffle. "It ain't human. I've noticed the varmint a-palaverin' round her frequent. And him a Marquis! Ain't that a title, Phony?"

"It's somethin' like a king," the Brushy Creek Kid hastened to explain, "only lower in the deck. Guess it comes in between the Jack and the ten-spot."

"Don't misconstruct me," went on Phonograph, "as undervaluatin' the a-risto-crats. Some of 'em air proper people and can travel right along with the Watson boys. I've herded some with 'em myself. I've viewed the elephant with the Mayor of Fort Worth, and I've listened to the owl with the gen'ral passenger agent of the Katy, and they can keep up with the percession from where you laid the chunk. But when a Marquis monkeys with the innocent affections of a cook-lady, may I inquire what the case seems to call for?"

"The leathers," shouted Dry-Creek Smithers.

"You hear'er, Charity!" was the Kid's form of corroboration.

"We've got your company," assented the cowpunchers, in chorus.

Before the Marquis realized their intention, two of them seized him by each arm and led him up to the log. Phonograph Davis, self-appointed to carry out the sentence, stood ready, with a pair of stout leather leggings in his hands.

It was the first time they had ever laid hands on the Marquis during their somewhat rude sports.

"What are you up to?" he asked, indignantly, with flashing eyes.

"Go easy, Marquis," whispered Rube Fellows, one of the boys that held him. "It's all in fun. Take it good-natured and they'll let you off light. They're only goin' to stretch you over the log and tan you eight or ten times with the leggin's. 'Twon't hurt much."

The Marquis, with an exclamation of anger, his white teeth gleaming, suddenly exhibited a surprising strength. He wrenched with his arms so violently that the four men were swayed and dragged many yards from the log. A cry of anger escaped him, and then Miss Sally, his eyes cleared of the tobacco, saw, and he immediately mixed with the struggling group.

But at that moment a loud "Hallo!" rang in their ears, and a buckboard drawn by a team of galloping mustangs spun into the campfire's circle of light. Every man turned to look, and what they saw drove from their minds all thoughts of carrying out Phonograph Davis's rather time-worn contribution to the evening's amusement. Bigger game than the Marquis was at hand, and his captors released him and stood staring at the approaching victim.

The buckboard and team belonged to Sam Holly, a cattleman from the Big Muddy. Sam was driving, and with him was a stout, smooth-faced man, wearing a frock coat and a high silk hat. That was the county judge, Mr. Dave Hackett, candidate for reelection. Sam was escorting him about the country, among the camps, to shake up the sovereign voters.

The men got out, hitched the team to a mesquite, and walked toward the fire.

Instantly every man in camp, except the Marquis, Miss Sally, and Pink Saunders, who had to play host, uttered a frightful yell of assumed terror and fled on all sides into the darkness.

"Heavens alive!" exclaimed Hackett, "are we as ugly as that? How do you do, Mr. Saunders? Glad to see you again. What are you doing to my hat, Holly?"

"I was afraid of this hat," said Sam Holly, meditatively. He had taken the hat from Hackett's head and was holding it in his hand, looking dubiously around at the shadows beyond the firelight where now absolute stillness reigned. "What do you think, Saunders?"

Pink grinned.

"Better elevate it some," he said, in the tone of one giving disinterested advice. "The light ain't none too good. I wouldn't want it on my head."

Holly stepped upon the hub of a hind wheel of the grub wagon and hung the hat upon a limb of a live-oak. Scarcely had his foot touched the ground when the crash of a dozen six-shooters split the air, and the hat fell to the ground riddled with bullets.

A hissing noise was heard as if from a score of rattlesnakes, and the cow-punchers emerged on all sides from the darkness, stepping high, with ludicrously exaggerated caution, and "hist"-ing to one another to observe the utmost prudence in approaching. They formed a solemn, wide circle about the hat, gazing at it in manifest alarm, and seized every few moments by little stampedes of panicky flight.

"It's the varmint," said one in awed tones, "that flits up and down in the low grounds at night, saying, 'Willie-wallo!' "

"It's the venomous Kypootum," proclaimed another. "It stings after it's dead, and hollers after it's buried."

"It's the chief of the hairy tribe," said Phonograph Davis. "But it's stone dead, now, boys."

"Don't you believe it," demurred Dry-Creek. "It's only 'possumin'.' It's the dreaded Highgollacum fantod from the forest. There's only one way to destroy its life."

He led forward Old Taller, the 240-pound cow-puncher. Old Taller placed the hat upright on the ground and solemnly sat upon it, crushing it as flat as a pancake.

Hackett had viewed these proceedings with wide-open eyes. Sam Holly saw that his anger was rising and said to him:

"Here's where you win or lose, Judge. There are sixty votes on the Diamond-Cross. The boys are trying your mettle. Take it as a joke, and I don't think you'll regret it." And Hackett saw the point and rose to the occasion.

Advancing to where the slayers of the wild beast were standing about its remains and declaring it to be at last defunct, he said, with deep earnestness:

"Boys, I must thank you for this gallant rescue. While driving through the arroyo the cruel monster that you have so fearlessly and repeatedly slaughtered sprang upon us from the tree tops. To you I shall consider that I owe my life, and also, I hope, reelection to the office for which I am again candidate. Allow me to hand you my card."

The cow-punchers, always so sober-faced while engaged in their monkey-shines, relaxed into a grin of approval.

But Phonograph Davis, his appetite for fun not yet appeased, had something more up his sleeve.

"Pardner," he said, addressing Hackett with grave severity, "many a camp would be down on you for turnin' loose a pernicious varmint like that in it; but, bein' as we all escaped without loss of life, we'll overlook it. You can play square with us if you'll do it."

"How's that?" asked Hackett, suspiciously.

"You're authorized to perform the sacred rights and lefts of matter-mony, air you not?"

"Well, yes," replied Hackett. "A marriage ceremony conducted by me would be legal."

"A wrong air to be righted in this here camp," said Phonograph, virtuously. "A a-ristocrat have slighted a 'umble but beautchoos female wat's pinin' for his affections. It's the jooty of the camp to drag forth the haughty descendant of a hundred—or maybe a hundred and twenty-five—earls, even so at the p'int of a lariat, and jine him to the weepin' lady. Fellows! round up Miss Sally and the Marquis, there's goin' to be a weddin'."

This whim of Phonograph's was received with whoops of appreciation. The cow-punchers started to apprehend the principals of the proposed ceremony.

"Kindly prompt me," said Hackett, wiping his forehead, though the night was cool, "how far this thing is to be carried. And might I expect any further portions of my raiment to be mistaken for wild animals and killed?"

"The boys are livelier than usual to-night," said Saunders. "The ones they are talking about marrying are two of the boys—a herd rider and the cook. It's another joke. You and Sam will have to sleep here to-night anyway; p'rhaps you'd better see 'em through with it. Maybe they'll quiet down after that."

The matchmakers found Miss Sally seated on the tongue of the grub wagon, calmly smoking his pipe. The Marquis was leaning idly against one of the trees under which the supply tent was pitched.

Into this tent they were both hustled, and Phonograph, as master of ceremonies, gave orders for the preparations.

"You, Dry-Creek and Jimmy, and Ben and Taller—hump yourselves to the wildwood and rustle flowers for the blow-out—mesquite'll do—and get the Spanish dagger blossom at the corner of the horse corral for the bride to pack. You, Limpy, get out that red and yaller blanket of your'n for Miss Sally's skyirt. Marquis, you'll do 'thout fixin'; nobody don't ever look at the groom."

During their absurd preparations, the two principals were left alone for a few minutes in the tent. The Marquis suddenly showed wild perturbation.

"This foolishness must not go on," he said, turning to Miss Sally a face white in the light of the lantern, hanging to the ridge-pole.

"Why not?" said the cook, with an amused smile. "It's fun for the boys; and they've always let you off pretty light in their frolics. I don't mind it."

"But you don't understand," persisted the Marquis, pleadingly. "That man is county judge, and his acts are binding. I can't—oh, you don't know—"

The cook stepped forward and took the Marquis's hands.

"Sally Bascom," he said, "I KNOW!"

"You know!" faltered the Marquis, trembling. "And you—want to—"

"More than I ever wanted anything. Will you—here come the boys!"

The cow-punchers crowded in, laden with armfuls of decorations.

"Perfidious coyote!" said Phonograph, sternly, addressing the Marquis. "Air you willing to patch up the damage you've did this ere slab-sided but trustin' bunch o' calico by single-footin' easy to the altar, or will we have to rope ye, and drag you thar?"

The Marquis pushed back his hat, and leaned jauntily against some high-piled sacks of beans. His cheeks were flushed, and his eyes were shining.

"Go on with the rat killin'," said he.

A little while after a procession approached the tree under which Hackett, Holly, and Saunders were sitting smoking.

Limpy Walker was in the lead, extracting a doleful tune on his concertina. Next came the bride and groom. The cook wore the gorgeous Navajo blanket tied around his waist and carried in one hand the waxen-white Spanish dagger blossom as large as a peck-measure and weighing fifteen pounds. His hat was ornamented with mesquite branches and yellow ratama blooms. A resurrected mosquito bar served as a veil. After them stumbled Phonograph Davis, in the character of the bride's father, weeping into a saddle blanket with sobs that could be heard a mile away. The cow-punchers followed by twos, loudly commenting upon the bride's appearance, in a supposed imitation of the audiences at fashionable weddings.

Hackett rose as the procession halted before him, and after a little lecture upon matrimony, asked:

"What are your names?"

"Sally and Charles," answered the cook.

"Join hands, Charles and Sally."

Perhaps there never was a stranger wedding. For, wedding it was, though only two of those present knew it.

When the ceremony was over, the cow-punchers gave one yell of congratulation and immediately abandoned their foolery for the night. Blankets were unrolled and sleep became the paramount question.

The cook (divested of his decorations) and the Marquis lingered for a moment in the shadow of the grub wagon. The Marquis leaned her head against his shoulder.

"I didn't know what else to do," she was saying. "Father was gone, and we kids had to rustle. I had helped him so much with the cattle that I thought I'd turn cowboy. There wasn't anything else I could make a living at. I wasn't much stuck on it though, after I got here, and I'd have left only—"

"Only what?"

"You know. Tell me something. When did you first—what made you—"

"Oh, it was as soon as we struck the camp, when Saunders bawled out 'The Marquis and Miss Sally!' I saw how rattled you got at the name, and I had my sus—"

"Cheeky!" whispered the Marquis. "And why should you think that I thought he was calling me 'Miss Sally'?"

"Because," answered the cook, calmly, "I was the Marquis. My father was the Marquis of Borodale. But you'll excuse that, won't you, Sally? It really isn't my fault, you know."

Out of Nazareth

Okochee, in Georgia, had a boom, and J. Pinkney Bloom came out of it with a "wad." Okochee came out of it with a half-million-dollar debt, a two and a half per cent. city property tax, and a city council that showed a propensity for traveling the back streets of the town. These things came about through a fatal resemblance of the river Cooloosa to the Hudson, as set forth and expounded by a Northern tourist. Okochee felt that New York should not be allowed to consider itself the only alligator in the swamp, so to speak. And then that harmless, but persistent, individual so numerous in the South—the man who is always clamoring for more cotton mills, and is ready to take a dollar's worth of stock, provided he can borrow the dollar—that man added his deadly work to the tourist's innocent praise, and Okochee fell.

The Cooloosa River winds through a range of small mountains, passes Okochee, and then blends its waters trippingly, as fall the mellifluous Indian syllables, with the Chattahoochee.

Okochee rose, as it were, from its sunny seat on the post-office stoop, hitched up its suspender, and threw a granite dam two hundred and forty feet long and sixty feet high across the Cooloosa one mile above the town. Thereupon, a dimpling, sparkling lake backed up twenty miles among the little mountains. Thus in the great game of municipal rivalry did Okochee match that famous drawing card, the Hudson. It was conceded that nowhere could the Palisades be judged superior in the way of scenery and grandeur. Following the picture card was played the ace of commercial importance. Fourteen thousand horsepower would this dam furnish. Cotton mills, facories, and manufacturing plants would rise up as the green corn after a shower. The spindle and the flywheel and turbine would sing the shrewd glory of Okochee. Along the picturesque heights above the lake would rise in beauty the costly villas and the splendid summer residences of capital. The naphtha launch of the millionaire would spit among the romantic coves; the verdured hills would take formal shapes of terrace, lawn, and park. Money would be spent like water in Okochee, and water would be turned into money.

The fate of the good town is quickly told. Capital decided not to invest. Of all the great things promised, the scenery alone came to fulfilment. The wooded peaks, the impressive promontories of solemn granite, the beautiful green slants of bank and ravine did all they could to reconcile Okochee to the delinquency of miserly gold. The sunsets gilded the burning. Okochee, true to the instinct of its blood and clime, was lulled by the spell. It climbed out of the arena, loosed its suspender, sat down again on the post-office stoop, and took a chew. It consoled itself by drawling sarcasms at the city council which was not to blame, causing the fathers, as has been said, to seek back streets and figure perspiringly on the sinking fund and the appropriation for interest due.

The youth of Okochee—they who were to carry into the rosy future the burden of the debt—accepted failure with youth's uncalculating joy. For, here was sport, aquatic and nautical, added to the meagre round of life's pleasures. In yachting caps and flowing neckties they pervaded the lake to its limits. Girls wore silk waists embroidered with anchors in blue and pink. The trousers of the young men widened at the bottom, and their hands were proudly calloused by the oft-plied oar. Fishermen were under the spell of a deep and tolerant joy. Sailboats and rowboats furrowed the lenient waves, popcorn and ice-cream booths sprang up about the little wooden pier. Two small excursion steamboats were built, and plied the delectable waters. Okochee philosphically gave up the hope of eating turtle soup with a gold spoon, and settled back, not ill content, to its regular diet of lotus and fried hominy. And out of this slow wreck of great expectations rose up J. Pinkney Bloom with his "wad" and his prosperous, cheery smile.

Needless to say J. Pinkney was no product of Georgia soil. He came out of that flushed and capable region known as the "North." He called himself a "promoter"; his enemies had spoken of him as a "grafter"; Okochee took a middle course, and held him to be no better nor no worse than a "Yank."

Far up the lake—eighteen miles above the town—the eye of this cheerful camp-follower of booms had spied out a graft. He purchased there a precipitous tract of five hundred acres at forty-five cents per acre; and this he laid out and subdivided as the city of Skyland—the Queen City of the Switzerland of the South. Streets and avenues were surveyed; parks designed; corners of central squares reserved for the "proposed" opera house, board of trade, lyceum, market, public schools, and "Exposition Hall." The price of lots ranged from five to five hundred dollars. Positively, no lot would be priced higher than five hundred dollars.

While the boom was growing in Okochee, J. Pinkney's circulars, maps, and prospectuses were flying through the mails to every part of the country. Investors sent in their money by post, and the Skyland Real Estate Company (J. Pinkney Bloom) returned to each a deed, duly placed on record, to the best lot, at a price, on hand that day. All this time the catamount screeched upon the reserved lot of the Skyland Board of Trade, the opossum swung by his tail over the site of the exposition hall, and the owl hooted a melancholy recitative to his audience of young squirrels in opera house square. Later, when the money was coming in fast, J. Pinkney caused to be erected in the coming city half a dozen cheap box houses, and persuaded a contingent of indigent natives to occupy them, thereby assuming the rôle of "population" in subsequent prospectuses, which became, accordingly, more seductive and remunerative.

So, when the dream faded and Okochee dropped back to digging bait and nursing its two and a half per cent. tax, J. Pinkney Bloom (unloving of checks and drafts and the cold interrogatories of bankers) strapped about his fifty-two-inch waist a soft leather belt containing eight thousand dollars in big bills, and said that all was very good.

One last trip he was making to Skyland before departing to other salad fields. Skyland was a regular post-office, and the steamboat, *Dixie Belle,* under contract, delivered the mail bag (generally empty) twice a week. There was a little business there to be settled—the postmaster was to be paid off for his light but lonely services, and the "inhabitants" had to be furnished with another month's homely rations, as per agreement. And then Skyland would know J. Pinkney Bloom no more. The owners of these precipitous, barren, useless lots might come and view the scene of their invested credulity, or they might leave them to their fit tenants, the wild hog and the browsing deer. The work of the Skyland Real Estate Company was finished.

The little steamboat *Dixie Belle* was about to shove off on her regular up-the-lake trip, when a rickety hired carriage rattled up to the pier, and a tall, elderly gentleman, in black, stepped out, signaling courteously but vivaciously for the boat to wait. Time was of the least importance in the schedule of the *Dixie Belle*; Captain MacFarland gave the order, and the boat received its ultimate two passengers. For, upon the arm of the tall, elderly gentleman, as he crossed the gangway, was a little elderly lady, with a gray curl depending quaintly forward of her left ear.

Captain MacFarland was at the wheel; therefore it seemed to J. Pinkney Bloom, who was the only other passenger, that it should be his to play the part of host to the boat's new guests, who were, doubtless, on a scenery-viewing expedition. He stepped forward, with that translucent, child-candid smile upon his fresh, pink countenance, with that air of unaffected sincerity that was redeemed from bluffness only by its exquisite calculation, with that promptitude and masterly decision of manner that so well suited his calling—with all his stock in trade well to the front, he stepped forward to receive Colonel and Mrs. Peyton Blaylock. With the grace of a grand marshal or a wedding usher, he escorted the two passengers to the side of the upper deck, from which the scenery was supposed to present itself to the observer in increased quantity and quality. There, in comfortable steamer chairs, they sat and began to piece together the random lines that were to form an intelligent paragraph in the big history of little events.

"Our home, sir," said Colonel Blaylock, removing his wide-brimmed, rather shapeless black felt hat, "is in Holly Springs—Holly Springs, Georgia. I am very proud to make your acquaintance, Mr. Bloom. Mrs. Blaylock and myself have just arrived in Okochee this morning, sir, on business—business of importance in connection with the recent rapid march of progress in this section of our state."

The Colonel smoothed back, with a sweeping gesture, his long, smooth, gray locks. His dark eyes, still fiery under the heavy black brows, seemed inappropriate to the face of a business man. He looked rather to be an old courtier handed down from the reign of Charles, and re-attired in a modern suit of fine, but raveling and seam-worn, broadcloth.

"Yes, sir," said Mr. Bloom, in his heartiest prospectus voice, "things have been whizzing around Okochee. Biggest industrial revival and waking up to natural resources Georgia ever had. Did you happen to squeeze in on the ground floor in any of the gilt-edged grafts, Colonel?"

"Well, sir," said the Colonel, hesitating in courteous doubt, "if I understand your question, I may say that I took the opportunity to make an investment that I believe will prove quite advantageous—yes, sir, I believe it will result in both pecuniary profit and agreeable occupation."

"Colonel Blaylock," said the little elderly lady, shaking her gray curl and smiling indulgent explanation at J. Pinkney Bloom, "is so devoted to business. He has such a talent for financiering and markets and investments and those kind of things. I think myself extremely fortunate in having secured him for a partner on life's journey—I am so unversed in those formidable but very useful branches of learning."

Colonel Blaylock rose and made a bow—a bow that belonged with silk stockings and lace ruffles and velvet.

"Practical affairs," he said, with a wave of his hand toward the promoter, "are, if I may use the comparison, the garden walks upon which we tread through life, viewing upon either side of us the flowers which brighten that journey. It is my pleasure to be able to lay out a walk or two. Mrs. Blaylock, sir, is one of those fortunate higher spirits whose mission it is to make the flowers grow. Perhaps, Mr. Bloom, you have perused the lines of Lorella, the Southern poetess. That is the name above which Mrs. Blaylock has contributed to the press of the South for many years."

"Unfortunately," said Mr. Bloom, with a sense of the loss clearly written upon his frank face, "I'm like the Colonel—in the walk-making business myself—and I haven't had time to even take a sniff at the flowers. Poetry is a line I never dealt in. It must be nice, though—quite nice."

"It is the region," smiled Mrs. Blaylock, "in which my soul dwells. My shawl, Peyton, if you please—the breeze comes a little chilly from yon verdured hills."

The Colonel drew from the tail pocket of his coat a small shawl of knitted silk and laid it solicitously about the shoulders of the lady. Mrs. Blaylock sighed contentedly, and turned her expressive eyes—still as clear and unworldly as a child's—upon the steep slopes that were slowly slipping past. Very fair and stately they looked in the clear morning air. They seemed to speak in familiar terms to the responsive spirit of Lorella. "My native hills!" she murmured, dreamily. "See how the foliage drinks the sunlight from the hollows and dells."

"Mrs. Blaylock's maiden days," said the Colonel, interpreting her mood to J. Pinkney Bloom, "were spent among the mountains of northern Georgia. Mountain air and mountain scenery recall to her those days. Holly Springs, where we have lived for twenty years, is low and flat. I fear that she may have suffered in health and spirits by so long a residence there. That is one potent reason for the change we are making. My dear, can you not recall those lines you wrote—entitled, I think, 'The Georgia Hills'—the poem that was so extensively copied by the Southern press and praised so highly by the Atlanta critics?"

Mrs. Blaylock turned a glance of speaking tenderness upon the Colonel, fingered for a moment the silvery curl that drooped upon her bosom, then looked again toward the mountains. Without preliminary or affectation or demurral she began, in rather thrilling and more deeply pitched tones, to recite these lines:

"The Georgia hills, the Georgia hills!—
Oh, heart, why dost thou pine?
Are not these sheltered lowlands fair
With mead and bloom and vine?

Ah! as the slow-paced river here
Broods on its natal rills
My spirit drifts, in longing sweet,
Back to the Georgia hills.
"And through the close-drawn, curtained night

I steal on sleep's slow wings
Back to my heart's ease—slopes of pine—
Where end my wanderings.
Oh, heaven seems nearer from their tops—
And farther earthly ills—
Even in dreams, if I may but
Dream of my Georgia hills.

"The grass upon their orchard sides
Is a fine couch to me;
The common note of each small bird
Passes all minstrelsy.
It would not seem so dread a thing
If, when the Reaper wills,
He might come there and take my hand
Up in the Georgia hills."

"That's great stuff, ma'am," said J. Pinkney Bloom, enthusiastically, when the poetess had concluded. "I wish I had looked up poetry more than I have. I was raised in the pine hills myself."

"The mountains ever call to their children," murmured Mrs. Blaylock. "I feel that life will take on the rosy hue of hope again in among these beautiful hills. Peyton—a little taste of the currant wine, if you will be so good. The journey, though delightful in the extreme, slightly fatigues me."

Colonel Blaylock again visited the depths of his prolific coat, and produced a tightly corked, rough, black bottle. Mr. Bloom was on his feet in an instant. "Let me bring a glass, ma'am. You come along, Colonel—there's a little table we can bring, too. Maybe we can scare up some fruit or a cup of tea on board. I'll ask Mac."

Mrs. Blaylock reclined at ease. Few royal ladies have held their royal prerogative with the serene grace of the petted Southern woman. The Colonel, with an air as gallant and assiduous as in the days of his courtship, and J. Pinkney Bloom, with a ponderous agility half professional and half directed by some resurrected, unnamed, long-forgotten sentiment, formed a diversified but attentive court. The currant wine—wine home made from the Holly Springs fruit—went round; and then J. Pinkney began to hear something of Holly Springs life.

It seemed (from the conversation of the Blaylocks) that the Springs was decadent. A third of the population had moved away. Business—

and the Colonel was an authority on business—had dwindled to nothing. After carefully studying the field of opportunities open to capital he had sold his little property there for eight hundred dollars and invested it in one of the enterprises opened up by the book in Okochee.

"Might I inquire, sir," said Mr. Bloom, "in what particular line of business you inserted your coin? I know that town as well as I know the regulations for illegal use of the mails. I might give you a hunch as to whether you can make the game go or not."

J. Pinkney, somehow, had a kindly feeling toward these unsophisticated representatives of by-gone days. They were so simple, impractical, and unsuspecting. He was glad that he happened not to have a gold brick or a block of that western Bad Boy Silver Mine stock along with him. He would have disliked to unload on people he liked so well as he did these; but there are some temptations too enticing to be resisted.

"No, sir," said Colonel Blaylock, pausing to arrange the queen's wrap. "I did not invest in Okochee. I have made an exhaustive study of business conditions, and I regard old settled towns as unfavorable fields in which to place capital that is limited in amount. Some months ago, through the kindness of a friend, there came into my hands a map and description of this new town of Skyland that has been built upon the lake. The description was so pleasing, the future of the town set forth in such convincing arguments, and its increasing prosperity portrayed in such an attractive style that I decided to take advantage of the opportunity it offered. I carefully selected a lot in the centre of the business district, although its price was the highest in the schedule—five hundred dollars—and made the purchase at once."

"Are you the man—I mean, did you pay five hundred dollars for a lot in Skyland?" asked J. Pinkney Bloom.

"I did, sir," answered the Colonel, with the air of a modest millionaire explaining his successes; "a lot most excellently situated on the same square with the opera house, and only two squares from the board of trade. I consider the purchase a most fortuitous one. It is my intention to erect a small building upon it at once, and open a modest book and stationery store. During past years I have met with many pecuniary reverses, and I now find it necessary to engage in some commercial occupation that will furnish me with a livelihood. The book and stationery business, though an humble one, seems to me not inapt nor altogether uncongenial. I am a graduate of the University of Virginia; and Mrs. Blaylock's really wonderful acquaintance with belles-lettres and poetic literature should go far toward insuring success. Of course, Mrs. Blaylock would not personally serve behind the counter. With the nearly three hundred dollars I have remaining I can manage the building of a house, by giving a lien on the lot. I have an old friend in Atlanta who is a partner in a large book store, and he has agreed to furnish me with a stock of goods on credit, on extremely easy terms. I am pleased to hope, sir, that Mrs. Blaylock's health and happiness will be increased by the change of locality. Already I fancy I can perceive the return of those roses that were once the hope and despair of Georgia cavaliers."

Again followed that wonderful bow, as the Colonel lightly touched the pale cheek of the poetess. Mrs. Blaylock, blushing like a girl, shook her curl and gave the Colonel an arch, reproving tap. Secret of eternal youth—where art thou? every second the answer comes—"Here, here, here." Listen to thine own heartbeats, O weary seeker after external miracles.

"Those years," said Mrs. Blaylock, "in Holly Springs were long, long, long. But now is the promised land in sight. Skyland!—a lovely name."

"Doubtless," said the Colonel, "we shall be able to secure comfortable accommodations at some modest hotel at reasonable rates. Our trunks are in Okochee, to be forwarded when we shall have made permanent arrangements."

J. Pinkney Bloom excused himself, went forward, and stood by the captain at the wheel.

"Mac," said he, "do you remember my telling you once that I sold one of those five-hundred-dollar lots in Skyland?"

"Seems I do," grinned Captain MacFarland.

"I'm not a coward, as a general rule," went on the promoter, "but I always said that if I ever met the sucker that bought that lot I'd run like a turkey. Now, you see that old babe-in-the-wood over there? Well, he's the boy that drew the prize. That was the only five-hundred-dollar lot that went. The rest ranged from ten dollars to two hundred. His wife writes poetry. She's invented one about the high grounds of Georgia, that's way up in G. They're going to Skyland to open a book store."

"Well," said MacFarland with another grin, "it's a good thing you are along, J.P.; you can show 'em around town until they begin to feel at home."

"He's got three hundred dollars left to build a house and store with," went on J. Pinkney, as if he were talking to himself. "And he thinks there's an opera house up there."

Captain MacFarland released the wheel long enough to give his leg a roguish slap.

"You old fat rascal!" he chuckled, with a wink.

"Mac, you're a fool," said J. Pinkney Bloom, coldly. He went back and joined the Blaylocks, where he sat, less talkative, with that straight furrow between his brows that always stood as a signal of schemes being shaped within.

"There's a good many swindles connected with these booms," he said presently. "What if this Skyland should turn out to be one—that is, suppose business should be sort of dull there, and no special sale for books?"

"My dear sir," said Colonel Blaylock, resting his hand upon the back of his wife's chair, "three times I have been reduced to almost penury by the duplicity of others, but I have not yet lost faith in humanity. If I have been deceived again, still we may glean health and content, if not worldly profit. I am aware that there are dishonest schemers in the world who set traps for the unwary, but even they are not altogether bad. My dear, can you recall those verses entitled, 'He Giveth the Increase,' that you composed for the choir of our church in Holly Springs?"

"That was four years ago," said Mrs. Blaylock; "perhaps I can repeat a verse or two.

"The lily springs from the rotting mould;
Pearls from the deep sea slime;
Good will come out of Nazareth
All in God's own time.

"To the hardest heart the softening grace
Cometh, at last, to bless;
Guiding it right to help and cheer
And succor in distress.

"I cannot remember the rest. The lines were not ambitious. They were written to the music composed by a dear friend."

"It's a fine rhyme, just the same," declared Mr. Bloom. "It seems to ring the bell, all right. I guess I gather the sense of it. It means that the rankest kind of a phony will give you the best end of it once in a while."

Mr. Bloom strayed thoughtfully back to the captain, and stood meditating.

"Ought to be in sight of the spires and gilded domes of Skyland now in a few minutes," chirruped MacFarland, shaking with enjoyment.

"Go to the devil," said Mr. Bloom, still pensive.

And now, upon the left bank, they caught a glimpse of a white village, high up on the hills, smothered among green trees. That was Cold Branch—no boom town, but the slow growth of many years. Cold Branch lay on the edge of the grape and corn lands. The big country road ran just back of the heights. Cold Branch had nothing in common with the frisky ambition of Okochee with its impertinent lake.

"Mac," said J. Pinkney suddenly, "I want you to stop at Cold Branch. There's a landing there that they made to use sometimes when the river was up."

"Can't," said the captain, grinning more broadly. "I've got the United States mails on board. Right to-day this boat's in the government service. Do you want to have the poor old captain keelhauled by Uncle Sam? And the great city of Skyland all disconsolate, waiting for its mail? I'm ashamed of your extravagance, J.P."

"Mac," almost whispered J. Pinkney, in his danger-line voice, "I looked into the engine room of the *Dixie Belle* a while ago. Don't you know of somebody that needs a new boiler? Cement and black japan can't hide flaws from me. And then, those shares of building and loan that you traded for repairs—they were all yours, of course. I hate to mention these things, but—"

"Oh, come now, J.P.," said the captain. "You know I was just fooling. I'll put you off at Cold Branch, if you say so."

"The other passengers get off there, too," said Mr. Bloom.

Further conversation was held, and in ten minutes the *Dixie Belle* turned her nose toward a little, cranky wooden pier on the left bank, and the captain, relinquishing the wheel to a roustabout, came to the passenger deck and made the remarkable announcement: "All out for Skyland."

The Blaylocks and J. Pinkney Bloom disembarked, and the *Dixie Belle* proceeded on her way up the lake. Guided by the indefatigable promoter, they slowly climbed the steep hillside, pausing often to rest and admire the view. Finally they entered the village of Cold Branch. Warmly both the Colonel and his wife praised it for its homelike and peaceful beauty. Mr. Bloom conducted them to a two-story building on a shady street that bore the legend, "Pinetop Inn." Here he took his leave, receiving the cordial thanks of the two for his attentions, the Colonel remarking that he thought they would spend the remainder of the day in rest, and take a look at his purchase on the morrow.

J. Pinkney Bloom walked down Cold Branch's main street. He did not know this town, but he knew towns, and his feet did not falter. Presently he saw a sign over a door: "Frank E. Cooly, Attorney-At-Law and Notary Public." A young man was Mr. Cooly, and awaiting business.

"Get your hat, son," said Mr. Bloom, in his breezy way, "and a blank deed and come along. It's a job for you.

"Now," he continued, when Mr. Cooly had responded with alacrity, "is there a bookstore in town?"

"One," said the lawyer. "Henry Williams's."

"Get there," said Mr. Bloom. "We're going to buy it."

Henry Williams was behind his counter. His store was a small one, containing a mixture of books, stationery, and fancy rubbish. Adjoining it was Henry's home—a decent cottage, vine-embowered and cosy. Henry was lank and soporific, and not inclined to rush his business.

"I want to buy your house and store," said Mr. Bloom. "I haven't got time to dicker—name your price."

"It's worth eight hundred," said Henry, too much dazed to ask more than its value.

"Shut that door," said Mr. Bloom to the lawyer. Then he tore off his coat and vest, and began to unbutton his shirt.

"Wanter fight about it, do yer?" said Henry Williams, jumping up and cracking his heels together twice. "All right, hunky—sail in and cut yer capers."

"Keep your clothes on," said Mr. Bloom. "I'm only going down to the bank."

He drew eight one-hundred-dollar bills from his money belt and planked them down on the counter. Mr. Cooly showed signs of future promise, for he already had the deed spread out, and was reaching across the counter for the ink bottle. Never before or since was such quick action had in Cold Branch.

"Your name, please?" asked the lawyer.

"Make it out to Peyton Blaylock," said Mr. Bloom. "God knows how to spell it."

Within thirty minutes Henry Williams was out of business, and

Mr. Bloom stood on the brick sidewalk with Mr. Cooly, who held in his hand the signed and attested deed.

"You'll find the party at the Pinetop Inn," said J. Pinkney Bloom. "Get it recorded, and take it down and give it to him. He'll ask you a hell's mint of questions; so here's ten dollars for the trouble you'll have in not being able to answer 'em. Never run much to poetry, did you, young man?"

"Well," said the really talented Cooly, who even yet retained his right mind, "now and then."

"Dig into it," said Mr. Bloom, "it'll pay you. Never heard a poem, now, that run something like this did you?—

"A good thing out of Nazareth
Comes up sometimes, I guess
On hand, all right, to help and cheer
A sucker in distress."

"I believe not," said Mr. Cooly.

"It's a hymn," said J. Pinkney Bloom. "Now, show me the way to a livery stable, son, for I'm going to hit the dirt road back to Okochee."

Hearts and Hands

At Denver there was an influx of passengers into the coaches on the eastbound B. & M. express. In one coach there sat a very pretty young woman dressed in elegant taste and surrounded by all the luxurious comforts of an experienced traveler. Among the newcomers were two young men, one of handsome presence with a bold, frank countenance and manner; the other a ruffled, glum-faced person, heavily built and roughly dressed. The two were handcuffed together.

As they passed down the aisle of the coach the only vacant seat offered was a reversed one facing the attractive young woman. Here the linked couple seated themselves. The young woman's glance fell upon them with a distant, swift disinterest; then with a lovely smile brightening her countenance and a tender pink tingeing her rounded cheeks, she held out a little gray-gloved hand. When she spoke her voice, full, sweet, and deliberate, proclaimed that its owner was accustomed to speak and be heard.

"Well, Mr. Easton, if you *will* make me speak first, I suppose I must. Don't you ever recognize old friends when you meet them in the West?"

The younger man roused himself sharply at the sound of her voice, seemed to struggle with a slight embarrassment which he threw off instantly, and then clasped her fingers with his left hand.

"It's Miss Fairchild," he said, with a smile. "I'll ask you to excuse the other hand; it's otherwise engaged just at present."

He slightly raised his right hand, bound at the wrist by the shining "bracelet" to the left one of his companion. The glad look in the girl's eyes slowly changed to a bewildered horror. The glow faded from her cheeks. Her lips parted in a vague, relaxing distress. Easton, with a little laugh, as if amused, was about to speak again when the other forestalled him. The glum-faced man had been watching the girl's countenance with veiled glances from his keen, shrewd eyes.

"You'll excuse me for speaking, miss, but, I see you're acquainted with the marshal here. If you'll ask him to speak a word for me when we get to the pen he'll do it, and it'll make things easier for me there. He's taking me to Leavenworth prison. It's seven years for counterfeiting."

"Oh!" said the girl, with a deep breath and returning color. "So that is what you are doing out here? A marshal!"

"My dear Miss Fairchild," said Easton, calmly, "I had to do something. Money has a way of taking wings unto itself, and you know it takes money to keep step with our crowd in Washington. I saw this opening in the West, and—well, a marshalship isn't quite as high a position as that of ambassador, but—"

"The ambassador," said the girl, warmly, "doesn't call any more. He needn't ever have done so. You ought to know that. And so now you are one of these dashing Western heroes, and you ride and shoot and go into all kinds of dangers. That's different from the Washington life. You have been missed from the old crowd."

The girl's eyes, fascinated, went back, widening a little, to rest upon the glittering handcuffs.

"Don't you worry about them, miss," said the other man. "All marshals handcuff themselves to their prisoners to keep them from getting away. Mr. Easton knows his business."

"Will we see you again soon in Washington?" asked the girl.

"Not soon, I think," said Easton. "My butterfly days are over, I fear."

"I love the West," said the girl, irrelevantly. Her eyes were shining softly. She looked away out the car window. She began to speak truly and simply, without the gloss of style and manner: "Mamma and I spent the summer in Denver. She went home a week ago because father was slightly ill. I could live and be happy in the West. I think the air here agrees with me. Money isn't everything. But people always misunderstand things and remain stupid—"

"Say, Mr. Marshal," growled the glum-faced man. "This isn't quite fair. I'm needin' a drink, and haven't had a smoke all day. Haven't you talked long enough? Take me in the smoker now, won't you? I'm half dead for a pipe."

The bound travelers rose to their feet, Easton with the same slow smile on his face.

"I can't deny a petition for tobacco," he said, lightly. "It's the one friend of the unfortunate. Good-bye, Miss Fairchild. Duty calls, you know." He held out his hand for a farewell.

"It's too bad you are not going East," she said, reclothing herself with manner and style. "But you must go on to Leavenworth, I suppose?"

"Yes," said Easton, "I must go on to Leavenworth."

The two men sidled down the aisle into the smoker.

The two passengers in a seat near by had heard most of the conversation. Said one of them: "That marshal's a good sort of chap. Some of these Western fellows are all right."

"Pretty young to hold an office like that, isn't he?" asked the other.

"Young!" exclaimed the first speaker, "why—Oh! didn't you catch on? Say—did you ever know an officer to handcuff a prisoner to his *right* hand?"